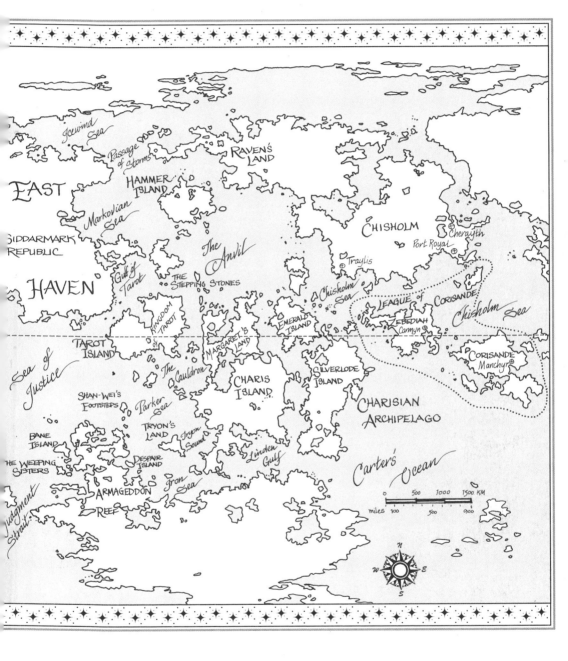

ICEWIND SEA

PASSAGE OF STORMS

RAVEN'S LAND

EAST

HAMMER ISLAND

CHISHOLM

Cherayth

Markovian Sea

Port Royal

SIDDARMARK REPUBLIC

The Anvil

Traylis

HAVEN

Gulf of Tarot

THE STEPPING STONES

Chisholm Sea

LEAGUE of CORISANDE

Chisholm Sea

KINGDOM of TAROT

EMERALD ISLAND

ZEBEDIAH Carmyn

Sea of Justice

TAROT ISLAND

MARGARET'S LAND

The Cauldron

CHARIS ISLAND

SILVERLODE ISLAND

CORISANDE Manchyr

SHAN-WEI'S FOOTSTEPS

Parker Sea

CHARISIAN ARCHIPELAGO

BANE ISLAND

TRYON'S LAND

Tryon Sound

Linden Gulf

Carter's Ocean

THE WEEPING SISTERS

DESPAIR ISLAND

Iron Sea

500   1000   1500 KM

Judgment Strait

ARMAGEDDON REEF

miles 100   500   900

N

W   E

S

OFF ARMAGEDDON REEF

OFF ARMAGEDDON REEF

✦

DAVID WEBER

TOR®

A TOM DOHERTY ASSOCIATES BOOK

NEW YORK

OFF ARMAGEDDON REEF

Copyright © 2007 by David Weber

This book is printed on acid-free paper.

Edited by Patrick Nielsen Hayden
Book design by Ellen Cipriano
Maps by Ellisa Mitchell

A Tor Book
Published by Tom Doherty Associates, LLC
175 Fifth Avenue
New York, NY 10010

www.tor.com

Tor® is a registered trademark of Tom Doherty Associates, LLC.

Library of Congress Cataloging-in-Publication Data

Weber, David, 1952–
    Off Armageddon Reef / David Weber.
        p. cm.
    ISBN-13: 978-0-765-31500-7
    ISBN-10: 0-765-31500-9
    1. Space warfare—Fiction. I. Title.

PS3573.E217O35 2007
813'.54—dc22
                                    2006025838

First Edition: January 2007

Printed in the United States of America

0   9   8   7   6   5   4   3   2   1

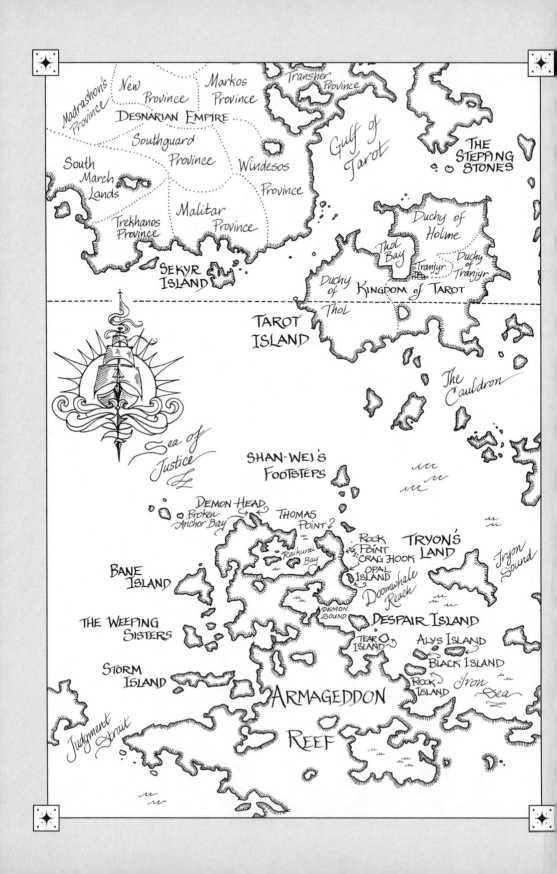

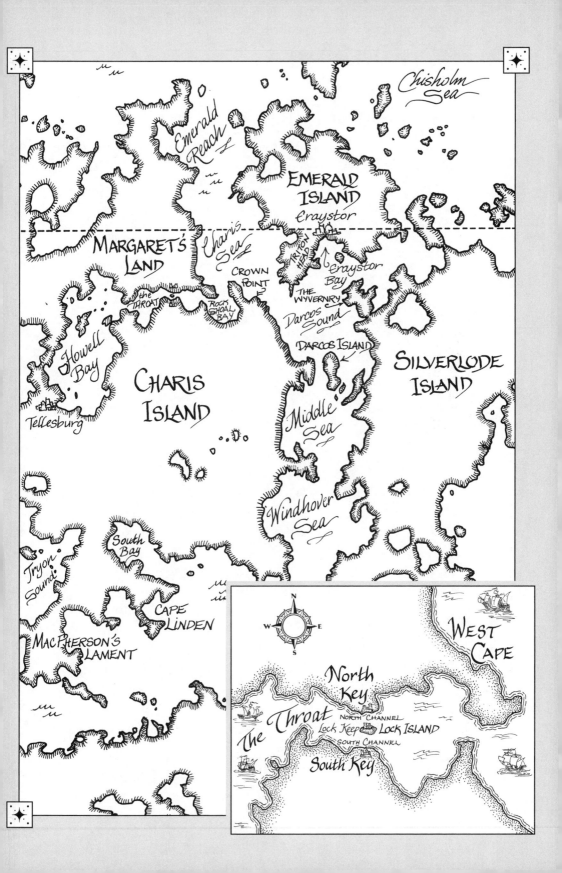

"Captain to the bridge! Captain to the bridge!"

Captain Mateus Fofão rolled out of bed as the urgent voice of the officer of the watch blared over the intercom, counterpointed by the high-pitched wail of the emergency General Quarters signal. The captain's bare feet were on the deck-sole and he was already reaching for the bedside com before his eyes were fully open, and he jabbed the red priority key purely by feel.

"Bridge." The response came almost instantly, in a voice flat with the panic-resisting armor of training.

"It's the Captain, Chief Kuznetzov," Fofão said crisply. "Give me Lieutenant Henderson."

"Aye, Sir."

There was a brief instant of silence, then another voice.

"Officer of the deck," it said.

"Talk to me, Gabby," Fofão said crisply.

"Skipper," Lieutenant Gabriela Henderson, the heavy cruiser's tactical officer, had the watch, and her normally calm contralto was strained and harsh, "we've got bogies. *Lots* of bogies. They just dropped out of hyper twelve light-minutes out, and they're headed in-system at over four hundred gravities."

Fofão's jaw clenched. Four hundred gravities was twenty percent higher than the best Federation compensators could manage. Which pretty conclusively demonstrated that whoever these people were, they *weren't* Federation units.

"Strength estimate?" he asked.

"Still coming in, Sir," Henderson replied flatly. "So far, we've confirmed over seventy."

Fofão winced.

"All right." He was astounded by how calm his own voice sounded. "Implement first-contact protocols, and also Spyglass and Watchman. Then take us to

Condition Four. Make sure the Governor's fully informed, and tell her I'm declaring a Code Alpha."

"Aye, aye, Sir."

"I'll be on the bridge in five minutes," Fofão continued as his sleeping cabin's door opened and his steward loped through it with his uniform. "Let's get some additional recon drones launched and headed for these people."

"Aye, aye, Sir."

"I'll see you in five," Fofão said. He keyed the com off and turned to accept his uniform from the white-faced steward.

▼   ▼   ▼

In actual fact, Mateus Fofão reached the command deck of TFNS *Swiftsure* in just under five minutes.

He managed to restrain himself to a quick, brisk stride as he stepped out of the bridge elevator, but his eyes were already on the master plot, and his mouth tightened. The unknown vessels were a scatter of ominous ruby chips bearing down on the binary system's GO primary component and the blue-and-white marble of its fourth planet.

"Captain on the bridge!" Chief Kuznetzov announced, but Fofão waved everyone back into his or her bridge chair.

"As you were," he said, and almost everyone settled back into place. Lieutenant Henderson did not. She rose from the captain's chair at the center of the bridge, her relief as Fofão's arrival relieved her of command obvious.

He nodded to her, stepped past her, and settled himself in the same chair.

"The Captain has the ship," he announced formally, then looked back up at Henderson, still standing beside him. "Any incoming transmissions from them?"

"No, Sir. If they'd begun transmitting the instant they dropped out of hyper, we'd have heard something from them about"—the lieutenant glanced at the digital time display—"two minutes ago. We haven't."

Fofão nodded. Somehow, looking at the spreading cloud of red icons on the display, he wasn't surprised.

"Strength update?" he asked.

"Tracking estimates a minimum of eighty-five starships," Henderson said. "We don't have any indications of fighter launches yet."

Fofão nodded again, and a strange, singing sort of tension that was almost its own form of calm seemed to fill him. The calm of a man face-to-face with a disaster for which he has planned and trained for years but never really expected to confront.

"Watchman?" he asked.

"Implemented, Sir," Henderson replied. "*Antelope* got under way for the hyper limit two minutes ago."

"Spyglass?"

"Activated, Sir."

That's something, a detached corner of Fofão's brain said.

TFNS *Antelope* was a tiny, completely unarmed, and very fast courier vessel. Crestwell's World was the Federation's most advanced colonial outpost, fifty light-years from Sol, too new, too sparsely settled, to have its own hypercom yet. That left only courier ships, and at this moment *Antelope*'s sole function was to flee Sol-ward at her maximum possible velocity with the word that Code Alpha had come to pass.

Spyglass was the net of surveillance satellites stretched around the periphery of the star system's hyper limit. They were completely passive, hopefully all but impossible to detect, and they weren't there for *Swiftsure*'s benefit. Their take—all of it—was being beamed after *Antelope*, to make certain she had full and complete tactical records as of the moment she hypered out. And that same information was being transmitted to *Antelope*'s sister ship, TFNS *Gazelle*, as she lay totally covert in orbit around the system's outermost gas giant.

Her task was to remain hidden until the end, if she could, and then to report back to Old Earth.

And it's a good thing she's out there, Fofão thought grimly, *because* we *certainly aren't going to be making any reports.*

"Ship's status?" he asked.

"All combat systems are closed up at Condition Four, Sir. Engineering reports all stations manned and ready, and both normal-space and hyper drives are online prepared to answer maneuvering commands."

"Very good." Fofão pointed at her normally assigned command station and watched her head for it. Then he inhaled deeply and pressed a stud on the arm of his command chair.

"This is the Captain," he said, without the usual formalities of an all-hands announcement. "By now, you all know what's going on. At the moment, you know just as much about these people as I do. I don't know if they're the Gbaba or not. If they are, it doesn't look very good. But I want all of you to know that I'm proud of you. Whatever happens, no captain could have a better ship or a better crew."

He released the com stud and swiveled his chair to face the heavy cruiser's helmsman.

"Bring us to zero-one-five, one-one-niner, at fifty gravities," he said quietly, and TFNS *Swiftsure* moved to position herself between the planet whose human colonists had named it Crestwell's World and the mammoth armada bearing down upon it.

Mateus Fofão had always been proud of his ship. Proud of her crew, of her speed, of the massive firepower packed into her three-quarters-of-a-million-tonne hull. At the moment, what he was most aware of was her frailty.

Until ten years earlier, there'd been no Terran Federation Navy, not really. There'd been something the Federation *called* a navy, but it had actually been little more than a fleet of survey vessels, backed up by a handful of light armed units whose main concerns had been search and rescue operations and the suppression of occasional, purely human predators.

But then, ten years ago, a Federation survey ship had found evidence of the first confirmed advanced nonhuman civilization. No one knew what that civilization's citizens had called themselves, because none of them were still alive to tell anyone.

Humanity had been shocked by the discovery that an entire species had been deliberately destroyed. That a race capable of fully developing and exploiting the resources of its home star system had been ruthlessly wiped out. The first assumption had been that the species in question had done it to itself in some sort of mad spasm of suicidal fury. Indeed, some of the scientists who'd studied the evidence continued to maintain that that was the most likely explanation.

Those holdouts, however, were a distinct minority. Most of the human race had finally accepted the second, and far more horrifying, hypothesis. They hadn't done it to themselves; someone else had done it to them.

Fofão didn't know who'd labeled the hypothetical killers the Gbaba, and he didn't much care. But the realization that they might exist was the reason there was a genuine and steadily growing Federation Navy these days. And the reason contingency plans like Spyglass and Watchman had been put into place.

And the reason TFNS *Swiftsure* found herself between Crestwell's World and the incoming, still totally silent fleet of red icons.

There was no way in the universe a single heavy cruiser could hope to stop, or slow down, or even inconvenience a fleet the size of the one headed for Fofão's ship. Nor was it likely he could have stayed away from hostile warships capable of the acceleration rate the unknowns had already demonstrated, but even if he could have, that wasn't *Swiftsure*'s job.

Even at their massive acceleration rate, it would take the bogies almost four hours to reach Crestwell's World, assuming they wanted to rendezvous with it. If all they wanted to do was overfly the planet, they could do it in less than three. But whatever their intention, it was *Swiftsure*'s job to stand her ground. To do her damnedest, up to the very last instant, to open some sort of peaceful communication with the unknowns. To serve as a fragile shield and tripwire which might just possibly, however remote the possibility might be, deter an attack on the newly settled planet behind her.

And, almost certainly, to become the first casualty in the war the Federation had dreaded for almost a decade.

▼   ▼   ▼

"Sir, we're picking up additional drive signatures," Lieutenant Henderson announced. "They look like fighters." Her voice was crisp, professionally clipped. "Tracking makes it roughly four hundred."

"Acknowledged. Still no response to our transmissions, Communications?"

"None, Sir," the com officer replied tautly.

"Tactical, begin deploying missiles."

"Aye, aye, Sir," Henderson said. "Deploying missiles now."

Big, long-ranged missiles detached from the external ordnance rings, while others went gliding out of the cruiser's midships missile hatches. They spread out in a cloud about *Swiftsure* on their secondary stationkeeping drives, far enough out to put the ship and their fellow missiles safely outside the threat perimeter of their preposterously powerful primary drives.

Looks like they want to englobe the planet, he thought, watching the bogies' formation continue to spread while his ship's unceasing communication attempts beamed towards them. *That doesn't look especially peaceful-minded of them.*

He glanced at the master plot's range numbers. The intruders had been inbound for almost a hundred and sixteen minutes now. Their velocity relative to Crestwell's World was up to just over thirty-one thousand kilometers per second, and unless they reversed acceleration in the next few seconds they were going to overfly the planet after all.

I wonder—

"Missile launch!" Gabriela Henderson announced suddenly. "Repeat, missile launch! Many missiles inbound!"

Mateus Fofão's heart seemed to stop.

They can't possibly expect to actually hit an evading starship at that range. That was his first thought as the thousands of incoming missile icons suddenly speckled his plot. *But they can sure as hell hit a* planet, *can't they?* his brain told him an instant later.

He stared at that hurricane of missiles, and knew what was going to happen. *Swiftsure*'s defenses could never have stopped more than a tithe of that torrent of destruction, and a frozen corner of his mind wondered what they were armed with. Fusion warheads? Antimatter? Chemical or biological agents? Or perhaps they were simply kinetic weapons. With the prodigious acceleration they were showing, they'd have more than enough velocity to do the job with no warheads at all.

"Communications," he heard his voice say flatly as he watched the executioners of Crestwell's World's half-million inhabitants accelerating towards him, "secure communication attempts. Maneuvering, bring us to maximum power, heading zero-zero-zero, zero-zero-five. Tactical"—he turned his head and met Lieutenant Henderson's eyes levelly—"prepare to engage the enemy."

FEBRUARY 14, 2421
TFNS EXCALIBUR, TFNS GULLIVER
TASK FORCE ONE

The scout ship was too small to be a threat to anyone.

The tiny starship was less than three percent the size of TFNS *Excalibur*, the task force's dreadnought flagship. True, it was faster than *Excalibur*, and its weapons systems and electronics were somewhat more advanced, but it could not have come within a light-minute of the task force and lived.

Unfortunately, it didn't have to.

▼   ▼   ▼

"It's confirmed, Sir." Captain Somerset's mahogany-skinned face was grim on Admiral Pei Kau-zhi's flag bridge com screen. *Excalibur*'s commander had aged since the task force set out, Admiral Pei thought. Of course, he was hardly alone in that.

"How far out, Martin?" the admiral asked flatly.

"Just over two-point-six light-minutes," Somerset replied, his expression grimmer than ever. "It's too close, Admiral."

"Maybe not," Pei said, then smiled thinly at his flag captain. "And whatever the range, we're stuck with it, aren't we?"

"Sir, I could send the screen out, try and push him further back. I could even detach a destroyer squadron to sit on him, drive him completely out of sensor range of the fleet."

"We don't know how close behind him something heavier may be." Pei shook his head. "Besides, we need them to see us sooner or later, don't we?"

"Admiral," Somerset began, "I don't think we can afford to take the chance that—"

"We can't afford *not* to take the chance," Pei said firmly. "Go ahead and push the screen out in his direction. See if you can get him to move at least a little further out. But either way, we execute Breakaway in the next half-hour."

Somerset looked at him out of the com screen for another moment, then nodded heavily.

"Very well, Sir. I'll pass the orders."

"Thank you, Martin," Pei said in a much softer voice, and cut the circuit.

"The Captain may have a point, Sir," a quiet contralto said from behind him, and he turned his bridge chair to face the speaker.

Lieutenant Commander Nimue Alban was a very junior officer indeed, especially for an antigerone society, to be suggesting to a four-star admiral, however respectfully, that his judgment might be less than infallible. Pei Kau-zhi felt absolutely no temptation to point that out to her, however. First, because despite her youth she was one of the more brilliant tactical officers the Terran Federation Navy had ever produced. Second, because if anyone had earned the right to second-guess Admiral Pei, it was Lieutenant Commander Alban.

"He *does* have a point," Pei conceded. "A very good one, in fact. But I've got a feeling the bad news isn't very far behind this particular raven."

"A *feeling*, Sir?"

Alban's combination of dark hair and blue eyes were the gift of her Welsh father, but her height and fair complexion had come from her Swedish mother. Admiral Pei, on the other hand, was a small, wiry man, over three times her age, and she seemed to tower over him as she raised one eyebrow. Still, he was pleased to note, in a bittersweet sort of way, it wasn't an incredulous expression.

After all, he told himself, *my penchant for "playing a hunch" has a lot to do with the fact that I'm the last full admiral the Terran Federation will ever have.*

"It's not some arcane form of ESP in this case, Nimue," he said. "But where's the other scout? You know Gbaba scout ships always operate in pairs, and Captain Somerset's reported only one of them. The other fellow has to be somewhere."

"Like calling up the rest of the pack," Alban said, her blue eyes dark, and he nodded.

"That's exactly what he's doing. They must have gotten at least a sniff of us before we picked them up, and one of them turned and headed back for help immediately. This one's going to hang on our heels, keep track of us and home the rest in, but the one thing he *isn't* going to do is come in close enough to risk letting us get a good shot at him. He can't afford to let us pick him off and then drop out of hyper. They might never find us again."

"I see where you're going, Sir." Alban looked thoughtful for a moment, her blue eyes intent on something only she could see, then returned her attention to the admiral.

"Sir," she asked quietly, "would I be out of line if I used one of the priority com circuits to contact *Gulliver*? I'd . . . like to tell the Commodore goodbye."

"Of course you wouldn't be," Pei replied, equally quietly. "And when you do, tell him I'll be thinking about him."

"Sir, you could tell him yourself."

"No." Pei shook his head. "Kau-yung and I have already said our goodbyes, Nimue."

"Yes, Sir."

▼   ▼   ▼

The word spread quickly from *Excalibur* as the Tenth Destroyer Squadron headed for the Gbaba scout, and a cold, ugly wave of fear came with the news. Not panic, perhaps, because every single member of the murdered Federation's final fleet had known in his heart of hearts that this moment would come. Indeed, they'd planned for it. But that made no one immune from fear when it actually came.

More than one of the officers and ratings watching the destroyers' icons sweep across the tactical displays towards the scout ship prayed silently that they would overtake the fleet little ship, destroy it. They knew how unlikely that was to happen, and even if it did, it would probably buy them no more than a few more weeks, possibly a few months. But that didn't keep them from praying.

Aboard the heavy cruiser TFNS *Gulliver*, a small, wiry commodore said a prayer of his own. Not for the destruction of the scout ship. Not even for his older brother, who was about to die. But for a young lieutenant commander who had become almost a daughter to him . . . and who had volunteered to transfer to *Excalibur* knowing the ship could not survive.

"Commodore Pei, you have a com request from the Flag," his communications officer said quietly. "It's Nimue, Sir."

"Thank you, Oscar," Pei Kau-yung said. "Put her through to my display here."

"Yes, Sir."

"Nimue," Pei said as the familiar oval face with the sapphire blue eyes appeared on his display.

"Commodore," she replied. "I'm sure you've heard by now."

"Indeed. We're preparing to execute Breakaway even now."

"I knew you would be. Your brother—the admiral—asked me to tell you he'll be thinking about you. So will I. And I know you'll be thinking about us, too, Sir. That's why I wanted to take this chance to tell you." She looked directly into his eyes. "It's been an honor and a privilege to serve under you, Sir. I regret nothing which has ever happened since you selected me for your staff."

"That . . . means a great deal to me, Nimue," Pei said very softly. Like his brother, he was a traditionalist, and it was not the way of his culture to be emotionally demonstrative, but he knew she saw the pain in his eyes. "And may I also say," he added, "that I am deeply grateful for all the many services you have performed."

It sounded horribly stilted to his own ear, but it was the closest either of them dared come over a public com circuit, especially since all message traffic was automatically recorded. And, stilted or no, she understood what he meant, just as completely as he'd understood her.

"I'm glad, Sir," she said. "And please, tell Shan-wei goodbye for me. Give her my love."

"Of course. And you already know you have hers," Pei said. And then, whatever his culture might have demanded, he cleared his throat hard, harshly. "And mine," he said huskily.

"That means a lot, Sir." Alban smiled almost gently at him. "Goodbye, Commodore. God bless."

▼　　▼　　▼

The destroyers did succeed in pushing the scout ship back. Not as far as they would have liked, but far enough to give Admiral Pei a distinct feeling of relief.

"General signal to all units," he said, never looking away from the master tactical display. "Pass the order to execute Breakaway."

"Aye, aye, Sir!" the senior flag bridge com rating replied, and a moment later, the light codes on Pei's display flickered suddenly.

Only for an instant, and only because his sensors were watching them so closely.

Or, he thought wryly, *that's the theory, anyway*.

Forty-six huge starships killed their hyper drives and disappeared as they dropped instantly sublight. But in the very same instant that they did, forty-six *other* starships, which had been carefully hidden away in stealth, appeared just as quickly. It was a precisely coordinated maneuver which Pei's command had practiced over and over again in the simulators, and more than a dozen times in actual space, and they performed it this one last time flawlessly. The forty-six newcomers slid quickly and smoothly into the holes which had abruptly appeared in the formation, and their drives' emissions signatures were almost perfect matches for those of the ships which had disappeared.

That's going to be a nasty surprise for the Gbaba, Pei told himself coldly. *And one of these days, it's going to lead to an even bigger and nastier surprise for them*.

"You know," he said, turning away from the display to face Lieutenant Commander Alban and Captain Joseph Thiessen, his chief of staff, "we came *so* close to kicking these people's asses. Another fifty years—seventy-five at the outside— and we could have taken them, 'star-spanning empire' or no."

"I think that's probably a little over-optimistic, Sir," Thiessen replied after a moment. "We never did find out how big their empire actually is, you know."

"It wouldn't have mattered." Pei shook his head sharply. "We're in a virtual dead heat with them technologically right now, Joe. Right now. And how old are their ships?"

"Some of them are brand new, Sir," Nimue Alban replied for the chief of staff. "But I take your point," she continued, and even Thiessen nodded almost unwillingly.

Pei didn't press the argument. There was no reason to, not now. Although, in some ways, it would have been an enormous relief to tell someone besides Nimue what was really about to happen. But he couldn't do that to Thiessen. The chief of staff was a good man, one who believed absolutely in the underlying premises of Operation Ark. Like every other man and woman under Pei's command, he was about to give his life to ensure that Operation Ark succeeded, and the admiral couldn't tell him that his own commanding officer was part of a plot against the people charged with making that success happen.

"Do you think we gave them enough of a shock that they may start actively innovating, Sir?" Thiessen asked after a moment. Pei looked at him and raised one eyebrow, and the chief of staff shrugged with a crooked smile. "I'd like to think we at least made the bastards sweat, Sir!"

"Oh, I think you can safely assume we did that," Pei replied with a humorless smile of his own. "As to whether or not it will change them, I really don't know. The xenologists' best guess is that it won't. They've got a system and culture which have worked for them for at least eight or nine thousand years. We may have been a bigger bump in the road than they're accustomed to, but the formula worked in our case, too, in the end. They'll probably be a little nervous for a century or three, if only because they'll wonder if we got another colony away somewhere without their noticing, but then they'll settle back down."

"Until the next poor dumb suckers come stumbling into them," Thiessen said bitterly.

"Until then," Pei agreed quietly, and turned back to the display.

Eight or nine thousand years, he thought. *That's the xenologists' best guess, but I'll bet it's actually been longer than that. God, I wonder how long ago the first Gbaba discovered fire!*

It was a question he'd pondered more than once over the four decades it had taken the Gbaba Empire to destroy the human race, for two things the Gbaba definitely were not were innovative or flexible.

At first, the Gbaba had clearly underestimated the challenge mankind posed. Their first few fleets had only outnumbered their intended victims three- or four-to-one, and it had become quickly and painfully obvious that they couldn't match humanity's tactical flexibility. The first genocidal attack had punched inward past Crestwell to take out three of the Federation's fourteen major extra-Solar star systems, with one hundred percent civilian casualties. But then the Federation Navy had rallied and stopped them cold. The fleet had even counterattacked, and captured no less than six Gbaba star systems.

Which was when the *full* Gbaba fleet mobilized.

Commander Pei Kau-zhi had been a fire control officer aboard one of the Federation's ships-of-the-line in the Starfall System when the real Gbaba Navy appeared. He could still remember the displays, see the endless waves of scarlet icons, each representing a Gbaba capital ship, as they materialized out of hyper like curses. It had been like driving a ground car into crimson snowflakes, except that no snow had ever sent such an ice-cold shudder through the marrow of his bones.

He still didn't know how Admiral Thomas had gotten any of her fleet out. Most of Thomas' ships had died with her, covering the flight of a handful of survivors whose duty had been not to stand and share her death, but to live with the dreadful news. To flee frantically homeward, arriving on the very wings of the storm to warn mankind Apocalypse was coming.

Not that humanity had been taken totally unawares.

The severity of the opening Gbaba attack, even if it had been thrown back, had been a brutal wakeup call. Every Federation world had begun arming and fortifying when the first evidence of the Gbaba's existence had appeared, ten years before Crestwell. *After* Crestwell, those preparations had been pressed at a frenetic pace, and a star system made an awesome fortress. The surviving fleet elements had fallen back on the fixed defenses, standing and fighting to the death in defense of humanity's worlds, and they'd made the Gbaba pay a hideous price in dead and broken starships.

But the Gbaba had chosen to pay it. Not even the xenologists had been able to come up with a satisfactory explanation for why the Gbaba flatly refused to even consider negotiations. They—or their translating computers, at any rate—obviously comprehended Standard English, since they'd clearly used captured data and documents, and the handful of broken, scarred human prisoners who'd been recovered from them had been "interrogated" with a casual, dispassionate brutality that was horrifying. So humanity had known communication with them was at least possible, yet they'd never responded to a single official communication attempt, except to press their attacks harder.

Personally, Pei wondered if they were actually still capable of a reasoned response at all. Some of the ships the Federation had captured or knocked out and been able to examine had been ancient almost beyond belief. At least one, according to the scientists who'd analyzed it, had been built at least two millennia before its capture, yet there was no indication of any significant technological advance between the time of its construction and its final battle. Ships which, as Alban had suggested, were brand-new construction had mounted identical weapons, computers, hyper drives, and sensor suites.

That suggested a degree of cultural stagnation which even Pei's ancestral China, at its most conservative rejection of the outside world, had never approached. One which made even ancient Egypt seem like a hotbed of innovation. It was impossible for Pei to conceive of any sentient beings who could go that long without any major advances. So perhaps the Gbaba no longer *were* sentient in the human sense of the term. Perhaps everything—all of this—was simply the result of a set of cultural imperatives so deeply ingrained they'd become literally instinctual.

None of which had saved the human race from destruction.

It had taken time, of course. The Gbaba had been forced to reduce humanity's redoubts one by one, in massive sieges which had taken literally years to conclude. The Federation Navy had been rebuilt behind the protection of the system fortifications, manned by new officers and ratings—many of whom, like Nimue Alban, had never known a life in which humanity's back was not against the wall. That navy had struck back in desperate sallies and sorties which had cost the Gbaba dearly, but the final outcome had been inevitable.

The Federation Assembly had tried sending out colony fleets, seeking to build hidden refuges where some remnants of humanity might ride out the tempest. But however inflexible or unimaginative the Gbaba might be, they'd obviously encountered that particular trick before, for they'd englobed each of the Federation's remaining star systems with scout ships. Escorting Navy task forces might attain a crushing local superiority, fight a way through the scouts and the thinner shell of capital ships backing them up, but the scouts always seemed able to maintain contact, or regain it quickly, and every effort to run the blockade had been hunted down.

One colony fleet *had* slipped through the scouts . . . but only to transmit a last, despairing hypercom message less than ten years later. It might have eluded the immediate shell of scout ships, but others had been sent out after it. It must have taken literally thousands of them to scour all of the possible destinations that colony fleet might have chosen, but eventually one of them had stumbled across it, and the killer fleets had followed. The colony administrator's best guess was that the colony's own emissions had led the Gbaba to them, despite all of the colonists' efforts to limit those emissions.

Pei suspected that long-dead administrator had been right. That, at any rate, was an underlying assumption of Operation Ark's planners.

"At least we managed to push their damned scout ship far enough back to give Breakaway a fighting chance of working," Thiessen observed.

Pei nodded. The comment came under the heading of "blindingly obvious," but he wasn't about to fault anyone for that at a moment like this.

Besides, Joe probably meant it as a compliment, he thought with something very like a mental chuckle. After all, Breakaway had been Pei's personal brainchild, the sleight-of-hand intended to convince the Gbaba they'd successfully tracked down and totally destroyed mankind's last desperate colonization attempt. That was why the forty-six dreadnoughts and carriers which had accompanied the rest of his task force in stealth had not fired a missile or launched a fighter during the fight to break through the shell of capital ships covering the Gbaba scout globe around the Sol System.

It had been a stiff engagement, although its outcome had never been in doubt. But by hiding under stealth, aided by the background emissions of heavy weapons fire and the dueling electronic warfare systems of the opposing forces, they had hopefully remained undetected and unsuspected by the Gbaba.

The sacrifice of two full destroyer squadrons who'd dropped behind to pick off the only scout ships close enough to actually hold the escaping colony fleet on sensors had allowed Pei to break free and run, and deep inside, he'd hoped they'd manage to stay away from the Gbaba scouts. That despite all odds, *all* of his fleet might yet survive. But whatever he'd hoped, he'd never really expected it, and that was why those ships had *stayed* in stealth until this moment.

When the Gbaba navy arrived—and it would; for all of their age, Gbaba ships were still faster than human vessels—it would find exactly the same number of ships its scouts had reported fleeing Sol. Exactly the same number of ships its scouts had reported when they finally made contact with the fugitives once again.

And when every one of those ships was destroyed, when every one of the humans crewing them had been killed, the Gbaba would assume they'd destroyed *all* of those fugitives.

But they'll be wrong, Pei Kau-zhi told himself softly, coldly. *And one of these days, despite everything people like Langhorne and Bédard can do to stop it, we'll be back. And then, you bastards, you'll—*

"Admiral," Nimue Alban said quietly, "long-range sensors have picked up incoming hostiles."

He turned and looked at her, and she met his eyes levelly.

"We have two positive contacts, Sir," she told him. "CIC makes the first one approximately one thousand point sources. The second one is larger."

"Well," he observed almost whimsically. "At least they cared enough to send the very best, didn't they?"

He looked at Thiessen.

"Send the Fleet to Action Stations, if you please," he said. "Launch fighters and began prepositioning missiles for launch."

SEPTEMBER 7, 2499
LAKE PEI ENCLAVE,
CONTINENT OF HAVEN,
SAFEHOLD

"Grandfather! Grandfather, come quickly! It's an angel!"

Timothy Harrison looked up as his great-grandson thundered unceremoniously through the open door of his town hall office. The boy's behavior was atrocious, of course, but it was never easy to be angry with Matthew, and no one Timothy knew could *stay* angry with him. Which meant, boys being boys, that young Matthew routinely got away with things which ought to have earned a beating, at the very least.

In this case, however, he might be excused for his excitement, Timothy supposed. Not that he was prepared to admit it.

"Matthew Paul Harrison," he said sternly, "this is my *office*, not the shower house down at the baseball field! At least a modicum of proper behavior is expected out of anyone here—even, or *especially*, out of a young hooligan like you!"

"I'm sorry," the boy replied, hanging his head. But he simultaneously peeped up through his eyelashes, and the dimples of the devastating smile which was going to get him into all sorts of trouble in another few years danced at the corners of his mouth.

"Well," Timothy harumpfed, "I suppose we can let it go without harping upon it . . . *this* time."

He had the satisfaction of noting what was probably a genuine quiver of trepidation at the qualifier, but then he leaned back in his chair.

"Now, what's this you were saying about an angel?"

"The signal light," Matthew said eagerly, eyes lighting with bright excitement as he recalled his original reason for intruding upon his grandfather. "The signal light just began shining! Father Michael said I should run and tell you about it immediately. There's an *angel* coming, Grandfather!"

"And what color was the signal light?" Timothy asked. His voice was so completely calm that, without his realizing it, it raised him tremendously in his great-grandson's already high esteem.

"Yellow," Matthew replied, and Timothy nodded. One of the lesser angels, then. He felt a quick little stab of regret, for which he scolded himself instantly. It might be more exciting to hope to entertain a visit from one of the Archangels themselves, but mortal men did well not to place commands upon God, even indirectly.

Besides, even a "lesser" angel will be more than enough excitement for you, *old man!* he told himself scoldingly.

"Well," he said, nodding to his great-grandson, "if an angel's coming to Lakeview, then we must make our preparations to receive him. Go down to the docks, Matthew. Find Jason, and tell him to raise the signal for all the fishing boats to return to harbor. As soon as you've done that, go home and tell your mother and grandmother. I'm sure Father Michael will be ringing the bell shortly, but you might as well go ahead and warn them."

"Yes, Grandfather!" Matthew nodded eagerly, then turned and sped back the way he'd come. Timothy watched him go, smiling for a moment, then squared his shoulders and walked out of his office.

Most of the town hall staff had paused in whatever they were doing. They were looking in his direction, and he smiled again, whimsically.

"I see you all heard Matthew's announcement," he said dryly. "That being the case, I see no need to expand upon it further at this time. Finish whatever you were doing, file your work, and then hurry home to prepare yourselves."

People nodded. Here and there, chairs scraped across the plank floor as clerks who'd already anticipated his instructions hurried to tuck files into the appropriate cabinets. Others bent over their desks, quill pens flying as they worked towards a reasonable stopping point. Timothy watched them for a few seconds, then continued out the town hall's front door.

The town hall stood upon a hill at the center of the town of Lakeview. Lakeview was growing steadily, and Timothy was aware that it wouldn't be long before it slipped over that elusive line dividing "town" from "small city." He wasn't certain how he felt about that, for a lot of reasons. But however *he* might feel about it, there was no doubt how God and the angels felt, and that made any purely personal reservations on his part meaningless.

Word was spreading, he saw. People were hurrying along the cobblestone streets and sidewalks, heads bent in excited conversation with companions, or simply smiling hugely. The signal light on the steeple of Father Michael's church was deliberately placed to be visible by as much of the town as possible, and Timothy could see its bright amber glow from where he stood, despite the brightness of the summer sun.

The bell in the church's high bell tower began to ring. Its deep, rolling voice sang through the summer air, crying out the joyous news for any who had not seen the signal light, and Timothy nodded around a bright, lilting bubble of happiness. Then he began walking towards the church himself, nodding calmly to the people he passed. He was, after all, Lakeview's mayor, which gave him a certain responsibility. More to the point, he was one of Lakeview's slowly but steadily declining number of Adams, just as his wife Sarah was one of the town's Eves. That left both of them with a special duty to maintain the proper air of dignified respect, adoration, and awe due one of the immortal servants of the God who had breathed the very breath of life into their nostrils.

He reached the church, and Father Michael was waiting for him. The priest was actually younger than Timothy, but he looked much older. Michael had been one of the very first of the children brought forth here upon Safehold in response to God's command to be fruitful and multiply. Timothy himself had not been "born" at all, of course. God had created his immortal soul with His Own hand, and the Archangel Langhorne and his assistant, the Archangel Shan-wei, had created Timothy's physical body according to God's plan.

Timothy had Awakened right here, in Lakeview, standing with the other Adams and Eves in the town square, and the mere memory of that first glorious morning—that first sight of Safehold's magnificent blue heavens and the brilliant light of Kau-zhi as it broke the eastern horizon like a dripping orb of molten copper, of the towering green trees, the fields already tilled and rich with the waiting harvest, the dark blue waters of Lake Pei, and the fishing boats tied up and waiting at the docks—still filled his soul with reverential awe. It was the first time he'd ever laid eyes upon his Sarah, for that matter, and that had been a miracle all its own.

But that had been almost sixty-five years ago. Had he been as other men, men born of the union of man and woman, his body would have begun failing long since. Indeed, although he was four years older than Father Michael, the priest was stoop-shouldered and silver-haired, his fingers beginning to gnarl with age, while Timothy's hair remained dark and thick, untouched by white, although there *were* a few strands of silver threading their way into his beard here and there.

Timothy remembered when Father Michael had been a red-faced, wailing babe in his mother's arms. Timothy himself had already been a man full grown— a man in the prime of early manhood, as all Adams had been at the Awakening. And being what he was, the direct work of divine hands, it was to be expected that his life would be longer than the lives of those further removed from the direct touch of the godhead. But if Michael resented that in any way, Timothy had never seen a single sign of it. The priest was a humble man, ever mindful that to be permitted his priestly office was a direct and tangible sign of God's grace, that grace of which no man could ever truly be worthy. Which did not absolve him from *attempting* to be.

"Rejoice, Timothy!" the priest said now, eyes glowing under his thick white eyebrows.

"Rejoice, Father," Timothy responded, and went down on one knee briefly for Michael to lay a hand upon his head in blessing.

"May Langhorne bless and keep you always in God's ways and laws until the Day Awaited comes to us all," Michael murmured rapidly, then tapped Timothy lightly on the shoulder.

"Now get up!" he commanded. "You're the Adam here, Timothy. Tell me I shouldn't feel this nervous!"

"You shouldn't feel this nervous," Timothy said obediently, rising to put one arm around his old friend's shoulders. "Truly," he added in a more serious tone, "you've done well, Michael. Your flock's been well tended since the last Visitation, and it's increased steadily."

"*Our* flock, you mean," Father Michael replied.

Timothy started to shake his head, then suppressed the gesture. It was kind of Michael to put it that way, but both of them knew that however conscientiously Timothy had sought to discharge his responsibilities as the administrator of Lakeview and the surrounding farms, all of his authority ultimately stemmed from the Archangels, and through them, from God Himself. Which meant that here in Lakeview, the ultimate authority in any matter, spiritual or worldly, lay with Father Michael, as the representative of Mother Church.

But it's like him to put it that way, isn't it? Timothy thought with a smile.

"Come," he said aloud. "From the pattern of the signal light, it won't be long now. We have preparations to make."

▼   ▼   ▼

By the time the glowing nimbus of the *kyousei hi* appeared far out over the blue waters of Lake Pei, all was ready.

The entire population of Lakeview, aside from a few fishermen who'd been too far out on the enormous lake to see the signal to return, was assembled in and around the town square. The families from several of the nearer farms had arrived, as well, and Lakeview's square was no longer remotely large enough to contain them all. They overflowed its bounds, filling the approach streets solidly, and Timothy Harrison felt a deep, satisfying surge of joy at the evidence that he and his fellow Adams and Eves had, indeed, been fruitful and multiplied.

The *kyousei hi* sped nearer, faster than the fastest horse could gallop, faster than the fastest slash lizard could charge. The globe of light grew brighter and brighter as it swept closer to the town. At first it was only a brilliant speck, far out over the lake. Then it grew larger, brighter. It became a star, fallen from the vault of God's own heaven. Then brighter still, a second sun, smaller than Kau-zhi, but brilliant enough to challenge even its blinding brightness. And then, as it flashed across the last few miles, swift as any stooping wyvern, its brilliance totally surpassed that of any mere sun. It blazed above the town, without heat and yet far too bright for any eye to bear, etching shadows with knife-edged sharpness, despite the noonday sun.

Timothy, like every other man and woman, bent his head, shielding his eyes against that blinding glory. And then the brilliance decreased, as rapidly as it had come, and he raised his head slowly.

The *kyousei hi* was still above Lakeview, but it had risen so high into the heavens that it was once more little brighter than Kau-zhi. Still far too brilliant to look upon, yet far enough removed that merely mortal flesh could endure its presence. But if the *kyousei hi* had withdrawn, the being whose chariot it was had not.

All across the town square, people went to their knees in reverence and awe, and Timothy did the same. His heart sang with joy as he beheld the angel standing on the raised platform at the very center of the square. That platform was reserved solely and only for moments like this. No mortal human foot could be permitted to profane its surface, other than those of the consecrated priesthood responsible for ritually cleansing it and maintaining it in permanent readiness for moments like this.

Timothy recognized the angel. It had been almost two years since the last Visitation, and the angel hadn't changed since his last appearance in Lakeview. He did have the appearance of having aged—slightly, at least—since the first time Timothy had ever seen him, immediately after the Awakening. But then, the *Writ* said that although the angels and Archangels were immortal, the bodies they had been given to teach and guide God's people were made of the same stuff as the mortal world. Animated by the *surgoi kasai*, the "great fire" of God's Own touch, those bodies would endure longer than any mortal body, just as the bodies of Adams and Eves would endure longer than those of their descendants, but they *would* age. Indeed, the day would ultimately come when all of the angels—even the Archangels themselves—would be recalled to God's presence. Timothy knew God Himself had ordained that, yet he was deeply grateful that he himself would have closed his eyes in death before that day arrived. A world no longer inhabited by angels would seem dark, shadowed and drab, to one who'd seen God's Own messengers face-to-face in the glory of that world's very first days.

In many ways, the angel looked little different from a mortal. He was no taller than Timothy himself, his shoulders no broader. Yet he was garbed from head to foot in brilliant, light-shimmering raiment, a marvelous garment of perpetually shifting and flowing colors, and his head was crowned by a crackling blue fire. At his waist, he bore his staff, the rod of imperishable crystal half as long as a man's forearm. Timothy had seen that rod used. Only once, but its lightning bolt had smitten the charging slash lizard to the earth in a single cataclysmic thunderclap of sound. Half the slash lizard's body had been literally burned away, and Timothy's ears had rung for hours afterwards.

The angel looked out across the reverently kneeling crowd for several seconds in silence. Then he raised his right hand.

"Peace be with you, My Children," he said, his voice impossibly clear and loud, yet not shouting, not raised. "I bring you God's blessings, and the blessing of the Archangel Langhorne, who is His servant. Glory be to God!"

"And to His servants," the response rumbled back, and the angel smiled.

"God is pleased with you, My Children," he told them. "And now, go about your business, all of you, rejoicing in the Lord. I bring tidings to Father Michael and Mayor Timothy. After I have spoken with them, they will tell you what God desires of you."

Timothy and Michael stood side by side, watching as the crowded square and surrounding streets emptied, quickly and yet without hurrying or pushing. Some of the farmers from outside town had ridden hard—or, in some cases, literally run for miles—to be here for the moment of the angel's arrival. Yet there was no resentment, no disappointment, in being sent about their business once again so quickly. It had been their joyous duty to welcome God's messenger, and they knew they had been blessed beyond the deserts of any fallible, sinful mortal to have beheld the angel with their own eyes.

The angel descended from the consecrated platform and crossed to Timothy and Michael. They went to one knee again before him, and he shook his head.

"No, My Sons," he said gently. "There will be time enough for that. For now, we must speak. God and the Archangel Langhorne are pleased with you, pleased with the way in which Lakeview has grown and prospered. But you may be called to face new challenges, and the Archangel Langhorne has charged me to strengthen your spirits for the tasks to which you may be summoned. Come, let us go into the church, that we may speak in the proper setting."

▼   ▼   ▼

Pei Kau-yung sat in the comfortable chair, his face an expressionless mask, as he listened to the debate.

The G6 sun they had named Kau-zhi in honor of his brother shone down outside. It was just past local noon, and the northern summer was hot, but a cool breeze off Lake Pei blew in through the open windows, and he grimaced mentally as it breathed gently across him.

The bastards couldn't heap enough "honors" on us, could they? Named the local sun after Kau-zhi. The lake after him, too, I suppose—or maybe they meant to name it after both of us. Maybe even Shan-wei, at the time. But that's as far as they're going to go. I wonder if Mission Control picked Langhorne and Bédard because the planners knew they were megalomaniacs?

He tried to tell himself that that was only because of the weariness almost sixty standard years—almost sixty-five *local* years—of watching the two of them in operation had made inevitable. Unfortunately, he couldn't quite shake the thought that the people who'd selected Eric Langhorne as the colony's chief administrator and Dr. Adorée Bédard as its chief psychologist had known exactly what they were doing. After all, the survival of the human race—at any cost—was far more important than any minor abridgments of basic human rights.

"—and we implore you, once again," the slender, silver-haired woman standing in the center of the breezy hearing room said, "to consider how vital it is that as the human culture on this planet grows and matures, it *remembers* the Gbaba.

That it understands *why* we came here, why we renounced advanced technology."

Kau-yung regarded her with stony brown eyes. She didn't even look in his direction, and he felt one or two of the Councillors glancing at him with what they fondly imagined was hidden sympathy. Or, in some cases, concealed amusement.

"We've heard all of these arguments before, Dr. Pei," Eric Langhorne said. "We understand the point you're raising. But I'm afraid that nothing you've said is likely to change our established policy."

"Administrator," Pei Shan-wei said, "your 'established policy' overlooks the fact that mankind has always been a toolmaker and a problem solver. Eventually, those qualities are going to surface here on Safehold. When they do, without an institutional memory of what happened to the Federation, our descendants aren't going to know about the dangers waiting for them out there."

"That particular concern is based on a faulty understanding of the societal matrix we're creating here, Dr. Pei," Adorée Bédard said. "I assure you, with the safeguards we've put in place, the inhabitants of Safehold will be safely insulated against the sort of technological advancement which might attract the Gbaba's attention. Unless, of course"—the psychiatrist's eyes narrowed—"there's some outside stimulus to violate the parameters of our matrix."

"I don't doubt that you can—that you have already—created an anti-technology mind-set on an individual and a societal level," Shan-wei replied. Her own voice was level, but it didn't take someone with Bédard's psychological training to hear the distaste and personal antipathy under its surface. "I simply believe that whatever you can accomplish right now, whatever curbs and safeguards you can impose at this moment, five hundred years from now, or a thousand, there's going to come a moment when those safeguards fail."

"They won't," Bédard said flatly. Then she made herself sit back a bit from the table and smile. "I realize psychology isn't your field, Doctor. And I also realize one of your doctorates is in history. Because it is, you're quite rightly aware of the frenetic pace at which technology has advanced in the modern era. Certainly, on the basis of humanity's history on Old Earth, especially during the last five or six centuries, it would appear the 'innovation bug' is hardwired into the human psyche. It isn't, however. There are examples from our own history of lengthy, very static periods. In particular, I draw your attention to the thousands of years of the Egyptian empire, during which significant innovation basically didn't happen. What we've done here, on Safehold, is to re-create that same basic mind-set, and we've also installed certain . . . institutional and physical checks to maintain that mind-set."

"The degree to which the Egyptians—and the rest of the Mediterranean cultures—were anti-innovation has been considerably overstated," Shan-wei said coolly. "Moreover, Egypt was only a tiny segment of the total world population of its day, and other parts of that total population most definitely were innovative. And despite the effort to impose a permanent theocratic curb on—"

"Dr. Pei," Langhorne interrupted, "I'm afraid this entire discussion is pointless. The colony's policy has been thoroughly debated and approved by the Administrative Council. It represents the consensus of that Council, and also that of myself, as Chief Administrator, and Dr. Bédard, as Chief Psychologist. It will be adhered to . . . by everyone. Is that clear?"

It must have been hard for Shan-wei not to even look in his direction, Kau-yung thought. But she didn't. For fifty-seven years the two of them had lived apart, divided by their bitter public disagreement over the colony's future. Kau-yung was one of the Moderates—the group that might not agree with everything Langhorne and Bédard had done, but which fervently supported the ban on anything which might lead to the reemergence of advanced technology. Kau-yung himself had occasionally voiced concern over the *degree* to which Bédard had adjusted the originally proposed psych templates for the colonists, but he'd always supported Langhorne's basic reasons for modifying them. Which was why he remained the colony's senior military officer despite his estranged wife's position as the leader of the faction whose opponents had labeled them "Techies."

"With all due respect, Administrator Langhorne," Shan-wei said, "I don't believe your policy does represent a true consensus. I was a member of the Council myself, if you will recall, as were six of my colleagues on the present Alexandria Board. All of us opposed your policy when you first proposed it."

Which, Kau-yung thought, *split the vote eight-to-seven, two short of the supermajority you needed under the colonial charter to modify the templates, didn't it, Eric? Of course, you'd already gone ahead and done it, which left you with a teeny-tiny problem. That's why Shan-wei and the others found themselves arbitrarily* removed *from the Council, wasn't it?*

"That's true," Langhorne said coldly. "However, none of you are current members of the Council, and the present Council membership unanimously endorses this policy. And whatever other ancient history you might wish to bring up, I repeat that the policy *will* stand, and it *will* be enforced throughout the entire colony. Which includes your so-called Alexandria Enclave."

"And if we choose not to abide by it?" Shan-wei's voice was soft, but spines stiffened throughout the hearing room. Despite the decades of increasingly acrimonious debate, it was the first time any of the Techies had publicly suggested the possibility of active resistance.

"That would be . . . unwise of you," Langhorne said after a moment, glancing sidelong at Kau-yung. "To date, this has been simply a matter of public debate of policy issues. Now that the policy has been set, however, active noncompliance becomes treason. And I warn you, Dr. Pei, that when the stakes are the survival or extinction of the human race, we're prepared to take whatever measures seem necessary to suppress treason."

"I see."

Pei Shan-wei's head turned as she slowly swept all of the seated Councillors with icy brown eyes so dark they were almost black. They looked even darker today, Kau-yung thought, and her expression was bleak.

"I'll report the outcome of this meeting to the rest of the Board, Administrator," she said finally, her voice an icicle. "I'll also inform them that we are required to comply with your 'official policy' under threat of physical coercion. I'm sure the Board will have a response for you as soon as possible."

She turned and walked out of the hearing room without a single backward glance.

▼   ▼   ▼

Pei Kau-yung sat in another chair, this one on a dock extending into the enormous, dark blue waters of Lake Pei. A fishing pole had been set into the holding bracket beside his chair, but there was no bait on the hook. It was simply a convenient prop to help keep people away.

We knew it could come to this, or something like it, he told himself. *Kau-zhi, Shan-wei, Nimue, me, Proctor—we all knew, from the moment Langhorne was chosen instead of Halversen. And now it has.*

There were times when, antigerone treatments or not, he felt every single day of his hundred and ninety standard years.

He tipped farther back in his chair, looking up through the darkening blue of approaching evening, and saw the slowly moving silver star of the orbiting starship—TFNS *Hamilcar,* the final surviving unit of the forty-six mammoth ships which had delivered the colony to Kau-zhi.

The gargantuan task of transporting millions of colonists to a new home world would have been impossible without the massive employment of advanced technologies. That had been a given, and yet it had almost certainly been the betraying emissions of that same technology which had led to the discovery and destruction of the only other colony fleet to break through the Gbaba blockade. So Operation Ark's planners had done two things differently.

First, Operation Ark's mission plan had required the colony fleet to remain in hyper for a minimum of ten years before even beginning to search for a new home world. That had carried it literally thousands of light-years from the Federation, far enough that it should take even the Gbaba scouting fleet centuries to sweep the thicket of stars in which it had lost itself.

Second, the colony had been provided with not one, but two complete terraforming fleets. One had been detached and assigned to the preparation of Safehold, while the other remained in close company with the transports, hiding far from Kau-zhi, as a backup. If the Gbaba had detected the ships actually laboring upon Safehold, they would undoubtedly have been destroyed, but their destruction would not have led the Gbaba to the rest of the fleet, which would then have voyaged onward for *another* ten years, on a totally random vector, before once more searching for a new home.

Hamilcar had been with that hidden fleet, the flagship of Operation Ark's civilian administration, and she'd been retained this long because the basic plan for Operation Ark had always envisioned a requirement for at least some technological presence until the colony was fully established. The enormous transport, half again the size of the Federation's largest dreadnought, was at minimal power levels, with every one of her multiply redundant stealth systems operating at all times. A Gbaba scout ship could have been in orbit with her without detecting her unless it closed to within two or three hundred kilometers.

Even so, and despite her enormous value as administrative center, orbiting observatory, and emergency industrial module, her time was running out. That was what had prompted the confrontation between Shan-wei and Langhorne and Bédard this afternoon. The Safehold colonial enclaves had been up and running for almost sixty standard years, and Langhorne and his Council had decided it was finally time to dispose of all the expedition's remaining technology. Or almost all of it, at any rate.

Hamilcar's sister ships were already long gone. They'd been discarded as quickly as possible, by the simple expedient of dropping them into the star system's central fusion furnace once their cargoes had been landed. Not that those cargoes had been used exactly as Mission Control had originally envisioned . . . thanks to Bédard's modifications to the psych templates.

A deep, fundamental part of Pei Kau-yung had felt a shudder of dismay when Mission Control first briefed him and his brother on everything involved in Operation Ark. Not even the fact that every one of the cryogenically suspended colonists had been a fully informed volunteer had been enough to overcome his historical memory of his own ancestors' efforts at "thought control." And yet he'd been forced to concede that there was an element of logic behind the decision to implant every colonist with what amounted to the detailed memory of a completely false life.

It almost certainly would have proved impossible to convince eight million citizens of a highly developed technological civilization to renounce all advanced technology when it came down to it. No matter how willing they all were before they set out for their new home, no matter how fit, young, and physically vigorous they might be, the reality of a muscle-powered culture's harsh demands would have convinced at least some of them to change their minds. So Mission Control had decided to preclude that possibility by providing them with memories which no longer included advanced technology.

It hadn't been an easy task, even for the Federation's tech base, but however much Kau-yung might despise Adorée Bédard, he had to admit the woman's technical brilliance. The colonists had been stacked like cordwood in their cryo capsules—as many as half a million of them aboard a single ship, in the case of really large transports, like *Hamilcar*—and they'd spent the entire ten-year voyage with their minds being steadily reprogrammed.

Then they'd stayed in cryo for another eight standard years, safely tucked away in hiding, while the far less numerous active mission team personnel located their new home world and the alpha terraforming crew prepared it for them.

The world they'd named Safehold was a bit smaller than Old Earth. Kau-zhi was considerably cooler than Sol, and although Safehold orbited closer to it, the planet had a noticeably lower average temperature than Old Earth. Its axial tilt was a bit more pronounced, as well, which gave it somewhat greater seasonal shifts as a result. It also had a higher proportion of land area, but that land was broken up into numerous smallish, mountainous continents and large islands, and that helped to moderate the planetary climate at least a little.

Despite its marginally smaller size, Safehold was also a bit more dense than mankind's original home world. As a result, its gravity was very nearly the same as the one in which the human race had initially evolved. Its days were longer, but its years were shorter—only a bit more than three hundred and one local days each—and the colonists had divided it into only ten months, each of six five-day weeks. The local calendar still felt odd to Kau-yung (he supposed it made sense, but he *missed* January and December, damn it!), and he'd had more trouble than he expected adjusting to the long days, but overall, it was one of the more pleasant planets mankind had settled upon.

Despite all of its positive points, there'd been a few drawbacks, of course. There always were. In this case, the native predators—especially the aquatic ones—presented exceptional challenges, and the ecosystem in general had proved rather less accommodating than usual to the necessary terrestrial plant and animal strains required to fit the planet for human habitation. Fortunately, among the units assigned to each terraforming task group, Mission Control had included a highly capable bio-support ship whose geneticists were able to make the necessary alterations to adapt terrestrial life to Safehold.

Despite that, those terrestrial life-forms remained interlopers. The genetic modifications had helped, but they couldn't completely cure the problem, and for the first few years, the success of Safehold's terraforming had hung in the balance.

That had been when Langhorne and Bédard *needed* Shan-wei, Kau-yung thought bitterly. She'd headed the terraforming teams, and it was her leadership which had carried the task through to success. She and her people, watched over by Kau-yung's flagship, TFNS *Gulliver*, had battled the planet into submission while most of the colony fleet had waited, motionless, holding station in the depths of interstellar space, light-years from the nearest star.

Those had been heady days, Kau-yung admitted to himself. Days when he'd felt he and Shan-wei and their crews were genuinely forging ahead, although that confidence had been shadowed by the constant fear that a Gbaba scout ship might happen by while they hung in orbit around the planet. They'd known the odds were overwhelmingly in their favor, yet they'd been too agonizingly aware of the stakes for which they played to take any comfort from odds, despite all the precautions Mission Planning had built in. But they'd still had that sense of purpose, of wresting survival from the jaws of destruction, and he remembered their huge sense of triumph on the day they realized they'd finally turned the corner and sent word to *Hamilcar* that Safehold was ready for its new inhabitants.

And that was the point at which they'd discovered how Bédard had "modified" the sleeping colonists' psychological templates. No doubt she'd thought it was a vast improvement when Langhorne initially suggested it, but Kau-yung and Shan-wei had been horrified.

The sleeping colonists had volunteered to have false memories of a false life implanted. They hadn't volunteered to be programmed to believe Operation Ark's command staff were gods.

It wasn't the only change Langhorne had made, of course. He and Bédard had done their systematic best to preclude the possibility of any reemergence of advanced technology on Safehold. They'd deliberately abandoned the metric system, which Kau-yung suspected had represented a personal prejudice on Langhorne's part. But they'd also eliminated any memory of Arabic numerals, or algebra, in a move calculated to emasculate any development of advanced mathematics, just as they had eliminated any reference to the scientific method and reinstituted a Ptolemaic theory of the universe. They'd systematically destroyed the tools of scientific inquiry, then concocted their religion as a means of ensuring that it never reemerged once more, and nothing could have been better calculated to outrage someone with Shan-wei's passionate belief in freedom of the individual and of thought.

Unfortunately, it had been too late to do anything about it. Shan-wei and her allies on the Administrative Council had tried, but they'd quickly discovered that Langhorne was prepared for their resistance. He'd organized his own clique, with judicious transfers and replacements among the main fleet's command personnel, while Shan-Wei and Kau-yung were safely out of the way, and those changes had been enough to defeat Shan-wei's best efforts.

Which was why Kau-yung and Shan-wei had had their very public falling out. It had been the only way they could think of to organize some sort of open resistance to Langhorne's policies while simultaneously retaining a presence in the heart of the colony's official command structure. Shan-wei's reputation, her leadership of the minority bloc on the Administrative Council, would have made it impossible for anyone to believe *she* supported the Administrator. And so their roles had been established for them, and they'd drifted further and further apart, settled into deeper and deeper estrangement.

And all for nothing, in the end. He'd given up the woman he loved, both of them had given up the children they might yet have reared, sacrificed fifty-seven years of their lives to a public pretense of anger and violent disagreement, for nothing.

Shan-wei and the other "Techies"—just under thirty percent of the original Operation Ark command crew—had retired to Safehold's southernmost continent. They'd built their own enclave, their "Alexandria Enclave," taking the name deliberately from the famous library at Alexandria, and rigorously adhered to the *original* mission orders where technology was concerned.

And, even more unforgivably from the perspective of Langhorne and Bédard's new plans, they'd refused to destroy their libraries. They'd insisted on preserving the true history of the human race, and especially of the war against the Gbaba.

That's what really sticks in your craw, isn't it, Eric? Kau-yung thought. *You know there's no risk of the Gbaba detecting the sort of preelectric "technology" Shan-wei still has up and running at Alexandria. Hell, any one of the air cars you're still willing to allow your command staff personnel to use as their "angelic chariots" radiates a bigger, stronger signal than everything at Alexandria combined! You may say that any indigenous technology— even the* memory *of that sort of tech—represents the threat of touching off more advanced, more readily detectable development, but that's not what really bothers you. You've decided you like being a god, so you can't tolerate any heretical scripture, can you?*

Kau-yung didn't know how Langhorne would respond to Shan-wei's threat of open defiance. Despite his own position as Safehold's military commander, he knew he wasn't completely trusted by the Administrator and the sycophants on Langhorne's Administrative Council. He wasn't one of *them*, despite his longstanding estrangement from Shan-wei, and too many of them seemed to have come to believe they truly were the deities Bédard had programmed the colonists to think they were.

And people who think they're gods aren't likely to exercise a lot of restraint when someone defies them, he thought.

Pei Kau-yung watched *Hamilcar's* distant, gleaming dot sweep towards the horizon and tried not to shiver as the evening breeze grew cooler.

▼   ▼   ▼

"Father. *Father!*"

Timothy Harrison muttered something from the borderland of sleep, and the hand on his shoulder shook him again, harder.

"Wake *up*, Father!"

Timothy's eyes opened, and he blinked. His third-born son, Robert, Matthew's grandfather, stood leaning over the bed with a candle burning in one hand. For a moment, Timothy was only bewildered, but then Robert's shadowed expression registered, despite the strange lighting falling across it from below as the candle quivered in his hand.

"What is it?" Timothy asked, sitting up in bed. Beside him, Sarah stirred, then opened her own eyes and sat up. He felt her welcome, beloved presence warm against his shoulder, and his right hand reached out, finding and clasping hers as if by instinct.

"I don't know, Father," Robert said worriedly, and in that moment Timothy was once again reminded that his son looked far older than he himself did. "All I know," Robert continued, "is that a messenger's arrived from Father Michael. He says you're needed at the church. Immediately."

Timothy's eyes narrowed. He turned and looked at Sarah for a moment, and she gazed back. Then she shook her head and reached out with her free hand to touch his cheek gently. He smiled at her, as calmly as he could, though she was undoubtedly the last person in the world he could really hope to fool, then looked back at Robert.

"Is the messenger still here?"

"Yes, Father."

"Does *he* know why Michael needs me?"

"He says he doesn't, Father, and I don't think it was just a way to tell me to mind my own business."

"In that case, ask him to return immediately. Ask him to tell Father Michael I'll be there just as quickly as I can get dressed."

"At once, Father," Robert said, not even attempting to hide his relief as his father took charge.

▼　　▼　　▼

"Michael?"

Timothy paused just inside the church doors.

The church, as always, was softly illuminated by the red glow of the presence lights. The magnificent mosaic of ceramic tiles and semiprecious stones which formed the wall behind the high altar was more brightly illuminated by the cut-crystal lamps, which were kept filled with only the purest oil from freshwater kraken. The huge, lordly faces of the Archangel Langhorne and the Archangel Bédard gazed out from the mosaic, their noble eyes watching Timothy as he stood inside the doors. The weight of those eyes always made Timothy aware of his own mortality, his own fallibility before the divinity of God's chosen servants. Usually, it also filled him with reassurance, the renewed faith that God's purpose in creating Safehold as a refuge and a home for mankind must succeed in the end.

But tonight, for some reason, he felt a chill instead. No doubt it was simply the unprecedented nature of Michael's summons, but it almost seemed as if shadows moved across the Archangels' faces, despite the unwavering flames of the lights.

"Timothy!"

Father Michael's voice pulled Timothy away from that disturbing thought, and he looked up as Michael appeared in a side door, just off the sanctuary.

"What's this all about, Michael?" Timothy asked. He paused to genuflect before the mosaic, then rose, touching the fingers of his right hand to his heart, and then to his lips, and strode down the central aisle. He knew he'd sounded sharp, abrupt, and he tried to smooth his own voice. But the irregularity, especially so soon after the Visitation, had him on edge and anxious.

"I'm sorry to have summoned you this way," Father Michael said, "but I had no choice. I have terrible news, *terrible* news." He shook his head. "The worst news I could possibly imagine."

Timothy's heart seemed to stop for just an instant as the horror in Michael's voice registered. He froze in midstride, then made himself continue towards the priest.

"What sort of news, Michael?" he asked much more gently.

"Come."

It was all the priest said, and he stepped back through the door. It led to the sacristy, Timothy realized as he followed, but Michael continued through another door on the sacristy's far side. A narrow flight of stairs led upward, and the priest didn't even pause for a candle or a taper as he led Timothy up them.

The stairs wound upward, and Timothy quickly recognized them, although it was over forty years since he'd last climbed them himself. They led up the tall, rectangular bell tower to the huge bronze bells perched under the pointed steeple at the very top.

Timothy was panting by the time they reached the top, and Michael was literally stumbling with exhaustion from the pace he'd set. But he *still* didn't speak, nor did he pause. He only put his shoulder under the trapdoor, heaved it up, and clambered through it.

A strange, dim radiance spilled down through the opened trapdoor, and Timothy hesitated for just a moment. Then he steeled his nerve, reached for his faith. He followed his friend and priest through the trapdoor, and the radiance strengthened as the one who had awaited them turned towards him and the power of his presence reached out.

"Peace be with you, My Son," the angel said.

▼　　▼　　▼

Fifteen minutes later, Timothy Harrison found himself staring at an angel with the one expression he had never expected to show one of God's servants: one of horror.

"—and so, My Children," the angel said, his own expression grave, "although I warned you only days before that new challenges might await you, not even I expected this."

He shook his head sorrowfully, and yet if it would not have been impious, Timothy would have called the angel's expression as much worried as "grave."

Perhaps it is, the Mayor thought. *And why shouldn't it be? Not even angels—not even* Archangels—*are God themselves. And to have something like* this *happen . . .*

"It is a sad and a terrible duty to bring you this word, these commands," the angel said sadly. "When God created Safehold for your home, the place for you to learn to know Him and to serve His will, it was our duty to keep it safe from evil. And now, we've failed. It is not your fault, but ours, and we shall do all in our power to amend it. Yet it is possible the struggle will be severe. In the end, we must triumph, for it is we who remain loyal to God's will, and He will not suffer His champions to fail. But a price may yet be demanded of us for our failure."

"But that's not—" Timothy began, then closed his mouth firmly as the angel looked at him with a small smile.

"Not 'fair,' My Son?" he said gently. Timothy stared at him, unable to speak again, and the angel shook his head. "The Archangel Shan-wei has fallen, My Sons, and we did not keep the watch we ought to have kept. Her actions should not have taken us by surprise, but they have, for we trusted her as one of our own.

"She *was* one of our own, but now she has betrayed us as she has betrayed herself. She has turned to the Darkness, brought evil into God's world through her own vaunting ambition, blind in her madness to the sure and certain knowledge that no one, not even an Archangel, may set his will against God's and triumph. Maddened by her taste for power, no longer content to serve, she demanded the power to *rule*, to remake this world as *she* would have it, and not as God's plan decrees. And when the Archangel Langhorne refused her demands and rebuffed her mad ambition, she raised impious war against him. Many lesser angels, and even some other Archangels, seduced to her banner, gathered with her. And, not content to damn their own souls, they beguiled and misled many of their mortal flock to follow in their own sinful path."

"But—but what shall *we* do?" Father Michael asked, in a voice which scarcely even quavered, Timothy noted. But was that because the priest had found his courage once again, or because the enormity of the sin the angel had described was simply too vast for him to fully take in?

"You must be prepared to weather days of darkness, My Son," the angel said. "The sorrow that she who was one of the brightest among us should have fallen so low will be a hard thing for your flock to understand. There may be those among that flock who require reassurance, but you must also be vigilant. Some even among your own may have been secretly seduced by Shan-wei's minions, and they must be guarded against. It is even possible that other angels may come here, claiming Visitation in Langhorne's name, when in fact they serve Shan-wei."

"Forgive me," Timothy said humbly, "but we're only mortals. How shall *we* know who an angel truly serves?"

"That is a just question, My Son," the angel said, his expression troubled. "And, in honesty, I do not know if it will be possible for you to tell. I am charged by the Archangel Langhorne, however, to tell you that if you question the instructions you are given by any angel in his name, he will forgive you if you hesitate to obey them until you have requested their confirmation from me, who you know serves his will—and God's—still.

"And"—the angel's expression hardened into one of anger and determination, almost hatred, such as Timothy had never expected to see upon it—"there will not be many such angels. The Archangel Langhorne's wrath has already been loosed, with God's holy fire behind it, and no servant of Darkness can stand against the Light. There is war in Safehold, My Children, and until it is resolved, you must—"

The angel stopped speaking abruptly, and Timothy and Father Michael wheeled towards the open side of the belfry as a brilliant, blinding light flashed upon the northern horizon. It was far away, possibly all the way on the far shore of the enormous lake, but despite the vast distance, it was also incredibly bright. It split the darkness, reflecting across the lake's waters as if they were a mirror, and as it blazed, it rose, higher and higher, like some flaming mushroom rising against the night.

The angel stared at it, and it was probably just as well that neither Timothy nor the priest could tear his own eyes away from that glaring beacon to see the shock and horror in the angel's expression. But then, as the column of distant flame reached its maximum height and began slowly, slowly to dim, the angel found his voice once more.

"My Children," he said, and if the words weren't quite steady, neither of the two mortals with him was in any shape to notice it, "I must go. The war of which I spoke has come closer than I—than we—expected. The Archangel Langhorne needs all of us, and I go to join him in battle. Remember what I have told you, and be vigilant."

He looked at them one more time, then stepped through the belfry opening. Any mortal would have plunged to the ground, undoubtedly shattering his body in the process. But the angel did not. Instead, he rose quickly, silently into the blackness, and Timothy summoned the courage to lean out and look up after him. A brilliant dot blossomed far above as he looked, and he realized that the angel's *kyousei hi* had lifted him up.

"Timothy?"

Michael's voice was soft, almost tiny, and he looked imploringly at the mayor, then back to the distant glare, still fading on the horizon.

"I don't know, Michael," Timothy said quietly. He turned back to the priest and put his arm about him. "All we can do is place our faith in God and the Archangels. That much I understand. But after that?"

He shook his head slowly.

"After that, I just don't know."

OCTOBER 1, 3249
THE MOUNTAINS OF LIGHT,
SAFEHOLD

She woke up. Which was odd, because she didn't remember going to sleep.

Sapphire eyes opened, then narrowed as she saw the curve of a glass-smooth stone ceiling above her. She lay on her back on a table of some sort, her hands folded across her chest, and she'd never seen this room before in her life.

She tried to sit up, and the narrowed eyes flared wide when she discovered she couldn't. Her body was totally nonresponsive, and something very like panic frothed up inside her. And then, abruptly, she noticed the tiny digital ten-day clock floating in one corner of her vision.

"Hello, Nimue," a familiar voice said, and she discovered she could at least move her head. She rolled it sideways, and recognized the holographic image standing beside her. Pei Kau-yung looked much older. He wore casual civilian clothing, not his uniform; his face was grooved with lines of age, labor, and grief; and his eyes were sad.

"I'm sorrier than I can ever say to be leaving this message for you," his image said. "And I know this is all coming at you cold. I'm sorry about that, too, but there was no way to avoid it. And, for whatever it's worth, you volunteered. In a manner of speaking, at least."

His lips quirked in an almost-smile, and his image sat down in a chair which suddenly materialized in the hologram's field.

"I'm getting a little old, even with antigerone, for standing around during lengthy explanations," he told her, "and I'm afraid this one's going to be lengthier than most. I'm also afraid you'll find you won't be able to move until I've finished it. I apologize for that, too, but it's imperative that you stay put until you've heard me completely out. You must fully understand the situation before you make any decisions or take any action."

She watched his expression, her thoughts whirling, and she wasn't surprised to discover she wasn't breathing. The digital display had already warned her about that.

"As I'm sure you've already deduced, you aren't really here," Commodore Pei's recorded message told her. "Or, rather, your biological body isn't. The fact that you were the only member of what I suppose you'd have to call our 'conspiracy' with a last-generation PICA was what made you the only practical choice for this particular . . . mission."

If she'd been breathing, she might have inhaled in surprise. But she wasn't, because, as Pei had just said, she wasn't actually alive. She was a PICA: a Personality-Integrated Cybernetic Avatar. And, a grimly amused little corner of her mind—if, of course, she could be said to actually *have* a mind—reflected, she was a top-of-the-line PICA, at that. A gift from Nimue Alban's unreasonably wealthy father.

"I know you won't recall any of what I'm about to tell you," the commodore continued. "You hadn't realized there'd be any reason to download a current personality record until just before we went aboard ship, and we didn't have time to record a new one before you transferred to *Excalibur*. For that matter, we couldn't risk having anyone wonder why you'd done it even if there'd been time."

Her eyes—the finest artificial eyes the Federation's technology could build, faithfully mimicking the autoresponses of the human "wetware" they'd been built to emulate—narrowed once again. For most people, PICAs had been simply enormously expensive toys since they were first developed, almost a century before Crestwell's World, which was precisely how Daffyd Alban had seen his gift to his daughter. For others, those with serious mobility problems not even modern medicine could correct, they'd been something like the ultimate in prosthetics.

For all intents and purposes, a PICA was a highly advanced robotic vehicle, specifically designed to allow human beings to do dangerous things, including extreme sports activities, without actually physically endangering themselves in the process. First-generation PICAs had been obvious machines, about as aesthetically advanced as one of the utilitarian, tentacle-limbed, floating-oil-drums-on-counter-grav, service 'bots used by sanitation departments throughout the Federation. But second- and third-generation versions had been progressively improved until they became fully articulated, full-sensory-interface, virtual doppelgangers of their original human models. Form followed function, after all, and their entire purpose was to allow those human models to actually experience *exactly* what they would have experienced doing the same things in the flesh.

To which end PICAs' "muscles" were constructed of advanced composites, enormously powerful but exactly duplicating the natural human musculature. Their skeletal structure duplicated the human skeleton, but, again, was many times stronger, and their hollow bones were used for molecular circuitry and power transmission. And a final-generation PICA's molycirc "brain" (located about where a flesh-and-blood human would have kept his liver) was almost half the size of the original protoplasmic model. It had to be that large, for although a PICA's "nerve" impulses moved literally at light speed—somewhere around a hundred times as fast as the chemically transmitted impulses of the human body—matching the interconnectivity of the human brain required the equivalent of a data bus literally trillions of bits wide.

A PICA could be directly neurally linked to the individual for whom it had been built, but the sheer bandwidth required limited the linkage to relatively short ranges. And any PICA was also hardwired to prevent any *other* individual from ever linking with it. That was a specific legal requirement, designed to guarantee that no one else could ever operate it, since the individual operating a PICA was legally responsible for any actions committed by that PICA.

Eventually, advances in cybernetics had finally reached the level of approximating the human brain's capabilities. They didn't do it exactly the same way, of course. Despite all the advances, no computer yet designed could fully match the brain's interconnections. Providing the memory storage of a human brain had been no great challenge for molecular circuitry; providing the necessary "thinking" ability had required the development of energy-state CPUs so that sheer computational and processing speed had finally been able to compensate. A PICA's "brain" might be designed around completely different constraints, but the end results were effectively indistinguishable from the original human model . . . even from the inside.

That capability had made the *remote* operation of a PICA possible at last. A last-generation PICA's owner could actually load a complete electronic analogue of his personality and memories (simple data storage had never been a problem, after all) into the PICA in order to take it into potentially dangerous environments outside the direct neural linkage's limited transmission range. The analogue could operate the PICA, without worrying about risk to the owner's physical body, and when the PICA returned, its memories and experiences could be uploaded to the owner as his own memories.

There'd been some concern, when that capability came along, about possible "rogue PICAs" running amok under personality analogues which declined to be erased. Personally, Nimue had always felt those concerns had been no more than the lingering paranoia of what an ancient writer had labeled the "Frankenstein complex," but public opinion had been adamant. Which was why the law required that any downloaded personality would be automatically erased within an absolute maximum of two hundred forty hours from the moment of the host PICA's activation under an analogue's control.

"The last personality recording you'd downloaded was made when you were still planning that hang-gliding expedition in the Andes," Commodore Pei's holograph reminded her. "But you never had time for the trip because, as part of my staff, you were tapped for something called 'Operation Ark.' For you to understand why we're having this conversation, I need to explain to you just what Operation Ark was . . . and why you, Kau-zhi, Shan-wei, and I set out to sabotage it."

Her eyes—and, despite everything, she couldn't help thinking of them as *her* eyes—widened, and he chuckled without any humor at all.

"Basically," he began, "the concept was—"

▼　　▼　　▼

"—so," Pei Kau-yung told her a good hour later, "from the moment we found out Langhorne had been chosen over Franz Halversen to command the expedition, we knew there was going to be a lot of pressure to dig the deepest possible hole, crawl into it, and fill it in behind us. Langhorne was one of the 'we brought this down on ourselves through our own technological arrogance' types, and, at the very least, he was going to apply the most stringent possible standard to the elimination of technology. In fact, it seemed likely to us that he'd try to build a primitive society that would be a total break with anything which had come before—that he might decide to wipe out all record that there'd ever *been* a technologically advanced human society. In which case, of course, all memory—or, at least, all *accurate* memory—of the Gbaba would have to be eliminated as well. He couldn't very well explain we'd encountered them once we attained interstellar fight without explaining how we'd done *that*, after all.

"None of us could question the necessity of 'going bush' to evade detection, at least in the short term, yet where Langhorne was determined to prevent any new confrontation with the Gbaba, *we* felt that one was effectively inevitable.

Someday, despite any effort to preclude the development of a high-tech civilization, the descendants of our new colony's inhabitants would start over again on the same road which had taken us to the stars and our meeting with them."

He shook his head sadly.

"In light of that, we began considering, very quietly, ways to prevent those distant descendants of ours from walking straight back into the same situation we were in. The only solution we could see was to ensure that the memory of the Gbaba wasn't lost after all. That our descendants would know they had to stay home without attracting attention, in their single star system, until they'd reached a level of technology which would let them defeat the Gbaba. The fact that the Gbaba have been around for so long was what suggested they'd still be a threat when mankind ventured back into space, but the fact that they've been around so long without any significant advances also suggested that the *level* of threat probably wouldn't be much higher than it was today. So if there was some way for our descendants to know what level of technological capability they required to survive against the Gbaba, they would also know when it ought to be safe—or relatively safe—for them to move back into interstellar flight.

"One way to do that would be to maintain a preelectric level of technology on our new home for at least the next three or four centuries, avoiding any betraying emissions while preserving the records of our earlier history and the history of our war with the Gbaba. Assuming we could convince Langhorne, or at least a majority of the Administrative Council, to go along with us, we would also place two or three of the expedition's ships in completely powered-down orbits somewhere in our destination star system, where they'd be only a handful of additional asteroids without any active emissions, impossible to detect or differentiate from any other hunk of rock without direct physical examination, but available for recovery once indigenous spaceflight was redeveloped. They would serve as an enormous bootstrap for technological advancement, and they'd also provide a yardstick by which to evaluate the relative capabilities of later, further developments."

His holographic face grimaced, his eyes bitter.

"That was essentially what the original mission plan for Operation Ark called for, and if Halversen had been in command, it's what would have been done. But, frankly, with Langhorne in command, we never gave it more than a forty percent chance of happening, although it would obviously have been the best scenario. But because the odds of achieving it were so poor, we looked for a second option. We looked hard, but we couldn't find one. Not until we were all sitting around after dinner on the very evening before our departure, when you and Elias Proctor came up with the idea which led to this conversation.

"You were the one who pointed out that the same technology which had gone into building the PICAs could have been used to build an effectively immortal 'adviser' for the colony. An adviser who actually remembered everything which ought to have been in the records we were all afraid Langhorne wouldn't want preserved and who could have guided—or at least influenced—the new colony's development through its most dangerous stages. Unfortunately, there was no time to implement that idea, even if there'd been any way Operation Ark's planners would have signed off on any such notion. And even if the mission planners had agreed to it, someone like Langhorne would almost certainly order the 'adviser's' destruction once he was out on his own.

"But Elias was very struck by your observation, and he pointed out, in turn, that the only thing preventing an existing, off-the-shelf PICA from being used to fulfill the same role were the protocols limiting PICAs to no more than ten days of independent operation. But those protocols were all in the *software*. He was relatively certain he could hack around them and deactivate them. And a single PICA, especially one with its power completely down, would be relatively easy to conceal—not just from the Gbaba, but from Langhorne."

The PICA on the table, which had decided she might as well continue to think of herself as the young woman named Nimue Alban, whose memories she possessed, would have nodded if she could have moved her head. Doctor Elias Proctor had been the most brilliant cyberneticist Nimue had ever known. If anyone could hack a PICA's software, he could. Of course, trying to would have been a felony under Federation law, punishable by a minimum of fifteen years in prison.

"Unfortunately"—Pei Kau-yung's expression turned sad once again—"the only last-generation PICA belonging to anyone we knew we could trust was yours, and there wasn't time to acquire another. Certainly not without making Mission Control wonder what in the world we wanted it for. In fact, you were the one who pointed that out to us. So I signed off on a last-minute cargo adjustment that included your PICA in your personal baggage allotment, on the basis that it might prove useful for hostile environment work somewhere along the line. And then, after all our personnel and cargo had been embarked, you volunteered to transfer to Kau-zhi's staff aboard *Excalibur*."

Nimue's eyes went very still, and he nodded slowly, as if he could see them.

"That's right. You volunteered for service on the flagship, knowing it would be destroyed if Operation Breakaway worked. And when you were transferred to *Excalibur*, the official manifest on your gear included everything you'd brought aboard *Gulliver*, including your PICA. But you didn't actually take it with you, and I personally transferred it to a cargo hold where it could be permanently 'lost.' It was the only way to drop it completely off all of the detailed equipment lists in Langhorne's computers."

His image seemed to look straight into her eyes for several seconds. Then he drew a deep breath.

"It wasn't easy to let you go," he said softly. "You were so young, with so much still to contribute. But no one could come up with a counterscenario that offered us as good a chance of success. If you hadn't been . . . gone before we reached Safehold, the master manifests would have shown you still holding the

PICA. You would have been forced to turn it over to Langhorne for destruction, and if you'd announced you'd 'lost' it somehow, instead, all sorts of alarms would have gone off, especially given how late in the process it was added to your allotment. So, in the end, we really had no choice. Yet to be perfectly honest, despite the fact that you'd chosen to deliberately sacrifice your life to give us this option, we all hoped we'd never actually need it.

"Unfortunately, I'm afraid we do."

He settled back in his chair, his face hard, set with an expression she'd seen before, as Gbaba warships appeared on his tactical display.

"Langhorne and Bédard have turned out to be not just fanatics, but megalomaniacs. I've left a complete file for you, with all the details. I don't have the heart to recite them all for you now. But the short version is that it turns out Langhorne and his inner clique never trusted me quite as completely as I thought they had. They deployed a complete orbital kinetic strike system without ever telling me, as their senior military officer, a thing about it. I never knew it was there, couldn't take any steps to neutralize it. And when Shan-wei and her supporters resisted their efforts to turn themselves into gods, they used it. They killed her, Nimue—her and all of the people trying to openly maintain any memory of our true history."

A PICA had no heart, not in any physical sense, but the heart Nimue Alban no longer possessed twisted in anguish, and he cleared his throat, then shook his head hard.

"To be honest, I thought about waking you up, having this conversation with you in person, but I was afraid to. I've lived a long time now, Nimue, but you're still young. I didn't want to tell you about Shan-wei. For a lot of reasons, really, including the fact that I know how much you loved her and I was . . . too cowardly to face your pain. But also because I know *you*. You wouldn't have been willing to 'go back to sleep' until you'd personally done something about her murder, and I can't afford to lose you. Not now. Not for a lot of reasons. Besides, you'd probably try to argue with me about my own plans. And when you come right down to it, no time will pass for you between now and when you actually see this message, will it?"

His bittersweet smile was crooked, but when he spoke again, his voice was brisker, almost normal-sounding.

"We did our best to give you at least some of the tools you'll need if you decide—if *you* decide, as the person you are *now*, not the Nimue Alban who originally volunteered for this—to continue with this mission. We didn't really think we'd be able to do that, since we hadn't known Langhorne would decide to keep *Hasdrubal* with the main fleet instead of personally overseeing Safehold's terraforming. We were delighted that he did, at the time, because it gave us a lot more freedom. Of course"—he smiled bitterly—"we didn't realize then *why* he was staying there. Even without him looking over our shoulder, though, we couldn't begin to give you everything I would have liked to. There were still limits to what we dared to 'disappear' from the equipment lists, but Shan-wei and I showed a little creativity during the terraforming operations. So you'll have some computer support, the most complete records we could provide, and at least some hardware.

"I've set the timer to activate this . . . depot, I suppose, seven hundred and fifty standard years after I complete this recording. I arrived at that particular timing because our best projections indicate that if the Gbaba didn't decide Kau-zhi's fleet was all of Operation Ark's units, and if their scout ships continued to sweep outward, it ought to take them a maximum of about five hundred years to pass within easy detection range of radio emissions or neutrinos from this system. So I've allowed a fifty percent cushion to carry you through the threat zone of immediate detection. That's how long you will have been 'asleep.'"

He shook his head again.

"I can't begin to imagine what it's going to be like for you, Nimue. I wish there'd been some way, *any* way, I could have avoided dropping this burden on you. I couldn't find one. I tried, but I couldn't."

He sat silent once more for several seconds, his holographic eyes gazing at something no one else had ever been able to see, then blinked back into focus and straightened in his chair.

"This is the final message, the last file, which will be loaded to your depot computer. Besides myself, only one other person knows of your existence, and he and I have an appointment with Administrator Langhorne and the Administrative Council tomorrow evening. I don't know if it will do any good, but Langhorne, Bédard, and their toadies are about to discover that they aren't the only people with a little undisclosed military hardware in reserve. There won't be any survivors. It won't bring back Shan-wei, or any of the rest of my—our—friends, but at least I'll take a little personal satisfaction out of it."

He seemed to look at her one last time, and he smiled once more. This time, it was an oddly gentle smile.

"I suppose it could be argued that you don't really exist. You're only electronic patterns inside a machine, after all, not a *real* person. But you're the electronic pattern of a truly remarkable young woman I was deeply honored to have known, and I believe that in every way that counts, you *are* that young woman. Yet you're also someone else, and that someone else has the right to choose what you do with the time and the tools we've been able to give you. Whatever you choose, the decision *must* be yours. And whatever you decide, know this; Shan-wei and I loved Nimue Alban very much. We honored her memory for sixty years, and we're perfectly satisfied to leave the decision in your hands. Whatever you decide, whatever you choose, we still love you. And now, as you once said to me, God bless, Nimue. Goodbye."

MAY, YEAR OF GOD 890

✦

The Temple of God's colonnade soared effortlessly against the springtime blue of the northern sky. The columns were just over sixty feet high, and the central dome which dominated the entire majestic structure rose higher yet, to a height of a hundred and fifty feet. It shone like a huge, polished mirror in the sunlight, plated in silver and crowned with the gem-encrusted, solid-gold icon of the Archangel Langhorne, tablets of law clasped in one arm, the scepter of his holy authority raised high in the other. That icon was eighteen feet tall, glittering more brilliantly even than the dome under the morning sun. For over eight centuries, since the very dawn of Creation, that breathtakingly beautiful archangel had stood guard over God's home on Safehold, and it and the dome under it were both as brilliant and untouched by weather or time as the day they were first set in place.

The Temple sat atop an emerald green hill which lifted it even further towards God's heavens. Its gleaming dome was visible from many miles away, across the waters of Lake Pei, and it glittered like a gold and alabaster crown above the great lakeside city of Zion. It was the city's crown in more than one way, for the city itself—one of the half-dozen largest on all of Safehold, and by far its oldest—existed for only one purpose: to serve the needs of the Church of God Awaiting.

Erayk Dynnys, Archbishop of Charis, strolled slowly towards the Temple across the vast Plaza of Martyrs, dominated by the countless fountains whose dancing jets, splashing about the feet of heroic sculptures of Langhorne, Bédard, and the other archangels, cast damp, refreshing breaths of spray to the breeze. He wore the white cassock of the episcopate, and the three-cornered priest's cap upon his head bore the white cockade and dove-tailed orange ribbon of an archbishop. The fragrant scents of the northern spring wafted from the beds of flowers and flowering shrubs the Temple's gardening staff kept perfectly maintained, but the archbishop scarcely noticed. The wonders of the Temple were a part of his everyday world, and more mundane aspects of that same world often pushed them into the background of his awareness.

"So," he said to the younger man walking beside him, "I take it we still haven't received the documents from Breygart?"

"No, Your Eminence," Father Mahtaio Broun replied obediently. Unlike his patron's, his priest's cap bore only the brown cockade of an upper-priest, but the white crown embroidered on his cassock's right sleeve marked him as a senior archbishop's personal secretary and aide.

"A pity," Dynnys murmured, with just a trace of a smile. "Still, I'm sure Zherald did inform both him and Haarahld that the documentary evidence was necessary. Mother Church has done her best to see to it that both sides are fairly presented before the Ecclesiastical Court."

"Of course, Your Eminence," Father Mahtaio agreed.

Unlike the prelate he served, Broun was careful not to smile, even though he knew about the private message from Dynnys to Bishop Executor Zherald Ahdymsyn instructing him to administratively "lose" the message for at least a five-day or two. Broun was privy to most of his patron's activities, however . . . discreet they might be. He simply wasn't senior enough to display amusement or satisfaction over their success. Not yet, at least. Someday, he was sure, that seniority *would* be his.

The two clerics reached the sweeping, majestically proportioned steps of the colonnade. Dozens of other churchmen moved up and down those steps, through the huge, opened bas-relief doors, but the stream parted around Dynnys and his aide without even a murmur of protest.

If he'd barely noticed the beauty of the Temple itself, the archbishop completely ignored the lesser clerics making way for him, just as he ignored the uniformed Temple Guards standing rigidly at attention at regular intervals, cuirasses gleaming in the sunlight, bright-edged halberds braced. He continued his stately progress, hands folded in the voluminous, orange-trimmed sleeves of his snow white cassock, while he pondered the afternoon's scheduled session.

He and Broun crossed the threshold into the vast, soaring cathedral itself. The vaulted ceiling floated eighty feet above the gleaming pavement—rising to almost twice that at the apex of the central dome—and ceiling frescoes depicting the archangels laboring at the miraculous business of Creation circled the gold and gem-encrusted ceiling. Cunningly arranged mirrors and skylights set into the Temple's roof gathered the springtime sunlight and spilled it through the frescoes in carefully directed shafts of brilliance. Incense drifted in sweet-smelling clouds and tendrils, spiraling through the sunlight like lazy serpents of smoke, and the magnificently trained voices of the Temple Choir rose in a quiet, perfectly harmonized a cappella hymn of praise.

The choir was yet another of the wonders of the Temple, trained and dedicated to the purpose of seeing to it that God's house was perpetually filled with voices raised in His praise, as Langhorne had commanded. Just before the morning choir reached the end of its assigned time, the afternoon choir would march quietly into its place in the identical choir loft on the opposite side of the cathedral, where it would join the morning choir's song. As the afternoon singers' voices rose, the morning singers' voices would fade, and, to the listening ear, unless it was very carefully trained, it would sound as if there had been no break or change at all in the hymn.

The archbishop and his aide stepped across the vast, detailed map of God's world, inlaid into the floor just inside the doors, and made their way around the circumference of the circular cathedral. Neither of them paid much attention to the priests and acolytes around the altar at the center of the circle, celebrating the third of the daily morning masses for the regular flow of pilgrims. Every child of God was required by the *Writ* to make the journey to the Temple at least once in his life. Obviously, that wasn't actually possible for *everyone*, and God recognized that, yet enough of His children managed to meet that obligation to keep the cathedral perpetually thronged with worshippers. Except, of course, during the winter months of bitter cold and deep snow.

The cathedral pavement shone with blinding brightness where the focused beams of sunlight struck it, and at each of those points lay a circular golden seal, two feet across, bearing the sigil of one of the archangels. Like the icon of Langhorne atop the Temple dome and the dome itself, those seals were as brilliant, as untouched by wear or time as the day the Temple was raised. Each of them—like the gold-veined lapis lazuli of the pavement itself, and the vast map at the entry—was protected by the three-inch-thick sheet of imperishable crystal which covered them. The blocks of lapis had been sealed into the pavement with silver, and that silver gleamed as untarnished and perfect as the gold of the seals themselves. No mortal knew how it had been accomplished, but legend had it that after the archangels had raised the Temple, they had commanded the air itself to protect both its gilded roof and that magnificent pavement for all time. However they had worked their miracle, the crystalline surface bore not a single scar, not one scuff mark, to show the endless generations of feet which had passed across it since the Creation or the perpetually polishing mops of the acolytes responsible for maintaining its brilliance.

Dynnys' and Broun's slippered feet made no sound, adding to the illusion that they were, in fact, walking upon air, as they circled to the west side of the cathedral and passed through one of the doorways there into the administrative wings of the Temple. They passed down broad hallways, illuminated by skylights and soaring windows of the same imperishable crystal and decorated with priceless tapestries, paintings, and statuary. The administrative wings, like the cathedral, were the work of divine hands, not of mere mortals, and stood as pristine and perfect as the day they had been created.

Eventually, they reached their destination. The conference chamber's door was flanked by two more Temple Guards, although these carried swords, not halberds, and their cuirasses bore the golden starburst of the Grand Vicar quartered with the Archangel Schueler's sword. They came smartly to attention as the archbishop and his aide passed them without so much as a glance.

Three more prelates and their aides, accompanied by two secretaries and a trio of law masters, awaited them.

"So, here you are, Erayk. At last," one of the other archbishops said dryly as Dynnys and Broun crossed to the conference table.

"I beg your pardon, Zhasyn," Dynnys said with an easy smile. "I was unavoidably delayed, I'm afraid."

"I'm sure." Archbishop Zhasyn Cahnyr snorted. Cahnyr, a lean, sparely built man, was archbishop of Glacierheart, in the Republic of Siddarmark, and while Dynnys' cassock bore the black scepter of the Order of Langhorne on its right breast, Cahnyr's showed the green-trimmed brown grain sheaf of the Order of Sondheim. The two men had known one another for years . . . and there was remarkably little love lost between them.

"Now, now, Zhasyn," Urvyn Myllyr, Archbishop of Sodar, chided. Myllyr was built much like Dynnys himself: too well-fleshed to be considered lean, yet not quite heavy enough to be considered fat. He also wore the black scepter of Langhorne, but where Dynnys' graying hair was thinning and had once been golden blond, Myllyr's was a still-thick salt-and-pepper black. "Be nice," he continued now, smiling at Cahnyr. "Some delays truly are unavoidable, you know. Even"—he winked at Dynnys—"Erayk's."

Cahnyr did not appear mollified, but he contented himself with another snort and sat back in his chair.

"Whatever the cause, at least you *are* here now, Erayk," the third prelate observed, "so let's get started, shall we?"

"Of course, Wyllym," Dynnys replied, not obsequiously, but without the insouciance he'd shown Cahnyr.

Wyllym Rayno, Archbishop of Chiang-wu, was several years younger than Dynnys, and unlike a great many of Mother Church's bishops and archbishops, he had been born in the province which had since become his archbishopric. He was short, dark, and slender, and there was something . . . dangerous about him. Not surprisingly, perhaps. While Dynnys, Cahnyr, and Myllyr all wore the white cassocks of their rank, Rayno, as always, wore the habit of a simple monk in the dark purple of the Order of Schueler. The bared sword of the order's patron stood out starkly on the right breast of that dark habit, white and trimmed in orange to proclaim his own archbishop's rank, but its episcopal white was less important than the golden flame of Jwo-jeng superimposed across it. That flame-crowned sword marked him as the Schuelerite Adjutant General, which made him effectively the executive officer of Vicar Zhaspyr Clyntahn, the Grand Inquisitor himself.

As always, the sight of that habit gave Dynnys a slight twinge. Not that he'd ever had any personal quarrel with Rayno. It was more a matter of . . . tradition than anything else.

Once upon a time, the rivalry between his own Order of Langhorne and the Schuelerites had been both open and intense, but the struggle for primacy within the Temple had been decided in the Schuelerites' favor generations ago. The Order of Schueler's role as the guardian of doctrinal orthodoxy had given it a powerful advantage, which had been decisively strengthened by the judicious political maneuvering within the Temple's hierarchy which had absorbed the Order of Jwo-jeng into the Schuelerites. These days, the Order of Langhorne stood clearly second within that hierarchy, which made the Schuelerite practice of dressing as humble brothers of their order, regardless of their personal rank in the Church's hierarchy, its own form of arrogance.

Dynnys sat in the armchair awaiting him, Broun perched on the far humbler stool behind his archbishop's chair, and Rayno gestured to one of the law masters.

"Begin," he said.

"Your Eminences," the law master, a monk of Dynnys' own order, said, standing behind the neat piles of legal documents on the table before him, "as you all know, the purpose of the meeting of this committee of the Ecclesiastical Court is to consider a final recommendation on the succession dispute in the earldom of Hanth. We have researched the applicable law, and each of you has received a digest of our findings. We have also summarized the testimony before this committee and the documents submitted to it. As always, we are but the Court's servants. Having provided you with all of the information available to us, we await your pleasure."

He seated himself once more, and Rayno looked around the conference table at his fellow archbishops.

"Is there any need to reconsider any of the points of law which have been raised in the course of these hearings?" he asked. Heads shook silently in reply. "Are there any disputes about the summary of the testimony we've already heard or the documents we've already reviewed?" he continued, and, once again, heads shook. "Very well. Does anyone have anything new to present?"

"If I may, Wyllym?" Cahnyr said, and Rayno nodded for him to continue. The lean archbishop turned to look at Dynnys.

"At our last meeting, you told us you were still awaiting certain documents from Bishop Executor Zherald. Have they arrived?"

"I fear not," Dynnys said, shaking his head gravely.

Zherald Ahdymsyn was officially Dynnys' assistant; in fact, he was the de facto acting archbishop for Dynnys' distant archbishopric and the manager of Dynnys' own vast estates there. Charis was the next best thing to twelve thousand miles from the Temple, and there was no way Dynnys could have personally seen to the pastoral requirements of "his" parishioners and also dealt with all of the other responsibilities which attached to his high office. So, like the vast majority of prelates whose sees lay beyond the continent of Haven or its sister continent, Howard, to the south, he left those pastoral and local administrative duties to his bishop executor. Once a year, despite the hardship involved, Dynnys traveled to Charis for a monthlong pastoral visit; the rest of the year, he relied upon Ahdymsyn. The bishop executor might not be the most brilliant man he'd ever met, but he was dependable and understood the practical realities of Church politics. He was also less greedy than most when it came to siphoning off personal wealth.

"But you did request that he send them?" Cahnyr pressed, and Dynnys allowed an expression of overtried patience to cross his face.

"Of course I did, Zhasyn," he replied. "I dispatched the original request via semaphore to Clahnyr over two months ago, as we all agreed, to be relayed by sea across the Cauldron. Obviously, I couldn't go into a great deal of detail in a semaphore message, but Father Mahtaio sent a more complete request via wyvern the same day, and it reached Clahnyr barely a five-day later. We also notified Sir Hauwerd's man of law here in Zion of our requirements and informed him that we were passing the request along to his client."

" 'Two months ago' doesn't leave very much time for any documentation to arrive from so far away. Particularly at this time of year, given the sort of storms they have in the Cauldron every fall," Cahnyr observed in a deliberately neutral tone, and Dynnys showed his fellow prelate his teeth in what might possibly have been called a smile.

"True," he said almost sweetly. "On the other hand, the message was sent *over* two months ago, which seems more than sufficient time for Zherald to have relayed my request to Sir Hauwerd and for Sir Hauwerd to have responded. And for a dispatch vessel from Charis to cross back to Clahnyr, weather or no weather, with at least a semaphore message to alert us that the documents in question were on their way. In fact, I've exchanged another complete round of messages with Zherald on other topics over the same time frame, so I feel quite sure the dispatch boats are surviving the crossing, despite any autumn gales."

Cahnyr looked as if he was tempted to launch another sharp riposte of his own. But if he was, he suppressed the temptation. Rayno and Myllyr only nodded, and Dynnys hid a mental smirk.

He often found Cahnyr's brand of personal piety rather wearing, although he had to admit it gave his rival a certain cachet in the Temple's hierarchy. He wasn't quite unique, of course, but most of the archbishops and vicars charged with administering God's affairs were too busy for the sort of simpleminded pastoral focus Cahnyr seemed to prefer.

Dynnys was prepared to admit that that was even more true in his case than in many others'. It could scarcely be otherwise, with Charis so far from Zion and the Temple. Cahnyr's archbishopric was less than half as distant, although, to be fair, most of the weary miles to Glacierheart were overland, and Cahnyr made two pastoral visits per year, not just one. But he could also make the journey without being totally out of touch with the Temple. Thanks to the semaphore chains the Church maintained across Haven and Howard, the two-way message time between Glacierheart and the Temple was less than three days.

Dynnys had occasionally wondered if a part of Cahnyr's enmity might not stem from the differences between their archbishoprics. He *knew* that at least a portion of the bad blood between them came from the fact that Cahnyr had been the son of a minor Dohlaran nobleman, whereas Dynnys was the son of an archbishop and the grandnephew of a grand vicar. Cahnyr stood outside the traditional great ecclesiastic dynasties which had dominated the Temple for centuries, and he'd never seemed to quite grasp how those dynasties played the game.

That game, as Dynnys was well aware, explained how he'd gotten Charis and Cahnyr . . . hadn't. Despite the other prelate's ostentatious piety, he couldn't be totally dead to ambition, or he would never have attained a bishop's ruby ring, far less his present rank, and Cahnyr's archbishopric was a mere province of the Republic of Siddarmark, whereas Dynnys' was the entire Kingdom of Charis. It was always possible that fact did, indeed, account for Cahnyr's hostility, although Dynnys rather doubted it in his calmer moments. Craggy, mountainous Glacierheart was barely a quarter the size of Charis proper, and sparsely populated compared with the rest of Haven, but it probably had almost as many inhabitants as the entire kingdom.

Although not, he reflected complacently, *a tenth as much wealth.*

Haven and Howard were the principal landmasses of Safehold, and Langhorne and his fellow archangels had planted humanity far more thickly across them than anywhere else. Even today, eight, or possibly even as many as nine, out of every ten inhabitants of Safehold were to be found there, so it was little wonder Mother Church's attention was so fully fixed there as well. The long chains of semaphore stations, reaching out from Zion in every direction, allowed the Temple to oversee its far-flung archbishoprics, bishoprics, cathedrals, churches, congregations, monasteries, convents, and ecclesiastical manors, as well as the intendants assigned to the various secular courts, parliaments, and assemblies. Those semaphores belonged to Mother Church, and although she permitted their use by secular authorities, that use was always subject to availability. And as more than one prince or king or governor had discovered, "availability" could be quite limited for anyone who had irritated his local ecclesiastical superiors.

But not even Mother Church could erect semaphore stations in the middle of the sea, and so the only way to communicate with such distant lands as Charis, or the League of Corisande, or Chisholm, was ultimately by ship. And ships, as Dynnys had long since discovered, were slow.

An additional semaphore chain had been extended across Raven's Land and Chisholm, on the far side of the Markovian Sea, but even there, messages must cross the Passage of Storms, a water gap of almost twelve hundred miles between the semaphore stations on Rollings Head and Iron Cape. That gave Zherohm Vyncyt, the Archbishop of Chisholm, a two-way message time of almost seventeen days, but the situation was even worse for Dynnys. It took only six days for a message to travel from the Temple to the Clahnyr semaphore station in southern Siddarmark, but then it had to cross over three thousand miles of seawater to reach Tellesberg. Which meant, of course, that it took twenty-five days—five five-days—on average for one of his messages just to reach his bishop executor.

The actual voyage from the Temple to Tellesberg, however, took two full months . . . one way. Which explained why Dynnys simply could not absent himself from Zion and the Temple for more than a single pastoral visit per year, usually in late autumn. That got him out of the Temple Lands before Hsing-wu's Passage froze over and let him spend the Temple's ice-blasted winter in Charis, which was not only in the southern hemisphere but less than thirteen hundred miles below the equator. Summer in Tellesberg was *ever* so much more pleasant than winter in Zion! Of course, that same distance from Zion (and the Temple) also explained why some of those more distant lands—like Charis itself, upon occasion—were sometimes just a bit more fractious then those closer to Zion.

"Erayk has a point, Zhasyn," Rayno said now. "Certainly everyone involved in this dispute has been arguing back and forth long enough to recognize how important it is to comply with any documentary requests we may have. If Breygart hasn't seen fit even to acknowledge the receipt of our request, that speaks poorly for him."

"It may speak more poorly of the quality of his purported evidence," Myllyr pointed out. "If he truly has proof Mahntayl's claims are false, he ought to be eager to lay that evidence before us."

Cahnyr shifted in his seat, and Rayno quirked one eyebrow at him.

"Yes, Zhasyn?"

"I only wanted to observe that from the very first, Sir Hauwerd Breygart—" the Archbishop of Glacierheart stressed the title and surname very slightly "—has maintained that Mahntayl's claim to descent from the fourteenth earl was false. And," he looked around the conference table, "he accompanied his initial arguments with depositions to that effect from over a dozen witnesses."

"No one is disputing that he did, Zhasyn," Dynnys pointed out. "The point under consideration is Breygart's assertion that he's uncovered proof—not depositions, not hearsay evidence, but documented *proof*—that Tahdayo Mahntayl is not Fraidareck Breygart's great-grandson. It was that 'proof' we asked him to share with us."

"Precisely," Rayno agreed, nodding solemnly, and Cahnyr clamped his lips firmly together. He glanced at Myllyr, and his lips thinned further as he read the other prelate's eyes.

Dynnys could read the others' expressions just as well as Cahnyr could, and he couldn't quite completely suppress his own smile. Myllyr's support for his position was hardly a surprise; not only were they both Langhornites, but the two of them had been scratching one another's backs for decades, and both of them knew how Mother Church's politics worked. Rayno had been a bit more problematical, but Dynnys had confidently anticipated his support, as well. The Inquisition and Order of Schueler had been less than pleased by Charis' growing wealth and power for almost a century now. The kingdom's obvious taste for . . . innovation only made that worse, and the energy the Charisian "Royal College" had begun displaying over the last ten or fifteen years rubbed more than one senior Schuelerite on the raw.

The view that religious orthodoxy waned in direct proportion to the distance between any given congregation and Zion was an inescapable part of most

Schuelerites' mental baggage. Rayno, despite his own sophistication and ecclesiastical rank, still regarded such distant lands as Charis with automatic suspicion. In Charis' case, the power of its trade-based wealth and apparent inventiveness, coupled with the "Royal College's" active support for that inventiveness and the Ahrmahk Dynasty's domestic policies, made him even more suspicious. And the fact that Haarahld of Charis, unlike the majority of Safehold's rulers, had stayed out of debt to the Temple's moneylenders was one more worry for those—like Rayno—who fretted over how to control him if the need should arise.

The Schuelerites' dominant position in the Church hierarchy would have been enough to put Charis under a cloud in the Church's eyes all by itself. But the kingdom's steadily growing wealth, and the influence its vast merchant fleet gave it in lands far beyond its own borders, made a bad situation worse in many respects. While most of the more mundane suspicion and ire of the Council of Vicars focused on the Republic of Siddarmark simply because of the Republic's proximity to the Temple Lands, there were those—including the Grand Inquisitor himself—who felt that Charis' attitudes and example were even more dangerous in the long run.

Dynnys' own view, buttressed by reports from Zherald Ahdymsyn and Father Paityr Wylsynn, the Order of Schueler's own intendant in Tellesberg, was that Rayno's suspicions of Charis' fidelity to Mother Church's doctrines were baseless. True, Charisians' willingness to find new and more efficient ways to do things required a certain degree of vigilance. And, equally true, the Charisian branch of the Church was rather more permissive on several issues than the Council of Vicars would truly have preferred. And, yes, it was even true that this "college" of Haarahld's was actively seeking new ways to combine existing knowledge, which could only enhance that national fetish for "efficiency." That, however, was exactly why Father Paityr was there, and his reports—like those of his immediate predecessors—made it quite clear that nothing going on in Charis came remotely close to a violation of the Proscriptions of Jwo-jeng.

As for domestic policies and dangerous examples, Dynnys was willing to grant that King Haarahld's great-grandfather's decision to legally abolish serfdom throughout his kingdom could be construed as a slap in Mother Church's face, if one were determined to view it that way. Dynnys wasn't, especially given the fact that there'd never been more than a relative handful of serfs in Charis even before the institution was officially abolished. Nor did he believe the claims—mostly from the Charisians' competitors—that his parishioners' focus on trade and the acquisition of wealth was so obsessive that it inspired them to ignore their obligations to God and Mother Church and skimp on the kingdom's tithe. Bishop Executor Zherald and his tithe-collectors would certainly have made their own displeasure known if they'd suspected there was any truth to *those* tales! Ahdymsyn might not be the most brilliant man ever to attain a bishop's ring, but he was no fool, either, and Mother Church had centuries of experience with every way kings or nobles might try to hide income from the tithe-assessors.

And the Church's—and Inquisition's—grip on the mainland populations was surely firm enough to suppress any dangerous notions which might creep across the seas aboard Charisian merchantmen.

No, Dynnys had no fear Charis was some sort of hotbed of potential heresy. Not that he hadn't been prepared to play upon Rayno's suspicions and the Council of Vicars' basic distrust and dislike for the kingdom.

Which, he reflected, *made the fact that Haarahld was clearly one of Breygart's strongest supporters the kiss of death as far as Wyllym was concerned.*

He supposed it was actually a sign of Rayno's moral integrity that it had taken him this long to come openly out in support of Tahdayo Mahntayl's claim.

His fraudulent but extremely well-paying *claim,* Dynnys reflected silently, allowing no trace of his inner satisfaction to show. And the fact that Lyam Tyrn, the Archbishop of Emerald, was going to owe him a substantial favor for supporting Prince Nahrmahn's candidate wasn't going to hurt, either.

"I think," Rayno, as the senior member of the court, continued, "that in light of Breygart's failure to provide his supposed proof, or even to respond to our request in a timely fashion, we must make our decision based upon the evidence already presented. Rather than rush to a conclusion, however, I would suggest we adjourn for lunch and afterwards spend an hour or so meditating upon this matter in privacy. Let us reconvene at about the fifteenth hour and render our decision, Brothers."

The others nodded in agreement—Cahnyr a bit grudgingly—and chairs scraped as the archbishops rose. Cahnyr nodded to Rayno and Myllyr, managed to ignore Dynnys completely, and strode briskly from the conference room. Rayno smiled slightly, like an indulgent parent with two sons who were continually at odds, then followed Cahnyr.

"Will you share lunch with me, Erayk?" Myllyr asked after the others had left. "I have a small matter which will be coming before the Office of Affirmation next five-day that I'd like to discuss with you."

"Of course, Urvyn," Dynnys replied brightly. "I'd be delighted to."

And it was true, he reflected. He actually looked forward to the inevitable dragon trading with Myllyr. It was part of the game, after all. The sizable "gift" about to land in his private purse, and the opportunity to remind Haarahld Ahrmahk where the true authority in Charis lay, would have been enough to place him firmly on Mahntayl's side, but even more seductive than mere wealth was the exercise of power. Not simply within his own archbishopric, but within the only hierarchy which truly mattered, right here in the Temple.

"I understand the kitchens have something special waiting for us this afternoon," he continued. "Shall we partake of it in the main dining hall, or would you prefer to dine on the plaza?"

F ather, you know as well as I do who's really behind it!"
Crown Prince Cayleb folded his arms across his chest and glared at his
father. King Haarahld, however, endured his elder son's expression with remarkable equanimity.

"Yes, Cayleb," the King of Charis said after a moment. "As it happens, I do
know who's really behind it. Now, just what do you suggest I do about it?"

Cayleb opened his mouth, then paused. After a moment, he closed it again.
His dark eyes were, if anything, even more fiery than they had been, but his father nodded.

"Exactly," he said grimly. "There's nothing I'd like better than to see Tahdayo's head on a pike over my gate. I'm sure he and his . . . associates feel the
same about mine, of course. Unfortunately, however much I'd like to see his
there, there's not much prospect of my collecting it any time soon. And since I
can't—"

He shrugged, and Cayleb scowled. Not in disagreement, but in frustration.

"I know you're right, Father," he said finally. "But we're going to have to find
some answer. If it were only Tahdayo, or even just him and Nahrmahn, we could
deal with it easily enough. But with Hektor behind the two of them, and with Erayk and Zherald sitting in their purses . . ."

His voice trailed off, and Haarahld nodded again. He knew, whether his son
chose to admit it or not, that at least half of Cayleb's frustration sprang from fear.
King Haarahld wasn't about to hold that against his heir, however. In fact, fear
could be a good thing in a monarch, or a future monarch, as long as it was not allowed to rule him. And as long as it sprang from the right causes. Cowardice was
beneath contempt; fear of the consequences for those one ruled was a monarch's
duty.

"If I had the answer you want, Cayleb," he said, "I wouldn't be a king; I'd be
one of the archangels come back to earth."

He touched his heart and then his lips with the fingers of his right hand, and
Cayleb mirrored the gesture.

"Since, however, I'm merely mortal," Haarahld continued, "I'm still trying to
come up with something remotely like an answer."

The king climbed out of his chair and crossed to the window. Like most
Charisians, Haarahld was a little above average height for Safehold in general,
with broader shoulders and a generally stockier build. His son was perhaps an

inch or two taller than he, and Cayleb's frame was still in the process of filling out. He was going to be a muscular, powerful man, Haarahld thought, and he moved with a quick, impatient grace.

I used to move like that, Haarahld reflected. *Back before that kraken tried to take my leg off. Was that* really *twenty years ago?*

He stopped by the window, dragging his stiff-kneed right leg under him and propping his right shoulder unobtrusively against the window frame. His son stood beside him, and they gazed out across the broad, sparkling blue waters of South Howell Bay.

The bay was dotted with sails out beyond the city's fortifications and the wharves. There were at least sixty ships tied up at the docks or awaiting wharf space. Most were the relatively small one- and two-masted coasters and freight haulers which carried the kingdom's internal trade throughout the enormous bay, but over a third were the bigger, heavier (and clumsier-looking) galleons which served Safehold's oceanic trade. Most of the galleons had three masts, and they loomed over their smaller, humbler sisters, flying the house flags of at least a dozen trading houses, while far beyond the breakwaters, three sleek galleys of the Royal Charisian Navy strode northward on the long spider legs of their sweeps.

"That's the reason we're not going to find many friends," Haarahld told his son, jutting his bearded chin at the merchant ships thronging the Tellesberg waterfront. "Too many want what we have, and they're foolish enough to think that if they league together to take it away from us, their 'friends' will actually let them keep it afterward. And at the moment, there's no one who feels any particular need to help *us* keep it."

"Then we have to convince someone to feel differently," Cayleb said.

"True words, my son." Haarahld smiled sardonically. "And now, for your next conjuration, who do you propose to convince?"

"Sharleyan is already half on our side," Cayleb pointed out.

"But only half," Haarahld countered. "She made that clear enough this past spring."

Cayleb grimaced, but he couldn't really disagree. Queen Sharleyan of Chisholm had as many reasons to oppose the League of Corisande as Charis did, and her hatred for Prince Hektor of Corisande was proverbial. There'd been some hope that those factors might bring her into open alliance with Charis, and Haarahld had dispatched his cousin Kahlvyn, the Duke of Tirian, to Chisholm as his personal envoy to explore the possibility.

Without success.

"You know how convincing Kahlvyn can be, and his position in the succession should have given any suggestion from him far greater weight than one from any other ambassador," the king continued. "If anyone could have convinced her to ally with us, it would have been him, but even if she'd been certain she wanted to support us fully, she'd still have had her own throne to consider. Corisande is as close to her as to us, and she has that history of bad blood between her and Hektor to think about. Not to mention the fact that the Temple isn't exactly one of our greater supporters just now."

Cayleb nodded glumly. However much Sharleyan might despise Hektor, she had just as many reasons to avoid open hostilities with him. And, as his father had just implied, she had even more reasons for not antagonizing the men who ruled the Temple . . . and few compelling reasons to come to the aid of what was, after all, her kingdom's most successful competitor.

"What about Siddarmark?" the crown prince asked after several seconds. "We do have those treaties."

"The Republic is probably about the most favorably inclined of the major realms," Haarahld agreed. "I'm not sure the Lord Protector would be especially eager to get involved in our little . . . unpleasantness, but Stohnar recognizes how valuable our friendship's been over the years. Unfortunately, he has even more reason than Sharleyan to be wary of irritating the Church's sensibilities, and those treaties of ours are all trade treaties, not military ones. Even if they weren't, what would Siddarmark use for a fleet?"

"I know." Cayleb pounded lightly on the window frame, chewing his lower lip.

"It's not as if this really comes as a surprise," his father pointed out. "Tahdayo's been pressing his so-called claim for years now. Admittedly, he was mostly trying to make himself enough of a nuisance for me to buy him off and be done with him, but is it really a surprise that he's suddenly started taking himself seriously now that he's finally found someone to back him?"

"It ought to be," Cayleb growled. "Tahdayo has no legitimate claim to Hanth! Even if that ridiculous lie about his grandmother's being Earl Fraidareck's bastard daughter had an ounce of truth in it, Hauwerd would still be the rightful heir!"

"Except that Mother Church is going to say differently." Haarahld's tone was light, almost whimsical, but there was nothing amused or lighthearted in his expression.

"Why shouldn't she when Nahrmahn and Hektor are so willing and eager to pour gold into Dynnys' purse?" Cayleb snarled. "Besides, the Council's always—!"

He broke off abruptly as his father laid a hand on his shoulder.

"Carefully, Cayleb," Haarahld said, his voice soft. "Carefully. What you say to me is one thing, but you are my heir. What you say where other ears can hear and use it against you—against *us*—is something else entirely."

"I know that, Father." Cayleb swung away from the window and looked into his father's eyes. "But you know, and I do, that it's exactly what's happened. And you know why the Council of Vicars is allowing it to stand, too."

"Yes," Haarahld admitted, and there was as much sorrow as anger in his eyes now. "If all Mother Church's priests were like Maikel, or even Father Paityr, it would never have happened. Or, at least, I wouldn't be worried that my son would be executed for heresy simply because he spoke the truth in the wrong ear. But they aren't, and I am. So guard your tongue, my son!"

"I will," Cayleb promised, then turned to look back out across the busy bay once more. "But you also know this is only the beginning, Father. Forcing you to accept Tahdayo as Earl of Hanth is only the first step."

"Of course it is." Haarahld snorted. "This is Hektor's doing. He's a sand maggot, not a slash lizard. Nahrmahn's too impatient to take any longer view than he absolutely must, but Hektor's always preferred to let someone else take the risk of making the kill. He's content to get fat on the leavings until, one day, the slash lizard looks over its shoulder and discovers it's strayed into the surf and the maggot's grown into a kraken."

"No doubt. But that doesn't change the fact that Tahdayo is only the opening wedge."

"Nor the fact that he's going to begin looting Hanth the instant he's confirmed as Earl," Haarahld agreed, his expression hard. "And I won't be able to protect 'his' people from him, either. Not when the whole world knows I was forced to accept him by Church decree. Any attempt I make to rein him in will be the same as openly defying the Church, once his agents in the Temple get done telling the tale to the Vicars, and many on the Council will be prepared to automatically believe them."

"But he and his masters aren't going to stop trying to undermine you, or our house, just because you can't crush him like the bottom-feeder he is."

"Of course not."

Haarahld turned away from the window and began limping back towards his chair. He seated himself heavily in it, and looked up at his son.

"I believe we still have some time," he said then, his expression somber. "How much, I can't say. At least a few months, though, I think. We're not entirely without advocates in the Temple even today, even if our own archbishop has ruled against us in this matter. And even our foes in Zion are eager to drape their actions in the mantle of fairness and justice. So for at least a little while, Tahdayo and his patrons are going to be leery of anything that could be construed as an open move against us. And while I'm seldom happy to see Dynnys, if he holds to his usual schedule, he'll be *here* by February or March, which should put a sea anchor on affairs in the Temple until he returns to Zion next fall. But once the situation's settled a bit, they're going to begin pushing again, even without him there to speak in their support."

"That's my thought, as well," Cayleb said. "I wish I felt more confident that I knew *how* they'll begin pushing, though."

"Not openly, I think," his father said slowly, lips pursed as his fingers drummed on the arms of his chair. "I almost wish they would. If it were only a matter of our fleet against that of the League, even with Nahrmahn's thrown in, I believe we could more than hold our own. But Hektor will know that as well as I do. Before he commits to any sort of open warfare, he'll find a way to strengthen their combined naval power."

"How?" Cayleb asked.

"I don't know—not yet. My guess, though, would be that he's already talking to Gorjah."

Cayleb frowned. King Gorjah III, ruler of the Kingdom of Tarot, was officially one of his father's allies. On the other hand . . .

"That *would* make sense, wouldn't it?" he murmured.

"Gorjah's never been all that happy with our treaty," Haarahld pointed out. "His father was another matter, but Gorjah resents the obligations he's found himself saddled with. At the same time, he recognizes the advantages of having us for friends rather than enemies. But if Hektor can work on him, convince him that with Corisande and Emerald both prepared to support him . . ."

The king shrugged, and Cayleb nodded. But then his eyes sharpened, and he cocked his head to one side.

"I'm sure you're right about that, Father. You usually are; you're one of the canniest men I know. But there's something else going on inside that head of yours."

Haarahld looked at him for several seconds, then shrugged again. It was a very different shrug this time, as if his shoulders had become heavier since the last one.

"Your mother is dead, Cayleb," he said softly. "She was my left arm and the mirror of my soul, and I miss her counsel almost as much as I miss *her*. Nor will I get any more heirs, and Zhan is barely eight years old, while Zhanayt is only two years older, and a girl child. If my enemies truly wish to cripple me, they'll take away my strong right arm as I've already lost the left."

He looked into his elder son's eyes, his own level, and Cayleb looked back.

"Remember the sand maggot," Haarahld told him. "The slash lizard might fling himself against us, fangs and claws first, but not the maggot. Watch your back, my son, and watch the shadows. Our enemies know us as well as we know them, and so they'll know that to kill you would take not simply my arm, but my heart."

.III.

The Mountains of Light,
The Temple Lands

Nimue Alban leaned back in the comfortable chair and frowned.

There was really no actual need for her to use the chair, just as there was no need—aside from purely "cosmetic" considerations—for her to breathe, but as she'd discovered the very first time she used a PICA, habits transcended such minor matters as simple physical fatigue. Although, she reflected with a wry smile, breathing the preservative nitrogen atmosphere with which Pei Kau-yung had filled the depot wouldn't have done a flesh-and-blood human much good.

She'd spent most of the last three local days sitting in this very chair, studying the data files Pei Kau-yung had left for her the hard way, because Elias Proctor's modifications to her software had inadvertently disabled her high-speed data interface. She was pretty sure Proctor hadn't realized he'd created the problem, and while she would have been confident enough about attempting to remedy it herself under other circumstances, she had no intention of fiddling around with it under these. If she screwed up, there was no one available to retrieve the error, and it would be the bitterest of ironies if, after all the sacrifices which had been made to put her here, she accidentally took herself permanently off-line.

In a way, having to wade through all the information the old-fashioned way had been something of a relief, really. Sitting there, reading the text, viewing the recorded messages and video instead of simply jacking into the interface, was almost like a concession to the biological humanity she'd lost forever. And it wasn't as if she were exactly in a tearing hurry to start making changes.

"Owl?" she said aloud.

"Yes, Lieutenant Commander?" a pleasant, almost naturally modulated tenor voice replied.

"I see here that Commodore Pei left us a ground-based surveillance system. Is it online?"

"Negative, Lieutenant Commander," Owl replied. That was all "he" said, and Nimue rolled her eyes.

"Why not?" she asked.

"Because I have not been instructed to bring it online, Lieutenant Commander."

Nimue shook her head. Owl—the name she'd assigned to the Ordoñes-Westinghouse-Lytton RAPIER tactical computer Pei Kau-yung had managed to "lose" for her—wasn't exactly the brightest crayon in the cybernetic box. The AI was highly competent in its own areas of expertise, but tactical computers had deliberately suppressed volitional levels and required higher levels of direct human command input. Owl wasn't precisely brimming with imagination or the ability—or desire—to anticipate questions or instructions. In theory, Owl's programming was heuristic, and something more closely resembling a personality ought to emerge eventually. On the other hand, Nimue had worked with a lot of RAPIERs, and none of them had ever impressed her as geniuses.

"What I meant to ask," she said now, "is whether or not there's any hardware problem which would prevent you from bringing the array up."

Again there was no response, and she pressed her lips rather firmly together.

"*Is* there any such hardware problem?" she amplified.

"Yes, Lieutenant Commander."

"*What* problem?" she demanded a bit more testily.

"The array in question is currently covered by approximately thirteen meters of ice and snow, Lieutenant Commander."

"Ah, now we're getting somewhere." Her sarcasm simply bounced off the AI's silence, and she sighed.

"Is it otherwise in operable condition?" she asked in a tone of deliberate patience.

"Affirmative, Lieutenant Commander."

"And can the ice and snow be removed or melted?"

"Affirmative, Lieutenant Commander."

"And you're connected to it by secure landline?"

"Affirmative, Lieutenant Commander."

"All right." Nimue nodded. "In that case, I want you to bring it up, passive systems only, and initiate a complete standard sky sweep for orbital infrastructure. And give me an estimate for time required to complete the sweep."

"Activating systems now, Lieutenant Commander. Time required to clear the array's receptors of ice and snow will be approximately thirty-one standard hours. Time required for a passive sweep after clearing receptors will be approximately forty-three standard hours, assuming favorable weather conditions. However, optical systems' efficiency may be degraded by unfavorable weather."

"Understood." Nimue's tight smile showed perfect white teeth. "What I'm looking for ought to be fairly easy to spot if it's really up there."

Owl didn't say anything else, and for just a moment Nimue tried to imagine what it must be like to be a genuine artificial intelligence rather than a *human* intelligence which had simply been marooned in a cybernetic matrix. She couldn't conceive of just sitting around indefinitely, patiently waiting for the next human command before doing *anything*.

She grimaced at the direction of her own thoughts. After all, she'd been sitting around doing absolutely nothing herself for the last eight standard centuries—almost nine Safeholdian centuries—counting all the years since Nimue Alban's biological death. Of course, it didn't seem that way to her. Not, at least, until she thought of all the people she'd never see again. Or the fact that while she'd slept the Gbaba had undoubtedly completed the destruction of the Terran Federation and all human life on every single one of its planets . . . including Old Earth.

A shiver ran through her, one which had absolutely nothing to do with the temperature of the "air" about her, and she shook her head hard.

That's enough of that, Nimue, she told herself firmly. *You may be a PICA, but your personality's still the same. Which probably means you're entirely capable of driving yourself crackers if you dwell on that kind of crap.*

She climbed out of the chair and clasped her hands behind her as she began to pace up and down. Aside from the fact that a PICA never experienced fatigue, it felt exactly the way it would have felt in the body nature had issued her, which was precisely how it was supposed to feel.

The polished-glass stone ceiling was a smoothly arched curve, almost four meters above the absolutely level, equally smooth floor at its highest point. She was in one of a dozen variously sized chambers which had been carved out underneath one of the planet Safehold's innumerable mountains during the terraforming process. This particular mountain—Mount Olympus, in what had become known as the Mountains of Light—was lousy with iron ore, and Commodore Pei and Shan-wei had thoughtfully tucked her hideaway under the densest concentration of ore they could find. She was barely forty meters above sea level, and Mount Olympus was almost a third again the height of Old Earth's Everest. There were twelve thousand meters of mountain piled on top of her, and that was more than enough to have made the tiny trickle of energy from the geothermal power tap keeping the depot's monitoring computers online completely undetectable after Langhorne and the main fleet had arrived.

She'd wandered through the rest of the complex, physically checking the various items she'd found on the equipment list stored in Owl's memory. Some of it seemed bizarre enough that she suspected that the Commodore and Shan-wei had added it simply because they could, not because they'd envisioned any compelling use for it, and exactly how they'd managed to drop some of it off of Langhorne's master lists was more than Nimue could imagine. The three armored personnel carriers, for example. And the pair of forward recon skimmers—not to mention the all-up assault shuttle, which was the size of an old pre-space jumbo jet. The small but capable fabrication unit in the cave complex's lowest (and largest) chamber made sense, and so, she supposed, did the well-stocked arms locker. Although exactly how Kau-yung had expected a single PICA to use two hundred assault rifles and two million rounds of ammunition all by herself was a bit of a puzzlement.

The fully equipped medical unit from the transport *Remus* was another puzzlement, given her cybernetic nature. It even had cryo-sleep and antigerone capability, and although she would have hesitated to use any of its drugs after eight centuries, even with cryonic storage, the nanotech portion of the therapies were still undoubtedly viable. Not that a PICA had any need for either of them, of course. She sometimes wondered if Kau-yung's and Shan-wei's emotions had insisted that they remember the flesh-and-blood Nimue Alban, rather than the being of alloys and composites which had replaced her. Whatever their reasoning had been, there was even a complete kitchen . . . despite the fact that a PICA had no particular need for food.

Other parts of the depot—which she'd found herself thinking of as Nimue's Cave—made a lot more sense. The library, for example. Kau-yung and Shan-wei had somehow managed to strip the library core out of the *Romulus*, as well, before the ship was discarded. They hadn't managed to pull the entire library computer, which was a pity in a lot of ways, since its AI, unlike Owl, had been specifically designed as an information processing and reference tool. Nimue wondered if that had been a size issue. The entire data core consisted of only three spheres of molecular circuitry, none larger than an Old Earth basketball, which could undoubtedly have been smuggled past others' eyes more easily than the entire computer system. But they'd still gotten the core down and connected it to Owl, which meant Nimue had access to the equivalent of a major Federation core world university's library system. That was undoubtedly going to be of enormous value down the road.

The hefty store of SNARCs—Self-Navigating Autonomous Reconnaissance and Communication platforms—were also going to be incredibly useful. The stealthy little fusion-powered robotic spies were only very slightly larger than Nimue herself, but they had decent AI capability, were capable of speeds of up to Mach 2 in atmosphere (they could manage considerably better than that outside it, of course), could stay airborne for months at a time, and could deploy recoverable, almost microscopic-sized remotes of their own. She had sixteen of them up at this very moment, hovering invisible to the eye, or to any more sophisticated sensors (had there been any), above major towns and cities.

For the moment, they were concentrating on recording the local languages and dialects. Without the PICA data interface, Nimue was going to have to learn the hard way to speak the considerably altered version of Standard English spoken by present-day Safeholdians. It looked as if the written language and grammar had stayed effectively frozen, but without any form of audio recording capability, the spoken form's pronunciation had shifted considerably . . . and not always in the same directions in all locations. Some of the dialects were so different now as to be almost separate tongues, despite the fact that virtually every word in them was spelled the same way.

Fortunately, she'd always been a fair hand with languages, and at least her present body didn't need sleep. Her human personality *did* need occasional down periods—she'd discovered that the first time she'd operated a PICA in autonomous mode—although the cybernetic "brain" in which that personality resided didn't. She didn't really know whether she was completely "shut down" during those periods, or if she was at some level of . . . standby readiness. Functionally, it was the equivalent of going to sleep and dreaming, although she needed no more than an hour of it every few days or so, and she suspected it was going to be rather more important to her in her present circumstances than it ever had been before. After all, no one had ever contemplated maintaining a PICA in autonomous mode indefinitely, which meant no one had any experience in doing that for more than ten days at a time.

Knack for language or not, it was going to take her a while to master the local version sufficiently for her to even consider attempting direct contact with any native Safeholdians. There was also the minor matter that she was female on a planet which had reverted, by and large, to an almost totally male-dominated culture.

There *was* something she could do about that, although she didn't really care for the thought particularly. But there was also the fact that almost all the skills she'd learned growing up in a society which took advanced technology for granted were going to be of limited utility in this one. She'd always been an enthusiastic sailor, when she had time, but only in relatively small craft, like her father's favorite ten-meter sloop. That might be useful, she supposed, but unlike some of her fellow military personnel, she'd never been particularly interested in survival courses, marksmanship, hand-to-hand combat training, blacksmithing, or the best way to manufacture lethal booby traps out of leftover ration tins and old rubber bands. True, Commodore Pei *had* gotten her interested in kendo several years before Operation Ark. She'd done fairly well at it, as a matter of fact, although she'd scarcely thought of herself as a mistress of the art. Still, that was about the only locally applicable skill she could think of, and she was none too sure just how useful even that one was going to prove.

Those were problems she was going to have to address eventually. In the meantime, however, she had plenty of other things to think about. Kau-yung's notes—almost a journal, really—had given her an insider's perspective on what Langhorne and Bédard had done to the colonists. With that advantage, she hadn't required any particular level of genius to begin discerning the consequences of their original meddling, despite her current imperfect understanding of the locals' conversations.

Safehold was unlike any other planet which had ever been inhabited by humans. Even the oldest of the Federation's colony worlds had been settled for less than two centuries when humanity first encountered the Gbaba. That had been long enough for the older colonies to develop strong local cultural templates, but all of those templates had begun from the frothy intermingling of all of Old Earth's cultural currents. There'd been enormously diverse elements bound up in all of them, and, of course, Old Earth herself had been the most diverse of all.

But whereas the cultures on all of those other planets had been created by blending different societies, belief structures, ideologies, philosophies, and worldviews into a pluralistic whole, Safehold had begun with an absolutely uniform culture. An *artificially* uniform culture. The human beings who made up that culture had all been programmed to believe *exactly* the same things, so the differences which existed here on Safehold were the consequences of eight standard centuries of evolution *away* from a central matrix, rather than towards one.

On top of that, there was the way Langhorne and Bédard had programmed the colonists into an absolute belief in the "religion" they'd manufactured. Nimue's library included the original text of the Safeholdian "*Holy Writ*" which Maruyama Chihiro, one of Langhorne's staffers, had composed, and she'd skimmed it with a sort of horrified fascination.

According to the Church of God Awaiting, God had created Safehold as a home where His children could live in simple harmony with one another, embracing a lifestyle uncomplicated by anything which might come between Him and them. Towards that end, He had selected archangels to help with the creation and perfection of their world, as well as to serve as mentors and guardians for His children. The greatest of the archangels (of course) had been the Archangel Langhorne, the patron of divine law and life, and the Archangel Bédard, the patron of wisdom and knowledge.

The version of the Church's scripture available to Nimue had almost certainly undergone significant revision following the events Commodore Pei had described in his final message. She had no way of knowing exactly what those revisions might have been until she could get her hands—or, rather, get one of her SNARCs' hands—on a more recent edition. But since the original version listed Pei Shan-wei as one of the archangels herself, the Archangel Langhorne's main assistant in bringing Safehold into existence in accordance with God's will, she was fairly sure that particular portion had seen some changes after Shan-wei's murder. Then there was the little matter of Kau-yung's intention to kill Langhorne and Bédard, as well. No doubt some judicious editing had been necessary to account for that, too.

But it was clear that the fundamentals, at least, of the plan Langhorne and Bédard had concocted had been put into effect. The Church of God Awaiting was a genuine universal, worldwide church. For all intents and purposes, the original colonists truly had been created in the instant they stepped onto Safehold's soil and the false memories implanted in them took effect. They hadn't simply believed Langhorne, Bédard, and the other members of the Operation Ark command crew were archangels; they'd *known* they were.

The fact that all of the original command crew would have continued access to the antigerone treatments had also been factored into Langhorne's original plan. The colonists had had those treatments themslves prior to leaving Old Earth, but in their new environment they would be unable to keep up the program of booster treatments. Since the command crew *would* be able to keep it up, they could expect total lifespans of as much as three centuries, and many of them had been as young as Nimue herself when they were assigned to the mission.

The original "Adams" and "Eves" would live far longer than any human who'd never received the base antigerone therapy, probably at least a century and a half, and the nanotech aspects of the original therapy would keep them disease- and infection-free. Given the colonists' average ages when Operation Ark was mounted, that would give them each at least a hundred and twenty years of fully adult life here on Safehold, more than enough to distinguish them from their shorter-lived descendants by giving them (Nimue made a moue of distaste) life spans of truly biblical proportions, coupled with immunity from disease. Yet the "angels" would live even longer, which meant the colonists, and the first five or six generations of their descendants, would have direct physical contact with "immortal" archangels.

The fact that literacy had been universal among the original colonists was yet another factor. The sheer mass of written, historically documentable firsthand accounts of their "creation" here on Safehold, of their later interaction with the archangels into whose care God had committed them, and of their enormously long lives must be overwhelming. Safehold's Church wasn't confined to the writings of a restricted number of theologians, or to a relatively small seminal holy writ. It had the journals, the letters, the inspired writings, of *eight million* people, all of whom had absolutely believed the accuracy of the events they'd set down.

No wonder Bédard felt so confident her theocratic matrix would hold, Nimue thought sourly. *These poor bastards never had a chance.*

And even if Kau-yung had succeeded in his plan to kill Langhorne and his senior followers, someone had clearly survived to take charge of the master plan. The Temple of God and City of Zion were evidence enough of that, she thought grimly, for neither had existed prior to Shan-wei's murder. And the Temple, especially, was the centerpiece of the physical proof of the *Holy Writ*'s accuracy.

She hadn't dared to let her SNARCs operate too freely in or around Zion after she'd realized there were still at least a few low-powered energy sources somewhere under the Temple, and she'd decided against using them inside the Temple itself at all, despite the hole she knew that was going to make in her information-gathering net. Unfortunately, she had no idea what those energy sources might be, and no desire to find out the hard way. But she hadn't had to get very close to the Temple to appreciate its undeniable majesty and beauty. Or the fact that it would probably outlast most of the local mountain ranges.

It was ridiculous. She'd seen planetary-defense command bunkers which had been flimsier than the Temple, and she wondered which brilliant lunatic had decided to plate that silver dome in armorplast? It looked as if the plating was at least seven or eight centimeters thick, which meant it would have been sufficient to stop an old, pre-space forty-centimeter armor-piercing shell without a scratch. It seemed just a little excessive as a way to keep the dome and that ludicrous statue of Langhorne bright and shiny. On the other hand, the simple existence of the Temple, and the "miraculous" armorplast and other advanced materials which had gone into it—not to mention the fact that its interior appeared to be completely climate-controlled even now, which *probably* explained those power sources—"proved" archangels truly had once walked the surface of Safehold. Surely no mere mortal hands could have reared such a structure!

And yet, for all its size and majesty, the Temple was actually only a tiny part of the Church's power. Every single monarch on the planet was ruler "by the grace of God and the Archangel Langhorne," and it was the Church which extended—or denied—that legitimacy. In theory, the Church could depose any ruler, anywhere, any time it chose. In fact, the Church had always been very cautious about exercising that power, and had become even more so as the great kingdoms like Harchong and Siddarmark had arisen.

But the Church was still the mightiest, most powerful *secular* force on Safehold, in her own right. The Temple Lands were smaller than Harchong or Siddarmark, with a smaller population, but they were larger and more populous than almost any other Safeholdian realm. And not even the Church truly knew how much of the planet's total wealth it controlled. Every single person on Safehold was obligated by law to deliver a tithe of twenty percent of his income every single year. Secular rulers were responsible for collecting that tithe and delivering it to the Church; the Church then used it for charitable projects, the construction of yet more churches, and as capital for a profitable business lending funds back to the local princes and nobility at usurious rates. Plus, of course, the lives of incredible wealth and luxury it provided to its senior clergy.

It was a grotesquely top-heavy structure, one in which the absolutism of the Church's power was matched only by its faith in its own right *to* that power, and Nimue hated it.

And yet, despite all of that, a part of her had actually been tempted to simply stand back and do nothing. The entire purpose of Operation Ark had been to create a refuge for humanity without the betraying high-tech spoor which might draw Gbaba scout ships to it, and so far, at least, Langhorne's megalomaniacal concoction seemed to be doing just that. But another part of her was both horrified and outraged by the monstrous deception which had been practiced upon the Safeholdians. And, perhaps more to the point, what her SNARCs had already reported to her indicated that the façade was beginning to chip.

It doesn't look like anyone's challenging the basic theology—not yet, she thought. *But the population's grown too large, and the Church has discovered the truth of that old saying about power corrupting. I wish I could get the SNARCs inside the Temple proper, but even without that, it's obvious this Council of Vicars is as corrupt and self-serving as any dictatorship in history. And even if it doesn't realize that itself, there have to be plenty of people outside the Council who do.*

It's only a matter of time until some local Martin Luther or Jan Huss turns up to demand reforms, and once the central matrix begins to crack, who knows where it may go? Any Safehold Reformation's going to be incredibly messy and ugly, given the universality of the Church and its monopoly on temporal power. And these people absolutely believe the archangels are still out there somewhere, watching over them. The believers will expect the "Archangel Langhorne" and his fellows to come back, come to the aid of the Church—or of the reformers. And when they don't, somebody's going to proclaim that they never really existed in the first place, despite all the "evidence," and that their entire religion has been a lie for almost a thousand local years. And when that happens . . .

She shuddered—a purely psychosomatic reaction, she knew—and her expression tightened.

AUGUST, YEAR OF GOD 890

✦

City of Tellesberg and Harith Foothills
near Rothar,
Kingdom of Charis

Your Highness, I don't think this is such a good idea," Lieutenant Falkhan said. "In fact, I think it's a very *bad* idea."

Crown Prince Cayleb looked at his chief bodyguard and raised one eyebrow. It was an expression of his father's which he'd been practicing for some time now. Unfortunately, it didn't seem to have quite the same effect when Cayleb employed it.

"It's all very well for you to give me that look," Falkhan told him. "You aren't the one who's going to have to explain to the King what happened to his heir if something unfortunate *does* happen. And with my luck, the instant I let you out of my sight, something will."

"Ahrnahld, it's only a hunting trip," Cayleb said patiently as he handed his tunic to Gahlvyn Daikyn, his valet. "If I take a great thundering herd of bodyguards along, how am I going to hunt anything?"

"And if it should turn out someone is inclined to be hunting *you?* Things are just a bit unsettled lately, you know. And the last time I looked, there were several people on Safehold who didn't cherish feelings of great warmth where your house is concerned."

Ahrnahld Falkhan, the youngest son of the Earl of Sharpset, was only nine years older than Cayleb himself. He was also an officer in the Royal Charisian Marines, however, and by tradition, the Marines, and not the Royal Guard, were responsible for the heir to the throne's security. Which meant young Falkhan hadn't exactly been picked for his duties at random. It also meant he didn't let his youth keep him from taking his responsibilities to keep the heir to the Charisian throne alive very seriously indeed, and Cayleb hated it when he resorted to unfair tricks like logic.

"They'd have to know where I was, to begin with," Cayleb said. "And I haven't said I'm not willing to take *any* bodyguards along. I just don't see any reason to drag the entire detachment up into the hills less than twenty miles from Tellesberg."

"I see. And just how large a *part* of the detachment were you thinking in terms of?"

"Well . . ."

"That's what I thought." Lieutenant Falkhan folded his arms and leaned his broad shoulders against the wall of his prince's airy, blue-painted sitting room, and Cayleb was almost certain he'd heard a snort of agreement from Daikyn as the valet left the room.

"The least I'll settle for is a minimum of five men," Falkhan announced.

"*Five?*" Cayleb stared at him. "We won't need to stand off a regiment, Ahrnahld! Unless you think Nahrmahn or Hektor can get an entire army past the Navy."

"Five," Falkhan repeated firmly. "Plus me. Any fewer than that, and you aren't going at all."

"Unless I'm mistaken, *I'm* the prince in this room," Cayleb said just a bit plaintively.

"And I'm afraid princes actually have less freedom than a lot of other people." Falkhan smiled with true sympathy. "But as I say, I'm not going to face your father and admit I let anything happen to you."

Cayleb looked rebellious, but there was no give in Falkhan's eyes. The lieutenant simply looked back, patiently, waiting until his youthful, sometimes fractious charge's basic good sense and responsibility had time to float to the surface.

"All right," Cayleb sighed at last. "But *only* five," he added gamely.

"Of course, Your Highness," Lieutenant Falkhan murmured, bowing in graceful submission.

▼　　▼　　▼

"Excuse me, Your Highness," Lieutenant Falkhan said the following day, as the crown prince, Falkhan, and five Marine bodyguards rode across a rolling valley through a winter morning which was working its way steadily towards noon.

This close to the equator, the weather was still quite warm, despite the official season, and the lieutenant was sweating in his cuirass's airless embrace. That wasn't the reason for his sour expression, however. *That* stemmed from the fact that the small town of Rothar, a prosperous farming village eighteen miles from Tellesberg, lay two hundred yards behind them . . . along with the local mayor, who'd just finished answering Prince Cayleb's questions.

"Yes, Ahrnahld?"

"It's just occurred to me that there seems to have been a small failure in communication here. Unless, of course, you ever mentioned to me exactly what you were going hunting for and I've simply forgotten."

"What?" Cayleb turned in his saddle and looked at the Marine officer with wide, guileless eyes. "Did I forget to tell you?"

"I rather doubt that," Falkhan said grimly, and Cayleb's lips twitched as he valiantly suppressed a smile.

The crown prince, Falkhan decided, had inherited every bit of his father's talent for misdirection. He'd gotten Falkhan so tied up in arguing about numbers of bodyguards that the lieutenant had completely forgotten to ask about the hunt's intended quarry.

"Certainly you don't think I deliberately failed to tell you?" Cayleb asked, his expression artfully hurt, and Falkhan snorted.

"That's exactly what I think, Your Highness. And I'm half inclined to turn this entire expedition around."

"I don't think we'll do that," Cayleb said, and Falkhan's mental ears twitched at the subtle but clear shift in tone. He looked at the prince, and Cayleb looked back levelly. "This slash lizard's already killed two farmers, Ahrnahld. It's got the taste for man flesh now, and more and more people are going to be out working the fields over the next few five-days. It's only a matter of time before it takes another one . . . or a child. I'm not going to let that happen."

"Your Highness, I can't argue with that desire," Falkhan said, his own tone and expression equally sober. "But letting you personally hunt something like this on foot comes under the heading of unacceptable risks."

Cayleb looked away for a moment, letting his eyes sweep over the foothills leading up to Charis' craggy spine. The dark green needles of the tall, slender pines moved restlessly, rippling like resinous waves under the caress of a strong breeze out of the south, and the white-topped, dark-bottomed anvils of thunderclouds were piling up gradually on the southern horizon.

Looking back to the west, towards Tellesberg, the green and brown patchwork of prosperous farms stretched across the lower slopes; above them to the east, the mountains towered ever higher. It was already noticeably cooler than it had been in the capital, and that would become steadily more pronounced as they climbed higher into the hills. Indeed, there was snow on some of the taller peaks above them year-round, and high overhead he saw the circling shape of a wyvern, riding the thermals patiently as it waited for some unwary rabbit or hedge lizard to offer itself as breakfast.

It was a beautiful day, and he inhaled a deep, fresh draught of air. The air of Charis, the land to whose service he'd been born. He let that awareness fill his thoughts as the air had filled his lungs, then looked back at the lieutenant.

"Do you remember how my father nearly lost his leg?"

"He was almost as young and foolish as you are at the time, I understand," Falkhan replied, rather than answering the question directly.

"Maybe he was," Cayleb conceded. "But however that may be, it didn't happen because he was running away from his responsibilities to his subjects. And there are at least a dozen children in Tellesberg today who have fathers because *my* father remembered those responsibilities." The crown prince shrugged. "I'll admit I didn't tell you about the slash lizard because I want to go after it myself. That doesn't change the fact that hunting it down—or, at least, seeing to it that it *is* hunted down—is my responsibility. And in this case, I think Father would support me."

"After he got done administering the thrashing of your life," Falkhan growled.

"Probably." Cayleb chuckled. "I'm getting a bit old for that sort of thing, but if you were to tell him about the way I threw dust into your eyes, he'd probably be just a *little* upset with me. Still, I think he'd agree that now that I'm here, I shouldn't be turning around with my tail between my legs."

"He wouldn't be any too pleased with me for *letting* you throw dust into my eyes, either," Falkhan observed glumly. Then he sighed.

"Very well, Your Highness. We're here, you fooled me, and I'm not going to drag you home kicking and screaming. *But* from this point on, you're under *my* orders. I'm not going to lose you to a slash lizard, of all damned things, so if I tell you to get the hell out of the way, you get the hell out of the way." He shook his head as the prince started to open his mouth. "I'm not going to tell you you can't hunt the thing, or how to go about doing it. But you're not taking any foolish chances—like walking into any thickets after a wounded lizard, for example. Clear?"

"Clear," Cayleb agreed, after a moment.

"Good." Falkhan shook his head. "And, just for the record, Your Highness, from now on I want to know *what* you're hunting, not just where and when."

"Oh, of course!" Cayleb promised piously.

▼   ▼   ▼

However Cayleb might have misled him in order to get here in the first place, Falkhan had to admit that the crown prince was in his element as they moved cautiously across the mountain slope. Cayleb's tutors had their hands full getting him to pay attention to his books even now. When he'd been younger, that task had been all but impossible, but the royal huntsmen and arms masters couldn't have asked for a more attentive student. And however much Falkhan would have preferred to see someone else—*anyone* else, actually—hunting this particular slash lizard, the prince was showing at least a modicum of good sense.

Slash lizards were one of Safehold's more fearsome land-going predators. A fully mature mountain slash lizard could run to as much as fourteen feet in length, of which no more than four feet would be tail. Their long snouts were amply provided with sharp, triangular teeth—two complete rows of them, top and bottom—which could punch through even the most tightly woven mail, and their long-toed feet boasted talons as much as five inches long. They were fast, nasty-tempered, territorial, and fearless. Fortunately, the "fearless" part was at least partly the result of the fact that they were pretty close to brainless, as well. A slash lizard would take on anything that moved, short of one of the great dragons, but no slash lizard had ever heard of anything remotely like caution.

Cayleb knew all of that at least as well as Falkhan did, and he was making lit-tle effort to stalk his quarry. After all, why go to the trouble of looking for the slash lizard when he could count on it to come looking for *him?* Falkhan didn't much care for the logic inherent in that approach, but he understood it. And, to be honest, he also accepted that Prince Cayleb was much handier with the lizard spears they all carried than any of his bodyguards were. The lieutenant didn't much care for *that*, either, but he knew it was true.

The crown prince was actually whistling—loudly, tunelessly, and off-key—as they wandered as obviously as possible through the heart of the slash lizard's ap-parent range. They were on foot, and Falkhan supposed he should at least be grateful Cayleb wasn't singing. King Haarahld had an excellent singing voice—a deep, resonant bass, well suited to the traditional Charisian sea chanties—but Cayleb couldn't have carried a tune in a purse seine. Which did not, unfortu-nately, prevent him from trying to on all too many occasions.

None of the bodyguards was trying to be particularly quiet, either. All of them, and the prince, were, however, staying as far away from any undergrowth as they could manage. Fortunately, the shade under the tall, straight-trunked pines creeping down from the higher slopes had choked out most of the tangled wire vine and choke tree which formed all but impenetrable thickets lower down in the foothills. That gave them—and the slash lizard—fairly long, relatively un-obstructed sight lines. And assuming the local farmers' reports about the slash lizard's recent habits were accurate, then they ought to be—

A sudden bloodcurdling scream came out of the woods on the slopes above them.

No one who'd once heard an enraged slash lizard could ever mistake its war cry for anything else. The high-pitched, wailing whistle somehow still managed to sound like the tearing canvas of a sail splitting in a sudden gale. It was the voice of pure, distilled rage, raised in furious challenge, and the entire hunting party wheeled towards the sound as the broad, low-slung creature who'd made it erupted from the woods behind it.

It wasn't a fully mature slash lizard after all, a corner of Falkhan's mind noted as he muscled his eight-foot lizard spear around. This one was barely eleven feet from snout tip to tail tip, but all six legs churned furiously as it charged, gaping maw spread wide to show all four rows of wetly shining fangs.

The lieutenant was still wrestling his spear into position when Prince Cayleb shouted back at the charging lizard. The prince's shout was as obscene as it was loud, accusing the creature's mother of certain physically impossible actions, but content was less important than volume. Although it shouldn't have been possi-ble for the slash lizard to hear *anything* through the sheer racket of its own bellow, it obviously heard Cayleb just fine. And, with the single-minded, territorial fury of its kind, it recognized the raised voice of a puny counterchallenge.

Falkhan swore even more obscenely than Cayleb as the hurtling predator's trajectory altered slightly. It thundered directly towards Cayleb, as fast as or faster than any charging horse, and not one of the prince's bodyguards was in position to intercept it.

Which, of course, was precisely what the crown prince had intended.

Cayleb turned his body almost at right angles to the slash lizard's charge. His lizard spear's long, broad, leaf-shaped head came down with the precision of a Siddarmark pikeman, his right foot extended slightly towards the lizard, and his left foot slid back and came down on the butt of his spear shaft to brace it. It all happened almost instantaneously, with the muscle-memory instinct of a swordsman and a polished perfection of form any of the prince's hunting mentors would have been proud to see. Then the lizard was upon him.

The creature's thick, squat neck stretched forward, the white lining of its opened mouth and gaping gullet shocking against the dark gray-green of its winter pelt as its jaws reached for the foolhardy foe who'd dared to invade *its* territory. And then the wailing thunder of its challenge turned into a high-pitched squall of anguish as the prince's razor-edged spearhead punched unerringly into the base of its throat.

The twenty-inch spearhead drove into the center of its chest, and its own hurtling weight hammered the knife-edged point home with a power no human arm could have achieved. The stout eighteen-inch crossbar a foot below the base of the spearhead prevented that same weight from driving it straight down the spear shaft to reach Cayleb. The shock of impact still nearly bowled the prince over, despite his impeccable form and braced position, but it didn't, and the slash lizard's squall turned into a choking scream as the spearhead punched straight into its heart.

The lizard slammed to a halt, writhing and thrashing in pinned agony, blood fountaining from opened mouth and nostrils. Its death throes almost accomplished what the force of its charge had failed to, shaking the crown prince like one of the port's mastiffs shaking a spider rat. It could still have killed Cayleb with a single blow from one of its massively clawed forefeet, but the prince clung to his spear shaft, using it to fend off the half-ton of mortally wounded fury.

To Lieutenant Falkhan, it seemed to take a brief eternity, but it couldn't actually have been anywhere near that long. The lizard's screams turned into bubbling moans, its frantic thrashing slowed, and then, with a last, almost pathetic groan, it folded in upon itself and went down in a twitching heap.

▼　　▼　　▼

"Shan-wei take it!" the shortest of the men lying belly-down on the ridgeline snarled in disgust. "Why couldn't that accursed lizard have done its job?"

"Never really much chance of that, Sir," his second-in-command observed dryly. "That was as pretty a piece of work as I've ever seen."

"Of course there wasn't," the leader acknowledged sourly. "Still, I could *hope*, couldn't I?"

His subordinate simply nodded.

"Well," the leader sighed after a moment, "I suppose it just means we'll have to do it the hard way after all."

▼   ▼   ▼

"Well," Ahrnahld Falkhan said, looking at his crown prince across the slash lizard's still shuddering carcass, "that was certainly exciting, wasn't it?"

Cayleb's answering laugh was exuberant, despite his chief bodyguard's less than fully approving tone. Then the prince braced one foot on the lizard's shoulder, gripped the spear shaft in both hands, bent his back, and grunted with effort as he pulled the long, lethal head free.

"Actually, it was," he agreed as he began scrubbing blood off the spear by wiping it through the low-growing near-heather.

"I'm glad you enjoyed it," Falkhan said repressively, and Cayleb grinned at him. The lieutenant tried to glower back, but despite his best efforts, his own grin leaked through. He started to say something else, then shook his head and looked at one of his subordinates instead.

"Payter."

"Yes, Sir?" Sergeant Payter Faircaster replied crisply, although he couldn't quite suppress a smile of his own. The prince's bodyguards might all deplore the way their charge's insistence on doing things like this complicated their own duties, but there was no denying that it was more satisfying to protect someone who wasn't afraid of his own shadow.

"Take someone back with you for the horses. And send someone else back to take a message to Rothar. Tell the Mayor to send out a cart to haul this—" he poked the lizard with the toe of one boot "—back with us. I'm sure," he gave the prince a sweet smile, "that His Majesty is going to be fascinated to see what sort of small game the Prince was out hunting this morning."

"Oh, that's a low blow, Ahrnahld!" Cayleb acknowledged, raising one hand in the gesture a judge used to indicate a touch in a training match.

"I know, Your Highness," Falkhan agreed, while the rest of the prince's bodyguards chuckled with the privilege of trusted retainers.

"Luhys," Faircaster said, pointing to one of the other troopers. "You and Sygmahn."

"Aye, Sergeant." Luhys Fahrmahn's broad mountain accent was more pronounced than usual, and he was still grinning as he touched left shoulder with right hand in salute and jerked his head at Sygmahn Oarmaster. "We'll do that thing."

He and Oarmaster handed their spears to Fronz Dymytree; then the two of them trotted off with Faircaster, leaving Dymytree and Corporal Zhak Dragoner with Falkhan and the prince.

▼   ▼   ▼

"Now isn't that handy," the short man on the ridgeline murmured in much more satisfied tones.

"It suits *me* right down to the ground, Sir," his second-in-command agreed feelingly. Charisian Marines had a well-earned reputation, and they didn't get assigned as royal bodyguards for their sweet dispositions and retiring ways.

"Well," the leader said after a moment, "I suppose we'd best get to it. And at least we've got ground we can work with."

He and his men had been shadowing the prince's party ever since it left Rothar, and while he would have preferred for the lizard to do their job for them, the opportunities the present terrain offered were obvious to his experienced eye.

"Let's go. And remember—" He glared at the rest of his men. "—I'll personally cut the throat of anyone who makes a sound until the crossbows are into position."

Heads nodded, and eleven more men, all dressed in the same gray-brown and green garments, two of them armed with crossbows, climbed to their feet behind him and his sergeant.

▼   ▼   ▼

"Just as a matter of curiosity, Your Highness," Lieutenant Falkhan asked as he paced the length of the slash lizard's outstretched body, "how did you come to hear about this?"

"Hear about it?" Cayleb repeated, eyebrows raised, and Falkhan shrugged.

"As a general rule, palace gossip spreads faster than a crown fire in a pinewood," he said. "In this case, though, I hadn't heard a whisper about this fellow." He jerked a thumb at the dead lizard. "That's why you were able to get this little expedition past me. I'm just curious about how you managed to hear about it before anyone else?"

"I don't really remember," Cayleb admitted, after considering it for a few seconds. He scratched one eyebrow, frowning thoughtfully. "I think it may have been from Tymahn, but I'm not really sure about that."

"Tymahn would've known about it if anyone did," Falkhan acknowledged. Tymahn Greenhill, one of King Haarahld's senior huntsmen for over eighteen years, had been Cayleb's chief hunting mentor, since the king's crippled leg had prevented him from filling that role himself.

"He does have a way of hearing about things like this," Cayleb agreed. "And he—"

"*Get* down, *Your Highness!*"

Ahrnahld Falkhan's head snapped up as a voice he'd never heard before in his life shouted the four-word warning.

▼   ▼   ▼

The short man whirled in shock as the deep, powerful voice shouted from be-hind him.

He and his men had gotten to within fifty yards of their intended prey. The thick carpet of pine needles had muffled any sound their feet might have made, and the steep-sided gully of a dry, seasonal streambed's twisting course had pro-vided cover for their approach. His two crossbowmen had just settled into firing position, bracing their weapons on the raised lip of the streambed and waiting pa-tiently for the moving Marine lieutenant to clear their line of fire to their target. Not surprisingly, every scrap of the leader's attention at that moment was con-centrated on the Charisian crown prince and his three remaining bodyguards.

Which was why he was totally unprepared to see the man charging across that same carpet of pine needles towards him with a drawn sword in his hands.

▼　　▼　　▼

Lieutenant Falkhan reacted out of instinct and training, not conscious thought. His right hand swept towards the hilt of his sword, but his left reached out si-multaneously. It caught Crown Prince Cayleb by the front of his tunic and yanked brutally.

The sudden heave took Cayleb completely by surprise. He unbalanced and went down in an ungainly sprawl . . . just as a crossbow bolt hissed through the space he'd occupied an instant before.

The same bolt could not have missed Falkhan by more than six inches, and a second bolt slammed into Zhak Dragoner's chest. The corporal crumpled back-ward without even a scream, and the lieutenant's blade hissed out of its sheath.

Fronz Dymytree tossed aside the lizard spears he'd been holding and snatched out his own cutlass almost as quickly as Falkhan's sword cleared the scabbard. The two surviving Marines, still reacting before conscious thought could catch up with them, moved to place themselves between the prince and the apparent source of the attack.

▼　　▼　　▼

The assassins' leader just had time to draw his own sword before the interfering madman came bounding down into the dry watercourse towards him.

"Finish the job!" the leader shouted to his second-in-command. "I'll deal with this bastard!"

His subordinate didn't even hesitate. The leader's reputation as a master swordsman was well deserved. It was also one of the reasons he'd been chosen for this mission in the first place, and the second-in-command heaved himself up out of the streambed on the side closest to the Charisians.

"Come on!" he barked.

▼   ▼   ▼

Falkhan swore viciously as at least ten men seemed to appear out of the very ground. Two of them carried crossbows, but all the rest had drawn swords, and the crossbowmen dropped their ungainly, slow-firing weapons and reached for their own swords.

"Run, Highness!" the lieutenant shouted as he sensed Cayleb bouncing back to his feet behind him.

"Fuck that!" the crown prince spat back, and steel scraped as he drew his own blade.

"God *damn* it, Cayleb, *run!*" Falkhan bellowed, and then the attackers were upon them.

▼   ▼   ▼

The assassin leader was confident in his own skill, but a faint warning bell rang somewhere inside him as his unexpected opponent's peculiar stance registered. The mysterious newcomer held the hilt of his weapon in both hands, just above eye level, with one foot advanced and his entire body turned at a slight angle.

It was unlike any stance the assassin had ever seen, but he had no time to analyze it. Not before the hovering weapon hissed forward like a steel lightning bolt.

The sheer, blazing speed of the stroke took the assassin by surprise, but he was just as good as his reputation claimed. He managed to interpose his own broadsword, despite his opponent's speed and even though he'd never encountered an attack quite like this one.

It didn't help.

He had one brief instant for his eyes to begin to widen in shocked disbelief as the newcomer's blade sliced cleanly through his own, and then his head leapt from his shoulders.

▼   ▼   ▼

Ahrnahld Falkhan parried frantically as the first sword came chopping in. Steel jarred on steel with an ugly, anvil-like clang, and he twisted aside as a second blade reached for him. He heard more metal clashing on metal, and swore with silent desperation as he realized Cayleb, instead of running while he and Dymytree tried to slow the assassins, had fallen into formation with them.

Only three things kept the crown prince and either of his Marines alive for the next few seconds. One was the two crossbowmen's need to discard one weapon and draw another, which slowed them and dropped them a little behind the other ten attackers. The second was the fact that all of the assassins coming at them had expected those crosswbows to do the job without any need to engage anyone hand-to-hand. They'd been just as surprised by the mysterious stranger's intervention as Falkhan had been by their own attack, and their rush towards the prince and his bodyguards was a scrambling, unorganized thing. They didn't come in together in a tightly organized attack.

And the third thing was that Cayleb had ignored Falkhan's order to run.

The first assassin to reach the crown prince leapt towards him, sword slashing, only to stumble back with a sobbing scream as Cayleb unleashed a short, powerful lunge. King Haarahld had imported a weapons master from Kyznetzov, in South Harchong, and while the Empire might be decadent, might be corrupt, and was definitely insufferably arrogant, it still boasted some of the finest weapons instructors in the world. Master Domnek was at least as arrogant as any Harchong stereotype, but he was also just as good at his craft as he thought he was . . . and a relentless taskmaster.

Most Safeholdian swordsmen were trained in the old school, but Cayleb had been taught by someone who recognized that swords had points for a reason. His savage, economic lunge drove a foot of steel through his opponent's chest, and he'd recovered back into a guard position before his victim hit the ground.

A second assassin came hurtling in on the crown prince, only to collapse—this time with little more than a gurgling moan—as Cayleb's second thrust went home at the base of his throat.

Falkhan was too heavily engaged against two other opponents to allow his attention to stray, but he was agonizingly aware that the assassins were concentrating their efforts against Cayleb. The fact that they were was probably the only reason Falkhan and Dymytree were still alive, yet he didn't expect to stay that way for long against three-to-one odds.

But then something new was added.

▼　　▼　　▼

The assassins' second-in-command heard a scream from behind him and grinned nastily at the evidence that his commander had dealt with the interfering busybody who'd spoiled their ambush. But then he heard a *second* scream, and he backed off a couple of paces from the confusion of blades and bodies around the Charisian prince and his outnumbered bodyguards and turned to look back the way he'd come.

He just had time to take in the crumpled bodies of his two crossbowmen, and then the man who'd killed both of them was upon him in a swirl of steel.

Unlike his late commander, this assassin had no time to register anything peculiar about his opponent's stance. He was too busy dying as the newcomer drove a two-handed thrust straight through his lungs and heart, twisted his wrists, and recovered his blade, all in one graceful movement and without ever breaking stride.

▼　　▼　　▼

Ahrnahld Falkhan got through to one of his attackers. The man fell back with a groan, dropping the dirk in his off hand as his left arm went limp, but then the lieutenant grunted in anguish as a sword got through his own guard and gashed the outside of his left thigh. He staggered, staying on his feet somehow, but his sword wavered, and another blade came driving at him.

He managed to beat the attack aside, carrying his attacker's sword to the left, but that left him uncovered on the right, and he sensed another assassin coming in on him.

And then that assassin went down himself, instantly dead, as a gory steel thunderbolt impacted on the nape of his neck like a hammer and severed his spinal cord.

Falkhan wasted no time trying to understand what had just happened. There were still armed men trying to kill his prince, and he used the distraction of the stranger's attack to finish off his wounded adversary. He heard Dymytree groan behind him, even as the dead man fell, and cursed as the Marine went down, uncovering Cayleb's left side. Falkhan knew the prince was exposed, but the wounded lieutenant was still too heavily engaged with his sole remaining opponent to do anything about it.

Cayleb saw Dymytree collapse from the corner of one eye. He knew what that meant, and he tried to wheel to face the man who'd cut down his bodyguard. But the two men already attacking him redoubled their efforts, pinning him in place. The prince's mind was clear and cold, focused as Master Domnek had taught him, yet beyond the shield of that focus was a stab of cold terror as he waited for Dymytree's killer to take him from the flank.

But then, suddenly, someone else was at his side. Someone whose flashing blade cut down two foes in what seemed a single motion.

The three surviving would-be assassins abruptly realized that the odds had somehow mysteriously become even. They fell back, as if by common consent, but if they'd intended to break off the attack, they'd left it too late.

Cayleb stepped forward, lunging in quarte. Another of his attackers folded forward over the bitter thrust of his blade, and the stranger who'd mysteriously materialized at his left side lopped off another head in almost the same instant. It was the first time Cayleb had actually heard of anyone managing that in a single, clean, one-handed blow—outside some stupid heroic ballad, at least—and the sole remaining assassin seemed as impressed by it as the crown prince. He whirled to flee, and Cayleb was in the act of recovering his stance, unable to interfere as the man turned to run. But the stranger's sword licked out with blinding speed, and the assassin shrieked as he was neatly hamstrung.

He collapsed, and the stranger stepped forward. A booted foot slammed down on the back of the wounded man's sword hand, evoking another scream as it crushed the small bones. The assassin twisted, his left hand scrabbling at the hilt of the dagger at his hip, and the stranger's sword licked out again, severing the tendons in his wrist.

It was over in a heartbeat, and then Cayleb found himself facing the stranger who had just saved his life across the sobbing body of the only surviving attacker.

"It occurred to me," the stranger said in an odd, clipped accent, strange sapphire eyes bright, "that you might want to ask this fellow a few questions about who sent him, Your Highness."

.II.
Harith Foothills Near Rothar,
Kingdom of Charis

Crown Prince Cayleb knew he was staring at his totally unanticipated rescuer, but he couldn't help it. The newcomer looked unlike anyone he'd ever seen before. His complexion was paler even than Father Paityr Wylsynn's, and Cayleb had never seen eyes of such a deep, dark blue. Yet while Father Paityr's complexion and gray eyes went with an unruly shock of bright red hair, this man's hair was as dark as Cayleb's own. And he was taller even than Cayleb by a full two inches.

He was also quite improbably handsome, in spite of the thin, white scar which seamed his right cheek. In some ways, his features were almost effeminate, despite his fiercely waxed mustachios and neat dagger beard, yet that, like the piratical-looking scar, only gave his face a certain exotic cast. All in all, a most impressive character, and one who'd arrived at the proverbial last second.

Which, of course, raised the question of just how he'd managed to do that. Cayleb might not have been the most bookish scholar his tutors had ever encountered, but he'd been well grounded in basic logic, history, and statecraft, and his father had personally undertaken his instruction in the essential suspicion any head of state required. While he was perfectly well aware that coincidences truly did happen, he was also aware that some "coincidences" were *made* to happen. Especially when the people responsible for them were engaged in a shadowy struggle for the highest stakes imaginable.

"I hope you'll forgive me for pointing this out," the prince said, without cleaning or sheathing his own blade, "but you appear to have a certain advantage. You know who *I* am, but I have no idea who *you* are, sir."

"Which must certainly appear suspicious under the circumstances, Your Highness," the stranger observed with a smile, and bowed ever so slightly. "I'm called Merlin, Prince Cayleb, Merlin Athrawes, and the reason the circumstances appear suspicious is because they are. I scarcely happened along by accident, and explaining exactly how I did come to arrive will require some time. For now, however—" He bent and ripped a handful of fabric from his last, whimpering victim's tunic, used it to wipe his blade, and sheathed the steel smoothly. "—both this fellow here and Lieutenant Falkhan would seem to require a little attention."

Cayleb twitched as he was reminded, and looked quickly at the lieutenant. Falkhan sat on the pine needles, his eyes glassy as he used both hands to stanch the flow of blood from his wounded thigh, and the crown prince took a quick step in his direction. Then he froze, his eyes whipping back to "Merlin," as he realized how thoroughly and effortlessly the stranger had redirected his attention.

But the other man simply stood there, arms folded across his chest, and raised one sardonic eyebrow.

Cayleb flushed. On the other hand, if the stranger had wished him harm, there'd been no reason to interfere in the ambush in the first place. That didn't mean he might not have some deeper, subtly inimical purpose in mind, but it seemed unlikely that burying a dagger in the prince's back was among his immediate plans.

The crown prince dropped to his knees beside Falkhan. Rather than waste time cleaning his own sword and returning it to the scabbard, he laid it on the pine needles, then drew his dagger and began slicing open the leg of the lieutenant's breeches.

The wound was ugly enough, and bleeding freely, but without the heavy, pulsing flow of arterial blood. He unbuttoned the huntsman's pouch on his left hip and quickly extracted the rolled bandage of boiled cotton. He covered the wound with a pad of fleming moss, then wrapped the bandage tightly around Falkhan's thigh, applying pressure to the wound. If pressure and the absorbent, healing moss didn't stop the bleeding, he had a packet of curved needles and boiled thread to close the wound with stitches, but he was scarcely a trained surgeon. He preferred to leave that sort of repair to someone who knew what he was doing.

The lieutenant had slumped back, eyes closed, while the prince worked on him. By the time Cayleb tied the bandage off, though, Falkhan's eyes were open once more.

The Marine turned his head, and his mouth tightened with more than the physical pain of his own wound as he saw Dragoner's and Dymytree's bodies. Then he looked outward, at the sprawled corpses of the assassins, and his eyes narrowed as he saw the mysterious Merlin kneeling beside the one surviving attacker. Merlin's hands had been busy attending to the other man's wounds even as Cayleb saw to Falkhan's, although it was apparent from the assassin's sounds that the stranger wasn't wasting a great deal of gentleness upon him.

Falkhan's head rolled back, his gaze met Cayleb's, and both eyebrows rose in question. Cayleb looked back at him, then shrugged. The lieutenant grimaced, then pushed himself up—with the prince's assistance and a grunt of pain—into a sitting position. Cayleb positioned himself unobtrusively to allow the Marine to lean back against him, and Falkhan cleared his throat.

"Excuse me," he said, looking up at the man who'd saved not only the prince's life, but his own, "but I think we need a few answers, sir."

▼   ▼   ▼

The man who'd introduced himself to Cayleb as "Merlin"—and who had decided he really needed to work on never thinking of himself as Nimue Alban—smiled. The expression was rather more confident than he actually felt, but he'd known this moment, or one very like it, was going to come.

Well, not exactly like this *one,* he amended. It was sheer serendipity that his SNARC had not only stumbled across the plot to assassinate Crown Prince Cayleb but that he'd actually managed to arrive in time to help foil it.

Good thing I did, too. I already knew Cayleb was a good-looking kid, but I hadn't realized quite how much presence he has. Especially for someone who's barely nineteen standard. If I can just get him to trust me, I can do something with him.

Assuming, of course, that I can figure out a way to go on keeping him alive.

"I am known," he told Falkhan, "as I've already informed Prince Cayleb, as Merlin Athrawes. And I'm not at all surprised you have questions, Lieutenant Falkhan. I certainly would, in your place. And while *I* may be confident I cherish no ill designs upon the Prince, there's no reason *you* should feel that way. So, if you have questions I can answer, ask them."

Falkhan cocked his head, his expression wary, then bought a little time by easing his wounded leg's position with a wince of pain which was not at all feigned. He was uncomfortably aware that his own light-headedness scarcely made this the ideal time for a probing, insightful interrogation. Unfortunately, this was the only time—and the only wit—he had. Besides, something about Merlin's manner made him suspect he would be outclassed in any battle of wits with him at the best of times.

"Since you've been courteous enough to acknowledge that my duty to my Prince requires me to be suspicious of apparent coincidences," he said, after a moment, "perhaps you might begin by telling me how you happened along at such an extremely . . . opportune moment."

Cayleb stirred slightly behind him, but stilled as Falkhan reached back unobtrusively and squeezed his ankle. He knew the crown prince well enough to be aware that, despite Cayleb's own recognition of the need to be cautious, he retained sufficient of childhood's romantic faith in heroic ballads—and how the characters in them ought to act—to feel uncomfortable at such a direct challenge.

But this Athrawes (and what sort of surname was that, anyway?) seemed more amused then offended. He took time to recheck his rough but efficient repairs to the crippled assassin, then folded down gracefully to sit tailor-fashion on the pine needles.

"To begin at the beginning, Lieutenant," he said then, in that strangely clipped accent, "I come from the Mountains of Light. Although I wasn't born there, I've made my home among their peaks for many years, and after long and careful study, I've been blessed with some, at least, of the powers of a *seijin.*"

Falkhan's eyes narrowed, and Cayleb inhaled audibly behind him. The Mountains of Light contained the second-holiest site of Safehold, the mighty peak of Mount Olympus, where the Archangel Langhorne had first set foot upon the solid earth of Safehold when God established the firmament in the misty dawn of creation. And the *seijin* were a legend in their own right—warriors, holy men, sometimes prophets and sometimes teachers. Only the archangels themselves could endure *surgoi kasai*, God's own mystic fire, but the *seijin* had been touched by *anshinritsumei*, God's "little fire," and it rendered them men forever set apart from other mortals.

To the lieutenant's knowledge, no authentic *seijin* had ever visited the Kingdom of Charis, and the mere fact that someone claimed to be one proved nothing. Although, he conceded, it would take more nerve than most people possessed to claim *seijin* status falsely.

"That's . . . an interesting statement, sir," Falkhan said slowly, after a moment.

"And one difficult to prove," Merlin agreed. "Believe me, Lieutenant, you can't be more aware of that fact than I am." He smiled wryly and leaned back, stroking one waxed mustachio with the fingers of his right hand. "In fact, I must admit that I never anticipated *I* might find myself called to such a role. Still, I believe the *Writ* warns us that our tasks in life will seek us out, wherever we may be, and whatever we may plan."

Falkhan nodded. Again, he had the distinct impression that Athrawes was amused by his questions, his suspicion. Still, he sensed no malice in the other man. His own current dizziness made him distrust his instincts, yet he found he felt more curious than threatened.

"For quite some time," Merlin continued, his expression more serious, "I've been gifted with the Sight. I sometimes see events which take place thousands of miles away, although I've never seen into the future or the past, as some have claimed to do. That ability to see distant events is what led me to Charis at this time. While I may not be able to see the future, I *have* seen other visions—visions concerning Charis, Crown Prince Cayleb and his father, and their enemies. Somehow I find it difficult to believe such visions would be given to me if I weren't meant to act upon them."

"Forgive me," Cayleb said, his expression intent, "but if, as you say, you can't see the future, then how did you know about this?"

He took one hand from Falkhan's shoulder and waved at the carnage all about them.

"Your Highness," Merlin said, almost gently, "surely you aren't so . . . naïve as to believe this attack simply materialized out of thin air this morning? You have enemies, Prince. Enemies who, whether they realize it or not, serve darkness, and I've seen many visions of their plans and plots, of correspondence and orders passing between them. I've known for almost half a year that they intended to bring about your death in any way they could. This isn't their first plan, but simply the first which came this close to success. I've been traveling from the Temple Lands to Charis for many five-days now, ever since I became aware that they were preparing to move from mere plans to actual execution, if you'll pardon the choice of words."

He smiled, showing improbably white, perfect teeth, and Cayleb frowned.

"Don't think me ungrateful," he said, "but I find it difficult to believe I'm so righteous that God Himself would send a *seijin* to save me."

"I suspect you're more righteous than many, Your Highness. Possibly even than most—after all, at your age, how much opportunity have you had to become *un*righteous?" Merlin chuckled and shook his head. "However, I'm not at all sure your personal righteousness has anything to do with it. You seem a nice enough young man, but I rather suspect that what brought me here has more to do with what you may accomplish in the future than anything you've already done."

"Accomplish in the future?" Cayleb stiffened, and Merlin shrugged.

"As I've already said, Your Highness, it's never been given to me to see the future. I do, however, see the patterns of the present, and what I've seen of your father's rule gives me a very good opinion of him. I know." He held up one hand with an easy smile. "I know! Presumptuous of me to judge the worth of any king, and especially of a king not my own! Still, there it is. His people are happy and prosperous and, until . . . certain other parties began actively plotting against him, they were secure, as well. And he's spent years training you, which suggests you would continue in the same mold as king. At any rate, and for whatever reason those visions have come to me, it seemed evident your enemies were prepared—or preparing—to strike directly at either you, your father, or both. There was nothing I could do about it from my home, and so I took ship for Charis. I arrived three days ago, aboard Captain Charlz' ship."

"Marik Charlz?" Falkhan asked more sharply than he'd intended to, and Merlin nodded.

"Yes. I traveled cross-country to Siddar, and I was fortunate enough to find *Wave Daughter* there with a load of Zebediahan tea. Captain Charlz had run into some sort of problem with the Customs officers which took several five-days to straighten out, but he'd finally gotten it taken care of just before I arrived. He was headed home with a cargo of Siddarmark brandy, and I needed a ride." Merlin smiled again. "If the good Captain is typical of the way you Charisians haggle, it's small wonder so many envy your trading ships' successes!"

"Captain Charlz drives a hard bargain," Falkhan agreed. "I suppose it comes from all the years he spent as a purser in the Navy."

"You need more practice at trapping liars, Lieutenant," Merlin told him with a chuckle. "Captain Charlz was never a purser. In fact, I believe he told me he holds a reserve commission in your navy. As a full ship master, if I recall correctly." Cayleb snorted behind Falkhan, and Merlin winked at the crown prince. "Besides," he added, "it would be particularly stupid of me to give you the name of both captain and ship if I were lying, wouldn't it?"

"Yes, it would," Falkhan acknowledged. "Still, given the . . . uncanny nature of your tale, I'm sure you realize we will be speaking to Captain Charlz?"

Merlin simply nodded, with another small smile, and Falkhan inhaled deeply.

"So. You arrived in Tellesberg three days ago. Why didn't you make your presence known sooner?"

"Oh, come now, Lieutenant!" This time Merlin laughed out loud. "Suppose I'd walked up to the palace gate three days ago, rung the bell, and informed the commander of the Palace Guard that I'd journeyed all the way from the Temple Lands to Charis because I had a vision that the Crown Prince was in danger, and could I possibly have a personal audience with him to explain all that, please? Given all the political currents and crosscurrents swirling about between Charis, Emerald, Corisande, and Tarot, how do you think Colonel Ropewalk would have reacted?"

"Not well," Falkhan admitted, noting once more that whoever and whatever else this Athrawes might actually be, he was fiendishly well informed about events and people here in Charis.

" 'Not well' is putting it mildly, Lieutenant." Merlin snorted. "I'm sure he would've been at least reasonably polite about it, but I'd still be sitting in a cell somewhere while he tried to figure out which of your many enemies had sent me." He shook his head. "I'm afraid Colonel Ropewalk doesn't have a very trusting disposition."

"Which is why he's the commander of the Palace Guard," Falkhan pointed out.

"I'm sure. But without any way to prove my bona fides, it seemed best to me to find myself an inn and take a room while I waited to see what would happen next. At that time, I had no knowledge of any immediate, specific threat to the King or to the Prince. Indeed," Merlin said with total honesty, "it was only late yesterday evening that I became aware of this particular plot. In my visions, I'd already seen these men's commander"—a jerk of his head indicated the bodies sprawled around them—"receiving instructions and passing on instructions of his own. But only last night did I 'see' him issuing the orders for this attack. And, by the way, it was he who saw to it that one of the Prince's huntsmen heard about this slash lizard, as well. I'm afraid he and his masters had a very good idea of how the Prince would react to the news.

"Thanks to my vision, I knew what was intended, but I had absolutely no evidence I could have presented to anyone. Had I been in your boots, Lieutenant, I would have been most suspicious of any total stranger who arrived on my doorstep this morning with tales of hidden assassins lurking in the forest. I would have had the stranger in question detained, at least until I could get to the bottom of his preposterous story. Which would just happen to have put the only person— other than the murderers, of course—who knew anything about the plan in a position from which he could accomplish nothing. So instead of trying to warn you, I came ahead, determined to do what I could to spoil their plans myself."

Merlin paused, and his strange sapphire eyes darkened as he gazed briefly at the two dead Marines.

"I regret that I couldn't find a way to do it which would have kept the rest of your men alive, Lieutenant. Perhaps if I *could* see the future, I might have been able to."

Falkhan sat silent for several minutes, gazing at the blue-eyed stranger. The lieutenant felt certain there were a great many things this Athrawes wasn't telling, or was glossing over. And yet he also felt oddly certain the mysterious foreigner truly did wish young Cayleb well. And whatever else he might be up to, without his intervention, the prince would most assuredly be dead at this moment. Moreover, it was Athrawes who'd seen to it that they had at least one of the assassins to interrogate, which he would hardly have done if that interrogation might implicate *him* in any plots.

It was always possible Athrawes, or someone he worked for, had designs of his own upon Charis. He might know exactly who'd sent the assassins and be working at cross-purposes to that particular enemy without being a friend himself. At the same time, however, he'd provided a wealth of detail about his own arrival in Charis which could be readily checked, and it might well be possible to test his claim to see "visions," as well.

For the moment, the lieutenant decided, he had no choice but to take the *seijin* claim at least tentatively seriously. Where that might lead if, indeed, it proved accurate was anyone's guess.

Except, of course, that those who wished his kingdom ill would not be at all pleased to hear about it.

.III.
Tellesberg,
Kingdom of Charis

WHAT happened?"

"How do I know?" Oskahr Mhulvayn replied irritably. He glowered at Zhaspahr Maysahn, his immediate superior. The two of them sat at a table in a street-side café only two blocks from the wharves, sipping cups of strong, sweet Dohlaran chocolate. The café was on the west side of the street, which had put it into cool shadow as the sun moved steadily towards evening (for which both men were devoutly grateful), and seabirds and sand wyverns foraged for scraps in a square across from it, where the produce hucksters had just closed their booths for the day. Despite the noise and bustle of a typical, busy Tellesberg day, the scene was reassuringly normal and calm. Which might well change in the next few hours, Mhulvayn thought, and shrugged one shoulder.

"Cayleb went out; he came back. Alive," he said.

"That much I've figured out for myself," Maysahn said sarcastically. "And I know two of his bodyguards came back dead, and another one came back wounded, too."

"Then you should also know the gate guard was told to expect a pair of wagons shortly. One's supposed to have a dead slash lizard in it; the other one's supposed to be piled up with dead assassins. A full wagonload—over a dozen." Mhulvayn bared his teeth in a caricature of a smile. "I don't suppose you'd care to guess just who all of those 'dead assassins' might be?"

"Shan-wei!" Maysahn muttered. "How could they screw up that badly against just five bodyguards?"

"Well," Mhulvayn said philosophically, "at least *we* don't have any explaining to do." He paused and looked at his superior closely. "We don't, do we?"

"Not likely!" Maysahn snorted. "You think I'd be sitting around here talking to you if there were any chance something like this might lead back to me?"

"It would seem a little foolish," Mhulvayn agreed.

"The only thing more foolish I could think of right off hand would be going home to tell *him* in person that I'd been involved in anything this stupid."

Mhulvayn chuckled, although, in truth, neither of them felt particularly amused. He started to say something else, then paused as the waiter stopped by their table to offer refills on their chocolate. Maysahn raised one eyebrow at him, and Mhulvayn nodded. The imported chocolate was expensive, but Mhulvayn's cover as the representative of a Desnairi banking house and Maysahn's cover as the owner of a small fleet of merchant ships gave them the resources to indulge themselves from time to time.

The waiter poured, then departed, and Mhulvayn waited until the young man was out of earshot before speaking again. Their table was right at the edge of the slightly raised sidewalk, which put them very close to the cobblestone street. It was hardly a preferred location for most of the café's patrons. The noise of horse hooves, the grating roar of iron-shod wheels over cobbles, the burbling whistles of draft dragons, and the constant surf of background voices made it difficult to carry on a comfortable conversation. That same racket, however, also made it extremely difficult for anyone to overhear what they might have to say to one another.

"Actually," Mhulvayn said in a more serious tone, when he was certain no one else was in earshot, "from the rumors I've heard, it ought to have worked."

"The rumors are already busy?" Maysahn looked amused, and Mhulvayn shrugged.

"The rumors are always busy. In this case, the mayor of Rothar sent a messenger ahead. The yokel he chose passed his message to the gate guards, then found himself a tavern and had a few beers." Mhulvayn raised one hand and waggled it back and forth. "By the time he had three or four of them inside him, he was waxing eloquent. How much of it was accurate, I don't know, of course."

"Of course." Maysahn nodded. Half a spy's job consisted of picking up rumors which might or might not be true and passing them along. If he was smart, he eliminated all the ones he could demonstrate were inaccurate and was honest with his employer about the ones whose veracity he doubted. Not that all spies were smart, in Maysahn's experience.

"Bearing that in mind," Mhulvayn continued, "it sounds like everything went pretty much according to plan. They had the Prince out in the woods, and he'd sent two or three of his bodyguards back for horses. And they'd brought along crossbows, so they shouldn't even have had to get into sword's reach of them."

Maysahn looked impressed, almost against his will. He cupped his chocolate in both hands, sipping thoughtfully, then shook his head.

"If they had a 'wagonload' of men, and they had the target just where they wanted him, what the hell went wrong?"

"That's the interesting part," Mhulvayn said. "According to our beer-loving messenger, everything was going exactly the way it should have until some mysterious stranger interfered."

" 'Mysterious stranger'?" Maysahn repeated.

"That's what he said. Some fellow with 'strange blue eyes' who killed at least a dozen assassins single-handedly."

"Of course he did!" Maysahn snorted sarcastically. "I may not have been overly impressed with the quality of our . . . associates' brains, Oskahr, but they were reasonably competent in their own limited area."

"Agreed, but this fellow was pretty insistent. According to him—and he stuck by it through at least three complete repetitions before I had to leave to make our appointment here—it was the stranger who warned Cayleb's bodyguards about the attack, and then he apparently slaughtered the attackers right and left himself. If we're going to believe the messenger's version of things, Cayleb and this 'stranger' were the only two still on their feet when it was all over."

"Really?" Maysahn leaned back, lips pursed. "That *is* interesting," he murmured, so softly even Mhulvayn could scarcely hear him through the background noise. "If this fellow was that insistent, then he was probably telling the truth, at least as far as he *knows* the truth. Did he have anything to say about how this stranger of his happened to be there?"

"According to him, the stranger was obviously sent by God," Mhulvayn said. The two of them looked at one another across the table, their eyes amused. "After all, how else could he have arrived at exactly the right moment to save the crown prince?"

"Somehow I doubt God had a great deal to do with it," Maysahn said dryly. "Which isn't to say someone else didn't. Were our friends indiscreet, do you think?"

"They must've been. Although," Mhulvayn frowned, "I wouldn't have expected it of them. Admittedly, they were basically blunt instruments, but they knew Haarahld's agents are watching everywhere for assassins these days, and they *were* experienced."

"Not the sort to blab about their plans where someone might hear, you mean?"

"Exactly. Besides, if that was what happened, why was only one 'stranger' involved? We're talking about Cayleb. If they'd truly believed someone meant to try to kill him, they'd have had an entire regiment out there, not just one man."

"Unless that one man was the only one who'd realized what our less adroit associates intended to do," Maysahn said thoughtfully.

"Even then, he should have gone straight to the Guard with it," Mhulvayn argued.

"Unless he truly *is* a stranger, not a Charisian at all, and he saw this as an opportunity to win the Prince's confidence."

"Ah?" Mhulvayn scratched one eyebrow, frowning thoughtfully out across the busy street, then looked back at Maysahn.

"That could be it," he conceded. "A rather risky strategy, though, I'd have said. One man would stand a pretty good chance of getting himself killed trying to play hero against a 'wagonload' of assassins. Assuming this really was the work of the people we think it was, and I'm pretty sure it was, there'd have been at least a dozen of them. Pretty steep odds, don't you think?"

"*I* certainly wouldn't care for them." Maysahn nodded. "On the other hand, I suppose a lot would depend on just how good with a sword you actually were. That's not my area of expertise, after all. Actually, the riskiest part of the entire strategy would be that the assassins might succeed despite your intervention. You wouldn't win much of Cayleb's confidence if he was dead. Besides, if he'd been killed, and you looked like you'd known about the attempt ahead of time, Haarahld would probably have had a few unpleasant things to say to you about your failure to bring it to someone else's attention."

"At the very least." Mhulvayn made a face at the oblique reminder of all of the "unpleasant things" King Haarahld and his interrogators might have to say to one Oskahr Mhulvayn under certain best not thought about circumstances.

"But," Maysahn continued thoughtfully, "if this 'stranger' did manage to stymie an attempt to kill the Prince, he's undoubtedly going to find himself cordially received at the palace. If he plays his cards properly, that could lead to all sorts of rewards. Or," he looked back across the table at his subordinate, "influence."

"Influence to accomplish what?" Mhulvayn wondered.

"Who knows?" Maysahn shrugged. "Still, I suspect our employer won't be overly pleased to discover that a new player's taken a hand. This broth's rich enough without adding another cook to the kitchen!"

"What do you want to do about it?" Mhulvayn asked.

"He's going to want to know about this as soon as possible," Maysahn replied. "Unfortunately, Captain Whaite's just sailed."

"Should we use one of the alternate couriers?"

"An interesting question." Maysahn took another sip of chocolate and considered Mhulvayn's query.

Captain Styvyn Whaite's merchant ship plied a regular trading route from

Tellesberg, up Howell Bay and The Throat, and across the Charis Sea to Corisande, picking up whatever cargo charters he could. That ought to be enough to make him a guaranteed object of suspicion to Haarahld's agents, but Whaite's vessel was a miserable, barely seaworthy tub, and Whaite himself was a drunk who spent most of his time in port cozied up to a cask of cheap wine. No one in his right mind would trust him or his ship with anything remotely important or confidential.

Unless, that was, they knew Captain Whaite was actually Lieutenant Robyrt Bradlai of the League Navy. Lieutenant Bradlai didn't even like the taste of cheap wine, and he was far from incompetent. He couldn't afford to be, since his *Sea Cloud* was almost as ramshackle as she looked. The Royal Charisian Navy was unlikely to be fooled by surface appearances, so she truly was as down-at-the-heels and poorly maintained as she seemed. Which made nursing *Sea Cloud* back and forth between Tellesberg and Corisande a nontrivial challenge even for a sober captain.

Bradlai and his counterpart, Lieutenant Fraizher Maythis (better known in Charis as Wahltayr Seatown), maintained Maysahn's communications with Prince Hektor. Voyage time was almost forty days each way at *Sea Cloud*'s best speed, however, and Maythis' equally disreputable *Fraynceen* wouldn't arrive back at Tellesberg for another three five-days. Which meant Hektor wouldn't have Maysahn's report for another seven, minimum, if he used the regular channels for it. There were arrangements for emergency alternates, but Maysahn was reluctant to use them, because none of the alternative couriers' covers were as good as Whaite's or Maythis'. Their best protection was that they'd never been used, and he had no desire to risk exposing them—or himself—to Charisian agents for something which wasn't demonstrably critical.

"I think we won't use any of the others," he said finally. "Not at once, at any rate. Better to use the time until 'Seatown's' return to see what additional information we can pick up." He shook his head slowly, eyes distant. "It's only a feeling, so far, but something tells me a new cook is indeed about to begin stirring this particular pot, whether we like it or not."

"Wonderful," Mhulvayn sighed. He finished his cup of chocolate and stood.

"In that case, I suppose I'd better get started picking up that information," he said, and nodded briskly to Maysahn before he turned away from the table.

Maysahn watched him go, then stood himself, tossed a handful of coins onto the table, and headed off in the opposite direction.

▼   ▼   ▼

"Stupid damned idiots!" Braidee Lahang muttered savagely as he watched Crown Prince Cayleb riding past below his second-story window vantage point.

The Royal Guards who'd been dispatched to meet the prince at the gate formed a solid, vigilant ring around him, and a Marine lieutenant rode in a stretcher suspended between two horses, while three other Marines rode tight-shouldered at Cayleb's back. That much Lahang had more or less expected, given the preliminary reports he'd already received. What he hadn't expected was the civilian riding with the prince, and his eyes narrowed as he gazed down at the dark-haired stranger.

So that's the bastard who screwed all of our plans to hell and gone, he thought sourly. He still didn't have a clue how the mysterious civilian had gotten wind of the operation in the first place, or how his highly paid mercenaries could have been so inept as to allow a single busybody to completely negate so many days of careful planning.

It ought to have worked—it would *have worked—if not for him.* Lahang kept his bitter anger out of his expression, but it was harder than usual to make sure his face said only what he wanted it to say. Prince Nahrmahn was going to be . . . displeased.

He watched the cavalcade move on up the street towards the palace, then turned away from the window. He crossed the main chamber of his modest, if comfortable, lodgings and climbed the stairs to the roof.

A chorus of whistling hisses and clicking jaws greeted him, and he smiled with genuine pleasure, his frustration and anger fading, and hissed back. The wyverns in the big, subdivided rooftop coop pressed against the latticework, crowding together as they whistled for treats, and he chuckled and reached through the lattice to rub skulls and stroke necks. It was, in many ways, a fool-hardy thing to do. Some of the wyverns in that coop had wingspans of over four feet. They could have removed a finger with a single snap of their serrated jaws, but Lahang wasn't worried.

He made a comfortable living, without ever having to touch the funds his prince could have made available to him, by raising and training hunting and rac-ing wyverns for the Charisian nobility and wealthier merchants. And the wyverns in these coops were not only his friends and pets, but also his cover, in more than one way. They provided his income, and his profession explained why he had a constant influx of new wyverns to replace those he sold. Which conve-niently hid the fact that two or three in each shipment he received were homing wyverns from Prince Nahrmahn's own coop in Eraystor.

Now Lahang took the enciphered report from his tunic pocket. It was writ-ten on the finest Harchong paper, incredibly thin and tough, and commensu-rately expensive, although that was the least of his concerns as he opened the coop door and crooned a distinctive sequence of notes.

One of the wyverns inside the coop whistled imperiously at its companions. A couple of them were slow to move aside, and it slapped them smartly with its forward wings until they bent their heads obsequiously and got out of its way. Then it stood in the coop door, stretching its long neck so that Lahang could scratch its scaly throat while it crooned back to him.

He spent a few moments petting the creature, then lifted it out of the coop and closed and carefully secured the door behind it. The wyvern perched on top of the coop, obediently extending one leg and watching alertly, head cocked, as he affixed the report to the message-holding ring. He made sure it was securely in position, then gathered the wyvern in both arms and walked to the corner of the roof.

"Fly well," he whispered in its ear, and tossed it upward.

The wyvern whistled back to him as it flew one complete circle around the rooftop. Then it went arrowing off to the north.

He gazed after it for a moment, then drew a deep breath and turned back towards the stairs. His preliminary report would be in Prince Nahrmahn's hands within the next six days, but he knew his master well. The prince was going to want full details of how the plan to assassinate the Charisian heir had failed, and that meant it was going to be up to Braidee Lahang to find out what had happened.

Hopefully without losing his own head in the process.

.IV.
Royal Palace, Tellesberg, Kingdom of Charis

The man called Merlin Athrawes looked around the sitting room of his guest suite in the royal palace of Tellesberg, capital of the Kingdom of Charis. It was a pleasant, airy chamber, with the high ceilings favored in warm climates, on the second level of Queen Marytha's Tower. It was also comfortably furnished and had an excellent view of the harbor, and a room in Queen Marytha's Tower was an indication of high respect. The tower, where foreign ambassadors were customarily lodged, lay on the boundary between the royal family's personal section of the palace and its more public precincts.

Of course, there were no doors which led directly from the tower into the royal family's quarters, and there just happened to be that permanently manned guard post at the tower's only entrance and exit. Solely, no doubt, to protect the ambassadors' highly respected persons.

Merlin smiled and strolled across to the mirror above the beautifully inlaid chest of drawers in the suite's bedchamber. The mirror was of silver-backed glass, and he studied the surprisingly clear, sharp reflection in its slightly wavery depths almost as if it were a stranger's.

Which, after all, it was in many ways.

He grimaced, then chuckled ruefully and ran a fingertip along one of his waxed mustachios. It was, he was forced to admit, a masterful disguise.

One of the features of a full-capability, last-generation PICA had been its owner's ability to physically reconfigure it. It wasn't a feature Nimue Alban had ever used, but, then, she hadn't used her PICA at all, very often. Certainly not as much as her father had hoped she would. To be honest, she'd known, he would have vastly preferred for her never to have joined the Navy in the first place, and he'd deeply resented the demands it had placed upon her time. He'd loved her very much, and a man of his wealth and position had known the truth about the ultimate hopelessness of the Federation's position early on. She'd suspected that he hadn't intentionally brought her into a doomed world in the first place. That her birth had been an "accident" her mother had arranged, which very probably helped explain their divorce when she was only a child. Even if her suspicions were correct, that hadn't kept him from loving her once she'd been born, but he'd been afraid that as a serving officer in the Navy, she would die sooner than she had to. He'd wanted her to live as long as she could, and to pack as much living as possible into the time she had, before the inevitable happened.

Well, Merlin thought, his smile going bittersweet, *it looks like your decision to give me a PICA worked out after all. I'm going to have a very long time to live, indeed, Daddy.*

He gazed deep into his own reflected blue eyes, looking for some sign of the biological person he once had been, then brushed that thought aside and gave his mustachio another twirl.

Nimue Alban had never been tempted to shift genders, either in her own biological case, or even temporarily, using her PICA. Others had been rather more adventurous, however, and PICAs had been designed to be fully functional in every sense. And since the technology had been available, the PICA designers had seen no reason not to allow their customers to reconfigure the gender, as well as the general physical appearance, of their marvelous, expensive toys.

Given the male-dominated nature of Safeholdian society, Nimue finally had used the capability.

There were, inevitably, some limitations for even the most capable technology. A PICA couldn't be made significantly shorter or taller than it already was. There was some flex, but not a great deal. Shoulders could be broadened, hips could be narrowed, genitalia and pelvic structures could be rearranged, but the basic physical size of the PICA itself was pretty much fixed by the size of its original human model. Fortunately, Nimue Alban had been a woman of rather more than average height even for her birth society, whose members had been blessed with excellent medical care and adequate diet from childhood. As a woman on Safehold, she would have been a giantess, and "Merlin" was quite a bit taller than most of the men he might meet.

Nimue had added several judiciously placed scars here and there, like the one on Merlin's cheek, as well. Merlin was a warrior, and she hadn't wanted anyone to wonder how someone had attained his years and prowess without ever even being wounded.

The decision to become male hadn't been an easy one, despite the logic which made it effectively inevitable. Nimue Alban had never *wanted* to be a man, nor had she ever felt any particular physical attraction to women, and looking at Merlin's nude, undeniably male—and very masculine—physique in a full-length mirror for the first time had left "him" with very mixed feelings. Fortunately, Nimue had allowed herself—or, rather, had allowed Merlin—two of Safehold's thirty-day months to become accustomed to "his" new body.

In light of the plan Nimue had evolved, Merlin was impressively muscled. Not so much for brute strength as for endurance and staying power. The fact that a PICA's basic frame and musculature were stressed to approximately ten times the strength and toughness of a normal human and that a PICA never tired were simply two of the little secrets Merlin intended to hold in reserve.

At the same time, accomplishing his mission would require him to earn the respect of those about him, and this was a muscle-powered society in which a man who aspired to influence must be prepared to demonstrate his own prowess. Enough wealth might buy respect, but Merlin couldn't simply appear with bags full of gold, and he certainly had no patent of nobility. His chosen *seijin's* role would help in that respect, but he would have to demonstrate its reality, and that meant living up to a *seijin's* reputation, which almost any flesh-and-blood human being would have found . . . difficult.

That was why Merlin had spent quite a bit of time experimenting with the governors on his basic physical capabilities. Nimue had never done a great deal of that, but Merlin was likely to find himself in much higher-risk environments than any into which Nimue had ever ventured in her PICA. More to the point, Merlin's survival was far more important than Nimue Alban's had ever been. So he'd set his reaction speed to a level about twenty percent higher than any human could have matched. He could have set it higher still—*his* nervous impulses traveled at light speed, through molecular circuitry and along fiber-optic conduits, without the chemical transmission processes upon which biological nerves depended—and he still had that extra speed in reserve for emergencies. But it was *only* for emergencies, and fairly dire ones, at that; even a *seijin* would be looked at askance if he seemed *too* quick and agile.

By the same token, Merlin had adjusted his strength to about twenty percent above what might have been expected out of a protoplasmic human with the same apparent musculature. That left him with quite a lot of literally superhuman strength in reserve, as well, and he'd set the overrides to let him call upon it at need.

It had taken him every day of the five-days Nimue had allowed to learn not simply to move like a man, but to adjust for his enhanced reaction speed and strength. Well, that and the fact that his body's center of gravity had moved vertically upward quite a bit.

He'd spent a lot of that time working out with the katana and wakazashi he'd used Pei Kau-yung's fabrication module to build. He'd had Owl design and actually fabricate the weapons, and he'd cheated just a little bit with them, too. The blades looked like the work of a Harchong master swordsmith, with the characteristic ripple pattern of what Old Earth had called "Damascus steel." They even carried the proof marks of Hanyk Rynhaard, one of the legendary swordmakers of Harchong, but they were actually made of battle steel, orders of magnitude harder and tougher than any purely metallic alloy. Merlin could have had Owl give them an edge which was literally a molecule wide, but he'd resisted that temptation. Instead, he'd settled for one which was "only" as sharp as a Safehold surgeon's finest scalpel for the katana. The wakazashi was quite a bit "sharper" than that, since he anticipated using it only in dire emergencies. The katana would be Merlin's primary weapon, and since it was made of battle steel, he could do little things like using his reserve strength to slice completely through the assassin leader's blade without worrying about nicking or dulling his own.

He intended to make very certain no one but he ever cared for either of those weapons. He also intended to spend quite a lot of time carefully inspecting their edges, honing them on a regular basis, seeing to it that they were properly oiled and guarded against rust, and everything else a blade made of true steel would have required. On the other hand, a *seijin* was supposed to be a mysterious figure, with more than merely mortal capabilities, and Merlin had no objection to carrying a sword which evoked at least a little awe. That was one reason he'd stayed with the katana, which had no exact counterpart on Safehold. The fact that it was specifically suited to the only style of fencing Nimue Alban had ever studied was another factor, but its exotic appearance should contribute to the image he needed to create.

He chuckled again, then turned away from the mirror with a final stroke for his absolutely genuine—in as much as *any* of him could be called "genuine"—mustachio. A PICA had fully functional taste buds and a "stomach," so that its owner could sample novel cuisine while running it in remote mode. And since it might well have organic material in the aforesaid stomach, the designers had seen no reason not to utilize that material as efficiently as possible. The nanotech built into what passed for Merlin's digestive tract was fully capable of converting any food he ate into naturally "growing" fingernails, toenails, and hair. It couldn't begin to use all of the food an organic human being consumed in a day, however, and if Merlin was going to be forced to eat regularly—which he undoubtedly was—he'd have to dispose of the unused material at regular intervals.

So I guess I'll still have to hit the head after all, from time to time, he thought with a grin as he strolled back across to the window.

Although Queen Marytha's Tower had long since been renovated into comfortable, modern guest quarters, it had been a portion of the original royal castle's outer walls when it had first been built. The wall of the tower itself was a good meter and a half thick—*five feet*, he corrected himself irritably, once again cursing that maniac Langhorne for abandoning the metric system—and he pushed the diamond-paned windows open and leaned his elbows on the immensely deep windowsill.

The city made an impressive sight. It was built mainly of stone and brick—

the Kingdom of Charis had far better uses for good timber than wasting it building houses—and the area near the waterfront was a vast sprawl of substantial warehouses, shipyards, ropewalks, chandlers, and business offices. Farther inland, away from the warren of taverns, bistros, and bordellos which served the mariners who manned the kingdom's merchant vessels, were the homes of the thousands of workmen who labored in those same warehouses and other establishments. And farther inland still, on the rising land moving away from the harbor along the banks of the Telles River towards the Palace itself, were the townhouses and mansions of noblemen and wealthy merchants.

The city's total population was in the vicinity of a hundred thousand, which made it huge for Charis and much more than merely respectable for Safehold generally. It also meant Tellesberg was completely ringed by farmland whose sole purpose was to keep the city's population fed. Even so, it was necessary to import vast quantities of food on a regular basis. The Charisian merchant marine was more than equal to the task, as long as the Royal Charisian Navy maintained control of Howell Bay, but a hundred thousand was still an enormous population for a city built by a civilization powered only by wind, water, and muscle.

It was also a remarkably clean city. Safeholdian notions of public hygiene and waste disposal were far more stringent than anything Old Earth had known at any comparable technology level. Merlin was delighted that they were, too. The sorts of pestilences and plagues which had routinely swept through preindustrial Old Earth cities were very rare occurrences on Safehold. Besides, it also meant Tellesberg *smelled* far better than its Old Earth counterparts ever had.

He smiled, but then the smile faded as he saw the church spires which dominated the city's low-lying skyline. He could see literally dozens of them from where he stood, and every one of them was part of the lie which had brought him to Charis in the first place.

On the other hand, he thought, *every single one of them has at least one bell in its tower, too. Big ones, at that, and that means foundries. Lots and lots of foundries. That's going to come in handy as hell in the not-too-distant.*

The dark blue waters of Howell Bay stretched northward as far as even his eyes could see. The bay was very nearly half the size of Old Earth's Mediterranean. If the body of water called "The Throat" were added, their combined length would have been eighty percent of the Mediterranean's, although they would also have been much narrower. Like the Mediterranean, The Throat and Howell Bay were almost completely landlocked, except where The Throat opened onto the Charis Sea, and they—and the Charis Sea—were utterly dominated by the Royal Charisian Navy.

At the moment.

Merlin pursed his lips and whistled tunelessly as he considered King Haarahld VII's dilemma.

The Kingdom of Charis was one of Safehold's more substantial kingdoms.

It had grown, although the local histories didn't remember it exactly that way, out of one of the original colonial enclaves. In fact, the original site for the city of Tellesberg had been chosen by Pei Shan-wei herself, during her terraforming operations.

Given Shan-wei's place in the revised version of Langhorne's religion, it wasn't surprising that no one remembered *that*, and Tellesberg hadn't been a very large enclave. Most of those had been located on the larger landmasses of Haven and Howard, where the bulk of the planet's population was located even today. Nor had Tellesberg received much in the way of outside support, possibly because of its "parentage." Yet it had grown anyway, slowly but steadily, and it had begun establishing colonies of its own about five hundred local years ago. Those colonies had quickly established their independence as feudal territories in their own right, but Tellesberg had always remained the largest and most powerful of the Charisian states—"first among equals," one might say.

Then, about two hundred local years ago, the House of Ahrmahk had risen to power in Tellesberg under Haarahld III, the present king's direct ancestor. Over the last two centuries, the Ahrmahk dynasty had gradually extended its control over the entire landmass known as Charis Island.

Personally, Merlin considered that something of a misnomer. The "island" in question would have been considered a continent on most planets. Of course, its sparsely inhabited upper third or so was almost completely severed from the rest of it by The Throat and Howell Bay. The mountainous isthmus which connected it to the lower two-thirds and formed the bay's western coast, between the bay and the Cauldron, was barely fifty-five kilometers (*thirty-four miles*, he corrected sourly) wide at its narrowest point. That upper portion had long been considered a completely separate landmass. In fact, it had been given its own name— Margaret's Land—and only added to the rest of the Kingdom of Charis about eighty local years ago.

Across the Charis Sea lay Emerald Island, about the size of Margaret's Land (and just as sparsely settled), but independent from—and resentful of—Charis. Prince Nahrmahn of Emerald walked carefully around Charis, but his hatred of Haarahld and the huge Charisian merchant marine which dominated the carrying trade of Safehold was both deep and profound. The House of Baytz had acquired title to Emerald less than two generations ago, following the unfortunate demise of every male member of the previous ruling house. As such, Narhrmahn had a lively awareness of how a ruler's fortunes could shift abruptly. That, coupled with the fact that he was, perhaps not unreasonably, suspicious that Charis's long, steady expansion meant the Ahrmahk Dynasty ultimately had designs upon Emerald, as well, only added fuel to his hatred for all things Charisian.

Silverlode Island, southeast of Emerald and directly across the smaller Middle Sea and Windhover Sea from Charis, was almost as big as Charis itself. Combined with Charis, Margaret's Land, and Emerald, Silverlode comprised the thoroughly inaccurately labeled Charisian Archipelago. Silverlode itself was even more sparsely settled than Charis, mostly because of its terrain, which was considered rugged even by Safeholdian standards. What population there was tended to be clustered along the long western coastline, sheltered from the dreadful storms which all too often blew in off of the Carter Ocean, to the southeast. Most of the Silverlode towns, cities, and petty nobles, although nominally independent of the Charisian crown, owed personal fealty of one sort or another to King Haarahld and his house, and, for all practical purposes, they were an integral part of the kingdom he ruled.

It had taken Charis centuries of patient effort to attain her present position, but today she was the unquestioned mistress of Safehold's oceans. Her merchant marine was the largest on the entire planet, by a very considerable margin. Her navy was at least equal to that of any two of her potential rivals, and her wealth reflected that. Yet, for all that, Charis was not quite in the top rank of Safehold's great powers. In many respects, she hovered on the cusp of crossing over to that status, but for the present, she was definitely not in the same league as the densely populated Harchong Empire, or the Republic of Siddarmark or the Desnairian Empire. Or, of course, the Temple Lands.

Fortunately for Charis, none of those great powers, with the possible exception of the Desnairians, had any extensive naval tradition or, for that matter, ambitions. *Unfortunately* for Charis, the League of Corisande, to the east of Emerald and Silverlode, and the steadily unifying corsair kinglets of Trellheim, even farther to the east, most certainly did. For that matter, so did the Kingdom of Chisholm, which dominated the somewhat larger continent of the same name, not to mention the Kingdom of Dohlar or the Kingdom of Tarot. The latter might be an official ally of long standing, but its present monarch resented the arrangement. Not without some reason, since he found himself virtually a tributary vassal of Haarahld's.

Oh, yes. There were lots of people who had their own reasons for resenting, envying, hating, or fearing Charis. Including, unfortunately, the Church.

Merlin frowned at that thought, watching the busy harbor unseeingly while he contemplated it. He remained unable—or, at least, unwilling—to risk inserting his SNARCs' listening devices into the Temple's precincts. There was simply too much danger that those unidentified power sources might connect to something he really, really didn't want to disturb. But that meant that the one set of meetings he most longed to snoop upon—those of the Council of Vicars—were beyond his reach. He could operate a bit more freely in Zion, farther away from the Temple, but it wasn't the same, because virtually all of the Vicars—the Church of God's equivalent of the college of cardinals—lived in the Temple itself, in the vast, comfortable suites which were part of the original structure.

Lesser prelates, like Charis' "own" Archbishop Erayk, had luxurious lodgings elsewhere in the city, and Merlin was able to listen in on *their* conversations in the restaurants, coffeehouses, gaming houses, and discreet brothels where much of their business was conducted. He was well aware of the advantages that gave him, but it also made his lack of access inside the Temple even more irritating.

From what he could pick up, however, it was obvious the Church cherished longstanding suspicions about Charis, and he sometimes suspected that dim memories of Shan-wei's initial sponsorship of Tellesberg still lingered. Whether that was so or not, the kingdom's distance from the Temple and Zion would probably have been enough to make the Church wary of its doctrinal reliability, and the local clergy was accustomed to a sort of benign neglect. When it took two months for the Temple to send a message to Tellesberg and receive a reply, there was simply no way the Council of Vicars could keep the local Church as firmly under thumb as it could the clergy of Haven and Howard.

From what Merlin had been able to discover, fears of Charisian heresy were unfounded, but Charisian attitudes were increasingly, if quietly, critical of the Vicars' flagrant abuses of power. No one was going to be stupid enough to say so openly—the Inquisition operated even here, after all—which made it difficult for even Merlin to judge what sort of resentment simmered beneath the surface. But it was enough to bring at least some softly spoken criticism out of the Church's own clergy here in the kingdom, which probably did amount to "heresy" in the Vicars' eyes, Merlin admitted. And it was obvious that the kingdom's steadily growing wealth and international prestige was another factor in the disfavor with which Mother Church regarded Charis.

But while there were many people prepared to resent or envy Charis, there were relatively few, with the probable exception of Greyghor Stohnar, Lord Protector of Siddarmark—effectively, the elective dictator of the Republic—who felt any particular urge to *help* the kingdom. And Siddarmark, unfortunately, despite the well-deserved reputation of its matchless pike-armed infantry, had no navy beyond a purely coast defense force which Nahrmahn of Emerald could handily have defeated all by himself.

All in all, Charis' future looked rather bleak. Not today. Not this five-day, or possibly even next year, or the year after. But her enemies were drawing the noose steadily tighter about her with what amounted to the Church's tacit approval.

So far, Haarahld's canny diplomacy had managed to stave off outright disaster, but his enemies' recent success in having Tahdayo Mahntayl's claim to the Earldom of Hanth confirmed over that of Hauwerd Breygart marked a serious downturn in his fortunes. Hanth was the largest of the feudal territories of Margaret's Land, and the one which had longest resisted Charisian authority. Having it handed to what everyone recognized, whether they were willing to admit it or not, as a usurper with no legitimate claim to the title would have been a blow to Haarahld at any time. At this particular time, that blow might well prove mortal. Or, at least, the first of the thousand cuts his enemies had in mind for him.

By Merlin's current estimate, it was likely Haarahld would manage to pass his throne and crown to Cayleb. It was unlikely Cayleb would ever pass them to a son or daughter of his own.

Unless something changed.

Merlin straightened, folding his arms as he watched the busy shipping along the wharves and docks of Tellesberg. There was power and vitality in Charis. Harchong was decadent, Desnair was too focused on conquest, and Siddarmark was too preoccupied with securing its own frontiers against the threat of Harchong and Desnair alike. But Charis . . .

There was wealth, art, and literature in Charis. In many ways, the kingdom reminded Merlin of what Nimue had read of Old Earth's England in the seventeenth or eighteenth centuries. Or perhaps Holland of roughly the same time period. There were no burgeoning scientists, for the Church of God Awaiting would never have permitted that, but at the same time, it was obvious to Merlin that Langhorne's plan had begun to slip, if ever so slightly. The critical, challenging mind-set of Old Earth's scientific revolution might not have arisen—yet—but that didn't mean all advances had been frozen.

Here in Charis, for example, there was a yeasty, bubbling ferment, and the Royal College Haarahld's father had founded had gathered together a body of truly formidable scholars. It might be true that none of them had ever heard of the scientific method, but they were deeply devoted to the collection and preservation of knowledge, as well as teaching, and the present king had begun quietly appointing some of his kingdom's best "mechanics" to the College's fellows. The College's collective work helped foster a sense of opening horizons, in applied techniques as well as the traditional humanities, which extended to other aspects of the kingdom's life.

Like the burgeoning industrial base—of sorts, at least—which underlay much of its growing wealth.

The *Holy Writ*'s proscriptions against any sort of advanced technology were unchallenged, even in Charis, but there'd already been a certain amount of . . . leakage. Safeholdian metallurgy, for example, was at the level of Old Earth's early eighteenth century, or even a bit further advanced. And the planet's agriculture—built around the "teaching" of the Archangel Sondheim, disk harrows, animal-drawn reapers, and terrestrial food crops genetically engineered for disease and parasite resistance, not to mention high yields—was productive enough to create a surplus labor force. It wasn't that huge a surplus, as a percentage of the total population, especially not in places like Harchong, where the social structure had stratified centuries ago around a serf-based agricultural economy. It still took a lot of farmers to keep people fed. But there were a lot of artisans almost everywhere, as well, and the situation was even worse, from Langhorne's perspective, here in Charis, whose climate permitted year-round agriculture in much of the island.

Charis was a land with a sparse population and a widespread trading empire. Those factors had conspired to create a degree of inventiveness which would have horrified Langhorne and Bédard, and the Royal College's interest in the mechanical arts had begun to shape and direct that inventiveness. That thought alone would have been enough to incline Merlin favorably towards Charis (and to explain the Church's suspicions of it), even if it hadn't suited the kingdom so well to his needs. If any of Langhorne's sycophants had studied history the way Shan-wei had, he suspected, the *Writ* would have incorporated far more stringent controls on things like the use of water power. But they appeared to have overlooked the fact that Old Earth's Industrial Revolution had begun with *waterwheels*, not steam engines, and Charis' "manufactories" were well on the road towards the same destination.

Nor was that the only thing which had slipped through the cracks of Langhorne's great plan. These people had gunpowder, for example. It wasn't very *good* gunpowder—it was still "meal" powder, weak and dangerous to work with—and they hadn't had it very long, but he rather suspected that the gunpowder genie alone would have been enough to topple Langhorne's neat little scheme, eventually. Merlin wondered exactly how its introduction had gotten past the Church. He suspected that the answer was a fairly massive bribe, probably from Harchong, where it had originally been introduced.

Approving it for any reason struck Merlin as an act of lunacy on the Church's part, given the system it was dedicated to maintaining. But in fairness, the Church might well not have recognized its military potential when it first arrived. As nearly as Merlin could tell so far, it had been introduced primarily for use in mining and engineering projects, not warfare. And even now, eighty or ninety years later, it was obvious Safehold was still feeling its way towards the compound's military applications.

At the moment, their firearms and artillery were about as primitively designed as their gunpowder. The best infantry firearm they had was a crudely designed matchlock, and no one appeared to have thought even of the wheel lock yet, much less the flintlock. Their artillery wasn't much more advanced, conceptually, but that wasn't because their metallurgy wasn't good enough to produce much better weapons . . . assuming someone were to suggest how that might be done. Coupled with the Charisians' manufacturing base, general inventiveness, and tightening circle of enemies, that offered all sorts of possibilities for opening the nascent cracks in Langhorne's foundations just a bit wider.

But even more importantly, there was a social openness in the Kingdom of Charis, as well. No one would ever confuse Charis with a representative democracy. King Haarahld would probably suffer an apoplectic attack at the very notion. But the Royal Charisian Navy had a centuries-long tradition of accepting only the service of freemen, outright serfdom had been abolished in Charis well over a century ago, and by the standard of any other Safeholdian state, Charisian commoners were undeniably "uppity."

Which, coupled with the centrality of trade and traders to Charisian prosperity, helped explain why Haarahld's parliament was an active, vital part of his government. For the most part, it did what it was told, but it zealously guarded its prerogatives, and Haarahld was wise enough to side with the Commons against the Lords sufficiently often to leave no doubt in anyone's mind where the true power lay. For that matter, most of the Charisian nobility was actively involved in trade, without the arrogant hauteur of the landed nobles of Harchong or Desnair. They recognized ability as being just as vital as blue blood. The mere possession of a title did not excuse sloth or indolence, and a Charisian commoner of ability and energy could expect to rise far higher than his counterpart in almost any other Safeholdian realm.

That was why Merlin was here. The basic matrix of Charisian politics and society offered the most fertile soil for the seed he had to plant. There was still the minor problem of Langhorne's insurance policy, which Owl had discovered in his orbital survey. Figuring out a way to deal with *that* was going to be . . . a challenge. But, even after it was overcome, it was obvious to Merlin that he couldn't possibly try to impose technology upon Safehold, any more than he could single-handedly overthrow the Church. The changes he had to induce must be organic, must grow out of a genuine shift in basic attitudes and belief structures.

Merlin had come to think of himself as a virus. The analogy wasn't perfect, but it worked. By himself, he could accomplish nothing. But if he found the proper cell, invaded it, made it over in the necessary image, it would spread the infection for him. And Charis was the perfect host.

Assuming, of course, that he could prevent its destruction.

Fortunately, he continued to share one common trait with Nimue Alban; both of them had always liked a challenge.

.V.
Royal Palace, Eraystor,
Emerald Island

What's so damned important?" Prince Nahrmahn demanded in a surly tone. The prince wore a light robe of Harchong cotton silk over his pajamas, and his expression was not happy as Hahl Shandyr, the fifth Baron of Shandyr, was shown into his breakfast parlor. Nahrmahn, as every male of the House of Baytz seemed to be, was short. Unlike his late father, however, he was also a corpulent man with a round baby face which was capable of beaming with the simple joy of human kindness whenever its owner required it to. At such times, the casual observer might be forgiven for failing to note the hard, calculating light which burned behind its apparently mild brown eyes.

At other times—like now—Nahrmahn's expression was a clear warning that he was in a foul mood, and when that was true no one would have called his eyes "mild."

"I crave your pardon for disturbing you so early, My Prince," Shandyr replied, bending in a deep and profound bow. "I wouldn't have done so had the situation not required your immediate attention."

Nahrmahn grunted. The sound managed to combine dubiousness and irritation in almost equal measure, Shandyr noted unhappily. Nahrmahn hated having his leisurely breakfast routine interrupted by business, especially when the business in question included things he wasn't going to like hearing about. And there were very few bits of news, Shandyr knew, which he was going to be less happy to hear about over the post-breakfast pastries. On the other hand, the Prince of Emerald recognized Shandyr's value. And however irritable and . . . demanding Nahrmahn could be, he also recognized the value of loyalty. Unpleasant scenes were far from rare for those unfortunates who found themselves bringing him bad news, but in the long run, he was a craftsman who cared for his tools, and he didn't *really* have the messenger beheaded.

Not often, at any rate.

The prince looked at him for several moments, keeping him standing. That wasn't a particularly good sign, in Shandyr's experience, but it wasn't necessarily a disastrous one, either. The baron stood as calmly as he could under his prince's scrutiny, waiting. Morning breeze blew gently through the wide, open window, stirring the sheer drapes, and the luxuriously furnished, room was quiet enough that Shandyr could hear the rattle of near-palm fronds and the twittering of birds from the palace gardens, the more distant whistle of wyverns from the palace mews, and the occasional zinging whine of a spider beetle as it droned past the window. Then the prince snapped his fingers at the servant standing behind his chair.

"A cup of chocolate for the Baron," he said, and the footman produced cup and chocolate pot as if by magic. Nahrmahn pointed at a chair at the foot of his table, and Shandyr seated himself and waited, with carefully hidden relief, until the cup arrived in front of him.

"Leave the pot," Nahrmahn directed the servant.

"Yes, Sire," the man murmured. He set the pot at Shandyr's elbow, then bowed himself out of the room. That was one thing about Nahrmahn's servants, Shandyr reflected as he sampled the delicious chocolate. They were well trained and knew the value of discretion.

"All right," Nahrmahn said as the dining parlor door closed behind the servant. "I don't imagine you came calling this early to bring me *good* news."

"I'm afraid not, My Prince," Shandyr admitted. In fact, the baron would vastly have preferred to wait. Unfortunately, while Nahrmahn was never in a good mood when business interrupted his morning routine, he would have been in an even worse mood whenever he eventually discovered that Shandyr had delayed bringing him this particular bit of information.

"Well, spit it out," Nahrmahn commanded.

"My Prince, we've received a report from Lahang. Cayleb is still alive."

Nahrmahn's round, chubby face tightened, and his eyes narrowed ominously. Shandyr, as the man ultimately responsible for the planning and execution of all of Nahrmahn's clandestine operations, had seen that expression on several occasions, and he ordered his own expression to remain calm.

"Why?" Nahrmahn asked coldly.

"Lahang wasn't certain when he wrote his report, My Prince," Shandyr replied, reminding himself that he and his network of agents succeeded in Nahrmahn's service far more often than they failed. "As you know," he added delicately, "Lahang wasn't completely free of constraints when he organized the assassination."

Nahrmahn's lips tightened further for just an instant, but then they relaxed, and he nodded curtly. He knew exactly why Shandyr had raised that point, but the semi-excuse had more than a little validity, and he recognized that, as well.

"Granted," the prince said after a moment. "On the other hand, I thought the people he'd chosen were supposed to be professionals."

"They were, My Prince," Shandyr said. "At least, they came highly recommended. And, under the circumstances, I have to agree with Lahang—and, for that matter, with the Duke—that using any of our own people would have been . . . unwise."

"Not if they'd succeeded," Nahrmahn growled. But then he shook his head. In fairness, Lahang had been against the operation from the outset, and not just because of the tactical difficulties of arranging it. But the duke had convinced Nahrmahn to overrule his agent on the spot, and Lahang hadn't been picked for that assignment at random. The fact that he'd initially opposed the attempt to kill Cayleb wouldn't have kept him from doing his very best to make the assassination succeed. And given the way things seemed to have worked out, he'd obviously been right about the need to maintain the greatest possible degree of deniability on Emerald's part.

"No. You're right, Hahl," he conceded at last. "Even if they'd succeeded, they might have been taken, made to talk."

"From Lahang's report, it sounds as if at least one of them was taken, My Prince," Shandyr said. Nahrmahn grimaced, and his spymaster shrugged. "At the moment, it appears unlikely the fellow knows much about who hired him. It sounds as if he was one of the common swordsmen."

"Thank Langhorne for small favors," Nahrmahn muttered, then inhaled deeply.

"What went wrong?" he asked in a calmer tone, reaching for his own chocolate cup and sipping with a delicacy which always seemed a bit odd in someone as rotund as he.

"Lahang is still working on the details." Shandyr gave another small shrug. "Obviously, he has to be particularly careful just now. Suspicion in Tellesberg has to be running high, and Wave Thunder's going to be looking very carefully at anyone who seems to be poking around for information at a time like this. From the preliminary reports and rumors he'd been able to pick up before dispatching his message, though, it sounds like something out of a children's tale."

Nahrmahn's eyebrows arched, and Shandyr chuckled humorlessly.

"According to Lahang, the story going around in Tellesberg is that the assassins almost succeeded. That they *would* have succeeded if not for the intervention of some mysterious stranger."

"Stranger?" Nahrmahn repeated.

"That's what Lahang says, My Prince. So far, there aren't any reliable details on just who this 'stranger' might be, but the gossip running around Tellesberg already has him bigger than life. Some of the wilder tales insist he's some sort of *seijin*, probably with a magic sword, to boot. But almost all of the rumors, even the more reasonable ones, agree it was he who warned Cayleb and his bodyguards at the very last moment. The attackers still managed to kill or wound all of Cayleb's guards, but between them, Cayleb, his guardsmen, and this stranger killed all but one of the assassins. Most of the gossip agrees that the stranger killed over half of them himself."

"It sounds like we should have hired *him*," Nahrmahn observed with bleak humor, and Shandyr allowed himself a small smile in response.

The prince sat back in his chair, nibbling on a pastry rich with nuts and sticky with honey, while he considered Shandyr's report. Shandyr often wondered how the man could savor such sweet, heavy treats, given the climate of a sea-level capital city almost directly upon the equator, but Nahrmahn's sweet tooth was proverbial. He chewed thoughtfully, steadily, for at least five full minutes, and the baron sat equally silent, sipping his own chocolate. Finally, Nahrmahn finished the pastry, wiped its stickiness from his fingers with a napkin, and drained his own cup.

"I assume you've told me everything we know so far," he said.

"I have, My Prince. As I've said, Lahang is working to get us more details, and I expect we'll hear from the Duke ... eventually." This time, he and Nahrmahn grimaced at one another. "Until then, however," the baron continued, "we really *know* nothing."

"Granted. Still, if the rumors and gossip all insist this stranger—whoever the Shan-wei he was—was responsible for whatever went wrong, I think we need to discover all we can about him. Somehow, I doubt he's just going to disappear—not after saving the Crown Prince's life!"

"You may well be right, My Prince. But it's also possible he's no more than a common adventurer who was lucky enough to be in the right place at the right time."

"If you truly believe that's likely, Hahl, then perhaps I need a new chief spy," Nahrmahn snorted.

"I didn't say it was likely, My Prince. I simply pointed out that it was possible, and it is. I agree that we need to discover all we can about him, especially how he may have learned about our plans ahead of time. At the same time, it's never wise to allow oneself to become too wedded to any set of assumptions before they can be confirmed or denied."

"A valid point," Nahrmahn conceded. "Still, I want to know everything we can about him."

"Of course, My Prince."

"And I think we need to consider our own exposure," Nahrmahn continued. "I know Lahang's links to the Duke are well hidden, but Wave Thunder's no fool, and well hidden isn't the same as invisible. Haarahld is bound to suspect us, and if they've figured out more than we think they have, they may know exactly who Lahang is and pull him in for questioning. How much damage can he do us if they do?"

"A great deal, I'm afraid," Shandyr admitted. "He's in charge of all our operations in Tellesberg, and he coordinates almost all of our agents outside the capital, as well. And although we never told him what our ultimate objectives might be, he's bound to have recognized, especially with the Duke's participation, that it was a direct attack on the monarchy, not just on Cayleb." The baron sighed. "To be effective, he has to know enough—and be intelligent enough—to be dangerous, My Lord."

"Should we consider his . . . retirement?"

"I honestly don't know." Shandyr frowned, one fingertip tracing circles in a brilliant patch of sunlight on the table's waxed and polished surface as he thought about it.

"I'm sure he has plans in place to quietly disappear at need," the baron said after a few seconds. "How good those plans may be is impossible to say, of course, especially from this distance. If the Charisians know or suspect who he really is, the chance of his managing to simply vanish probably isn't very good. They'd have to be prepared to pounce the instant he looked as if he might be trying to get out of town. Given the fact that it's what he knows that makes him dangerous to us, ordering him to try to leave Tellesberg might be the worst thing we could do, if it did cause them to go ahead and arrest him for interrogation.

"It would probably be simpler, and safer, to simply have him removed, My Prince. That would be relatively straightforward, and there are enough Charisians we could hire through a proper intermediary to kill him for any number of ostensible reasons without implicating ourselves. But he *is* our chief agent in Charis, and he's always been effective for us. Losing him, and all of his contacts and background knowledge, would be a serious blow. It would take months, probably years, for anyone else to develop the same capabilities and sources."

"I know, but if Wave Thunder arrests him, we lose him anyway, with the added risk that they may be able to prove we were involved."

"My Prince, Haarahld needs no proof of your enmity," Shandyr pointed out. "From that perspective, what happens to Lahang is completely beside the point."

"Not if it inspires him to respond in kind," Nahrmahn observed dryly.

"Agreed. But if they aren't certain we were directly behind the attempt, they have to suspect everyone else, as well. Hektor must be on their list of suspects, for example. Even Mahntayl *could* have been responsible for it. If Wave Thunder has connected Lahang to us, then killing him would probably convince them we were the primary movers. After all, if we weren't, why would we want to remove him?"

"Decisions, decisions," Nahrmahn sighed.

"There is one other aspect to consider, My Prince," Shandyr said. Nahrmahn looked at him, then gestured for him to continue.

"There's always the Duke to bear in mind," the spymaster pointed out. "I don't trust his ultimate reliability any more than I feel sure he trusts ours, but he has had direct contact with Lahang. If Lahang is interrogated, the Duke is just as exposed as we are, and also right where Haarahld can get at him. I feel confident he's keeping his own eye on Lahang, and that he has his own plans already in place to ensure Lahang never has the opportunity to betray him. Which means—"

"Which means," Nahrmahn interrupted, "that we can rely on his self-interest." He nodded. "That doesn't mean his plans will *work*, of course, but he's right there in Tellesberg, while we're two thousand miles away."

"Exactly, My Prince." Shandyr nodded. "And if he should have Lahang killed, and if Wave Thunder *hasn't* identified Lahang as our agent, then any investigation would lead to the Duke before it led to us."

Nahrmahn plucked at his lower lip, then nodded.

"A good point," he agreed. "I'd really prefer to tie off that particular loose end ourselves, if it becomes necessary, but I think we'll have to rely on the Duke to worry about that for us. Of course, that leaves the problem of the Duke himself, doesn't it?"

Shandyr's eyes widened ever so slightly at the prince's biting tone, and Nahrmahn chuckled coldly.

"It's not as if I've ever *trusted* him, Hahl. And we both know that, even now, he could probably make some arrangement with Haarahld if it came to it. Which, given how much he knows, could be . . . unfortunate for our other arrangements in Charis."

"My Prince," Shandyr began very carefully, "are you suggesting—?"

He broke off, allowing the question to hover, and Nahrmahn snorted.

"Part of me would like nothing better, but, no," he said. "Not yet, at any rate. And at least"—he smiled thinly and coldly—"if the time *does* come, we already have our own man in place to do the job."

He considered for several more seconds, then sighed.

"All right. I suppose that's about all we can decide right now. In the meantime, however, I want you to brief Trahvys and Gharth, as well."

Shandyr nodded. Trahvys Ohlsyn, Earl of Pine Hollow, was Nahrmahn's cousin and chief councillor, and Gharth Rahlstahn, the Earl of Mahndyr, was the commander of the Emerald Navy.

"Shall I brief them *fully*, My Prince?" the baron asked, arching one eyebrow, and Nahrmahn frowned.

"Tell Trahvys everything we know or suspect," he directed after a moment. "Tell Gharth that we have to assume Haarahld will suspect we were involved, whether or not we actually were, and that I want him to be thinking about ways we can improve our own preparedness just in case."

"Yes, My Prince."

"In addition, I want you to put together reports for Tohmas and Hektor, as well," Nahrmahn continued. "In Tohmas' case, I'll write a letter of my own to go with it. For Hektor, though, I think, we'll just let you send your own report— purely as a professional courtesy, since we obviously don't have any firsthand information—to Coris."

Shandyr nodded again. Grand Duke Tohmas of Zebediah was the closest thing Prince Hektor of Corisande had to a rival for control of the League of Corisande. Unfortunately for Tohmas' dreams of glory, he wasn't very much of a rival. Although he was the preeminent noble of the island of Zebediah and the hereditary leader of the Council of Zebediah, the entire island was firmly under Hektor's thumb. Tohmas functioned as little more than the governor of Zebediah in Hektor's name, and however much he might aspire to greater heights, it was most unlikely he would ever attain them. Still, Nahrmahn had been careful to cultivate the man. One never knew when one might need any counterweight one could get, after all.

Phylyp Ahzgood, the Earl of Coris, on the other hand, was Shandyr's own counterpart in Hektor's service. Shandyr had a lively respect for Coris' native ability, and he didn't for a moment think the earl would believe Nahrmahn hadn't been a primary mover behind the attempt on Cayleb. Still, appearances had to be maintained, and Hektor was scarcely likely to press the point as long as Nahrmahn chose to maintain the fiction. After all, Hektor wouldn't exactly have shed any tears if the assassins had succeeded.

"Of course, My Prince," he murmured aloud, and Nahrmahn grunted in satisfaction.

"In that case, I think you should probably be on your way," he said, and Shandyr rose, bowed respectfully, and backed his way out of the dining parlor.

Neither he nor his prince had noticed the almost microscopic "insect" hanging from the ceiling above the table. Even if they had noticed it, they would have paid it no attention, of course, for neither of them had ever heard of something called a SNARC, and certainly not of the remote sensors one of them could deploy.

S*eijin* Merlin, Your Majesty," the chamberlain said quietly as he stepped through the open doorway and bowed. Merlin followed him into the small presence chamber—more of a working office, really, it seemed—and bowed a bit more profoundly than the chamberlain. King Haarahld's court was looked down upon by the courtiers of such sophisticated lands as Harchong because of its casual informality and ability to get along without a veritable horde of servitors. Still, Haarahld was a king, and one of the more powerful ones on the face of Safehold, whatever others might think.

"*Seijin*," Haarahld said, and Merlin looked up.

He saw a man of middle years, stocky, for a Charisian, and taller than most, although shorter than his son and considerably shorter than Merlin. Haarahld wore the traditional loose-cut breeches and thigh-length linen over-tunic of the Charisian upper class, although *his* tunic was bright with bullion embroidery and beadwork. The belt about his waist was made of intricately decorated, seashell-shaped plaques of hammered silver, the golden scepter badge of one who'd made his required pilgrimage to the Temple gleamed on his shoulder brooch, and the glittering fire of the emerald-set golden chain which was his normal badge of office glowed upon his chest. He had a neatly trimmed beard, somewhat more luxuriant than Merlin's own, and the slight epicanthic fold common to most of Safehold's humanity.

Haarahld VII was fifty-two local years old, just over forty-seven standard, and he'd sat on his throne for just over twenty local years. In that time, he'd come to be known—by his own subjects, at least—as "Haarahld the Just," and his level eyes considered Merlin thoughtfully. He was putting on a bit of extra flesh these days, Merlin noticed. Judging from his chest and shoulders, he'd been a man of heroic physique in his youth, but maintaining that sort of fitness, especially at his age, must have been the next best thing to impossible given his immobile right knee. His leg stretched out straight in front of him, his heel resting on a footrest, as he sat in a comfortable but not particularly splendid armchair behind a desk cluttered with documents and slates.

One other person was present. A bishop of the Church of God Awaiting with silvering dark hair and a splendid patriarchal beard stood at the king's right shoulder. His three-cornered cap bore the white cockade of a senior bishop, but lacked the ribbon of an archbishop. His eyes were bright as they considered Merlin, and his white cassock bore the oil-lamp emblem of the Order of Bédard.

The sight of that lamp set Merlin's teeth instantly on edge, but he made himself suppress the instinctive reaction firmly. Much as he hated to admit it, the order which bore Adorée Bédard's name had changed over the years into something far different from anything its ostensible patron would have wanted to see. Besides, he'd "seen" this bishop often enough through his SNARCs to strongly suspect what impelled Haarahld to trust him so totally.

"Your Majesty," he murmured in reply to the king's greeting after only the briefest of pauses. "You do me honor to receive me privately."

"Perhaps," Haarahld said, studying his visitor intently. "Some might feel I've slighted you by not greeting you and thanking you for my son's life in a more public audience."

"But at that more public audience, Your Majesty, I would undoubtedly have been uncomfortably aware of all of the spanned crossbows watching me so alertly. Here," Merlin smiled charmingly, "I need worry only about the two bodyguards behind that screen."

He nodded towards the exquisitely detailed lacquered Harchongese screen behind the king, and Haarahld's eyes narrowed. The bishop's, however, only considered Merlin with a sort of calm curiosity.

Interesting, Merlin thought, but his attention was mainly focused on the king, waiting for *his* reaction. Which came after a heartbeat in a single word.

"Indeed?" Haarahld said, and Merlin smiled again.

"This is Thursday, Your Majesty. Assuming you've stuck to your regular duty schedule, it should be Sergeant Haarpar and Sergeant Gahrdaner."

The chamberlain stepped quickly to one side, right hand falling to the dagger sheathed at his hip, the bishop touched the golden scepter of Langhorne hanging upon his breast, and even Haarahld sat up straighter in his chair. But the king also raised one hand, and shook his head sharply at the chamberlain.

"No, Pawal," he said. "After all, our guest *is a seijin*, is he not?"

"Or something else, Sire," the chamberlain said darkly. He glowered at Merlin with eyes full of suspicion, and his hand left his dagger hilt only reluctantly.

"Your Majesty," Merlin said, "my weapons have all been left in my chamber. Your guardsmen were extremely courteous, but they also searched me very carefully before permitting me into your presence. Surely, one unarmed man is no threat to a monarch whose servants are as loyal to him as yours are to you."

"Somehow, *Seijin* Merlin, I doubt a man such as you is ever unarmed, as long as he has his brain," Haarahld said with a slow, appreciative smile of his own.

"One tries, Your Majesty," Merlin conceded.

The bishop's lips twitched in what might almost have been a stillborn smile, and Haarahld leaned back in his chair once more, considering the blue-eyed stranger even more thoughtfully than before. Then he nodded and looked at the chamberlain.

"Pawal, I believe we might offer *Seijin* Merlin a chair."

Pawal Hahlmahn looked moderately outraged, but he also carried a straight-backed but upholstered chair from the corner of the room and set it down facing Haarahld's desk.

"Please, *Seijin*," Haarahld invited. "Be seated."

"Thank you, Your Majesty."

Merlin settled into the chair and cocked his head, his eyebrows raised.

"Yes, *Seijin*," Haarahld said with a suspiciously grin-like smile, "the interrogation will now begin."

"I'm at your service, Your Majesty." Merlin inclined his head again, politely, and Haarahld chuckled.

"I find that difficult to believe, *Seijin*," he said. "Somehow, I have the distinct impression that it's more a case of Charis finding herself at *your* service."

Merlin smiled, but behind that smile he winced. Haarahld VII, in person, was even more impressive than he'd been observed from afar via SNARC.

"Before we begin," Haarahld said more seriously, "allow me to extend my personal thanks for your intervention on Cayleb's behalf. Without you, he would be dead, and for that I and my house stand in your debt. How may I reward you?"

"Your Majesty," Merlin said with matching seriousness, "while I'm sure some token of your gratitude is in order, it might be as well to draw as little attention to me as possible."

"And why might that be?" Haarahld asked.

"Because I'll be far more useful to Charis if my presence here doesn't become general knowledge."

"And why should you care to be of use to me?"

"Your pardon, Your Majesty," Merlin said almost gently, "but I didn't say of use to *you*. I said of use to *Charis*. The two are closely related, but not, I fear, identical."

"The King *is* the Kingdom!" Hahlmahn snapped, then flushed darkly as he realized he'd spoken out of turn. But despite the flush, there was no hiding the fresh anger in his eyes.

"No, My Lord Chamberlain," Merlin disagreed. "The King is the heart and soul of the Kingdom, but he is *not* the Kingdom itself. Were that true, then the Kingdom would perish with his death."

"The Church teaches that King and Crown are one," the bishop observed, speaking for the first time, and his voice and expression were both carefully neutral.

"And I don't dispute that point with the Church, Bishop Maikel," Merlin said, and the priest's head cocked to one side as the stranger named him correctly. "I simply observe that the King who is the heart of the Kingdom isn't merely a single individual, but all individuals who hold that office and discharge those duties in the name of the Kingdom. And so, while the King and the Kingdom are one, the mortal man who holds that office is but one man in an endless chain of men who hold their crowns in trust for those they are charged to guard and protect."

Haarahld glanced up at Bishop Maikel, then returned his attention to Merlin and gazed at him without speaking for the better part of a full minute. Finally, he nodded slowly.

"A valid distinction," he said. "Not one all monarchs would agree with, but one I can't dispute."

"And the fact that you can't, Your Majesty, is the reason I'm here," Merlin said simply. "While all kings may be ordained by God, all too few prove worthy of their coronation oaths. When one sees the visions which I've been given to see, that fact becomes sadly evident."

"Ah, yes, those 'visions' of yours." Haarahld pursed his lips, then chuckled and raised his voice slightly. "Charlz, you and Gorj may as well come out and join us."

A moment later, the lacquered screen shifted to one side, and two Royal Guard sergeants stepped out from behind it. Both wore black cuirasses, the breastplates emblazoned with the golden kraken of Charis. They also carried spanned, steel-bowed arbalests, and they regarded Merlin warily as they took their places at their king's back.

"I must admit," Haarahld said, "that I found your performance rather impressive, *Seijin* Merlin. As, no doubt, you intended I should. Of course, it's always possible sufficiently good spies could have provided you with that information. On the other hand, if my personal household is that riddled with spies, my house is already doomed. So, since you obviously want me to ask the question, I will. How did you know?"

Despite his whimsical tone, his brown eyes sharpened and he leaned slightly forward in his chair.

"Your Majesty," Merlin replied, "these three men"—he waved one hand, taking in the two Guardsmen and the chamberlain—"are, I believe, loyal unto death to you, your son, and your house. I trust them as fully as I trust you, yourself. And Bishop Maikel has been your confessor for—what? Fifteen years now? But while what I'm about to tell you may prove difficult to believe, I hope to be able to offer you proof I speak the truth. And I believe that if I can prove that to you, you'll understand why it must be kept as secret as possible for as long as possible." ·

He paused, and the king nodded without even glancing at his retainers. The three of them continued to regard Merlin with wary eyes, but Merlin saw how their shoulders straightened and their expressions firmed at the king's obvious confidence in their trustworthiness. Bishop Maikel simply moved a half-step closer to Haarahld's chair and rested one large, powerful hand lightly on its back.

"As I'm sure Prince Cayleb and Lieutenant Falkhan have already told you, Your Majesty," he began, "I've lived for many years in the Mountains of Light, and in the process I've developed some, though far from all, of the reputed powers of the *seijin*. It isn't a title I would lightly claim for myself, yet it may be that it fits.

"At any rate, it's been given to me to see visions of distant places and events, to hear the voices of distant people. It's as if an invisible bird perched on the wall there," he pointed at a spot on the plastered wall not far from an open window, "or on the branch of a tree, and I saw through its eyes, heard through its ears. I've never seen the future, and I can't call up the past. I see only the present, and no man can see *all* that transpires everywhere in the entire world. But the things which I have seen have focused more and more tightly upon Charis, upon your house, and upon Cayleb. I don't believe that would happen by accident."

Haarahld's eyes seemed to bore into Merlin's. The King of Charis had a reputation for being able to pull the truth out of any man, but Merlin gazed back levelly. After all, everything he'd said was completely truthful. If eight standard centuries at the same address didn't count as "living for many years" in the Mountains of Light, he couldn't imagine what would. And his "visions" *had* focused more and more upon Charis, and definitely not by accident.

"What sorts of visions?" Haarahld asked after a long, still moment. "Of whom?"

"As I've said, I see and hear as if I were physically present. I can't read a page, if it isn't turned; I can't hear a thought, if it isn't spoken. I can't know what passes in the secret places of someone's heart, only what they say and do.

"I've seen visions of you, Your Majesty. I've seen you in this chamber with your personal guards, seen you with Chamberlain Hahlmahn. I've seen you discussing the Hanth succession with Cayleb and matters of policy with Earl Gray Harbor. I saw and heard you discussing the new patrols off Triton Head with High Admiral Lock Island when you instructed him to reinforce *Falcon* and *Warrior* with *Rock Shoal Bay* and her entire squadron."

Haarahld had been nodding slowly, but he froze abruptly at the mention of Lock Island. Not surprisingly, Merlin thought, given that he and the high admiral had discussed those reinforcements—and the reasons for them—under conditions of maximum security. None of their precautions, however, had been directed at a SNARC which could deploy reusable parasite spy bugs.

"I've seen visions of Cayleb," Merlin continued. "Not just in conversation with you, but riding to the hunt, with his arms master, even at his books." Merlin smiled slightly and shook his head at that. "And I've seen him sitting in council with you, and on shipboard.

"And just as I've seen those visions, I've seen your people. I told Cayleb that what I've seen gives me a good opinion of you, Your Majesty, and it does. In all honesty, and without seeking to curry favor with you, I haven't been given a vision of any other king of Safehold who comes as close as you do to the ideal the Church proclaims. You aren't perfect. Indeed, if you'll forgive me, you're far from it. But you also know you aren't, and, perhaps even more importantly, you've taught your heir to know the same thing. Those qualities, that sense of responsibility, are too rare and precious for me to see them lightly cast aside. I believe the reason I've seen what I've seen has been to bring me here to offer my services, such as they are, to the preservation of this kingdom and the tradition of service its monarchs strive to uphold."

"The praise of the praiseworthy is especially welcome," Haarahld said, after another long, thoughtful pause. "I trust you'll forgive me, however, for pointing out that praise and flattery sometimes blur."

"Especially when the one offering them desires something," Merlin agreed. "And, to be honest, Your Majesty, I *do* desire something." Haarahld's eyes narrowed, and Merlin smiled. "I desire to see Charis become all she may become," he said.

"All she may become," Haarahld repeated. "Why Charis? Even if everything you've said about my myriad good qualities were accurate, why pick *this* kingdom? It can't be because of any sense of loyalty to my house, since the one thing you obviously aren't is a Charisian. So, if you'll forgive me, *Seijin* Merlin, it must be because of something you want out of Charis. Some goal or objective of your own. And while I'm deeply grateful for your part in saving my son's life, and although only a fool could fail to recognize the value of an adviser who sees what you appear to see, no king worthy of his crown could accept such services without knowing that what *you* want is also what *he* wants."

Merlin leaned back in his own chair, gazing thoughtfully at the Charisian monarch, then nodded mentally. Haarahld VII was just as tough-minded as Merlin had expected, but there was a hard core of honesty, close to the king's surface. This was a man who could play the game of deception, of bluff and counterbluff, with the best of them, but it wasn't the game he preferred.

Of course, it remained to be seen if Bishop Maikel was equally tough-minded and resilient. Normally, Merlin wouldn't have been very optimistic about that where a bishop of the Church of God Awaiting was concerned, but Maikel was hardly typical of the breed.

For one thing, the king's confessor was a Charisian. So far as Merlin had been able to determine, he'd never left the kingdom in his entire life, except to make his own pilgrimage to the Temple, and he was the highest-ranking native Charisian in the entire archbishopric's hierarchy. Haarahld's choice, ten years before, of Maikel Staynair to be Bishop of Tellesberg, as well as his confessor had, *not* been popular with Archbishop Erayk's predecessor. But Haarahld had clung stubbornly to his prerogative to nominate the priest of his choice to the capital's see, and over the years, Maikel had become a member of the king's inner circle of advisers.

Which could be a good thing . . . or a very bad thing, indeed.

"Your Majesty," Merlin said finally, "why did your great-grandfather abolish serfdom here in Charis?"

Haarahld frowned, as if surprised by the question. Then he shrugged.

"Because it's what he believed God wanted of us," he said.

"But serfdom exists in Emerald," Merlin pointed out, "and in Tarot, Corisande, and Chisholm. In Harchong, the lot of a serf is little better than that of a beast of the field. Indeed, they treat their draft animals better than they do their serfs, because those animals are more expensive, and in Desnair and Trellheim, they practice outright slavery. Even in the Temple Lands"—he looked up from the king's face to meet Bishop Maikel's eyes with just a hint of challenge—"men are bound to the land of the great church estates, although they aren't *called* serfs. Yet not here. Why not? You say it's not what God wants of you, but why do you believe that?"

"The *Writ* teaches that God created every Adam and every Eve in the same instant, the same exercise of His will through the Archangel Langhorne," Haarahld said. "He didn't create kings first, or nobles, or wealthy merchants. He breathed the breath of life into the nostrils of *all* men and *all* women. Surely that means all men and all women are brothers and sisters. We may not be born to the same states, in this later, less perfect world. Some of us are born kings now, and some are born noble, or to wealth, or all three. Yet those born more humbly are still our brothers and sisters. If God sees men that way, then so must we, and if that's true, then men aren't cattle, or sheep, or horses, or dragons. Not something to be owned."

He half-glared at Merlin, and Merlin shrugged.

"And would *you* agree with that, Bishop Maikel?" he asked quietly.

"I would."

The priest's voice was deep and powerful, well suited to preaching and prayer, and there was a glitter in his eyes. They weren't quite as hard as Haarahld's, but there was no retreat in them, either, and Merlin nodded slowly. Then he looked back at the king.

"Other rulers would appear to disagree with you, Your Majesty," he observed. "Even the Church feels differently, to judge by her own practices in her own lands, at any rate. But you do believe it. And that, Your Majesty, is my goal, my objective. I believe the same thing you do, and I see no other powerful kingdom which does. I respect you, and in many ways, I admire you. But my true loyalty?" He shrugged once more. "That belongs not to you, or to Cayleb, but to the future. I *will* use you, if I can, Your Majesty. Use you to create the day in which no man owns another, no man thinks men born less nobly than he *are* cattle or sheep."

Hahlmahn glared angrily at him, but Haarahld only nodded slowly, his expression thoughtful.

"And that's the true reason I want Charis not simply to survive, but to prosper," Merlin said. "Not because I love empire, and not because I crave wealth, or because I confuse military might with the true strength of a kingdom. But while it may not be given to me to see the future, I know what future I would *like* to see. I know what values, what laws, what sort of monarchy, I believe God wants called forth. And at this time, Your Majesty, Charis offers the best hope for the future I would like to see to ever come to pass. Which is why I said from the very beginning that I came not to serve you, specifically, but to serve Charis. The *idea* of Charis, of her future."

Haarahld drummed lightly on one arm of his chair with the fingers of his right hand, then glanced up at Bishop Maikel.

"Maikel?" he said quietly.

"Sire," the bishop said without hesitation, "I can quarrel with nothing this man has said. I know your hopes, your aspirations. And I know what it is you most fear." His fingers stroked his pectoral scepter again, apparently unconsciously, and his nostrils flared. "If I might, Sire?"

Haarahld nodded, and the bishop looked back at Merlin.

"I've never met an actual *seijin*," he said. "Once in my life I met a man who *claimed* to be a *seijin*, but what he was in reality was a charlatan."

"Your Eminence," Merlin said when the bishop paused, "I haven't claimed to be a *seijin*; I've claimed only that I have some of the powers ascribed to *seijin*."

"I observed that," Maikel said with a small smile. "Indeed, while I would never claim to be the equal of my esteemed colleagues in the Temple as a theologian, I've engaged in my share of theological debate. And, perhaps as a consequence of that, I was struck by *several* things you didn't say."

"You were?" Merlin's politely attentive expression never wavered, but internal alarms began to sound as the bishop gazed at him levelly for several seconds.

"According to many of the tales I read when I was younger," Maikel said finally, "a true *seijin* frequently is known only after the fact, by the nature of his deeds. Others may give him the title; he seldom claims it for himself. The nature of these 'visions' of yours, however, will strike many as ample evidence that whatever else you may be, you are *not* as other mortal men. So perhaps we can all agree '*seijin*' is the word best suited—for now, at least—to describing whatever it is you are.

"But having agreed to that, what are we to make of you and your purposes? That, I'm sure you will agree, is the critical question. And my answer to it is that the *Writ* teaches that the true nature of any man will be shown forth in his actions. It matters not whether that man is a king, a merchant, a *seijin*, or a peasant; in the end, he cannot conceal what he truly is, what he truly stands for. So far, you've saved Cayleb's life. Whether or not God sent you to us for that specific purpose, I don't know. But, in my judgment, it was not the act of one who would serve darkness."

The bishop looked at his monarch and bent his head in a curiously formal little bow.

"Your Majesty," he said, "I sense no evil in this man. I may be wrong, of course—unlike the Grand Vicar or the Chancellor, I'm merely a humble, unlettered, provincial bishop. But my advice to you is to listen to him. I know the darkness which is settling about us. Perhaps this man and the services he offers are the lamp"—he touched the embroidered sigil of his order on the breast of his habit—"you require."

Had Merlin been a being of flesh and blood, he would have let out a long, quiet exhalation of relief. But he wasn't. And so he simply sat, waiting, while Haarahld looked deeply into his confessor's eyes. Then the king returned his attention to Merlin once again.

"And how would you serve Charis?" he asked intently.

"With my visions, as they're given to me. With my sword, as I must. And with my mind, as I may," Merlin said simply. "For example, I'm certain you've interrogated the one assassin we managed to take alive."

"That *you* managed to take alive," Haarahld corrected, and Merlin shrugged.

"Perhaps, Your Majesty. But while I've had no vision of his interrogation—as I say, I see much, but not all—I do know who sent him."

Hahlmahn and the two Guardsmen leaned slightly forward, eyes intent. Bishop Maikel's bearded lips pursed thoughtfully, and Merlin's smile was cold.

"I know it must have been tempting to lay the blame on Hektor of Corisande," he said, "but in this case, it would be an error. The men who attempted to kill Prince Cayleb were mercenaries, Desnairians hired by Prince Nahrmahn and . . . certain others, but Prince Hektor wasn't even consulted, so far as I'm aware.

"Which isn't to say he isn't involved in plots of his own. Indeed, his objection to your assassination, Your Majesty, or Cayleb's, is purely tactical, not a matter of any sort of personal qualm. From what he's said to his own closest advisers and servants and what I've read of his letters to Nahrmahn, he simply believes assassins are unlikely to succeed. And, I think, fears how your kingdom might react if an attempt *did* succeed. He has no desire to meet you ship-to-ship at this time, not yet, and he believes that if Cayleb were killed and you believed Corisande was behind it, that's precisely what he would face. Which is why he prefers to undermine your strength at sea in order to weaken you for a decisive blow by more conventional means. You once called him a sand maggot, not a slash lizard, when you and Cayleb discussed him, and I believe it was an apt description. But in this case, the sand maggot is thinking in more . . . conventional terms than his allies."

Haarahld's eyes had grown more and more intent as he listened to Merlin. Now he sat back in his chair, his expression one of wonder.

"*Seijin* Merlin," he said, "when I summoned you to this audience, I didn't honestly expect to believe you. I wanted to, which is one reason I was determined not to. But the finest spies in the world couldn't have told you all you've just told me, and every word you've said has been accurate, so far as my own sources are able to confirm. I know someone who's said what you've said here today will understand that despite all of that, your sincerity and trustworthiness must be tested and proved. For myself, as an individual—as Haarahld Ahrmahk—I would trust you now. As King Haarahld of Charis, I can give no man the trust I must give you if I accept the services you offer until he be proven beyond question or doubt."

"Your Majesty," Merlin said quietly, "you're a king. It's your duty to remember men lie. That they deceive, and that often revealing a little truth makes the final deception all the more convincing. I don't expect you to accept my services, or even the truth of my visions, without testing thoroughly. And as you test, I beg you to remember this. I've said my service is to Charis and what Charis may become, not to you personally, and I meant it. I'll give you all the truth that lies in me, and the best council I may, but in the end, my service, my loyalty, is to a future which lies beyond your life, beyond the life span of this person you call Merlin, and beyond even the lifespan of your son. I would have you understand that."

"*Seijin* Merlin, I do." Haarahld looked deep into those unearthly sapphire eyes, and his voice was soft. "It's said the *seijin* serve the vision of God, not of man. That any man who accepts the advice of a *seijin* had best remember the vision of God need not include his own success, or even survival. But one of the duties of a king is to die for his people, if God requires it of him. Whatever God's vision for Charis may demand, I will pay, and if you are a true *seijin*, if you truly serve His vision, that's more than sufficient for me, whatever my own future may hold."

.VII.
Tellesberg and Styvyn Mountains,
Kingdom of Charis,
Armageddon Reef

Merlin sat once more in his chamber.

A humid, windless night pressed heavily against its window. Nimue Alban, born and raised in Old Earth's NorEurope, would have found that night uncomfortably warm, despite the season, but a PICA was unconcerned by such minor matters. Merlin was more struck by the moonless night's impenetrable blackness, which was still one of the most alien aspects of Safehold for the man whose mind had been Nimue Alban's. Nimue had been a child of a technological civilization, one of illumination, of light and energy that drove back the darkness and domed its cities in reflected cloud-glow on the darkest of nights. Tellesberg was well lit for a city of Safehold, but the only illumination on *this* planet came from the simple flames of burning wood or wax, of tallow or oil, far too feeble to drive out the night.

Like Tellesberg itself, Merlin's chamber was well lit by Safeholdian standards. It was illuminated not by candles, but by the fine, clear flame of lamps filled with kraken oil and equipped with the comparatively newfangled notion of polished reflectors, placed behind their chimneys to concentrate and direct their light. Despite that, the available light was scarcely sufficient for comfortable reading, especially of the intricate calligraphy in the hand-lettered volume on Merlin's desk. It could be done, and had been, by generations of Safehold-born humans, but not without a stiff penalty in eyestrain.

Merlin, however, had certain advantages. For one, his artificial eyes were immune to strain. They were also equipped with light-gathering technology, which made the room—and, indeed, the bottomless night outside it—daylight clear.

He'd deleted the standard PICA ten-day countdown clock from his visual field, and there was nothing to distract him as he skimmed rapidly and steadily through the thick leather-bound copy of the *Holy Writ* of the Church of God Awaiting.

It was far from the first time he'd perused the *Writ*, yet he found the book continually fascinating, in the way a homicide detective might have been fascinated by the autobiography of a sadistic serial killer he'd known as a boyhood friend. There were many aspects of its moral teachings with which Merlin could not take issue, however badly he wanted to. Maruyama Chihiro had borrowed heavily from existing religions, and the core of his "*Writ*'s" moral teachings would have been familiar to almost any Old Earth theologian. For the most part, Merlin reflected, that was undoubtedly inevitable, for a stable society required an underlying framework of rules and laws which those living within it accepted. Throughout human history, religion had been one of the primary wellsprings of that legitimacy, and it was that portion of the *Writ* which produced priests like Bishop Maikel.

But the religions from which Maruyama had lifted his core commandments and moral precepts had been the product of a genuine effort to understand, or at least conceptualize, God or whatever higher power their adherents had sought. The Church of God Awaiting's seminal scripture wasn't. It was a deliberate fraud, perpetrated upon its followers by individuals whose actions had directly contradicted the principles and beliefs of the religions in which so many of them had been raised. It was a lie, using the hunger within human beings which had driven them to seek God, by whatever name, or in whatever form, throughout the human race's entire history, not simply to control, but to program. To stifle any sense of inquiry which might threaten the fraudulent template Eric Langhorne and Adorée Bédard had manufactured to hammer any future human society into the pattern *they* had found good.

Merlin had to admit that, between them, Langhorne, Bédard, and Murayama had managed to kill quite a few birds with the single stone of the *Writ*. He turned back to the beginning of the volume and grimaced as he glanced once more at the table of contents. *The Book of Langhorne, The Book of Bédard, The Book of Pasquale*, the books of Sondheim, Truscott, Schueler, Jwo-jeng, Chihiro, Andropov, Hastings.

The list went on and on, each book attributed to one of the "archangels." The *Writ* contained no gospels written by mere mortals. Such human-produced writings existed, in *The Commentaries* and *The Insights*, not to mention *The Testimonies*, which were also part of the Church of God Awaiting's central scripture and authority. But none of those merely human writings could compare to the legitimacy and centrality of the *Writ*, for unlike them, *its* every word had been handed down directly from the mouth of God through his immortal angels.

The *Writ* wasn't just an instrument of social control, either. True, *The Book of Langhorne* dealt with the "law of God" as taught by the Church of God Awaiting. Merlin had gagged mentally, more than once, as he waded through the love-cloaked half-truths and outright falsehoods from which Langhorne—or Murayama, writing for Langhorne, at any rate—had woven the straitjacket into which he'd laced the inhabitants of Safehold. And *The Book of Bédard* was at least as hard for Merlin to take, a masterpiece of psychology in the service of deception and mind control that rejoiced in the subtitle of *"The Book of Wisdom and Self-Knowledge."*

But many of its other books were, in fact, a practical guide to terraforming and the colonization of an alien planet.

The Archangel Hastings' "book," for example, was actually an atlas—a very *detailed* atlas of the entire planet, based upon the meticulous maps Shan-wei's crew had made at the time of its original terraforming. The maps in Merlin's copy of the *Writ* were on far too small a scale to be very useful, and quite a bit of distortion had crept in when the printer's engravings were made, but the master maps had been carefully preserved in the Temple. Indeed, those master maps were some of the Church's holiest artifacts. The advanced synthetics of their "paper" were fireproof, waterproof, about as tough as a five-millimeter sheet of hammered copper, and virtually immune to the effects of age—all of which, of course, amply proved their "miraculous" nature.

Almost equally importantly, however, *The Book of Hastings* required that copies of those maps be made available, to the public as well as the Church, in the cathedral of every bishop. Safeholdians knew *exactly* what the geography of their world looked like, which had been of enormous importance when they set about deciding where to plant additional enclaves, and the *Writ*'s other books had given them a guide for how those enclaves were to be established.

It was a guide that deliberately falsified the basis for many of the lessons it taught and the religious laws it handed down, but it had provided the basic framework under which humanity had expanded from its initial enclaves on this planet. *The Book of Sondheim* dealt with agronomy and farming, including, especially, the necessary steps to prepare Safehold's soil for the essential terrestrial plants humanity required. *The Book of Truscott* did the same thing for animal husbandry—for native Safeholdian species, as well as imports from Earth. *The Book of Pasquale* contained "religious laws" to provide sanitation, good hygiene and diet, the treatment of wounds, and basic preventive medicine. Even *The Book of Bédard*, despite the purpose for which it had been written, contained quite a lot of sound psychological advice and insight, and the members of "her" order—like Bishop Maikel—had taken its precepts in very different directions from anything she might have intended. The order's successes in ministering to the mental and emotional needs of Safeholdian humanity were little short of amazing in many cases, and it was the Bédardites who administered the majority of the Church's charitable works.

Yet all of the *Writ*'s directives were couched as religious laws, proper rituals and sacrifices to be performed by the devout. *The Book of Pasquale*'s injunctions never mentioned germs or the scientific basis on which his "laws" rested, for example. And if a healer failed to wash his hands in one of the "holy waters," properly prepared and blessed by a priest, before treating a wound, and that wound became septic, or before delivering a baby, and that mother died of childbed fever, then it was not infection or disease which was to blame, but sin.

And the maps of *The Book of Hastings*, which conclusively demonstrated that their world was a sphere, also explicitly taught Safeholdians the Ptolemaic theory of the universe . . . and turned gravity itself into yet another of the Archangel Langhorne's miraculous gifts to man, through God's grace. Indeed, Langhorne had created the world as a round ball at the center of the crystal spheres of the moon, sun, stars, and God's own Heaven expressly as a means to demonstrate to Man that God could accomplish anything He willed. After all, did it not require an act of divine will and power to keep people from falling off the bottom side of the world and crashing into the moon?

And so, in addition to providing the directions by which the original enclaves had followed the Archangel Langhorne's direction to be fruitful and multiply and inhabit the world God had given them, the *Writ* had aided powerfully in the systematic abortion of anything resembling the scientific method while simultaneously reinforcing the power of the Church as preceptor and governor of humanity.

Then there were *The Book of Jwo-jeng* and *The Book of Schueler*. Neither of them were as long as some of the others, but they went to the very heart of Langhorne's ultimate purpose here on Safehold. Jwo-jeng handed down the official descriptions and definitions of that technology which God found acceptable, and that which He rejected as unclean, or tainted, or reserved solely for His archangels and angels. And Schueler, whose "book" was both the shortest and the most horrifying of them all, defined the punishment to be visited upon those who violated the proscriptions of Langhorne and Jwo-jeng. The thought that anyone raised in the same society as Nimue Alban could have resurrected so many nightmares from the horrific closet of mankind's savagery to his own was enough to turn even Merlin's alloy and composites stomach. Schueler must have spent endless hours poring over the history texts to come up with such a detailed catalog of atrocities to be visited upon the "unbeliever" in "God's most holy Name."

But the most fascinating—and infuriating—of all, in many ways, was *The Book of Chihiro*. The book which had been added later, after the close of the original copy of the *Writ* which had been stored in the computers in Nimue's cave.

It seemed apparent that Pei Kau-yung's vengeance for his wife and friends had eliminated almost all of Langhorne's leadership cadre. Indeed, from the sudden dearth of "angelic" visitations recorded in *The Testimonies* following his attack, it seemed likely he'd gotten a huge chunk of Langhorne's lower level personnel, as well. Unfortunately, Maruyama Chihiro hadn't been among the casualties, and he and his fellow survivors had managed to keep most of Langhorne's plan on track. The Archangel Chihiro, revered as the patron of personal protection and called the Guardian of Cities in the hagiography of the Church of God Awaiting, had been the official historian of God. He was the one who had recorded the miracle of Safehold's creation . . . and he was also the recorder of how Shan-wei, Dark Mother of Evil, had tainted the purity of that creation in the name of ambition and greed.

Murayama had tied it all together well, Merlin thought bitterly. Shan-wei, brightest of all the Archangel Langhorne's assistants, had viewed Safehold not as a work of God which she had been privileged to help bring into existence, but as the work of her own hands. And from that hubris, that twisted sense of her own self-worth and that vaunting pride, had flowed all of the evil in Safehold.

She had set herself against her rightful overlord, the Archangel Langhorne, and against God Himself, and she'd gathered to herself the Archangel Proctor, who had opened the seals on temptation and forbidden knowledge. The Archangel Sullivan, who had taught humanity gluttony and self-indulgence. The Archangel Grimaldi, whose twisted version of the healing teachings of the Archangel Truscott had been the father and mother of pestilence. The Archangel Stavrakis, who had preached the avarice of personal gain over the godly yielding to the Church of God Awaiting that first fruit of every harvest which was God's due. The Archangel Rodriguez, who had preached the arrogant, seductive lie that men were actually capable of setting their own fallible hands to the creation of the law under which they might live. The Archangel Ascher, Father of Lies, whose so-called history's twisted version of the true *Writ* had led those mortals foolish enough to believe anything Shan-wei said into equally dark damnation.

And, of course, the fallen archangel who was, in so many ways, the darkest of them all—the Archangel Kau-yung, Father of Destruction, Lord of Treachery, who had smitten the Archangel Langhorne and the Archangel Bédard, traitorously and without warning, after the grieving Langhorne had been compelled to unleash the *Rakurai*, the lightning bolt of God, upon Shan-wei and her fallen followers. Kau-yung, who had been the most trusted of all Langhorne's subordinates, the warrior charged with guarding all that Safehold stood for, who had turned to Shan-wei's evil. It was Kau-yung's monumental treachery, darker even then Shan-wei's original sin, which had so terribly wounded the perishable bodies of the Archangels Langhorne, Bédard, Pasquale, Sondheim, and their most loyal followers, those closest to God Himself, that they were forced to leave Safehold with their work unfinished.

Merlin had no personal memory of the majority of Shan-wei's "fallen archangels." Nimue had found most of them in the computers in her caves, but if the original Nimue had ever met or known them, that knowledge had never been uploaded to her PICA. Yet some of them she *had* known, and especially Kau-yung and Shan-wei herself. To see them so vilified, to know that fifty generations of men and women they had died to free reviled them not as heroes but as the darkest of devils, the source of all evil and unhappiness, was like a knife in Merlin's heart.

Part of him longed desperately to denounce the *Writ*, to break out his assault shuttle and his recon skimmers and turn the Temple into a glowing crater to prove Langhorne's entire religion was built on lies. But he couldn't. Not yet, at any rate. But someday, he told himself yet again. Someday the people of Safehold would be ready to hear the truth and to accept it, and when that day came, Shan-wei and Kau-yung and everyone who had died with them would be remembered for who they'd truly been, all they'd truly stood for.

Merlin felt the anger stirring deep inside his molycirc heart and mind and closed the book. He supposed he really shouldn't allow himself to dwell on it this way, but when it came right down to it, the *Writ* and the so-called church it served were his true enemies. Prince Hektor, Prince Nahrmahn, and all of the others plotting against Charis were impediments to his real struggle, nothing more.

Still, he thought, lips quirking in a mustachioed smile, *they're certainly the* immediate *problem, aren't they? So I suppose I ought to be getting on with it.*

He brought up the digital clock at the corner of his vision and checked the time. He'd recalibrated it to match Safehold's twenty-six-and-a-half-hour day, and it was two hours past the thirty-one-minute period Safeholdians knew as Langhorne's Watch. On any other human-colonized planet, it would have been known as "compensate," or simply "comp," the adjustment period required to tweak an alien world's day into something neatly divisible into mankind's standard minutes and hours. On Safehold, anyone who found himself awake at the midnight hour was supposed to spend Langhorne's Watch in silent meditation and contemplation of all God had done for him, by Langhorne's intervention, in the day just past.

Somehow, Merlin had never gotten around to spending the Watch on just that purpose.

He snorted at the thought, and boosted the sensitivity of his hearing. The enhancing software sorted through the incoming sounds, confirming the slumbering quiet of Marytha's Tower. Given the guard post at the tower's entrance, there was no need for guards or sentries elsewhere, and given the limitations of their nighttime lighting, Safeholdians tended to be early to bed and early to rise. By now, all the tower's small population of honored guests sounded to be deeply asleep, and even the attendant servants had retreated to the workrooms and waiting rooms set aside for them on the tower's lowest levels to await the ringing bell if some insomniac should require their services.

Which was precisely what Merlin had been waiting for.

"Owl," he subvocalized.

"Yes, Lieutenant Commander?" the AI's voice replied almost instantly over his built in communicator.

"I'm ready," Merlin said. "Send the skimmer in as previously directed."

"Yes, Lieutenant Commander."

Merlin rose, extinguished the wicks of his lamps, and opened the chamber window. He clambered up onto the thick window ledge and sat there, dangling his legs into the night, leaning one shoulder against the wide embrasure, while he gazed out over the harbor.

The waterfront was a scene of activity, even this late at night, as longshoremen worked to finish loading cargoes for skippers eager to catch the next tide. There was also, inevitably, activity among the taverns and brothels, and Merlin's boosted hearing carried him snatches of laughter, music, drunken song, and quarrels. He could also hear—and see—the sentries standing alertly at their posts, or walking their beats, on the palace's walls, and by zooming in on the guard towers of the harbor fortifications and defensive batteries, he could see the sentries standing watch there, as well.

He sat there for several minutes, waiting patiently, before Owl spoke again.

"ETA one minute, Lieutenant Commander," it said.

"Acknowledged," Merlin subvocalized back, although he supposed it wasn't really necessary.

The transmission from the compact, long-ranged communicator, built into his PICA chassis about where a biological human would have carried his spleen, bounced off the SNARC hanging in geosynchronous orbit over The Anvil, the large sea or small ocean north of Margaret's Land, to Owl's master array fourteen thousand kilometers—*no, eighty-seven hundred miles, damn it,* he corrected himself—distant in the Mountains of Light. The SNARC, like the array itself, was heavily stealthed (which might not be quite as excessive a precaution as Merlin had thought when he originally arranged it), and so was the vehicle coming silently out of the north above him after loitering safely out at sea all day.

Merlin reached out and up, hooking the fingers of his left hand into a crevice between two of Marytha's Tower's massive stones for balance. Then he pulled himself into a half-standing position in the window opening.

"All right, Owl. Collect me," he said.

"Yes, Lieutenant Commander," the AI replied, and a tractor beam reached down from the recon skimmer hovering a thousand meters above Tellesberg and scooped Merlin neatly off his window-ledge perch.

He rose effortlessly and silently through the darkness, watching the city beneath his boots. This was exactly how Langhorne and his so-called angels had managed to come and go so "miraculously," and Merlin had been bitterly tempted to make open use of the same capability. His recon skimmer was configured for maximum stealth at the moment, which meant its smart-skin fuselage was faithfully duplicating the night sky above it. Effectively, it was as transparent as the air in which it hovered, as invisible to the human eye—or even to Merlin's—as its stealth systems had already rendered it to the vast majority of more sophisticated sensors. But that same smart skin and its normal landing light systems could have been used to produce the blinding brilliance of the "*kyousei hi*" the "angels" had used. Coupled with the literally inhuman capabilities built into Merlin's PICA, not to mention the other bits and pieces of advanced technology Kau-yung and Shan-wei had been able to hide away, he could easily have duplicated any feat the "angels" had ever performed.

But Nimue had rejected that possibility almost immediately. Not only had she been instantly and instinctively revolted by the notion of following in Langhorne's and Bédard's footsteps, but there'd been more practical objections, as well. Sooner or later, she was going to have to tell someone the truth, which was precisely the reason Merlin had never told an outright lie. Continuing to avoid lies was going to become both easier and harder, he suspected, but when the time came that the truth had to be openly revealed, he could not afford to have told a single lie of his own. Not if he wanted whoever it was to believe him when he told them of the far greater lie which had been perpetrated upon their entire planet for so many hundreds of years.

Even more to the point, simply replacing one superstition, one false religion, with another would never accomplish the task to which Nimue Alban had set her hand. "Decrees from God," to be obeyed without question, wouldn't engender the widespread independent, inquiring mind-set and attitudes which would be required in the decades and centuries to come. And the appearance of an "angel" preaching a doctrine fundamentally at odds with that of the Church and the *Writ* could not help but raise all sorts of accusations of demonic origin. Which, in turn, would almost certainly lead to the religious war she'd feared was inevitable anyway, but hoped to at least minimize and hold off for a generation or two.

The hovering skimmer's thick armorplast bubble canopy slid back, and the tractor beam deposited Merlin on the extended, built in ladder. He climbed it quickly, and settled into the comfortable, if not exactly spacious, cockpit's forward flight couch as the ladder retracted back into the fuselage. The canopy slid itself shut over his head, locking with the quiet "*shuuuusssh*" of a good seal, enclosing him in the cool, safe cocoon of the cockpit, and he felt the gentle, unbreakable embrace of the flight couch's activating tractor field as he reached out and laid his hand on the joystick.

"I have control, Owl," he said.

"Acknowledged, Lieutenant Commander. You have control," the AI replied, and Merlin took the skimmer out of hover and eased back on the stick, angling upward as he goosed the throttle.

The skimmer accelerated smoothly, and he watched the airspeed indicator climb to seven hundred kilometers per hour. He could have taken it higher—the atmospheric indicator was calibrated to a speed in excess of Mach 6—but he had no intention of creating sonic booms. Once or twice, it might be taken for natural thunder, even on a cloudless night like tonight, but that wouldn't be the case if he made a practice of it. The time might well come when he wouldn't have a choice about that; in the meantime, however, he wasn't about to let himself get into bad habits.

He headed northwest from Tellesberg, almost directly away from the site of

Cayleb's encounter with the slash lizard—and Nahrmahn's assassins—crossing the waterfront and sweeping out over the waters of South Howell Bay. From his increased altitude, he could see the dim lights of the fortresses on Sand Shoal Island and Helen Island, hundreds of kilometers out into the Bay, but he wasn't interested in them tonight. Instead, he continued onward, swinging further to the west, until the steep-shouldered peaks of the Styvyn Mountains loomed ahead of him.

The Styvyns rose like a rampart, a wall across the southern end of the isthmus connecting Charis proper to Margaret's Land. The pronunciation shift in the mountain range's name indicated that it had been christened long after "the Archangel Hastings" had prepared his maps, probably not more than a few hundred years earlier, and it was only lightly populated, even now. Its higher peaks rose to as much as three thousand meters—*ten thousand feet*, Merlin corrected himself irritably; he *had* to get used to thinking in the units of the local measuring system—and population pressure hadn't been sufficient to push settlers up into its inhospitable interior.

Which suited it quite well to Merlin's requirements.

He reached his objective, just under two hundred miles from the Charisian capital, and brought the skimmer back into a hover over the high alpine valley.

It didn't look a great deal different from any other stretch of the uninhabited mountains. There were a handful of clusters of terrestrial vegetation, but they were few and far between, lost among the native "pines" (which really did look quite a bit like the Earth tree of the same name, he reflected, aside from their smooth, almost silky bark and even longer needles) and tanglewood thickets. Without terrestrial plants to provide them with habitat, there were none of the transplanted animals and birds whose ranges were still washing steadily outward from the areas of the planet humanity had claimed. There were plenty of examples of Safehold's native fauna, however, and Merlin reminded himself that a slash lizard or a dragon wouldn't realize a PICA was indigestible until after it had made the mistake of devouring one.

He smiled at the thought of one of the native predators straining to pass the undigested chunks of an unwary PICA, and punched up the skimmer's terrain display of the detailed topographical map Owl had generated from the SNARC's overflights several five-days earlier. There. *That* was what he wanted, and he sent the skimmer sliding slowly and gently forward.

The cave entrance was a dark wound in the mountainside. It looked even bigger now that he was here in person, with the skimmer to use as a visual referent, and he guided the slender reconnaissance vehicle through the opening. It was over twice as wide as the skimmer's fuselage and stub wings and widened still further once he was inside. The vertical stabilizer had ample clearance, as well, and he took the skimmer almost a hundred meters—*three hundred and thirty feet*, he reminded himself as he made the conversion, this time almost automatically—

farther in, then pivoted the vehicle in place, until its nose pointed once more towards the open night beyond the cave.

Not bad, he thought. *Not bad at all.*

In fact, it was almost perfect. Less than half an hour from Tellesberg even at the relatively modest velocity he'd allowed himself tonight, it was at least thirty or forty of the Safeholdians' miles from the nearest human habitation, and the cave was more than large enough to serve as the skimmer's hangar. It was a little on the damp side, with quite a bit of seepage on the southern wall, despite its elevation, but that wouldn't be a factor. Once the skimmer set down and sealed its ports, Merlin could have submerged the thing in salt water and left it there without damaging it.

There were signs that something large—probably a dragon, he thought, studying the leavings, and not one of the vegetarian variety—had laired here, but that was all right, too. In fact, it was another plus. Not even a great dragon was going to be able to damage the heavily armored recon skimmer very easily, and should some wandering hunting party actually penetrate into this high, mountain valley, they were . . . unlikely to go poking about in a cave which had been claimed by one of Safehold's most fearsome land-going predators.

The rest of the gear isn't as tough as the skimmer, though, he reflected. *Probably be a good idea to leave the sonic system on, anyway.*

His copies of Shan-wei's original terraforming notes and progress reports contained enormous amounts of information on the planet's native ecology, and she and her teams had determined the sonic frequencies most effective at repelling the local wildlife. If he played with the power levels a little, he ought to be able to come up with a sonic field which would keep even a dragon safely away from his local equipment depot without driving it into finding another lair.

He hovered there, a meter or so—*three feet*—off the cavern's reasonably flat floor. The skimmer's adjustable landing legs were more than long enough to compensate for the inevitable irregularities, and he nodded to himself, pleased by the cave's suitability.

"Owl."

"Yes, Lieutenant Commander?"

"This is going to work very well," he said. "Go ahead and run the air lorry in tomorrow night. But don't unload anything until I've been able to get back here and fiddle with the skimmer's sonic fences."

"Yes, Lieutenant Commander."

"And don't forget to avoid any population centers on its flight in, either."

"Yes, Lieutenant Commander."

For just a moment, Merlin thought he'd heard something like a trace of exaggerated patience in the AI's voice. But that was ridiculous, of course.

"Do you have the take from the day's surveillance?"

That's another redundant question, he told himself. *Of* course *Owl has the day's take!*

"Yes, Lieutenant Commander," the AI said.

"Good. Anything more from Nahrmahn and Shandyr about Duke Tirian's involvement in the assassination attempt?"

"No, Lieutenant Commander."

Merlin grimaced unhappily at that. He had nowhere near as much information on the Duke of Tirian as he would have liked. He'd identified the noble as a player only relatively late in the game, and the duke was very cautious about the people with whom he met and what he discussed when he met them. He couldn't prevent Merlin from eavesdropping on almost any meeting Merlin knew about, but there didn't seem to *be* very many meetings of any sort. Almost as irritating, the care he exercised in what he said to his human henchmen when he did meet with one or more of them made analysis difficult.

There was no question that he was deep in bed with Nahrmahn, although Merlin had been unable to determine the exact point at which he intended to plant his own dagger in the Emerald prince's back. Unfortunately, given the duke's rank, relatives, and in-laws, accusing him of treason was going to be a . . . delicate proposition. Which was one reason Merlin hadn't brought it up with Haarahld. And equally a reason he'd hoped to acquire additional corroborating evidence before he sat down to talk to the king's most trusted councilors in the morning.

"I don't suppose the Duke gave us anything new from *his* end, did he?" he asked.

"No, Lieutenant Commander."

Merlin grimaced again, this time with a chuckle. According to the manufacturer's manual, a RAPIER tactical computer's AI had a vocabulary of over a hundred thousand words. So far, he estimated, Owl must have used at least sixty of them.

"All right, Owl. Go ahead and burst-transmit the take to the skimmer's onboard systems. I'll have time to skim through it before I head back to Tellesberg."

"Yes, Lieutenant Commander."

Owl was perfectly capable of maintaining the critical bugs Merlin had emplaced in various and sundry locations about Safehold. At the moment, they were concentrated in Charis, Emerald, and Corisande, but he wasn't neglecting Zion or the Kingdom of Tarot. For that matter, Queen Sharleyan had one permanently parked on the ceiling of her throne room and another in her privy council chamber.

Despite the fact that Merlin required far less "sleep" than any biological human, he couldn't possibly have found time to monitor all of those stealthy spies himself. But Owl had been carefully instructed about the names, places, and events in which Merlin was interested. The AI had also been given a list of more generalized trigger words and phrases—like "assassinate," for example, or "bribe"—and unlike Merlin, it was both designed to monitor multiple inputs simultaneously and immune to boredom.

The transmission took only a handful of seconds. Then a green light blinked, indicating completion of the transmission. Merlin nodded in satisfaction, then cocked his head.

"Anything more on your analysis of the *Rakurai* platforms, Owl?" he asked.

"Affirmative, Lieutenant Commander," the AI replied, then fell silent, and Merlin rolled his eyes.

"In that case, tell me what you've come up with on how to take them out."

"I have not been able to devise a plan to destroy them, Lieutenant Commander," Owl said calmly.

"What?" Merlin sat straighter in his couch, eyes narrowing. "Why not, Owl?"

"The kinetic bombardment and solar energy platforms are nested in the center of a sphere of area defense systems and passive scanners which no weapons at my disposal can hope to penetrate," the AI told him. "Analysis suggests that most of those defenses were emplaced after Commodore Pei's destruction of the original Lake Pei Enclave."

"*After* Langhorne was dead?"

"Yes, Lieutenant Commander." Owl's response actually surprised Merlin a bit. The AI wasn't usually very good at recognizing questions—especially what might be rhetorical ones—appropriate for it to answer unless they were specifically directed to it.

"Do you have any hypothesis for why they might have been added at that time?"

"Without better historical data, no reliable, statistically significant hypotheses can be offered," Owl said. "However, modeling of the apparent strategy of the Langhorne administration prior to that time, particularly in light of the fact that Commodore Pei was kept in complete ignorance of the bombardment system's existence before its use against the Alexandria Enclave, would suggest the Administrator's successors were concerned that there might be other 'disloyalists,' particularly among the military units the Commodore had commanded. Assuming that to be true, it would perhaps have seemed logical to bolster the platforms' defenses against additional attacks."

Merlin frowned—not in disagreement, but in thought—for several seconds, then nodded slowly.

"That does make sense, I suppose," he mused aloud. "Not that it helps our problems very much."

Owl said nothing, and Merlin chuckled harshly at its lack of response. Then he thought some more.

The kinetic bombardment platforms which had been used against Shan-wei were still there, sweeping silently in orbit around the planet. It was impossible to be certain, but Merlin was virtually positive the platforms were tasked to bombard and destroy any ground-based energy signature which might indicate that Safeholdians were straying from the dictates of *The Book of Jwo-jeng's* limitations on technology. The energy footprint of an electrical generating plant, for example.

The exact level of emissions necessary to activate them was impossible to estimate, but *The Book of Chihiro* clearly warned that the same *Rakurai* which had smitten the evil Shan-Wei waited to punish anyone so lost to God as to attempt to follow in her footsteps. According to the *Writ,* the lightning associated with natural thunderstorms was God's reminder of the destruction awaiting those who sinned, a sort of inverted mirror image of the symbology of the rainbow's promise to Noah following the Deluge.

Owl had been able to get fairly good imagery of the platforms using purely passive systems, but the one SNARC which had gone active to probe for additional information had been picked off almost instantly by a laser-armed antimissile platform. Another SNARC had attempted to penetrate the defended perimeter under maximum stealth, only to be detected and destroyed while it was still thousands of kilometers from the platforms. That had rather conclusively answered the question of whether or not the solar power-powered systems were still active. At the same time, the defensive systems had shown absolutely no interest in any stray emissions Merlin's other SNARCs, skimmer flights, or com transmissions might have let slip.

Probably would have been just a bit of a problem for their own operations if it had gone around shooting the "angels" in the ass because of their emissions, he thought mordantly. *So the damned thing almost certainly is waiting to kill the first sign of emerging technology outside the Jwo-jeng parameters. Which doesn't mean it couldn't be used for something else if those damned power sources hiding in the Temple told it to. And it's got six loaded cells, each capable of covering half a continent at need, by Owl's best estimate. Not good. Not good at all.*

"We can't get *anything* close enough to do the job, Owl?" he asked after the better part of a full minute.

"Negative, Lieutenant Commander."

"Why not?"

"Because none of the weapons stockpiled for your use have the range to engage the platforms from outside the range at which the platforms' defensive systems can destroy them, Lieutenant Commander. Nor do any of the platforms available to you have the stealth capability to get deep enough into the defended zone to change that fact."

"I see." Merlin grimaced, then shrugged. "Well, if that's the way it is, that's the way it is. We'll just have to cross that bridge when we come to it, and I'm sure that between us we'll be able to come up with a solution eventually."

Owl said nothing, and Merlin chuckled again. Tact or obtuseness? he wondered. Not that it mattered. But whichever it was, there was no point in beating his head against that particular wall right now.

He put the problem aside and leaned back in the flight couch once more as he took the skimmer high and allowed its airspeed to climb to Mach four on a southwesterly heading. The flight he had in mind would take over an hour, even at that speed, and he punched up the first of Owl's recordings.

▼   ▼   ▼

The local night was much younger as Merlin switched off the playback from the surveillance bugs five thousand kilometers and almost an hour and a half later. As always, most of the recorded surveillance data had been boring, irritatingly cryptic, or both. But, equally as always, there were more than a few nuggets tucked away amid all the background noise.

At the moment, though, that wasn't really foremost in Merlin's thoughts, and his expression tightened as he gazed down at the terrain below him.

Armageddon Reef, the locals called it. Once, it had been called Alexandria, but that had been long ago, and its new name was grimly appropriate.

Just under a thousand miles, east to west—that was the width of Rakurai Bay, the bay at the heart of Armageddon Reef, the most accursed spot on Safehold, which had once been home to the Alexandria Enclave. The island upon which that enclave had stood was still there, but it wasn't as large as it had been, and it had been battered into a near-lunar landscape by overlapping impact craters.

Langhorne hadn't been content just to destroy Shan-wei's enclave and murder all of her friends and associates. There'd been colonists in that enclave, as well. Some in Alexandria itself; others scattered across the minor continent surrounding the vast bay. They, too, had had to be destroyed, for they might have been infected by Shan-wei's "heretical" teachings.

Besides, Merlin thought harshly, *the bastard wanted to make a statement. Hell, he wanted to play with his goddamned toy, that's what he wanted.* "Rakurai," *my ass!*

He realized his hand was tightening dangerously on the stick. Even with the governors he'd set on his PICA strength, he could damage the controls if he really tried, and he forced himself to relax.

It was . . . difficult.

From his altitude, it was easy for his enhanced vision, despite the darkness, to see how the kinetic bombardment had shredded a roughly circular zone over eighteen hundred kilometers across. Not just once, either. Nimue had had plenty of time to run the reports from the SNARCs she'd dispatched to the site of that long-ago mass murder through Owl's analyzing software. It was readily apparent from the overlapping impact patterns that Langhorne had sent three separate waves of artificial meteors hammering across the continent. And he'd given Alexandria itself even more attention than that. At least five waves of kinetic strikes had marched back and forth across the island. Even now, almost eight hundred standard years later, the tortured, broken ruin he'd left behind was brutally evident from Merlin's present height.

But he didn't kill quite *everyone, did he?* Merlin told himself bitterly. *Oh, no! He needed someone to bear* witness, *didn't he?*

For that was exactly what Langhorne had done. He'd spared a single settlement from destruction, so that its stunned and terrified inhabitants could testify to the rain of fiery thunderbolts—the *Rakurai* of God—which had punished Shan-wei and her fallen fellows for their evil. The "archangels" who'd swooped down upon that surviving village in the aftermath of the bombardment had borne them away, distributing them in family groups to other towns and villages across Safehold. Officially, they'd been spared because, unlike their fellows, they had been free of sin. As Lot and his family had been spared from the destruction of Sodom and Gomorrah, *they* had been spared because they'd remained faithful to God and His revealed laws. In fact, they'd been spared solely so that they could testify to the might and fearsome power of God's fury . . . and the fate of any who rebelled against His viceroy on Safehold, the Archangel Langhorne.

There'd been no reason Merlin had to make this flight. Not really. He'd already known what had happened here, already seen the SNARCs' imagery. There wasn't really any difference between that imagery and what his own artificial eyes reported to the electronic ghost of Nimue Alban who lived behind them. Yet there was. Oh, but there was.

PICAs were programmed to do anything humans could do, and to react naturally, with appropriate changes of expression, to their operators' emotions, unless those operators specifically instructed them not to. Merlin had not so instructed himself, for those natural, automatic reactions, like the scars Nimue had been careful to incorporate into his appearance, were a necessary part of convincing those about him that he was human. And, electronic analog or not, perhaps he truly was still human, a corner of his cybernetic brain reflected as a tear trickled down his cheek.

He hovered there, far, far above the scene of that ancient carnage, that long-ago murder which had happened only months ago, as far as he was concerned. He didn't stay long, actually, though it seemed far longer. Just long enough to accomplish the thing he'd come here to do—to mourn his dead, and to promise them that however long it took, whatever challenge might arise, the purpose for which they had died *would* be achieved.

Langhorne and his adherents had named this place Armageddon Reef, the place where "good" had triumphed over "evil" for all time. But they'd been wrong, Merlin thought coldly. The atrocity they'd wreaked here had been not the final battle of that struggle, but its first, and the end of the war it had begun would be very different from the one *they* had envisioned.

He hovered there, feeling that promise sinking into his alloy bones, and then he turned the skimmer's nose back into the east, towards the approaching dawn, and left that place of sorrow once again.

Your Majesty," the distinguished-looking man said, bending his head in a respectful bow as he entered the council chamber.

"Rayjhis," King Haarahld responded.

The distinguished-looking man straightened and crossed to the chair at the foot of the long table. He paused and stood beside it, waiting, until Haarahld's waving hand invited him to be seated. He obeyed the gesture, then, and settled into the elaborately carved armchair.

Merlin studied him from behind impassive eyes. His SNARCs and their parasite bugs had observed and listened to this man often over the past few months, but that wasn't quite the same as finally meeting him face-to-face.

Rayjhis Yowance, Earl of Gray Harbor, was Haarahld VII's first councillor, the senior member of the Privy Council—effectively, Charis' prime minister, although the term (and office) hadn't been invented yet on Safehold. He was of less than average height for a Charisian, but he carried his neat, compact frame with the confidence of a man who knew his worth. He was a few years older than Haarahld, and, unlike the king, he was clean-shaven. The long hair pulled back in the old-fashioned sort of ponytail favored by the more rustic members of the minor nobility and serving sea officers was liberally streaked with silver, but his dark eyes were bright and alert. The chain of office around his neck was less elaborate than Haarahld's, without the glittering gem sets of the king's, and his tunic's embroidery was more subdued, although its fabric was just as rich and he, too, wore the golden scepter of the Pilgrimage.

Despite the superb tailoring and obvious cost of his clothing, he carried an air of physical toughness, as well as the mental toughness one might expect out of the kingdom's first councillor. Which probably owed something to the twenty years he'd spent as an officer in the Royal Navy before his childless older brother's death had dropped the Gray Harbor title on him and forced his resignation. The present earl had gone to sea as a midshipman officer cadet at the ripe old age of eleven and risen to command his own ship by the age of twenty-eight, and he'd seen his share of sea fights and bloodshed before he'd become an effete politician.

Gray Harbor looked back at Merlin, his face equally impassive, and Merlin smiled mentally. The first councillor had to be alive with curiosity, given all the rumors about the assassination attempt and the crown prince's mysterious rescuer which had been swirling about the Palace. No doubt Gray Harbor had been considerably better informed than almost anyone else, but that wasn't saying a great deal.

The king had just opened his mouth to say something more when the council chamber door opened again. Another man came through it, his step considerably more hurried than Gray Harbor's had been.

The newcomer was at least a head taller than the earl, and although his clothing was made of rich fabric and jeweled rings glittered on his fingers, he lacked the first councillor's air of polish. He was also younger than Gray Harbor, and considerably more weathered-looking, and he was already going bald. His hooked beak of a nose was high-arched and proud, and his eyes were a lighter shade of brown—almost amber—than most Charisians'.

"Your Majesty," he said just a bit gruffly. "I apologize. I came as quickly as I could when my secretary gave me your message."

"There's no need to apologize, Bynzhamyn," Haarahld said with a smile. "I understood you wouldn't return from Sand Shoal until late this evening or tomorrow. I didn't expect you to be able to attend at all, or we would have waited for you."

"I've just returned, Your Majesty," Bynzhamyn Raice, Baron Wave Thunder, replied. "The matter I'd gone to attend to required considerably less time than I'd anticipated."

"I'm glad to hear it," Haarahld told him. "It will be much more convenient to discuss this with you and Rayjhis at the same time. Please, be seated."

Wave Thunder obeyed the polite command, seating himself in what was obviously his regular place, two chairs down from Gray Harbor, to the earl's left. Haarahld waited until he'd settled fully into position, then waved his right hand in Merlin's direction.

"Rayjhis, Bynzhamyn, this is the mysterious Merlin the two of you have undoubtedly heard so much about. *Seijin* Merlin, the Earl of Gray Harbor and the Baron of Wave Thunder."

Gray Harbor's eyes grew narrower and even more intent as Haarahld gave Merlin the "*seijin*" title, but the king continued calmly.

"Rayjhis manages the Privy Council for me and does most of the hard work of running the kingdom. Bynzhamyn, not to put to fine a point on it, is my spymaster. And very good he is at it, too."

The three men nodded courteously, if warily, to one another, and Haarahld smiled.

"I realize all sorts of rumors about *Seijin* Merlin have been running around the palace ever since Cayleb got home. Fortunately, no one seems to have realized Merlin really *is* a *seijin* . . . or what that implies, at least. And for reasons I believe will become clear, I very much want to keep it that way. Given what happened out there in the woods, and the stories—many of them far wilder than the palace gossip, I'm sure—which have to be running about the city, as well, people will expect him to receive a certain amount of preference here at Court. That's only natural, yet it's important we not show him too *much* preference. In order to make best use of his services, however, I believe, it will be important for him to have access not simply to me, but also to the Council. Exactly how to reconcile those two opposed considerations puzzled me for a time, but I think I've come up with a solution.

"I intend to name *Seijin* Merlin to the Royal Guard expressly to serve as Cayleb's personal guardsman and bodyguard. Lieutenant Falkhan will remain in command of Cayleb's normal Marine detail, but Merlin will be assigned directly to Cayleb, with the understanding that he'll be cooperating with Falkhan but not directly responsible to the Lieutenant. I'm sure some in the Marines will resent that, even see it as a slap in their service's face, but I also expect them to learn to live with it. And, after such a close escape, no one will be surprised if we make some changes in our long-standing security arrangements.

"Assigning him permanently to Cayleb will keep him physically close at all times without officially admitting him to my inner circle of advisers. It's unlikely we'll be able to keep the fact that he's a *seijin* from leaking out, of course. When it does, I suggest we all emphasize the tales of the *seijin's* martial abilities . . . and downplay any reference to any other unusual talents."

Gray Harbor and Wave Thunder nodded, almost in unison, although it seemed to Merlin that it was more in acknowledgment of Haarahld's instructions than from any understanding of why the king might have given those instructions in the first place. Which, he reflected, wasn't very surprising, after all.

"As part of the effort to divert attention from him," Haarahld continued, "the two of you are the only members of the Council who will know he's anything more than the exceptionally capable warrior assigned to protect Cayleb which he appears to be. Maikel also knows, of course, but I intend to restrict that information as much as possible to the three of you, Cayleb and myself, and our personal bodyguards. In time, we'll have to broaden that circle, but I want the minimum possible number of people admitted to the secret. In addition to keeping any of our . . . less friendly neighbors, shall we say, from suspecting the true extent of his talents, that should also prevent him from becoming an object of the sorts of court suspicion and jealousy which would be inevitable if a complete stranger rose abruptly to a position of high power here in Charis."

The king's expression turned briefly grim.

"Nonetheless, the truth is that his talents extend far beyond the field of battle," he said. "I'm strongly of the opinion that those other talents will be of far greater importance to us in the long run, and I expect the three of you are likely to spend quite a bit of time working together."

He paused, as if to allow that to sink in, then looked directly at Gray Harbor.

"Rayjhis, *Seijin* Merlin managed to impress me even more during our interview yesterday morning than his intervention to save Cayleb's life had already done. I went to that meeting prepared to be both skeptical and suspicious; I emerged from it with the belief that *Seijin* Merlin both means Charis well and has the ability to be of great service to us. I'm sure you'll form your own opinion of him—I value you and Bynzhamyn for your independence of thought as much as for your loyalty and ability—but I want the two of you to listen very carefully to what he has to say. Before I turn all of you loose together, though, let me tell you exactly why he's impressed me as much as he has.

"To begin with—"

▼　　▼　　▼

"—and since every single thing he told me matched perfectly with everything you've been able to confirm, Bynzhamyn," the king finished his briefing of his councillors several minutes later, "I had no choice but to accept that he truly does possess the Sight. Of course, as I told him at the time, both his abilities and his trustworthiness must be proven before I can consider relying upon him as I already rely on the two of you. *Seijin* Merlin was courteous enough to accept that without rancor."

He paused, and both of the councillors looked at Merlin with thoughtful expressions. Wave Thunder looked fascinated, if still faintly skeptical, which wasn't much of a surprise. Gray Harbor also looked skeptical, but unless Merlin was seriously mistaken, at least half of the first councillor's skepticism was reserved for the mysterious stranger's *real* motives and ambitions.

"Since *Seijin* Merlin is clearly much better informed about events and the people behind them here in Tellesberg and in Charis generally than most newcomers," the king continued dryly after a few moments, "it seemed to me that the first thing for us to do would be for the three of you to discuss our concerns about our less friendly neighbors' . . . representatives among us. I want you and Bynzhamyn to combine what we already know with what *Seijin* Merlin can tell us, Rayjhis. This attempt to murder Cayleb wasn't exactly completely unexpected, but it does represent a decision on someone's part to significantly raise the stakes. I think it's time we considered suggesting to them that attempts to murder the heir to the throne are . . . unwise."

The king's tone was light, almost whimsical; his eyes were not.

"I understand, Your Majesty," Gray Harbor replied with a nod that was half a bow. Then he cocked his head slightly. "Just how firmly would you like that message delivered, Sire?"

"*Very* firmly where the individuals actually involved in this attempt are concerned," Haarahld said in a rather colder tone. "That much, I think, everyone will expect, assuming we can determine just who was responsible. And, frankly, I intend to take quite a bit of personal satisfaction out of seeing to it no one's disappointed in that respect. For the rest of our local spies, a somewhat more restrained reaction may be in order. I still want them made nervous, you understand."

"I believe we do, Your Majesty," Wave Thunder said gruffly. "But just to be completely clear, you aren't instructing us to reverse our policy on known spies?"

"Probably not," Haarahld said, and shrugged slightly. "Leaving the ones we know about in place to discourage their masters from sending in new ones has served us well so far. On the other hand, what almost happened to Cayleb indicates they can still circumvent our surveillance. Besides, they have to know we've identified at least some of their agents, and after something like this, they'll expect us to devote some attention to housecleaning. If we *don't* move against at least a few of them, they'll wonder why we didn't. For now, assume anyone on the secondary list is fair game and use your own judgment as to which of them will be most useful removed from play and which left in place. On the primary list, get my approval before moving against anyone."

"And what shall we do with the information provided by *Seijin* Merlin?" Gray Harbor asked in an almost painfully neutral tone.

"I'll trust your and Bynzhamyn's judgment when it comes to deciding which list to put any new names on," Haarahld told him. "Take no action against anyone you put on the primary list without first discussing it with me. As far as anyone on the secondary list is concerned, I'm prepared to rely on your judgment."

"Understood, Your Majesty," Gray Harbor said.

"Thank you." Haarahld pushed back his chair and stood, and the other three quickly stood in turn, bending their heads respectfully. The king watched them, then smiled at his first councillor and shook his head slightly.

"I know exactly what you're thinking, Rayjhis," he said. "I suspect *Seijin* Merlin does, too. Still, you're much too intelligent to allow that ingrained suspicion of yours to cloud your judgment. Besides, I predict you're going to be just as surprised by the *seijin's* . . . talents as I was."

"It's not *Seijin* Merlin's talents which concern me, Sire," Gray Harbor said with a thin smile which acknowledged the accuracy of his monarch's observation.

"Oh, I know that." Haarahld chuckled. "And so does the *seijin*. But I still think you're going to be surprised."

He smiled again, this time at all three of them, and limped out of the council chamber.

▼　　▼　　▼

"—and Mhulvayn is running an entire ring of agents out of the Crossed Anchors for Maysahn," Merlin finished up his basic report the better part of an hour later. "The tavernkeeper is one of Mhulvayn's people, but most of the agents he's overseeing really think they're working for the representative of a legitimate foreign banker whose interests are firmly entwined with your own merchant houses. They think they're providing basically commercial information, without realizing how useful that information could be to Hektor, or what can be deduced from it."

Wave Thunder nodded without looking up from the several sheets of paper on which he was still busily jotting notes. Unlike Gray Harbor, the baron had not been born to the nobility. His father had been a common ship's master, and Bynzhamyn Raice had earned his patent of nobility by rising from that beginning to become one of Tellesberg's great business magnates. He'd trained as a clerk along the way, and still had the fast, clearly legible handwriting he'd developed then. It continued to serve him well, since his duties as the head of Haarahld's intelligence apparatus left him disinclined to trust secretaries when it came to taking sensitive notes.

Now he sat back finally, studying what he'd written, then glanced at Gray Harbor before looking at Merlin.

"I'm as impressed as His Majesty predicted, *Seijin* Merlin," he said, gathering up the dozen-plus sheets of closely written notes. "By all the information you've just provided, of course, but also by your ability to keep track of all that without notes of your own."

"I, too, am impressed," Earl Gray Harbor agreed, lounging back in his own chair, regarding Merlin from hooded eyes.

"I'm also impressed," Wave Thunder continued, "by the fact that so far as I'm aware, every single major foreign agent we've been able to identify is on your list, as well. As I'm sure you're aware, that sort of corroboration is always valuable. And, to be honest, it lends additional weight to your information about agents we *haven't* been able to identify. Like this entire secondary ring Lahang is running in North Key." He shook his head. "I suppose I should have realized he'd have to have someone else to act as his eyes and ears that far from Tellesberg, but we've never had as much as a sniff of who it might actually be."

"I wouldn't feel too badly about that, Baron," Merlin said with a shrug. "I have certain advantages your regular investigators don't. If I'd had to investigate the same way they do, I'd never have been able to discover as much as I'm sure you already know."

"No doubt," Gray Harbor said thoughtfully. "At the same time, *Seijin* Merlin, I must admit I'm curious as to just how it happens that you've 'seen' so much about Charis." Merlin arched one eyebrow, and the first councillor shrugged. "It just seems . . . odd that a *seijin* from the Mountains of Light should be granted such detailed 'visions' of events this far from the Temple Lands that you can identify individual tavernkeepers working for Prince Hektor."

Wave Thunder frowned slightly, sitting back in his own chair and looking back and forth between the other two men. Merlin, on the other hand, smiled slightly.

"It's not as odd as you might think, My Lord," he said. "I do have some control over the sorts of things I see, you know."

"Indeed?" Gray Harbor sounded politely skeptical. "In all the tales I've ever heard or read, the visions of a *seijin* seem to be . . . cryptic, one might say. Or, perhaps, nonspecific. Yet *your* visions, *Seijin* Merlin, appear to be extremely specific."

"I would suspect," Merlin said, "that quite a few of those 'nonspecific' visions from the tales you've heard were works of fiction." He leaned back in his own chair with an amused smile. "Either they never happened at all, or else they were . . . embroidered, let's say, by the people who reported them. While it pains me to admit it, I'm sure more than one 'seijin' was little more than a common charlatan. In a case like that, the more 'cryptic' a so-called vision, the better. A little space for loose interpretation would go a long way towards maintaining someone's credibility."

"That's certainly true enough." Gray Harbor seemed a bit taken aback by Merlin's direct response.

"My Lord," the blue-eyed stranger said, "when I first began having these visions of mine, they came from all over Safehold. Indeed, they were quite bewildering, in a great many ways. But I soon discovered that by concentrating on places and people of special interest, I could redirect, or possibly 'focus' would be a better word, subsequent visions."

"And you chose to focus them here, on Charis?"

"Yes, I did. I don't blame you for being skeptical, My Lord. That's one of your duties to the King. However, I've already explained to His Majesty exactly what it was which attracted to me to Charis in the first place. And, to be frank, at this particular moment Charis needs all the advantages she can get."

"That's true enough, Rayjhis," Wave Thunder said. He began jogging his sheets of notes into a tidy sheaf. "And while I'm as suspicious as the next man," the baron continued, "so far, at least, *Seijin* Merlin's credentials seem to be standing up quite well. I had my suspicions about who was behind that assassination attempt on the Prince, but none of my people had picked up the connection between Lahang and his mercenaries. Now that it's been pointed out, though, I expect we'll be able to confirm it. It makes sense, anyway."

"I know." Gray Harbor sighed. "I suppose it's just—"

The first councillor grimaced, then looked at Merlin with an odd little half-smile.

"You're certainly right about our needing every advantage we can get," he said in a more open tone. "Perhaps it's just that I've felt we were trying to stave off krakens with a bargepole for so long that I simply find it hard to believe this sort of help could just fall into our laps, as it were."

"I can understand that." Merlin looked at him for several moments, then glanced back at Wave Thunder. "I can understand that," he repeated, "and because I do, I've hesitated to mention one more name to you."

"You have?" Gray Harbor's eyes narrowed, and Wave Thunder frowned.

"There's one more highly placed spy," Merlin said slowly. "Highly placed enough that I'd originally intended not to mention him at all until after you'd had the opportunity to evaluate the reliability of the other information I could provide."

"Where? Who are you talking about?" Gray Harbor leaned forward, his voice once more edged with suspicion.

"My Lord, if I tell you that, it will cause you great distress."

"I'll be the best judge of that, *Seijin* Merlin," the earl said with the crisp, hard-edged authority of the kingdom's first councillor.

"Very well, My Lord." Merlin bent his head in a small bow of acknowledgment, not in submission. "I'm afraid the Duke of Tirian is not the man you think he is."

Gray Harbor sat back abruptly. For a moment, his expression was simply shocked. Then his face darkened angrily.

"How *dare* you say such a thing?" he demanded harshly.

"I dare a great many things, My Lord," Merlin said flatly, his own expression unyielding. "And I speak the truth. I told you it would distress you."

"That much, at least, was the truth," Gray Harbor snapped. "I greatly doubt the rest of it was!"

"Rayjhis," Wave Thunder began, but Gray Harbor cut him off with a sharp, abrupt wave of his hand, never taking his own furious eyes off of Merlin.

"When the King told us to work with you, I doubt very much that he ever suspected for a moment that you would tell us his own cousin is a traitor," he grated.

"I'm sure he didn't," Merlin agreed. "And I'm not surprised by your anger, My Lord. After all, you've known the Duke since he was a boy. Your daughter is married to him. And, of course, he stands fourth in the succession, and he's always been King Haarahld's staunch supporter, both in the Privy Council and in Parliament, as well. You've known *me* less than two hours. It would astonish me if you were prepared to take my unsupported word that a man you've known and trusted for so long is in fact a traitor. Unfortunately, that doesn't change the truth."

"*Truth?*" Gray Harbor hissed. "Is that what this has been all about? Who sent you to discredit the Duke?!"

"No one sent me anywhere except my own will," Merlin replied. "And I seek to discredit no one except those whose own actions have already discredited them."

"Not one more lie! I won't—"

"Rayjhis!" Wave Thunder looked unhappy, but the sharpness in his voice pulled Gray Harbor's eyes back to him. The first councillor glared, and Wave Thunder shook his head.

"Rayjhis," he said again, his voice much closer to normal, "I think we need to listen to what he has to say."

"*What?*" Gray Harbor stared at his fellow councillor in disbelief.

"My own people have reported a few . . . irregularities where the Duke is concerned," Wave Thunder said uncomfortably.

"What sort of 'irregularities'?" Gray Harbor demanded incredulously.

"Most of them were small things," Wave Thunder admitted. "Company he kept, a few instances in which known Emerald agents slipped through our hands in Hairatha when we'd alerted the authorities to take them, trading ventures that proved unusually profitable for him and in which Emerald merchant interests were deeply involved. And the fact that he's been Lahang's best customer for wyverns, as far as we can tell."

"Don't be ridiculous," Gray Harbor said coldly. "The Duke—my *son-in-law*, I remind you—is addicted to the hunt. His wyvern coop is the biggest, most expensive one in the entire Kingdom! Of course he's Lahang's 'best customer'! For God's sake, Bynzhamyn—we've known all along that Lahang's cover was chosen expressly to give him access to people just like Kahlvyn! If you're going to accuse him on that basis, you'll have to accuse half the nobles in Charis!"

"Which is why I *haven't* accused him of anything yet," Wave Thunder said rather more sharply. "I said it was small things, and no one is going to accuse someone in the Duke's position of treason on the basis of such flimsy evidence. Not when he's so close to the Crown, and when he's so openly and strongly supported the King for so long. But that doesn't change the reports I've received, and it doesn't necessarily make *Seijin* Merlin a liar. Which"—the baron looked Gray Harbor straight in the eye—"is exactly what you're accusing him of being."

"Hasn't he just accused the Duke of far worse?" Gray Harbor snapped back.

"Yes, he has," Wave Thunder said, his voice even flatter than Merlin's had been. "And what if he's right?"

"The very idea is preposterous!"

"Which doesn't mean it can't be true," Wave Thunder said unflinchingly. "This is *my* area of responsibility, Rayjhis. I don't want *Seijin* Merlin to be right about the Duke, but it's my responsibility to consider the possibility that he might be. And it's *your* responsibility to let me do my job and find out."

Gray Harbor glared at him for several taut seconds. Then he looked back at Merlin, and his dark eyes were bitter with fury.

"Very well," he gritted. "*Do* your job, Bynzhamyn. And when you've proved there isn't a single word of truth in it, 'do your job' and investigate *this* man, too! As for me, I'm afraid I have other duties at the moment."

He stood, jerked an angry bow at Wave Thunder, and stalked out of the chamber without even glancing in Merlin's direction again.

.IX.
Baron Wave Thunder's Office,
Tellesberg

I'm afraid it looks as if there . . . may be something to it, My Lord."

Bynzhamyn Raice leaned back in his chair, his expression unhappy. Sir Rhyzhard Seafarmer, his second-in-command, looked equally unhappy. Sir Rhyzhard had primary responsibility for Wave Thunder's counterintelligence operations (although that, too, was a term which had not yet been reinvented on Safehold). He was Wave Thunder's most trusted subordinate, both for his loyalty and his judgment, and he was also a very intelligent man. Wave Thunder hadn't told him the identity of the duke's accuser, but the baron felt confident Seafarmer had deduced his identity. Sir Rhyzhard, however, had half a lifetime of experience in not asking questions about things he wasn't supposed to know, and Wave Thunder trusted his discretion completely.

At the moment, Seafarmer was also the man who'd just spent the last two days going back over every scrap of information they had on the Duke of Tirian. The duke had worked closely with Wave Thunder—and Seafarmer—on more than one occasion, given his rank and his duties. Tirian was inside many of the kingdom's critical strategies, privy to most of the king's secrets, both personal and political, and he'd been there literally for decades. Which, because Seafarmer was as experienced as he was intelligent, meant he understood precisely where this particular pocketful of worms could lead.

"I don't like admitting that for several reasons," Seafarmer continued after a moment. "First, of course, because of how messy this could turn out to be, and for how much it's going to hurt His Majesty. But I'm almost equally unhappy about the fact that without this new information—wherever it came from," he added dutifully—"we probably never would have realized there could be anything serious to look at in the first place."

"Not too surprising, really, I suppose," Wave Thunder sighed. He pinched the bridge of his proud nose, balding scalp gleaming in the sunlight streaming in through the window behind him, and shook his head. "No one wants to be the first to point a finger at the Kingdom's second-ranking noble, Rhyzhard. And no one wants to believe someone who stands that high in the succession could be a traitor in the first place."

"It's happened other places," Seafarmer pointed out grimly. "I should have borne in mind that it could happen here, as well, My Lord."

"You should have, I should have." Wave Thunder waved his hand. "Neither of us did. And now that we have, I don't want us jumping to hasty conclusions of guilt because we feel like we ought to have been suspicious all along."

"Point taken, My Lord."

Seafarmer nodded, and Wave Thunder reached out to toy with a paperweight on his desk while he considered his subordinate's report.

Wave Thunder himself was proof of how open the Kingdom of Charis' nobility was, compared with those of most other kingdoms of Safehold, and he—and King Haarahld—believed in using the best talent available, regardless of how blue (or not blue) that talent's blood might be. That policy had served them well over the years, but it had its drawbacks, too. And one of them was that, however open the Charisian aristocracy might be, commonly born men still hesitated to accuse great nobles of wrongdoing.

Partly that was the result of innate respect, the belief that certain people simply had to be above suspicion. That, Wave Thunder felt sure, was the category to which Seafarmer (just as Wave Thunder himself) had assigned Kahlvyn

Ahrmahk, the Duke of Tirian, in his own mind. After all, the present duke was the only living son of the king's only uncle. Although his father, Ahryn, had been Haarahld VI's younger brother, he was actually a few years older than Haarahld, since Ahryn, like Kahlvyn himself, had married late. He and Haarahld had been raised more like brothers than like cousins, and he was Cayleb's godfather, as well as his cousin.

He was also Constable of Hairatha, the key fortress city on Tirian Island. Hairatha was arguably the second or third most important naval base of the entire kingdom, placed to dominate the northern half of Howell Bay, and its constable was traditionally considered the senior Charisian military officer after High Admiral Lock Island himself. Not only that, but Tirian was one of the senior leaders of the king's party in the House of Lords, an unwavering advocate of King Haarahld's policies, one of the king's most trusted diplomatic representatives, *and* the son-in-law of the kingdom's first councillor. Surely he, of all people, simply could not be a traitor!

But, as Seafarmer had just pointed out, it had happened other places. Which was where the fact that so many of Wave Thunder's best investigators were common-born might well come into play. It was possible that someone who was nobly born himself might have been more willing to cherish suspicions about a fellow aristocrat. More to the point, however, he might have been more likely to risk voicing any suspicions he did cherish about such a powerful potential enemy. Even in Charis, a commoner who made an enemy among the high aristocracy was unlikely to prosper, and the same held true for his family.

It was a potential blind spot Wave Thunder was going to have to pay more attention to in the future, because although he'd just cautioned Seafarmer against leaping to any conclusions, the baron himself felt a sinking surety of the duke's guilt. Merlin Athrawes had provided too much other information whose veracity could be tested. And so far, every single thing he'd told them—and which Wave Thunder's agents had been able to test—had proved accurate.

It was always remotely possible that Gray Harbor's suspicion that it was all part of some elaborate, convoluted plot to damage the crown's faith in the duke was correct. The very factors which had placed Tirian "above suspicion" made him vitally important to the kingdom and its security. If, in fact, he was as loyal as everyone had always believed him to be, then discrediting him—possibly even driving him into rebellion as his only defense against false accusations—would be a tremendous coup for any of Charis' many enemies.

But Wave Thunder didn't believe it for a moment. And had Gray Harbor been even a little less closely associated with Tirian, the baron suspected, the first councillor wouldn't have believed it, either.

Unfortunately, the earl *was* that closely associated with the duke. And then there was the little matter of the fact that Tirian was also King Haarahld's first cousin, and that both the king and the crown prince held him in deep affection.

"We have to move very cautiously here, Rhyzhard," the baron said finally. Seafarmer didn't reply, but his expression was one of such emphatic agreement that Wave Thunder's lips twitched. Clearly that was one of the more unnecessary warnings he'd ever issued.

"Do you have any thoughts on how best to approach the problem?" he continued.

"That depends upon the answer to a rather delicate question, My Lord."

"I'm sure it does," Wave Thunder said dryly. "And, no, I don't think we want to tell the King about this until we're more confident there actually is something to tell him. He's going to be badly hurt, if there's any truth to it. And he's going to be angry, whatever happens, even if it all proves to be a false alarm. But if we tell him about this before we're sure, it's likely to . . . adversely affect our investigation's secrecy. His Majesty is one of the canniest men I know, but I'm not certain how well he'd be able to dissemble if he thought the Duke was a traitor."

And, he chose not to add aloud, *as long as we keep it just between ourselves, something I authorized without His Majesty's knowledge or approval, he'll have someone to throw to the krakens if it turns out the Duke is innocent after all.*

Wave Thunder didn't find contemplating that possibility especially cheering, but it came with his job. And if the duke was in fact innocent, his importance to the kingdom would make placating his possible fury at having been wrongly suspected a high priority for King Haarahld.

"That limits the possibilities, My Lord," Seafarmer pointed out respectfully. He wasn't complaining—obviously, he'd followed the same chain of logic—but simply considering the practical implications. "The Duke's own guardsmen are very, very good, and they're intimately familiar with how we go about things. They ought to be—they've helped us do it, often enough! So if we try anything like sneaking one of our people inside his household, we're more likely to alert him to the fact that we're suspicious than we are to succeed."

"And we can't get at his private correspondence, either," Wave Thunder agreed.

The duke's public correspondence, associated with the offices he held by royal appointment, like his position as Constable of Hairatha, was another matter. *That,* the baron was confident, he could gain access to without undue difficulty. And he was quite confident it would do him absolutely no good after he'd done it. He'd do it anyway, of course, just in case, but he'd be astonished if anything were to come of it.

"If we knew exactly what he's doing—assuming, of course, that he *is* doing something," Seafarmer qualified scrupulously, "—it would make things a lot easier. If we knew he was passing information, and suspected who he was passing it to, we could try planting false information on him and see how the other side reacted. But all I can really tell you is that he seems to be spending an inordinate amount of time with people we've determined are in Nahrmahn's pocket, one way or another. Like Baron Black Wyvern. And Lahang, of course. And"—Seafarmer's expression turned grimmer—"there's that little matter of those Emerald agents who seem to keep getting lost in Hairatha."

Wave Thunder nodded, but he hadn't missed the way Seafarmer's eyes narrowed. Two of the suspected Emerald agents who'd somehow managed to elude apprehension in Hairatha had cut the throats of a pair of Seafarmer's most trusted investigators before making their escape. Investigators who'd come to Hairatha with what should have been perfect covers . . . and the duke's knowledge of their identities and mission.

In fact, the duke had been the *only* person in Hairatha who'd been informed of their presence, precisely because Nahrmahn's agents there had so persistently escaped arrest in the past. Seafarmer had double- and triple-checked to be certain of that, which meant the duke was also the only person in Hairatha who could have given their identities away. That didn't necessarily prove anything. The secret might have been compromised at the Tellesberg end when Seafarmer first sent them out, or one of the investigators might have been known to the other side from a previous case. Unlikelier things had happened in the past, and would again. And even if the duke was responsible for the information leakage, he might well have revealed it inadvertently. For that matter, Nahrmahn might have succeeded in getting a spy inside the duke's official household, in a position to compromise the information without his knowledge.

The problem was finding out whether or not that was what had happened. And until Wave Thunder managed to do that, he couldn't really afford to act on any of the rest of Merlin's information. Certainly not on any of that information he couldn't independently confirm.

"All right," the baron said after a moment. "I think we need to go about this in two separate ways. First, I want the people we have watching him to be reinforced. And I'm sure I don't need to tell you how important it is to be absolutely sure of the loyalty of anyone we assign to this, Rhyzhard."

"Of course not, My Lord."

"And, second," Wave Thunder said grimly, "I think we need to set a little trap."

"A trap, My Lord?" Sir Rhyzhard repeated, and Wave Thunder nodded again.

"As you say, if we knew who he was passing information to, we could try feeding him false information to pass them. Well, perhaps we *do* know, in a general sense, someone to whom he's passing it."

Seafarmer looked puzzled, and Wave Thunder snorted harshly.

"You just said it yourself, Rhyzhard. Nahrmahn's people in Hairatha seem to have become rather more elusive than those anywhere else in the kingdom."

"Ah, I see, My Lord," Seafarmer said, and his eyes began to gleam.

You can't be serious, Bynzhamyn!" the Earl of Gray Harbor protested.

"I know you don't want to hear this, Rayjhis," Wave Thunder said, "but I can't justify not taking it seriously."

"And have you told His Majesty about it?" Gray Harbor demanded.

"Not yet," Wave Thunder conceded. "His Majesty and Cayleb are even closer to the duke than you are. Until and unless I'm certain there's a fire somewhere under all this smoke, I'm not going to tell them anything which could hurt them this badly on a personal level. Surely you don't think I enjoy telling *you* that someone I know is this close to you and your daughter, the father of your grandchildren, could be a traitor?"

Gray Harbor looked across at him with narrow eyes. The two of them sat in facing armchairs in a private sitting room in Gray Harbor Hall, the earl's Tellesberg mansion. Each of them held a half-filled glass, and a bottle of excellent Siddarmark whiskey sat on a table at the earl's elbow. It was late afternoon, and heavy weather was rolling in from the southwest, sweeping through the passes of the Styvyn Mountains and in from the Cauldron, that shallow, current-wracked stretch of seawater between Charis and Tarot Island. The rising wind drove heavier waves against the harbor's breakwaters, and all along the waterfront crews were battening down in preparation for heavy weather. Overhead, the morning's sunlight had turned into the heavy dimness of cloudy early evening, and thunder muttered ominously. The clouds which had obscured the sun were black-bottomed and thick, and lightning flickered here and there among them.

The weather, Wave Thunder thought, was an unfortunately apt mirror of the tension inside this sitting room.

"No, of course I don't think you enjoy telling me," Gray Harbor said finally. "Which doesn't mean I think you're right, however."

"Believe me," Wave Thunder said with the utmost sincerity, "in this case, I would far, far rather discover my suspicions are misplaced. And I have no intention of damaging the King's relationship with his cousin until and unless I'm certain there's a reason to."

"But you're not quite that concerned about *my* relationship with Kahlvyn?" Gray Harbor said with a wintry smile.

"You know better than that, Rayjhis." This time there was a bit of bite in Wave Thunder's voice, and he met the earl's eyes very levelly. "I wouldn't have told you anything until I knew one way or the other, either, if the law didn't require me to."

Gray Harbor gazed at him again for a second or two, and then, unhappily, nodded.

The law was very clear, and had been since Haarahld's great-grandfather's day. In Charis, unlike most other lands, not even the most commonly born man could simply be seized and hauled off to prison. Not legally, at any rate, although Gray Harbor knew as well as any that the law had been bent, and even outright violated, upon occasion. Legally, however, any citizen of Charis must be charged with some specific offense before a King's Magistrate before he could be imprisoned, even on suspicion, by the secular authorities. And he must be convicted of that offense before the King's Bench before he could be kept there. The Church's courts were another matter entirely, of course, and there was a certain tension between Crown and Church as a result, but both Haarahld and Bishop Executor Zherald attempted to minimize it as much as possible.

Nobles enjoyed considerably greater protection, however, even in Charis. Which, Gray Harbor would have said (if he'd ever bothered to consider the point at all), was the way it ought to be. In the case of a noble of Kahlvyn Ahrmahk's stature, even the Crown was required to move carefully. Wave Thunder could not legally initiate the sort of investigation he obviously intended to propose without the express approval of the king . . . or of his first councilor. In fact, it was entirely possible, if Gray Harbor wanted to be a stickler about it, that Wave Thunder had already exceeded his legal authority in this case.

A part of the earl was tempted to make that point, but he put the temptation aside. The very idea that Kahlvyn could possibly be a traitor was beyond ridiculous, yet Wave Thunder was right. He did have a responsibility to examine even the most ludicrous allegations. And the fact that Kahlvyn was Gray Harbor's son-in-law only made the situation more painful for both of them.

"I know you wouldn't have told me if you hadn't had to, Bynzhamyn," Gray Harbor sighed after a moment. "And I know this is damned awkward. I think the entire idea is preposterous, and more than a little insulting, but I know where the original . . . accusation came from. Personally, I think this so-called *seijin* has overreached himself, and I'm looking forward to seeing him try to explain to His Majesty why he's seen fit to falsely impugn the honor of a member of His Majesty's own family. But I realize you need my authorization before you can continue. So, tell me what you suspect and how you intend to prove or disprove your suspicions. Unless, of course," he smiled thinly, " '*Seijin* Merlin' has seen fit to accuse *me* of treason, as well."

"Of course he hasn't," Wave Thunder said gruffly, then looked down into his whiskey glass. He considered the clear, amber depths for a moment or two, then took a sip and looked back up at his host.

"Very well, Rayjhis," he said. "Here's what we have so far. First—"

▼   ▼   ▼

Thunder rumbled, loud and harsh, crashing across the heavens, and Rayjhis Yowance, Earl of Gray Harbor, stood looking out an open window across the immaculate garden of his townhouse. Wind whipped branches and flowering shrubbery, flogging the dark, glossy leaves to show their lighter under surfaces; the air seemed to prickle on his skin; and he smelled the sharp, distinctive scent of lightning.

Not long, he thought. *Not long until the storm breaks.*

He lifted his whiskey glass and drank, feeling its hot, honeyed fire burn down the back of his throat as he gazed into the darkness. Lightning flared suddenly out over the whitecapped harbor, flaming through the clouds like the braided whip of Langhorne's *Rakurai*, etching the entire world ever so briefly in livid, blinding light, and fresh thunder exploded, louder than ever, in its wake.

Gray Harbor watched for a few more seconds, then turned away and looked around the comfortable, lamplit sitting room Wave Thunder had left a little more than two hours ago.

The earl walked back across to his armchair, poured more whiskey, and sat. His mind insisted upon replaying everything Wave Thunder had said, and he closed his eyes in pain.

It can't be true, he thought. *It can't be. There has to be some other explanation, some other answer, whatever Seafarmer and Bynzhamyn may think.*

But he was no longer as confident of that as he had been, and that lost assurance hurt. It hurt far worse than he'd believed it possibly could when he'd been so certain it could never happen.

He opened his eyes once more, staring out the window, waiting for the first crashing waterfall of the gathering storm.

He'd been prepared to reject any possibility of his son-in-law's guilt. Not simply because Kahlvyn was the king's cousin, next in line for the throne after Haarahld's own children and the designated regent for his minor children, should something happen to Haarahld and Cayleb. Not simply because of Kahlvyn's importance to the kingdom. And not simply because of the undoubted additional power and influence which his daughter's marriage to the duke had brought to Gray Harbor's own position, or because Kahlvyn had always been his staunch ally on the Privy Council and in Parliament.

No. He'd been prepared to reject that possibility because Kahlvyn had always been a kind and loving husband to his daughter, Zhenyfyr, and a doting father to her two children. Because he'd stepped into the place of Gray Harbor's long-dead son Charlz.

Because the Earl of Gray Harbor loved his son-in-law.

But, he admitted grimly to himself, if it had been anyone else, he would have found Wave Thunder's suspicions . . . persuasive.

Not conclusive! he told himself, rallying gamely. But then his shoulders sagged again. *No, not conclusive, but suggestive enough that they have to be investigated. Suggestive enough that they have to affect the way Haarahld feels about him, the extent to which Haarahld can trust him.* Damn *that so-called* seijin!

He could have dismissed all of it without a qualm, but for the deaths of Seafarmer's investigators in Hairatha . . . and Kahlvyn's association in ventures with known Emerald trading interests. Like many nobles, Kahlvyn sometimes found the expense involved in maintaining the appearances expected of a man of his rank punishing, and his own taste for expensive hunting hounds, wyverns, and lizards, and for occasional high-stakes wagers, put even more demands on his purse. He was far from a poor man, yet the financial strain was undeniable, upon occasion, and although that was scarcely common knowledge, Gray Harbor had known about it for years. But somehow, whenever funds seemed to be growing a bit tight, one or another of his trading ventures always succeeded. And just a few too many of them, the earl knew now, involved partnerships with men whose ultimate loyalty was suspect, to say the very least.

But there's no evidence Kahlvyn knows he's dealing with people like that, Gray Harbor thought. *His duties are mainly military, and he's not anywhere near as deeply involved as Bynzhamyn and I in the day-to-day effort to ferret out Nahrmahn's agents. He's never been briefed as thoroughly as I have. As far as I know, he's never had any reason to question the loyalty of his partners . . . or wonder if some of them have been using him without his knowledge.*

The earl brooded over his whiskey glass as thunder rolled and rumbled again. The blue-white flicker of lightning flared once more, driving eye-searing fury across storm-purple heavens, and he heard the first few raindrops pelt down on the townhouse's slate roof.

Was it truly possible that Kahlvyn—his son-in-law, the king's first cousin—was a traitor? Could he have fooled *everyone* that completely for so long? Or was it all still a mistake? Only a matter of circumstantial evidence which ultimately meant nothing? Nothing but appearances manipulated into something suspicious by "*Seijin* Merlin's" accusations?

The earl drained his glass and refilled it. He knew he shouldn't. Knew he'd already drunk enough to impair his judgment. But it helped with the pain.

He ran back over Wave Thunder's proposal, and his jaw tightened. The most damning evidence—if it could be called that—against Kahlvyn were the deaths of Seafarmer's investigators in Hairatha. The investigators whose identities only he had known. So Seafarmer proposed to give him the identity of another of his investigators, along with the information that the man in question was hot on the heels of a highly placed Emerald agent. From Seafarmer's description of the suspected agent, it would be apparent to Kahlvyn (assuming he was actually guilty) that the agent was one of Kahlvyn's own business partners.

And if he is guilty, Gray Harbor thought grimly, *Seafarmer's new investigator will go the same way as his predecessors. Or that's what would happen without the dozen additional men Kahlvyn* won't *know about.*

If there was an attempt on Seafarmer's man, or if the suspect in question abruptly disappeared, it still wouldn't *prove* anything. But the circumstances would be utterly damning, and a full-scale investigation would become inevitable.

Gray Harbor emptied the whiskey glass yet again, and refilled it. He was halfway through the second bottle, he noticed, and grimaced.

.XI.
The Duke of Tirian's Mansion, Kingdom of Charis

Your Grace, I'm sorry to disturb you, but you have a visitor."

Kahlvyn Ahrmahk, Duke of Tirian, looked up from the correspondence on his desk and raised one eyebrow at his majordomo.

"A visitor, Marhys? At this hour?" The duke waved elegantly at the window of his study and the pelting sheets of rain running down its diamond panes. "In this weather?"

"Yes, Your Grace." Marhys Wyllyms had been in Tirian's service for the better part of sixteen years. His expression was almost serene, but Tirian saw something else in his eyes, and straightened in his chair.

"And who might this 'visitor' be?" he asked.

"It's Earl Gray Harbor, Your Grace."

"*What?*" Despite himself, Tirian was unable to keep the astonishment out of his voice, and Wyllyms bowed slightly.

"The Earl himself?" Tirian pressed, and Wyllyms bowed again. "Did he—?"

Tirian cut himself off. Nothing he could think of would have brought his father-in-law out on a night like this one. Certainly not without having so much as previously hinted he might come to call! Which meant it had to be some sort of dire emergency, but the earl obviously—and not surprisingly—hadn't confided the nature of that emergency to Wyllyms.

"The Earl," the majordomo said after a moment, "came by carriage, Your Grace. He is accompanied only by a single personal guardsman. I showed him and his man into the library and offered him refreshment before I came to announce his presence to you. He declined the offer."

Tirian's eyebrows went up again, this time in genuine alarm. The first councillor of Charis had no business wandering about with only a single guard at any time, and especially not on a night like this! He started to speak quickly, then made himself stop and think for a moment first.

"Very well, Marhys," he said after a moment. "I'll go to him immediately." He paused long enough to jot a few hastily scribbled words on a sheet of paper, then folded it and handed it to Wyllyms. "I can't imagine what brings the Earl out in this sort of weather, but I'm sure he didn't set out lightly. Have his coach and coachmen sent to the stables. I have no idea how long the Earl will be staying—overnight, if I can convince him not to go back out into the storm—but at the least, let's get his horses and his coachmen out of the rain for as long as they're here."

"Of course, Your Grace."

"And after you've given instructions for that, please personally deliver that note to Captain Zhahnsyn."

Frahnk Zhahnsyn was the commander of Tirian's personal guard, the only one of his senior servants who'd been with him even longer than Wyllyms.

"Of course, Your Grace," the majordomo murmured yet again, and withdrew from the study at the duke's gesture.

Tirian sat a moment longer, gazing unseeingly at the rain-lashed window. Then he drew a deep breath, stood, and walked out of the room.

▼   ▼   ▼

"Father!" Tirian said as he stepped briskly into the library.

Tellesberg's temperatures virtually never dropped below freezing, but they could get a bit on the cool side, especially in the winter, and a night with weather like this was sufficiently chill for a fire to have been kindled. It was as much for emotional comfort as to drive off the physical chill, and the Earl of Gray Harbor stood in front of the hearth, holding out his hands to the crackling flame.

The library was much larger than Tirian's study. In fact, if Wyllyms hadn't already ushered the earl into it, Tirian would have chosen a smaller, more intimate setting. The vast room had been added to the Tirian townhouse by the present duke's maternal grandfather, who'd been all but illiterate, as a wedding gift for his daughter. The old man had spared no expense to give his beloved oldest child the most impressive library collection in Tellesberg, and he'd insisted on providing proper housing for it, as well.

Many-paned skylights were set into both sides of the vast chamber's vaulted ceiling. They ran in a wide circle around the look-through fireplace's stone chimney, arranged to provide natural sunlight for the reading desks at the library's heart. Now deluging rain beat on the thick glass with endless, waterfall patience while thunder rumbled and crashed overhead, and fresh lightning glared beyond the skylights, like the very fury of Schueler, as the earl looked up at his son-in-law's entrance.

Tirian was shocked by Gray Harbor's expression. The earl's face was drawn, clenched around some heavy burden, and his eyes were laden with misery. The duke crossed to him quickly, holding out both hands, and his own concern deepened as he got close enough to smell his father-in-law's breath.

"Father," he said more gently, putting his hands on the shorter, more slightly built earl's shoulders, "what is it? What brings you out on a night like *this*?"

He jerked his head at the water-streaming skylights, and his alarm clicked up another notch as he noted the water dripping from the earl's soaked ponytail. Had his father-in-law charged out into a raging storm like this one without so much as a hat?

"I—" the earl began, then stopped, staring up into his son-in-law's face, seeing the powerful family resemblance to King Haarahld. There was less of Cayleb in Tirian's features, but he could almost have been a slightly older mirror of the king.

"What?" Tirian asked gently, his eyes dark with concern and affection. Surely, Gray Harbor thought, that concern—that love—had to be genuine. He *couldn't* be mistaken about that! And yet . . . and yet . . .

"Tell me," the duke commanded in a soft voice, simultaneously urging the earl away from the hearth and towards a leather upholstered armchair. He pushed his father-in-law gently down into the chair, just as Marhys Wyllyms knocked lightly at the library door and entered, personally carrying a silver tray laden with a bottle of the duke's finest Harchong brandy and two glasses.

Tirian hadn't ordered the brandy, but he nodded in approval as the major-domo set the tray on a small table by the earl's chair, and then withdrew as quietly as he'd appeared.

The duke unstoppered the brandy and poured two glasses, giving the obviously distraught Gray Harbor a few moments. Then he extended one glass to the earl, took the other, and settled into the facing armchair.

"Father," he said firmly as Gray Harbor accepted his brandy glass. The earl simply held it, not even sipping, and Tirian continued in that same, firm tone. "You obviously didn't come out in weather like this on a whim. So tell me what brings you here. Tell me what I can do to help."

To his astonishment, his father-in-law's eyes abruptly filled with tears.

"I shouldn't have come," Gray Harbor said finally, and his voice was hoarse, his words more than a little slurred. Obviously, Tirian realized, he'd been drinking even more heavily than the duke had guessed.

"I shouldn't have come," the earl repeated, "but I had to. I had to, Kahlvyn."

"Why, Father? What's happened?"

"Kahlvyn, you've been . . . involved with some people you shouldn't have been," Gray Harbor said. Tirian's eyes narrowed, and the earl shook his head. "I know you had no reason to suspect them," he continued, "but some of the men with whom you've been doing business are . . . They aren't what you think they are."

"Father," Tirian said slowly, "I'm afraid I don't understand what you're talking about."

"I know, I know."

Gray Harbor looked away, staring into the crackling fire while Zhorzh Hauwyrd, his personal guardsman, stood uncomfortably behind his chair. Hauwyrd had joined Gray Harbor's service over twelve years ago. He'd become the earl's personal guardsman two years later, following his predecessor's accidental drowning on a fishing trip, and he'd long since proven his loyalty. Yet it was obvious Hauwyrd had no idea what had so perturbed the earl, although Gray Harbor's longtime retainer was clearly concerned about whatever it was.

Well, that was fair enough. *Tirian* was concerned, too. Despite the heavy smell of whiskey on the earl's breath, his sentences came out almost normally. The consequences, no doubt, of all of his years of political and diplomatic experience. That clarity of phrase could have fooled many people into underestimating the extent of his inebriation, but Tirian knew him better than that. It was obvious to him that Gray Harbor was unfocused, searching not simply for words, but for the thoughts he wanted to put *into* words.

Tirian had never seen him like this, and he reached out and laid one hand on the older man's knee.

"What do you know, Father?" His gentle question was all but lost in the next crash of thunder, and Gray Harbor looked back from the fire to focus a bit owlishly on his face.

"Kahlvyn," he said, "some of your business partners, some of the men you think are friends, aren't. They're spies. Traitors." He shook his head, eyes no longer filled with tears, but still dark with concern. "You shouldn't be associated with them."

"Spies?" Tirian sat back in his chair abruptly, his eyebrows lowering. "Traitors?" He shook his head. "I don't know what you're talking about, Father!"

"I'm talking about men you do business with who also work for Nahrmahn of Emerald," Gray Harbor said. "I'm talking about the man you buy hunting wyverns from. You're dealing with people who are the enemies of the King and the Kingdom, Kahlvyn. And," he drew a deep breath, "there are some who suspect that you know you are."

"People suspect *me* of treason?" Tirian demanded sharply. Behind the earl's chair, Hauwyrd's face went abruptly and totally expressionless. Clearly, the guardsman wasn't at all happy about the turn the conversation had just taken.

"Some people, yes," Gray Harbor said.

"Who?" Tirian asked harshly. "Who are they?"

"I can't tell you that, you know that. I shouldn't have said as much as I already have. But I'm telling you, Kahlvyn, you have to disassociate yourself from those men."

"I don't even know which men you're talking about!" Tirian protested.

"I can tell you that much," Gray Harbor said. "Lahang, the wyvern trainer. He's one of Nahrmahn's people. And Tairehl and Thorsyn, the merchants—they are, too. And there are others."

"*Which* others?" Tirian set his own brandy glass back on the tray, and his eyes were narrow, intent, as they focused on the earl's face.

"Those are the most important three," Gray Harbor told him, waving his left hand. "Oh, there are a few others, but those are the ones we *know* are important to Nahrmahn's operations here in Charis."

"Who knows?"

"Wave Thunder, of course," Gray Harbor said a bit impatiently. "Seafarmer, others. Does it really matter, Kahlvyn?"

"Of course it matters, if they think *I'm* a traitor, too, simply because of men I know, men I do business with!"

"The point is to demonstrate that you *aren't* a traitor."

"The point is that I want to know who would dare to accuse me of such a crime!" Tirian said hotly. "I'm Haarahld's cousin, for Langhorne's sake!"

"I don't blame you for being angry," Gray Harbor replied, "but no one *wants* to believe anything but the best about you. You must know that! It's just that—"

He broke off, shaking his head, and Tirian glowered at him.

"Just what, Father?" he demanded.

"There's been an . . . accusation," Gray Harbor said, after a moment, glancing back at the fire. "It's ridiculous, of course. But there it is. And given the . . . person from whom it came, Bynzhamyn had no choice but to consider it seriously."

" 'The person from whom it came,' " Tirian repeated slowly, his eyes intent and thoughtful. Then he nodded to himself.

"It was the foreigner," he said. "This 'Merlin.' The one some people are calling a '*seijin*'? Wasn't it?"

"I can't tell you that. I won't." Gray Harbor shook his head. "I think it's nonsense, that it may well be politically motivated, but I can't tell you its source, at least until Bynzhamyn's disproved the charges. And," he looked back at Tirian, his own eyes narrowing, "the best way for you to help disprove them is to voluntarily disassociate yourself from Nahrmahn's known agents and tell Bynzhamyn and Seafarmer everything you know about them."

"Everything I know? You make it sound as if you think I *have* been consorting with traitors!"

"Damn it, Kahlvyn!" Gray Harbor said, his voice sharper than it had been. He set his own untouched glass back onto the tray forcefully enough to slop brandy over the rim, and glared at his son-in-law. "You *have* been! Whether you knew you were doing it or not is immaterial, as far as that's concerned. We *know* they're Nahrmahn's men. What matters now is for you to demonstrate that, now that you've been told who they are, you want to help us prove they are."

"Why?" Tirian asked harshly. "If Wave Thunder already knows they're traitors, what am I supposed to add to his knowledge about them?"

"Anything you can," Gray Harbor said slowly, his eyebrows tightening. "Anything that might help." He sat back in his chair, gazing at the duke narrowly.

"Surely you don't need me to tell you how it works, Kahlvyn. I would have thought you'd be as eager as I am to do that!"

"Why should I be? *You* aren't the one some unknown foreigner is accusing of *treason*." Tirian snorted angrily and pushed himself up out of his armchair. He stamped over to the fire and glared down into the crackling flames, his back to his father-in-law, his hands clasped behind him and his shoulders tight.

"Why should I be so eager to defend my name—my family's name—against that sort of accusation?"

"To discredit him in turn," Gray Harbor said, still speaking slowly, staring at the younger man's rigid spine.

"Shan-wei with *him!*" Tirian growled. "I'm the King's cousin, not some wretched little backcountry baron! Why should I care about the charges of some ragged adventurer?"

"You shouldn't," the earl said, more slowly yet, ". . . unless they're true."

Tirian wheeled back to face him, just that little bit too quickly, and saw it in his father-in-law's eyes. Saw that Gray Harbor hadn't been quite as drunk as Tirian had thought he was. Saw the concern in those eyes turning into something else—something both far sadder and much harder—as the speed of his turn, or some flicker of his own expression, abruptly confirmed what Gray Harbor had so desperately wanted not to believe.

"Langhorne," the earl said softly. "They *are* true, aren't they? You already knew Lahang is Nahrmahn's chief agent here in Tellesberg."

Tirian opened his mouth, obviously to deny the accusation. But then he paused. He stood for a moment, looking at the earl, then glanced at Hauwyrd.

"Yes," he said then, his voice clipped but composed. "Yes, Father. I knew Lahang was one of Nahrmahn's spies. And I'll admit he approached me, wanted to recruit me into a plot against Haarahld."

"And you never told anyone." Gray Harbor's words were no longer slurred. They came crisp, cold. There was anger in them, and sorrow, and Tirian shrugged.

"No, I didn't," he agreed. "Why should I? If Lahang wanted to use me in some plot against Haarahld, he'd have to give me some of the details, wouldn't be? How better to position myself to discover what Nahrmahn was up to?"

"If that's what you were really thinking, you should have taken the information to Bynzhamyn the instant Lahang approached you."

"And risk having the secret get out before I'd had the opportunity to actually learn anything?" Tirian began. "I hardly think—"

"Spare me," Gray Harbor interrupted sharply. Tirian looked at him, and the earl shook his head. "I've known Bynzhamyn Raice for more than twenty-five years; you've known him almost that long. We both know that secrets entrusted to him don't 'get out.'" He shook his head again, slowly, sadly. "No, Kahlvyn. The only reason you wouldn't have told Bynzhamyn would be that you were considering accepting Lahang's offer."

Despite the thunder grumbling overhead, despite the rain pounding on the skylights, and the crackle of the fire, silence seemed to hover in the library. And then, finally, the Duke of Tirian nodded.

"I was," he conceded. "And why not? My blood's the same as that in Haarahld's veins. My grandfather was his grandfather. If that kraken had taken his life, and not simply his knee, the throne would have been mine. Why shouldn't I consider the possibility that it still could be?"

Gray Harbor stared at him, as if seeing him for the very first time.

"I thought I knew you," the earl said at last, so softly his voice was all but drowned by the sound of the furious winter rain. "But if you can ask me that, then I never knew you at all, did I?"

"Of course you did." Tirian made a throwing away gesture. "I've been your son-in-law for fourteen years. You've become my father in truth, not just in name. Anything I may have thought, may have done where Haarahld is concerned, doesn't change that."

"It changes *everything*, Kahlvyn," Gray Harbor said. "Can't you even *see* that? I was the King's man, his servant, before I was ever your father-in-law. I swore an *oath* to him—the same one you swore—and I can't break it. Not for you, not for Zhenyfyr or the boys. Not even for me, for *my* love for my daughter's husband."

"I see."

Tirian stood gazing at him for endless seconds, hands clasped behind him once again, then shrugged slightly.

"So, I assume I can't talk you into forgetting about this, or throwing your lot in with mine?" The duke smiled crookedly. "We'd make a formidable team, Father. Think about it. The Kingdom's ranking duke and the First Councillor? We could do it, if you could just forget about that oath of yours."

"Never," Gray Harbor said firmly, sadly.

"Which leaves . . . what?"

"Bynzhamyn's already more than half convinced Merlin's accusations were accurate," the earl said. "Seafarmer's already investigating. And now, *I* know the truth, Kahlvyn. It's only a matter of time, and not much of that, until the King knows, as well. I think you have only one chance to salvage anything from this, and that's to turn King's Evidence."

"Confess what I've done? Throw myself on Haarahld's mercy and promise to tell him everything I know?"

"What else can you hope for?"

"I can still hope to *win*, Father," Tirian said softly.

"*Win?*" Gray Harbor repeated incredulously. "How? It's over, Kahlvyn! All you can do now is try to minimize the damage. You're Haarahld's cousin, and he and Cayleb both love you. Of course they'll be angry—furious! But you're also the most important nobleman in the entire kingdom, after Cayleb himself. Obviously this is going to change everything where their trust in you is concerned, but if you admit what you've done, do your best to help undo it, Haarahld will do all he can to keep the entire thing quiet. You know that!"

"Dear, loving Cousin Haarahld," Tirian said, his voice harder, an ugly light glittering in his eyes. "Father, it should be *me* on the throne, not him!"

Gray Harbor's expression hardened. He looked at his son-in-law, and he saw the man he'd always known . . . and a total stranger. A stranger so soured by ambition and resentment that he'd become both traitor and would-be usurper, yet somehow been able to conceal the depths of that bitter emotion from everyone.

Even from those who loved him.

"Kahlvyn," the first councillor said coldly, "the throne is *not* yours. It never will be. Accept that now, and do what you can to make amends with Haarahld while the opportunity still exists."

"I don't think so," Tirian said.

Gray Harbor stiffened in his chair, and Hauwyrd's hand dropped to the hilt of his sword, but the duke ignored the guardsman, gazing straight into Gray Harbor's eyes.

"It seems I can't convince you to join me," he said, "but I'm afraid you can't convince *me* to join *you*, either, Father. Which leaves us with a bit of a problem, doesn't it?"

"You can't win, Kahlvyn."

"I disagree." Tirian reached up to rest one hand on the mantelpiece of the fireplace beside him and smiled at his father-in-law.

"I know you, and I know Wave Thunder," he said easily, almost lightly. "You wouldn't have blabbed about this to anyone else—not yet. Seafarmer, yes." He nodded. "I'll give you that, and Seafarmer may have spoken to one or two people he knows and trusts. But that's all, so far."

"And it's enough," Gray Harbor said flatly.

"No, Father, it isn't," Tirian disagreed. "I'm afraid events are going to force me to do something I wanted to avoid, but this isn't exactly something I never planned for."

"What do you mean?" Gray Harbor demanded, his voice suddenly taut.

"I mean I'd hoped the only person I'd have to kill would be Cayleb." Tirian shook his head in what appeared to be genuine regret. "I didn't want to do even that much. Maybe if I had, I would have planned better."

"You admit you planned to murder your own cousin? Your Crown Prince?" Gray Harbor sounded as if he couldn't believe it, even now.

"It was my idea," Tirian acknowledged. "Lahang was nervous. He and Nahrmahn didn't want anything to do with it at first. But Nahrmahn came around when I pointed out that I was Zhan and Zhanayt's regent."

"And the King?" Gray Harbor's voice was no longer taut. It was leached of emotion, flattened and yet fascinated.

"That would have been more difficult," Tirian admitted. "On the other hand, I felt reasonably confident Nahrmahn would be so . . . enthusiastic, shall we say, after Cayleb's death that I could trust him to make a respectable effort to remove Haarahld, as well. I'd have preferred that, actually."

"Well, it isn't going to happen now," Gray Harbor said.

"No, not that way. But I do have my own friends in the Palace, and I am the King's cousin. I'm afraid it's going to be much messier this way, but this Merlin fellow of yours will help make it work for me."

"What are you talking about?"

"It's simple." Tirian smiled thinly. "I'm afraid there are about to be several murders here in Tellesberg tonight. Wave Thunder, Seafarmer, most of Seafarmer's senior investigators—since I don't know which of them he's talked to, I'll have to attend to all of them. And Lahang will have to go, too. I can't have anyone who knows about my . . . association with him or Nahrmahn."

Gray Harbor's expression was appalled. Less because of what he was hearing than because of who he was hearing it *from.*

"Everyone will be horrified when they hear the news," Tirian continued. "Fortunately, you will have come to me tonight and warned me of your suspicions about this Merlin. Your fear that he's actually in the employ of Nahrmahn, himself, part of some plot against the Crown. Your concern that the King has given his trust too quickly, allowed this stranger too close to him and to Cayleb by naming him one of Cayleb's personal guards.

"Given your obvious concern about him, the moment I hear about the murder of Wave Thunder and so many of his most senior investigators, I'll immediately go to the Palace with my own most trusted guardsmen. Obviously, if Merlin really is guilty of all you think he is, it will be essential to arrest him before he can do any more damage. Unfortunately, as everyone knows from his rescue of Cayleb, he's a very gifted swordsman and, as it turns out, assassin. His entire reason for 'saving' Cayleb from his own employer's 'assassins' was to get him inside the Palace, where he could kill *all* of Haarahld's immediate family. By the time my guardsmen and I can reach him, he and the other members of Haarahld's own Palace Guard he's managed to suborn will have murdered the King and the Crown Prince. My guardsmen and I will, of course, kill the traitors in the Guard and manage to save Zhan and Zhanayt's lives, and I'll immediately proclaim a regency in Zhan's name."

"That's insane," Gray Harbor said almost conversationally. "No one would believe it."

"I think differently." Tirian smiled again. "Some of my friends at court would be prepared to support me, whatever happened. Others, even if they doubt all the circumstances, will see Haarahld and Cayleb dead, Zhan a mere child, and enemies surrounding us on every side. If not me, then who? Or do you think they'll embrace a dynastic civil war with Nahrmahn and Hektor waiting to pounce? And who knows anything about this 'Merlin'? He's a stranger, a foreigner who appeared under mysterious circumstances and who's been busily worming his way into the King's favor! Half the nobles at court probably already fear the influence he might come to wield, and none of them *know* him. They'll be happy enough to see the last of him. Especially"—his smile disappeared, and his eyes narrowed—"when Haarahld's own First Councillor confirms the reasons for *my* suspicion of him."

"I won't do it," Gray Harbor said flatly.

"I think you should reconsider that, Father." There was no threat in Tirian's voice, only a tone of reason. "Who *will* you support, if Haarahld and Cayleb are dead? Will *you* stand father to a civil war? Simply hand the Kingdom over to Hektor and Nahrmahn? Or will you do what's best for Charis and support the only person who can hold the Kingdom together? You told me my only chance was to turn King's Evidence for Haarahld. Well, I'm telling *you* that your only chance to serve the Kingdom is to turn King's Evidence for me."

"Never."

"Never is a long time, Father. I think you'll probably reconsider, given enough time to think about it."

Gray Harbor started to stand up, then gasped in astonishment as a heavy hand pushed him firmly back down in his chair. His head snapped around, and he looked over his shoulder, eyes widening, as Zhorzh Hauwyrd looked back at him.

"I'm sorry, Father," Tirian said, and Gray Harbor's eyes whipped back around to him. The duke shook his head, and continued with that same note of sincerity. "I'm afraid I realized a day like this might come. Have you forgotten Zhorzh was in my service before yours? That I was the one who recommended him to you when you first retained him, not to mention putting in a good word for him when your last guardsman suffered his . . . accident."

"My God," Gray Harbor half-whispered. "You've been planning this *that* long?"

"In a manner of speaking, I suppose. And when you appeared so unexpectedly in this sort of weather, I took a few additional precautions." Tirian took a small bell from the mantelpiece. "I didn't truly expect to need them, but I believe in being prepared."

He shook the bell once. Its voice was sweet, rising clear and sharp in an interval between thunderclaps, and the library door opened instantly.

Frahnk Zhahnsyn and fourteen other members of Tirian's personal guard filed in through it. The library was a huge room, but it was well populated with bookshelves and scroll racks, and the fifteen armed and armored men completely filled one end of it.

"I never planned for this actual moment," Tirian continued, "and, whether you believe this or not, Father, I love you. I'll admit that I never planned on that in the beginning, either. Zhenyfyr, yes, but you were already First Councillor. I had to think of you in tactical terms, and, as I say, I believe in being prepared. Since I couldn't take a chance on how you might jump at a moment like this, I took precautions—wisely, it would appear."

"It doesn't change anything," Gray Harbor said. "Your entire so-called plan is insane, but even if it works, I won't support you. I can't."

"We'll see about that. And I hope, for many people's sake, that you're wrong. In the meantime, however I'm afraid it's time to—"

Lightning flared, thunder crashed again, and on the heels of that deep, rumbling roar came another crash. The crash of breaking glass as the skylight above Gray Harbor shattered into a thousand glittering pieces and a rain-soaked, black-clad figure in the cuirass and mail of the Royal Guard came plunging through it.

The intruder landed with impossible grace, as if the twenty-five-foot plunge from the roof above had been a mere two feet. His knees straightened, and the drawn sword in his hands hissed.

Zhorzh Hauwyrd staggered back with a high-pitched sound of shocked agony, left hand clutching the stump of his blood-spouting right forearm as the hand which had been on Gray Harbor's shoulder thumped to the library's floor.

"Your pardon, Your Grace," Merlin Athrawes said politely, "but I trust you'll understand if I take exception to your plans."

▼　　　▼　　　▼

Kahlvyn Ahrmahk stared in shock at the dripping apparition before him. Merlin's abrupt, totally unexpected arrival had stunned every person in that library, Gray Harbor not least, and Merlin smiled thinly.

He hadn't planned on this confrontation—hadn't wanted anything remotely like it, in fact. Nor had he anticipated any likely need for it. But at least he'd been worried enough over how his accusation of Tirian might work out that he'd kept an eye on Wave Thunder. He'd planted SNARC-deployed parasite bugs in several places in Tellesberg by now, and he'd monitored the one in Wave Thunder's office on a real-time basis. That was the only reason he'd known about Seafarmer's conclusions . . . or the fact that Wave Thunder would discuss those conclusions with Gray Harbor.

He'd maneuvered the office bug onto Wave Thunder's shoulder for the trip to Gray Harbor's townhouse, then dropped it off onto the earl, instead. But he'd been slow to realize what Gray Harbor intended to do. In fairness, the *earl* probably hadn't known what he was going to do before he started drinking so heavily, and he'd already summoned his carriage for the trip before Merlin realized where he was going.

The fact that Merlin had been dining with Cayleb at that moment had made things even more difficult. Fortunately, it had been a private dinner, and he'd managed to disengage himself from the prince rather more hastily than protocol would normally have permitted by claiming—accurately, as it happened—that he was even then receiving a "vision." The crown prince had accepted his newest bodyguard's excuse that he needed to retreat to his chambers to meditate upon the vision, and Merlin had retired with a hasty bow.

He'd also instructed Owl to retrieve the recon skimmer even before he took leave of the prince, and given the quantity of thunder rumbling around the sky to disguise any sonic booms, the skimmer had made the trip at better than Mach four. The moment it arrived, the AI, at his command, had used its tractor to snatch Merlin from his chamber window and deposit him on the roof of Tirian's Tellesberg mansion instead. The trip through the wind-lashed rain and thunder, supported only by the tractor while lightning flared and hissed, had been an experience Merlin could have done without indefinitely. Unfortunately, he'd had no choice but to make it.

He'd arrived, still listening to the bug on Gray Harbor, about the time Tirian handed his father-in-law the brandy glass, and he'd been almost as dumbfounded as Gray Harbor himself by Tirian's calm admission of guilt . . . and by how long the duke had been an active traitor. As Merlin himself had told Haarahld and Cayleb, he couldn't see the past, and he'd had no idea Tirian had been plotting against his cousins for so long.

Which brought him to the present rather ticklish moment, confronting the King of Charis' first cousin and fifteen of his handpicked guardsmen in the Duke of Tirian's library.

▼   ▼   ▼

"—take exception to your plans."

The Earl of Gray Harbor sat paralyzed in his chair, looking at the back of the man who'd exploded out of the night. The man he'd distrusted and resented . . . who stood now between him and fifteen armed men in the service of a traitor and would-be regicide.

"It would seem," his son-in-law said after what seemed a small eternity, "that I've underestimated you, *Seijin* Merlin."

Gray Harbor could scarcely believe how calm Kahlvyn sounded. The duke couldn't possibly really be that collected, that poised. Or possibly he could. Whatever else, the earl knew now that the man he'd thought he knew was in fact a total stranger to him.

"I could say the same, Your Grace," Merlin replied with another of those thin smiles.

The *seijin* stood quite still, his body language almost relaxed, ignoring the man whose hand and wrist he'd amputated as Hauwyrd went to his knees and his blood spread in a coppery-smelling pool. The *seijin*'s own sword remained ready in his hands, in a stance Gray Harbor—no mean swordsman himself—had never before seen, and danger radiated from him like smoke as thunder rumbled and rolled overhead yet again.

"Certainly," Tirian said, "you're not foolish enough to believe you can somehow rescue my father-in-law and get out of this house alive?"

"I'm not?" Merlin sounded almost *amused*, Gray Harbor realized with a fresh sense of disbelief.

"Come now!" Tirian actually chuckled as his guardsmen moved slowly and

carefully, placing themselves between him and Merlin. "There's no point pretending, I suppose. The way I see it, the only two choices you have are to join me,
or to die. I'll admit, in light of my previous underestimation of your capabilities,
that you'd make a formidable ally. On the other hand, I'd already planned on
killing you, so"—he shrugged—"it won't break my heart to stay with that solution if you choose to prove stubborn. Before you make that decision, though, I'd
suggest you consider it carefully. After all, what do you think the odds are of your
managing to defeat fifteen of my best?"

"Better than average," Merlin replied, and attacked.

▼   ▼   ▼

Frahnk Zhahnsyn was a veteran of the Royal Charisian Marines. He'd served for
over eight years before he'd been recruited by a much younger Kahlvyn
Ahrmahk to become a sergeant in the Duke of Tirian's personal guard. He was as
hard-bitten, capable, and dangerous as he was loyal to his patron, and the men
he'd assembled in response to Tirian's hasty note—armored in the same cuirasses
and mail hauberks as the Royal Guard—were his best. Every one of them was a
veteran, as well, and there were fifteen of them.

They'd heard the wild rumors about Merlin's rescue of Crown Prince
Cayleb. They'd listened to all the tales, all the gossip, but they'd dismissed them
as the sorts of absurdity to be expected when ignorant farmers or soft city merchants got together to discuss the shivery-shuddery details of such gory goings-
on. They'd seen too much, done too much themselves, to be taken in by that sort
of heroic fantasy.

That was unfortunate, because it meant that despite all the potential warnings, they had not the least idea what they faced in that moment. And because
they didn't, the last thing they'd expected was for a single, outnumbered madman to *attack*.

▼   ▼   ▼

Gray Harbor lunged up out of his chair in disbelief as the lunatic sprang forward.

The earl, too, was a veteran of far more combat than most, and the man
who'd captained his own cruiser had summed up the odds against Merlin as
quickly as Tirian or Zhahnsyn. Which meant the *seijin*'s sudden attack surprised
him just as badly.

But however insane it might be, the earl couldn't let Merlin face such odds
alone. Not when he knew it was his own unforgivable stupidity which had led
the *seijin* here to his death. And not when Gray Harbor's own survival might
prove one more weapon against the king whose trust he'd betrayed by coming
here in the first place.

His hand fell to the hilt of the gem-encrusted dress dagger at his hip. It was a pretty toy, but no less lethal for its decoration. The finely tempered steel scraped from its sheath, and then he froze, jaw dropping.

▼   ▼   ▼

Merlin released the governors he'd set on his reaction time and strength, and his katana flashed with literally inhuman speed as he bounded a single long pace forward.

The first guardsman never had time to grasp what was happening. His head leapt from his shoulders before he realized he'd seen the blade move, and Merlin's wrists turned as he brought the blade flashing back across in a flat figure-eight. Another head flew before the first victim's knees had even begun to buckle, and then Merlin recovered, still with that impossible speed and precision, and drove the katana's chisel point straight through a third guardsman's cuirass—breast and backplate alike.

He twisted his blade, withdrew it, and leapt backward, recovering his original position and stance, all in the same flashing movement, before the first corpse had hit the floor.

▼   ▼   ▼

Kahlvyn Ahrmahk's eyes went wide in disbelief as Merlin Athrawes savaged his guardsmen like a kraken rising hungry from the depths. One instant, the *seijin* was standing there, smiling at him. The next, the library exploded in blood, and then, suddenly, Merlin was back exactly where he'd been two seconds before . . . but he faced only twelve opponents.

Zhahnsyn and the other guardsmen froze. It wasn't cowardice, wasn't panic. It was simple surprise, and even that wasn't their fault. For just a moment, they stared at their three dead fellows, the water-dripping apparition which had killed them, and the blood spreading across the library's parquet floor in a tide of crimson. Then—

"*Spread out!*" Zhahnsyn barked, and the survivors moved forward, fanning out to envelop their single opponent.

▼   ▼   ▼

Gray Harbor was at least as astonished as anyone else. He'd never imagined such speed and power, but he realized almost instantly that however lethal the *seijin* might be, he faced one fatal disadvantage.

He was trying to protect Gray Harbor.

He was like a single war galley, anchored to the defense of a fat, lumbering merchantman while a dozen scruffy pirates lunged and dashed at his charge. Not one of them could hope to face him in single combat, but they didn't need to do anything so foolish. As long as he was tied down protecting the earl, Tirian's men could choose their moment and coordinate their attacks, and there was nothing Gray Harbor could do about it. Even if he'd been properly armed, he would only have gotten in Merlin's way, and he knew it, however humiliating admitting it might be. But if he couldn't help, then surely there had to be some way he could at least—

"Look to yourself, *Seijin!*" he barked, and leapt directly away from the cautiously advancing guardsmen.

▾   ▾   ▾

Tirian cursed as his father-in-law sprang for the wrought-iron spiral stair to the balcony catwalk that served the library's upper rows of shelves. The duke had installed that whimsically ornate creation as a gift for his wife on their third anniversary. Zhenyfyr Ahrmahk loved books at least as much as her husband or father ever had, and she'd laughed in delight at the absurdity of his surprise. Not that it hadn't been practical, as well; certainly it was more convenient for someone in long skirts than the steep, rolling ladders it had replaced.

One of the duke's guards recognized the earl's intent quickly enough to lunge forward, trying to grapple with the older man before he reached the stair. But his effort brought him into Merlin's reach, and the *seijin's* sword licked out with that same blinding speed. It bit effortlessly through flesh and bone, blood exploded in a hot, stinking fan, and the guardsman went down with a wailing scream as razor-sharp steel sheared through the thick bone of his femur as cleanly as an ax and amputated his left leg three inches above the knee.

The other guards were slower to react, and Gray Harbor raced up the ornamental treads, dagger shining in his hand. From its top, he could hope to hold off even a sword-armed opponent at least briefly. More importantly, it got him out of the reach of any immediate threat.

Tirian's remaining guardsmen realized what that meant almost as quickly as the duke had, and their cautious advance became a sudden rush. They surged forward through their fallen fellows' shrieks, seeking to engulf Merlin before he took advantage of his sudden mobility.

But quick as they were, they weren't quick enough. Merlin made no effort to evade them; he came to *meet* them.

▾   ▾   ▾

Captain Yowance of the Royal Charisian Navy had been no stranger to combat, and the Earl of Gray Harbor recognized carnage when he saw it. But he'd never imagined anything like this.

Tirian's guardsmen tried to swarm over Merlin, but it was like a school of herring trying to swarm a kraken. The *seijin* seemed to stride forward almost casually, but his peculiar sword was a blur of motion. It moved literally too quickly for the eye to follow, and armor meant nothing before its impossible sharpness. Bodies—and bits of bodies—flew away from him in gory sprays of blood, and the peaceful library became an abattoir. Men screamed and cursed and died, and Merlin Athrawes moved through the chaos untouched, dealing death like the Archangel Schueler himself.

▼   ▼   ▼

Kahlvyn Ahrmahk was no coward, but an icy wave of fear washed through him. Like his guards, he'd discounted the wild rumors and speculation about Merlin. Now, as he watched his men go down—some of them screaming in agony; most dead before they hit the floor—he knew he'd been wrong. He knew the ridiculous rumor that the mysterious foreigner was a *seijin* was true, after all . . . and that all the preposterous tales, all the stupid heroic ballads and children's stories, about *seijin* and their superhuman powers weren't preposterous at all.

His surviving guardsmen—all six of them—were no longer advancing to envelop Merlin. They were falling back, huddling together. None of Tirian's guards had ever lacked courage, but this was too much, something beyond their experience or comprehension. They hadn't panicked, even now—there hadn't really been *time* for that—but the deadly sense of how totally outclassed they were had driven them completely onto the defensive, and even as Tirian watched, another of them fell to Merlin's implacable blade.

He's not human!

The thought flashed through the duke's mind, and he shook himself, fighting to throw off his own incipient panic. His brain raced, and he drew a deep breath.

There was still a way, if he could only get out of the library before Merlin reached him. Wyllyms was out there somewhere, and surely the clash of steel, the screams, had to have alerted the majordomo. He *must* have already sounded the alarm for the rest of Tirian's personal guards! If the duke could reach those guards first, he could tell them how Merlin had exploded out of the night in an effort to assassinate him, how the supposed *seijin* had taken Gray Harbor hostage. However deadly Merlin might be, Tirian had the next best thing to another sixty men ready to hand, and most of them were as well trained with bows or arbalests as with swords. And if, in the process of retaking the library, there should be a tragic accident, or if Merlin should cut the earl's throat rather than allow him to be rescued, or—

Yet another guardsman folded up around the bitter steel buried in his belly, and Tirian turned.

▼   ▼   ▼

A corner of Merlin's attention saw the duke turn and race for the library's door. He realized instantly what Tirian had in mind, but there were still four guardsmen between him and the traitor. He couldn't kill them quickly enough to—

The Earl of Gray Harbor's belt dagger flashed in the lamplight as it flew across the library. It was heavy, awkward, and not really properly balanced for throwing, but the earl's hand had not forgotten the captain's skill entirely, and grief and terror had burned the alcohol out of his system.

Kahlvyn Ahrmahk, Duke of Tirian, rose on his toes like a dancer, arms flung wide, spine arched, and mouth open in agony, as ten lethal inches of steel drove into his back. A jeweled hilt blossomed between his shoulder blades, blood sprayed from his lips, and he crashed facedown to the floor.

.XII.
Braidee Lahang's Lodgings, Tellesberg

The pounding on Braidee Lahang's door was furious enough to wake him despite the tumult of the storm.

His immediate reaction was one of panic. No spy wanted to hear an official fist battering on his door in the middle of the night, and he could think of very few *non*official errands which might bring someone out on a night like this one. But then his panic eased just a bit. When Baron Wave Thunder's agents came to call on a suspected spy, they were seldom so polite as to bother to knock. Doors had a way of becoming splinters in the course of their visits, although on the (rare) occasions when they demolished the wrong person's door, they were very good about replacing it, later.

Still, it was unlikely that whoever was knocking at his door was here in any official capacity, and he felt his heartbeat slow just a bit as he climbed out of bed.

He'd selected his lodgings not simply because they were close to the heart of the city, or even because of the roof space available for his wyvern coops. Those were factors, of course, yet an even more important one was the fact that the building's ground-floor was occupied by a ship chandler during the day but empty at night. That gave Lahang a certain degree of anonymity on the occasions when he was expecting callers after hours. He'd made a few additional judicious modifications without benefit of discussion with his landlord, as well, and he paused well to one side of his second-story door and peered through the inconspicuous peephole he'd bored through the wall.

There was no lamp in the hallway or on the stairs. Since there wasn't normally any traffic after dark, there was no point risking the accidental fire an unattended candle or lamp might lead to. But Lahang's visitor had brought a bull's-eye lantern, and Lahang's eyebrows rose as he recognized the other man by the light streaming from its opened slide.

His initial alarm returned, if in a rather less acute version. Marhys Wyllyms had delivered several messages to him over the past few years, and Lahang was aware that Duke Tirian trusted his majordomo's discretion implicitly. But Wyllyms had never arrived in the middle of the night without warning, or without any of the signals Tirian and Lahang had devised to alert one another that they needed to make contact. Unexpected messages like this, especially ones which carried such a risk of exposure, were only marginally more welcome to a spymaster than the heavy-handed minions of the Crown.

He drew a deep breath, opened the door part way, leaving the safety chain latched, and peered out.

"What?" he asked, his voice harsh.

"I have a package from the Duke," Wyllyms replied.

"Well, hand it over," Lahang said briskly, extending his hand through the gap.

"It won't fit," Wyllyms said reasonably, and drew a fat package, wrapped in oilskin against the weather, out from under his streaming poncho.

"What is it?" Lahang asked, already reaching to unlatch the chain.

"He didn't tell me." Wyllyms shrugged. "There's been some trouble at the townhouse, though. I wouldn't be surprised if it's documents he needs to get rid of."

"Trouble?" Lahang's eyes sharpened, and he opened the door fully. "What kind of trouble?"

"Nothing we can't handle, I think," Wyllyms said, handing him the package. The spy took it almost absently, his eyes so focused on Wyllyms' face that he never noticed the majordomo's hand sliding back under his poncho until it reemerged with the dagger.

Even then, Lahang didn't really *notice* the blade. In fact, he still hadn't seen it when it severed his throat in a steaming gush of blood.

Prince Nahrmahn's chief agent in Charis thudded to the floor with a dying gurgle, and Wyllyms stepped back, grimacing as he regarded the spray pattern on the front of his poncho.

Well, no matter, he thought. The rain would wash away the stains quickly enough . . . just as Lahang's death would wash away the information about Wyllyms true patron which he might have provided to Wave Thunder's investigators.

Now all Wyllyms had to do was get back to Emerald, himself.

Haarahld VII's face was hard and grim, a mask of angry discipline over grief. His son sat beside him at the huge table in the lamp-lit council chamber, and Cayleb's expression was even more mask-like than his father's. Both of them watched, silent and hard-eyed, as Merlin and the Earl of Gray Harbor stepped through the chamber's door.

Bynzhamyn Raice also sat at the table, accompanied by Sir Rhyzhard Seafarmer. Neither Bishop Maikel, nor any of the Privy Council's other members were present, and Merlin wondered whether that was a good sign or a bad one. At least the king seemed prepared to maintain Merlin's low profile for the moment.

The Royal Guards had been courteous when they'd followed Gray Harbor's coachman back to Tirian's mansion in obedience to the earl's urgent summons, but they'd also been very, very firm. It was hard to blame them, really, considering the blood-spattered and body-littered scene which had greeted them in the recently deceased Duke of Tirian's library. Being found standing over the bodies of the king's first cousin and fifteen of his personal guardsmen had to come under the heading of suspicious conduct, after all.

At least they *had* been summoned by the earl, and Lieutenant Huntyr, the youthful officer who'd accompanied the squad which had responded, had been willing to at least tentatively assume the first councillor knew what he was doing. That willingness had taken a hit when Huntyr discovered just exactly whose dagger was planted in the duke's back. But it had been sufficient to at least ensure that the house would be sealed and that the entire matter would be kept secret until the king himself had been informed.

That was as far as the lieutenant had been willing to go, however, and first councillor or not, Gray Harbor had found himself placed ever so politely under arrest. To Merlin's amusement—as much as anything could be amusing, under the circumstances—the young guardsman had been almost as courteous to him as to the earl. Both of them, however, had been relieved of all weapons before they were "escorted" to the council chamber.

"Owl," Merlin subvocalized now. "Communications and telemetry check."

"Communications link confirmed in normal operation, Lieutenant Commander," the AI replied. "All skimmer telemetry links are nominal," it added, and Merlin nodded mentally. He hoped things weren't going to turn out badly, but that didn't mean they weren't. It was always possible, however unlikely, that Haarahld might order their immediate execution, and Merlin couldn't let that happen. Not only would it be very inconvenient for him personally, but it would also mean the complete failure of Nimue Alban's mission on Safehold.

That was why the recon skimmer was hovering directly above the Royal Palace despite the rumbling thunderstorm. And it was also the reason the skimmer's weapons were fully online under Owl's control.

"Your Majesty," Lieutenant Huntyr said quietly, "Earl Gray Harbor and Lieutenant Athrawes."

"Thank you, Lieutenant." Haarahld's voice was harsh-edged, the courtesy automatic, and he never so much as glanced at the Guardsman. "Leave us, please. And see to it we're not disturbed."

"As you command, Your Majesty," Huntyr murmured.

He withdrew, and the massive council-chamber door closed quietly behind him. The metallic clack of the latch was loud in the stillness, and then, as if on cue, another thunderous rumble of thunder shook the Palace.

"So," Haarahld said after a long, still moment. "I've spoken to Bynzhamyn. I've spoken to Lieutenant Huntyr. I've spoken to the most senior of Kahlvyn's guardsmen we could find. Now I want to know what in Shan-wei's name happened."

His voice was hard, colder than Merlin had ever heard it, in person or through one of his SNARCs, and his eyes were chips of brown ice.

"Your Majesty." Gray Harbor went down on one knee and bent his head before his monarch. Merlin saw Cayleb's eyes widen, but Haarahld's expression didn't even flicker.

"Whatever happened was my fault," the first councillor said, his voice low-pitched and sad, but firm.

"*I* will determine who was at fault," Haarahld told him, "not you."

"Your Majesty—" Wave Thunder began, but Haarahld held up a hand abruptly.

"No, Bynzhamyn," he said coldly. "I'm not exactly pleased with *you* at this moment, either, you know. But I want to hear what Rayjhis and *Seijin* Merlin have to say for themselves without any excuses from you."

Wave Thunder settled unhappily back in his chair, mouth shut, and the king's eyes bored into the kneeling Gray Harbor.

"Why do you say it was your fault?" he demanded.

"Because it was my stupidity which created the situation from which *Seijin* Merlin was forced to rescue me," Gray Harbor said unflinchingly. "The *seijin* warned Bynzhamyn and me that Kahlvyn was a traitor. I refused to believe it. Indeed, I went so far as to believe—to insist—that Merlin was lying for purposes of his own. Even when Bynzhamyn came to me, told me what Sir Rhyzhard had already discovered, I refused to believe. And because I did, I violated my oath as First Councillor. Instead of maintaining the secrecy of the information Bynzhamyn had shared with me, I went to Kahlvyn to tell him he was under suspicion. That he had to disassociate himself from the men we knew were Emerald agents. That he had to come to you, Your Majesty—tell you everything, *prove Seijin* Merlin's accusations were lies. But—" He looked up at last, his face wrung with pain and his eyes glistening with unshed tears. "—they weren't lies."

The chamber was still, a frozen tableau, as the kneeling father-in-law met the cousin's eyes. The silence stretched out for several seconds, almost a full minute, and more distant thunder grumbled quietly in the background. Then, finally, Haarahld's nostrils flared as he inhaled deeply.

"How do you know they weren't?" he asked very, very softly.

"Because Kahlvyn admitted it to me, Your Majesty." Gray Harbor's voice wavered at last, frayed by remembered pain.

"He *admitted* it?" Haarahld repeated as if even now he simply could not believe his own ears.

"Your Majesty, he admitted that the attempt to assassinate Cayleb was *his* idea originally, not Nahrmahn's. He told me *he* should have been King, not you. And because I'd revealed that he was under suspicion, he planned to murder you and Cayleb this very night rather than face the disgrace and dishonor his crimes had earned. He actually believed he could steal the throne for himself, if only you, Cayleb, and Bynzhamyn and his senior investigators were dead, and he invited me to join him in his treason."

"I don't believe it," Haarahld said flatly, but Merlin heard the tiny tremor in that hard voice's depths.

"Your Majesty, I'm talking about my *son-in-law*," Gray Harbor said, his own voice and eyes wretched. "My daughter's husband, the father of my grandchildren. I loved him as if he'd been the son of my own body. Loved him so much I violated my oath to you to warn him he was under suspicion. Do you think I would *lie* about something like this? Something which will hurt Zhenyfyr so terribly? Do you think I would kill my own grandchildren's *father* if I'd had any choice at all?"

Haarahld stared down at him, and the king's frozen expression began to change. His jaw muscles clenched into hard-defined lumps, then relaxed as his cheeks sagged and he closed his eyes at last. A single tear trickled down his right cheek, and the hard, angry shoulders sagged.

"Why, Rayjhis?" he asked hoarsely. "Why didn't you and Bynzhamyn come to me as soon as *Seijin* Merlin spoke?"

"Bynzhamyn because he didn't want to hurt you, Your Majesty," Gray Harbor said softly. "And I because I refused to believe."

"And now this." Haarahld opened his eyes once more and shook his head. "Now *this*, Rayjhis. You're right, it *is* your fault, and you did violate your oath when you went to warn a possible traitor he was suspected. If you hadn't, if you'd waited—as you should have—Kahlvyn would still be alive. We might yet have learned a great deal from him, and he would have been *alive*. My cousin, almost my brother, would have been alive."

The earl bent his head once more, and his shoulders shook, but he said nothing in his own defense.

"May I speak, Your Majesty?" Merlin asked quietly, and the king's eyes darted to his face. For a moment, they flashed with fiery anger, but then Haarahld made himself stand back from that instant, automatic rage.

"Speak," he said curtly.

"Your Majesty, I told Baron Wave Thunder and Earl Gray Harbor I had no positive proof of my suspicion of the Duke. Yet had I possessed that proof, I would have laid it in their hands. I would not have laid it in yours."

Haarahld's eyes glittered dangerously, but Merlin continued steadily, meeting the king's angry glare.

"He was your cousin, Your Majesty. You loved him, and I knew it. It wasn't my place to tell you something which would cause you so much pain, and even if it had been, I had no idea of the true depth of his treason. I told your ministers what I knew, what I suspected, but even I suspected only a fraction of the full truth, and I had no proof even of that. If they erred in the fashion in which they responded to what I told them, they did so out of concern and out of love of their own. Neither of them was prepared to shirk his duty to the Crown to investigate any charge, however absurd, and both of them acted as they did out of their love for you and their desire to spare you pain.

"Baron Wave Thunder initiated that investigation without telling you because he knew how much it would hurt you if the charges proved well-founded, and because he wanted to spare you that pain until and unless he knew they were. And also, at least in part, to protect your relationship with your cousin, should those charges *not* prove valid, by arranging things so that you could blame him for proceeding without your authority if the Duke proved innocent and learned he'd been suspected. And while the Earl flatly refused to believe the Duke could possibly be a traitor, he agreed with Baron Wave Thunder, out of his duty to you, that the charges must be investigated. If he acted . . . unwisely in other ways, that, too, was out of love—love for you, and for his own son-in-law.

"Perhaps they should have told you immediately. Perhaps *I* should have. But if we had, how would you have reacted? Would you have believed it? Or would you have done precisely what the Earl did? Given the cousin you loved the opportunity to disprove the ridiculous allegations being made against him by a foreigner about whom you truly know almost nothing?"

The king continued to glare at him for a few moments, but then the fire in his eyes ebbed once again.

"Precisely, Your Majesty," Merlin said softly. "You did love him, as did the Earl. Neither of you would have wanted to believe. And because the Earl refused to believe, he was nearly killed by his own son-in-law—*would* have been killed, if the Duke had decided his death was necessary to advance his own plans. Do not deceive yourself, Haarahld of Charis; the cousin you loved planned your son's murder, and yours. Had he become regent for Zhan, he would undoubtedly have arranged his death, as well, and possibly even Zhanayt's, if it had proven necessary to secure his own claim to the throne. If you'd given him the opportunity to clear his name, he would have responded in precisely the same way he responded to Earl Gray Harbor's offer, and quite possibly have succeeded."

Silence hovered once again, and then the king shook himself. He looked away from Merlin, away from the still-kneeling Gray Harbor.

"What have you discovered so far, Bynzhamyn?" he asked harshly.

"I fear everything *Seijin* Merlin's told us about the Duke was true, Sire," Wave Thunder said heavily. "His majordomo and at least twenty-three more of his personal guardsmen managed to disappear before Lieutenant Huntyr and his men arrived at the Duke's mansion. The only reason I can think of for them to have done that was because they *knew* the Duke was a traitor and they were implicated in his treason. And I fear that at least one of them may have served two masters, and not just the Duke, alone."

"What do you mean?" Haarahld demanded, and Wave Thunder nodded to Seafarmer.

"I received a report from one of my agents just before *Seijin* Merlin and the Earl arrived here at the Palace, Your Majesty," Sir Rhyzhard said. "A man who *may* have matched the description of the Duke's majordomo, Marhys Wyllyms, went to Braidee Lahang's lodgings this evening. The weather is so bad tonight my man couldn't make a positive identification, but because it's so bad, he was also suspicious about why someone might be out in the storm. So after the visitor left, he decided he should quietly check to be sure Lahang was still there, that he hadn't crept out a back way as the first step in disappearing. What he discovered instead was that Lahang had been murdered."

"Murdered?" Haarahld repeated, and there was an almost bemused note in his voice. As if even someone as tough-minded as the King of Charis was beginning to feel overloaded.

"Yes, Your Majesty." Seafarmer nodded.

"I don't believe the Duke ordered his execution, Sire," Wave Thunder said. "I suspect that just as the Duke had inserted his own guardsman into Rayjhis' service, Nahrmahn had inserted this Wyllyms into the Duke's. He was probably the hidden dagger waiting to remove the Duke at a time of Nahrmahn's choosing, but it would seem he was also charged with removing the one man who could have given us complete details on Nahrmahn's network of spies here in the Kingdom. Especially if it appeared the Duke's downfall might lead us to Lahang in turn."

"Langhorne," Haarahld sighed, and covered his eyes with his hand. He sat that way for quite some time, then made himself straighten once more, lowered his hand, and looked at Gray Harbor.

"Oh, stand up, Rayjhis!" he half-snapped.

The earl's head came up once more, and Haarahld made an unhappy sound, halfway between a snort and something angrier.

"The *seijin's* right," he said. "Yes, you were stupid and you violated your oath. And if you'd told me the way you should have, I would have done something equally stupid. Because, as *Seijin* Merlin says, I loved Kahlvyn. God forgive me, but I *still* love him. And he *would* have used that love to kill me and Cayleb, and probably Zhan and Zhanayt, as well."

"Your Majesty, I—" Gray Harbor began, but Haarahld shook his head sharply.

"No. Don't say it. You're too valuable to me—to the Kingdom—to be permitted to resign your post. And however . . . unwisely—" The king smiled thinly, tightly at Merlin. "—you may have acted in this instance out of love, certainly you've also given me the strongest possible proof of your own loyalty. Terrible as this has been for me and for Cayleb, it will be even worse for you in the days to come. I can't do without a man willing to shoulder that much pain in the service of the oaths he swore to me and to my crown. So stand up, come over here, and sit where you belong. Now."

Gray Harbor hesitated an instant longer, then stood a bit unsteadily, walked across to take his place at the council table, and seated himself. That left Merlin standing alone before the table, and Haarahld leaned back in his chair and gazed at him.

"And so to you, *Seijin* Merlin," he said softly. "You carry deadly gifts."

"I regret that," Merlin said unflinchingly, "but I told you I'd give you the truth, Your Majesty."

"You did, and you have." Haarahld raised one hand in a little throwing-away gesture. "I thought truth was what I wanted to hear; now I know better. It isn't what I want to hear; it's only what I *need* to hear. It will be a long time before I can truly forgive you, or Rayjhis, or Bynzhamyn, or—especially—myself for what's happened tonight. But the truth is that you, and Rayjhis, have quite possibly saved my life, and my children's lives. And whether Kahlvyn's plans would have succeeded ultimately or not, you've unmasked and destroyed the most dangerous traitor in the entire Kingdom. And so, even though my heart cries out in anger, you aren't the proper target of that anger."

Merlin bent his head, bowing silently, and Haarahld gave himself another shake.

"In addition," he continued more briskly, "it would appear you've once again saved a valued servant of the Crown from assassination. And against even more formidable odds than before."

He regarded Merlin with an intent expression, his eyes much closer to their normal piercing sharpness.

"I've glanced over Lieutenant Huntyr's preliminary report, *Seijin* Merlin. Fifteen armed and armored guardsmen, I believe he said. And while Kahlvyn may have been a traitor, he was an excellent judge of fighting men. Yet according to Lieutenant Huntyr, you went through fifteen of his picked men like a scythe through grass. Not to mention arriving—once again—at a most . . . opportune moment."

He paused, obviously awaiting a response, and Merlin shrugged slightly.

"As I already told Prince Cayleb during supper, Your Majesty, I had a vision of the Earl. It was sufficient to alert me to the danger in which he was about to place himself, but I feared it would be impossible to convince anyone else the Duke was a threat to him or to the Crown. Or, at least, to convince anyone in time. So I went myself to do what I could."

Cayleb stirred slightly at his father's side. Merlin glanced at him, one eyebrow slightly quirked, and the young man settled back into stillness.

"You went yourself," Haarahld murmured, his attention so focused on Merlin that he paid no heed to the silent exchange with Cayleb. "And how, pray, did you manage to get out of Marytha's Tower and off the Palace grounds without so much as a single challenge from my reasonably competent Guards?"

"Your Majesty," Merlin replied with an easy smile, "the night is dark, it's pouring down rain by the bucketful, I'm dressed entirely in black, and I came to you from the Mountains of Light, where there are many steep cliffs upon which to practice climbing. And, in all fairness to your Guards, none of them have the training and other advantages I have."

Haarahld cocked his head to one side, and if he'd still been a being of protoplasm, Merlin would probably have held his breath. So far, nothing he'd said had been an actual lie, and he wanted badly to keep it that way.

"I suppose," the king said finally, slowly, "that when a man can come crashing down through a skylight to a floor twenty-five feet below him and kill not just fifteen armed guardsmen but *sixteen*, including Rayjhis' supposed guardsman, it shouldn't be surprising if he can also scale palace walls like some sort of human fly. I feel, however, that I really ought to point out that you seem to be establishing a very difficult example for the next *seijin* to live up to."

"That isn't my intention, Your Majesty," Merlin replied. "In fact, I think it would be a very good thing if we could minimize my own part in this evening's events."

"That might be just a bit difficult," Wave Thunder observed dryly.

"And possibly pointless, as well," Haarahld added.

"Difficult, perhaps, My Lord," Merlin replied to the baron, "but not 'pointless,' Your Majesty. If I may explain?"

"By all means, Master Traynyr," Harold said, his tone even drier than Wave Thunder's had been, and Merlin surprised himself with a small chuckle.

"Master Traynyr" was a stock character out of the Safeholdian puppet theater tradition, a sort of symbol of yin and yang, although the terms were unknown on Safehold. The name was given to a character within the play who was usually a bumbling conspirator, someone whose elaborate plans always miscarried. But, in a sort of backhanded joke, it was also the traditional *nom de theatre* of the master puppeteer who controlled all of the marionette "actors."

"Perhaps not Master Traynyr, Your Majesty," he said, "but a conspirator of sorts, nonetheless. With the revelation of the Duke's treason and Lahang's murder by Nahrmahn's own man, all of Nahrmahn's and Hektor's other agents here in Charis are going to be in what might charitably be called a state of consternation. All of them, I'm certain, will be wondering if Baron Wave Thunder's agents are about to pounce on *them*, as well. And they're undoubtedly going to be wondering exactly how the Baron and his investigators tumbled to the Duke's involvement in the first place.

"I believe all of us are in agreement that concealing the existence and accuracy of my visions from Nahrmahn and Hektor is desirable on a great many levels. On the level of grand strategy, keeping your enemies unaware of the advantage those visions offer you will only make them even more advantageous. And it would probably be a very good idea to keep those who wish you ill from looking too closely at any of my other activities, as well. On a purely personal level, I would vastly prefer not to have to be perpetually on guard against the horde of assassins I'm sure the two of them would send after me to . . . negate that advantage."

"I rather doubt any 'horde of assassins' is going to succeed in killing *you*," Haarahld observed. "So far, it's been rather the other way around, after all."

"Any mortal man can be killed, Your Majesty. I'd like to think it would be somewhat harder to kill me than some, but at the very least, slaughtering assassins in job lots would be fatiguing. Not to mention a . . . distraction from all the other things I really ought to be doing."

"I see." For the first time since Merlin and Gray Harbor's arrival, there might actually have been a small flicker of amusement in the king's eyes. "And I'd hate to have you inconvenienced in that fashion, of course. But that brings us to the minor matter of Bynzhamyn's observation about the difficulty in concealing your modest part in this evening's activities."

"I'd prefer not so much to conceal it as to downplay it, Your Majesty," Merlin said in a more serious tone, "and your decision to name me as Cayleb's personal guard may make that easier. If you and Earl Gray Harbor are willing, I would prefer for the official version to be that Baron Wave Thunder's investigators became suspicious of the Duke after interrogating the single assassin we captured alive, not because of anything *I* may have said. After that, the Baron began a cautious investigation, and the Earl reacted much as he actually did, by going to the Duke and suggesting that it was imperative for him to clear his name of any suspicion. However, instead of taking only his personal guardsman, he requested that I accompany him, as well, which I did."

"And why, precisely, did he request that?" Haarahld asked.

"Partly to help convince the Duke of the serious nature of the charges, Your Majesty. I was, after all, present when the assassination attempt failed. As such, my presence tonight might have helped to . . . rattle the Duke's nerve, if he'd been involved even peripherally with Nahrmahn. And also as an additional witness to anything which transpired."

"That sounds a little thin to me," Haarahld mused, then shrugged. "On the other hand, if we all say the same thing—and manage to keep our faces straight while we do it—we can probably make it stand up. So. Rayjhis has gone to visit Kahlvyn, and he's taken you along. And then?"

"When the Duke was confronted, he responded exactly as he actually did, Your Majesty, except that he'd brought only five of his own guardsmen into the library at that time. When they attempted to seize the Earl, his guardsman and I managed to prevent them from doing so and, in the process, killed or wounded most of them. At which point the Duke summoned the other ten men he'd had waiting outside the library door. In the ensuing fight, the Earl's guardsman was killed, but not before he, the Earl, and I—fighting together—had defeated the Duke's men. In the general chaos of the fight, the Duke himself was killed, after which the Earl summoned the Royal Guard—not surprisingly, considering that a member of the royal house had been killed—and Lieutenant Huntyr and his men responded."

"Master Traynyr, indeed," Haarahld said after a moment, then looked at Wave Thunder and Gray Harbor and raised both eyebrows.

"It cuts against the grain to turn Zhorzh into one of the heroes of this piece of fiction," Gray Harbor said heavily, and shook his head. "I believed for years that he truly was that loyal to me. It would be hard to maintain a straight face knowing he was actually a traitor and died a traitor's death."

"It may cut against the grain, Rayjhis," Wave Thunder said, "but it also might just work. Aside from you and *Seijin* Merlin, the only one left alive who knows what *actually* happened is probably this Wyllyms, the Duke's majordomo. Even he wasn't there for the actual fight, although he does know you arrived without *Seijin* Merlin. He'll undoubtedly report that to Nahrmahn, but there's nothing we can do to prevent that, unless we manage to catch him before he gets back to Emerald, which, frankly, is unlikely, to say the least. All the same, I suspect Nahrmahn and Baron Shandyr are going to tend to discount the more outrageous rumors about the *seijin*, just as we would in their place. So they're going to know we're covering up *something*, but they won't know exactly what. And *Seijin* Merlin and the King are quite correct when they say his ability to see these 'visions' of his will be even more valuable to us if no one else knows he can do it."

"I think Merlin and Bynzhamyn have a point, Rayjhis," Haarahld said. "And if it helps, think of it this way. Your man may have been a traitor, but this way his death will actually strike a blow against the very men for whom he actually worked."

"Very well, Your Majesty." Gray Harbor inclined his head once more, then gave Merlin a lopsided smile. "And I suppose, under the circumstances, that it's the very least I can do for *Seijin* Merlin in return for his saving my life after I'd openly accused him of being a traitor himself."

"Then that's settled," Haarahld said. "Bynzhamyn, I'll have a few words with Lieutenant Huntyr myself, just to ensure that his final report doesn't disagree with Merlin's . . . creativity."

"That would probably be wise, Sire. In the meantime, I think Rhyzhard and I need to get back over to the office and decide which of Nahrmahn's other spies the Duke—or something we found in his papers—might have implicated. With your permission, I intend to prune back Nahrmahn's network rather severely."

"Consider my permission granted," Haarahld said grimly, then sat back in his chair and gazed speculatively at Merlin.

"Your Majesty?" Merlin said politely after several seconds, and Haarahld snorted.

"I was just thinking, *Seijin* Merlin."

"Thinking, Your Majesty?" Merlin prompted obediently when the king paused.

"Thinking about how predictable and orderly life was before your arrival here in Tellesberg. I'm sure that, in time, we'll all adjust, but I hope you won't take it wrongly if I tell you I find myself more than a little terrified when I contemplate the future and reflect upon what's followed in your wake in the space of less than a single five-day. Especially because a part of me suspects the *real* chaos and confusion is yet to come."

Merlin smiled crookedly and shook his head without speaking. There wasn't much other response he could have made.

After all, the king was right.

.XIV.
A Private Audience Chamber,
Royal Palace,
Tellesberg

The small presence chamber's door opened.

A woman in formal court attire stepped through it, accompanied by two small boys. She was in her mid-thirties, possibly a little older, but her figure was firm and trim. The light, flowing drape of the cotton gowns enforced by Tellesberg's climate made that abundantly clear, but her face was tight-clenched, her eyes suspiciously swollen under the cosmetics which helped to mask their redness.

She walked down the runner of carpet across the cool, stone floor, holding the hands of her two sons as they walked beside her. The younger of them—perhaps five years old, standard—looked more confused than anything else. He kept glancing up at his mother, worried and concerned by the emotions he sensed from her.

The older boy, twice his younger brother's age, was different. He appeared shocked, almost like someone trapped in a terrible nightmare from which he could not awake. Like his mother and his brother, he was perfectly attired, complete to the dress dagger hanging at his right hip, but his eyes were as swollen as his mother's, and Merlin could almost physically feel the concentration it took to keep his lower lip from quivering.

King Haarahld VII watched the small, pathetic procession coming towards him for perhaps three heartbeats. Then he pushed himself up out of his throne and, in a total violation of every rule of court protocol, stepped down from the dais and went to meet them. He moved so quickly his habitual limp was far more evident than usual—so quickly neither of the bodyguards standing behind his throne could keep up with him. Then he reached the widowed mother and the grieving son, and went awkwardly, awkwardly, to his good knee, his right leg stretched painfully behind him.

"Rayjhis," he said to the older boy, and reached out one hand to cup the back of the boy's head.

"Y-Your Majes—" the boy began, but then he stopped, eyes gleaming with tears, as his voice cracked and he had to fight for control.

"No titles, Rayjhis," the king told his first cousin once removed gently. "Not yet."

The boy nodded mutely, his face crumbling with the grief the king's tone told him it was all right to display, and Haarahld looked up at his mother.

"Zhenyfyr," he said softly.

"Your Majesty," she half-whispered. Her voice was more controlled then her son's, Merlin thought, but it was still husky, shadowed by sorrow and tears. Haarahld looked up at her for a moment, then began to push himself up off of his knee.

"Sire."

Sergeant Charlz Gahrdaner's voice was quiet, but he'd caught up with his king, and he held out a mailed arm. Haarahld grimaced, but he also took it and used it to pull himself back erect. He towered above the two boys, looking down at them for a moment, then scooped the younger up into his own arms. The boy clung to his neck, pressing his face into the king's tunic, and Haarahld held him with one arm while he extended the other hand to Rayjhis.

The older boy looked at that hand for a moment. Then he took it, and Haarahld limped more slowly back to his throne. The king's mouth, Merlin noticed from his place at Cayleb's left shoulder, behind the crown prince's flanking throne, tightened each time his weight came down on his right leg.

Haarahld reached the dais, followed by Lady Zhenyfyr Ahrmahk, who had just become the Dowager Duchess of Tirian. He paused, setting the younger boy gently back on his feet, then lowered himself back into his chair and used both hands to lift his right leg until his foot rested once more on the stool before it.

"Zhenyfyr, Rayjhis, Kahlvyn," he said then, softly. "You know why you're here, but before we face the Council and all the official details we have to deal with, I need to speak to all three of you as members of my family, not as a king to his subjects."

Duchess Tirian flinched slightly at the word "family," and Haarahld held out his hand to her. She took it a bit hesitantly, and he drew her closer to his throne.

"Don't feel guilty for grieving," he told her very gently. "Don't think I blame you for that, or that *anyone* ought to. And don't think Cayleb and I aren't grieving, as well."

She looked into his eyes, her mouth quivering, and his grip on her fingers tightened comfortingly as tears trickled slowly down her cheeks.

"It's going to take us a long time to understand exactly what happened, where the Kahlvyn we knew and loved turned into the man who could have done the things we know now that he did," the king continued. He looked back into Zhenyfyr's eyes for a moment longer, then looked down at her older son.

"Rayjhis," he said, "this is going to be hard for you, the hardest thing you've ever done. Some people are going to say horrible things about your father. Others are going to insist those things couldn't have been true. And there are going to be a great many men who believe that because of the things your father may have done, *you* may somehow become a threat or a danger to the Crown someday."

Rayjhis' effort to control his expression wavered, and the king's free hand reached out to cup the back of his head gently once more.

"What's going to make it hurt worst of all," he told the boy, "is that so many of those horrible things are going to be true. If I could protect you from hearing them, I would. But I can't. You're young to be faced with all of this, but no one else can face it for you."

Rayjhis looked back at him mutely for several seconds, then nodded in tight-mouthed understanding.

"In just a few minutes," the king continued, "we're all going to appear before the Council, and before Bishop Maikel and Bishop Executor Zherald, as the Church's representatives. They're going to ask you—and your mother—" He looked up at Zhenyfyr briefly. "—a lot of questions. Some of them are going to make you angry. A lot of them are going to hurt and make you sad. All you can do is answer them as honestly as you can. And I want you to remember—I want all three of you to remember—that you are my cousins. Nothing anyone—not your father, not the Council—could do will ever change that. Do you understand that, Rayjhis?"

The boy nodded again, tightly, and Haarahld drew a deep breath.

"There's one more thing, Rayjhis," he said. "One thing that's going to hurt worse than anything else, I'm afraid."

Zhenyfyr Ahrmahk made a soft, inarticulate sound, and her hand twitched, as if she wanted to reach out, stop the king. But she didn't, and Haarahld continued, speaking slowly and carefully, his eyes on both her sons.

"People are going to tell you," he said, "that your grandfather killed your father."

Kahlvyn, the younger of the two, jerked, his eyes suddenly huge. Rayjhis only looked back at the king, but *his* eyes were suddenly darker and filled with even more pain, and Merlin's heart twisted in silent sympathy for the heartbroken boy who'd just become a duke.

"The reason they're going to say that," Haarahld went on, "is because it's true. He didn't want to, because he loved your father, just as I did, just as Cayleb did. But he had no choice. Sometimes even people we love do bad things, Rayjhis, Kahlvyn. Sometimes it's because there's a part of them we never knew was there—a secret part, that wants things they shouldn't have and tries to take them.

"Your father and I were raised as if we were brothers, not cousins. I loved him the same way Kahlvyn loves you, Rayjhis. I thought he loved me the same way. Some people will say I was wrong to believe that, because in the end, he wanted to steal the Crown from me, and he tried to murder Cayleb to do it. That was a terrible, terrible thing for him to do. But despite all of that, I wasn't wrong to love him, and I wasn't wrong to believe he loved me.

"People change, sometimes, boys. There are sicknesses that don't affect our bodies, but our hearts and our minds. I believe that's what happened to your father. He wanted the Crown so badly it became a sickness, one that twisted things deep down inside him. When he and I were your ages, when we were growing up together here in the Palace, before that . . . hunger for the Crown poisoned him inside, he did love me. And he did love Cayleb, I believe, just as your grandfather loved *him*.

"But when he did what he did, and when he refused to step back from the plans he'd set in motion, your grandfather had to make a choice. He had to decide whether he was going to do the things his oaths to the Crown and his own honor required, or whether he was going to join your father in doing the terrible things your father's ambition had driven him to do. And when your grandfather decided he couldn't support treason, no matter how much he loved the person committing it, your father ordered his personal guardsmen to seize him and hold him prisoner until after Cayleb and I, and quite a lot of other people, had all been killed."

Kahlvyn was shaking his head again and again, slowly, with a five-year-old's expression of pain and loss and confusion. Rayjhis was old enough to understand, however imperfectly, what the king was saying, and his chin quivered as the words sank home.

"Your grandfather couldn't let that happen," Haarahld said, his voice soft but unflinching. "Your grandfather is my First Councillor. He's one of my vassals. He was an officer in my Navy. And your grandfather understands what honor means. What oaths mean. And so, as much as he loved your father—and he *did* love him, Rayjhis, I swear that to you—when it came to open fighting, and your father's guards tried to seize or kill him, he honored those oaths and killed the man he loved for the crimes that man had committed."

Both boys were weeping now, and so was their mother. Haarahld pushed himself back up out of his throne and drew Zhenyfyr into his embrace. A moment later, two five-year-old arms locked around his left thigh, and he felt Kahlvyn pressing his face into his hip. Rayjhis stared up at him, his face working with desolation and loss, and the king reached one hand to him.

The boy who had just become a duke, and in the process learned how hideously expensive a title could be, looked at his monarch through a veil of tears. And then he took the offered hand in both of his, clutching at it as a drowning man might cling to a spar.

"There's a reason your grandfather wasn't here to tell you this himself," Haarahld said, looking down and speaking to Zhenyfyr as much as to her sons. "He wanted to be. As painful as he knew it would be, he wanted to tell you himself, Rayjhis. But I wouldn't let him. I'm your King, and you're one of my dukes now. There are obligations between kings and their nobles, and the fact that you're also part of my family makes those obligations stronger than ever. It was *my* duty to tell you. And I wanted you to hear it from me because I wanted you to know—to know in your heart, as well as your mind—that nothing that's happened, nothing your father could have done, will ever change the way I feel about you and your mother. God judges all men in the end. Kings are sometimes required to judge men, too, but a wise king judges any man or woman only on the basis of their own actions, not those of anyone else. I'm not always wise, however hard I try, however much I pray for guidance. But this much I promise you. When I look at you through the eyes of your cousin and remember your father, it will be the boy I loved, the good man I treasured, that I see in you. And when I look at you through the eyes of your King, it will be the boy you are and the man you become that I see, not the father who betrayed his trust."

Merlin watched Zhenyfyr's face, saw the pain and the loss mingled with acceptance of Haarahld's words. And as he saw those things, Merlin knew he'd been right; kings like Haarahld VII *were* what had made Charis a kingdom worth saving.

"Whatever your father may have done at the end of his life," Haarahld finished gently, "he and your mother—and your grandfather—taught you and Kahlvyn well, first. Remember those lessons, Rayjhis. Always remember them, and honor the man he was when he taught them to you, and you'll grow into a man worthy of anyone's love."

The boy stared up at him, weeping freely, now, and the king gave Zhenyfyr one more squeeze, then released her so he could bend over and gather the youthful, brokenhearted Duke of Tirian into a crushing hug of comfort.

He embraced Rayjhis for several seconds, then released him and straightened.

"And now, Your Grace," he said quietly to his cousin, "let us go and meet the Council."

The mighty organ's rich, powerful voice filled Tellesberg Cathedral with music. The organist's assistants pumped strongly, steadily, fueling its voice, and Merlin Athrawes—Lieutenant Athrawes, now, of the Royal Guard—stood at one corner of the Royal Box as it flowed over him.

The circular cathedral was awash in a polychromatic sea of light as the morning sunlight streamed in through the stained-glass clerestory which completely encircled it, and the magnificent mosaic of the Archangel Langhorne and Archangel Bédard looked out over the congregation with stern eyes. Merlin gazed back at it, meeting those majestic eyes, outwardly calm and composed despite his internal rage.

One day, he promised Pei Shan-wei's ghost . . . and theirs. *One day.*

He looked away from the mosaic, more to distract himself from the anger he dared not display than for any other reason. Even here, and even today—or perhaps *especially* today—Cayleb and Haarahld could not be left unguarded, and Merlin was scarcely the only armed and armored Guardsmen present. Lieutenant Falkhan and four of his Marines stood between the box and the central aisle, as well, and their eyes were just as hard, just as alert as Merlin's as they surveyed the huge crowd filling the cathedral's pews.

As always, the aristocracy and upperclass were heavily represented, glittering with jewels and bullion embroidery. At a guess there had to be at least two thousand people in the cathedral, enough to strain even its enormous capacity, and there was something odd about their mood.

Well, of course there is, he thought. *Given Tirian's death, and the wave of arrests Wave Thunder's launched, everybody in the entire Kingdom is probably feeling a little . . . anxious. And none of the nobility could possibly risk missing this service without absolutely ironclad proof that it was literally impossible for them to be here. But still . . .*

Word of the king's cousin's treason—and death—had spread like wildfire. Things like that simply didn't happen in Charis, and no one doubted for a moment that they wouldn't have happened now if someone from outside the kingdom hadn't made them. King Haarahld and his council might not be prepared to name names, but Charisians in general were far more aware of political realities than the subjects of most Safeholdian realms. That was probably inevitable, given the way international politics routinely affected the trade relationships upon which Charis' prosperity depended. Haarahld might have chosen not to point any fingers, but there was no question in his subjects' minds about who'd been responsible, and Merlin could almost physically taste their rage, like acid on his tongue.

Yet there was more to it than anger. There was . . . fear.

No, he thought. *"Fear" isn't the right word for it, either. That's part of it, but there's more to it. These people know there's more going on here than just the routine power games between rival princes, and they're turning to their Church for reassurance.*

A sudden shift in the organ music drew his mind away from its thoughts, and he turned his head as the cathedral's doors swung wide. An acolyte stepped through them, bearing the golden scepter of Langhorne upright before him on a gleaming, night-black staff of ironwood bound in rings of engraved silver. Two candle bearers flanked him, and two under-priests followed them, swinging censers that trailed fragrant strands of incense, like white, drifting ribbons in the light of the stained-glass windows.

Behind the under-priests came the massed choir in its green cassocks and white surplices. As the first rank passed through the open doors, the entire choir burst into song, and despite Merlin's hatred for all the Church of God Awaiting represented, the beauty of those superbly trained voices washed through him like the sea.

It took a long time for the choir to pass through the doors and wend its way to the choir lofts on either side of the archangels' mosaic. Behind them, following them through the storm of music, came Bishop Maikel, another dozen acolytes, and half that many priests and under-priests, followed by yet another scepter bearer and two more thurifers.

The bishop paced slowly down the central aisle, his vestments glittering with gems, his usual priest's cap replaced by the simple golden coronet of his ecclesiastic rank. Heads bent in reverent courtesy as he passed, and his expression was serene as he reached out, touching shoulders, heads, the hair of children, in quiet benediction as he walked past them.

That, Merlin knew, was scarcely standard practice on the part of "Mother Church"'s bishops, and one eyebrow arched slightly as he saw people daring to touch the bishop in return. He'd known Maikel Staynair was deeply respected here in Tellesberg; until this morning, he hadn't realized how deeply the bishop was loved.

The bishop entered the sanctuary and genuflected before the altar and its mosaic. Then he stood, turning to face the congregation while his assistants made their way to their own places. It was all as precisely choreographed as any formal ball, and the last acolyte found his position at the same instant the final note of the processional hymn died.

There was utter silence for a moment, and then Bishop Maikel's superbly trained voice rang out in the stillness.

"May Langhorne be with you, My Children."

"And with you, My Father," rumbled back at him.

"Let us pray for the intercession of Langhorne and the guidance of God upon our worship this day," Maikel said, and turned once more to face the altar and dropped to his knees.

"Our Father, who is in heaven," he began, "blessed be Your name. May the Day Awaited come. May the law proclaimed in Your name by the Blessed Langhorne be done on Safehold, as it is in Heaven. Give us—"

Merlin tuned it out. He had to.

Nimue Alban had been raised in the church. She had not, perhaps, been as observant as her parents and religious instructors might have desired, but she'd discovered here on Safehold that it had stuck. Now, as he listened to the utter sincerity in Maikel Staynair's voice, Merlin reminded himself the bishop had been taught from childhood to believe in the teachings of the Church of God Awaiting. It was hard to remember as the words which had meant so much to Nimue were perverted to Langhorne's purposes, and yet it was true. And how could Merlin condemn a manifestly good and caring man for honoring the belief system in which he had been raised?

None of which made it any easier to stand by and watch. Merlin was just as glad Langhorne had decided to build the Safeholdian year around a five-day "week" which no longer included Saturday or Sunday and established the middle day of those five as his church's "holy day," instead. Simply attending at all was hard enough without doing so on Sunday.

It had to be the greatest irony in the history of mankind, he thought. The last Christian in the entire universe was a machine. Legally, that was all even an autonomous PICA had ever been, although Merlin had long since ceased to apply that legal definition to himself. Still, it was a question he wished he could have discussed with someone else. Was he, in fact, the human being whose memories he possessed? Or was he simply an echo, a recording—an AI with delusions of grandeur? And did *he* have the immortal soul in which Nimue Alban had always believed? Or had Nimue taken that soul with her at the moment of her biological body's death?

He had no answer to any of those questions. For a time, he'd even wondered if a being of molycircs and alloy had any right to so much as ask God about them. Then he'd decided God must be able to understand what impelled his questions, just as he'd decided that the fact that the Church of God Awaiting was an enormous, obscene lie could never shut God's ears to the sincerity of the prayers rising about him even now.

But he did know he had another responsibility, over and beyond any duty to prepare the surviving human race to meet the Gbaba again one day. He was the last surviving Christian. In a sense, he was also the last surviving Muslim. The last Jew. The last Buddhist, Hindu, Shintoist. The library computer in Nimue's cave was the final repository for millennia of human religious thought, of human striving for divine inspiration, and Merlin Athrawes was the only being who knew it was there.

Someday, that repository would be opened, for that, too, was Merlin's responsibility. He was the protector and guardian of Christianity, Islam, Judaism, Buddhism, all of them, and whether he was merely a machine or not, it was one of his tasks to restore that rich, varied heritage to the humanity from whom it had been stolen.

He only hoped that when that day came, the human race's ability to believe would not have been destroyed by the realization of the lie which had enslaved it for almost a thousand years.

▼   ▼   ▼

It was a mass of thanksgiving, not a funeral mass.

Under the doctrine of the Church of God Awaiting, traitors were forbidden burial in holy ground. Or, at least, Merlin corrected himself, *proven* traitors were forbidden, which was probably just as well. From his own observations to date, at least a quarter of Safehold's aristocracy—and probably as much as half its vicars— would otherwise have been buried outside the cemetery wall. But the definition of traitor, unfortunately, by his own admission, applied to Kahlvyn Ahrmahk, once Duke of Tirian.

That had been hard on Haarahld and Cayleb. Despite everything, as Haarahld had told Zhenyfyr Ahrmahk and her sons, they'd loved their cousin. To be denied the right to bury him in the Church, to be forced to have his body interred in unconsecrated ground, had caused them both enormous pain. Yet they'd had no choice. Not even Bishop Maikel could change that for them, however much he might have longed to. But what he could do, he had. The mass thanked God for preserving the lives of the King, the Crown Prince, and the Kingdom's First Councillor, but the sermon which accompanied it focused on the fallibility of humans and the cost of sin to others.

"—and so, Shan-wei did not lead men into evil by appealing to their evil nature." Merlin gritted his teeth, his expression calm, as Maikel's voice reached out to every corner of the vast cathedral with a projection any trained actor would have envied. "The *Writ* tells us that not even Shan-wei herself was evil to begin with. Indeed, she was one of the brightest of all the archangels. And when she herself had fallen into evil, it was not man's evilness to which she appealed, but his goodness. She tempted him not with power over his fellows, not with dominion, but with the promise that all men everywhere would partake of the power of the archangels themselves. That their children, their wives, their fathers and mothers, their friends and neighbors, would all become as God's own angels if they simply reached out their hands to what she promised them.

"And so it is that even good men can unwittingly open the door to evil. I do not tell you, My Children, that there are no evil men. I do not tell you that those who turn to betrayal, to theft, to murder and treason, do so only because they are good men who have been led astray. I tell you only that all men *begin* as good men. What they are taught as children, what is expected of them as young men, is either the armor about that goodness or the flaw that allows evil in."

Merlin rested one hand on the scabbard of his katana and gazed straight ahead. The bishop's voice was compassionate, caring, and yet everything he'd said was straight out of the Church of God Awaiting's doctrine and theology. But then—

"Yet we must not forget our responsibility to teach them correctly. To discipline when discipline is required, yes, but also to use gentleness and love whenever we may. To be sure that that which we discipline is, indeed, a wrongful act. And to teach our children to know wrong from right themselves. To teach them to judge with clear eyes and unclouded hearts, fearlessly. To teach them it does not matter who *tells* them something is right or wrong, but whether or not it *is* right or wrong. To teach them the world is a vast and wondrous place, one which holds challenges, promises, and tasks fit to test the mettle of any mortal. To teach them that to truly know God, they must find Him in themselves and in the daily lives they live."

A stir went through the cathedral, more sensed than seen, and Merlin twitched at the unanticipated direction of Maikel's text. It was a small thing, in many ways, but not here, not in a sermon from the third-ranking prelate in all of Charis.

The Church of God Awaiting acknowledged a personal relationship between God and each of His children, but it did not encourage those children to *seek* that relationship. It was the function of the Church to teach and inform, to decree to the faithful what God's will for them was and define their "personal" relationship with Him for them. The *Writ* did not specifically proclaim the infallibility of the Church as it had that of the "archangels," but the Church's *doctrine* did extend that same infallibility to the vicars who were heirs to the archangels' authority.

Maikel had not openly assailed that doctrine, what he'd said was simply an argument that even the best teachers could fail. But that was also an argument that those teachers could be wrong. And so his words could be *interpreted* as an attack upon the infallibility of the Church which was every Safeholdian's teacher. Especially here in Charis, where independence of thought was openly encouraged.

"We strive to teach all our children those lessons," the bishop continued calmly, as if completely unaware he'd said anything at all out of the ordinary, "and sometimes, despite all our efforts, we fail. There *is* evil in the world, My Children. It can be found anywhere, among any men, and it waits patiently and its snares are cunning. Men—powerful or weak, nobly born or common, wealthy or poor—fall into those snares, and thus into sin, and it is our responsibility as God's people, to hate sin. To reject it, and cast it out when it arises among us. Yet it is also the responsibility of God's people to love one another. To hate the sin, but love the sinner, and not to feel guilt or self-hatred because we *do* love the sinner.

"It is meet and right that we should give thanks this day for the preservation of our King, our Crown Prince, and our First Councillor. It is meet and right for us to condemn and hate the crime of treason which threatened them, and through them, all of us. Yet even as we give thanks, let us remember that the evil which threatened them and was thwarted still claimed its victims from among us. Those who fell into temptation's grasp and lent themselves to these evil actions are as lost to us as Crown Prince Cayleb would have been had their plans succeeded. What they've done will forever mark their memory among those who loved them, and the price for their immortal souls will be higher than any of God's children should be called to pay. And so, I beseech you all, as you join me in our closing prayer of thanks, to pray also for the souls of *all* who have perished, and for the wounded hearts of those who loved them."

He gazed out over the cathedral's silent pews for perhaps ten seconds, then drew a deep breath and turned back to face the altar and the enormous faces of Langhorne and Bédard as he raised his hands in prayer.

Merlin looked at the bishop's sword-straight spine as the words of Maikel's prayer flowed over him. He hardly even heard the actual words, although a PICA's perfect memory would recall them later, if he wanted to. But the important words had already been said, and Merlin wondered if Haarahld and Cayleb had suspected where their bishop's sermon was headed.

.XVI.
Archbishop's Palace,
Tellesberg

P erhaps you would care to explain the text of your sermon, Bishop?" Bishop Executor Zherald Ahdymsyn inquired icily, turning from the window of his study to face his "guest."

"Forgive me, Your Eminence," Maikel Staynair said calmly, "but I'm not certain what part of the text you're referring to."

His eyes met the bishop executor's stony gaze levelly, and Ahdymsyn's fists clenched in the flowing sleeves of his cassock. He'd never been happy about Staynair's accession to the capital see. The man was too . . . too . . . too *Charisian*. But Haarahld's stubborn insistence on nominating the priest of his own choice to the empty throne in Tellesberg Cathedral had given the previous archbishop pause. He could have rejected the nomination. As far as Ahdymsyn was concerned, he damned well *ought* to have rejected it, and the bishop executor had said so at the time.

But the archbishop had flinched from the King of Charis' adamantine will. Archbishop Rojyr had been old and tired, already fading. He'd wanted only peace for his final years in the archbishopric, and perhaps he'd feared that if he pressed Haarahld too hard, it would create a situation which would force the Council of Vicars and the Inquisition to act.

And so, instead of dealing with it himself, he left it to fall onto my *plate,* Ahdymsyn thought bitterly.

"I have been told," he said to Maikel now, "that your sermon called into question the primacy and authority of Mother Church."

"Your Eminence," Maikel said, his expression one of total innocence, "I'm afraid I simply can't conceive of how anything I may have said might have called Mother Church's legitimate primacy and authority into question! What portion of my sermon could have led anyone to think for a moment that such was my intention?"

Ahdymsyn's fists clenched more tightly and his nostrils flared as he inhaled deeply.

"Did you, or did you not, say that it was the responsibility of any godly individual to decide *for himself* what constitutes right or wrong?"

"Of course I did, Your Eminence." Maikel's surprised tone couldn't have been improved upon by the most skilled of actors, Ahdymsyn thought. "Isn't that what both the *Writ* and *The Commentaries* teach us? That God and the archangels," his fingers touched his heart, then his lips, "expect all of us to be armored against evil? That it's our duty as godly men and women to be eternally upon our guard, and to recognize evil for ourselves when we see it?"

Ahdymsyn's teeth grated as his jaw muscles tightened. He wanted to reach out and slap the bland-faced Charisian in front of him. Both of them knew what Maikel had really been saying, yet the bishop's glib response was drawn directly from the Church's most central doctrines.

"I don't disagree with the statement that God and the archangels—" It was Ahdymsyn's turn to touch his heart and then his lips. "—expect us to recognize evil when we see it. But it's dangerous, both in a doctrinal sense and in terms of maintaining Mother Church's legitimate authority, both in this world and the next, to suggest her teachings may be in error."

"With all due respect, Your Eminence, but I said nothing of the sort," Maikel asserted firmly. "I spoke of a parent's responsibility to teach his children to recognize right from wrong. And to be wary, alert to the fact that others, less responsive to their obligations, or for their own evil and corrupt purposes, may attempt to mislead them. To couch false arguments in terms of acceptable beliefs. I never suggested that *Mother Church* might fall into the error of false teaching. If you believe I've done so, I beg you to instruct me as to where and how I might have set forth such an unforgivable accusation!"

Ahdymsyn glared at him for a moment, then wheeled back to the window while he fought to get his own expression—and temper—back under control.

"Whether or not you intended that . . . 'accusation,'" he said finally, "your words, as reported to me, could be interpreted in that sense by those inclined to set up their own judgment in opposition to that of Mother Church."

"I assure you, Your Eminence, that I've never had any intention of questioning Mother Church's legitimate authority. If any words of mine could be interpreted in that fashion, I do most humbly apologize."

Ahdymsyn continued to glower out the window. The sun was settling steadily into the west. The western horizon was a solid mass of crimson coals, reaching out to paint Howell Bay with an ominous tinge of red, and the bishop executor drew another deep breath.

"I am most displeased with the evident . . . carelessness of your choice of words, Bishop Maikel. You are, after Archbishop Erayk and myself, the senior bishop of the entire Kingdom of Charis. You have a responsibility, to God and to Mother Church, to remind the sheep of your flock where their duty and the safety of their souls lie. And it follows that you have an equal responsibility to avoid . . . inadvertently driving potential wedges between them and the safety afforded by Mother Church's authority."

He made himself speak calmly, reasonably, although he knew perfectly well that neither he nor Staynair had any doubt that the Charisian bishop had done precisely what Ahdymsyn had accused him of doing. But, by the same token, Staynair had covered himself. His interpretation of what he'd meant, however inaccurate and self-serving it might be, sounded both plausible and reasonable. Or would have, anywhere except here in Charis.

"I regret that you have reason to feel displeased with me, Your Eminence," Staynair said.

"I'm sure you do." Ahdymsyn smiled out the window without any humor at all.

Technically, he had the authority to remove Staynair temporarily from his see. Without Archbishop Erayk's agreement, he couldn't remove the Charisian permanently, however, and he wasn't at all certain the Archbishop *would* support him.

And that's partly your own fault, Zherald, he told himself coldly. *You've known for years how stubborn these Charisians are, and yet you've persistently assured the Archbishop that the situation was under control. You've downplayed the reports of people like Hektor and Nahrmahn as exaggerations—because they* are *exaggerated, wildly, damn it!—for too long. If you simply report Staynair's words now, after all that, and accuse him on that basis of seeking to undermine the Church's authority, you'll sound as if you're starting to exaggerate, as well. Without seeing the man's face, listening to his tone, sensing the mood of his parishioners, everything he's said will sound completely reasonable. And any allegations you may lay against him will sound hysterical and alarmist.*

The bishop executor's smile turned into a glare as he gazed at the smoldering horizon and wondered if that crimson pile of cloudy embers was an omen of some sort. Staynair was worrisome, of course, but that was at least partly because of the composition of the Charisian priesthood in general.

One huge reason reason Staynair's elevation to the Tellesberg see stuck in Ahdymsyn's craw was that it flew in the face of the Church's normal policy of moving and assigning senior clergy, especially bishops and auxiliary bishops, so that they served outside the kingdoms or provinces of their birth. It was never a good idea, in Ahdymsyn's opinion, to allow the leadership of the local Church to develop a feeling of loyalty to the secular realm it served. As far as he was concerned, that was particularly true in lands such as Charis, which were so far from the Temple and Zion.

But convincing members of the priesthood to move to such distant and isolated hinterlands was always difficult. Those with patrons of their own could always find some way to weasel out of it. While Charis' wealth offered a certain level of enticement, the truth was that assignment here was regarded as exile. At the best, it would be a severe blow to the potential career of anyone sent here.

Ahdymsyn's own case was atypical. He'd amply demonstrated his reliability, but he lacked that necessary patronage at the very highest level to ever become an archbishop in his own right. Since that was the case, Charis had suited him just fine, when it was offered. It was far enough from the Temple and Zion to give him a degree of independence and autonomy, plus manifold opportunities for acquiring personal wealth.

But better than nine out of every ten members of the Church's clergy here in Charis were Charisian-born, just like Staynair. The numbers were higher in the lower ranks of the priesthood, and among the various monastic orders, of course. But that was the very thing which made admitting a Charisian to the third-highest church office in the entire kingdom so . . . worrisome. Those lower-ranking priests and under-priests were undoubtedly listening to anything "their" bishop said.

"I'll accept your assurance that you didn't intentionally assail Mother Church's authority and right to declare error," he said finally, turning back to face Staynair after several silent moments. "That doesn't abate my displeasure, however. Nor, I feel sure, would the Council of Vicars or the Inquisition be pleased by the potential for error contained in your . . . unfortunately chosen words. You aren't some simple parish priest. You're a bishop, one of Mother Church's bishops, and as such you will be rightly held to a higher standard. Is that understood, · Bishop Maikel?"

"It is, of course, Your Eminence," Staynair said, bowing his head very slightly.

"These are perilous times," Ahdymsyn continued levelly. "Danger threatens Charis on many levels, as, indeed, the treason of the King's own cousin clearly illustrates. Do not increase that peril."

"I'll take your warning to heart, Your Eminence," Staynair said with another slight bow.

"See that you do," Ahdymsyn said. "Be very *careful* to see that you do. Neither my patience, nor the Archbishop's, nor the Office of Inquisition's, is without limit. If your failure in your duties leads to consequences for others, then the weight of those consequences will be upon your own immortal soul, and Mother Church will demand an accounting of you."

Staynair said nothing, but neither did he flinch, and there was no give in his steady eyes. Well, he'd been warned. And whatever else the man might be, he wasn't a fool. That would have to be enough . . . for now, at least.

"You may go," Ahdymsyn said coldly, and extended his ring for Staynair to kiss.

"Thank you, Your Eminence," the Bishop of Tellesberg murmured as he brushed his lips lightly across the golden scepter inlaid into the blood-red ruby of the ring. "I assure you that I'll remember everything you've said to me today."

SEPTEMBER,
YEAR OF GOD 890

✦

A rchbishop Erayk Dynnys smiled happily as he bade Madame Ahnzhelyk Phonda a heartfelt good night.

"As always, it's been a delightful evening, Ahnzhelyk," he said, patting her delicate, perfumed fingers between both of his own well manicured hands.

"You're always too kind, Your Eminence," Madame Ahnzhelyk said with the gracious smile which had been so much a part of her success during her own working days. "I'm afraid you flatter us more than we really deserve."

"Nonsense. Nonsense!" Dynnys said firmly. "We've known one another far too long for me to stand on ceremony or worry about polite nothings with you and your charming ladies."

"In that case, thank you, Your Eminence." Madame Ahnzhelyk bent her head in a small bow. "We're always delighted to see you. Especially now. We weren't certain we'd have the chance to entertain you again before your departure for Charis."

"*Not* something I'm looking forward to, to be honest," Dynnys sighed with a small grimace. "Of course, I can't delay much longer. In fact, I should already have left. The first snows have fallen in the mountains, according to the semaphore's reports. It won't be much longer before Hsing-wu's Passage starts to freeze, and I'm afraid the voyage itself won't be very much fun at this time of year, even after we clear the Passage."

"I know, Your Eminence. Still, they say summer in Tellesberg is much more pleasant than winter here in Zion, so at least you have something nice to look forward to at journey's end."

"Well, *that's* certainly accurate enough," Dynnys agreed with a chuckle. "In fact, I sometimes wish the archangels hadn't been quite so immune to the effects of waist-deep snow when they chose the Temple's site. I love Zion's climate in the *summer*, you understand, but winter is something else again entirely. Even, alas, despite your own charming company."

It was Madame Ahnzhelyk's turn to chuckle.

"In that case, Your Eminence, and in case I don't see you again before you leave, allow me to wish you a comfortable voyage and a safe return to us."

"From your lips to the archangels' ears." Dynnys touched his heart and then his lips, smiling into her eyes, and she rose on tiptoe to kiss him chastely on the cheek.

It was, he reflected through a pleasant glow of memory, the only chaste thing which had happened to him since entering her door, several hours before.

Madame Ahnzhelyk's door was one of the more discreet portals in all of Zion. While the *Holy Writ* recognized that human beings were fallible, and that not all of them would seek the approval of Mother Church's clergy upon their . . . relationships, it was quite strict on the subjects of fornication and infidelity. Which complicated Erayk Dynnys' life somewhat, since both the *Writ* and the Church's own regulations also required that any churchman who aspired to the ranks of the episcopate must have married. How else could he understand the physical and emotional needs of the wedded believers for whose spiritual well-being he was responsible?

Dynnys himself had, of course, met that requirement, although he very seldom saw his wife. Adorai Dynnys was neither surprised nor particularly unhappy about that. She'd been only twelve when the Dynnys and Laynohr families arranged the marriage, and she'd been raised to understand as well as Dynnys did how such matters were handled among the Church's dynasties. Besides, she hated Zion's world of social activity almost as much as she disliked the complex maneuvering of the Temple's internal factions. She lived quite happily on one of Dynnys' estates, raising horses, chickens, draft dragons, and the two sons she had dutifully borne for him in the early years of their marriage.

That left Dynnys, like many of his peers, at loose ends for feminine companionship. Fortunately for him, Madame Ahnzhelyk and her unfailingly lovely and exquisitely trained young ladies were available to fill the void. Always, of course, with the utmost discretion.

"Ah, well, Ahnzhelyk!" he sighed now, as she escorted him the last few feet to the door and the dignified porter opened it at their approach. "I'm afraid I truly do have to go. Not," he added with a shudder which wasn't entirely feigned as he gazed out the open door at a fall night's cold, drizzling rain, "without more regrets than you can possibly imagine."

"Flatterer!" Madame Ahnzhelyk patted him on the shoulder with a peal of laughter. "Of course, if the weather is *too* bad, you could always stay the evening, Your Eminence."

"'Get you behind me, Shan-wei!'" Dynnys quoted with an answering chuckle, then shook his head. "Seriously," he continued, watching the steamy plumes of his coachmen's and horses' breath rise into the rainy night under his coach's lamps as they awaited him at the curb, "I'd be most tempted to take up your gracious offer. Unfortunately, there are a great many matters which require attention before I can depart for Charis, and I have several meetings scheduled early in the morning. But for that, I feel sure, you could easily convince me."

"In that case, Your Eminence, I accept my defeat." Madame Ahnzhelyk gave his hand another squeeze, then released it and watched him step out the front door.

No one, least of all Dynnys, was entirely certain later exactly what happened next. The porter bowed the archbishop through the door, accepting the heavy golden weight of a coin with a murmur of thanks. From his perch high on the carriage's box, Dynnys' senior coachman watched his employer's approach with undisguised gratitude. However pleasant the archbishop's visit might have been for *him*, the long wait had been cold, wet misery for the driver, his assistant, and the blanketed horses. The assistant coachman holding the horses' heads felt much the same thing, plus a twinge of envy for the way his seated senior partner's voluminous cloak formed a well-draped tent about him. Madame Ahnzhelyk's footman and lantern boy went scurrying ahead of the archbishop, lighting his way and ready to open the coach door for him. And Dynnys himself settled his thick, fur-lined cloak and started down the broad, smooth steps with his eyes half-squinted against the blowing rain.

That was when his feet went out from under him.

Literally.

Dynnys had never experienced anything quite like the sudden tugging, almost *snatching* sensation. It was as if a hand had reached out, grasped his right ankle, and pulled on it powerfully. It staggered him, and he was not, unfortunately, a particularly athletic man.

The archbishop flailed his arms with a most un-archbishop-like squawk of astonishment as he fought for balance. But that tugging sensation didn't let go, and he squawked again—louder—as his feet went out from under him and he tobogganed down the steps.

Had he considered it, he might have found it odd that he went down *feet*-first, instead of headfirst. Which, in turn, might have caused him to think rather harder about that peculiar pulling sensation. At the moment, however, he was too busy falling to ponder such matters as they, perhaps, deserved, and he cried out as he hit the cobbled walkway at the bottom of the tall steps. He slammed across it until the avenue's raised, granite-slab curb abruptly stopped him and sent a bolt of anguish ripping through his right leg and shoulder.

Madame Ahnzhelyk's horrified servants raced after him, and the assistant coachman abandoned his place at the horses' heads to dash towards him. The archbishop shook his head groggily, scraped and bleeding and more than half-stunned by the ugly, slithering tumble. Then he tried to stand up, and cried out again, more loudly, as the injudicious attempt sent waves of pain washing through him.

"Don't move, Your Eminence!" the assistant coachman said urgently, going to his knees beside the prelate. "You've broken at least one leg, sir!"

The young man had already ripped off his own cloak. Now he spread it over his fallen patron and looked at Madame Ahnzhelyk's footman.

"Fetch a healer!" he snapped. "His Eminence is going to need a bonesetter, at least!"

The white-faced servant gave a single, jerky nod and went dashing off into

202 / DAVID WEBER

the night even as Madame Ahnzhelyk came scurrying down the steps. Her face
was twisted with genuine concern and dismay as she held a filmy evening cloak
over her elaborately coiffured hair and knelt beside the coachman in her flow-
ingly draped silk gown.

"Don't move, Erayk!" she said, not realizing his servant had already given
him the same command. She let one hand rest lightly on his chest. "I can't *believe*
this happened! I'll never forgive myself for it! Never!"

"Not . . . not your fault," Dynnys told her through gritted teeth, touched by
her manifestly sincere worry despite his own pain. "Slipped. Must have been the
rain."

"Oh, your poor leg!" she said, staring at the obviously badly broken limb.

"I sent for a bonesetter, My Lady," the assistant coachman told her, and she
nodded jerkily.

"Good. That's good." She looked up over her shoulder at her porter, who
had followed her down the steps and now stood at her shoulder, wringing his
hands. "Styvyn," she said sharply, "don't stand there like a ninny! Get back in the
house. I want blankets out here at once! And a pillow for the Archbishop's head.
Now, go!"

"Yes, ma'am!" the porter said, and turned to flee back into her establishment
in obedience to her commands.

▼　　▼　　▼

Merlin Athrawes stood atop the roof of an elegant townhouse across the street
from Madame Ahnzhelyk's. He'd been waiting there for the better part of three
hours, and he'd come to the firm opinion that he spent entirely too much time
loitering on rooftops in the rain. Since he seemed to have acquired the habit,
however, he was just as glad that at least a PICA didn't have to feel the cold and
wet if it didn't want to.

He was also glad no one—and no*thing*—appeared to have noticed him so far.
He'd hoped it would work that way, yet he'd had significant reservations about this
entire operation. Unfortunately, he'd also come to the conclusion it was necessary.

His recon skimmer hovered discreetly out of sight, well to the north of the
City of Zion, hiding under every stealth system it possessed while its passive sensors watched over the emission signatures Nimue Alban and Owl had detected in
their first sweep of the Temple and its environs. The fact that those emission signatures existed still made Merlin extremely uneasy, but he'd come to the conclusion that Nimue's initial hypothesis—that most of the signatures his skimmer was
reading were those of the Temple's still-functioning environmental systems—
had been correct. Certainly the Temple was "mystically" warm and inviting, despite the increasingly unpleasant weather outside it. Given the local winter
climate, that particular "miracle" had to be one of the archangels' more welcome
dispensations, he reflected.

There were still a few other, more powerful signatures Merlin couldn't account for, though, and a part of him wanted to get even closer, take a better look. But prudence suggested otherwise. Whatever they were, they were buried beneath the Temple itself, and while he devoutly hoped they were merely more of the Temple's heating and cooling systems, there was simply no way to tell that. And until he had at least some clue about exactly what those emissions represented—or until he had absolutely no other choice—he wasn't prepared to push for additional information. There were always those orbiting kinetic bombardment platforms to think about. Poking his nose, even by electronic proxy, where any computer controlling the platforms might decide it didn't belong could have unfortunate consequences.

It was frustrating, to say the very least. If there was one organization he needed to keep close tabs on, it was the Council of Vicars. But unless he'd been prepared to deploy SNARCs—or, at least, their parasites—dangerously close to those unidentified emissions signatures, there was no way to snoop upon the Council's meetings.

What made that especially worrisome was that even from his less risky coverage of the more junior archbishops and bishops living in Zion, it was clear the Council was growing increasingly restive about Charis. So far, it seemed, that restiveness had yet to attain critical dimensions, but Merlin was coming to the conclusion that he'd rather badly underestimated its underlying strength in the first place. He'd gradually become aware that discussion of Charis cropped up much too often in his SNARCs' coverage for his peace of mind. In private conversation between the Church's senior prelates, as well as in more official settings, and there was a hard edge to many of the discussions he'd overheard.

In point of fact, the Church hierarchy's apparent level of concern was out of all proportion to the size and population of the kingdom. He was beginning to suspect the Church was better aware than he'd originally believed of the potentialities he himself had sensed in Charis, and Charis' many enemies, led by Prince Hektor and Prince Nahrmahn, were fanning the fire as energetically as they dared.

The fact that the Church's suspicions of Charis seemed to be at least as much emotional as reasoned played into Hektor's and Nahrmahn's hands. They had to exercise some caution—their own distance from the Temple left their own orthodoxy open to a certain degree of automatic suspicion of its own, especially in the eyes of the Office of the Inquisition—but neither Hektor's Corisande nor Nahrmahn's Emerald had produced anything like Charis' innovativeness. Their agents in the Temple were carefully emphasizing that fact as they spread exaggerated tales of King Haarahld's willingness to "skirt the fringes of the Proscriptions of Jwo-jeng," coupled with observations about Haarahld's willingness to "overturn the existing social order," all backed by sizable cash donations.

Somewhat more sophisticated (or at least discreet) techniques might be required to sway the Vicars themselves, but the more junior ranks of the episcopate and, perhaps even more importantly, the priests and under-priests who provided the Council's staff functions—and who were thus ideally positioned to shape the way those tales were presented to their superiors—responded quite well to simple bribery. So did more than one of the Council's own members, apparently, and Hektor and Tohmas' efforts were slowly but steadily gaining ground.

Archbishop Erayk was as aware of that as anyone. It had been apparent from his discussions with his fellows and the instructions he'd been issuing to Father Mahtaio that he'd recognized he would be expected to look very closely at the situation in Tellesberg during his annual pastoral visit. The Council of Vicars obviously wanted to hear his personal assurance either that the rumors it was hearing were wildly overblown, or that the Archbishop of Charis had taken the necessary steps to correct any problems.

That, unfortunately, couldn't be permitted, because just this once, Haarahld's enemies were *under*estimating exactly what one Merlin Athrawes had in mind for the Kingdom of Charis. He had no intention of actually violating the Proscriptions—not yet—but that distinction might well be lost upon an archbishop intent on satisfying the demands of his ecclesiastical superiors.

Which was why Merlin came to be standing on this miserable, rainswept roof on a bone-chilling autumn night.

Fortunately, Zion was a very large city, and Madame Ahnzhelyk's establishment was in an expensive and exclusive section of it, almost five miles from the Temple proper. That gave him a certain comfort zone where unidentified energy signatures were concerned, as long as he was discreet, and he'd discovered he could be very, very discreet when the need arose.

Now he listened via the remote riding in a fold of Dynnys' cloak and nodded with satisfaction. He had nothing personally against Dynnys—yet, at least—and he felt pleased satisfaction as he eavesdropped on Ahnzhelyk and Dynnys' assistant coachman. The archbishop's injuries were undoubtedly painful, he reflected as he packed away the handheld tractor unit he'd used on Dynnys' feet, but it didn't sound as if they were life-threatening. That was good. Merlin didn't want to get into the habit of casually killing people he didn't *have* to kill, and overall, he preferred Dynnys to a potentially more doctrinaire and . . . rigorous replacement.

On the other hand, it was obvious the archbishop's right leg, at least, was badly broken. Probably his right shoulder, as well, judging by what Merlin's light-gathering systems could see from here and what he could overhear. Dynnys would be a long time recovering. By the time he did, Hsing-wu's Passage would certainly be frozen over for the winter, and Merlin rather doubted anyone in the Temple would expect the archbishop to make the arduous winter overland journey to Clahnyr and cross the Cauldron, especially so soon after such a nasty accident and injury. Which ought to delay Dynnys' pastoral visit for at least another five or six Safeholdian months.

Long enough for me to get things up and running and erase my own fingerprints, anyway . . . I hope, he reflected. *At any rate, it's the best I can do for right now. And I need to be getting back "home."*

He chuckled inside at the thought. It was broad daylight in Charis at the moment. He'd told Haarahld and Cayleb (truthfully enough) that he needed some time in privacy to deal with certain aspects of his visions. The king had agreed to allow him to seek solitude in the mountains near Tellesberg while he did so, although it was obvious Haarahld was none too happy about the thought of allowing Merlin out on his own and unprotected. Cayleb, on the other hand, had merely looked thoughtful—*extremely* thoughtful—when Merlin made his request, and Merlin wondered exactly what was going on in the crown prince's mind.

Whatever it was, the sooner Merlin got home to deal with it—or to divert the prince's suspicions, as the case might be—the better.

He climbed very quietly down from his rooftop perch, arranged his poncho about himself, pulled up its hood, and strode briskly away. Owl would be waiting to collect him with the skimmer's tractors, but not until he'd put at least ten more miles between himself and the Temple. At least, he reflected sardonically, he'd have the city streets pretty much to himself on a night like this.

.II.
Royal Palace,
Tellesberg

Crown Prince Cayleb raised his hand to knock courteously, then paused just outside the half-open chamber door. One eyebrow rose as he listened to the quiet, crisp clicking sound. It came again, then ceased, then began yet again.

The prince frowned, wondering what fresh novelty he was about to encounter, then shrugged and continued his interrupted knock on the door frame.

"Come in, Your Highness," an amused voice invited an instant before his knuckles actually contacted the wood, and Cayleb shook his head with a crooked grin and pushed the door fully open. He stepped through it into Merlin Athrawes' comfortable, sunlit sitting room and paused just inside the threshold.

In keeping with his official position as Cayleb's personal bodyguard, the *seijin* had been moved from Marytha's Tower to quarters in the royal family's section of the palace. In fact, they were quite near Cayleb's own, with a view of the harbor that was almost as good as the one from the prince's bedchamber, although they were considerably more modest.

The *seijin* had risen respectfully from his chair behind a desk at Cayleb's entry. Now he stood there, clad in the kraken-badged livery of the House of Ahrmahk, head cocked, with a quizzical smile of his own. His sword and the matching shortsword were racked on the wall behind him, and Cayleb smiled slightly as he glanced at them. The longer of the two swords was unlike anything anyone in Charis had ever seen before. It was also, apparently, unlike anything anyone had ever seen in Harchong, judging from Master Domnek's reaction, at least. The arms master was obviously being eaten alive with curiosity about the *seijin* and his weapons, but his Harchongese pride refused to let him ask the questions burning within him.

The crown prince shook his head and looked away from the sword rack, and one of his eyebrows quirked. There was a peculiar device on Merlin's desk—a rectangular wooden frame, about two feet long and six inches tall. Twenty-one vertical rods connected the upper and lower sides of the frame, and there were six flattened beads on each rod, five below and one above a wooden dividing strip near the outer frame's upper side. The beads on the rods were arranged to slide up and down, and their present configuration formed an obviously deliberate—if incomprehensible—pattern.

There were also several sheets of paper on the desk, covered with the *seijin's* strong, clear handwriting, but also with columns of some sort of symbols or characters Cayleb had never seen before.

"Oh, sit down, Merlin!" the prince said, crossing the chamber to him. The *seijin* only smiled more quizzically still, then waited until Cayleb had seated himself in the chair in front of the desk before sitting once more behind it. Cayleb shook his head and snorted.

"I thought we were supposed to be leaving for Helen this afternoon?" he said.

"We are, Your Highness," Merlin agreed. "*Catamount*'s been delayed, though. The page taking you a copy of his note probably passed you on your way here. We won't be leaving for at least another hour or so, so I thought I'd spend the time jotting down a few notes."

"Is that what those are?" Cayleb nodded to the neatly inscribed sheets of paper, and Merlin nodded. "What sort of notes?"

"Most of them are for High Admiral Lock Island—today, at least," Merlin replied. "I've got some I've already worked up for Doctor Mahklyn and Master Howsmyn. I was just completing some calculations on manpower and tonnages—Hektor's and Nahrmahn's, not your father's—for the High Admiral."

"Calculations?" Cayleb leaned back in his chair, then gestured at the rectangular frame on the desk. "Since you knew it was me outside the door without even looking, you must know I was eavesdropping shamelessly. I imagine that clicking sound I heard came from this thing?"

"Indeed it did, Your Highness," Merlin said gravely, his peculiar sapphire eyes glinting with amusement while the notes of distant birdsong floated through the open window.

"Yet another of your little surprises, I suppose. Just what does this one do, if I might ask?"

"It's called an 'abacus,' Your Highness," Merlin replied. "It's a device for doing mathematical calculations."

"It's what?" Cayleb blinked.

"It's a device for doing mathematical calculations," Merlin repeated.

"How does it work?" Cayleb could hardly believe he'd asked that question, and he felt a momentary stab of panic as he realized he'd laid himself open to the sort of "explanation" Frahnklyn Tohmys, his tutor, had always delighted in administering.

"Actually," Merlin said with a wicked smile, "it's quite simple." Cayleb shuddered at the dreaded "simple" word, but the *seijin* continued mercilessly. "Each vertical rods represents one integer, Your Highness. Each bead in this group here, above the divider, represents the value of five when lowered. Each bead in this group here, *below* the divider, represents a value of one when it's *raised*. At the moment"—he waved a finger at the device's first four rods—"the setting of the beads represents the number seven thousand four hundred and thirteen."

Cayleb had opened his mouth to disavow any interest in further explanation, but he paused, disavowal unspoken. He had no idea what an "integer" was, but he'd spent more than enough time working his laborious way through the endless numbers contained in the sort of report Merlin had been preparing for Admiral Lock Island. Surely it wasn't possible to represent a number that high with only four rods and twenty-four beads!

"You can keep track of numbers that high on something that size?" he asked almost incredulously.

"Or much higher," Merlin assured him. "It takes practice, but after you've learned to do it, it's quick and simple."

Cayleb only looked at him for several seconds, then reached out and drew one of the sheets of notes across in front of him. He glanced down the page, and made a soft sound in the back of his throat as he reached one of the columns of peculiar symbols. From the context, it was obvious that they represented the results of some of the calculations Merlin had been making, but they made absolutely no sense to Cayleb.

"Admittedly, I've never been the most enthusiastic scholar my family ever produced," he said with masterful understatement, looking up at Merlin. "Still, it occurs to me that I've never seen anything like this." He tapped the column with a fingertip.

"It's simply another way of writing numbers, Your Highness." Merlin's tone was almost casual, yet Cayleb had the definite impression that there was something watchful and focused behind those odd sapphire eyes, almost as if the *seijin* had deliberately arranged this moment of explanation.

It was a feeling the prince had had before.

"Another way of writing numbers," he repeated, and chuckled. "All right, I'll grant you that. Somehow, though, I don't think 'simply' really enters into it," he observed, and in that moment, although he didn't realize it himself, he looked remarkably like his father.

"Well," Merlin said, sliding a blank sheet of paper across to Cayleb and handing him the pen with which he'd been writing, "why don't you write down the number set here on the abacus? Seven thousand four hundred and thirteen," he reminded helpfully.

Cayleb looked at him for a moment, then took the pen, dipped it in the desk's inkwell, and began scribbling down the number. When he'd finished, he turned the sheet around and showed it to Merlin.

"There," he said just a bit suspiciously, tapping the number with the end of the wooden pen holder.

Merlin glanced at it, then took the pen back and jotted four of his incomprehensible symbols under it. Then he turned the sheet back around to Cayleb.

The prince looked down at it. There was the number he'd written—"MMMMMMMCDXIII"; and under it were Merlin's odd symbols—"7,413."

"It's the same number," Merlin told him.

"You're joking," Cayleb said slowly.

"No, I'm not." Merlin leaned back in his chair.

"That's ridiculous!" Cayleb protested.

"Not ridiculous, Your Highness," Merlin disagreed. "Only different . . . and simpler. You see, each of these symbols represents a specific value from one to ten, and each column—" He tapped the symbol "3" with the end of the pen holder, then tapped the first of the rods on his "abacus," as well. "—represents what you might think of as a holding space for the symbol. The wise woman who taught them to me many years ago called them 'Arabic numerals,' which I suppose is as good a name as any for them. There are only ten symbols, including one which represents nothing at all, called 'zero,' "—he drew another symbol, which looked for all the world like the letter "O," on the sheet of paper—"but I can write any number you can think of using them."

Cayleb stared at him. The prince often joked about his own aversion to "book learning," but he was far from stupid, and he was also the crown prince of his world's leading maritime power. Recordkeeping and accounting were critical to Charis' traders and shippers, and they were also functions which ate up the efforts of huge numbers of clerks with a voracious appetite. It didn't require a genius to recognize the huge advantages of the system Merlin was describing, assuming it actually worked.

"All right," the prince challenged, taking back the pen briefly. "If you can write 'any number' using these numerals of yours, write *this* one."

The steel nib of the pen scratched across the paper as he wrote "MMMMM-MMMMMMMMMMMMMMMDCCII." Then he passed both of them back across to the *seijin.*

Merlin looked it over for a moment, then shrugged. The pen scratched again, and Cayleb's eyes narrowed as Merlin wrote simply "19,702."

"There you are, Your Highness," he said.

Cayleb stared down at the sheet of paper for several long, silent seconds, then looked back up at Merlin.

"Who are you, really?" he asked softly. "*What* are you?"

"Your Highness?" Merlin's eyebrows rose, and Cayleb shook his head.

"Don't play with me, Merlin," he said, his voice still soft, his eyes level. "I believe you mean me, my father, and my kingdom well. But even though I may still be young, I'm not a child any longer, either. I'll believe you're a *seijin*, but you're more than that, too, aren't you?"

"Why do you say that, Your Highness?" Merlin countered, but his own voice was level, taking Cayleb's question seriously.

"The legends and ballads say *seijin* may be teachers, as well as warriors," the prince replied, "but none of the tales about them mention anything like this." He tapped the sheet of paper between them, then gestured at the "abacus" lying to one side. "And," he looked very steadily at the other man, "I've never heard any tale about even a *seijin* who could cross an entire unfamiliar city through the middle of the winter's worst thunderstorm as quickly as you did."

"As I told your father, Your Highness, I was alerted by my vision. You were there at the time I experienced it, yourself."

"Yes, I was," Cayleb agreed. "And you seemed . . . distracted enough by it that I followed you to your rooms to be certain you'd reached them safely. I got there only seconds behind you, and I thought I heard something from inside your chamber. So I knocked. There was no answer, so I knocked again, then opened the door, but you'd already disappeared. The only way you could have done that was to go out the window, Merlin. I noticed that you never actually specifically answered Father's question when he asked you how you'd done it, but I saw no rope ladder you might have climbed down, and the sheets were all still on your bed."

"I see." Merlin leaned back in his chair, gazing steadily at the prince, then shrugged. "I told you—and your father—I possess some of the powers the tales say *seijin* possess, and I do. I also possess some the tales don't mention. Some which must be kept secret. I think—hope—I've demonstrated that I do, indeed, mean you and Charis well. That I'll serve you—and Charis—in any way I can. And someday, perhaps, I'll be able to tell you more about those powers and abilities I must keep secret for now. I promised your father the truth, and I've never lied, although as you've obviously noticed, that isn't necessarily the same thing as telling *all* the truth. I'm not free to tell all the truth, however. I regret that, but I can't change it. So I suppose the question is whether or not you can accept my service with that limitation."

Cayleb looked back at him for several seconds, then inhaled deeply.

"You've been expecting this conversation, haven't you?" he asked.

"Or one like it," Merlin agreed. "Although, to be honest, I'd expected to have it with your father, or possibly Bishop Maikel, first."

"Father is more confident of his ability to judge men's hearts and intentions than I am." Cayleb shrugged slightly. "He's been doing it a lot longer than I have.

I think some of the same questions have occurred to him, and he's simply chosen not to ask."

"And why should he have made that choice?"

"I'm not sure," Cayleb admitted. "But I think perhaps it's because he truly believes—as I do—that you mean Charis well, and because he's already guessed there are questions you can't, or won't, answer. He knows how desperately we need any advantage we can find, and not just against Hektor and Nahrmahn, and he's unwilling to risk losing your services by pressing the point."

"And Bishop Maikel?"

"Much the same, I think." Cayleb shook his head. "I'm never really certain what Maikel thinks, in a lot of ways. He's a Charisian, and he loves this Kingdom. He also loves my father and our family. And even though he's never expressly said it to me, I think he actually fears the Temple. He—"

Cayleb paused a moment, then shook his head.

"Let's simply say he's well aware of the way our enemies could use the Temple and the Church against us, and why. Like Father, he knows the trap we're in, and if he says he senses no evil in you, then he doesn't. Which isn't exactly the same thing as saying he has no reservations at all."

"And do *you* agree with your father?"

"Yes . . . to a point." Cayleb looked Merlin in the eye. "But I will require one answer from you, *Seijin* Merlin. This"—he gestured at the sheet of paper and the "abacus" once again—"goes beyond visions and attempted assassinations. The 'services' you're offering now will change Charis forever, and eventually, they're going to spread beyond Charis and change the entire world. I suspect there are going to be even more changes than I can imagine at this moment, changes some will fear and hate. Changes some may even argue violate the Proscriptions of Jwo-jeng, with all the dangers that would entail. I think the thunderstorm you disappeared into was no more than a spring shower beside the typhoon following on your heels. So the one question I have, the one answer I require, is why? You once said many of our enemies 'serve darkness,' whether they realize it or not. But which do *you* serve, Merlin? Darkness or light?"

"Light, Your Highness," Merlin said promptly, unflinchingly, looking straight into Cayleb's eyes. "There's enough darkness in the world already," the *seijin* continued, "and more is gathering. Charis stands in its way, and so I stand with Charis. And I tell you this, Cayleb Ahrmahk, Crown Prince of Charis—I will die before I permit darkness to triumph, whatever its source."

Cayleb looked deep into those level sapphire eyes for at least thirty measured seconds, and then, slowly, he nodded.

"That's enough for me," he said simply, and tapped the piece of paper once more.

"Now," he invited, "try explaining these 'numerals' of yours to me again, if you would."

King's Harbor,
Helen Island

Helen Island lay a hundred and fourteen miles northeast of Tellesberg in South Howell Bay. It was shaped roughly like a triangle with a bite taken out of its eastern side and measured about seventy-five miles in its longest dimension. That wasn't particularly huge for a planet like Safehold, where islands were an everyday fact of life, but this island's craggy mountains rose to a spectacular height above sea level. More to the point, perhaps, Helen Island was a vital part of the ancestral Ahrmahk lands, and it had been heavily fortified for centuries.

Howell Bay had been the key to the evolution of the Kingdom of Charis. Waterborne transportation was faster, easier, and far cheaper than trying to haul the same goods and materials overland, and Howell Bay had provided Charis the equivalent of a broad, straight highway at its heart. Swift galleys and sailing vessels had tied the growing power of the kingdom together and provided the impetus and seagoing mind-set for the oceanic expansion of trade which had followed. And Howell Bay had been dominated by three islands—Sand Shoal, Helen, and Big Tirian. The fact that the House of Ahrmahk had managed to secure control of all three of them had a great deal to do with the fact that it had also eventually secured the Charisian throne.

That had been centuries ago, but the Kingdom of Charis had maintained the fortifications on all three islands, and King's Harbor, Helen's major port, was the site of one of the Royal Navy's main shipyards. King's Harbor was also an ancient fortress whose walls had been steadily expanded for centuries, which made the shipyard what might be considered a secure location. And the fact that most of the island's usable supply of ship timbers had been logged off long ago wasn't much of a drawback. Timber could always be shipped in, and Helen *did* offer substantial deposits of copper and iron plus, despite its relatively small size, enough mountain-born rivers and streams to drive a great many of Charis' overshot water-wheels. The King's Harbor shipyard had installed its first water-powered sawmill over a century before, and a very respectable complex of supporting installations had grown up since.

Over the years, more than one project about which the kings of Charis wanted the rest of the world kept in ignorance had been carried out at King's Harbor. The shipyards at Hairatha on Big Tirian were bigger and more capable, in some ways, but Big Tirian's population was also far higher, which meant security was commensurately more difficult to maintain there. And the Royal Navy's Tellesberg shipyard—the biggest and most capable of all—was also the most public.

All of which helped to explain why Merlin Athrawes stood on the foredeck of the Royal Charisian Navy galley HMS *Catamount* as she rowed steadily into King's Harbor, past the towers guarding either side of the opening in the seawall.

It was the first time Merlin had seen the harbor with his own eyes, as it were, and he was forced to admit the looming fortifications, standing stark and tall against the dark green and brown of their mountainous backdrop, were impressive, to say the least, when viewed from sea level. On the other hand, they were also about to become hopelessly obsolete, although no one else had any way to know that.

He gazed at the sheer stone curtain walls, crenelated and tall, with regularly spaced towers and platforms for catapults and ballistae. Cannon crouched on some of those platforms now, he noted, crudely designed yet well made, then turned his attention to the shipyard itself. Half a dozen galleys like *Catamount* were under construction, their partially completed hulls already showing the rakish gracefulness of their breed. They, too, were about to become obsolete, and Merlin felt a brief—very brief—stab of regret at the thought of the passing of such lithe, beautiful craft. The fact that he felt unhappily certain he was going to have no end of difficulty convincing some navy officers that their passage would be a good thing helped to account for some of that regret's brevity.

He snorted in amusement at the thought and turned to glance at the young men standing beside him.

"Impressive," he said, and Cayleb chuckled and looked over his shoulder.

"Merlin says it looks 'impressive,' Ahrnahld," he observed. "Do you think we should feel flattered?"

"At this point, Your Highness, I sometimes doubt *anything* truly impresses *Seijin* Merlin," Lieutenant Falkhan said dryly. The Marine had returned to duty less than a five-day after the assassination attempt, and he'd adjusted remarkably well to Merlin's constant presence at the prince's side. Some men in his position might have resented the public appearance that such a "special reinforcement" had been required. Falkhan, however, knew the real reason for the arrangement, and he seemed remarkably impervious to "public appearances." Now he only grinned.

"I've noticed, however, that the *seijin* is always polite and careful not to hurt his hosts' feelings," he added.

"That's about what I thought, too," Cayleb said with another chuckle, and turned back to Merlin.

"In this case, I meant exactly what I said, Your Highness," Merlin said. "It *is* impressive, and I can see how it must have aided your ancestors' efforts to unite the Kingdom."

"My, you *are* polite." Cayleb smiled broadly. "My 'ancestors' began as the most successful pirates on the Bay, as I'm sure you're quite well aware, Merlin. And I'm afraid their efforts to 'unite the Kingdom' had a great deal more to do with improving their opportunities to loot and plunder than with high and noble motivations."

"I'm not sure that's quite the way *I'd* put it, Your Highness," Falkhan interjected with a slightly pained expression.

"Of course it isn't. You're a loyal servant of the House of Ahrmahk; I, on the other hand, am the house's heir. As such, I can afford to tell the truth."

"And I'm sure it amuses you no end," Merlin said dryly. "Nonetheless, Your Highness, I do find the sight impressive. And I think it should suit our purposes quite well."

"You're probably right," Cayleb said more seriously, and pointed off to the right, where several columns of smoke rose from behind another stretch of curtain wall. "You'll want to look it over for yourself, I expect, but there's a fairly respectable foundry back there. If I recall correctly, something like half the Navy's guns have been cast there over the years. I realize from what you were saying the other night," he smiled tightly, "that we're going to need to expand it—a lot—but it's still a start."

"I'm sure it will be," Merlin agreed, without mentioning that he undoubtedly had a far better notion of that foundry's capacity than Cayleb himself did. The prince was right about how useful it was going to be, though.

"There's the *Mahry Zhayn*, Your Highness," Falkhan put in, pointing at another ship—one of the heavier, clumsier, square-rigged merchant ships which constituted the kingdom's true wealth—and Cayleb nodded in acknowledgment.

"Was it really necessary to haul *everyone* clear out here, Merlin?" the prince asked as their own galley altered course slightly to steer for the same anchorage.

"Probably not, from a security perspective," Merlin acknowledged. "On the other hand, I think your father was absolutely right about all the other reasons. It's not as if Helen were on the other side of the world, but it's far enough from Tellesberg to make the point that he's dead serious about the need to keep this entire meeting secret. And bringing all of them together at once, where they can see how all the bits and pieces fit together, is going to make them all realize how critical it is that they *pull* together."

"But it's also going to mean all of them *do* know 'how all the bits and pieces fit together.'" Cayleb's voice and expression alike were both suddenly darker, more somber. "If it turns out we're wrong about any one of them, he's going to be able to hurt us much worse than if each of them only knew about his own particular piece of it."

Merlin turned fully towards the prince, his own expression grave as he studied Cayleb's. Cayleb, like his father, had been very close to Kahlvyn Ahrmahk. After all, the duke had been his godfather, not just his cousin. Given the difference in their ages, Cayleb had always regarded Tirian more as an uncle—and, in many ways, a true second father—than as a cousin. It had been Kahlvyn who'd taught Cayleb to ride when Haarahld's crippled leg prevented him from doing so, just as it was Kahlvyn who'd overseen the beginning of Cayleb's training with sword and bow. The prince had loved his cousin, and more than a little of the adoration of a very young boy for a magnificent uncle had stayed with him.

Which meant the proof of Kahlvyn's treason had hit Cayleb even harder than it had hit Haarahld. In some ways, that was probably a good thing, for someone who would face the burden of kingship himself one day. But it had been a painful, painful lesson, the sort that left scars, and Merlin hoped it hadn't permanently damaged the boy's ability to trust those who truly deserved his trust.

"Your Highness," he said gently, after a moment, "these men are *loyal*. Baron Wave Thunder's vouched for all of them, and so do I. No man's judgment is perfect, but I have no fear that any of the people your father's 'invitation' has summoned to Helen today will ever betray you or Charis."

Cayleb scowled for a second or two. Then he snorted as he realized what Merlin had really said, and his expression eased slightly as he accepted the lesson.

"I know they won't," he said. "I've known some of them all my life, for that matter! But it's still hard—"

He broke off with an uncomfortable little shrug, and Merlin nodded.

"Of course it is," he said. "And it will be . . . for a while, at least. But I think you can rely on the Baron to keep what's left of Nahrmahn's spies on the hop for the next little bit. And I doubt Prince Hektor's going to be particularly pleased about what's happened to *his* spies, for that matter."

"No, he isn't, is he?" Cayleb agreed with a nasty smile, and Lieutenant Falkhan chuckled from behind him.

"I think that's a comfortable understatement, Your Highness," the prince's chief bodyguard observed with a certain relish. He'd never been privy to all the details of the hostile espionage networks in and around Tellesberg, but his position as Cayleb's guardian meant that, despite his relatively junior rank, he'd been better informed than most, and he was delighted by what the *seijin*'s arrival had done to them. His only real regret was that the decision had been made to leave so much of Hektor's spy rings effectively intact.

It probably didn't feel that way to Zhaspahr Maysahn and Oskahr Mhulvayn, of course. Mhulvayn, in particular, had gone into hiding when the warrant for his arrest was issued. He had no way of knowing Sir Rhyzhard Seafarmer had personally instructed the Crown's chief investigators that he was not to be successfully taken under any circumstances. Not that Seafarmer had had any objection to making Mhulvayn's life a living hell until the Corisandian managed to find transportation out of Tellesberg. But apprehending the man and interrogating him had been no part of Wave Thunder's plans. They might have been forced to go after Maysahn, as well, if they'd done that; as it was, they could pretend to have no suspicions at all where Maysahn was concerned, as long as Mhulvayn successfully "slipped away" from them.

In the meantime, Hektor's information-gathering capability in Charis had sustained a major blow, with the elimination at one stroke—for a time, at least—

of all of Mhulvayn's contacts. And Maysahn was undoubtedly going to operate very cautiously for the next several months himself, at least until he once again felt certain that *he* wasn't under suspicion, which was going to prevent him from rebuilding quickly, too. Most of the groundwork for the plans King Haarahld and Merlin had hatched would be firmly in place by the time Nahrmahn and Hektor were able to build back to anything approaching their previous capabilities.

Personally, Falkhan would have greatly preferred to take both Mhulvayn and Maysahn into custody and execute them for the snakes they were. Since he couldn't, he was just as happy he was a simple Marine, responsible for protecting the heir to the throne from direct attack, and not a spymaster himself. He understood that there were perfectly valid reasons to leave a known spy in place. He simply didn't like doing it.

"At any rate," Cayleb said after a moment, "we'll have an opportunity to start explaining things to them soon enough now."

▼   ▼   ▼

"Your Highness, welcome to King's Harbor," High Admiral Bryahn Lock Island, ninth Earl Lock Island, said as Cayleb walked into the large chamber high in the citadel. Wave Thunder, Merlin, and Falkhan were at his heels, and the spartanly furnished room was like a cool, welcoming cave after the brilliant brightness and heat of the day outside. A single, deep-walled window looked out over the harbor, and Merlin saw *Catamount* far below, gleaming in the sunlight like a child's toy, as she lay to her moorings.

There was more than a trace of family resemblance between the earl and the crown prince, and Merlin watched Cayleb closely but unobtrusively as the prince crossed to the admiral and extended his right hand. Lock Island clasped arms with him, and the older man's expression seemed to ease somehow.

So he was worried about the kind of scars Tirian might have left, too, Merlin thought.

"It's always good to be here, just as it is to see you, Bryahn," Cayleb said warmly. "Not that Helen isn't just a bit inconveniently placed for quick visits."

"That's certainly true enough," Lock Island agreed, and grimaced humorously. "Some of us, on the other hand, find ourselves required to make the trip just a bit more often than others of us."

"And others of us are just as glad we aren't part of the 'some of us' anymore," Cayleb agreed with a chuckle, looking past his kinsman at the other men who'd risen from the chairs around the chamber's large table at his entrance.

"If you'll permit me, *Seijin* Merlin," the prince continued, "I'll get the introductions out of the way, and then we can sit down and get started."

Most of the waiting faces showed surprise at Cayleb's obvious courtesy to his "bodyguard," and Merlin was pleased to see it. If *these* men were buying Haarahld's cover story, it might hold against the rest of the world far better than he'd feared it might.

"Of course, Your Highness," he murmured.

"In that case, let's begin with Doctor Mahklyn."

Merlin nodded, and followed the prince across to the five men at the table. He listened with half an ear, bowing, smiling, murmuring appropriate responses, as Cayleb made the introductions, but he didn't really need them. He'd already "met" every one of them through the interface of his SNARCs.

Doctor Rahzhyr Mahklyn was the Dean of the Royal College of Charis. He was a bit above average in height, gray-haired, with sharp brown eyes that were more than a little myopic. He was slightly stoop-shouldered, and he walked around with what the unwary might have thought was a perpetual air of mild bemusement.

Ehdwyrd Howsmyn was Mahklyn's physical opposite. Short, stout, with twinkling eyes and a cheerful smile, he was barely forty years old—less than thirty-seven standard. He was also one of the wealthiest men in the entire Kingdom of Charis, the owner of two of the kingdom's three largest foundries and of one of Tellesberg's larger shipyards, as well as a small fleet of merchant ships under his own house flag. Although he was a commoner by birth and hadn't bothered with acquiring any patents of nobility yet, everyone knew it was going to happen as soon as he found the time to get around to it. For that matter, four years ago he'd married the eldest daughter of an earl, and his noble father-in-law had been delighted by the match.

Raiyan Mychail, bald as an egg and at least sixty-five or seventy standard years old, was a sharp-eyed man who'd partnered with Howsmyn in a dozen or so of the younger man's most successful ventures. Mychail was a quiet man, whose apparently unassuming demeanor masked one of the sharpest business minds in Tellesberg. He was almost certainly the kingdom's largest single producer of textiles, and he was definitely the Royal Navy's primary sailmaker. Not to mention owning Tellesberg's largest ropewalk.

Sir Dustyn Olyvyr was about midway in age between Howsmyn and Mychail. Although he was a wealthy man by anyone else's standards, his personal worth didn't even approach that of the other two. He was physically unremarkable in many ways, but he had powerful shoulders, and his hands, although well manicured these days, carried the scars of his youthful apprenticeship as a ship's carpenter. That apprenticeship was far behind him now, and although he'd never owned (and never wanted to own) a shipyard of his own, he was always busy. He was one of Tellesberg's two or three top ship designers, and also the chief naval constructor of the Royal Charisian Navy.

The fifth man at the table wore the same sky-blue uniform tunic and loose, black trousers as High Admiral Lock Island. But Sir Ahlfryd Hyndryk, Baron Seamount, was only a captain, and while Lock Island was long, lean, and heavily tanned, with the crow's-feet and weathered complexion of a lifelong mariner, Seamount was a pudgy little fellow. He looked almost ludicrous standing beside the tall, broad-shouldered admiral, at least until one saw his eyes. Very sharp, those eyes, reflecting the brain behind them. He was also missing the first two fingers off his left hand, and there was a peculiar pattern of dark marks on his left cheek. A powder burn, Merlin knew, received from the same accidental explosion which had cost him those fingers. However unprepossessing Seamount might look, he was the closest thing to a true gunnery expert the Royal Charisian Navy (or any *other* navy) possessed.

Cayleb completed the introductions and took his place at the head of the table. The others waited until he'd been seated, then settled back into their own chairs. They didn't waste time worrying about who took precedence over whom, Merlin noticed with satisfaction, although Seamount did wait for Lock Island to seat himself. Clearly, though, that was in deference to the high admiral's superior naval rank, not to the precedence of this title. All of them obviously knew one another well, which might help explain their comfort level, but it was impossible to imagine grandees from, say, Harchong or Desnair accepting the social equality of any commoner.

Cayleb waited until everyone had settled, then looked around the table. Despite his relative youth, there was no question who was in command of this meeting, and Merlin rather suspected that there wouldn't have been even if Cayleb hadn't been the heir to the throne.

"There's a reason why my father commanded all of us to meet here today," the prince began. "As a matter of fact, there are several reasons. The fact that it's imperative that we prevent our enemies from discovering what we're up to—especially with you and Sir Ahlfryd, Bryahn—helps to explain why we're way out here at Helen.

"It's also the reason Father delegated this meeting to me. I'm still young enough that people may not expect me to be doing anything important without 'adult supervision.'" His smile was droll, and most of his listeners chuckled. Then his face sobered a bit. "More importantly, I can disappear to meet with all of you here without anyone noticing much more readily than he could. But I want it clearly understood that at this moment I am speaking for him."

He paused for a heartbeat or two, letting that sink in, then waved one hand at Merlin.

"I'm sure all of you have heard all sorts of fantastic tales about *Seijin* Merlin. Our problem is that most of those tales, despite their fantastic nature, actually fall short of the reality."

One or two of his listeners stirred, as if they found that difficult to accept, and Cayleb smiled thinly.

"Believe me, it's true. In fact, the reason Father's gone to considerable lengths to keep anyone with good sense from believing such ridiculous stories is because they happen to be true. Only two members of the Royal Council, Bishop Maikel, and a handful of our most trusted people—like Ahrnahld, here—know the truth about the *seijin* and his abilities. To everyone else, he's simply my new, personal guardsman and bodyguard—and, one whose imposition I've rather publicly complained about on several occasions—assigned to keep me from sticking my foolish nose into any more ambushes. A trusted and valuable retainer, but only that.

"There are several reasons for that, and one of the reasons for the secrecy of this meeting is to keep . . . certain other people, shall we say, from realizing just how important to us he is. As we all know, according to the old tales, *seijin* are sometimes teachers, as well as warriors, and that's exactly what *Seijin* Merlin is. He has things to teach us which may very well give us the advantages the Kingdom needs to defeat our enemies. But Father believes it's vital that people like Nahrmahn of Emerald and Hektor of Corisande, among others, don't realize he's the one teaching us. If for no other reason, because they would spare no effort or expense to assassinate him if they did."

All eyes had swung to Merlin as Cayleb spoke. Merlin looked back, his face carefully expressionless, and Cayleb smiled again.

"The purpose of this meeting is to accomplish several things," he continued. "First, *Seijin* Merlin's going to begin by sketching out how what he knows and what all of you already know can fit together to accomplish our objectives. But second, and just as important, we're going to discuss ways in which the six of you can take credit for what Merlin is teaching us."

Lock Island straightened in his chair, glancing around the table, then looked at Cayleb.

"Excuse me, Your Highness, but did you say *we're* to take credit for *Seijin* Merlin's knowledge?"

"If I may, Your Highness?" Merlin asked diffidently before Cayleb could reply, and the prince nodded for him to take the earl's question.

"High Admiral," Merlin said, turning to face Lock Island squarely, "much of what I know—of what I can 'teach you,' as Prince Cayleb's put it—would be of limited value without the practical experience which you and these other men possess. In many—most—cases, it's going to take what you already know to make what I can show you effective.

"Each of you is also an acknowledged master of your own trade, your own specialized area of knowledge, if you will. That means that when you speak, people will listen, and that will be important, because many of the things we're going to have to do will fly in the face of tradition. Change makes most people uncomfortable, even here in Charis, and your people will take more kindly to change that comes from men they know and trust than they will to change that comes from a mysterious outlander, whatever his credentials.

"And on top of those factors, there's the need to introduce the changes we're going to have to make on the broadest possible basis. They can't all come from one man, for a lot of reasons. One personal reason of my own is that what I can tell you comes from the teachings of many others, some of whom I knew personally, some of whom I never met myself. It isn't *my* work, and I'd prefer not to be known as some sort of mysterious, possibly sinister, and definitely foreign 'genius' just because I happen to be the person in a position to pass it on to the rest of you.

"On a more pragmatic basis, if a single stranger suddenly appears and becomes a fount of all knowledge, it's going to create both more resistance from those who cling to tradition and an unavoidable tension. It's always dangerous for a stranger to become too great, too powerful. It destabilizes things, creates jealousies and resentments. It can even lead to a fragmentation of authority, and Charis simply cannot afford anything like that when so many external enemies are already gathering around you.

"Besides, I feel quite confident that even though something I teach you may be what starts you in a given direction, where you finally arrive will, indeed, be the result of your own energy and work."

"And," Mychail said with a thin smile of his own, "if you'll pardon me for pointing this out, it will also help keep *you* alive, *Seijin* Merlin."

"Well, there *is* that minor consideration, Master Mychail," Merlin acknowledged with a chuckle.

"I trust," Howsmyn said, his tone carefully neutral, "that none of this 'teaching' of yours is going to infringe upon the Proscriptions, *Seijin* Merlin."

"You have my solemn oath that it will not, Master Howsmyn," Merlin replied gravely. "In fact, the King intends to involve Bishop Maikel and Father Paityr from the beginning to make certain of that."

A few tense sets of shoulders seemed to relax ever so slightly, and Merlin hid an inner chuckle. He'd come to the conclusion that Cayleb's estimate of Bishop Maikel was correct. There was no question about the bishop's personal piety, but he was also a Charisian patriot. And one, Merlin was coming to believe, especially after that cathedral sermon, who had few illusions about the nature of the Council of Vicars and the rest of the Church's senior hierarchy.

Father Paityr Wylsynn, on the other hand, was no Charisian. In fact, he'd been born in the Temple Lands, and he was Archbishop Erayk's chief intendant in Charis. Like many intendants, he was also a priest of the Order of Schueler, which made him the local representative of the Inquisition, as well. The prospect of coming to the Inquisition's attention was enough to make any Safeholdian nervous, and none of the men seated around that table was unaware of how the Schuelerites' wariness automatically focused on their own kingdom.

Despite that, Father Paityr was deeply respected in Charis generally, and in Tellesberg in particular. No one could doubt the strength of his personal faith, or the fervor with which he served the responsibilities of his priestly office. At the same time, no one had ever accused him of *abusing* his office—which, unfortunately, could not be said about a great many other inquisitors and intendants—and he was scrupulous about ensuring that the Proscriptions of Jwo-jeng were applied fairly. Schuelerites in general had a reputation for erring on the side of conservatism, but Father Paityr seemed less inclined in that direction than many of his brethren.

"*Seijin* Merlin is correct," Cayleb said. "Bishop Maikel has already been consulted and given his blessing to our efforts. Father Paityr hasn't yet, and Bishop Maikel has advised Father that it would be wisest to avoid . . . embroiling Father Paityr in all of the details of what we're doing."

He didn't go into all of the reasons for that; there was no need to.

"Bishop Maikel also strongly supports," the crown prince continued, "Father's belief that the degree to which *Seijin* Merlin is involved in all of this should be minimized. Not just for the reasons we've already discussed, although Bishop Maikel agrees all of them are valid, but also because the involvement of a *seijin* would automatically trigger a much more thorough—and time-consuming—preliminary inquisition if Father Paityr were forced to take formal cognizance of it. Bishop Maikel would prefer to avoid that, and he believes Father Paityr would, as well. After all, the critical point, as the *Writ* itself makes clear, is the substance of that which is tested, not its origin."

He paused until heads nodded solemnly, and Merlin resisted the temptation to smile cynically. All of those nodding men were perfectly well aware that Bishop Maikel was effectively advising Haarahld on how best to "game the system." But that was all right with them, because "gaming the system," whether it was called that or not, had been an everyday fact of the Church's life for as long as anyone could remember. As long as Mother Church formally approved a new concept or technique, its originators were covered, and at least in Father Paityr's case, approval wouldn't depend on the size of the bribe offered.

And every one of the men in this chamber also understood that one major unstated reason for them to take credit for the things Merlin was about to begin teaching them was to spread out the responsibility for those innovations. To avoid having so many simultaneous new ideas come at Father Paityr from a single, possibly suspect, source that he was driven to focus on where they came from, rather than upon their content.

"There's one more initial point Father wanted me to stress," Cayleb continued after a moment. "Nothing that *Seijin* Merlin is about to share with us can be kept indefinitely as our exclusive property. Once others have seen the advantages, it won't take them long to start trying to duplicate those same advantages for themselves. Some of what we're going to be talking about today, like what *Seijin* Merlin calls 'Arabic numerals' and an 'abacus,' are going to have to spread widely to be of any use to us. As such, their advantages are bound to be recognized, and they're bound to be adopted by others very quickly. Others will have exclusively, or at least primarily, military implications, involving ways to make the Navy and Marines more effective. The results of those changes are going to be quickly apparent to our adversaries if and when they encounter them in battle, but Father would be much happier if people like Nahrmahn and Hektor had no idea what we're doing *until* they encounter those changes in battle."

Heads nodded again, much more emphatically, and Cayleb nodded back soberly.

"In that case, *Seijin* Merlin," he said, "why don't you go ahead and begin."

▼　　▼　　▼

"Is it really that simple?" Baron Seamount asked several hours later, staring at the coarse black grains on Merlin's palm and shaking his head slowly. His expression was a curious mixture of awe and chagrin.

"It's really that simple," Merlin confirmed. "Of course, producing 'corned' powder like this has its own set of problems. It's easy to strike a spark, or even set it off from simple friction heat, especially during the grinding process. But overall, it's a lot safer, and more powerful, too."

He and the navy officer stood in Seamount's office in a squat stone structure beside the King's Harbor citadel. The office was a wide, low-ceilinged chamber, newer than much of the rest of the fortifications, since it sat squarely atop the fortress's main powder magazine.

Location is everything, Merlin thought dryly. *Although, now that I think about it, maybe it does make sense to put the officer in charge of the magazine's safety directly on top of it. If nothing else, it should make sure he pays attention to his duties!*

"I doubt any of those problems can begin to compare to the ones we've always had," Seamount said now. He held out his own hand—the mangled one—and Merlin turned his wrist to tip the black powder into the captain's palm.

Seamount raised it to his nose and sniffed, then stuck out his tongue and tasted the powder delicately.

"I can see why this . . . 'corned' powder of yours is going to be a lot safer to handle, *Seijin* Merlin," he said. "But why is it going to be more powerful?"

Merlin frowned thoughtfully and stroked his mustachios while he considered how best to answer the question.

As Seamount said, the safety advantages were obvious. Safeholdian gunpowder hadn't been around that long, and it was still a very crude proposition. The exact proportions of sulfur, saltpeter, and charcoal remained a matter of hot debate among the practitioners of the artillerist's art, such as it was and what there was of it. Worse, and much more dangerously, it was still "meal powder"—made by simply mixing the finely crushed ingredients into a powder with a consistency very close to that of flour. It worked, more or less, but the ingredients didn't *stay* mixed. They separated out, especially if the mixture was jostled or agitated. Which, given the state of most of Safehold's roads, meant a powder cart often found itself moving in a fine fog of highly flammable, highly explosive dust.

No one on Safehold had yet thought of the expedient of moistening the powder, pressing it into solid cakes, and then grinding it to a uniform consistency. The process bound the component ingredients together, preventing them from separating back out, which explained both Seamount's awe and his chagrin. The implications for the safe, efficient use of artillery and small arms were profound, yet the solution was so absurdly simple that it was difficult for him to forgive himself for not having already thought of it.

Which still left the the problem of how to explain the increase in propellant force.

"It's more powerful for several reasons, as I understand it, Sir Ahlfryd," Merlin said, after moment. "First, I've adjusted the . . . recipe just a bit. The one you were using had too much charcoal in it. But the main reason, as it was explained to me, is that basically what gunpowder does is simply to burn very, very quickly in a confined space. When the powder is made into grains this way, there's more space between each grain, which means the fire can burn even more quickly and completely. I'm sure you've seen the same sort of process when you've 'poked up' a fire on your hearth."

It was Seamount's turn to frown. He stood gazing down into his palm, gently stirring the powder grains with the index finger of his other hand, then nodded.

"Yes," he said slowly, thoughtfully. "Yes, I can see how that might be. I never considered it before, but then again, I never had 'corned' powder to experiment with."

He frowned some more, then looked back up at Merlin.

"But if it's more powerful, will our existing guns be up to firing it?"

"That's an excellent question, and I don't have a good answer," Merlin admitted. "From what I've seen of your artillery, it's well made, but it was all designed for meal powder, not corned powder. I think you're going to have to experiment to find out."

"I can see that." Seamount nodded. "We've always proofed our guns by firing them with double or triple charges and loads of shot. I suppose we should start by firing some of them with standard charges, by weight, of corned powder, then increase the loading until they fail."

"That sounds reasonable to me," Merlin agreed. "One thing, though. You may have to thicken the walls of the gun tubes to stand up to the power of the new powder, but you can probably reduce the barrel length."

Seamount raised an eyebrow, and Merlin chuckled.

"The main reason you've needed as much length as you've got now is to give the powder time to burn before the ball leaves the bore," he pointed out. "Since corned powder burns more quickly, you won't need the same barrel length to get the same effect."

"You're right." Seamount's eyes gleamed as he considered the implications. "So we could reinforce the thickness and might still end up saving weight, overall. And"—his eyes glowed even more brightly as his agile mind raced onward—"a shorter gun can be reloaded more quickly can't it?"

"Yes, it can." Merlin nodded, then stroked his mustachios again. "In fact, I just had another thought. One that would probably increase your rate of fire even more."

"What sort of thought?" Seamount's eyes narrowed into hawk-like intensity.

"Well," Merlin said slowly, frowning as he obviously worked through the implications himself, "you've always loaded each round using ladles of loose powder, haven't you?"

Seamount nodded quickly with an "of-course-we-have" sort of expression, and Merlin shrugged.

"Well," he said again, "suppose you were to pre-measure the charge for each shot? You could sew each charge into a cloth bag. Then you could just ram the bag home each time you load. And if the bag's weave was loose enough, the primer would burn a hole through the cloth and ignite the main charge."

"Langhorne!" Seamount muttered. He closed his eyes for a moment, thinking hard, then began to nod. Slowly, at first, then faster and harder.

"You're absolutely right!" he said, reopening his eyes, still nodding. "I'll bet we could at least double—probably triple—our rate of fire if we did that! And—" His nodding stopped abruptly. "—I don't see any reason we couldn't do the same thing for our field artillery. Or even—Langhorne! We could come up with a way for musketeers with this new 'flintlock' of yours to do the same kind of thing instead of using powderhorns!"

Merlin blinked in apparent astonishment. And, truth be told, he *was* just a little astonished. He'd known Baron Seamount had a first-class brain, but he was delighted by how quickly the naval officer was grappling with the new possibilities. The *"seijin"* had hoped introducing the basic concepts would produce this sort of synergy, but he hadn't expected even Seamount to grab them and run this quickly.

On the other hand, he reminded himself, *one reason the Charisians are so tough at sea is that they've invented the concept of a professional navy. Everybody else still insists on sticking army officers—preferably nobly born ones, whether they have any brains are not—aboard a ship to command it in battle. The professional sailors are only along to steer the thing where their landlubber "commanders" tell them to go; aside from that, they're supposed to keep their big mouths shut. But not in Charis. I wonder if Seamount really realizes just how big an advantage that gives his people?*

The professional naval officer in question turned to look at the diagrams chalked on one wall of his office. That entire wall was paneled in slabs of slate, turning it into one huge blackboard, and when they'd first entered the office, it had been covered by half a dozen sketches and jotted reminders to himself. But Seamount had swept them impatiently away and begun creating new ones with sharp, crisp strokes of his chalk as they spoke. Now he considered those newly created sketches and notes and shook his head slowly.

"Some of our officers are going to resist all this, you know, *Seijin*," he said.

"Why do you say that?"

"*Seijin* Merlin," Seamount replied with something trapped halfway between a snort and a chuckle, "you've been very tactful this afternoon. I'm fairly confident, though, that most of my own brilliant notions had already occurred to you before we began."

Merlin felt his face smooth into momentary, betraying non-expression, and the Charisian laughed.

"That wasn't a complaint," he said. "And while I have my own suspicions about just why you might prefer for us to 'figure it all out' for ourselves, I'm not going to worry about confirming them, either. But when you take all of this together—the new powder, these 'trunnions' of yours, the new gun carriages, this idea of premeasured charges, the shorter barrel length—it's going to stand every established notion of how naval battles are fought on its head. I haven't had time to consider all of it yet, of course, but one thing is obvious; every war galley in the Navy just became useless."

"I don't know if I'd go quite *that* far," Merlin said cautiously, but Seamount shook his head again, this time crisply, decisively.

"It won't work with galleys," he said, and his chalk rapped on slate with tack-hammer sharpness as he tapped the rough schematic of the new-style gun carriage with it. "We're going to have to come up with something else, and a whole new set of tactics and tactical formations. At the moment, the only real possibility I see is some development of the galleon, even though Langhorne knows we don't have many of them to play with! I suspect—" He gave Merlin another sharp-eyed glance. "—that you and Sir Dustyn are going to be discussing that shortly. But it's obvious a galley simply doesn't have anyplace to put enough guns, not if we can design and mount cannon that fire as quickly as I think we'll be able to fire now. They'll have to be mounted along the broadside of the ship, not just in the bowcastle and sterncastle, and you can't do that in a galley. The rowers would be in the way. And they don't have the loadbearing capability for that much weight of metal."

"But unless there's a fairly strong wind, a galley is faster than a sailing ship, and galleys are almost always more maneuverable," Merlin pointed out. "And all of those rowers are more Marines when it comes to the boarding melee."

"Doesn't matter," Seamount said almost brusquely. "As long as the sailing ship has enough way on her to keep her broadside pointed at the galley, no galley will survive to board her. Not with a dozen or so heavy cannon firing round shot straight into the galley's teeth, anyway! And battles between cannon-armed ships won't be settled by boarding most of the time, either. Oh," he waved his maimed hand, "it'll probably happen from time to time, anyway, but usually?" He shook his head again, sharply. "Usually, the business will be settled one way or the other well before anyone gets close enough to board."

Merlin looked at him for a moment, then tossed his head in a gesture of agreement.

Although, he thought, *Seamount may just be getting a bit ahead of himself. There were plenty of boarding actions during the canvas-and-cannon era on Old Earth. Still, he's headed in the right direction. And he's right that the old-fashioned land-battle-at-sea is about to become a thing of the past.*

"I see what you mean," he said aloud. "And, you're right. I had realized we'd need to come up with a new design for warships with the new guns even before you and I started talking. That's one reason I was going to suggest you sit in with

Sir Dustyn and me when *we* begin talking. You've undoubtedly got a better appreciation of how things are going to have to change than I do, and we might as well get it right from the beginning."

"I certainly agree with that." Seamount nodded emphatically. "And I imagine Sir Dustyn is going to explain to me why I can't build the ship I'd really like to. Just putting this much weight onto its decks is bound to create all sorts of problems. And even after he and I—and you, of course, *Seijin*—come to some sort of compromise agreement on that, we're going to have to figure out how to sell it to the rest of His Majesty's officers, as well."

"*And*, just to make your life even a little bit more complicated," Merlin said with a grin, "you're going to have to figure out how to convince them without letting Nahrmahn and Hektor realize what's coming."

"Oh, *thank* you, *Seijin* Merlin!"

"Don't mention it. But now, I believe, it's time for my first conversation with Master Howsmyn and Master Mychail. We've got quite a few things to discuss, including the best way to make your new cannon. After that, I'm supposed to meet with Sir Dustyn for the first time about three hours from now, and we'll have several other things to discuss, in addition to your new warship design. So, if I might suggest, perhaps I should leave you to consider exactly what ingredients you want incorporated into it while I go and discuss those other things with Master Howsmyn, Master Mychail, and him. Could you join us in the Citadel in, perhaps, four hours or so?"

"I'll be there," Seamount promised, and turned his rapt attention back to the chalk diagrams as Merlin quietly left the office.

▼   ▼   ▼

"I can see what you've got in mind, *Seijin* Merlin," Ehdwyrd Howsmyn said, sitting back from the conference table and gazing at the side-by-side pencil sketches. "And I imagine Sir Ahlfryd was drooling by the time you showed him these 'trunnions' of yours."

He reached out and tapped the closer of the two drawings with an index finger. It showed one of the new, modified artillery pieces Merlin was proposing. There were several differences between it and the standard type currently carried aboard the Royal Charisian Navy's galleys, but the most significant one was the way the gun itself was mounted.

Current cannon were basically simply huge muskets—a hollow tube of metal, tightly affixed to a long, straight, heavy wooden timber by metal bands. When the gun was fired, the timber recoiled across the deck until the combination of friction and the heavy tackle anchoring the gun to the gunport through which it fired brought it to a halt. The crew then reloaded and dragged the massive timber back into position by sheer brute strength.

There was no way to elevate or depress the gun's point of aim, dragging the ponderous timber across the deck required a *lot* of muscle power (at least if the gun was heavy enough to actually damage another ship's hull), and even a well-trained gun crew did well to get off a single shot every five minutes or so.

But the new piece Merlin had sketched had something called "trunnions," which were no more than cylindrical protrusions cast into the barrel and set at right angles to the gun's bore. They were long enough and thick enough to support the gun's weight, and they fitted into cutouts in the "gun carriage"—the *wheeled* gun carriage—which went under the piece. It was a ridiculously simple concept, Howsmyn reflected, but the implications were huge. The gun pivoted up and down on the "trunnions," which meant it could be elevated or depressed with ludicrous ease. The carriage's wheels (or "trucks," as Merlin insisted upon calling them for some reason), meant it could be brought back to battery far more quickly—and with a smaller gun crew for a given weight of weapon. And because of all that, and the fact that the pieces were so much shorter and handier, the rate of fire had to go up hugely.

"The problem, as I see it," the foundry owner continued, "is twofold. First, we're going to need a *lot* of these guns of yours. It won't do us much good to have two or three ships armed with them if the rest of the fleet isn't, and the whole point is to put enough of them aboard each ship to make that ship's weight of fire *decisive*. That means we're going to need more bronze than anyone's ever needed before, and somebody's going to have to mine and smelt the stuff. Either that, or we're going to have to figure out how to make them out of iron, and that's a much riskier proposition. But, second, even if we get our hands on the metal, just casting and boring the guns is going to take time—lots of time—and be sort of hard to conceal from someone like Hektor's eyes."

"I agree those are going to be problems, Ehdwyrd," Mychail said, leaning back in his own chair and tapping his front teeth with the knuckle of his right index finger. "I don't think they're insurmountable ones, though. Not if His Majesty's prepared to invest enough gold in the project, at any rate."

"Doing it in secret?" Howsmyn shook his head. "We don't have enough capacity here at Helen for *half* the guns Sir Ahlfryd's going to want, Raiyan! I know we could increase it, but we're going to need hundreds of workers to produce as many new guns as we're going to require. And even if we had those, I don't even know if there's enough space here at King's Harbor for the facilities we'll need in the long term."

"Agreed." Mychail nodded. "On the other hand, what about Delthak?"

Howsmyn started to shake his head, then paused with an arrested expression.

"There's nothing there yet," he said after a moment, and Mychail shrugged.

"And your point is?" The older man stopped tapping his teeth and jabbed his index finger at Merlin's sketches. "You just said we might need to consider iron guns. And that we'd have to expand the capacity here at Helen, assuming there were enough space for it, which there isn't. How much harder would it be to *build* the capacity from scratch somewhere else? And you certainly planned to do exactly that when you bought the land up there in the first place, didn't you?"

"Well, yes," Howsmyn said slowly, then glanced at Merlin. "Just how freely does His Majesty intend to spend in this effort, *Seijin* Merlin?"

"He hasn't told me that," Merlin replied. "I don't know if he's discussed it with Prince Cayleb yet, either, but he may well have. My impression is that he regards all of these projects as critical, but the treasury isn't exactly bottomless. May I ask why?"

"Raiyan has just reminded me about an investment of mine over near Big Tirian. I picked up quite a bit of land from Earl High Rock a few years go. It's near Delthak, right on the river, and High Rock's been trying to get someone to develop the iron deposits on the other side of the river." The foundry owner shrugged. "It's an excellent location, in a lot of ways, but there aren't many people in the area—no labor force to recruit from. And Delthak's a tiny little village, not much more than a wide, muddy spot in the road. I've got a smallish operation in place there, but it's not much yet. I've had to import my entire workforce, and we'd have to start essentially from scratch to develop it further."

"But the very fact that there aren't many people there already might work for us from the secrecy aspect," Merlin said thoughtfully.

"That's what Raiyan had in mind," Howsmyn agreed. "But at this particular moment, there's no real reason or need to develop the property further." He grimaced. "Trade's down generally since the dispute over the Hanth succession started making people jittery. I've got plenty of unused capacity in my Tellesberg foundries."

"That may be about to change, even without the new artillery," Merlin told him. Howsmyn sat a bit straighter in his chair, eyebrows arching, and Merlin snorted.

"Charis is about to experience a period of rapidly growing trade, I suspect," he said. "In fact, Master Mychail, you're going to be a major part of that."

"I am, am I?" Mychail chuckled and crossed his legs. "I admit, I like the sound of that, *Seijin* Merlin. I've always been partial to that nice, musical sound gold coins make falling into my purse."

"There are a couple of new machines I'm hoping you'll introduce for us," Merlin told him. "One is called the 'cotton gin,' and another is called the 'spinning jenny.'"

"And what do these machines do?" Mychail asked.

"The first one removes the seeds from raw cotton and cotton silk without requiring people to pick them out by hand. The 'spinning jenny' is basically a spinning wheel set up with multiple spindles, so one person can spin several yarns at the same time," Merlin said calmly.

Mychail's legs uncrossed, and Merlin smiled as the merchant leaned forward in his chair, his eyes suddenly intent.

"You can separate the seeds without hand labor?" the Charisian asked, and

Merlin nodded. "What sort of capacity are you talking about?" Mychail pressed. "And could it separate the seeds from steel thistle?"

"I don't really know the answer to either of those questions," Merlin admitted. "I've never actually built one, or seen one, for that matter. I know the principles around which it works, though, and on the basis of what I do know, I can't see any reason why it shouldn't work for steel thistle, as well."

Mychail pursed his lips, his mind racing, and Merlin hid a smile. Cotton silk was very similar to terrestrial cotton, except that the native Safeholdian plant produced a fabric which was even lighter and stronger than cotton and was widely used for clothing in climates like Charis'. It was expensive, because removing its seeds was even harder than removing them from regular cotton, yet Safehold's weavers had worked with it from the very beginning of the colony.

The potentials of steel thistle, another Safeholdian plant, on the other hand, had always tempted and frustrated local textile makers in almost equal measure. Steel thistle looked a lot like branching bamboo, with the same "segmented" looking trunks, and it grew even more quickly than the terrestrial plant. It also produced seed pods which were filled with very fine, very strong fibers which could be woven into a fabric even stronger than silk. Indeed, stronger than anything Old Earth's humanity had been able to produce before the days of synthetic fibers.

Unfortunately, the pods also contained very small, very spiny seeds. They were a nightmare to extract by hand, and the tiny wounds the seeds' spines inflicted had a nasty habit of turning septic. That was why no one outside Harchong and the Desnairian Empire, which practiced what was for all intents and purposes slave labor, had ever managed to produce useful quantities of woven steel thistle. It also explained the stuff's incredible cost. So if this cotton gin could remove *its* seeds without the need for hand labor . . .

"Given all of your own experience," Merlin continued, and Mychail blinked and refocused on him, "I'm sure you'll be able to develop a far more effective version of it than I could. And it occurs to me that Master Howsmyn would make an excellent partner for you. The two of you are already accustomed to working together, and his foundries already use a lot of water power. His master mechanics could undoubtedly come up with a way to power cotton gins and spinning jennies the same way . . . and all of his equipment has already been approved by the Church."

Mychail and Howsmyn looked at one another, their eyes brightly speculative, and Merlin smiled.

"While you're thinking about that," he added, "why don't the two of you—and Master Howsmyn's artificers—spend some time thinking about how to design a powered loom, as well? Once you get the cotton gin and spinning jenny up and running, you'll have yarn coming out of your ears. Besides, the Navy's going to need a lot more sail cloth. And I imagine a powered loom would let you manufacture canvas with a tighter weave, don't you think, Master Mychail?"

"Langhorne," Mychail muttered. "He's right, Ehdwyrd. And if this 'spinning jenny' works the way he seems to think it will, especially if you can figure out a way to power it, we can use it for wool and flax, as well." He shook himself and looked back at Merlin. "No wonder you're expecting an upturn in trade, *Seijin* Merlin!"

"Shipbuilding, too," Merlin assured them. "For the Navy, of course, but I suspect you're going to see a lot of new merchant ship construction, as well, once Sir Dustyn and I finish discussing something called a 'schooner rig.' *That* one I actually have some personal experience with, which is why I'm certain it's going to create quite a sensation when Sir Dustyn—and you, of course, Master Howsmyn—trot it out. It may take a few months for people to realize its advantages, but once they do, you're going to be swamped with orders. I suspect the sudden infusion of capital's going to make the development of a new foundry at Delthak much more feasible."

"And if we're that busy, it'll also explain why I suddenly need to be developing new foundries at all," Howsmyn said enthusiastically.

"And," Mychail added, "given the fact that all of these new ideas are really coming from you, *Seijin* Merlin, and from His Majesty, it's only fitting that that 'sudden infusion of capital' should go into building up the Navy."

"The King is considering the establishment of something called a 'patent office,'" Merlin told them. "It's something that's going to have to be approached cautiously, for a lot of reasons. But if we can get it organized, people who come up with new and better ways to do things will be able to file for a 'patent' on their new ideas. That means they'll *own* the idea, and that no one else—in Charis, at least—can use it without their permission . . . and, usually, the payment of a modest fee to the person who created it. At the moment, His Majesty plans for each of you to file for patents on the new ideas you introduce as a result of our conferences."

"I'm as selfish as the next man, *Seijin* Merlin," Howsmyn said, his expression troubled, "but I don't feel comfortable at the thought of owning a—what did you call it? a 'patent'?—on an idea *you* provided."

"Master Howsmyn," Merlin said with a smile, "I have absolutely no idea how to turn most of these ideas into practical devices. The cannon, yes. And the new rigging designs I'll be discussing with Sir Dustyn. But foundries, textile manufactories, investment arrangements—those are at least as foreign to me as anything I may know could possibly be to you. It's going to require a partnership, in every sense of the word, for us to make all of this work. So, my thought is that the simplest solution would be for each of you, as patriotic Charisians, to announce that you're assigning half of any patent fees you receive to the Crown. That, coupled with the duties the people buying your new goods will be paying, ought to recompense the King quite handily."

"And what about *you?*" Mychail asked, and Merlin shrugged.

"A *seijin* has little use for worldly wealth, they say. Personally, I've always enjoyed a few minor luxuries, but King Haarahld is providing me with quite comfortable living quarters, and I expect he'll be happy to provide those 'minor luxuries' if I ask him to. Beyond that, what would I do with money if I had it?"

"You actually mean that, don't you?" Howsmyn said, and Merlin nodded.

"I most certainly do, Master Howsmyn. Besides, I'm going to be far too busy for the next few years to worry about spending money on anything."

"Apparently *seijin* are even more different from other men than I'd always heard," Mychail said with a small smile. Then the smile faded, and he nodded solemnly to Merlin. "Nonetheless, *Seijin* Merlin, whatever else happens, Ehdwyrd and I—and all of Charis—are going to owe you far more than we could ever pay with mere money. Most of Charis won't know that; we will. For myself, and I feel sure for Ehdwyrd, as well, if we can ever serve you in any way, with gold or steel, you have only to call."

Howsmyn nodded firmly.

"I thank you for that—both of you," Merlin said, and meant every word of it. "But for now, I'm afraid it's about time for me to meet with Sir Dustyn. Prince Cayleb, Baron Seamount, and Earl Lock Island are going to be joining the two of us in about another hour. If I could impose upon you, Master Howsmyn, I would be very grateful if you would join us then, as well. There's one point, especially, I'm going to need your input on."

"Oh?" Howsmyn looked at him for a moment, then snorted suddenly. "Let me guess. It has to do with Dustyn's crazy idea about covering the bottoms of all the Navy's ships in copper?"

"I wouldn't call it a 'crazy idea,'" Merlin replied with a smile, "but that is what I wanted to discuss."

"It's going to cost a fortune," Howsmyn objected.

"It's going to be expensive, true," Merlin agreed. "But Sir Dustyn is on to something very important here, Master Howsmyn. Not only will sheathing the ships in copper below the waterline protect them from the borers, but it will cut down enormously on fouling. Which means the ships will be faster, more maneuverable, and last a lot longer."

Howsmyn continued to look dubious, and Merlin cocked his head.

"The way things are now," he said, "by the time a galley's been in the water for a month, its hull has already become foul enough to significantly reduce speed and make its rowers work much, much harder. Which means that exhaustion sets in sooner, and maneuverability goes down steadily. Now, we're talking about *sail*-powered ships, not galleys, but the same considerations apply."

"All right," Howsmyn said, a bit grudgingly, and Mychail grunted a laugh. Howsmyn looked at him, and Mychail shook his head.

"Admit it, Ehdwyrd! Your real problem is, first, that *you* didn't think of it instead of Dustyn, and, second, that you haven't been able to figure out a way to *do* it without the copper falling right back off!"

"Nonsense!" Howsmyn replied. The denial came out just a bit huffily, Merlin thought, and spoke up quickly.

"I think I know how to solve the problem of keeping it on the ships," he said. He had no intention of getting into the explanation of terms like "electrolytic solutions" and "galvinic action" between the copper and the iron nails Howsmyn had been using to attach it. Nor would he have to, once he'd demonstrated how to avoid it. Of course, coming up with that many copper fastenings to avoid the electrolytic corrosion of dissimilar metals was going to be a problem in its own right, but it would still be simpler than trying to explain the concept of "anodes."

"You do?" Howsmyn looked at him speculatively, and Merlin nodded.

"Yes. But coming up with that much sheet copper, not to mention the fastenings we're going to need, is going to put in even greater demand on your foundry capacity. So I'd be grateful if between now and then, you and Master Mychail could put a little more thought into the possibilities of developing Delthak. It occurs to me that you might consider turning it not simply into a new foundry, but into a shipyard. We'd like to keep anyone else from realizing that we're coppering our hulls. It's probably going to get out eventually, but the longer we can keep that from happening, the better. And if you're going to build a foundry and a shipyard, anyway, you might think about adding a textile manufactory, as well, if there's enough water power available from the river you mentioned."

The two Charisians nodded, and Merlin pushed his chair back, stood, and bowed slightly to them. Then he strode briskly out of the chamber.

Howsmyn and Mychail had their heads close together before he was completely out the door.

OCTOBER, YEAR OF GOD 890

M y Prince."

Oskahr Mhulvayn went down on one knee as Prince Hektor of
Corisande entered the small private council chamber and crossed to the ornately
carved chair at the head of the table. Phylyp Ahzgood, the Earl of Coris, followed
the prince, seating himself at Hektor's left hand. Neither of them said anything
for several seconds, and Mhulvayn reminded himself that wiping sweat from his
forehead would be . . . inadvisable.

"You may stand," Hektor said after a moment in the melodious tenor which
always seemed just a bit odd coming from one of the most cold-blooded political
calculators on the face of the planet.

Mhulvayn obeyed, rising and clasping his hands behind him as he met the
eyes of the ruler in whose service he had spied for almost twenty years.

Hektor hadn't changed a great deal over those two decades. The dark brown
hair was lightly frosted with silver at the temples. There were a few more wrin-
kles at the corners of the eyes, and a few strands of white in the neatly trimmed
beard. But he was still tall, straight, and broad-shouldered, and unlike the majority of rulers, he continued to work out regularly with his court arms master.

Beside him, Coris seemed somehow washed out, faded. Unlike his prince,
the earl was fair-haired, and if he was almost as tall as Hektor, he lacked the
prince's breadth of shoulder and muscularity. There was something about the
eyes, too, Mhulvayn thought, not for the first time. They weren't weaker than
Hektor's, but they were the eyes of a man who knew he would always be someone else's servant.

Which he was, of course.

"So, Master Mhulvayn," the prince said after several more seconds of fresh
silence. "What went wrong?"

"My Prince," Mhulvayn said, "I don't know."

He wasn't at all happy about making that admission, but it was far better to
be honest and avoid excuses.

"That doesn't seem to speak very well of your sources, Master Mhulvayn,"
Coris observed with a thin smile. The fact that not even a flicker of annoyance
crossed Hektor's face as the earl inserted himself into the conversation told
Mhulvayn quite a lot.

"Perhaps not, My Lord," he replied. "But, while I make no excuses, I would point out, if I might, that we weren't the only people Wave Thunder's men were after."

"Forgive me if I seem obtuse, but that sounds as if you *are* making excuses," Coris remarked.

"Not precisely, My Lord." Mhulvayn was a bit surprised his own voice sounded as calm as it did. "What I meant to suggest was that either Wave Thunder's known a great deal more than anyone thought he knew for a very long time, and chosen not to act upon it, or else something radically new has been added to the pot in Charis. If Wave Thunder did already know everything he finally acted upon, there's no excuse anyone could offer. If, however, some completely new factor has suddenly intruded, there was no way anyone could have predicted it and prepared against it ahead of time."

Coris grimaced and made a brushing-away gesture with his left hand, but Hektor cocked his head and contemplated Mhulvayn with a slightly more interested eye.

"We have only a fragmentary report from Master Maysahn," the prince said after a moment. "It's apparent from what he was able to tell us that something new has, indeed, been added. The question is what? And a second question is how you would suggest that whatever it is led Wave Thunder to *you?*"

"My Prince," Mhulvayn said, deciding to regard the fact that Hektor had chosen to reenter the conversation personally as a good sign, "I don't know what Zhaspahr may have already reported. By the time Lieutenant Maythis and the *Fraynceen* reached Tellesberg and I made contact with him, Zhaspahr and I had been out of touch for almost two five-days. It was clear Wave Thunder's agents were looking for me, and neither of us wanted their hunt for me to lead them to him. Certain . . . elements of the situation became evident only in the last day or so before Lieutenant Maythis sailed for home, however, and Zhaspahr may not have been aware of them when he wrote his report. I will, of course, tell you anything I can, but if I may, I would like to ask one question first."

Coris' eyebrows drew down in a frown, but Hektor only pursed his lips thoughtfully for a second, then nodded.

"Ask," he said.

"My Prince," Mhulvayn gathered his nerve in both hands, "did you know the Duke of Tirian was working with Prince Nahrmahn?"

Despite the fact that he was the official spymaster for the League of Corisande, the Earl of Coris failed to conceal his twitch of surprise. Hektor's expression never flickered, but there was something in the depths of those sharp, dark eyes. Silence lingered for perhaps ten seconds, then the prince shook his head.

"No," he said. "I wasn't aware of that. Why?"

"Because according to the rumors running about Tellesberg just before Lieutenant Maythis and I sailed, Tirian was not only working with Prince Nahrmahn, but was actually the one responsible for the attempt to assassinate Cayleb."

"What?" The single-word question came out calmly, almost conversationally, but there was a flare of genuine surprise in Hektor's eyes.

"Obviously, there was no time for me to confirm the stories one way or the other, even if I'd still dared to contact any of my people," Mhulvayn said. "Nonetheless, I believe them to have been true."

"What stories?"

"Apparently, My Prince, Tirian had been working with Nahrmahn for quite some time. While Nahrmahn's man Lahang undoubtedly arranged the actual attempt, the suggestion for it seems to have come from Tirian. It would appear he saw it as the first step in placing himself upon Haarahld's throne."

"And why"—Hektor's eyes were narrow, his expression intense—"do you believe these . . . stories were accurate?"

"Because I'd already known for over a five-day that Tirian was dead," Mhulvayn said simply.

"Tirian is *dead?*" The question was startled out of Coris, who glanced instantly and apologetically at Hektor, but the prince scarcely seemed to notice as he looked at Mhulvayn with the closest thing to consternation Mhulvayn had ever seen from him.

"Yes, My Lord." Mhulvayn chose to answer Coris, but his eyes were on Hektor. "That much had leaked out much earlier. So had the fact that he'd been involved in *something* treasonous, but Wave Thunder and Haarahld had been remarkably successful at concealing most of the details, presumably while they completed their investigation. It wasn't until after *Fraynceen's* arrival that I heard the first rumors that he not only was dead, but had been killed by Earl Gray Harbor himself."

Coris' jaw dropped, and Hektor sat back in his chair, laying his forearms along the armrests.

"As I'm sure Zhaspahr did include in his last report to you, My Lord," Mhulvayn continued, "the actual attempt to kill Cayleb was frustrated by the intervention of a stranger, a man named 'Merlin,' who apparently claims to be a *seijin.* I have no way to judge whether or not he truly is one, but he's obviously a dangerous man with a sword. One of the assassins was captured alive—again, according to the rumors, because of this Merlin. According to one of my contacts inside the Palace, the man they took was little more than a common soldier, and one wouldn't have thought such as he would have had access to any truly important information.

"Unfortunately for Duke Tirian, he apparently knew more than anyone believed he did. At any rate, under interrogation he said something which caused Wave Thunder to suspect that Tirian himself was involved with Nahrmahn in some way. Gray Harbor was unwilling to believe such a thing of his son-in-law—not to mention of the King's cousin—but the evidence must have been fairly compelling, whatever it was, because Gray Harbor went to personally confront Tirian. According to most versions of the tale that came to me, he hoped to convince Tirian to throw himself on Haarahld's mercy, which suggests that whatever they knew, they didn't begin to suspect the whole.

"No one I spoke to was quite certain exactly what happened that night, but Gray Harbor had gone to Tirian's townhouse accompanied by his own personal guardsman and this same Merlin. When he confronted Tirian, fighting broke out. Gray Harbor's guardsman was killed, as were at least ten or fifteen of Tirian's men—the majority of them, apparently, once again by Merlin—and Gray Harbor himself killed Tirian."

"Langhorne," Coris murmured, touching his heart and then his lips.

"And you believe these stories were accurate?" Hektor asked intently.

"My Prince, they must have been," Mhulvayn said simply. "There's no question that Gray Harbor killed Tirian. The Palace itself confirmed that the afternoon before we sailed, and the man was King Haarahld's cousin, fourth in line for the throne itself. If there were any question in *Haarahld's* mind of Tirian's guilt, Gray Harbor would, at the very least, have been stripped of his offices and imprisoned while the facts were investigated. None of that's happened, and this so-called *seijin* is still an honored guest in Haarahld's palace. Indeed, he's become a member of the Royal Guard and been assigned as Cayleb's personal guardsman, despite his involvement in whatever happened."

Hektor nodded slowly, obviously considering Mhulvayn's logic carefully. Then he once again cocked his head to one side.

"Is it your opinion that whatever happened to Tirian somehow explains what happened to *you?*"

"I don't know, My Prince. On the one hand, there was no connection between Zhaspahr or me and the assassination attempt. On the other hand, both of us knew Lahang was Nahrmahn's man in Tellesberg. I would say it's quite probable that, in turn, he knew I was one of your agents, and what he knew might have been passed on to Tirian or one of his own senior agents.

"It's obvious Gray Harbor must have gotten *something* out of Tirian before the Duke was killed. And more than just confirmation of his involvement in the assassination attempt, I suspect. Lahang was either killed or arrested that very same night. No one's certain which; he simply disappeared. My own belief is that he was taken and interrogated, probably quite . . . rigorously in light of the attempt to kill Cayleb."

"And you believe this because?"

"Because of the way Wave Thunder and his agents have devastated Nahrmahn's network in Charis since his disappearance, My Prince. Dozens of his senior people have been arrested, including several prominent Charisian merchants and more than a few members of the nobility. Some of them had already been executed before I left Tellesberg, and there were scores of additional arrests. You know Haarahld's reputation, and Wave Thunder's. They seldom arrest anyone unless they're completely confident of their evidence. These arrests—and, especially, the executions—would seem to me a clear indication that *somebody* in Nahrmahn's employ who knew all the important details about his network talked. The only two candidates I can see would be Tirian, who I doubt had time to reveal that much detailed information before he was killed, or Lahang himself."

"And you believe whoever it was who talked also knew about your own activities?" Hektor asked.

"It's the only explanation I've been able to think of, My Prince," Mhulvayn said frankly. "So far as I'm aware, they have no suspicion at all of Zhaspahr. And, also so far as I'm aware, although they've issued warrants for my own arrest, they haven't arrested any of the sources and contacts I've cultivated. I suppose it's possible they're leaving those contacts alone, waiting to see who replaces me, but I believe it's more likely that someone in Nahrmahn's organization who'd become aware of my activities mentioned my name under interrogation. Wave Thunder knows enough to suspect *me*; I doubt he knows about the rest of our organization in Charis, or he would have moved against more of our agents, not me alone."

"I see." Hektor leaned further back in his chair, his expression thoughtful. He sat that way for at least three full minutes, then nodded.

"It may be you're correct in your assumptions," he said at last. "It's also possible, of course, that you aren't. However, there's no need to act hastily."

He picked up a small, silver bell and shook it. Its voice was clear and sweet, and the chamber door opened almost instantly.

"Yes, My Prince?" a captain in the uniform of Hektor's personal guard said.

"Escort this man back to his quarters, Captain," the prince said. "See to it that he's treated well and with respect, and that any of his reasonable needs and desires are met. Is that understood?"

"It is, My Prince."

"Good." Hektor looked back at Mhulvayn. "At the moment, I'm very much inclined to believe that whatever happened wasn't your fault, and that your service there was as loyal and efficient as it's always proved in the past. Until I can be certain of that, however, precautions must be taken."

"Of course, My Prince."

"Good," Hektor said again, and made a small waving gesture with his right hand. The Guard captain bowed respectfully to Mhulvayn, holding the door open for him, and Mhulvayn stepped out of the chamber into the hall beyond with a cautious sense of optimism.

▼   ▼   ▼

"What do you think?" Prince Hektor asked, glancing at Earl Coris as the door closed behind Mhulvayn and the Guard captain.

"I think we don't have any independent information to confirm a single thing he's said, Sire," Coris replied after a moment.

"So you think he's lying?"

"I didn't say that, Sire," the earl said with a calm self-confidence rather at odds with the attitude he normally projected in Hektor's presence when anyone else was present. "What I said is that we don't have any independent corroboration, and we don't. It's certainly possible he *is* lying—the notion that his organization was broken through some sort of fluke circumstance beyond anyone's control would be one way to cover his ass, after all—but I don't know that he is. I'm simply not prepared to automatically assume he isn't. And even if he is, it doesn't necessarily follow that his analysis of what happened is correct."

"I think," Hektor said after a long, thoughtful moment, "that I believe him. We didn't pick fools to send to Tellesberg, and only a fool would spin a tale like that, knowing that sooner or later we'd find out he'd lied to us. And I suspect his theory about what happened is also substantially accurate."

The prince pushed back his chair, stood, and crossed to the chamber window. It was a wide window, set into a thick wall of heat-shedding stone, and it was also open to any breath of breeze, for Corisande's capital of Manchyr was closer to the equator even then Tellesberg, and the midday sun was hot and high overhead. He leaned on the sill, gazing out over the brilliant tropical flowers of his palace gardens, listening to the occasional twitter of birdsong from the flocks of songbirds maintained in the palace aviary.

"Nahrmahn is a fool," he said quietly, with a dispassion which might have fooled most people, but did *not* fool Phylyp Ahzgood. "Langhorne knows Tohmas is no genius, but he knows better than to cross me, and he's not a total idiot, either. Nahrmahn, on the other hand, can give a very convincing imitation of one. We've always known that. But one works with the tools one has, and, to be honest, I'm afraid, I never realized just how big a fool he is."

"We already knew his people were involved in the assassination attempt, Sire," Coris pointed out, and Hektor nodded, never looking away from the gardens beyond the window.

"Agreed. But to have involved himself with Tirian was incredibly stupid. Eventually, one of them would have *had* to turn on the other, and to let himself be talked into attempting to assassinate Cayleb—!"

The prince turned back to face Coris at last, shaking his head, his square jaw tight with anger.

"If the attempt had succeeded, it would only have meant Tirian would betray him even sooner. Surely even he should have recognized that!"

"I agree Nahrmahn isn't especially bright, Sire. At the same time, he has displayed a certain ruthlessness about disposing of tools which become liabilities. I wouldn't be surprised to discover that he'd placed someone with a knife close to Tirian as an insurance policy."

"You're probably right." Hektor sounded as if he were conceding the possibility considerably against his will, but then he shrugged and shook his head angrily.

"Even assuming you are, however, any insurance policy he had obviously failed, didn't it? And it would appear from what Mhulvayn has to say that Haarahld is reacting very much as I would have anticipated. This idiot attempt must have cost Nahrmahn the better part of ten years of building up his own network in Charis! Not to mention the effect it's having on our own efforts! And I'm afraid the possibility Mhulvayn raised—that they do know the identities of at least some of his agents and Wave Thunder is simply choosing to leave them in position and watch them now that their master's had to flee for his life—also has to be very seriously considered."

He glanced back out the window again for a moment, then walked back across to his chair and sat down once more.

"And," he continued more grimly, "if Haarahld chooses to view this direct attack on the monarchy as an act of war, he may not stop with Nahrmahn's *spies*."

"Do you really think that's likely, Sire?"

"I don't know." Hektor drummed the fingers of one hand on the table. "Everyone knows how he dotes on Cayleb and his other children. Obviously, from what he's already done, he doesn't take this little affair lightly. And if he's got sufficient solid evidence, and if he chooses to treat this as an act of war, Nahrmahn may suddenly find the Charisian Navy sailing into Eraystor Bay. At which point we'll have to decide whether to support the idiot—which, by the way, will also associate us with the assassination attempt itself, at least after the fact—or else see a major component of our master plan go out from under us."

Coris considered the prince's words thoughtfully, eyes hooded.

"I think, Sire," he said finally, "that if Haarahld were likely to take direct military action, he'd already have taken it. Charis has gnough galleys in permanent commission to annihilate Nahrmahn's entire fleet in an afternoon, without our support, and Haarahld wouldn't give him the time to even try to activate his alliances with us."

"Maybe he would, and maybe he wouldn't," Hektor said. "Haarahld has to be a bit cautious himself, you know. He's not particularly popular in Zion or the Temple, and he knows it. Besides, everyone knows Nahrmahn—and I, of course—backed Mahntayl against Breygart in Hanth. There are those in the Temple, like Clyntahn and the rest of the Group of Four, who might choose to interpret any action he takes against Nahrmahn as retribution for that. So he's unlikely to launch any quick attacks without first establishing with very convincing evidence that he's completely justified."

Coris nodded.

"You may very well be right about that, Sire. If so, how do we proceed?"

"We protest our innocence, if he tries to associate us with Nahrmahn's attack." Hektor smiled thinly. "And we'll actually be telling the truth for a change. That should be a novel experience. And I think we ought to invite several of the more important of our other nobles to a personal meeting . . . without mentioning it to Nahrmahn. I need to be certain they understand what we're doing—or as much of it as they need to know about, at any rate. And I want Tohmas here, where I can look him in the eye."

"Sire?" Coris' eyebrows arched. "Do you think Tohmas is thinking about climbing into bed with Nahrmahn?"

"No," Hektor said slowly. "Not that. But I wouldn't be at all surprised if Nahrmahn isn't trying to *convince* him to. It would be like Nahrmahn to try to weaken my authority here in the League in order to increase his own bargaining strength. I don't think Tohmas is stupid enough to fall for it, but I need to be sure."

"And if Nahrmahn learns the two of you have met separately, Sire? And that he wasn't invited to send a representative to any of your meetings?"

"It might not be a bad thing if he did." Hektor smiled coldly, his eyes bleak. "First, Tohmas is one of the highest-ranked nobles in the League, and Emerald isn't even a League member. Nahrmahn has no right to a seat at our table unless we invite him to join us. And, second, it would please me to make the fool sweat a little. Besides," Hektor snorted, "given his part in the assassination plot, he can hardly hope to switch sides and betray us to Haarahld even if we do hurt his feelings, now can he?"

"I suppose not," Coris conceded with a thin smile of his own.

"In the meantime, we should probably decide what steps we can take to ratchet up the pressure on Charis while Haarahld's still distracted by his concentration on Emerald. And, of course," the prince added a touch bitterly, "to keep ourselves occupied while we recover from the damage Nahrmahn's little fiasco's done to our own organization in Tellesberg."

"What sort of steps did you have in mind, Sire?"

"I don't know that we have all that many opportunities for direct action," Hektor admitted, "and even if we did, I might avoid them for now. After all, it was Nahrmahn's notion of 'direct action' that created this mess in the first place! But it occurs to me that one thing we definitely ought to do is immediately step up our efforts to influence the Council of Vicars."

"Risky, Sire," Coris observed. Hektor's eyes flashed, but he took the earl's caution far more calmly than most of his courtiers would have expected.

"I know it is," he agreed after a second or two. "But, I think, riskier for Haarahld than for us. He's got that damned College of his hanging around his neck. With a little luck, we may be able to convince the Group of Four to turn it into an executioner's halter."

Coris nodded, but the gesture expressed more acceptance than agreement, and Hektor knew why. Corisande was even farther from the Temple than Charis, and the same automatic suspicion that attached to Charis in the Church's eyes also attached to Corisande. But Hektor had been very careful to do absolutely nothing to encourage that suspicion, whereas Haarahld's support for his father's "Royal College," and for the social policies his great-grandfather had set in motion, did the reverse. And Hektor and Nahrmahn between them had spread a great deal more gold around a great many more hands in the Temple than Haarahld had. Still, Coris had always been rather more ambivalent than his prince about playing the Temple card.

"What do you make of this 'Merlin' of Mhulvayn's, Sire?" the earl asked, and Hektor smiled thinly at the tactful change of subject.

"At the moment, not very much," he said. "I don't doubt the fellow really is good with a sword, but it seems fairly evident from what happened to

Nahrmahn's organization in Charis that it wouldn't have taken a genius—or a 'seijin,' assuming they actually exist, outside the old fables—to penetrate it. It sounds like he stumbled over something that gave away the attempt on Cayleb, and he's probably been riding it for all it's worth ever since."

"An adventurer, then, you think, Sire?"

"I think that's the most likely explanation," Hektor agreed. "At the same time," he went on a bit grudgingly, "Haarahld, unlike Nahrmahn, is no fool. Given the fact that the man clearly saved, or helped save, his son's life, I'd expect a man like Haarahld to treat the fellow as an honored guest. Probably find him some fairly comfortable slot at court for the rest of his life, for that matter, which is what this 'personal guardsman' business sounds like. But if this Merlin steps into the inner circle of Haarahld's advisers, then I'll be tempted to believe there's more to him than just an adventurer."

"Should we take steps to . . . remove him, Sire?"

"After the way Nahrmahn bungled the attempt on Cayleb?" Hektor shook his head with a hard, sharp crack of laughter. "The last thing we need is to get *our* people—assuming we still *have* any people in Tellesberg by this time, of course—involved in a second assassination! If it worked, Haarahld would probably suspect Nahrmahn, but we've just had rather convincing evidence that assassinations don't always work out as planned, haven't we?"

"I suppose we have, at that, Sire," Coris conceded with another thin smile.

"No," Hektor said. "I think we'll wait a while before we decide to have the good *seijin* eliminated. Unless he begins to make himself a significant threat, there are far better targets for us to expend our effort upon."

.II.
The Schooner *Dawn*,
Off Helen Island

"Well, Captain Rowyn? What do you think now?"

Merlin had to shout to make himself heard over the rushing sound of wind and water. Seagulls and sea wyverns swirled in raucous clouds of white feathers and glistening, many-hued hide under the brilliant springtime sun. They dipped and dove about the fifty-foot twin-masted schooner *Dawn* as she drove through the brilliant blue water of South Howell Bay in explosions of scattered, rainbow-hewed spray and left a straight, white wake behind her.

Dawn was the first schooner ever seen on Safehold. Sir Dustyn Olyvyr was the official designer of the rig, and *officially* Merlin was simply a passenger aboard her. But Horahs Rowyn, the skipper of Olyvyr's personal yacht, the *Ahnyet*, was one of the small but steadily growing handful of people who'd had to be told at least part of the truth about the sudden flood of new innovations. Rowyn knew who'd really come up with the converted coaster's new sail plan, and despite his faith in his patron, he'd been openly skeptical about Merlin's claims.

That was obviously changing.

The captain—a stocky, balding man with a fringe of gray hair around a bare, sun-bronzed scalp and a spectacularly weathered face—stood on the schooner's short, cramped quarterdeck staring in something very like disbelief at the masthead pendant which showed the wind's direction.

Dawn was sailing close-hauled on the port tack. In itself, that was nothing particularly unique, but as she leaned stiffly to starboard under the press of her brand-new, snowy-white canvas, she was doing it better than anyone else had ever dreamed of.

Even the best square-rigged sail plans yet devised on Safehold were little more weatherly than Columbus' ships had been in 1492, and their version of "close-hauled" was quite different from *Dawn*'s. The galleons which plied Safehold's seas could steer no closer than within seventy degrees of directly into the wind, what Nimue Alban would have called little better than a close reach, under even ideal conditions. Indeed, a more realistic figure would have been closer to eighty degrees, and most Safeholdian sailing masters would have settled for that without complaint.

But *Dawn* was sailing within just under *fifty* degrees of the true wind. Even that was far from spectacular by the standards of the sailing yachts Nimue had known on Old Earth's salt water, but *Dawn* had been converted from a typical Howell Bay coaster. She was relatively shoal-hulled and broad-beamed, without the fin keel or centerboard of one of those yachts. Merlin and Sir Dustyn had added leeboards to give her better hydrodynamics, but it was an awkward, makeshift fix, and the schooner rig itself was inherently less weatherly than the sloops or yawls Nimue had once sailed for recreation.

Yet however disappointed Nimue Alban might have been by *Dawn*'s performance in those long-ago days on Old Earth's North Sea, Merlin was delighted, and Rowyn was astounded. No ship he'd ever seen could have matched that performance, and if twenty or thirty degrees might not have sounded like all that much to a landsman, it meant a great deal to an experienced seaman.

The only way for a sail-powered vessel to travel to windward was to beat, to sail as close-hauled as possible and swing back and forth across the wind. At the best of times, it was a slow, laborious, hideously inefficient business compared to sailing with or on the wind, or to what a powered vessel could have accomplished. Or, for that matter, a galley . . . while her rowers' endurance lasted.

Tacking, which was essentially a matter of turning the ship across the wind, was the more efficient way of going about it, but that required the vessel doing the tacking to maintain forward speed—and steerage way—long enough to swing across the eye of the wind. Given how far a typical Safeholdian square-rigger had to turn to swing across the wind, that was usually a . . . problematic venture at the best of times. Far more frequently, especially in moderate or light winds, a current-generation square-rigger had to wear ship, instead, turning *downwind*, away from the direction it actually wanted to go, through an effective arc of well over two hundred degrees, until it could settle onto its new heading. In the process, it had to give up a heartbreaking amount of hard-won progress as the wind pushed it to leeward during the maneuver.

It was hardly surprising that tacking was the preferred technique, but even there, the square-rigger had to swing through a total heading change of a hundred and forty degrees across the wind each time it tacked. *Dawn's* total heading change, on the other hand, would be little more than ninety degrees. That left her a much shorter "no-sail zone" to cross, and her basic rig was what a sailor would have called much faster in the stays than any Safeholdian square-rigger. Which, basically, simply meant she came about more rapidly, and her sails could be reset on the new tack much more quickly.

Even completely ignoring the fact that she could get around on to the new tack so much more speedily, *Dawn's* twenty-degree advantage over the very best Safeholdian square-rigger ever built (it was actually closer to twenty-five degrees) meant that to reach a point sixty miles directly to windward of her start position, all other things being equal, she would have to sail the next best thing to ninety miles, while the square-rigger would have to travel a hundred and eighty. And that was assuming the square-rigger was able to tack at all, instead of wearing.

Unlike pre-metric Old Earth, Safehold's sea miles and land miles were the same length, which meant that if both *Dawn* and the square-rigger were traveling at speeds of six knots, *Dawn* would make the sixty miles dead to windward in fifteen hours, while the square-rigger would require thirty. Over a voyage of several hundred or even thousands of miles, that would represent a significantly shorter overall voyage time. It also meant the square-rigger could never *catch* the little schooner in a chase to windward, which would be a handy insurance policy against pirates. By the same token, the square-rigger couldn't *evade* the schooner to windward, which had interesting implications for potential warships . . . or pirates.

It was obvious to Merlin, and—he felt sure—to Horahs Rowyn, that *Dawn's* present sail plan was far from perfectly balanced, and she required far more lee helm than she should have to hold her present course. But no one on Safehold had any notion of how to make proper displacement and stability calculations, far less how to calculate appropriate sail areas. Merlin had access to the necessary formulas, thanks to the library computer tucked away in Nimue's Cave, but despite Nimue's yachting experience, he had only the most limited possible practical experience in applying them. More to the point, there was no way he could possibly hand something like that over to Olyvyr or Rahzhyr Mahklyn without raising all sorts of questions none of them would have wanted answered.

But imperfect or not, it was doing its job, and a designer with Olyvyr's years of experience would soon hit upon a workable rule of thumb for designing proper sail plans for the new rig.

Which, Merlin thought with a smile, *will only make* Dawn's *successors perform even better.*

Rowyn was still staring up at the masthead pendant. Obviously, he hadn't heard a word Merlin had said, so Merlin thumped him on the shoulder. The Charisian jerked, then turned his head quickly with a questioning expression.

"I asked what you think now?" Merlin repeated loudly, and Rowyn grinned hugely.

"I think I want one of my very own," he half-shouted back, "and so will everyone else who sees this. Langhorne! Just look at that heading! And the reduction in sail handlers is going to be another big advantage for your typical clutch-fisted shipowner."

"Agreed." Merlin nodded vigorously. Any square-rigger was a manpower-intensive proposition, and a schooner-rigged vessel like *Dawn* required a much smaller crew. Conversely, the square-rigger could carry an enormous sail area, and because her sails tended to be individually smaller in proportion to her total sail plan, she could absorb more damage aloft than most schooner rigs could.

"Sir Dustyn tells me he wants *Ahnyet* re-rigged, too," Rowyn continued, cocking an eyebrow at Merlin, and Merlin chuckled.

"*Dawn*'s an experiment, Captain. Now that Sir Dustyn has his hand in, as it were, he's ready to do it right with *Ahnyet*. The fact that he designed her himself should give him a much better feel for modifying her rig, too. And then, of course, he's going to be inviting potential ship buyers aboard for a little cruise outside the Tellesberg breakwater. Just as a purely social occasion, of course."

"Oh, of course!" Rowyn agreed with a deep, rolling belly laugh. "He's been using that ship for 'purely social occasions' like that for as long as I've captained her for him. But this—"

He reached out and stroked the quarterdeck rail almost reverently, gazing back up at the masthead pendant and the set of the sails once again, then shook his head and looked back at Merlin.

"I think I'd best be getting a feel for the way she handles, Lieutenant Athrawes."

It was technically a statement, but actually a request, a recognition that *Dawn* was truly Merlin's ship . . . and that Merlin would be his real tutor over the next few days.

"I think that's an excellent idea, Captain," Merlin agreed, and hid another mental smile.

I wonder how Sir Dustyn would react if he knew the real reason I argued in favor of a pure fore-and-aft rig for our prototype?

Despite himself, he laughed out loud, and Rowyn looked at him with an interrogatory expression. But Merlin only shook his head. Eventually, he was certain, the topsail schooner would emerge as the rig of choice. With the addition of square-rigged topsails on both masts, and even a square-rigged course on the foremast, it was probably the most powerful two-masted schooner rig ever devised. It could be driven harder and faster on the wind without sacrificing a great deal of its weatherliness, which would make it highly attractive to anyone looking for speedy passages, although the manpower demands would rise. But Merlin had no more intention of explaining to Rowyn than to Sir Dustyn Olyvyr that the fellow responsible for showing them this marvelous new rig had absolutely no idea how to manage a square-rigger.

That probably wouldn't have done a lot for their confidence in my "suggestions," Merlin thought sardonically, then gave himself a mental shake and grinned at Rowyn.

"Why don't you step over here and take the helm yourself for a few minutes, Captain Rowyn?" he invited.

NOVEMBER,
YEAR OF GOD 890

Archbishop Erayk's Quarters,
City of Zion

G ood morning, Erayk."
    Erayk Dynnys sat a bit straighter in the comfortable armchair. Well, the chair *would* have been comfortable, if anything could have been. It was heavily upholstered, the cushions deep enough that it took Dynnys' valet and a Temple guardsman to boost him out of it when it was time to rise.

Unfortunately, with a leg broken in three places and a shoulder broken in at least two, there was no such thing as a comfortable place to sit.

At the moment, however, that was definitely in third or fourth place amongst his concerns as he found himself confronting a man in the unadorned orange priest's cap of a vicar.

"Good morning, Your Grace," he said. "Forgive my appearance. I . . . wasn't expecting a visitor this morning."

"I'm aware of that," Vicar Zahmsyn Trynair said with a gentle smile. "I was in the vicinity on another matter, however, and I thought I'd just drop in and see how you were doing."

Dynnys nodded with a smile of his own, although he was perfectly well aware that Trynair intended for him to realize he'd just been lied to. The Chancellor of the Council of Vicars didn't "just happen" to drop in on a mere archbishop. Especially not at this time of year, when the visit required the Vicar in question to leave the mystically heated precincts of his luxurious personal quarters in the Temple itself.

"May I?" Trynair gestured gracefully at another chair in Dynnys' sitting room, the sapphire ring of his office flashing in the lamplight, and the archbishop gave himself a shake.

"Please, be seated, Your Grace!" he said hastily. "And please forgive my lack of manners, as well. I truly wasn't expecting you, and I'm afraid the healers are still prescribing poppy juice."

"Don't concern yourself about it," Trynair said graciously. "After a fall such as yours, we're indeed fortunate your injuries weren't even more severe."

"I appreciate your understanding, Your Grace."

Dynnys waited while Trynair settled himself into the indicated chair. The Chancellor was taller than Dynnys, leaner, with an angular face, deep, intelligent eyes, and a closely trimmed beard. He wore the orange cassock of his exalted rank, badged with the blue quill sigil of the Order of Chihiro, and the hem of his cassock was damp with melted snow to above midcalf.

"May I offer you something to drink, Your Grace?" Dynnys asked once the Chancellor had seated himself and extended his hands to the coal fire crackling cheerfully on the hearth.

"Some hot chocolate would be most welcome on a day like this," Trynair agreed, and Dynnys nodded to his valet, who scurried off to deal with the request.

"I haven't been out myself, of course, Your Grace," Dynnys said, "but people tell me the weather's unusually severe this year."

"They tell you correctly, Erayk." Trynair chuckled and shook his head. "The snow's over three feet deep out there, and it's only November—not even full winter yet! I've seldom seen so many snowfalls so early in the season. And," his expression turned graver, "I'm afraid it's had a predictable effect on the semaphore."

Dynnys nodded glumly. The greatest single weakness of the Church's semaphore system was that it was visibility-limited. Darkness, snow, rain, fog—any and all of them could and did shut down Mother Church's communications relays. There was a system to send signals through simple darkness, but it was less reliable—more vulnerable to errors in transcription at the various semaphore stations—and much slower, and it still couldn't cope with typical winter weather's decreased visibility.

"It's always that way, isn't it, Your Grace?" he said after a moment, with an air of resignation.

"Yes, yes it is. Those in other lands who envy us our high office seldom think about the penance we pay each winter here in Zion and the Temple. Although," Trynair allowed himself a chuckle which struck Dynnys' ear as not quite truly spontaneous, "you yourself have been spared that particular penance for the past several years, haven't you?"

"I suppose I have," Dynnys replied, just a bit slowly, while his poppy-fumed brain raced. "And," he acknowledged with a chuckle of his own, "I suppose I ought to admit I've scheduled my pastoral visits expressly to avoid winter here in Zion, Your Grace."

"I'm not surprised," Trynair said dryly, then snorted. "Anyone but a village idiot *would* schedule them that way, if he had the option! *I* certainly would."

"Well, perhaps this"—Dynnys' left hand indicated the plaster the bonesetter had used to immobilize his shattered right leg and the sling supporting his right arm—"is all of those years of missed penances catching up with me at last."

He managed to keep his voice almost normal, but it was difficult. The pain was bad enough, but the healers had already warned him he would require a cane, at best, for his right leg would never be the same again.

"Oh, I doubt that." Trynair spoke in a voice so deliberately jovial that Dynnys suspected the Vicar had already heard the same healers' reports. "None of us is perfect, Erayk, but I rather doubt you could be *imperfect* enough to have laid up a debt quite that severe. On the other hand"—the Chancellor's eyes sharpened—"it may, perhaps, be . . . unfortunate that you suffered your accident at this particular time."

"Your Grace?" Dynnys felt his own eyes narrow slightly as he realized Trynair was finally approaching the true point of his visit.

"I'm sure you're aware that certain . . . concerns have been expressed about Charis," the Chancellor said. He held Dynnys' gaze until the archbishop nodded.

"I am, Your Grace. Indeed, I've passed those concerns on to Bishop Executor Zherald and Father Paityr, and I'd intended to devote quite a bit of my own attention to them while I was in Tellesberg. Now, though—"

His left hand indicated the heavy weight of plaster once again, and his left shoulder shrugged.

"I understand, of course." Trynair leaned forward to pat Dynnys lightly on his good knee, then straightened once more as the valet returned with an exquisitely glazed cup of tissue-thin Harchong porcelain filled with steaming hot chocolate.

The Chancellor accepted the cup with a murmur of thanks and sipped deeply and appreciatively while the valet set the matching chocolate pot and a second cup on the small table between him and Dynnys. The valet raised one eyebrow, indicating the unused cup, but the archbishop shook his head slightly. The valet bowed in acknowledgment and withdrew as silently as he had arrived.

"I understand—we all understand—why your usual pastoral visit had to be canceled this year," the Chancellor resumed after a moment. "It's regrettable, naturally, but given the nature and extent of your injuries, it was also unavoidable."

"I appreciate your understanding, Your Grace. I'd be less than honest, however, if I didn't say I would far rather be in Tellesberg right now than here."

He waved at the sitting room window. The glass was well sealed into its frame, and the cozy sitting room was free of any of the icy drafts which plagued so many homes here in Zion, yet the windowpane was heavily frosted, despite the fire on the hearth. Elsewhere in the city, he knew, people less fortunate than he were huddled around any source of heat they could find, and fall and winter always produced hunger, as well. Ships could still make it across Lake Pei, with food from the huge granaries and farms in the southern Temple Lands, but eventually, that route, too, would be closed. The city would become totally dependent upon its own granaries and storehouses, and somehow, huge as those were, they always ran short before spring in a city this size. When the present snow melted or was removed, the inevitable bodies would be found where the combination of cold, hunger, and lack of shelter had overtaken the most vulnerable of the city's poor.

"And I," Trynair said, his eyes very level, "would be less than honest if I didn't say I would far rather *have* you there than here at this moment, as well."

"Your Grace, forgive me, but I believe you didn't just happen to 'drop in' on me this morning. I'm deeply honored by your visit, of course, but I can't avoid the suspicion that you have something rather more serious than the weather on your mind."

"I suppose I was guilty of a little white lie," Trynair agreed with a smile. He sipped more hot chocolate for a moment, then lowered the cup. "I did have other business in the city today—that much was quite true, Erayk. But you're right. I do have certain concerns of my own which I wish to bring to your attention."

"Of course, Your Grace. Please tell me how I can serve you and the Church."

Dynnys heard the edge of wariness in his own voice, but Trynair ignored it. No doubt the Chancellor was accustomed to that reaction. As the acknowledged senior member of the vicars known (unofficially, of course) as the "Group of Four," he was the single most powerful man in the entire Temple.

Everyone knew Grand Vicar Erek XVII had been elevated to the grand vicarate only because Trynair had been too busy to seek the Throne of Langhorne for himself. Nor had there been any reason he had to. Erek XVII was little more than a figurehead, completely dominated by Trynair and the Grand Inquisitor, the dominant members of the Group of Four. It was said—very quietly, with carefully hidden snickers—that the Grand Vicar routinely demonstrated his independence of Trynair's direction by choosing which pair of shoes he would wear.

"No one is dissatisfied with the service you've already rendered, Erayk," Trynair said in reassuring tones. "However, as I'm sure you're aware, many members of the Council have felt increasingly . . . uneasy over Charis' growing wealth and influence for quite some time. There are those persistent rumors that the Kingdom is dabbling in proscribed techniques and knowledge. And the equally persistent rumors that Haarahld and his ministers have succeeded in evading their rightful tithes. Then there was that matter of the dispute over Hanth. And, of course, there's always that 'Royal College' of Haarahld's."

The Chancellor shook his head, his expression pensive, and Dynnys drew a deep, surreptitious breath.

"Your Grace," he began, "I realize the rumors and accounts of which you've spoken have to be weighed and considered carefully. However, I've made all of Bishop Executor Zherald's and Father Paityr's reports available to the Council. And my own observations on my past pastoral visits have been that—"

"Erayk." Trynair interrupted him, raising one hand and shaking his head with a slight, crooked smile, and the archbishop paused.

"No one's accusing you, or Bishop Executor Zherald, of any wrongdoing or inattention to your responsibilities. I've personally read many of your reports, and I've reviewed other sources of information. I trust your intelligence and your attention to the duties of your archbishopric, and I believe your observations have been substantially accurate in the past."

"Thank you, Your Grace," Dynnys said into the silence as Trynair paused. "I appreciate that."

"It's no more than your due," Trynair assured him. But then the Chancellor continued gravely. "However, the reports we've been receiving over the past months are different from earlier ones. They appear to be coming from many additional sources, and too many of them agree in form and content."

"I've fallen somewhat behind in my own correspondence over the past few five-days, Your Grace," Dynnys said slowly, cautiously. "Has there been some additional change in that time period?"

"To some extent, there has," Trynair confirmed. Dynnys sat up straighter, wincing at the pain of his injudicious movement, and Trynair shook his head quickly. "It's more a matter of volume then changes in content, Erayk," he said. "And, to be fair, I think it's entirely possible the seasonal loss of the semaphore has all of us in the Temple paying more attention to past correspondence than we might otherwise have done. After all," he smiled ruefully, "it's not as if there's a great deal of *new* correspondence to distract us from our chilblains!"

Dynnys chuckled dutifully, but his eyes remained serious, and Trynair shrugged.

"I've also read Father Paityr's reports on all of these new 'innovations' coming out of Charis, as have Vicar Zhaspyr and several other members of the Council. While Father Paityr appears to be comporting himself in his usual conscientious and hardworking fashion, Vicar Zhaspyr isn't entirely satisfied with all of his conclusions."

Dynnys felt genuine alarm. He tried to keep it from getting as far as his expression, but it was obvious he hadn't completely succeeded in the effort, and he cursed the befuddling effect of the poppy juice.

"No one is arguing that we have a genuine infraction of the Proscriptions, Erayk," Trynair said soothingly. But any reassuring effect was wiped away by his next words. "Yet, at least. There's some decided concern about where your Charisians may end up if they continue along this road, however."

"Your Grace, I assure you that as soon as I'm fit to travel, I'll—"

"Erayk, Erayk!" Trynair shook his head. "No one expects you to leap up out of your sickbed and go galavanting off to Charis through the middle of a Haven winter! As I say, we've seen no evidence that the Proscriptions have already been violated. Our concerns are for the future, and I'm sure there's no need for you to slog off through the snow to deal with them at this time. We would like you to schedule your next pastoral visit for as early in the year as possible, but no one's suggested packing you off to your archbishopric before the ice melts in Hsing-wu's Passage in the spring."

"Thank you, Your Grace. I . . . appreciate that, and of course I'll arrange to make the journey as soon as practical."

"Good. In the meantime, however, you need to be aware of how the Council is thinking," Trynair said more gravely. "Just last night, Vicar Zhaspyr, Vicar Rhobair, Vicar Allayn, and I were discussing this very point at an informal little dinner."

Despite the sitting room's warmth, Dynnys felt the marrow of his bones try to freeze. Zhaspahr Clyntahn was the Grand Inquisitor. Rhobair Duchairn was the Church's Treasurer General, Allayn Magwair was the Church's Captain General, and Trynair himself was the Council's Chancellor. Which meant Trynair's "informal little dinner" had actually been a working session of the Group of Four. *All* of the Group of Four.

"The problem, Erayk," Trynair said in that same grave tone, "is that, whether Haarahld of Charis intends it that way or not, his kingdom has the potential to become a serious threat. Whatever Father Paityr may be reporting about their current innovations, the sheer pace of the changes they're introducing is dangerous. We have many reports—not all, admittedly, from impartial sources—that the danger we fear in this regard may well be closer at hand than we'd originally thought. The *Writ* itself teaches that change begets change, after all, and that it is in times of change that Mother Church must be most watchful.

"Yet, even leaving that issue aside for the moment, there are other issues, issues which affect the Church's power in the secular world, as well. I realize Mother Church and we who serve her are supposed to be above the concerns of this world, but you know as well as I do that it's necessary, sometimes, for God's Church to have the power to act decisively in *this* world in order to protect men's souls in the next.

"Charis has grown too wealthy. Its ships travel too broadly, and its ideas spread too widely. Other nations will be quick to adopt Charisian innovations, if they appear to offer significant advantages. If that happens, then our concerns about the possible destination to which Charis' taste for . . . new things may lead will perforce spread to all of those other nations, as well. And we must not forget Charis' social restiveness. That, too, is being exported aboard its ships. When other kingdoms see the wealth which Charis has attained, it would be strange, indeed, if they weren't tempted to follow in Charis' wake. And, as your own reports have made evident"—Trynair's gaze bored into Dynnys' eyes—"King Haarahld is a stubborn man, as witness his insistence on naming his own man Bishop of Tellesberg. A king whose stubbornness, I fear, makes him altogether too likely to rule himself and his kingdom by his own judgment . . . even if that judgment conflicts with that of Mother Church."

Silence hovered for endless seconds, broken only by the whine of wind outside the window and the crackle of coal on the hearth.

"Your Grace," Dynnys said finally, "I thank you for bringing the Council's concerns to my attention. I understand the reasons for them, I believe, but I beg you and the other Vicars not to rush to judgment. Whatever else Charis may be, it's only a single kingdom. Despite the size of its merchant fleet, and its navy, it's basically a small land, with only a small population. Surely any danger it may represent isn't so pressing that we can't dispel it by taking timely action against it."

"I hope and believe you're right, Erayk," Trynair said, after a moment. "But remember, the Archangel Pasquale teaches us corruption can spread from even a tiny wound, if it isn't properly cleansed and purified. It's not the individual size and strength of Charis that gives us concern. It's what may grow and spread from it in the fullness of time. And, to be frank, from my own perspective, the possibility that the fundamental . . . defiance of Charis' attitude may combine with that of Siddarmark."

Dynnys had begun to open his mouth once more, but he closed it abruptly. So that was it—for Trynair, at least.

For the past five decades, the princes of the Church had been increasingly concerned over the republic of Siddarmark's growing power. The Republic dominated the eastern third of the continent of Haven, and while it was less populous than the Harchong Empire, its infantry were a terrifying force on the field of battle. And unlike the Harchongese or Desnairi, the Republic's highest offices were elective, not purely hereditary.

The Republic was separated from the Temple Lands by the so-called Border States which stretched almost twenty-five hundred miles from Hsing-wu's Passage in the north to the Gulf of Dohlar in the south. At their southern end, the Border States provided a buffer almost thirteen hundred miles across, but in the extreme north, northeast of the Mountains of Light, along the southern edge of Hsing-wu's Passage, the Republic's provinces of Tarikah and Iceland actually shared a common border with the Temple Lands.

And the Republic of Siddarmark, unlike the Kingdom of Charis, had the population—and the army—to pose a genuine threat to the Temple Lands' security.

The likelihood that the Republic would be mad enough to actually challenge Mother Church might not be very great, but it wasn't one the Church's great magnates were prepared to ignore, either. That was one reason Trynair and his predecessors as Chancellor had played the Kingdom of Dohlar and the Desnairian Empire off against the Republic for the past thirty years.

But if Charis' wealth and naval power were to suddenly find themselves allied with the matchless pikemen of Siddarmark, the counterpoised tensions the Church had arranged in Haven might find themselves abruptly destabilized. And if the Charisian "social restiveness" Trynair had just complained of melded with the Siddarmarkian version of the same thing, the Church might find herself facing the greatest threat to her primacy of her entire history.

"Your Grace," he said "I understand. These are grave matters, not really suited to open transmission over the semaphore, even if weather permitted it. However, I'll immediately draft new instructions to Bishop Executor Zherald and dispatch them overland by courier. I'll make him aware of your concerns and charge him to be particularly vigilant. And as soon as Hsing-wu's Passage clears in the spring, I'll personally journey to Tellesberg."

"Good, Erayk. That's good," Trynair said, and smiled as he reached for his chocolate cup once again.

Hold!"

Merlin stepped back instantly, lowering his wooden training sword, and cocked his head inquiringly.

"Yes, Your Highness? Was there a problem?"

Crown Prince Cayleb took his left hand from his own hilt, reached up, and dragged off his fencing mask. His face was streaked with sweat, and he was breathing more than a little hard as he glowered at "Lieutenant Athrawes."

"You," he puffed, ". . . don't sweat . . . enough."

Merlin quirked an eyebrow politely. It was quite visible, since, unlike the prince, he wore neither a mask nor training armor.

"Sweat," Cayleb told him severely, "is good for you. It opens the pores. Helps get rid of poisons."

"I appreciate your concern, Your Highness." Merlin inclined his head in a small bow. "But some of us take sufficient care with what we eat that we don't find it necessary to sweat out poisons."

"Oh, yes," Cayleb snorted. "I've noticed what a picky eater you are!" He shook his head. "You do your share at the table, Merlin."

"One tries, Your Highness. One tries."

Cayleb chuckled, and Merlin smiled, although the prince's observation wasn't entirely humorous as far as Merlin was concerned.

The fact that a PICA was designed to allow its user to savor the taste of food and drink did, in fact, let him hold his own at meals. Unfortunately, a PICA's . . . waste-disposal arrangements would have been more than enough to raise Safeholdian eyebrows, since he didn't have any digestive processes in the usual sense of the word. While the mechanics were essentially identical, what was left after his nannies had scavenged whatever they needed meant Merlin had to be careful to empty any chamber pots himself. It was, perhaps, fortunate that Safehold had developed indoor plumbing, at least in royal palaces.

Then there was another minor technical difficulty which Cayleb's humorous comment about sweating had put a finger squarely upon. PICAs *could* "sweat," but it wasn't exactly an ability of which most of their users had ever availed themselves, for fairly obvious reasons. Which meant producing that sweat in appropriate quantity and locations had acquired some finicky adjustments to Merlin's internal programming. And, as Cayleb had noted, he still "sweated" extraordinarily lightly for a flesh-and-blood human being. Fortunately, the fact of his supposed *seijin*hood and the physical and mental disciplines which attached to it gave him a degree of cover, even at times like this.

"Actually, Your Highness," he said, "I can't escape the feeling that you're criticizing *my* sweat level to distract attention from your own."

"Oh, a low blow, Merlin!" Cayleb laughed and shook his head. "A low blow, indeed."

"With all due respect, Your Highness," Ahrnahld Falkhan observed from where he stood to one side of the training ground, "Merlin has a point. You do seem just a bit, ah, *damper* than he does."

"Because *I'm* not a *seijin*, which he, obviously, *is*," Cayleb pointed out. "I don't see you being willing to stand out here and let him humiliate *you*, Ahrnahld."

"Because I'm quite satisfied with the sword techniques I already know, Your Highness," Falkhan replied cheerfully, and this time all three of them chuckled.

"Well, it really is just a little humiliating," Cayleb said, looking Merlin up and down. Unlike the prince's protective gear, Merlin had stripped to the waist while he instructed Cayleb in the art of kendo.

He felt just a little bit guilty about that. Cayleb needed every bit of protection against Merlin's occasionally punishing "touches" that he could get, whereas the prince had yet to get a single stroke through Merlin's guard unless Merlin chose to let him do so. Which wasn't really all that surprising, even though he strongly suspected that Cayleb's natural aptitude considerably outclassed that of the flesh-and-blood Nimue Alban. The Crown Prince, however, wasn't up against Nimue; he was up against Merlin Athrawes, whose nervous impulses moved a hundred times faster than his own. Merlin's reaction speed was, quite literally, inhuman, and he took full advantage of it while training Cayleb.

It wasn't simply to embarrass the prince, either, as Cayleb understood perfectly. Cayleb had expressed an interest in Merlin's fighting style almost the first day after Merlin had been officially assigned as his bodyguard, and Merlin wasn't at all averse to teaching the young man a technique no one else on the entire planet could possibly be familiar with.

Having agreed to teach him, though, and having produced a "spare" katana for the prince from his baggage (this one made out of regular steel), Merlin had deliberately used a PICA's reactions and strength to put Cayleb up against someone faster and stronger than any possible human opponent. The prince was a highly competitive youngster. He took his complete inability to pierce Merlin's guard as a challenge, not as a discouragement, and training against someone with Merlin's abilities ought to make taking on any mortal opponent seem like a casual stroll through the park.

Besides, Merlin thought with a mental smile, *I'm a seijin. I'm supposed to be better than he is*. Just a trace of his inner smile touched his lips as he recalled Pei Kau-yung teaching Nimue Alban the same moves, the same techniques. *"When you can snatch the pebble out of my hand, Grasshopper,"* Kau-yung had said like some ritualistic phrase at the beginning of each bout, then proceeded to whack the holy living daylights out of her.

Merlin still didn't know where he'd gotten the quotation from. He'd promised to tell Nimue the first time she outpointed him in a formal competition, and that day had never come.

His smile faded, and he shook his head, looking at Cayleb, remembering Kau-yung and Nimue.

"If you'd been doing this as long as I have, Grasshopper," he said, "you'd be just as good at it as I am."

" 'Grasshopper'?" Cayleb repeated, raising both eyebrows. There was a Safeholdian insect analogue called a "grasshopper," although this one was carnivorous and about nine inches long. "Where did *that* come from?"

"Ah," Merlin told him. "When you score three unanswered touches in a row, I'll tell you, Your Highness."

"Oh, you will, will you?" Cayleb glowered at him, and Falkhan laughed.

"You aren't helping here, Ahrnahld," Cayleb told him, and Falkhan shrugged.

"I think it's a perfectly reasonable stipulation, Your Highness. Think of it as a . . . motivator."

"Instead of an insurmountable challenge, you mean?"

"Oh, I'd never call it *that*, Your Highness."

Merlin's smile returned as he watched them. In experiential terms, he wasn't actually all that much older than Falkhan. Nimue Alban had been only twenty-seven standard years old when the Federation mounted Operation Ark, after all. Yet, as he looked at them, he felt far, far older. Perhaps some of the centuries which had trickled past while Nimue's PICA slept had left some sort of subliminal impress upon his molycirc brain?

"You'd *better* not call it that," Cayleb told Falkhan ominously, then scrubbed the back of one training gauntlet across his sweaty forehead.

"If you don't mind, Merlin," he said, "I'm thinking I'd just as soon call it a day. In fact, I'm thinking that since Ahrnahld here is so full of himself this afternoon, we might just try a little game of rugby."

"Are you sure you want to go there, Your Highness?" Falkhan asked, and Cayleb smiled nastily.

"Oh, I'm *quite* sure, Ahrnahld. Especially since I pick Merlin for the first member of my team."

Falkhan looked suddenly much more thoughtful, and Cayleb chuckled.

"Does Merlin know the rules?" the Marine inquired.

"Rules? In *rugby?*"

"Well, there is that," Falkhan acknowledged, then shrugged. "Very well, Your Highness. Challenge accepted."

▼   ▼   ▼

Charisian "rugby," it turned out, wasn't *quite* the game Merlin had expected.

Nimue Alban had never actually played rugby, which had remained a "thug's game played by gentlemen," in her father's estimation. She had, however, seen it played, and Merlin had felt reasonably confident of holding his own.

But *Charisian* rugby was a water sport.

Merlin had no idea who'd invented it, or retained the name of the Old Earth game for it, but he could see certain similarities to the only rugby matches Nimue had ever seen. The object was to get the ball—actually, the somewhat asymmetrical inflated bladder of a sea cow, a ten foot long, roughly walrus-like aquatic mammal—into the other team's net while playing shoulder-deep in the sea. Apparently, any tactic, short of actually drowning one of your opponents, was acceptable, as long as your intended victim had possession of the ball. Merlin was certain there had to be at least some rules, although it quickly became apparent there couldn't be very many. And strategy appeared to consist of swarming whoever had the ball and holding him under until he agreed to give it up.

Normally, that wouldn't have posed any difficulty for Merlin. After all, he had ten times the strength of any of his opponents, his reaction speed was faster, and he had no particular need to breathe. Unfortunately, there were still a few minor technical problems.

First, it seemed the Charisian custom when swimming, at least as long as only one sex was present, was to swim nude. Second, Charisian rugby was most definitely a "contact sport." Third, PICAs were designed to be *fully* functional. Fourth, Nimue Alban had been a woman.

Merlin had already observed that simply switching genders hadn't made women magically sexually attractive to him. He hadn't quite followed through to the corollary of that discovery, however. But when he abruptly found himself in the middle of a wet, splashing, *slithery* swirl of seventeen other naked male bodies—all of them extraordinarily physically fit, *young* male bodies—he discovered that PICA or no, he was, indeed, "fully functional."

Nimue had never really considered just how embarrassing her male friends and acquaintances must have found certain physiological responses to arousal, especially on social occasions. Merlin supposed the present occasion might be considered a social one, however, and he found that response *extremely* embarrassing. The fact that he'd never experienced it before only added to the . . . interesting nature of the phenomenon.

It also meant he spent the entire game very carefully staying in water which was at least chest-deep, and that he was the last person out of the water, *and* that he deployed his towel very carefully when he finally did emerge.

"They don't play rugby where you come from?" Cayleb asked him, vigorously toweling his hair, and Merlin—whose towel was knotted around his waist, *not* drying his hair—shook his head.

"The water's just a bit colder up in the Mountains of Light," he pointed out. It was a non sequitur, although there was no way for Cayleb to know that, and he smiled. "We did play a game we *called* 'rugby' when I was a child. It wasn't like this one, though. It was played on land."

"Ah, *that* explains it." Cayleb chuckled. "I was afraid there for a few minutes that Ahrnahld's team might actually win. But you seemed to get the hang of it after all."

"Oh, I certainly did, Your Highness," Merlin said.

"Good. Because, next time, I want to really pin his ears back."

"I'll certainly try," Merlin promised.

.III.
Vicar Rhobair Duchairn's Suite,
The Temple of God

I told you it wouldn't do any good," Zhaspahr Clyntahn said grumpily. The Grand Inquisitor was a portly man, with a head of carefully brushed silver hair and the substantial jowls of a man well accustomed to good food and drink. There were a few gravy spots on his orange cassock as he sat back from the table in Rhobair Duchairn's dining room at last and reached for his wineglass once more.

"Oh, come now, Zhaspahr," Duchairn said chidingly. He was taller than Clyntahn, and rather more acetic in appearance. "What, exactly, do you expect Dynnys to do? The man's got a broken leg and a broken shoulder, for God's sake! He's scarcely going to go out, hop on a horse or a dragon, and go plowing off through the winter!"

"If he'd been doing his job properly *before* he broke his leg," Allayn Magwair said harshly, "we wouldn't have this problem now, would we?"

"If we actually have a problem at all, of course," Duchairn replied in a rather more pointed tone.

"Now, now, Rhobair," Zahmsyn Trynair said. "Allayn and Zhaspahr may be a bit overly inclined to dwell on the negative, but I think you'd have to admit that *you* have a vested interest in overemphasizing the positive."

"If you mean I'm aware of the contributions Charis makes to the Treasury each year, you're quite correct," Duchairn conceded unapologetically. "For that matter, I think all of us are also aware that it's substantially cheaper for our bailiffs and stewards to buy Charisian goods than it is to buy from the Republic or the Empire."

Clyntahn's snort sounded remarkably porcine, but both Magwair and Trynair nodded, if only grudgingly in Magwair's case.

Any one of the men seated around that table in the comfort of the Temple's warmth was more powerful, even in purely secular terms, than the vast majority of Safehold's dukes and grand dukes. Most of them controlled vast Church estates in other lands and kingdoms, as well, but all of them were the masters of wealthy, powerful fiefdoms in the Temple Lands themselves. In addition to their membership on the Council of Vicars, all of them also held seats on the ruling council of the Knights of the Temple Lands, the official governing body of the Temple Lands. And whether they wanted to admit it or not, all of them were aware that the Charisian manufactories and the Charisian merchant marine could provide the goods—and luxuries—they required at a much lower price than anyone else.

Not to mention the fact that Charis paid at least three or four times as much per capita in tithes every year than any other Safeholdian kingdom.

"None of us wants to kill the wyvern that fetches the golden rabbit, Rhobair," Trynair said. "But the truth is—and you know it as well as I do—that the time is coming when Charis is going to have to be seen to. It's getting too powerful, too successful, and it's too damned in love with its 'innovations.'"

"Hear, hear," Clyntahn muttered, and drank deeply from his wineglass.

Trynair grimaced, but neither he nor either of his other two companions were fooled. Zhaspahr Clyntahn was a glutton by nature, and not just for food and drink, but he was also a dangerously intelligent man, and a very complex one. His was an odd fusion of ambition, laziness, cynicism, and a genuine fervor for the responsibilities of his high office. He could demonstrate furious energy one day and utter lethargy the next, but only a fool took him lightly.

"Zahmsyn's right, Rhobair," Magwair said after a moment. "Haarahld and his fleabite kingdom are useful. No one questions that. But they're also a danger, and one we can't allow to grow much greater."

Duchairn grunted in sour agreement. Then he cocked his head with a nasty little smile.

"There are those reports from Father Paityr, Zhaspahr," he pointed out provocatively.

"Bugger 'Father Paityr,'" Clyntahn growled. "He and that whole Wylsynn bunch are all pains in the arse!"

Trynair hastily picked up his own wineglass, using it to hide his sudden smile. Magwair was less tactful and let out a sharp crack of laughter. One of the reasons Father Paityr Wylsynn had been packed off to Charis, as all of Clyntahn's allies were aware, was that his father had been Clyntahn's closest competitor for the post of Grand Inquisitor. It had been a very close-run contest, and, in the end, Clyntahn had won primarily because the Wylsynn reputation for reformatory zeal had made a slim majority of the Council nervous.

"If 'Father Paityr' were doing his job properly, we wouldn't have to pussyfoot around this way," Clyntahn grumbled.

"Then call him home and replace him," Duchairn suggested sweetly.

"*Ha!* That'd be a *wonderful* idea, wouldn't it?" Clyntahn half-sneered. "Can't you just see him and his daddy standing up in the Council to complain that I was pressuring him to falsify his reports?"

Duchairn started to launch another jab, then stopped himself and shrugged. After all, Clyntahn was right. That was precisely what young Father Paityr would do, and his father and the other members of his unfortunately powerful family would undoubtedly support him. Reputation for piety or no, most of them wouldn't care one way or the other about the grounds for the dispute. But they would never pass up the opportunity to whittle away at the Group of Four's powerbase in any way they could.

"You probably have a point, Zhaspahr," he conceded instead, after a moment. "On the other hand, we *are* stuck with his reports."

"You're right about that," Magwair agreed moodily.

No one suggested undertaking a little judicious editing of the reports in question, although all of them knew it had been done in the past. But the same political considerations which put simply recalling young Wylsynn out of consideration would have applied to any . . . liberties they might take with his written reports.

Besides, Duchairn thought, *the sanctimonious little twerp's almost certainly sent duplicate copies of his reports to his father.*

"So *I'm* not going to be able to deal with the problem," Clyntahn pointed out. "Not anytime soon, anyway."

"And without being called in by Zhaspahr, *I* can't, either," Magwair added bitterly.

As if we had the naval power to attack Charis ourselves in the first place! Duchairn thought.

"Direct action may not be our best course, anyway," Trynair said. All eyes turned to him, and the Chancellor shrugged. "We've already been . . . encouraging Hektor and Nahrmahn. Perhaps it's time we began considering who *else* we might encourage."

Duchairn grunted unhappily at the thought. It wasn't as if the Council hadn't used similar approaches in the past. Nor, as much as he would have preferred to, could he simply dismiss his colleagues' worries over Charis out of hand. As they said, it wasn't so much the *direct* threat Charis represented as it was the threat of Charis' *example*.

"Who did you have in mind?" Magwair asked Trynair.

"We know Hektor's been working on Gorjah of Tarot," Trynair pointed out. "We could lend our weight to his efforts there. It might be wise to establish at least some preliminary contacts with Rahnyld of Dohlar, as well. And it may be time to at least alert Zherohm Vyncyt in Chisholm."

"Isn't it a bit early for that sort of thinking? At least where Dohlar and Chisholm are concerned?" Duchairn asked, and Trynair shrugged.

"It may be," he conceded. "On the other hand, arranging this sort of thing takes time. The distance between the Temple and Charis, or between the Temple and Corisande, for that matter, works against us. If we do decide we need to throw Dohlar's and Chisholm's weight into the scales, it would be wise, I think, to have done the preliminary spadework well ahead of time."

"Who would you use?" Clyntahn inquired, emerging from his wineglass just long enough to ask the question.

"Zhoshua Makgregair is already in place in Tarot, and he and I discussed this eventuality before I sent him. In fact, I gave him fairly detailed contingency directives. As soon as we get a break in the weather long enough for us to get semaphore messages out, I can instruct him to dust off those directives and get to work on Gorjah.

"In Chisholm's case, Vyncyt is actually making his pastoral visit right now, and he had plenty of experience in the diplomatic service as an upper-priest. He'd understand exactly what our thinking is, and having him broach the subject personally with Sharleyan would certainly carry additional weight, if we decided to do that. Even if we only warned *him* about it, he could give personal contingency instructions to his bishop executor in case we decide we need to bring Chisholm in later. As for Dohlar, I'm thinking about sending Young Harys to Gorath."

"Ahlbyrt Harys?" Magwair leaned back in his chair with a frown. "Isn't he perhaps a bit *too* young for something like this?"

"I think he's ready," Trynair disagreed. "And he's already demonstrated a remarkable sensitivity to this aspect of diplomacy. Besides, using someone as young as he is gives us certain alternatives if we decide we don't want to proceed. For one thing, he's young—and inexperienced—enough that we could put down any preliminary exploration of the possibilities to over enthusiasm on his part. And the season gives us an excellent excuse to send him instead of someone more senior. After all, he's got the youth to undertake a trip that long through this kind of winter."

Heads nodded, Duchairn's among them. A young, inexperienced diplomat who'd misunderstood his instructions, or possibly simply exceeded them in a burst of youthful exuberance, represented a ready-made way out if Trynair should need to disavow any suggestions to Rahnyld IV. Rhobair Duchairn understood that perfectly.

Which wasn't the same thing as saying that he thought it was a good idea. Unfortunately, his hesitance to unleash the Church's full wrath on Charis put him in a clear minority of one, and the Group of Four could not afford to show its many enemies on the Council of Vicars any appearance of internal dissension.

"I understand your concerns," he said after several seconds, addressing all three of the others. "And, to be honest, I suppose I do share them, myself. But Charis really is the wyvern that catches golden rabbits. If we destroy its maritime power, we destroy the basis for its wealth, and all the advantages that wealth offers to *us*, as well as to Haarahld and his house."

"So?" Magwair shrugged. "Hektor and Nahrmahn seem eager enough to take Haarahld's place."

If they could do that, Duchairn thought acidly, *then they'd already be serious competitors of his, wouldn't they? There's more to Charis' success than simply owning a few ships!*

But that wasn't something anyone was prepared to say out loud around this table, was it?

"Then I'll see to setting up the preliminary briefing for Father Ahlbyrt and composing the proper messages to Father Zhoshua and Archbishop Zherohm tomorrow morning," Trynair said, picking up his own wineglass and extending it to Duchairn.

"But for now, could I trouble you for a little more of that really excellent wine, Rhobair?"

.IV.
Marine Training Area,
Helen Island

Bryahn Lock Island, Earl of Lock Island, climbed down from the saddle with a sense of profound gratitude which was only slightly flawed by the knowledge that he would have to climb back up *into* it for the return journey. The high admiral was reasonably fit for a man of his years, but he spent too much time on shipboard. There wasn't room aboard a galley for anyone—and especially for an officer of his rank—to get the sort of exercise which kept a man from feeling short winded.

Worse, he thought as he massaged his aching buttocks with a grimace, sea officers spent very little time riding horses. Even those who'd been thoroughly schooled in horsemanship as youngsters—as he himself had been—got precious little opportunity to maintain the necessary skills.

Or the tough arses to avoid saddle sores, he reflected wryly.

He finished the massage and took a couple of trial steps. Everything seemed to be working more or less the way it ought to be, and he turned to his aide.

"It appears I'm going to survive after all, Henrai."

"Of course you are, My Lord," Lieutenant Henrai Tillyer replied gravely, although amusement glinted in his eyes. Lock Island smiled back, even as he reminded himself not to take vengeance on Tillyer for his youthful tolerance for sillinesses like horseback riding.

"I just hope this is all worth the exercise," the high admiral grumbled.

"Oh, I believe you'll be suitably impressed, My Lord," Tillyer assured him. "If you'll come this way?"

Lock Island followed in his aide's wake, stumping along the steep path with an air of resignation. Actually, little though he was prepared to admit it to anyone else, it was a pleasant enough walk, despite the steepness. They were over a thousand feet above sea level, and the additional height, coupled with the breeze blowing in off of Howell Bay, was a cool interlude in a typically warm Charisian spring.

The path topped out on a high ridgeline, and a mountain valley stretched out before them. There was an observation tower at the western edge of the valley, where the mountains broke steeply downward towards the bay, so far below. From that vantage point, a lookout could see for the better part of forty miles, and a lookout on the King's Harbor citadel could look straight up the mountain and see any signals from the tower.

Maintaining the observation post was a responsibility of the Royal Charisian Marines, and had been for years. Largely as a consequence, the Marines had gotten into the habit of using the valley and surrounding mountains as exercise areas. Unfortunately, Lock Island acknowledged to himself, they didn't use them for exercises as much as, perhaps, they really ought to.

The Kingdom of Charis had no standing army. The Charisian nobility had its personal retainers, whom the Crown could summon to the national colors in an emergency. But even the most powerful of them had no more than a hundred or so men under his direct, personal command nowadays, and an army of feudal levies had become increasingly anachronistic (and of increasingly dubious value) over the last century or so, anyway. There was also a national militia, of course, but it was undermanned and not particularly well drilled. Confronted by something like a company of Siddarmark pikemen or Desnairi cavalry, a Charisian militia unit wouldn't have been even a *bad* joke.

What the kingdom did have, however, were the Royal Charisian Marines. There were never as many of them as Lock Island would have liked, but they were tough, professional, well-trained, and confident. Indeed, if anything they were *over*confident. Like the Navy, the Marines were accustomed to winning, even against steep odds, and there was no seagoing infantry force in the world which could match them.

Overall, that had served Charis well over the years. The Navy was the kingdom's true defense. Nothing could threaten its people and its territory without first getting past the fleet, after all. But it would have been a serious mistake to think of the Marines as any sort of field army. They seldom if ever deployed in greater than battalion strength, they had no experience at all in large-scale land combat, and they were equipped and trained for the close-quarters fighting aboard ship, not for open field maneuvers.

Yet that, too, was going to have to change. If not tomorrow or the next day, it was still going to have to change soon enough, and that was what brought Lock Island to this cool valley this morning.

"Well, there you are, Bryahn!" a youthful voice called, and the high admiral turned to find Crown Prince Cayleb walking towards him. Merlin Athrawes and Ahrnahld Falkhan followed at the prince's heels, along with a Marine major Lock Island had never seen before, and the earl grimaced.

"I still don't see why we couldn't have done this in a civilized setting, like the deck of a ship," he complained to his crown prince. "After all, we're already test-firing the first of Ahlfryd's new guns out at sea, so maintaining secrecy wouldn't have been a problem. And, meaning no disrespect, Your Highness, but I'd much rather be standing on my own quarterdeck than here, with my arse burning and that never-to-be-sufficiently-damned horse waiting to take me back down the mountain later."

"Just getting you up here for a little exercise would be worthwhile all by itself," Cayleb said with a grin as he reached Lock Island and held out his right hand. The two of them clasped arms, and the crown prince chuckled. "You really ought to make time to spend a few hours in a saddle here and there. Maybe even join me on a slash-lizard hunt or two. You're getting soft, Bryahn."

"And when you're my age, so will you," Lock Island retorted.

"Nonsense!" Cayleb disagreed with the cheerfully arrogant confidence of youth. Then his expression sobered.

"Actually, there are some perfectly valid reasons for bringing you up here to show you this particular new toy of Merlin's, Bryahn. For one thing, we've got plenty of room and don't have to worry about targets that sink before we can examine them. For another thing, you can't really appreciate what Merlin's about to show you if you're on a moving deck. And for another, this is where Major Clareyk is going to be working out the best way to use it."

The crown prince nodded to the Marine major who had followed him and his two bodyguards. The major came quickly to attention and saluted, touching his left shoulder with his right fist. Lock Island studied him for a moment, then returned the salute.

Major Kynt Clareyk was on the young side for an officer of his rank, but he looked both tough and intelligent. And perhaps even more important than that, Lock Island knew, he—like every single man of his command—had been selected for his total loyalty and discretion, as well.

"Well, I'm here now, anyway, Your Highness," the high admiral said, turning back to the crown prince.

"Yes you are, and so *cheerful* about it, too," Cayleb observed with another grin. "And since you are, I suppose we might as well get started."

He turned and began walking towards the parade ground in front of the modest block of barracks built against the valley's steep northern wall. A platoon of Marines waited there under the supervision of a lieutenant and his grizzled sergeant, and all of them snapped to attention and saluted as Cayleb and Lock Island approached.

They looked like any other platoon of Marines Lock Island had ever seen, with one exception. They were smartly turned out in their blue tunics and trousers and broad-brimmed black hats, and they had the typical almost arrogant confidence of men who knew they were elite troops. They were armed with the standard cutlass and boarding ax of the Charisian Marines, but they were also armed with something else, and that was the exception.

"Here, Bryahn." Cayleb reached out, and a corporal handed him his weapon.

"Take a look," the crown prince invited, handing the same weapon across to the high admiral.

Lock Island took it a bit gingerly. He'd seen matchlock muskets in plenty, of course. They were used on shipboard in the preliminary stages of a boarding action, although they were utterly useless once an opponent with a cutlass or boarding ax got within a few yards. But while it was obvious the weapon in his hands was at least related to a matchlock, it was like no other musket Lock Island had ever seen.

For one thing, it was lighter, despite its length, and the stock and forestock were much sleeker. In fact, the entire weapon had a smooth, slim, wicked look to it, and as he hefted it in his hands, he realized it was enough lighter that it probably wouldn't need the crutch-like brace from which musketeers normally fired their weapons.

All of those aspects, however, were secondary to the difference between a matchlock and *this* weapon's firing mechanism. Instead of the long serpentine arm and lever designed to hold the length of smoldering slow match which was lowered into a matchlock's priming pan when it was fired, it had a much smaller, odd-looking lock. An S-shaped striker held a lump of shaped flint clamped between its jaws, and Lock Island shook his head as he contemplated the elegant simplicity of the concept which had never occurred to anyone else.

He turned the musket over, noting the ramrod—made of steel, not the usual wood—in its carrying well in the forestock. Then he frowned as he found the odd lug protruding from the right side of the barrel behind the muzzle, just in front of the leading edge of the forestock and offset far enough to clear the end of the ramrod easily. He had no idea what *that* was for, but he felt confident he was about to find out, and he handed the weapon back to Cayleb.

"It looks impressive, Your Highness," he admitted.

"Yes, it does," Cayleb agreed, returning the musket to its owner. "And it's even more impressive in action. Major?"

"Of course, Your Highness!" Clareyk replied, and nodded to the lieutenant. "Firing positions, Lieutenant Layn, if you please."

"Aye, aye, Sir," Lieutenant Layn acknowledged, and nodded in turn to his sergeant.

That gray-bearded worthy had been waiting patiently, and only the merest hint of a curled upper lip and an exposed canine were sufficient to send the men of Lieutenant Layn's platoon double-timing across the parade ground to the shooting range along its eastern side.

Cayleb and the other senior officers followed at a more leisurely pace. By the time they got there, Lieutenant Layn and his sergeant had the forty-man platoon arranged in two twenty-man lines. The Marines stood spaced about a yard apart, staggered so that the men in the second rank lined up with the spaces in the first rank, facing downrange towards a line of thirty or so human-sized mannequins at least a hundred and fifty yards away.

The mannequins were obviously made of straw, but each of them wore a standard Marine-issue cuirass and helmet.

"What's the best range for aimed fire you've ever seen out of a matchlock, Bryahn?" Cayleb asked, and the high admiral snorted.

"You mean the longest range where I've ever actually seen them *hit* something? Or the longest range at which I've seen them wasting powder *trying* to hit something?"

"Let's stick with actually hitting something," Cayleb said dryly. "In fact, let's be a little more specific. What's the longest range at which you've ever seen someone with a matchlock actually hit a particular man-sized target?"

"Well," Lock Island said thoughtfully, his expression much more serious, "that's not really such an easy question. For one thing, I've mostly seen them used at sea. The range is usually fairly low by the time they come into action, and the fact that all the ships involved are moving doesn't help much. Probably the longest range I've ever actually seen a hit scored at would be about, oh, forty yards. I understand volley fire can score hits out to a hundred, even a hundred and fifty yards, in a land engagement, on the other hand. I don't imagine the *percentage* of hits is very high even there, though. And as I understand it, no one's even trying to aim at a specific target at that range; they're simply blazing away in the enemy's general direction."

"That's about right," Cayleb agreed. "Generally speaking, effective musket range is about eighty yards. Which is exactly half the range from Lieutenant Layn's front line to the targets down there."

The crown prince let the high admiral think about that for a moment, then nodded to Clareyk.

"Proceed, Major," he said, and glanced back at Lock Island. "You might want to put your fingers in your ears," he suggested.

Lock Island only looked at him for a moment, suspecting a joke. But Cayleb was already putting his own fingers into his ears, and the high admiral decided to follow suit as Clareyk stepped up beside the nearer end of the first of Lieutenant Layn's two lines.

"Load!" he commanded.

Each Marine grounded the butt of his musket, holding it just behind the muzzle with his left hand while his right unbuttoned the cover of the hard leather case on his right hip. He reached into the case and extracted a rolled up twist of paper, raised it to his mouth, and bit off the end. He tipped the truncated paper up, spilling the granulated black powder it held down the muzzle of his weapon, then spat the bullet he'd bitten off after the powder. The empty cartridge paper was stuffed into the muzzle, the ramrod came out of its well and shoved the wadded paper, bullet, and powder charge home with a single strong stroke. Then the rod went back into its place, and the Marine raised his musket, turned it up on its side so that the "flintlock" was down, and struck it sharply once. Then the musket came back upright, held in a port-arms position.

The entire evolution couldn't have taken more than fifteen seconds, Lock Island thought, which was far, far faster than he'd ever seen a matchlock loaded, yet their smooth drill hadn't seemed especially hurried.

"Front rank, take aim!" Clareyk commanded, and the front rank's muskets rose. The brass butt plates pressed into their shoulders, and their right hands cocked the flintlock strikers, which automatically raised the priming pan lids, before settling into place with the index finger curved about the ridiculously tiny trigger.

"Fire!" Clareyk barked, and twenty muskets exploded as one.

Lock Island's ears cringed, despite the fingers he'd thrust into them, and a choking cloud of powder smoke billowed up.

"First rank, reload!" he heard through the ringing in his ears. "Second rank, present!"

The first rank stepped back a pace, right hands already reaching for their cartridge boxes once again. The second rank stepped *forward* a pace at the same moment, so that the two lines essentially exchanged positions.

"Second rank, take aim!" the major snapped, and the new first rank's muskets rose to their shoulders and cocked. Clareyk waited perhaps another five seconds. Then—

"Fire!" he ordered, and a fresh twenty-musket volley cracked out.

"Second rank, reload! First rank, present!"

Lock Island could hardly believe it. The first rank had actually already reloaded. Now they stepped back into their original positions while the second rank retired into *their* initial positions. Again, the brief pause—until, Lock Island realized, the second rank's Marines were halfway through their own reloading cycle—and then the first rank's muskets fired.

The process repeated a total of three times, with a fresh blast of musketry smashing downrange every ten seconds. In less than one minute, the forty men of Lieutenant Layn's platoon fired one hundred and twenty rounds. The same number of matchlock musketeers would have gotten off a single shot apiece in that same interval, and Lock Island suspected that Layn's men could have reloaded even more rapidly.

"Cease fire!" Clareyk shouted, his voice sounding tinny and distorted in the wake of the concentrated musket fire.

"Safe your weapons," the major added at a more conversational level, and the platoon grounded its musket butts smartly. Clareyk looked at them for a moment, then turned to Cayleb and Lock Island.

"Would you care to inspect the targets, Your Highness? High Admiral?" he asked.

"Bryahn?" Cayleb invited, and Lock Island gave himself a shake.

"I certainly would, Your Highness," he said, and he, Cayleb, Merlin, Major Clareyk, and Lieutenant Falkhan hiked across to the mannequins.

"Sweet Langhorne!" Lock Island murmured as he got close enough to the targets to see what the half-inch musket balls had done to them. He'd seen breastplates pierced by muskets at relatively short ranges, but he'd seen at least as many dished in and splashed with lead where they'd turned balls, instead, especially at longer ranges. These breastplates hadn't done that, and the high admiral's eyes widened as he saw the holes punched clear through them.

That was impressive enough, but almost equally impressive, each of those breastplates had been hit at least three times. That was a minimum of ninety hits out of a hundred and twenty shots fired, and no matchlock musketeers in the world could have matched that percentage of hits at such a range.

He reached out, running the tip of one finger around the rim of a bullet hole, then turned to look not at Cayleb, but at Merlin.

"How?" he asked simply.

"The rate of fire's fairly self-explanatory, I think, My Lord," Merlin replied gravely. "One thing which may not have been too obvious is that the flintlock touchhole is cone-shaped. The opening's wider on the inside, so it acts as a funnel. Instead of having to prime the pan in a separate operation, all they have to do is give the musket a sharp whack to shake powder from the main charge into the pan. That, the cartridges, and the steel ramrods mean they can simply reload faster—much faster—than anyone's ever been able to before.

"As far as the *accuracy* is concerned," he continued, indicating the multiple holes in each breastplate, "these aren't just muskets, My Lord. They're also rifles."

Lock Island's eyebrows rose. The principle of spinning a projectile to stabilize it in flight had been known to archers and crossbowmen for centuries. It hadn't taken all that long for someone to figure out that cutting rifling grooves into a musket barrel could impart the same stabilization to a musket ball. But no one had ever suggested using rifled muskets as serious weapons of war, because they took so long to load. In order to force the bullet into the rifling, it was necessary to use an oversized ball and literally hammer it down the barrel, which reduced the musket's already arthritic rate of fire to complete battlefield uselessness.

"Rifles?" he repeated, and Cayleb nodded.

"Look at this," he invited, and held out a musket ball.

But, no, it wasn't a "ball" at all, Lock Island realized as he accepted it. It was a slightly elongated cylinder, rounded at one end, but hollow at the other.

"When the powder charge explodes," Cayleb explained, "it spreads the hollow end of the bullet and forces it into the rifling. It also seals the bore, which traps more of the powder's power behind the ball. It may not be too obvious, but the barrels on these 'flintlocks' are actually longer than most matchlocks. Coupled with the way the balls seal the bore, that extra length gives each shot more velocity and power."

Lock Island looked up from the bullet and shook his head slowly.

"It's really that simple?"

"It's really that simple," Cayleb confirmed.

"How far does it extend the effective range?" the high admiral asked. "I remember watching Earl Pine Mountain on a hunt a few years ago. He had a rifled matchlock—from Harchong, I think—and took down a prong lizard at almost two hundred yards."

"Well," Cayleb said, "let's go back to the firing line, shall we?"

He led the way back to where Lieutenant Layn and his platoon stood waiting. Then he looked at Merlin.

"Would you care to do the honors?" he asked with a wicked gleam in his eye.

"Of course, Your Highness," Merlin murmured, and turned to the same corporal whose musket Lock Island had examined earlier.

"If I may?" he asked, holding out his hand, and the corporal handed the weapon over with a broad grin, followed by his cartridge box.

Merlin accepted both of them and calmly loaded the rifle. He shook powder into the pan, then turned back to Cayleb.

"May I assume you had a target in mind, Your Highness?" he asked mildly.

"As a matter of fact, I do," Cayleb assured him with a grin even broader than the corporal's. "In fact, I think I may have found one that will challenge even you, Merlin."

Merlin merely raised an eyebrow, and Cayleb turned and pointed downrange. Not at the mannequins which had served as the Marines' targets, but beyond them. *Well* beyond them, Lock Island realized, as he saw the additional mannequin standing all by itself at least four hundred yards away from them.

"That does seem rather a long shot, Your Highness," Merlin observed.

"Oh, I'm certain you can do it!" Cayleb said encouragingly. Merlin gave him a moderately reproving look, then stepped slightly out in front of the front rank of Marines.

He gazed downrange, sapphire eyes intent. None of the people watching him realized he was using a PICA's built-in laser-ranging capability to determine the exact distance to his target. It worked out at four hundred and twelve yards, and he nodded to himself.

Unlike any of the flesh-and-blood humans about him, Merlin knew the average muzzle velocity of the new rifles. No one on Safehold had yet gotten around to developing the chronograph which someone on Old Earth would have used to measure the muzzle velocity of a firearm, but Merlin didn't need one. Or, rather, he had one already built in.

Now he cocked the lock and raised the rifle into firing position. A red crosshair superimposed itself on his vision, well above the mannequin, as his CPU calculated the bullet's trajectory and indicated the proper point of aim, and he captured the front sight in the open V of the simple rear sight and aligned both of them on the glowing icon only he could see.

The crosshair steadied itself. In fact, it steadied with literally inhuman precision, for no flesh-and-blood human could have held that rifle so utterly, completely still. And then Merlin smoothly and steadily squeezed the trigger.

The striker snapped forward, the pan flashed, and the rifle spewed out the usual cloud of powder smoke as it slammed thunderously back against his shoulder with the brutal recoil of any large-caliber black-powder weapon. Then, four hundred and twelve yards downrange, the mannequin's helmet leapt off its head and spun flashing in the sunlight before it thudded to the ground.

"Oh, dear," Merlin murmured, turning to Cayleb with a smile. "I'm afraid we're going to need another new helmet, Your Highness."

▼   ▼   ▼

"I see why you wanted to keep all this out of sight, Your Highness," Lock Island conceded two hours later.

He stood with the crown prince, Merlin, and Lieutenant Tillyer, waiting while a couple of Marines fetched his and Tillyer's horses for the return journey to King's Harbor.

"It is something we'd like to keep under wraps," Cayleb replied. "And Major Clareyk and Lieutenant Layn have been doing some interesting things working out the best tactics. It's not just as simple as standing in place and blazing away, although that's probably going to be effective enough at first, given our range advantage and rate of fire. Eventually, though, both sides are going to have rifles, and when that happens, standing out in the open is going to be a good way to get lots and lots of people killed very quickly."

"I can well believe *that*," Lock Island said, with a shudder which wasn't at all feigned.

"The fact that every rifleman becomes his own pikeman as soon as he fixes his bayonet is also going to have a major impact in any boarding action, My Lord," Lieutenant Falkhan pointed out diffidently, and Lock Island nodded.

He understood the reason for the odd-shaped lugs on the rifle barrels now. The thing Merlin called a "ring bayonet" was essentially a knife with a fourteen-inch, two-sided blade and an open ring formed into one end of its cross guard. The ring fitted down over the muzzle in front of the front sight, and a simple half-twist locked a cutout in the knife's hilt over the lug to hold it firmly in place. The weapon could still be loaded and fired, although the rate of fire slowed drastically, and, as Falkhan had said, it literally turned each musket into a boarding pike. Which meant it would no longer be necessary for Marine musketeers to drop their firearms once the melee began.

"At the same time, Bryahn," Cayleb said very seriously, "one reason I wanted you to see this is that we have a decision to make, and I want your views on it before we do. Specifically, do we really want to begin issuing *rifles* to all our Marines?"

"What?" The high admiral felt his eyebrows arch in surprise at the question. "Why *shouldn't* we want to, Your Highness?" he asked after a moment.

"I can think of two main reasons," Cayleb replied. "First, it takes much longer to make a rifle than it does to make a smoothbore musket. We can probably produce as many as three or even five smoothbores for each rifle. Master

Howsmyn's going to move musket production to his new Delthak foundry as soon as he can. He ought to be able to begin producing them there sometime late next month, and putting it all under one roof will let him be sure all the interchangeable parts are really interchangeable."

The prince made a face, and Merlin hid a smile. Over the past few months, Cayleb had become aware of the disadvantages inherent in the absence of a truly uniform system of measurements. The notion of using interchangeable parts wasn't a totally new one, but if two different manufactories' "inches" weren't actually identical, the parts one of them produced wouldn't work in the muskets the other one produced. Which was why Howsmyn was making certain that all of *his* facilities used the same-sized units of measurement used at King's Harbor.

"Once he has his rifle shop fully set up there, which is going to take a month or so longer, he'll have two or three times as many rifling benches as he has now," Cayleb continued. "The overall production rate will go up, and the production ratio will shift a bit in the rifles' favor, but rifling barrels takes time and represents an entire additional stage in the process. Which means we'll always be able to produce smoothbores more rapidly than rifles. And while the range advantage of a rifle is really nice to have, we've also got to think in terms of having *enough* of them to do the job.

"Second, once we begin issuing them, and once they're used in action, everyone's going to want the same sorts of weapons for *their* infantry. And, let's face it, it's not going to be that difficult to duplicate them. We're not introducing any new principles or processes in the weapon itself, aside from the flintlock, which isn't an especially complicated proposition."

"So you're thinking about holding the new bullets in reserve," Lock Island said slowly, and Cayleb nodded.

"We'll be able to rifle the barrels of existing muskets a lot faster than we could build them as rifles from scratch," he pointed out. "If we hold the new bullets 'in reserve,' as you put it, we can take advantage of the superior rate of fire and the new bayonets immediately and *still* have a decisive advantage up our sleeves once other people begin duplicating flintlock muskets. And all the smoothbores we've built in the meantime will be available for rifling when the time comes."

"But even that's going to be a fairly fleeting advantage, Your Highness," Lock Island pointed out.

"Oh, I know that." Cayleb nodded again. "I'm not saying I'm wedded to the concept of delaying the introduction of the rifles. I'm simply saying that I think it's something we need to consider. Either way, Major Clareyk needs to go ahead developing tactics for both the smoothbores and the rifles, of course."

"You're certainly correct about that, Your Highness," Lock Island said a bit grimly. Cayleb cocked his head, and the high admiral snorted. "Your Highness, dealing with Nahrmahn, and probably Hektor, isn't going to be the end of this, you know. In fact, it's only going to be the beginning. So whether we introduce the rifles immediately or not, we're going to need them soon. Probably *very* soon."

Prince Nahrmahn sat back in his chair, resting his forearms on the carved wooden armrests, and watched without expression as an extraordinarily ordinary-looking man followed Baron Shandyr and Trahvys Ohlsyn, the Earl of Pine Hollow, into the meeting chamber of his Privy Council.

The bodyguards outside the meeting-chamber door braced to attention as Nahrmahn's first councillor and spymaster walked past them; the two guardsmen standing behind Nahrmahn's chair did not.

"So," the prince said as the door closed behind the new arrivals. "I understand you have some fresh report for me?"

His tone wasn't encouraging. Not that any of them were surprised.

"We do, My Prince," Pine Hollow said, speaking to his cousin rather more formally than was his wont. "And, no," he continued, in a drier tone "it's not news you're really going to want to hear."

Something almost like a smile flickered at the corner of Nahrmahn's mouth, and Shandyr allowed himself a feeling of cautious relief. The prince's mood had been . . . difficult ever since the first intimations of the disaster Shandyr's organization in Charis had suffered. Pine Hollow understood that, and the baron was grateful to the first councillor for his willingness to help divert the brunt of Nahrmahn's displeasure from Shandyr's own shoulders. The fact that Trahvys Ohlsyn was probably the one man on Safehold whom Nahrmahn unreservedly trusted didn't hurt a thing, either.

"Well, that certainly has the virtue of frankness," the prince said after a moment. Then the almost-smile, if that was what it had been, vanished, and he switched his gaze to Shandyr.

"You may as well go ahead and tell me," he half-growled.

"Yes, My Prince." Shandyr bowed and indicated the man who'd accompanied him and Pine Hollow. "My Prince, this is Marhys Wyllyms." Nahrmahn's eyes narrowed slightly, and the baron nodded. "Yes, My Prince. Master Wyllyms has finally managed to reach home."

"So I see."

Nahrmahn regarded Wyllyms thoughtfully as the man went to one knee and bent his head. The prince let him kneel there for several seconds, then waved one hand.

"Rise, Master Wyllyms," he said, and waited until Wyllyms had obeyed the command. Then he cocked his head to one side and pursed his lips. "I'm relieved to see you," he continued, "if not exactly delighted by the fact that you're here. I trust you can give us some firsthand information as to exactly what went wrong?"

"I'll do my best, Your Highness," Wyllyms replied respectfully. "All the same, Sire, please remember that I've been trying to find my way home without being taken by Wave Thunder's agents for over two months. The information I have is certainly out of date by now."

"That's understood," Nahrmahn said brusquely. "Just tell us what you *do* know."

"Well, Your Highness, as I've already reported to Baron Shandyr, I'm not at all sure what originally caused them to suspect the Duke. When Gray Harbor came to the townhouse, he and the Duke met privately in the library, and I was unable to overhear any of their discussion. I do know the Duke had ordered fifteen of his guardsmen to stand ready for his summons outside the library, though, because I personally took his note to his Guard captain. After he and Gray Harbor had been alone in the library, except for Gray Harbor's personal guardsman, for perhaps fifteen minutes, I heard the bell ring and his men entered the library."

Wyllyms paused for a moment, then shook his head with the expression of a man who wasn't certain his next few words were going to be believed.

"Your Highness, I knew the quality of the guardsmen the Duke had summoned, and I personally ushered Earl Gray Harbor into the library. After handing the Duke's note to Captain Zhahnsyn, I took it upon myself to deliver brandy to the library, as well, in order to pick up whatever information I could. At that time, the Duke, the Earl, and the Earl's guardsman were the only ones in the room, and although I wasn't supposed to know it, I also knew that the Earl's guardsman had been placed in his service years earlier by the Duke himself. Knowing all of that, I felt confident the Duke's men would easily take Gray Harbor into custody, if that was what he intended. What might have happened then was more than I could begin to predict, although I suspect the Duke was prepared to act upon the contingency plans for a coup he'd made long ago. I can't believe he might have had anything else in mind after ordering his men to seize the Kingdom's first councillor, at any rate!

"But what did happen was that I heard the sound of fighting from inside the library. *Lots* of fighting, Your Highness. It couldn't have lasted more than a very few minutes, but there shouldn't have been *any*, not with Gray Harbor alone against what amounted to sixteen of the Duke's men.

"With the lateness of the hour, there'd been very few other servants in that wing of the house when Gray Harbor arrived. Those who had been present had been sent away by Captain Zhahnsyn, presumably on the Duke's orders to avoid any unfortunate witnesses. So, what with the noise of the storm and all, I doubted anyone else had heard the fighting.

"I didn't know what was happening, myself, but from the sound of things, they weren't going the way the Duke had planned. So I positioned myself behind a door to one of the servants' passages from which I could watch the library door. If the Duke's men had prevailed, I was certain he'd come out of the library soon. He didn't. Instead, the library door opened, and a man I'd never seen before stepped out of it."

"A man you'd never *seen* before?" Nahrmahn repeated, leaning forward in his chair with a frown of confusion.

"Exactly, Your Highness." Wyllyms nodded as if for emphasis. "I knew exactly who was in the library—or I'd thought I did, at least. I suppose it's possible someone else could have arrived while I was taking the Duke's note to Captain Zhahnsyn, but he would have had to somehow enter the townhouse and find his way to the library without any of the other servants seeing him. Besides, *I* should have seen him when I served the brandy, and I didn't. Yet, there he was."

"What sort of man?" Nahrmahn asked intently. Baron Shandyr was cautiously pleased by the prince's expression. It was certainly better than the sour, half-accusatory glowers which had been coming the spymaster's way of late.

"Apparently an officer of the Royal Guard, Your Highness."

"The *Royal Guard?*"

"Yes, Your Highness. He wore the Guard's livery, with a lieutenant's insignia."

"You say he came out of the library?" Nahrmahn asked, and Wyllyms nodded. "What did he do then?"

"He called for a servant, Your Highness. So I opened the door and went to him."

Nahrmahn's eyes widened ever so slightly, and he sat back once more.

"You went to him," he repeated, an edge of respect in his voice, and Wyllyms shrugged.

"I was a servant, Your Highness, and it was a servant he was calling for. It seemed unlikely he intended to arrest or attack whoever responded, and it was my best—possibly my only—opportunity to find out what had happened."

"And what *had* happened?" Nahrmahn pressed.

"At the time, Your Highness, I didn't really know. The stranger had pulled the library door mostly closed behind him, and I could see little. What I did see, however, was a great deal of blood and at least two bodies, both in the Duke's colors. As nearly as I could tell, every one of the Duke's men had been killed."

"*All* of them?"

"That was my impression then, Your Highness, and the rumors I managed to collect on my way north all agree that they were."

Nahrmahn looked at Shandyr and his cousin for a moment, then back at Wyllyms.

"What happened then?"

"The Guardsman ordered me to summon a section of the Royal Guard, with an officer, from the Palace on Earl Gray Harbor's authority. I was to take the summons personally and directly, to return with the Guardsmen, and to have no discussion with anyone else along the way. I said I would, of course, and hurried off.

As soon as I found one of the Duke's under-footmen, I passed the same instructions to him and left the townhouse."

"And?"

"And, Your Highness"—for the first-time Wyllyms' voice and body language showed a hint of trepidation—"because I had no way of knowing what might have passed between the duke and the Earl, or if the Duke had been taken alive, I executed my contingency instructions from Baron Shandyr. I went to Braidee Lahang's quarters and killed him."

Nahrmahn sat very still for a moment, long enough for the apparently unflappable Wyllyms to begin sweating, then nodded.

"That was well done, Master Wyllyms," the prince said. "Indeed, it sounds as if you did very well that evening."

"Thank you, Your Highness." Wyllyms' taut shoulders relaxed perceptibly, and Nahrmahn smiled slightly.

"But returning to this 'stranger' in the library," he continued, smile fading into a faint frown of concentration. "You have no idea how he came to be there?"

"None, Your Highness." Wyllyms shook his head.

"Do you have any idea who he was?"

"According to the gossip I managed to pick up while making my way out of Tellesberg, it was the same man who broke up the attempt to assassinate Crown Prince Cayleb, Your Highness," Wyllyms said. "The most persistent rumor was that this man—a 'Merlin,' or something of the sort—had been given a commission in the Royal Guard as a reward for saving the Prince's life."

Nahrmahn's upper lip curled in what no one could ever have mistaken for a smile.

"It would appear we have a great deal to thank this . . . 'Merlin' for," he said softly.

"Yes, My Prince," Shandyr said, inserting himself into the interview. Nahrmahn's eyes moved to him, and he shrugged. "The most interesting thing to me, in many respects, My Prince, is that according to the reports we've received so far from Tellesberg, this Merlin *accompanied* Gray Harbor to the Duke's townhouse. Master Wyllyms' information is the first firsthand account we've received, and the damage Wave Thunder's done to Lahang's network means we're unlikely to get any more reports like it. But my people here in Emerald have been pumping every ship's company from Charis for information. And while there's a great deal of confusion and obvious nonsense in most of what we've been able to ferret out, there seems to be general agreement that the official story is that Gray Harbor took 'Merlin' with him when he went to call upon the Duke."

"Which he obviously didn't, if Master Wyllyms didn't see him arrive," Nahrmahn said thoughtfully.

"Your Highness," Wyllyms put in diffidently, "as I say, I didn't see him arrive, and he wasn't present when I delivered the brandy. I didn't personally take the instructions to Gray Harbor's coachmen to take the Earl's carriage and horses to the stable, though; I sent the word via one of the under-footmen. So it's possible he was with the carriage at that time, and somehow managed to enter the library in the interval between my delivery of the brandy and Zhahnsyn's arrival."

"But from your tone, you don't think it was likely," Nahrmahn observed.

"No, Your Highness, I don't. It's *possible*, however. I didn't waste any time talking to any of the other servants when I left. It may be that one of them admitted this 'Merlin' and he somehow got past me to the library without my seeing him. But I don't think that's what happened."

"Then how *did* he get there?"

"Your Highness, I don't know. All I can say is that I never saw him, and that there were rumors in Tellesberg that this 'Merlin' is some sort of *seijin*."

"Lahang reported the same rumor in his message immediately after the assassination attempt, My Prince," Shandyr reminded Nahrmahn, and the rotund prince nodded.

"But why should they put it about that he accompanied Gray Harbor if, in fact, he didn't?" Pine Hollow put in, his expression perplexed.

"A moment, Trahvys," Nahrmahn said, raising one hand, and looked back at Wyllyms.

"Have you anything else to report, Master Wyllyms?"

"Not about events in Tellesberg, Your Highness." Wyllyms bowed once more. "I'm still working on my report to Baron Shandyr concerning my journey to Eraystor and what I saw and heard along the way, but I believe that's all I can tell you about what happened in the capital."

"Then I thank you, both for your service and for your information. I'm sure Baron Shandyr will have many more tasks for a man of your proven capabilities. In the meantime, I assure you that you'll soon receive a more substantial token of my appreciation."

"Thank you, Your Highness," Wyllyms murmured.

"Leave us now, if you please, Master Wyllyms."

"Of course, Your Highness." Wyllyms bowed yet again and retired, walking backward out of Nahrmahn's presence as protocol required.

"Wait for me in the antechamber, Wyllyms," Shandyr said quietly, and Wyllyms nodded as he stepped through the door and it closed behind him.

"Now, Trahvys," Nahrmahn said to his cousin. "You were saying?"

"I was just wondering why Haarahld and Wave Thunder should be telling everyone this 'Merlin' character went to Tirian's townhouse with Gray Harbor if that's not what really happened?"

"I don't know," Nahrmahn conceded, and looked at Shandyr. "Hahl?"

"All any of us can do at this point is guess, My Prince," the baron said. "At first glance, I can't really see a reason for them to do so. Unless . . ."

"Unless what?" Nahrmahn prompted.

"My Prince," Shandyr said slowly, "this isn't the first time we've heard someone claim this man is a *seijin*."

"No, it isn't," Pine Hollow agreed. "But surely you're not suggesting he really *is* one, Hahl?"

"I don't know." Shandyr gave a shrug of frustrated ignorance. "I just know that apparently he specializes in hacking up large numbers of people working for us. And that the destruction of our entire Charis network coincides with his arrival in Tellesberg. If you can tell me how a single man could kill or disable *sixteen* picked guardsmen *and* either kill or capture Duke Tirian—never mind how he got into the library in the first place—I'll be delighted to hear it. At the moment, it sounds to me like all the bad ballads about *seijin* I've ever heard."

"He has a point, Trahvys," Nahrmahn said. "But there's another point that interests me, as well."

Both his nobles looked at him, and he shrugged.

"Wyllyms carried out his orders and killed Lahang before he could be taken into custody, correct?" The others nodded, and he snorted. "In that case, where did they get the information they obviously had to have for Wave Thunder to completely demolish our spy rings?"

"That point had occurred to me, as well, My Prince," Shandyr said. "I know we'd assumed initially that they must have started with Lahang—or with Tirian *and* Lahang—and worked their way down the chain after breaking one of them. Based on what we know so far, it's still possible they did take the Duke prisoner, but he shouldn't have known enough for them to identify so many of our other agents."

"So they must have identified Lahang already," Pine Hollow suggested. "If they already had him under surveillance, they might have identified at least some of his people, as well. And if something—like that assassin they took alive—started them sniffing around the Duke, then when Wyllyms carried out his instructions to remove Lahang, they probably started snapping up everyone they already knew about and questioning them pretty damned severely. If that's what happened, then each one they broke might have led them to others until the entire mess unraveled."

"That's certainly one possibility," Shandyr acknowledged. "There's no way for us to tell either way from here, of course, and it's going to take us time to even begin rebuilding in Charis. Still, I think we need to keep a close eye on this 'Merlin' of theirs. Whether or not he's really a *seijin*, things do seem to start happening when he's around. Which suggests to me, My Prince"—the baron smiled coldly— "that we might want to consider seeing to it that he *isn't* around much longer."

FEBRUARY,

YEAR OF GOD 891

King's Harbor,
Helen Island

I still say you don't sweat enough, Merlin."

Merlin opened one eyelid and glanced at Cayleb.

Nimue Alban had come from a culture—and a genetic heritage—which had thoroughly digested the perils of skin cancer and the advantages of sunblockers. Cayleb hadn't. He was extraordinarily fond of sunbathing, and there was no good way for Merlin to explain the downside of soaking his epidermis in sunlight to him. Nor could Merlin very well turn down the honor, and it *was* a genuine honor, of being invited to share the sun with the kingdom's crown prince.

Fortunately, he could adjust his skin's coloration at will, which meant his own complexion had become almost as bronzed as Cayleb's own. And he'd *also* gone into his programming after that . . . exciting rugby game and disabled certain functions. As a result, that particular problem hadn't recurred, although Merlin had to admit—*very* privately—that Cayleb Ahrmahk really was an extraordinarily attractive young man.

"And I still say that some of us don't need to sweat as much as others of us," he replied, and Cayleb chuckled.

"What do you think of Howsmyn's proposal?" the prince asked after a moment, and Merlin opened both eyes at the change of subject. He sat up, reached for a towel, and mopped the (relatively) meager sweat to which Cayleb had referred from his face.

"I think it makes excellent sense," he said then, and reached for the flask of chilled fruit juice they'd brought with them when they headed for the top of the harbor manager's office.

That office was at the very end of one of the main wharves in the Citadel Basin, the purely military anchorage under the looming walls of King's Harbor's main fortifications. It was an excellent perch for hopeful fishermen, and its location exposed it to a cooling breeze when the wind was in the southwest. That made it a popular sunbathing spot with the garrison's senior officers, as well, and there were special attractions in Cayleb's case. Specifically, his bodyguards liked the fact that they could make sure the office was empty, then throw a cordon across the wharf between it and the shore and allow the prince at least the illusion of privacy. Cayleb treasured it for the same reasons, which made the invitation to accompany him this afternoon even more of an indication of his high regard for Merlin.

Now Merlin took a swig of juice which was at least still cool, if no longer chilled. He didn't really need it, of course, but that didn't keep him from savoring the taste before he passed the flask across to Cayleb.

"One of our main worries has always been the manufacturing time for the artillery," he continued as the crown prince drank gratefully. "I assumed all along that we'd have to cast every gun we needed if we wanted them to have trunnions." He shrugged. "The only way I could see to do it was to melt the existing guns down to reclaim the bronze and recast them from scratch."

He stood and stretched, draping the towel around his neck, and walked across to the waist-high wall which ran around the top of the flat office roof. His neatly folded clothing and weapons were stacked on the bench seat which ran around the inside of the parapet, with his sheathed wakazashi weighting the pile, and an awning provided a band of shade as he leaned on the wall and gazed out across the harbor.

The unoccupied office's wall fell sheer to the wharf's outer end, and the water was an almost painful blue, shading to equally bright green as it shallowed. There wasn't very much breeze today, even this far above water level. A gentle swell rolled lightly across the sun-bright water, and six or seven children in a four-oared launch were rowing steadily, if not exactly in a straight-line, towards the wharf. The fishing poles sticking out of the boat at various angles indicated what they'd been doing, and Merlin felt a twinge of wistful envy as he remembered fishing trips from Nimue's childhood.

They were still the better part of a hundred yards out, but the seven- or eight-year-old girl sitting on the forwardmost thwart saw him looking at them and waved.

He waved back, then turned his back to the harbor as Cayleb rose and joined him in the shade.

"It never occurred to me," Merlin continued the thread of their conversation, "that it might be possible to add trunnions to *existing* guns."

Cayleb grunted in agreement. There was an intriguing jumble of odds and ends on the roof, presumably left by other sunbathers and fishermen, and one of the prince's eyebrows arched as he discovered the harpoon propped in one corner. He picked it up, trying its balance idly, and looked across at Merlin.

"What was that phrase you used the other day?" he asked. " 'Thinking outside the box,' wasn't it?" Merlin nodded, and the prince shrugged. "Well, I guess we should just feel fortunate Howsmyn is so good at it."

"That's putting it mildly, Your Highness," Merlin said with a grin, and turned to glance back at the launch. The girl in the bows waved again, and he chuckled.

Cayleb was right, he thought. Ehdwyrd Howsmyn had come at the problem from a completely different angle. He'd pointed out that the gun the Royal Charisian Navy called the "kraken"—a six-and-a-half-inch cannon roughly eleven feet long and throwing a round shot which weighed just under thirty-five pounds—came close to meeting the requirement Merlin and Captain Seamount had settled upon. It also happened to be the closest thing the Navy had to a "standard" heavy gun, which meant it was available in greater numbers than most other types.

There were others, some much heavier—like the "doomwhale," which weighed over four and a half tons and threw a sixty-two-pound shot. Or the even vaster "great doomwhale," a six-ton monster which threw a seventy-five-pound shot. Those, however, were far *too* heavy for their purposes. Eventually, all of them undoubtedly would be melted down to provide the bronze for sensibly sized replacements, but for now they were effectively useless.

What Howsmyn had suggested was standardizing on the kraken and welding an iron band around the gun tubes of as many of them as they could get their hands on. The *band* would be cast with trunnions, which could be done far faster than casting and boring an entire new gun. It wouldn't be as strong as casting the trunnions into the gun itself, but it would do as a temporary quick-fix, and as time allowed, the guns would, indeed, be melted down and recast.

It wasn't a perfect solution. The supply of krakens was scarcely unlimited, after all. But it would save a *lot* of time and resources, and given the new carronade design he and Seamount had worked out, it meant—

A sudden scream jerked him out of his thoughts, and he wheeled back towards the harbor.

The launch was no more than seventy yards from the wharf, now, but one of the older girls was screaming, one hand pressed to her mouth, while the other pointed wildly at the trio of triangular fins sweeping towards the boat.

"*Kraken!*" Cayleb spat. He was suddenly leaning out across the roof parapet towards the boatload of children. "Don't," he said, and it was obvious he wasn't talking to Merlin. "Don't panic!"

But the children in the launch couldn't hear him. The oldest of them could not have been more than fourteen, and their sudden terror was evident in the ragged disorder of their oars. The boat rocked in the water as the screaming girl shrank back against the gunwale on the side away from the krakens, then began to list as two more of the children joined her.

The fins slashed through the water, closing on the boat, and suddenly one of the krakens rose out of the water close alongside.

It was the first time Merlin had actually seen one of the fearsome predators, which normally preferred water deeper than that of most harbors. A fully mature sea kraken was up to twenty or twenty-two feet of voracious appetite. Roughly similar in body form to an elongated terrestrial shark, its head was quite different. It had the round, many-toothed mouth of a lamprey eel, but with a difference; over a foot across—almost three feet on fully mature krakens—it was fringed with a cluster of ten powerful tentacles. Those tentacles were from four to six feet long, and normally lay flat back against the torpedo-shaped body as it swam. But when the kraken attacked, they reached out and seized its prey, holding it while the mouth savaged it.

That would have been enough to explain the terror the creature evoked in any reasonably sane human being, but they were also intelligent. Nowhere near as intelligent as a terrestrial dolphin, perhaps, but smart enough to cooperate when they hunted. And smart enough to know boats contained food.

The terrified children shrieked as the first kraken lifted its head, then shrieked again, even more loudly, as the second slammed into the launch from below. The boat leapt madly in the water rocking so violently it almost capsized, and one of the boys went over the side.

There was a swirl in the water. His head came up and his mouth opened, screaming in terrified agony, as one of the krakens took him from below and dragged him under.

"*Shan-wei!*" Cayleb cursed helplessly, pounding the parapet with his fist, and the unbalanced launch heaved crazily as it was rammed again. This time, it went all the way up and over, spilling all of the children into the water.

Merlin didn't stop to think. Before Cayleb even realized his "bodyguard" had moved, Merlin hand flashed out with literally inhuman speed and snatched away the harpoon with which the prince had been toying. His arm cocked, and then Cayleb's eyes flew wide in disbelief, despite his horror, as the harpoon snapped out in a flat, vicious arc that ended a full seventy yards away.

One of the krakens rose two-thirds out of the water, standing on its thrashing tail, tentacles releasing the mangled body of its victim, as the harpoon struck it. No, Cayleb realized, the weapon hadn't simply *struck* its target; it had driven completely through that massive barrel of solid muscle and bone.

At least one of the wounded kraken's fellows turned upon it as its blood stained the water. But Cayleb's heart froze within him as another screaming child, a girl this time, disappeared forever into the churning, bloody horror which had enveloped the peaceful harbor.

And then he saw fresh movement out of the corner of his eye and reached out frantically. But he was too late to stop Merlin as he went over the roof parapet, thirty feet above the surface of the water.

Time seemed to have slowed impossibly, even as it flashed by. The crown prince saw everything, realized exactly what was happening, but he was a spectator. He could only watch as Merlin launched himself in a flat trajectory that carried him an impossible twenty yards before he hit the water.

▼   ▼   ▼

Merlin was already in midair before he realized what he was doing, by which time it was just a bit late for second thoughts. He hit the water and drove deep, despite his shallow trajectory. A flesh-and-blood human would have been forced to surface to regain his bearings, not to mention breathe, but Merlin was a PICA. His built-in sonar told him exactly where the boat, the thrashing, screaming children, and the krakens were, and his legs propelled him towards the chaos with a powerful flutter kick no biological human could have produced.

He'd snatched up his wakazashi without consciously considering it. Now he held its hilt in both hands, reversed seventeen-inch blade flat against the inside of his right arm to minimize drag, as he drove through the water. It took him less than twenty seconds to reach the capsized launch. Twenty seconds in which the kraken he'd harpooned wrenched frantically free of its attacking fellow and swam brokenly, erratically, towards shallower water. Twenty seconds in which a third shrieking child was dragged into the depths.

But then he was there.

The surviving children kicked and flailed frantically, fighting to climb on top of the overturned boat in search of even a few more moments of safety. An older boy snatched up one of the younger girls and literally threw her up onto the wet, slick boat bottom even as one of the two remaining krakens knifed towards him with lethal grace. The tentacles reached out, snapping towards him like striking serpents. One wrapped around his ankle, yanking his leg towards a tooth-filled maw, but a human-shaped hand closed on the tentacle, in turn. It locked down with the force of a hydraulic vise, and a battle steel wakazashi drove downward directly behind the creature's bulging eyes. It slammed hilt-deep into the kraken's head, and the impossibly sharp blade sliced effortlessly through bone, cartilage, and muscle.

The kraken's own movement added to the strength of the PICA's arm, and the wakazashi continued its forward trajectory straight through the creature's brain and back out through its snout in a fan of blood. The tentacle death-locked around the boy's ankle would have dragged him under with the still-thrashing carcass, but a second quick slash of the wakazashi severed it two feet from the kraken's opened skull.

The harpooned kraken's struggles were weakening as it writhed and twisted around the weapon driven through its body, but Merlin's sonar reached out, seeking the third. He found it, twenty feet beneath the surface, circling slowly as it ripped and tore at the remnants of its second victim.

He curled into a ball, oriented himself, and snapped straight, driving himself towards the feeding monster. Had it realized something as insignificant as he might pose a threat to it, it could easily have fled at a speed not even a PICA could have hoped to match. But it probably never even realized he was coming.

Even at this depth, his light-enhancing vision could see clearly, but he refused to let himself look at the mangled ruin clasped in the kraken's tentacles. He had eyes only for the kraken itself, and his left hand darted out and grasped the dorsal fin.

The kraken started to raise its head, as if in surprise, and the wakazashi drove down yet again. It sliced vertically through the thickest part of the creature's spine, directly in front of the fin, all but cutting the huge body in half, and it convulsed madly. It fell away from him, already dead, but still thrashing violently while its muscles tried to grasp the fact of its death, and he broke for the surface.

The surviving children were still screaming, fighting desperately to climb onto the boat, and he drove the wakazashi to the hilt into the launch's keel for safekeeping.

"It's all right!" he shouted. "It's all right—you're safe now!"

They didn't seem to notice him, and he reached out for the youngest child still in the water. It was the girl who'd waved to him, he realized, and she screamed in terror, writhing desperately, until she realized it was arms about her, not a kraken's tentacles. Then she reached back for him, her own arms ready to lock strangulation-tight about his neck. But he'd expected that and, his artificial muscles were more than a match even for her panic-driven strength as he boosted her up onto the overturned boat as gently as he could. She snatched at the keel, holding herself there, and he turned to pluck another child from the water.

"*You're safe now!*" he shouted again, and this time someone actually seemed to have heard him.

He heard another voice repeating the reassurance and realized it belonged to the boy who'd thrown the girl clear of the water. The familiar voice seemed to get through to the survivors where his own had not, and the worst of their panic began to subside. At least enough for all five of them to crawl up onto the boat and huddle there.

Three of them clung to the keel with white-knuckled fingers, weeping in terror that twisted Merlin's heart. But worse than that were the two children, one of them the first girl he'd lifted out of the water, who kept calling out frantically for two brothers and a sister they would never see again.

He stayed in the water, talking to them, trying to comfort them, and even as he did, a corner of his mind wondered how he was possibly going to explain *this* to Cayleb.

▼   ▼   ▼

"That was . . . impressive," Crown Prince Cayleb said quietly some hours later.

He and Merlin sat in facing chairs in Cayleb's quarters in the Citadel. The sun had set, and the room was comfortably cool, dim in the lamplight, as Merlin looked at him expressionlessly.

"I don't believe," Cayleb continued, "that I've ever heard of anyone killing a kraken, much less two of them, armed only with a short sword. Oh, and let's not forget the one you harpooned . . . at seventy yards. *Seijin* or no, Merlin, that was a remarkable feat."

Still, Merlin said nothing, and Cayleb leaned back in his chair, his face shadowed. Silence stretched out for several seconds, and then the crown prince sighed.

"Would you care to explain just how you managed all of that?"

The prince's voice sounded extraordinarily calm and reasonable, under the circumstances, Merlin thought.

"I can't, Cayleb," he said after a moment. "I wish I could. Truly, I do. But I can't."

"Merlin," Cayleb said quietly, "I don't care if you're a *seijin*. No mortal man could do what I saw you do this afternoon. No one, not even a *seijin*. I asked you once before what you truly were, and you promised me you serve light. But what sort of servant *are* you?"

"Cayleb—Your Highness," Merlin said softly, "I can't tell you that. Not 'don't want to'; not 'refuse to'; but *can't*."

"You're asking a great deal of me, Merlin," Cayleb said in that same, quiet voice. "My father trusts you. Trusts you enough to commit his entire kingdom to accepting your 'services'—your 'visions' and all the knowledge and suggestions you've brought us. And *I've* trusted you, as well. Were we wrong? If you can do what mortal men can't, that makes you more than mortal. And how am I to know if someone who must be either angel or demon speaks the truth?"

"I'm neither angel nor demon," Merlin replied. "I swear that. I simply can't tell you what I *am*. Not now—possibly never. And I suppose you're just going to have to decide for yourself whether or not you can trust someone who can't answer those questions for you."

He looked straight across at Cayleb, and Cayleb looked back into those strange sapphire eyes. The crown prince gazed deeply into them without speaking for at least a full minute. Then he inhaled deeply.

"You didn't have to do what you did this afternoon." His conversational tone sounded so normal it was almost bizarre, under the circumstances. "If you hadn't, I wouldn't have known what I know now, would I?"

"No," Merlin agreed. "You wouldn't. But that doesn't mean I didn't have to do it."

"No, it doesn't," Cayleb said. And then, to Merlin's astonishment, he smiled. It was an almost gentle expression, and the prince shook his head. "And that, Merlin, is the reason I *do* trust you."

"You do?" Despite himself, Merlin couldn't quite keep the surprise out of his own tone, and Cayleb chuckled softly.

"You showed me what you can do, the proof you're more than even a *seijin*, to save a pack of harbor urchins you didn't even know. You risked all the trust you've built up with me and my father for that. And I believe you did it without ever once considering *not* doing it."

"You're right. I didn't consider not doing it." Merlin shook his head. "I probably should have, but it never even crossed my mind."

"And that's why I trust you," Cayleb said simply. "A man—or even *more* than a man—who served darkness would never have let the lives of a handful of harbor brats weigh against his purposes. But you did. If you're prepared to risk throwing away all you've already achieved in order to save the lives of children, that tells me all I really need to know. Which isn't"—he flashed a sudden smile, suspiciously like a grin—"to say that I wouldn't *like* to know more, of course!"

"Your Highness," Merlin said, not even trying to keep the relief out of his voice, "on the day I can tell you more, *if* it comes, I will. I swear."

"I hope that day comes," Cayleb replied. "For now, though, I think you and I need to spend some time coming up with some sort of explanation for this afternoon. The good news is that no one on the shore, besides me, was in a position to see what actually happened. The bad news is that the *children's* version of what happened is pretty outrageous."

"You know how excitable children are, Your Highness." Merlin smiled. "I'm not a bit surprised if it all seemed even more impressive to them than it actually was!"

"All well and good," Cayleb said rather more soberly. "They've already brought in the carcass of one kraken, though. The one you harpooned. Trust me, there were more than a few raised eyebrows over that, even after I, ah . . . understated the range for the cast somewhat, let's say. Are there going to be even more if they bring up the other two?"

"Oh, I believe you can safely say there would be," Merlin admitted.

"And would that have something to do with the knife you stuck completely through the keel of that launch?" Cayleb asked politely.

"As a matter of fact, it would."

"Wonderful." Cayleb puffed his cheeks thoughtfully, then shrugged. "At least they were still in the main ship channel. The one you harpooned found its way into shallower water before it finally died, but the water's deep out there, and I understand there's a nasty tidal scour. We can at least hope the other two won't be recovered at all."

"That would undoubtedly be best," Merlin agreed, and sat for several seconds, gazing at the prince.

"Are you sure you're comfortable with this, Cayleb?" he asked finally.

" 'Comfortable' isn't the word I'd choose." Cayleb's smile was crooked. "In fact, it's not remotely *close* to the word I'd choose. But if you mean am I going to have second thoughts, the answer is no."

"I appreciate that," Merlin said gently. "Deeply."

"Well, let's look at it," Cayleb suggested. "So far, you've saved my life, saved Rayjhis' life, dealt with what was probably the most dangerous traitor in the Kingdom's history, broken both of the major spy rings in Charis, taught us the things which may actually save us from destruction, and now rescued five of my father's subjects from certain death. I'd say you've built up a considerable positive balance with me. So far, at least."

"I hadn't quite thought about it that way."

"Then you should have. As a matter of fact—" Cayleb broke off as someone knocked at the door.

He grimaced and shook his head irritably.

"I left instructions that we weren't to be disturbed," he said, then stood and faced the door.

"Enter!" he called in a voice which boded ill, in the absence of a very good excuse, for whoever was on the other side of the door.

It opened, and Ahrnahld Falkhan looked at the prince apologetically.

"I realize you left orders not to disturb you, Your Highness," he said. "But there's a courier boat from Tellesberg."

He held out an envelope sealed with crimson wax bearing King Haarahld's personal seal. Cayleb took it, his face suddenly expressionless, and broke the wax. Stiff, heavy paper crackled as he unfolded the brief message inside and read it. Then he looked up and met Merlin's gaze with a thin smile.

"It seems you and I are required in Tellesberg, Merlin," he said. "The Church's Intendant has . . . expressed a desire to speak to us."

.II.
Royal Palace,
Tellesberg

It was the first time Merlin had ever met Father Paityr Wylsynn, and as the upper-priest was ushered into the throne room, he devoutly wished that the meeting might have come under other circumstances. Almost *any* other circumstances.

Wylsynn was a young man, older than Cayleb but probably no older than Nimue Alban had been at the time of her biological death. He was slender, with red, curly hair, and a lively intelligence seemed to hover behind the gray eyes which, along with that hair, would have marked him as a foreigner to any Charisian.

He also wore the purple habit of the Order of Schueler, and the embroidered sword and golden flame on his sleeve marked him as the Church's Intendant in Charis, as well.

He followed the chamberlain to the foot of the dais and bowed gravely. First to Haarahld, then to Bishop Maikel, who stood at the king's shoulder, and finally to Cayleb.

"Your Majesty." His voice was a pleasant tenor, his accent that of the Temple and the City of Zion's elite.

"Father," Haarahld returned, his own soft Charisian accent sounding stronger than usual in contrast to the upper-priest's.

"I thank you for agreeing to see me on such short notice," Wylsynn continued. "And I thank you for joining us, Your Eminence," he added, with another small bow to Bishop Maikel.

"You're most welcome, Father," the bishop said. "And allow me to thank *you* for notifying me you intended to seek this interview. The courtesy is deeply appreciated."

Wylsynn smiled and waved his hand in a tiny gesture of dismissal, as if his notification to Staynair had been a matter of no consequence. But it most definitely had not been any such thing. As the Church's Intendant, Father Paityr had the authority to go anywhere, at any time of his choosing, and interrogate anyone he chose without advance notice to anyone in the entire kingdom, including Bishop Executor Zherald.

"Your message requested the presence of Crown Prince Cayleb and Lieutenant Athrawes," Haarahld observed after a moment. "As you observe, both of them are present. May we now know the reason for which you wished to see us?"

"Of course, Your Majesty." Wylsynn inclined his head in what was not quite a bow this time, but was still a gesture of respect.

"I fear certain reports have reached the Temple concerning matters here in Charis," he said calmly. "Most, I suspect, are the product of natural exaggeration. Some, alas, may be maliciously intended by those whose interests are . . . not identical to those of your kingdom, let us say. However, when there's this much smoke, the Council of Vicars and the Office of the Inquisition feel an obligation to be certain there's no fire underneath it. Hence my request for this interview."

Haarahld sat silent for several seconds, gazing at the young upper-priest, his own expression thoughtful. Merlin kept his own face completely expressionless as he stood behind Cayleb's chair, but his mind was busy considering Wylsynn's explanation. The upper-priest's tone was calm and measured, but there was an undertone, a hint of something which might almost have been exasperation, and Merlin remembered a brief conversation with Bishop Maikel about the reasons Wylsynn might have been assigned to Charis.

"Forgive me, Father," Haarahld said after a moment, "but I must assume any such reports would be in reference to the new processes and devices which have been introduced here in Charis over the past few months. It was my impression all of those had been examined and found free of taint."

"You're quite correct, Your Majesty," Wylsynn agreed. "I have, indeed, personally examined all the processes and devices which were submitted, exactly as they ought to have been, to the Office of the Intendant for approval. And it was, indeed, my determination that none of them even approached a violation of the Proscriptions. That remains my opinion."

Had Merlin still been a being of flesh and blood he would have inhaled a deep breath of relief. But Wylsynn wasn't finished, and he raised one hand slightly towards the king in a semi-apologetic gesture.

"Unfortunately, Your Majesty, I've been directly instructed by Archbishop Erayk to reconfirm my original determination. His semaphore message was, of course, quite terse, and didn't include the reasons he felt made such a reconfirmation desirable. I can only surmise that it's the result of those exaggerated reports I've already mentioned."

"I see. And I understand your responsibility to obey the Archbishop's instructions, of course. However," Haarahld allowed an edge of concern to creep into his voice, "since we'd been assured all these things were acceptable, we've already begun moving ahead with many of them. If we have to begin the examination process all over again, it's going to cause great hardship—and not a little financial loss—for many of our subjects who have acted in good faith."

"Believe me, Your Majesty, I'm well aware of that," Wylsynn said. "I've given this matter a great deal of thought since receiving the Archbishop's message. I'm entirely comfortable in my own mind with my original ruling on everything which has been submitted to my office. While I certainly owe the Archbishop my zealous obedience, I truly see no point in repeating the examination and testing process, as I feel confident my conclusions would be the same at the end of the effort. At the present time, however, I'm inclined to doubt that any remonstrance to the Archbishop on my part would . . . be of service to your kingdom's interests."

Merlin's eyes narrowed, and he sensed the stiffening of Cayleb's shoulders. Young Father Paityr was widely regarded as disdainfully oblivious to the political realities of the Church of God Awaiting's internal factions and how secular rulers tried to use them to advantage. Which made his last sentence even more interesting than it might otherwise have been.

"While I may feel the Archbishop's concerns, assuming they are in fact *his* concerns and not those of the Council of Vicars, are misplaced," Wylsynn continued, "I'm bound by both my formal vows and my duty as one of God's priests to fulfill his instructions to the very best of my ability. After much thought, I've concluded that the true nature of the concerns being expressed has less to do with the actual processes and devices I've already approved in Mother Church's name, than with the future to which they may lead."

Which, Merlin thought more than a little apprehensively, *shows even more "political" insight on his part. And cuts right to the chase in one simple sentence.*

"The *Writ* does warn us that change begets change, and that Shan-wei's temptations find their way into our hearts one step at a time," Wylsynn said gravely. "In that respect, I understand the Archbishop's legitimate concerns. And, to be totally honest, I find I share them, in some small degree. Your people here in Charis are a . . . boisterous lot, Your Majesty. I've come to like and admire them, but it may be that those within Mother Church who feel some apprehension about their taste for constantly improving how they do things have some justification for their worries.

"Because of that, and as a means of addressing what I believe was the Archbishop's intent, I've decided, after much prayer and meditation, how I believe I ought to proceed. I propose to cut directly to the heart of the Archbishop's concerns."

"In what way, Father?" Haarahld asked just a bit warily.

"In this way, Your Majesty," Wylsynn replied, and reached for his pectoral scepter of Langhorne. It was larger than most, and exquisitely gemmed, exactly the sort of scepter which might have been expected from someone of Wylsynn's familial wealth and prominence. But no one else in the throne room expected what happened when Wylsynn took it in both hands and twisted.

The scepter's crowned head came off, exposing the fact that the end of its staff projected into a gold-lined hollow inside the head.

Wylsynn released the head, letting it hang from the golden chain about his neck, and touched the staff's projecting end with the tip of his right index finger. And as he touched it, it began to glow.

Haarahld, Bishop Maikel, Cayleb, and the king's bodyguards all stared transfixed at that steadily strengthening blue glow. So did Merlin, but for completely different reasons.

"This," Wylsynn said softly, "is a treasure of Mother Church which was entrusted to my family centuries ago. According to the traditions which have been passed down with it, it was placed with us by the Archangel Schueler himself."

He touched his heart and then his lips, and everyone else in the throne room, including Merlin, did the same.

"The nature of the Stone of Schueler," Wylsynn continued, "is that if any lie is spoken by someone while touching it, the Stone will turn the color of blood. With your permission, Your Majesty, I propose to ask each of you in turn a few simple questions. The Stone will confirm for me the truth of your responses, and that, coupled with the examinations I've already carried out, will allow me to respond to the Archbishop's concerns in good faith."

He met Haarahld's gaze directly, his expression and manner radiating sincerity, and placed his own hand on the glowing blue crystal.

"No one outside a few members of my own family knows where the Stone has been bestowed in this generation," he said. "In fact, most in the Church believe it was lost forever at the time of Saint Evyrahard's death. I do not lightly reveal it to you at this time, but I have . . . concerns of my own about the nature of the allegations being made against Charis from within the Temple."

It was obvious to Merlin that it was almost physically painful for the young upper-priest to admit that, but the crystal burned steadily blue, and Wylsynn continued unflinchingly.

"I believe God sent the Stone to me for this very moment, Your Majesty. I believe He intends me to answer my own concerns so that I may know how best to answer those of others."

He stopped speaking, and Merlin held his mental breath as Haarahld VII of Charis looked deep into the young upper-priest's eyes.

Unlike Haarahld, Merlin knew exactly what had been hidden inside Wylsynn's reliquary, not that he'd ever expected to see it.

It was a verifier—the ultimate development of the old, clumsy pre-space lie detector. Unlike earlier attempts to produce a reliable means of determining truthfulness, the verifier used the brain waves of the individual being questioned. Under the law of the Terran Federation, verifiers could not be used without an explicit court order, and even then, there'd been stringent safeguards, limitations on the questions which could be asked, to prevent fishing expeditions or witch-hunts.

Even the verifier hadn't been a perfect guardian of truth. In almost a century of use, no instance of a verifier's inaccurately reporting a knowing lie as the truth had ever been reported, but it could only tell an interrogator whether or not the person he was questioning was telling the truth *as he knew it*. It didn't magically uncover truths no one knew . . . and certain mental disorders could return contradictory readings.

The one in Wylsynn's hand might well really have come from Schueler. At any rate, it had to have come from one of Langhorne's command crew, and it had clearly been intended to continue functioning indefinitely. The crystal itself was basically a solid chunk of molecular circuitry, which could have been pounded on with a sledgehammer without suffering undue damage, but there had to be some provision for *powering* the thing. Merlin couldn't be certain, but it seemed likely that the same "angel" who'd given the "relic" to Wylsynn's family had instructed them in the ritual required to keep it charged, probably via a simple solar power converter built into the thing.

None of which really mattered at this particular moment. What *mattered* was that the local representative of the Inquisition in Charis had it.

"I'm honored by your willingness to reveal this relic's existence, Father. And by both your trust in our discretion and your determination to judge these matters justly," Haarahld said finally. "For myself, I fear no just question." He didn't even look at the others.

"We will answer what you ask," he said.

▼　　▼　　▼

Merlin stood very still behind Cayleb's chair as Wylsynn approached the king. The upper-priest extended the verifier, and Haarahld touched it firmly, without hesitating, despite its unearthly glow. He looked across the blue light which turned his fingers almost translucent and met Wylsynn's eyes levelly.

"I'll keep my questions as brief as I may, Your Majesty," the upper-priest promised.

"Ask, Father," Haarahld replied steadily.

"Very well, Your Majesty." Wylsynn cleared his throat. "Your Majesty, of your knowledge, do any of the new processes, devices, or concepts which have been or will be introduced here in Charis violate the Proscriptions of Jwo-jeng?"

"They do not," Haarahld said in formal, measured tones, and the verifier glowed steady blue.

"Do you know of any individual here in Charis who would oppose God's will for Safehold?" Wylsynn asked, and Merlin held his mental breath.

"I know of no one here in Charis who would act in opposition to the will of God," Haarahld said. "I don't doubt there are some, for there are always those who prefer evil to good, but if they exist, I do not know who they may be, or where."

Again, the verifier continued to glow.

"Do you, as an individual and a monarch, accept God's plan for Safehold's salvation?" Wylsynn asked, and this time Haarahld's face tightened, as if with a flicker of anger. But he replied in that same measured tone.

"I accept God's plan for this world, for my Kingdom, and for myself," he said, and the verifier burned clear blue.

"Do you intend ill to any who do not intend ill to you?" Wylsynn asked very quietly, and Haarahld cocked his head slightly.

"Forgive me, Father," he said across the blue glow of the verifier, "but that question would seem to me to go just a bit far afield."

Wylsynn began to open his mouth, but the king shook his head before he could.

"Nonetheless," Haarahld continued, "I'll answer it. You've extended your trust to me, and so I'll extend mine to you. In answer to your question, I intend ill to no man who does not intend ill to me or the subjects for whose lives and safety I am responsible."

The verifier continued to glow, and Wylsynn bowed profoundly to the king and stepped back.

"I thank you, Your Majesty," he said, and looked at Cayleb.

"Your Highness?" he said, and Cayleb stretched out his hand as fearlessly as his father had.

"You heard the King's answers to my questions, Your Highness," Wylsynn said. "May I ask if you are in accord with his responses?"

"I am."

"Do you share your father's beliefs on these matters?"

"I do."

"Thank you, Your Highness," Wylsynn said as the verifier continued to glow brightly. Then he looked at Merlin.

"In addition to his concern about allegations of violations of the Proscriptions, the Archbishop informed me there have been reports of malign influences in the King's councils. He named no specific names, but I would imagine any such rumors probably focus on *you*, Lieutenant Athrawes. You are, after all, a stranger, and there are persistent rumors that you're also a *seijin*. The Archbishop didn't specifically instruct me to investigate those rumors, but it would be of great value to me—and a relief to my own mind—if you would permit me to do so."

Merlin looked back at him for several seconds, sensing the tension which suddenly ratcheted higher in Cayleb. Then he smiled crookedly and bowed to the upper-priest.

"I never anticipated anything quite like this, Father," he said with perfect honesty. "But if I can be of service, of course you have my permission."

He reached out his own hand, and settled it over the verifier. As he did, a small green icon glowed in the corner of his vision, and he drew a deep mental breath at the confirmation that the verifier was fully functional. Its circuitry and programming had detected the fact that he was a PICA operating in autonomous mode. It had no way to realize he was operating under hacked software, nor would it have had any way to report that fact to Wylsynn. But it had been designed to interface with a PICA's molycirc brain, as well as with a human one, and it had dropped automatically into the proper mode.

Which meant it would know if *he* lied to the upper-priest.

"Are you a *seijin*, Lieutenant?" Wylsynn asked.

"I have some, but by no means all, of the abilities *seijin* are reputed to have," Merlin replied calmly, choosing his words with deadly care. "I acquired them after many years in the Mountains of Light, but none of my teachers or instructors ever actually called me a *seijin*."

Wylsynn looked at the verifier's steady blue glow, then back up at Merlin's face.

"Why have you come to Charis?"

"For many reasons," Merlin said. "Specifically, I came to this kingdom to place my services and my sword at its disposal because I admire and respect King Haarahld, and because I believe Charis offers men the best chance to live as God would truly have them live."

"May I assume from your last answer that you believe in God's plan for Safehold?"

"Father," Merlin said very steadily, "I believe in God, I believe God has a plan for all men, everywhere, and I believe it's the duty of every man and woman to stand and contend for light against the darkness."

The verifier didn't even flicker, and Wylsynn's intent expression eased unexpectedly into a slight, crooked smile.

"I was going to ask you several more questions, Lieutenant," he said, "but you seem to believe in comprehensive answers."

"One tries, Father," Merlin murmured, and he and the upper-priest bowed to one another as Wylsynn stepped back from the dais, carefully deactivated the verifier, and returned it to its place of concealment.

"I thank you, Your Majesty, Your Highness. And you, Lieutenant Athrawes. I believe I know now what I needed to know in order to respond to the Archbishop's concerns."

"You're most welcome," Haarahld replied, and Merlin wondered if the king's calm voice concealed as much relief as *he* felt.

"And now, Your Majesty, Your Eminence, I know you have many duties to attend to. With your permission, I'll leave you to them."

"Of course, Father," Haarahld said, and Bishop Maikel raised one hand in benediction.

"You've done well here today, Father," the bishop said. "Would that all Mother Church's priests were as faithful, zealous, and careful in discharging their responsibilities. The blessings of God and the Archangels go with you."

"Thank you, Your Eminence," Wylsynn replied quietly. Then he bowed once again, and he was gone.

"S teeeeerike *three!*"

The capacity crowd in King Haarahld V Stadium roared its disapproval of the call, but the white-clad umpire behind the plate ignored the shouts coming his way. Umpires, after all, were the only branch of Mother Church's hierarchy who were *accustomed* to catcalls and vociferous disagreement.

Bishop Executor Zherald Ahdymsyn sometimes regretted that they were. It offended his sense of propriety for any of Mother Church's servants to be the subject of such abuse, although at least the Archangel Langhorne had been careful, when he established the *Writ's* commandments for the game, to reserve the office of umpire for the laity. It wasn't as if the crowd were booing a consecrated priest, after all. And this time around, even the most violently protesting fan probably understood that the umpire's call had been the correct one.

It would have been expecting a bit much out of them to *admit* it, though. The annual Kingdom Championship Series—yet again this year between the Tellesberg Krakens and their traditional, hated rivals, the Hairatha Dragons—was all tied up at three games each, and they were into the seventh inning of the deciding game with the Krakens trailing by two runs and the bases loaded, which made the second out on a called strike particularly painful.

The crowd noise subsided to its normal background surf, with only an occasional voice still shouting speculative comments on the quality of the umpire's vision, and the next batter advanced to the plate. A derisive cheer went up from the spectators as he stepped into the batter's box. Zhan Smolth was one of the most dominating pitchers in the league, especially in the post-season, and he was normally immensely popular. But like most pitchers, his batting performance was at best mediocre. Not only that, but he'd hit into an inning-ending double play in his last at-bat, and the home crowd clearly expected to be . . . disappointed by this one.

Which circumstances, Ahdymsyn thought, had made the preceding batter's strikeout even more excruciating for the spectators.

The bishop chuckled at the thought, then, as Smolth dug his cleats firmly in and tapped the plate with his bat, sat back in his comfortable, well-shaded seat in the box reserved for the Church's use in every major baseball stadium. Everyone else in the stadium was focused on the drama unfolding on the sun-drenched field, but Ahdymsyn's smile faded. He himself had other, more weighty matters on his mind.

In Haarahld V Stadium, the Church Box was located immediately to the right of the Royal Box. Zherald had only to turn his head to see King Haarahld and Crown Prince Cayleb watching the beautifully manicured field intently, and he frowned, ever so slightly, at the sight. It was a troubled frown, but it had nothing to do with the current game.

Zherald Ahdymsyn hadn't served as bishop executor for the Kingdom of Charis for so many years without gaining a certain sensitivity, even at this remove, to the political currents flowing about inside the Temple. No one actually told him anything about them in so many words, as a rule, but he'd had a lot of experience reading Archbishop Erayk's letters, and the latest set of dispatches had been even . . . franker than usual. It was apparent to Ahdymsyn that his temporal masters were unusually anxious over the reports they were receiving—not all from him—about Charis. That was never a good thing, and the freak accident which had prevented the archbishop from making his scheduled pastoral visit left his bishop executor responsible for dealing with it. Which, in Zherald Ahdymsyn's opinion was an even worse thing.

He chewed that unpalatable thought for a moment, then looked at the younger priest sitting beside him.

Father Paityr Wylsynn was a dark slash of purple amid the episcopal white and brown and green earth tones of the other bishops and priests filling the box. Competition for seating at the Kingdom Series was always ferocious, and technically, Wylsynn was considerably junior to some of the upper-priests of other ecclesiastical orders who'd failed to win places in the Church Box this year. But that didn't matter. As Mother Church's (and the Inquisition's) Intendant in Charis, the only member of the Charisian hierarchy *functionally* senior to the young, intense Schuelerite was Ahdymsyn himself.

Which made the bishop executor more than a little uneasy. Priests like Wylsynn often posed problems for their administrative superiors even under normal circumstances. Which, unless Ahdymsyn much missed his guess, these circumstances were not.

"Tell me, Father," he said after a moment, "have you had any fresh thoughts on the matter we discussed Thursday?"

"I beg your pardon, Your Eminence?" Wylsynn turned his head to face the bishop. "I was concentrating on the field, and I'm afraid I didn't quite hear your question."

"That's perfectly all right, Father." Ahdymsyn smiled. "I simply asked if you'd had any additional thoughts on that matter we talked about the other day."

"Oh." Wylsynn cocked his head, his expression suddenly much more thoughtful, then shrugged ever so slightly.

"Not really, Your Eminence," he said then. "I've pondered the Archbishop's latest despatches and instructions very carefully, and, as you know, I've personally interviewed the King and the Crown Prince in light of them. I've also exhaustively reviewed my original notes from my initial examination of all the new processes and devices. And, as I told you I would, I've spent quite a few hours in my chamber, praying earnestly over the matter. For the present, neither God nor the

Archangels—" He touched the fingers of his right hand to his heart, then to his lips. "—have vouchsafed me any additional insight, however. I—"

"Strike one!" the umpire called as the Dragons' pitcher grooved a fastball right through the center of the strike zone. Smolth's late, awkward swing didn't even make contact, and several fans groaned only too audibly. Wylsynn was one of them, and then he blushed as he realized he'd allowed the game to distract him from the conversation with his ecclesiastical superior.

"I'm sorry, Your Eminence." His sudden smile made him look even younger, almost boyish. "I know I'm a good northern boy from the Temple Lands, but I'm afraid the Krakens have seduced my allegiance away from the Slash Lizards. *Please* don't tell Father! He'd disinherit me, at the very least."

"Don't worry about it, Father." For all the somberness of his own thoughts and concerns, Ahdymsyn found himself smiling back. Despite the often ominous reputation of the Order of Schueler and Wylsynn's own frustrating insensitivity to the Temple's internal political dynamic, the intendant was a very likable young man. "Your secret is safe with me. But you were saying?"

"I believe I was going to say—before the umpire so rudely interrupted us— that despite all of my prayers and meditation, or perhaps because of them, I feel quite comfortable with my original judgment on these matters."

"Then you remain unconcerned about any violations of the Proscriptions?"

"Your Eminence," Wylsynn said gravely, "as a member of the Order, and as Mother Church's Intendant in Charis, I'm always concerned about possible violations of the Proscriptions. Indeed, the Order clearly recognizes the need to be particularly vigilant here in Charis, this far from the Temple, and I assure you I've attended to both the Grand Inquisitor's and the Archbishop's instructions in that regard most carefully. Nothing in any of the recent developments here in the Kingdom, however, has even approached the threshold of a Proscribed offense."

"I realize this is properly the Schuelerites' sphere of responsibility, Father Paityr," Ahdymsyn said. "And if it seemed I cherished any doubts about the zeal with which you discharge those responsibilities, that wasn't my intent." He frowned thoughtfully. "I suppose it's just the sudden appearance of so many . . . innovations in such a short span of time which causes me some disquiet."

And it would appear they're doing even worse than that for certain other people, now that word of them's gotten back to the Temple, he thought.

"*Strike two!*"

The crowd's groans were louder as the ball smacked into the catcher's mitt. Not that anyone particularly blamed Smolth this time. The Dragons' pitcher knew what even a bloop single could do to the scoreboard, and he wasn't pitching Smolth the way he normally would have pitched to someone with Smolth's regular-season batting performance. That nasty, late-breaking slider would have tied almost any hitter up in knots.

"I can certainly understand why you might be feeling some concern, Your

Eminence," Wylsynn said, smiling and shaking his head wryly as he watched Smolth step out of the batter's box to reorganize his thoughts. Then the Schuelerite turned back to face Ahdymsyn squarely.

"As matter of fact," he said rather more seriously, "I was quite taken aback by them myself, even here in Charis! While I've seen no evidence of demonic intervention during my years here, I must confess that the energy with which Charisians seek better ways to do things is often quite daunting, and this Royal College of theirs only makes it worse. I've had my own moments of doubt about them, and to have so many new ideas surfacing at once was something of a shock.

"Having said that, however, it seems apparent that all the innovations we've been considering over the past few months are actually no more than the application of already existing, approved techniques and practices in novel ways. Every one of those techniques and practices, in turn, was thoroughly tested by Mother Church before it received the Order's approval in the first place. And the *Writ* contains no injunctions against using approved practices for new ends, so long as those ends don't threaten God's plan."

"I see." Ahdymsyn considered the younger man for several seconds and wished he could ask the question he really wanted to ask.

With most other intendants, he probably could have, but Wylsynn had been shuffled off to Charis for a reason. For several of them, actually, including his obvious disapproval of the way in which Mother Church's senior prelates, even in his own order, allowed . . . pragmatism to color the decision-making process. His equally obvious disapproval of what he considered the "decadence" of the lifestyle embraced by those same senior prelates was just as pronounced, and his birth had made the possible consequences of his attitude potentially ominous.

The Wylsynn family had provided no less than six Grand Vicars. The last had been only two grand vicarates before, and one of them—Grand Vicar Evyrahard the Just—had been a fervent reformer of Temple "abuses" a hundred years earlier. His grand vicarate had lasted less than two years before he'd somehow mysteriously fallen from his balcony to his death, but it was still remembered with shudders of horror in the senior ranks of the episcopate. As Saint Evyrahard's direct heir—in more than one way—young Paityr might easily have become a major power in the Temple, if he'd chosen to play the game. And that would have posed an intolerable threat to too many cozy Temple relationships.

Fortunately, he was about as disinterested in politics as he could possibly have been, and those same family connections had preserved him from the worst consequences of his superiors' disapproval. On the other hand, given his family, his present rank as a mere upper-priest could well be construed as punishment for his tendency to make waves. As could his posting to Charis, for that matter.

But no man living could question Father Paityr Wylsynn's piety or intellectual prowess. Indeed, that was part of Ahdymsyn's problem. Wylsynn was far too fiercely focused on his order's duty to protect the Church's orthodoxy to waste time on things like the Temple's internal factions or the strife between them, and no one in his entire order was better informed on what that duty included. That might have as much to do with his assignment to Charis as any desire to get him out of Zion, but all those factors together combined to preclude any possibility of Ahdymsyn's discussing with him the potential consequences of so many Charisian innovations on the political calculations of the Temple.

Or the follow-on consequences for the career of one Bishop Executor Zherald.

"Would you say," the bishop asked instead, "that Doctor Mahklyn's new 'numerals' and this 'abacus' device of his fall into that same category?"

"Which category, Your Eminence?" Wylsynn looked puzzled, and Ahdymsyn managed not to sigh.

"The category of resting upon approved practices, Father," he said patiently.

"Forgive me, Your Eminence," the Schuelerite replied, "but the question really doesn't arise. While I readily admit I'm less well versed in mathematics than many, it's obvious from my study of Doctor Mahklyn's work that it's going to be hugely beneficial. The merchants who are already adopting these new 'numerals' of his have clearly demonstrated that much.

"Of course, as the *Writ* teaches, the mere fact that something appears to be beneficial in a worldly sense doesn't necessarily make it acceptable in the eyes of God. That was how Shan-wei tempted her original followers into evil and damnation, after all. But the Proscriptions say nothing, one way or the other, about ways to count or to record numbers. I assure you, after our previous conversations, I spent quite some time with my concordances, searching for any reference in the *Writ* or *The Insights*. I found none.

"The Proscriptions are concerned with unclean knowledge, the sort which opens doors to the kinds of temptation which lead men into Shan-wei's web. The Archangel Jwo-jeng is very specific on that point, as are *The Insights*, but the temptation lies in impiously seeking to profane that knowledge and power which are reserved for God and his angels. Within the sphere of knowledge appropriate to mortal men, the mere fact that a way of doing established tasks is more efficient and works better scarcely threatens men's souls with damnation. So long, at least, as none of the Proscriptions' thresholds are crossed."

"I see," Ahdymsyn repeated, although he was well aware that Wylsynn's views were not universally shared, even in the Order of Schueler. On the other hand, there was something about Wylsynn's voice, or perhaps it was his eyes. The young intendant's replies came quickly and easily, with the confidence of one who had, indeed, spent many hours reflecting upon them. But there was also an edge of . . . challenge. Not defiance, and not disrespect. Never that. Yet Ahdymsyn had the sinking sensation that the young man had made his decision in the full understanding that it was not the one his Archibishop or possibly even the Council itself wanted.

The bishop executor watched Smolth step back into the box and resume his batting stance, waiting while the pitcher and catcher tried to get together on what they wanted to do next. Although, Ahdymsyn thought, the decision shouldn't have been that complex. With two outs already and a count of two strikes and no balls, Smolth had to be feeling defensive, and the Dragons had three free pitches with which to work. Everyone in the stadium had to know it was time for something unhittable, well out of the strike zone, that they might possibly entice him into chasing for the strikeout.

Apparently the man on the pitcher's mound was the only person in Tellesberg who didn't realize that, the bishop observed sardonically. He watched the pitcher shake off sign after sign from the catcher, then glanced back at Wylsynn.

"Then I suppose that's all that needs to be said, Father," he said. "May I assume your own report on these matters will be completed within the next day or two? I have a dispatch vessel about ready to depart for Clahnyr. If your report will be available, I can hold her in port long enough to include it with my own correspondence to Archbishop Erayk."

"I can have it to you by tomorrow afternoon, Your Eminence."

"Excellent, Father. I'll look forward to reading it myself, and—"

CRACK!

The sudden sharp sound of wood meeting leather stunned the crowd into an instant of silence. The Dragons' pitcher had finally made his pitch selection, and it was a nasty one. In fact, the ball had been almost in the dirt and at least ten inches off the plate. But somehow the Krakens' pitcher had actually made contact. And not just "contact." His lunging swing looked impossibly awkward, yet it lifted the ball out of the infield, just out of reach of the leaping second baseman, and put it on the centerfield grass. It landed with a wicked spin, then seemed to hit something which imparted a nasty hop that sent it bounding past the diving centerfielder. It shot by him, no more than a foot beyond his desperately stabbing glove, and with the bases loaded and two strikes, the runners had been off the instant Smolth made contact.

The crowd's disbelieving roar of delight was ear-stunning, and even Zherald came to his feet as the ball rolled almost all the way to the centerfield wall before the Dragons' rightfielder managed to chase it down and scoop it up. The first Kraken had already crossed the plate by the time he got his throw off, and he threw it over the cutoff man's head. Given the distance it had to cover and how quickly he managed to get it off, it wasn't that bad a throw. But it wasn't a good one, either. It pulled the catcher a quarter of the way up the first-base line, well off of home plate, and he fumbled the catch slightly as the second Kraken crossed home with the tying run.

The Dragons' pitcher had charged in to cover the plate, but he'd started late, as if he couldn't believe Smolth had actually hit the ball. He arrived just after the second runner, but he was still in the process of turning towards the catcher, who was still juggling the ball and trying to set himself for a throw, when the *third* Kraken came thundering down the third-base line, all the way from first. The catcher finally got his throw off—a bullet, perfectly delivered to the plate—but the pitcher wasn't even looking in the runner's direction when the Kraken charged straight into him, knocked him over, and touched home base with the go-ahead run. The ball squirted away from the bowled-over pitcher, and Smolth—running harder than he ever had in his life before—found himself on third base, panting for breath, while the stadium went crazy.

"Well," Ahdymsyn said with a chuckle several minutes later, as the tumult died and he resumed his own seat, "it seems miracles do happen, don't they, Father?"

"Of course they do, Your Eminence!"

Wylsynn's tone pulled Ahdymsyn's eyes to his face. The youthful priest seemed startled by the levity of the bishop's observation. No, Ahdymsyn thought, not "startled." Disapproving, perhaps, although that wasn't exactly the right word either. Maybe the one he wanted was "disappointed."

Whatever, I need to remember it, Ahdymsyn told himself. *He's not here just to get him out from underfoot in the Temple. And he's not interested in . . . administrative compromises. I hope that doesn't turn into a problem.*

"Yes, they do, Father," the bishop executor agreed, his own voice and expression more serious. "Indeed they do."

▼　　▼　　▼

Zhaspahr Maysahn sat several hundred seats away from Bishop Zherald and Father Paityr. Like many individuals and firms which did business in Tellesberg, the small shipping house which he ostensibly owned held season tickets to the Krakens' games. His seat wasn't as good as those in the Royal Box or the Church Box, but it was almost directly behind third, and he shook his head in disbelief as Smolth wound up on that base.

"That's going to hurt," Zhames Makferzahn observed cheerfully from the seat beside him, and Maysahn glowered at him.

"It's only the seventh inning," he growled, and Makferzahn chuckled.

"Of course it is," he said soothingly, and rubbed his thumb and index finger together.

Maysahn managed to retain a suitably defiant expression, but he was afraid Makferzahn was right. The Dragons' devastating offensive lineup had made them the odds-on favorite to take the Series this year. Even the Tellesberg bet-takers had agreed on that one, however disgruntled they might have been by the notion. But Makferzahn had argued—and been willing to bet—that the Krakens' pitching, which had been very strong down the stretch, would carry the home team to victory. Maysahn had covered that bet, at two-to-one odds, and he was beginning to suspect that in this respect, at least, his new subordinate's judgment had been better than his own.

And it was like Makferzahn to have backed his judgment to the tune of several Charisian marks, despite the relatively brief time he'd been here. He'd arrived in Tellesberg as Oskahr Mhulvayn's replacement less than a month ago, but he'd gotten a quick grasp of much more than the way kingdom's baseball teams matched up. It was already obvious he was at least as capable as his predecessor. He was also self-confident and even more industrious . . . and, undoubtedly, ambitious, as well. Best of all, he was clearly not on Baron Wave Thunder's list of suspected foreign agents.

All of those—except, possibly, the ambition—were good things from Maysahn's perspective. Unfortunately, Makferzahn was still in the very early stages of assembling his own intelligence sources. Maysahn had considered putting his new subordinate into contact with some of the senior members of Mhulvayn's old web as a way to speed the process, but he'd rejected the temptation firmly.

It seemed unlikely Wave Thunder had managed to identify many of Mhulvayn's agents, despite the baron's obvious suspicion of Mhulvayn himself, since not one of them had been arrested. It was also possible, however, that Wave Thunder knew exactly who'd been working for Mhulvayn and had left them unmolested in hopes that Mhulvayn's replacement would identify himself by contacting them. But given the fact that Nahrmahn of Emerald's web of spies had been totally gutted, as far as Maysahn could tell, Maysahn's own organization had become the only window Prince Hektor and his allies had in Charis. Under those circumstances, he'd decided, it was far better to take a little longer getting Makferzahn fully up to speed than to risk walking into a Wave Thunder trap and losing that window, as well.

Not to mention risking the one and only skin of a certain Zhaspahr Maysahn.

He watched as the celebration of backslapping and mutual congratulation died down in the Krakens' dugout. The next batter—Rafayl Furkal, the Krakens' leadoff man—eventually advanced to the plate, while the Dragons' catcher trotted out to the mound to confer with the pitcher. Probably more in an effort to settle the pitcher down again than for any serious discussion of strategy. The Dragons had studied the scouting reports on the Krakens intensively, and they knew Furkal's power was almost exclusively to left field. The infielders were already shifting around to the left—indeed, the second baseman had become almost a second shortstop, and the first baseman had moved halfway to second—while the catcher was still talking soothingly to his pitcher.

I wish there'd been someone around to settle me *down over the past few months,* Maysahn thought moodily. It had been maddening to realize all sorts of things were clearly happening under the surface at the very moment when prudence and future survival had required him to operate so cautiously. He'd done his best, but his own sources had been much more strongly developed among the merchants operating in Tellesberg. Until Oskahr was forced to run for it, he hadn't truly realized how much he'd relied upon Mhulvayn's judgment and fieldwork where political and military matters were concerned. The good news was that Prince Hektor's dispatches made it clear the prince understood the constraints under which his Charisian spymaster had been forced to operate.

Or he says *he does, at least,* Maysahn couldn't quite help reflecting. He'd wondered, more than once, especially given Makferzahn's obvious capability, if Hektor might have sent the new man in with the intention of eventually elevating *him* to the top position in Charis. It was a distinct possibility, and if it happened, Maysahn's recall to Corisande would not bode well for his own career. Although, at least, Hektor was far less likely than Nahrmahn to simply have one of his agents eliminated.

For the moment, Maysahn had decided to take his prince's assurances of his continued confidence at face value and concentrate on finding out whatever it was Haarahld and Wave Thunder were working so diligently to conceal.

The pitcher delivered his first pitch, and Furkhal swung hard . . . and missed.

"Strike one!" the umpire announced, and Furkhal shook his head in obvious self-disgust. He stepped out of the box for a moment, clearly settling himself back down, then stepped back into it without even glancing at the Krakens' third-base coach for any fresh signs. He settled himself, and the pitcher came set and delivered his second pitch.

At which point, Furkhal astounded every single person in the stadium by dropping an almost perfect drag-bunt onto the first-base line. It wasn't—quite—a suicide squeeze, but it *was* a high-risk move, even for someone with Furkhal's speed. Despite that, its very audacity took the defense completely by surprise. The fact that he'd swung away at the first pitch probably helped, but it was obviously a preplanned ploy, despite the lack of any sign from the third-base coach, because Smolth had broken for home at the exact same instant Furkhal squared around to bunt.

The infield shift left the pitcher responsible for covering first, but he was left-handed, and his natural motion carried him towards the third-base side of the mound. It took him one critical instant to recover, charge over, and scoop up the ball. He was too late to tag Furkhal out, and by the time he whirled to throw home, Smolth had gotten just enough of a head start to beat the throw and score while the capacity crowd shouted, whistled, and stamped its feet in approval.

There was an analogy there, Maysahn decided.

He was only too well aware that he still didn't know everything the Charisians were up to. Most of what he did know was more disquieting than threatening. Unless Maysahn missed his bet, the new rigging design Sir Dustyn Olyvyr had come up with—this "schooner rig" of his—represented the most direct challenge anyone knew anything about. Maysahn rather doubted all of the fantastic tales about its efficiency and advantages could be accurate, but it was obvious those advantages were still substantial. They were bringing Olyvyr dozens of orders for new ships, the first of which which were already coming out of the yards to swell the ranks of the huge Charisian merchant marine. A merchant marine which was already far too big and had entirely too many advantages.

On the other hand, the "secret" of how it worked could scarcely be maintained for long, not if it was going to be used where anyone else could see it, anyway. And the same thing was true of Rahzhyr Mahklyn's new way of counting. Indeed, Maysahn had already personally acquired one of Mahklyn's "abacuses" and dispatched it to Corisande. He and Makferzahn were also following up the rumors of still more innovations among Charis' textile producers, and he expected to be able to deliver a preliminary report on them, as well, within the next few five-days.

A part of him was tempted to decide all of that meant he was getting back on top of the situation, but somewhere deep inside, a small, nagging voice warned that he wasn't. That what he knew about—what the rest of the world had been allowed to see—was only a part. A deliberate screen thrown up in an effort to convince everyone else to concentrate on the clearly visible part of the iceberg, the same way Furkhal's first swing had distracted everyone from the possibility of a bunt.

And I wonder, Maysahn thought, *if all of these fathers of innovation are* really *responsible for their "own" work?*

It was a question he'd pondered more than once. All the evidence suggested that Mahklyn, Olyvyr, and Raiyan Mychail truly had come up with their spate of new ideas all on their own. The fact that Haarahld's college had brought them all together, where their ideas could strike sparks off of one another, really could explain how so many new concepts had flowered in such a short period of time. But Maysahn couldn't quite shake the suspicion that Merlin Athrawes' abrupt arrival in Tellesberg had had more than a little to do with it, too, and that was what made him so nervous.

Don't borrow trouble, Zhaspahr, he told himself firmly. *Even if there's any truth to the story that the man really is a* seijin, *it doesn't make him some sort of all-around superhuman! If he was truly behind all of this, they'd have done something better with him than making him a lieutenant in the Royal Guard, for Langhorne's sake! Instead of worrying about him, why don't you worry about what the rest of the world* hasn't *been allowed to see yet? If they're so willing to tell us about the things we do know about, just what might they be hiding* behind *the things they've made public knowledge?*

He didn't know the answers to those questions, but he did know Wave Thunder and High Admiral Lock Island had strengthened the already tight security they maintained at Helen and Sand Shoal Islands. Since Kahlvyn Ahrmahk's death, security at Hairatha had also been stepped up significantly. All of that could be readily enough explained as a routine precaution after the attempt to assassinate Cayleb and the discovery that someone as highly placed as the Duke of Tirian had been in league with the kingdom's enemies. But it also just happened to provide a screen behind which almost anything might have been going on, and Zhaspahr Mhulvayn didn't like that.

No, he didn't like that at all.

APRIL, YEAR OF GOD 891

✦

Signal from the flagship, Sir!"

The Earl of Gray Harbor turned from his place at the quarterdeck rail as the shout floated down from the senior of the two midshipmen perched in the mizzentop. He folded his hands behind him, adjusting to the easy movement of the deck with the remembered reflexes of twenty-plus years at sea, and watched HMS *Typhoon*'s captain look up at the teenaged midshipman who'd announced the signal.

That young man had his eyes glued to the flagship. The noises of a ship at sea—wind humming through the rigging, the rhythmic surge of water past the hull, the creak of timbers and masts, the high-pitched cries and whistles of seabirds and wyverns following in *Typhoon*'s wake—flowed around Gray Harbor while he watched the senior middy straining to read off the signal flags streaming from HMS *Gale*'s mizzen yard. The other youngster sat with his back against the mast, holding the outsized book in his lap firmly against the insistent wind while he waited to turn its pages.

"*Well*, Master Mahgentee?" Captain Stywyrt prompted, glowering up at the mizzentop as the seconds trickled past.

"I can't quite make out the hoist, Sir, and—" Midshipman Mahgentee began, then broke off. "I've got it now, Sir! Numbers Nine and Thirty-Seven—form line of battle on the port tack, Sir!"

"Very good, Master Mahgentee," Captain Dahryl Stywyrt said, and looked at yet another midshipman, this one standing expectantly on the quarterdeck with him.

"Hoist the acknowledgment, Master Aymez," the captain said. "Lively, now!"

"Aye, aye, Sir!" Midshipman Aymez responded, and began barking orders to the seamen of his detail.

Gray Harbor watched without any temptation to smile, despite the fact that Aymez's thirteen-year-old voice had yet to break and that the youngest of the seamen under his command had to be twice his own age. The earl had once stood in Aymez's shoes, and the youngster clearly knew what he was about.

Balls of brightly colored bunting spilled out of the flag bags, and four of them were bent on to the signal halyards in the proper sequence. Aymez watched carefully, making certain of that, then gave a final order, and the flags rose swiftly.

The topmost flag reached the yardarm, and a quick jerk broke them to the wind. They streamed out, duplicating the signal at *Gale*'s yardarm, simultaneously indicating receipt of the flagship's signal and repeating it to show it had been properly read.

Mahgentee had never taken his eyes off the flagship. A few more moments passed, and then, as *Gale*'s signal officer hauled down the original hoist, he shouted down to the quarterdeck once again.

"Execute, Sir!"

"Very well, Master Ahlbair," the captain said to his first officer. "Lay the ship on the port tack, if you please."

"Aye, aye, Sir!" Lieutenant Ahlbair replied, and lifted his leather speaking trumpet to his lips. "Hands to sheets and braces!" he barked.

Gray Harbor watched Stywyrt's well-drilled crew as petty officers bellowed and seamen scampered to their stations. The evolution was more complicated than it had been aboard Gray Harbor's own final command, but *Typhoon* was a galleon, not a galley. At a hundred and twenty feet, she was thirty feet shorter than a typical galley, and she was also both beamier and taller, which made her look undeniably stubby. And she had three masts, compared to a typical galley's single one, of course, but some additional changes had been made, as well.

The most immediately apparent change—and the one which, Gray Harbor had discovered, had actually most offended his view of the way ships were supposed to look—was the disappearance of the towering forecastle and aftercastle. Those castles had provided the advantage of height both for defense against boarders and for pouring fire from matchlocks, crossbows, and light cannon down onto the decks of an opponent. Their disappearance seemed . . . wrong, somehow. Which, he knew, was a foolish attitude. They were no longer needed, and he'd already noticed how much more weatherly *Typhoon* had become without their wind resistance helping to push her to leeward. Besides, their removal had been an important part of Merlin's and Olyvyr's efforts to reduce top weight and displacement. But however he might feel about the way the castles had been cut down to the upper deck level, the alterations in her sail plan were actually a far more profound change.

Her square-rigged spritsail had been replaced with three of Sir Dustyn Olyvyr's new "jibs"—triangular staysails set "fore-and-aft" on the forward-leading stays supporting the foremast, and the mizzenmast's lateen sail had been replaced by a "spanker," a gaff-rigged fore-and-aft sail, with its foot spread by a heavy boom. They looked decidedly . . . odd to Gray Harbor's eye, but he had no intention of complaining. Nothing was likely to change the fact that square-rigged vessels always had been (and would remain) clumsy and awkward to maneuver. The improvement the new headsails and spanker made possible, however, had to be seen to be believed.

It wasn't enough to match the nimbleness and weatherliness of the "schooners" Olyvyr was producing, of course, but *Typhoon*'s jibs and spanker still gave her a huge maneuver advantage over more conventionally rigged ships. They were located well forward and aft of *Typhoon*'s natural pivot point, which gave them far more leverage than their sail area alone might suggest, and they helped her sail far closer to the wind than any square-rigger had ever before managed. That meant she had a shorter distance to go across the eye of the wind when it came time to tack, and the headsails' and spanker's leverage imparted a powerful turning moment as she began her turn, as well. The combination brought the vessel through the maneuver much more quickly and reliably. It was still easy for an unwary skipper to be caught aback and end up in irons, head-on to the wind and drifting to leeward, but it had become *less* easy, and the new sail plan helped a vessel regain way much more quickly if it did happen.

Personally, Gray Harbor knew, he would always be a galley captain at heart, but he was far too experienced not to grasp the enormous changes Lock Island, Seamount, and Merlin had wrought.

Typhoon completed her maneuver, settling onto her new heading, and Gray Harbor stepped back to his position at the rail, admiring the precision with which Commodore Staynair maneuvered his squadron's vessels.

In addition to all his other innovations, Merlin had radically overhauled the Navy's signal procedures, as well. The Royal Charisian Navy had evolved its own set of signals over the years, but they'd been restricted to fairly simple, straightforward messages. Hoisting a single red flag to the masthead, for example, as an order to engage the enemy. Adding the golden kraken on black of the Charisian ensign above it to order an attack on the enemy's van, or below it, to order an attack on his rear. Hoisting a black and yellow striped flag below the national flag as an order to "form line astern of me," or above it, as an order to form line abreast. There simply hadn't been a way to transmit more complicated orders . . . until Merlin stepped in, that was.

Baron Seamount had been too deeply involved in producing the new, modified artillery to deal with the signals issue himself, so he'd delegated that particular responsibility to Sir Domynyk Staynair. Staynair, the younger brother of Bishop *Maikel* Staynair, had been handpicked by High Admiral Lock Island to command Seamount's "Experimental Squadron."

He'd been chosen in part because his superiors' faith in his loyalty—and ability to protect the Navy's secrets—was absolute. But he'd also been chosen because of his raw ability. At thirty-seven, with over twenty-five years of seagoing experience, Staynair was young enough to remain flexible, yet more than experienced enough to help the *seijin* construct a comprehensive vocabulary of just under eight hundred standard commands. Those commands were listed in the signal book clasped so firmly by Midshipman Mahgentee's assistant in the top, and each of them had been assigned a numerical value.

Using the new signal flags, based on Merlin's "arabic numerals," each of those commands, which dealt with the overwhelming majority of possible evolutions, could be transmitted using a simple hoist of no more than three flags. The simple inclusion of a plain black flag—already called the "stopper" by the signals parties—between numerical flags served as punctuation. By inserting it to indicate breaks between individual values, multiple commands—such as Staynair's order to form line, followed by the order to do so on the port tack—could be hoisted simultaneously.

Staynair's vocabulary also contained a thousand of the words most commonly needed by seamen, each also represented by a single numerical hoist, to permit more complicated signals to be exchanged. And, if it should happen that a required word wasn't in the vocabulary, the letters of the alphabet had also been assigned flag values. *Any* word could be spelled out, although that was a laborious, time-consuming process.

The result was a vast increase in tactical flexibility . . . before battle was joined, at least. The amount of gunsmoke even old-style naval battles produced was quite sufficient to reduce the utility of any visual signaling system to virtually nothing once the actual shooting began. But any professional sea officer knew the ability to send quick, positive orders to the units of a squadron during the *approach* to battle was still a priceless advantage.

"Excuse me, My Lord."

Gray Harbor looked up, shaking himself out of his reverie, as a diffident young officer appeared beside him.

"Yes, Lieutenant?"

"Captain Stywyrt's respects, My Lord, but we're coming up on the target."

"Ah, of course! Thank you, Lieutenant. And please thank the Captain for me, as well."

"Of course, My Lord."

The lieutenant touched his left shoulder with his right fist in salute, then returned to his duties while Gray Harbor carefully inserted the cotton Seamount had provided into his ears.

"Beat to quarters, Master Ahlbair!" Stywyrt's voice sounded muffled through the cotton, but the order was clear enough, and the traditional deep-voiced drums began to boom.

Once again, bare feet pattered over wooden decks as the crew scurried to their stations. It wasn't necessary actually to clear for action—Stywyrt had seen to that long since—but the galleon's decks offered a seething flood of humanity in what seemed like utter chaos.

Gray Harbor's experienced eye saw through the apparent chaos to the intense, disciplined order underneath it. Where a landsman would have seen only confusion, he saw the precise choreography of a formal ball, and the fact that so much of what *Typhoon*'s crew was doing was completely new only made that precision even more impressive.

"Load starboard, Master Ahlbair," Stywyrt said.

"Starboard batteries, run in and load!" Lieutenant Ahlbair shouted, and

Gray Harbor stepped closer to the quarterdeck rail to gaze down and watch the gundeck gun crews casting off the breeching ropes which secured the newfangled gun carriages to the ship's side. Men tailed onto the side tackles, grunting with effort as they heaved, and their massive charges moved backward in a thunderous squeal of wooden gun trucks across deck planks which had been sanded to improve the gun crews' traction. The guns on *Typhoon's* main deck were krakens which had been rebored by Ehdwyrd Howsmyn. They weighed two and a half tons each, and they moved heavily, reluctantly, despite their carriages' wheels.

"Avast heaving!" gun captains shouted, announcing their satisfaction as their ponderous charges moved far enough inboard. The Number Three from each gun crew removed the wooden tampion which normally sealed the bore against spray, and the Number Two removed the sheet-lead "apron" which protected the secured gun's vent so Number One could attach the gunlock.

Powder monkeys—boys, some of them as young as seven or eight—dashed up to each gun with their wooden cartridge buckets. Each bucket contained a single flannel bag, filled with gunpowder and then stitched shut, and each monkey dumped his cartridge on deck at his assigned gun, then went racing back for another.

The gun's Number Five picked up the cartridge and passed it to Number Three, who slid it down the muzzle of the gun. Number Six had already selected a round shot from the garland along the bulwark. He passed it to Number Three while Number Four rammed the powder charge home. The gleaming round shot—just under six and a half inches in diameter and weighing over thirty-eight pounds—went down the bore next, followed by a fat, round wad of rope yarn to keep it from rolling around inside the gun as the ship moved, and Number Four tamped everything down with another stroke of his rammer.

Gun trucks squealed again as the cannon were run back into firing position. They snouted out of their gunports all down the galleon's starboard side as *Typhoon* bared her claws, and the Number Eight and Number Nine of each crew slid stout wooden handspikes under the gun tube. The gun carriage had been designed with "steps" cut out of the brackets—the heavy side timbers which supported the main weight of the gun—and the crewmen used those steps as purchase points, grunting with effort as they levered the breech of the gun upward.

The trunnions were placed so that the gun was slightly breech-heavy, and as the handspikes heaved the breech to the desired elevation, the gun captain inserted the elevation wedge—a simple wooden shim, designed to fit under the breech and hold it there. More work with handspikes levered the guns around, training them as far forward as possible, and then the gun captains drove priming irons—small iron skewers—down the guns' touchholes, piercing the cartridges, and reached for the primer boxes each wore at his belt.

That, too, was a new innovation. Before Merlin's intervention, each gun had been primed with loose powder from the gun captain's powderhorn and, when the moment came, it had been touched off with a red-hot iron rod or a length of slow match. But burning matches and glowing irons had never been the safest things to have around loose gunpowder, especially on a narrow, pitching deck filled with moving men, so still more changes had been made.

Now the gun captains took goose quills packed with fine-grained gunpowder from the cases at their waists, and inserted them into the vents. They stripped away the wax-covered paper seals to expose the powder filling, and metal clicked as their Number Twos cocked the gunlocks. The firing mechanism was an adaptation of Merlin's "flintlock," which was essentially identical to the lock used on the new muskets, but without a priming pan. Instead, when the striker came forward, the flint struck a milled steel surface and showered sparks over the powder-charged quill.

The entire evolution of running in, loading, and running back out took less than two minutes. Intellectually, Gray Harbor had already known it could be done that quickly with the new guns and carriages, but actually seeing it drove home the enormity of the changes about to transform naval warfare. Bringing a kraken into action on an old-style wheelless carriage, without cartridges, and with powderhorn priming, would have taken at least four times that long.

The earl stepped across to the bulwark, careful to keep well clear of the recoil paths of the lighter "carronades" which Seamount had cast specifically for the quarterdecks and fore decks of ships like *Typhoon*. They threw the same weight of shot as the rebored krakens, but they weighed less than half as much, they were less than half as long, and they required only half the crew. They also used a much lighter charge and were shorter ranged, although the care Seamount had taken in boring them out meant they—like the refurbished krakens—had substantially smaller windages than any previous artillery piece and were correspondingly more accurate across the range they did have.

Gray Harbor looked forward. The old galley *Prince Wyllym* and three equally old, worn out merchantmen had been anchored at two hundred-yard intervals in the relatively shallow water just off the Trhumahn Bank. The extensive sandbank lay far enough off the normal shipping routes to allow the Navy to train unobserved, and the water shoaled enough in its vicinity to make it practical to anchor the target vessels. Now Commodore Staynair's flagship led the other four ships of his squadron in line-ahead towards his targets under topsails, jibs, and spankers alone.

Compared to Gray Harbor's old galley command, *Typhoon* seemed to crawl under so little sail, and, in fact, despite the breeze, she was making good no more than two knots, at best, with barely a fifth of her total canvas set. But those sails were what Merlin and Seamount had designated "fighting sail"—yet *another* change from Gray Harbor's day, when galleys had struck their yards and canvas completely below before engaging.

Even at their slow, dragging pace, the ships of the meticulously dressed line were covering almost seventy yards every minute, and the waiting targets drew closer and closer. Gray Harbor was almost as impressed by the station-keeping displayed by Staynair's captains as he was by any of Merlin's innovations. In his experience, even galleys found it difficult to maintain precise formation, and sailing ships were still less prone to staying where they were supposed to be. On the other hand, by the time fleets of galleys smashed into each other for the hull-to-hull melee which resolved their battles, formation-keeping was seldom an issue any longer. That wasn't going to be the case for gun-armed galleons, and Seamount and Staynair had drilled their crews mercilessly with that in mind.

There!

Gale drew even with *Prince Wyllym* and the early afternoon was filled with a sudden bellow of smoky thunder. Even at this range—two hundred yards astern of the flagship—the abrupt, simultaneous detonation of eighteen heavy guns was like a hammer blow across the top of Gray Harbor's head. The flagship disappeared into a sudden, dense cloud of powder smoke, and Gray Harbor's eyes widened as a hurricane of shot slammed into the anchored galley.

Splinters and broken bits of timber flew. The galley shuddered visibly as the tempest of iron blasted into it, and something deep inside Gray Harbor cringed as he visualized—or tried to—what it would have been like for *Prince Wyllym*'s crew, had she had one aboard.

He knew he'd failed. He'd seen battles enough during his own Navy days, but even the heaviest galley carried no more than ten or twelve guns, of which no more than four or five could normally be brought to bear upon a single target. And broadside weapons were seldom much bigger than the three-inch piece called a "falcon," which threw only an eight-and-a-half-pound ball. He'd seen what *single* heavy cannon balls could do, as they demolished hulls and smashed through the fragile bodies of human beings in hideous sprays of blood, torn tissue, and flying limbs. But he'd never seen what the next best thing to *twenty* of them could do in a single one of Seamount's new "broadsides."

Gale was a hundred and fifty yards from her target. That was long range by most naval gunnery standards, although her krakens had a theoretical maximum range of three thousand yards. The chances of actually hitting something from a moving ship's deck at anything over a quarter-mile or so were remote, to say the least, however. Indeed, most captains reserved the single salvo they were likely to have time to fire before closing for the melee until the very last moment, when they could hardly have missed if they'd tried and might hope to sweep their opponents' decks with grapeshot and wreak carnage among the other ship's boarders. The number of guns *Typhoon* and her consorts carried, coupled with their rate of fire, changed that calculation, however.

Even at the squadron's slow rate of advance, and even given its rate of fire, there was just time at this range for each gun in *Gale*'s broadside to fire twice before her own movement carried her beyond the zone in which it could be trained far enough aft to bear on *Prince Wyllym*.

The second "broadside" was a much more ragged affair as the guns fired independently, each going off as quickly as its own crew could reload and run out again. The first broadside's billowing smoke, rolling downwind towards the anchored targets, more than half-obscured the crews' line of vision, as well, yet both of those broadsides smashed home with devastating effect. The actual holes the round shot punched in the galley's hull weren't all that large, but Gray Harbor knew exactly what was happening *inside* that hull. Splinters— some of them four and five feet in length, and as much as six inches across at the base—were being blasted loose. They were scything across the ship like screaming demons which would have clawed down any unfortunate seaman in their paths.

Other shots went home higher up the galley's side, smashing down entire sections of her stout bulwarks, sending yet more lethal clouds of splinters howling across her upper deck. Commodore Staynair had thoughtfully placed straw-stuffed mannequins here and there about the target ships' decks, and Gray Harbor saw huge clouds of straw flying in the sunlight, like a golden fog bank which would have been a ghastly red under other circumstances, as splinters and round shot tore them apart.

Then *Gale* was past *Prince Wyllym*, ready to fire upon the first of the anchored merchantships, while *Typhoon*, following in the flagship's wake, approached the battered galley.

"Stand ready, Master Ahlbair. We'll fire by sections, I believe," Captain Stywyrt said conversationally through the rumbling crash of *Gale*'s last few shots.

"Stand ready to fire by sections!" Ahlbair shouted through his speaking trumpet in turn, and *Typhoon*'s captain stepped up beside Gray Harbor at the bulwark as the gun captains took tension on the lanyards attached to the gunlocks. Stywyrt gazed thoughtfully at his approaching target, shoulders relaxed, eyes intent. This might be the first time *Gray Harbor* had actually seen the new weapons in action, but Stywyrt and the other members of the Experimental Squadron had been drilling with them for five-days now. The captain clearly knew what he was about, and his left hand rose slowly. He held it level with his left ear for several seconds, then brought it slashing down.

"*By sections, fire as you bear!*" Ahlbair bellowed, and the forward guns thundered almost as he spoke.

Gale had fired every gun which would bear in a single, massive broadside. *Typhoon*'s guns fired in pairs, gundeck and upper deck together, as soon as the gun captains could see their target in front of their muzzles, and she mounted nineteen broadside weapons to *Gale's* eighteen. It was a long, drawn out, rumbling roll of thunder, not a single brazen bellow, and the ship's fire was even more accurate than *Gale's* had been. So far as Gray Harbor could tell, not a single shot missed, despite the range, and *Prince Wyllym* shuddered in agony as round shot after round shot smashed into her splintering timbers.

The guns themselves lurched back, wooden trucks thundering across the planking, muzzles streaming smoke and embers. The stink of burning powder clawed at Gray Harbor's nose and lungs, and he coughed, more than half-deafened despite the cotton stuffed into his ears. The deck seemed to leap up underfoot, battering the soles of his feet, and *Typhoon* twitched as each pair of guns recoiled and the breeching tackle transmitted the force of three and a half tons of recoiling bronze directly to her timbers. The thick, choking clouds of smoke turned the deck into twilight before they went rolling slowly away from the ship on the breeze.

By allowing his gunners to fire independently, as soon as they bore upon the target, Captain Stywyrt had bought them a few precious moments of extra time to reload. As in *Gale's* case, each gun crew was responsible for reloading and firing as rapidly as it could, and Gray Harbor watched them as they launched into yet another choreographed burst of chaos.

The Number Four on each gun drove home the soaking wet sponge on one end of his rammer. It slid down the bore, hissing as it quenched any lingering embers from the previous charge. The gun captain stopped the vent, pressing his thumb—protected from the heat by a thick leather thumbstall—over the vent hole to prevent air from entering the bore and fanning any embers the sponge might have missed as a fresh cartridge was rammed home, followed by another round shot and wad. Gun trucks squealed as the gun was run back out. Handspikes clattered as it was trained farther aft, priming quills went down vent holes, gunlocks cocked, the gun captains drew the firing lanyards taut, looked to be certain every member of their crews were clear of the recoil, and yanked. The flint strikers snapped down, sparks showered over the priming quills, and the guns bellowed yet again.

It was ear-stunning, a bedlam which had to be experienced to be believed, and *Prince Wyllym's* battered side began to literally cave in.

Ahead of *Typhoon*, *Gale's* broadside thundered again as she took the first of the anchored merchantmen under fire. The merchant vessel was more lightly built than the galley, and the effect of the flagship's concentrated fire was even more horrific. Gray Harbor could make out few details, thanks to the obscuring gun smoke, but he saw the target's mainmast suddenly quiver, then topple slowly over the side. Even as it toppled, he heard a crashing rumble from HMS *Tempest*, *Typhoon's* next astern, as *her* forwardmost guns came to bear on *Prince Wyllym*, and he shook his head.

Thank God Merlin is on our *side*, he thought.

I'm impressed," Earl Gray Harbor said.

He, Cayleb, and Merlin stood atop the King's Harbor Citadel, looking down at the anchored ships of the Experimental Squadron in the basin below. Ahrnahld Falkhan and the rest of Cayleb's Marine bodyguards waited for them on the uppermost floor of the stone keep. It was much cooler there, for the summer sun was hot overhead, and it gave the crown prince and his companions privacy as they stood under a canvas awning that popped quietly in the breeze blowing over the fortress.

"Sir Ahlfryd told you you would be, Rayjhis," Cayleb replied now, and Gray Harbor chuckled.

"Baron Seamount told me I would, true," he acknowledged, and glanced at Merlin. "He also told me I shouldn't pay much attention to your efforts to give him the credit for it, Merlin."

"I suppose there's some truth to that," Merlin acknowledged, turning to face the earl fully. His relationship with Gray Harbor was very different from what it had been, and the first councillor raised a sardonic eyebrow.

"I did provide the original impetus," Merlin said in response. "And I suppose many of the underlying concepts came from me, too. But I would never have had the practical knowledge and experience to put those concepts into effect without Sir Ahlfryd and Sir Dustyn. And the work on tactical formations has been almost entirely Sir Domynyk's and Sir Ahlfryd."

Which, he reflected, was truly the case. The Royal Charisian Navy had developed a sophisticated tactical doctrine for its galleys, along with standard formations and an entire conceptual framework. As Baron Seamount had noted that very first day, however, none of those formations or tactics had been built around broadside armaments. But his navy was accustomed to thinking in terms of developed doctrine, not the sort of free-for-all brawl most other navies seemed prepared to settle for, and he and Staynair had sat down and essentially reinvented the line-of-battle tactics of the late eighteenth and early nineteenth centuries before the first conversion had been completed for the Experimental Squadron. They'd been practicing and refining them ever since, and Merlin was frankly awed by their accomplishments.

"As I say," he went on, "we really needed that experience. And Cayleb's had more than a little to do with making things work, for that matter."

"That much, I can believe," Gray Harbor said, and smiled approvingly at his crown prince. "Cayleb's always been mad about the Navy."

"Oh, no, he hasn't!" Cayleb said with a chuckle. "Not since you and Father sent me to sea, at any rate!" He looked at Merlin and shuddered dramatically. "There's this unfortunate tradition, here in Charis," he explained. "For some reason, people seem to feel the heir to the throne ought to know how the Navy works, so they send him off to sea as a midshipman. *And*," he added feelingly, "his superior officers are expressly forbidden to treat him differently from any other midshipman. I got to 'kiss the gunner's daughter' more than once."

" 'Kiss the gunner's daughter,' Your Highness?" Merlin repeated with raised eyebrows, and it was Gray Harbor's turn to chuckle.

"The bosun's responsible for disciplining the midshipmen," he explained. "That means miscreants find themselves bent over one of the guns while the bosun thrashes them firmly enough even a midshipman might think twice about repeating his offense."

"Oh, I always thought twice," Cayleb said cheerfully. "I just went ahead and did it anyway."

"Somehow, I find that depressingly easy to believe," Merlin said.

"So do I." Gray Harbor did his best to produce a properly disapproving glower. Unfortunately, it bounced off the crown prince's unrepentant grin without even a scuff mark.

"All the same," the earl continued more seriously, "that 'unfortunate tradition' exists for a reason, Your Highness, and the way you've taken hold out here shows why. I'll be honest, Cayleb. When your father first assigned this to you, a part of me thought it was solely a way to get *Merlin* out here without raising any questions. But I was wrong. He gave you this job because he knew how well you'd do it, too."

Cayleb waved one hand, still enough of a boy at heart to be embarrassed by anything which sounded like praise, but Merlin shook his head.

"The Earl is right, Your Highness," he said, rather more formally than he normally spoke to Cayleb these days. "In fact, I've been very impressed watching you and Baron Seamount in action. I think you have a natural feel for this sort of thing."

And, Merlin thought, *you're young enough not to have too many preconceptions to overcome in the process.*

"So do I," Gray Harbor agreed. "And I can understand why the two of you wanted me out here to see all this firsthand. I've read your reports to the King, and, of course, Cayleb's briefed the senior members of the Council several times, but until you've actually seen it, you can't really believe it or grasp all of the implications."

Merlin nodded. Cayleb had handled those briefings because even now Gray Harbor and Wave Thunder were the only councillors who knew the truth about Merlin's contributions. But even though Gray Harbor had been privy to the full details from the very beginning, this had still been his first chance to actually see the new hardware. The demonstration had been carefully planned to show the new artillery in action under near-perfect conditions, as the earl understood perfectly well, but his genuine enthusiasm pleased Merlin enormously. It wasn't really a surprise—the first councillor was a highly intelligent man who also happened to be an experienced naval commander—but that made it no less welcome.

"At the same time," the earl said, turning to look back out over the squadron's anchored ships, "I'm worried about how much time we have. Hektor's obviously getting more and more nervous about what we're up to, and I'm afraid our time may be running out more quickly than we'd hoped. Especially"—he turned his eyes back to Merlin's face—"in light of the reports we're getting out of the Temple and Bishop Zherald's offices right here in Tellesberg."

"I know," Merlin sighed. He leaned forward, bracing his folded arms on the battlements, and his sapphire eyes were distant, unfocused as he gazed across the harbor.

"I'm hoping," he continued, "that the Temple's . . . agitation will settle down a bit once Father Paityr's latest reports have a chance to circulate."

"In a reasonable world, that's probably what would happen," Gray Harbor told him. "In a world where Hektor and our *good* friend Nahrmahn are pouring their lies into the Church's ear, it probably won't."

The first councillor's expression was grim, and Cayleb nodded in bitter agreement.

"Do you think the Council of Vicars is likely to take an official position?" Merlin asked.

Even with his unwillingness to risk putting bugs inside the Temple proper, he had an excellent feel for what the Church's hierarchy was saying, thanks to his ability to eavesdrop on the Vicars' subordinates living in Zion. But he'd discovered that knowing what it was saying wasn't the same thing as knowing what it was *thinking*. Just as he'd come to realize that Gray Harbor and Haarahld had far more insight into the realities of Safehold's theocratic politics than he did.

"Probably not," Gray Harbor said after a moment. "Not openly, at least. Their own intendant is reporting that we've violated none of the Proscriptions, which is only true, after all. The Church can issue whatever decrees and commandments she chooses, and no one has the authority to gainsay her, but the Council's usually cautious about appearing capricious. That doesn't mean the Vicars—or, at least, the 'Group of Four'—won't do whatever they believe they have to, but, traditionally, they've preferred to act deliberately, after considering all of the evidence. Officially, at least."

It was Merlin's turn to quirk an eyebrow, and Gray Harbor chuckled. The sound was both cynical and rather sad.

"Mother Church is supposed to be above issues of political power and greed, Merlin. Some of her clergy truly are—like Father Paityr, for example, or Bishop Maikel. But others—like Chancellor Trynair and his allies in the Group of Four—aren't. I wouldn't say this before any other ears, but the truth is that the episcopate and even the Council of Vicars is more concerned with the wielding of power than with the salvation of men's souls these days." He shook his head slowly, brown eyes distant, and Merlin sensed how much it cost him to admit his own cynicism where the keepers of his religious beliefs were concerned. "Calculations are made in the Temple, and in the brothels and gaming houses of Zion, on the basis of political expediency and greed, as often as on the basis of doctrine or the *Writ*, I'm afraid."

"*More* often," Cayleb said harshly. Merlin looked at him, and the crown prince's eyes were deep and dark with bitter memory. "There was a time," the prince continued, "when Mother Church truly *was* a mother to all of her children. That day is gone."

Merlin managed to keep his expression tranquil, but this was the most frankly he'd ever heard Cayleb or Gray Harbor express themselves on the subject of the Church, even after the interview with Father Paityr, and Cayleb's bitter observation hit him like a splash of cold water. He hadn't truly realized until this moment just how fully justified the Council of Vicars' concerns over Charisian restiveness under the Church's oppressive control actually were.

"Cayleb's right, I'm afraid, Merlin," Gray Harbor said heavily. "On the other hand," he continued, "probably exactly because of the way those political factors have come to influence the Council's decisions, the Vicars are extraordinarily careful to avoid drawing attention to them. The Group of Four will be very certain that any decision—any *official* decision—the Council or the Grand Inquisitor may hand down is carefully written. It will make the Council's orthodoxy and devotion to truth crystal clear. And, so long as Father Paityr insists on reporting we haven't fallen into error, haven't violated the Proscriptions by thought or deed, the Council has no justification for moving openly against us.

"That, unfortunately, doesn't mean the Group of Four *won't* move against us. Never forget, Merlin, that the Temple Lands are one of Safehold's great kingdoms. The Vicars aren't simply the princes of the Church; they're secular princes, as well. As such, they're as subject to political pressures and calculations—and ambitions—as any other ruler. Whether or not Mother Church openly condemns Charis for doctrinal error, the Council may well choose to put forth its secular power against us. We have not, perhaps," he smiled faintly, "appeared sufficiently pliant for the Council's taste."

Merlin looked at the first councilor, and Gray Harbor shrugged.

"Don't misunderstand me, Merlin. The King—and Cayleb and I—doubt neither the power nor the love of God. Nor do we doubt the Church was created and ordained to safeguard the salvation of men. But the Vicars are also men, and if those responsible for the salvation of others fall into error, into the snares of ambition, greed, and corruption, who will redeem *them?*"

"I don't know, My Lord," Merlin said after a moment, his voice soft. If Cayleb's bitterness had been eye-opening, the implications of the earl's analysis were breathtaking.

"Neither do I," Gray Harbor said sadly. "But, whether or not any of us dare to admit it openly, much of the Kingdom's current danger is the direct result of the Church's encouragement of Hektor and Nahrmahn. Charis has grown too wealthy, too powerful, for the Council's taste. There are many reasons for that, but the consequence is that the Group of Four has quietly and quite unofficially supported Hektor's ambition to . . . reduce our power. I suspect Hektor, for all his cunning, fails to grasp that having used him to humble us, the Council is scarcely likely to allow *him* to assume our present position. Nor does that matter at the moment.

"What matters is that, to date, the Group of Four has had only to support our enemies' natural ambitions. That, without your arrival, would have been quite sufficient for the Vicars' purposes, in the fullness of time. But you *have* arrived, and I very much doubt that the Council has any concept of how radically the conflict between us and Hektor and his allies is about to change as a consequence. When the Group of Four does realize the truth, it *will* act. Not officially, perhaps—or not as Mother Church, at least. But there are many avenues open to it, and I feel quite confident it will find one of them."

The earl's voice was even grimmer than his expression, and Merlin turned to face him fully.

"My Lord," Merlin said quietly, "if this 'Group of Four' chooses to act against Charis with all of the Church's resources, can Charis survive?"

"I don't know," Gray Harbor said softly. "I truly don't know. Before your arrival, I would have said we couldn't—that no single kingdom could possibly hope to. Now, I see some possibility we might, but only a possibility."

"It wasn't my intention to bring Charis into direct conflict with the Church," Merlin said. *Not yet, at least,* he added to himself with painful honesty. *Not until we'd built the kingdom up into something which might survive the confrontation.*

"I never said—or thought—it was," Gray Harbor replied. "But the truth is, Merlin, that I'd long ago accepted that the best we could hope for was to stave off disaster for a time. For my lifetime, probably. Possibly for Cayleb's. But not any longer than that."

Merlin glanced at the bitter-faced crown prince, and Cayleb nodded. For just a moment, the crown prince's mask slipped, and Merlin saw through the young man's habitual cheerful humor to the ultimate despair which had hidden behind it.

It seemed to be a day for revelations, he reflected, as Gray Harbor continued.

"It's certainly possible the things you've done will bring the Council's suspicion and distrust of the Kingdom to a head sooner, but that day would have come eventually, with or without you. The King's decision to insist upon a Charis-born priest as Bishop of Tellesberg wasn't made lightly, and Bishop Maikel's seen the coming storm as clearly as any of us. The only thing which has changed is that you may have made it possible for us to survive that storm. And, if you haven't—if my Kingdom and my King and Prince and what we believe God requires of us all go down into ruin anyway—that will still be a better fate than to live as the gelded slaves of someone like Hektor. Or"—the earl looked directly into Merlin's eyes—"of a Council of Vicars so corrupted by its own secular power that it uses the authority of God Himself for its own gain in this world."

"Father agrees," Cayleb said softly. "And so do I, Merlin." The crown prince looked straight into Merlin's sapphire eyes. "Perhaps you're beginning to understand why Father was so ready to listen when you appeared. Don't think either of us—or Bishop Maikel—have failed to notice how careful you've been never to openly criticize the Church. And don't think we haven't recognized that *you* recognize that, ultimately, what we believe, what we see as our responsibility to our subjects, is a threat to the Council."

There were shadows in the prince's own eyes, and in those shadows Merlin saw Cayleb's memory of their conversation following the kraken attack, as well.

"I won't," he said after a moment.

"Good," Gray Harbor said, his voice as soft as Cayleb's had been. But then he drew a deep breath and spoke much more briskly.

"That, however, brings us back to this Experimental Squadron of yours. While I would never wish misfortune upon a prince of the Church," his smile, Merlin noted, was downright nasty, "I must admit that the way Archbishop Erayk's accident's prevented him from visiting us as scheduled has provided a useful cushion. By the time he actually gets here, Father Paityr's reports probably will have made it even more difficult for the Council to contemplate any official action against us. And," he gave Merlin a piercing glance, "we'll have had time to further obscure the fact that so many of 'our' recent innovations have come from a single man. Trust me, Merlin—*seijin* or no, the Inquisition would look very closely at you if the Temple realized everything you've shown us over the past few months."

"That it would," Cayleb agreed.

"But whatever the Council's position," Gray Harbor continued, "Hektor, and Nahrmahn aren't going to react well if—when—they realize just how you, Cayleb, and Sir Ahlfryd are in the process of increasing the fleet's fighting power. At the moment, Bynzhamyn shares your confidence that they haven't tumbled to what's going on out here at King's Harbor, but they have to be aware of the other changes you and the College have been introducing."

"I know," Merlin agreed. *And,* he thought, *Wave Thunder's right about what Hektor and his buddies know . . . so far. The SNARCs' bugs make that clear enough. How long we can keep it that way, though, is another question, isn't it?*

"They've been careful to avoid open warfare with us this long, Rayjhis," Cayleb pointed out, and Gray Harbor nodded.

"That's true. But that's been because our fleet is almost equal in numbers to Hektor's and Nahrmahn's, combined, and they know our captains and crews are better than theirs. As Merlin's visions have shown, however, they're working hard to acquire new allies to increase their own naval strength. If they succeed in doing so, and especially if they should realize how things like the new cannon are going to increase our existing strength, they may well choose to strike quickly, in an effort to destroy us before we can complete our plans and preparations."

"The Earl's right, Cayleb," Merlin said soberly. "At the moment, they believe they've got time—that our present strength is effectively the greatest we can sustain. That means time favors them, if they can acquire those allies Rayjhis is talking about. If they decide time's no longer on their side, though, their plans are likely to change."

"Precisely." Gray Harbor nodded energetically. "Which brings me back to the point I wanted to raise originally. How quickly *can* we complete our planned expansion?"

"In a lot of ways, that's really a question Sir Ahlfryd and Master Howsmyn could answer better than we can," Cayleb replied after glancing at Merlin.

"That's true," Merlin agreed. "I think we could probably make a fairly accurate guess, though."

"Please do, then," Gray Harbor invited, and Merlin shrugged.

"The problem is how few galleons the Navy had in commission when we began," he said. "That, and the fact that your galleys carried so few heavy guns, which means we don't have that many existing weapons to work with."

Gray Harbor nodded patiently, and Merlin grimaced internally. As he'd told the earl earlier, the combined experience and knowledge of Ehdwyrd Howsmyn, Sir Ahlfryd Hyndryk, and Sir Dynnys Olyvyr had been priceless. There'd been countless difficulties inherent in taking the conceptual knowledge Merlin had been able to provide through to a practical hardware stage which would never even have occurred to him. And because of that, unfortunately, he'd underestimated how long it was going to take to put that hardware into production in adequate numbers.

Except, he reflected wryly, *for the coppering technique. The one thing that's gone perfectly is also the one that's the hardest to conceal when we put it on, and the one that has the least immediate effect on our ships' firepower. Of course,* his amusement faded, *there's more to combat effectiveness than gunpower alone.*

Still, even—or, perhaps, especially—coppering the hulls in adequate numbers was taking longer than he'd originally let himself allow for. Especially in light of the numbers of ships Charis' enemies could muster between them.

Traditional Safeholdian navies counted their strength in galleys. Those galleys—or most of them, at any rate—might no longer mount old-fashioned beaked rams, but aside from that, they would have been right at home when the Athenian navy went up against Xenophon at Salamis. Well, that was probably unfair, but they would certainly have been familiar to Don Juan of Austria at the Battle of Lepanto. They had evolved from purely coastal craft into something which at least had aspirations to a true seagoing warship, especially in the case of Charis, but they would never have survived typical Atlantic weather conditions on Old Earth.

Fortunately, Safehold's seas tended to be smaller than those of Old Earth, and the crude state of Safeholdian navigation meant that until relatively recently, even the most daring mariners had tended not to stray far from sight of the coast. One of the things which had fueled Charis' rise to maritime supremacy had been her captains' iron-nerved willingness to undertake longer voyages, like the two-thousand-mile voyage across the heart of the sea known as the Anvil, steering by the stars and pure dead-reckoning.

Surviving such journeys had been more than the traditional coastal ship types could manage, and the galleon—like the ships of Commodore Staynair's squadron—represented a relatively new type which had evolved in response to the new challenges. Merlin found himself thinking of the galleys as "Mediterranean types," and the galleons as the prototypes—crude, and far from fully developed so far—of the "Atlantic type." They were less maneuverable than galleys, slower in light airs, and immobile in calms, but far more survivable than any galley in heavy weather.

Most of Safehold's navies felt no great pressure to adopt the galleon as a warship, however. Partly out of ingrained conservatism, but also for some very practical reasons. Every major naval battle in Safehold's history had been fought in coastal waters, and naval strategy focused on control of strategic straits, passages, and seaports. Deep-water survivability was scarcely a major factor for that sort of warfare, and the galley's maneuverability, ability to move even in a dead calm, and large crew made it a far more suitable platform for the boarding actions which climaxed virtually all naval engagements in the absence of truly effective artillery.

But as Baron Seamount had recognized that very first day, the galley was about to become hopelessly obsolete, regardless of where battles were fought. The unavoidable fact that a ship which depended upon long banks of oars as its primary means of movement simply could not mount the sort of broadside which could be mounted by a sail-powered ship doomed it as a type.

Unfortunately, the Royal Charisian Navy had possessed only a few more galleons than anyone else . . . and every one of them was anchored in King's Harbor as part of Commodore Staynair's squadron.

That was bad enough, but the fact that the Navy's galleys had mounted so few cannon was almost equally bad. Staynair's ships each carried between thirty-six and forty guns. The five of them mounted a total of a hundred and eighty-four . . . which represented the kraken armament of almost fifty galleys.

Matters weren't quite as bad as that might have seemed to suggest, given that over a third of the squadron's total artillery consisted of the newly designed and cast carronades, but he, Cayleb, and Seamount had still exhausted the Navy's entire reserve stockpile of krakens.

The eighty galleys the Royal Navy kept in permanent commission could have provided the krakens for another seven or eight galleons, and there were also the fifty galleys of the reserve fleet, which he and Cayleb were already planning on stripping of guns. But fifteen or sixteen gun-armed galleons weren't going to be sufficient to take on the combined fleets of Charis' enemies.

It was fortunate Charis had both copper and substantial deposits of tin. Merlin was aware that sooner or later—and probably sooner—they would have no choice but to begin using iron (especially given the voracious appetite for copper of the new anti-borer and anti-fouling sheathing), but bronze was actually a better alloy for smoothbore artillery. It was too soft to stand up to the wear of rifled shells, but it was more elastic and much less brittle than iron, which made bronze pieces less likely to burst, with catastrophic results for everyone in the vicinity.

Unfortunately, even bronze guns still had to be manufactured, and that took time. Howsmyn's welded trunnions had helped enormously as far as the existing guns were concerned, and he'd used some of the saved time for his reboring project, as well. That had finally produced a genuinely standardized gun caliber, and by reaming out the krakens' often irregular bores, he'd been able to reduce windage, which had simultaneously improved accuracy and increased both muzzle velocity and shot weight. It had also allowed him to use the same shot for the long guns and the new carronades, which greatly simplified ammunition requirements.

"We have to make some decisions," Merlin told Gray Harbor now. "We've pretty much exhausted the existing supply of krakens, and we can't afford to call in the existing fleet and strip it of artillery to get more of them. Even if that wouldn't make Hektor and Nahrmahn suspicious, we're going to need the existing ships to back up the new types whatever happens.

"We can produce almost three carronades for the same amount of metal that goes into a single kraken, and we've got large numbers of lighter artillery pieces—and quite a few heavier ones—we can melt down and recast. In fact, we're already doing that, partly because reclaiming the existing bronze lets us reserve more of the available copper for hull sheathing. But even if carronades can be cast and bored faster than long guns, it still takes at least half or two-thirds as long to produce one. And they're shorter ranged."

"Range would concern me less than many other factors, for now, at least," Gray Harbor said thoughtfully. "As I understand it, these 'carronades' are accurate out to at least two or three hundred yards, true?"

"Close to twice that, actually," Cayleb agreed.

"Well, most naval battles—most *old-fashioned* naval battles—are resolved at somewhat shorter ranges than that." Gray Harbor's tone was desert-dry. "Actually, they're usually resolved at sword's length. If you can stand off to a range of fifty or a hundred yards and pound them the way Staynair's squadron pounded its targets today, that should be more than sufficient."

"I tend to agree, My Lord." Merlin nodded. "And there's another advantage to the carronade: the weight of the individual pieces. No one's ever designed ships to carry this weight of artillery. Despite everything Sir Dustyn and I have have been able to do to reduce topweight, Staynair's galleons are still overloaded by the weight of their own guns."

It was Gray Harbor's turn to nod soberly.

"If we use carronades instead of krakens, we'll cut the weight of the guns by almost two-thirds for the same broadside," Merlin continued. "That, in turn, would mean not only that the new ships we're building could carry a more powerful armament, but also that we could convert more existing merchant ships. In some ways, I don't really like the thought of conversions. Merchant ships aren't built as heavily as warships; they can't take as much pounding or carry the same weight of artillery. On the other hand, if any battles we fight work out the way we hope they will, that shouldn't be a decisive factor."

"And the carronades weigh almost exactly the same as falcons," Cayleb pointed out. "If we've got time to cast enough of them, we can replace our galleys' broadside weapons, as well."

"Good points, all of them," Gray Harbor said. "Still, I think the range problem is one we're going to have to address in the long term. Eventually, our enemies are going to discover most of what we're up to, even if we manage to keep the surprise concealed until the first time they face the new ships in combat. When they do discover it, anyone but an utter idiot—which, unfortunately, neither Hektor nor Nahrmahn is—is going to realize they need the same sorts of ships. And when they have them, we won't be able to choose our own ranges. That means longer guns, eventually, so we'll have to find a way to solve the topweight problem."

"That's certainly true, Rayjhis," Cayleb said. "Most of the squadron's ships are already beginning to hog at least a little."

"I'm not surprised." Gray Harbor grimaced. The phenomenon known as "hogging" was scarcely unknown among galleys, after all. When you put heavy weights at the ends of a wooden hull (which was where most of a galley's guns happened to be mounted), it inevitably put a severe strain on a ship's keel. The usual result was that the ship's ends drooped downward and its keel "hogged"—literally warped and bent upward in the middle, sometimes severely enough to threaten the ship's safety.

"Sir Dustyn and I have been discussing that very problem with Baron Seamount . . . in our copious free time, of course," Merlin said dryly. "I believe Sir Dustyn may be on the track of a solution, but for right now, none of us want to make any changes in existing building practices unless we absolutely have to. It's more important to get the ships built than that we build the very best ships we possibly could."

"I agree," Gray Harbor said again, firmly. "Even if it does offend my sensibilities to build so many ships out of green timber."

Cayleb made a face which mirrored the earl's unhappiness. Ships made out of unseasoned timber rotted quickly. The Safeholdian teak tree, which really did resemble the terrestrial tree of the same name, was the most favored shipbuilding timber on the planet. It was very strong, very hard, and remarkably resistant—when properly seasoned—to rot. But they weren't using teak for most of the new ships. Charis had large stands of teak, at least half of which were owned outright by the Crown and the Royal Navy. But not even teak could resist rot effectively without time to season properly, and Haarahld and Cayleb had flatly refused to use up their precious reserves of teak on ships whose life spans were inevitably going to be short, to say the very least.

They'd be lucky if they got more than five years of service out of any of the vessels whose construction Olyvyr was currently overseeing here at King's Harbor, Merlin knew. Unfortunately, the available supply of seasoned ship timber was limited, and a ship which rotted into uselessness five years down the road but could be available this year was far preferable to one which wouldn't rot but couldn't be built in time. Which meant they didn't have a lot of choice.

"Sir Dustyn believes we should be able to find most of the timber we'll need for several dozen ships by breaking up the reserve galleys," Merlin offered. "We can't do that until we have enough newly built galleons, of course, but we'll begin as soon as we safely can, with your and the King's permission, My Lord."

"My permission you already have," Gray Harbor told him. "I feel confident the king will also agree."

"We're still going to be hard-pressed to build the new ships," Cayleb warned the first councillor. "I'm delighted by Master Howsmyn's success in providing the sheet copper for the hulls, but just finding the spars to mast them is going to be a genuine problem. And you can't roll spars out in a private foundry the way you can sheet copper. When the Navy starts buying up all of the suitable timber for that, it's going to make someone like Hektor start asking questions, anyway."

"And spars and copper are only part of it," Merlin agreed. "We need canvas, cordage, pitch—everything you can think of."

He shook his head ruefully. On the one hand, he'd been astounded by how quickly Sir Dustyn Olyvyr could get new ships laid down and built. The naval constructor's estimate—and it looked accurate—was that he could complete a new galleon's hull in no more than ninety days from the moment the green timbers arrived at the King's Harbor shipyard. From Merlin's research, that compared favorably with the construction times for eighteenth-century shipbuilders on Old Earth under emergency pressure. Unfortunately, Olyvyr could build only about half a dozen of them at a time, and however quickly he could build the *hulls*, the ships, as Cayleb had just pointed out, still needed to be masted and rigged. Not to mention finding the guns to put aboard them and the men to crew them.

"That's another place where converting merchant ships will help," Gray Harbor pointed out. "Surely we can cut gunports and modify existing sail plans more quickly than we can build from scratch."

"I'm sure you're right, My Lord," Merlin said, "although we have to think about strengthening their hulls against the recoil forces, as well. Still, I'm afraid our most optimistic estimates suggest that it's going to take us at least another full year to reach our original target numbers."

Gray Harbor looked grim.

"I don't think we're going to be able to keep all of this secret that long," he said.

"I agree," Cayleb said. "In fact, I think we need to reconsider laying down additional ships at Hairatha."

Gray Harbor's eyes narrowed unhappily at the suggestion, and the crown prince shrugged.

"I'm not blind to what Merlin calls the 'security aspects' of the idea, Rayjhis. As soon as the Navy starts building large numbers of galleons someplace people know we're doing it, someone's going to start wondering why. I know that. But after Tellesberg itself, Hairatha has our biggest shipyards. We could build a dozen in the royal dockyard at Hairatha alone."

"That's true, I realize, Cayleb," the first councillor said. "And once we're within striking range of our final projected numbers, finishing up the final ships 'in public,' as it were, won't be a problem, I suppose. But still . . ."

He let his voice trail off, and Cayleb nodded in glum agreement. But then the crown prince's eyes narrowed as Merlin stroked one of his waxed mustachios thoughtfully.

"What?" the prince asked. Merlin looked at him, and Cayleb snorted. "You're pulling on your mustache again. Are you going to tell us what new deviousness you've thought of this time, or not?"

"I don't know that I'd call it 'devious,'" Merlin said mildly, "but I *have* just had a thought."

"Well," Gray Harbor said with a grin, "in that case, while Cayleb may have spoken with the impetuosity of youth, he does have a point. Spit it out, man!"

"It's just occurred to me," Merlin said, "that there's no reason we can't build additional ships right out in the open, if we really want to. I think we've all been forgetting that Sir Dustyn is one of the Kingdom's best known *private* ship designers. He's already taken orders to build at least a dozen schooners I know of in Tellesberg, all for different owners. There's no reason we couldn't have him lay down another dozen or so galleons for the Navy in privately owned yards without telling anyone who he's actually building them for."

"But—" Cayleb began, only to stop as Gray Harbor held up one hand.

"You're suggesting we announce—or, rather, that he and the shipyard owners announce—to everyone that he's building them as merchant vessels for private owners?"

"Exactly." Merlin shrugged. "They won't look exactly like existing galleons, even on the building ways, but they won't look all *that* different, either. We couldn't copper them as they were built without giving away the game, but once they were launched and rigged, we could sail them to King's Harbor or Hairatha, drydock them, and copper them there. That would probably actually save time. And if the hulls look a little odd compared to standard merchantmen, everybody knows Sir Dustyn's just introduced a brand-new type with the schooner, and he's rigging two galleons he already had under construction with the new square-rigger sail plan, as well. Given that everyone knows he's experimenting, why shouldn't he be building galleons with hulls that don't look quite like those of existing ships?"

"And," Cayleb said, any initial temptation to object vanishing into sudden enthusiasm, "the very fact that we were building them openly would actually help keep anyone from suspecting what we were up to! How likely is Hektor or Nahrmahn to expect us to be building 'secret weapons' right out in front of everyone?"

"Hmmm." Gray Harbor tapped his chin for a moment, then nodded. "I think you have a point, Merlin. Both of you have points, in fact. I'll recommend to the King that he seriously consider authorizing the suggestion. But I think I'll also suggest that we don't bring the shipyard owners into the secret unless we absolutely have to. Better, I think, to pick a handful of shipowners we know we can trust and act through them. They can place the orders for us, with the Treasury to actually pay for the ships when they're completed."

"If that's practical, I think it would be a very good idea, My Lord," Merlin agreed.

"Very well, then." Gray Harbor looked back out across the anchored squadron once more, then drew a deep breath.

"I think it's time I was returning to Tellesberg," he said. "The King and I will have quite a lot to discuss, but at least I can tell him"—he looked back at Merlin and Cayleb and smiled broadly—"that our efforts out here are in excellent hands."

.III.
Royal Palace,
Eraystor

I don't much care for Hektor's tone lately," Trahvys Ohlsyn said.

The Earl of Pine Hollow sat across the dining table on the covered terrace from Prince Nahrmahn, watching his cousin pry shellfish out of their shells with gusto. Hahl Shandyr had joined them, but the spymaster's appetite obviously hadn't accompanied him. He'd done little more than nibble at the salad on his plate.

"I don't care for it, either," Nahrmahn grunted around a mouthful. He swallowed, then sipped fastidiously at a glass of fruit-juice-laced water.

"I don't care for his tone," the prince continued, setting the glass down, "and I'm rapidly coming to the conclusion that I don't much care for *him*, either."

"Unfortunately, My Prince," Shandyr said, "the feeling appears to be mutual."

Nahrmahn glowered at the baron. Shandyr wasn't exactly basking in his prince's admiration at the moment. The fact that Nahrmahn knew as well as Shandyr did that his current problems weren't entirely his fault didn't make the prince any happier. Unfortunately, he couldn't disagree with what Shandyr had just said.

"It's never been more than an alliance of convenience," he said, after a moment, reaching for another shellfish and the silver tongs. "It's not exactly as if we have to love one another."

"No," Pine Hollow agreed. "But what bothers me is this attitude of his. Look at this, for example." He tapped one of the letters he'd brought to the working lunch. "He's not *discussing* things with us; he's telling us what he's already *decided*. It's the kind of letter I might have sent the bailiff on one of my secondary estates!"

"It's not quite that bad," Nahrmahn disagreed. His cousin snorted, and the prince shrugged. "I'm not saying you're wrong, Trahvys. I'm just saying Hektor's always seen himself as the senior member of our little partnership. As nearly as we can tell, things aren't going a lot better for him in Tellesberg than they are for us right now, so he may be getting just a little testier as a result."

"It's not the *insult* that bothers me, Nahrmahn. Or, not much, at least. It's the mind-set behind it. If he's talking to us this way while the two of us are still allied against Charis, what's his attitude going to be after Charis goes down? And just who do you think he envisions getting the lion's share of the spoils?"

"I'm sure he plans on it being him," Nahrmahn said comfortably. "Of course, his calculations may just prove to be slightly in error."

Pine Hollow's eyes narrowed. He sat back for a moment, gazing at his cousin in intense speculation. Then he cocked his head to one side.

"Is there something going on here that I ought to know about?" he asked.

"Well," Nahrmahn said, opening up another shell and inspecting its contents thoughtfully, "actually, there are two things going on. First, there's a little side conversation I've been having with Bishop Executor Wyllys. It seems Archbishop Lyam is already sounding out support in the Temple for granting us a Church mandate over Margaret's Land on the basis of our historic association with its people. From what the Bishop Executor says, the Archbishop's meeting with a fairly favorable reception on that point. After all we're already on excellent terms with the new Earl of Hanth. And our orthodoxy is much firmer than Haarahld's. Or, for that matter, Hektor's."

He scooped out the shellfish and popped it into his mouth, managing to chew and smile sardonically at the same time.

Pine Hollow frowned thoughtfully. Lyam Tyrn, the Archbishop of Emerald, was greedier than most archbishops. Which was saying quite a lot, actually. Of course, Tyrn hadn't drawn the most lucrative of archbishoprics, either. Emerald wasn't exactly poverty-stricken, but compared to someplace like Charis—or Corisande, for that matter—its tithes were decidedly on the penurious side. And

Tyrn's holdings outside Emerald weren't precisely the most prosperous imaginable. Still, the man came from one of the more powerful of the Church dynasties, and his name and family connections gave him considerably more influence than his lack of wealth might indicate. And that lack of wealth made him much more willing to use that influence in return for suitable consideration.

"All right," the earl said after a moment. "I can see that. After all, presumably the Church will incorporate any new territory into his archbishopric. But that still leaves Silver and Charis Island itself."

"The Church isn't going to let anyone snap up all of Charis, Trahvys," Nahrmahn replied. "The Council of Vicars is perfectly willing to let Hektor and me *break* Charis, but the vicars aren't about to let either of us gobble up everything that's made Haarahld so . . . irritating to them. Hektor has visions of sneaking around them somehow, and I suppose it's possible he may get them to sign off on a mandate over Silver. For that matter, he may even manage to acquire outright title to it. But Silver's worth a lot less than Margaret's Land, and the people living there are even more firmly attached to the Ahrmahks. Controlling them's going to be a fairly strenuous pastime—one I'd just as soon avoid.

"As for Charis proper, I'll be very surprised if the Church doesn't step in and establish either direct rule—possibly in the name of Haarahld's minor children, assuming either of them survive—or else install a suitable puppet of its own. Possibly both. A regency for Haarahld's younger son might give them enough transition time to accustom Charis to direct Church rule, and there'd always be plenty of opportunities for him to suffer one of those tragic childhood accidents when he was no longer necessary. Either way, neither Hector nor I is going to get possession of Tellesberg. The difference between us is that I *know* I'm not, and I'm already making arrangements to be sure I do get the *second* most desirable slice of the pie."

"Fair enough." Pine Hollow nodded. "On the other hand, I *am* your First Councillor, Nahrmahn. I think it might be a good idea to keep me informed on these little side negotiations of yours. Just to keep me from stepping on any toes because I didn't know they were there."

"A valid point," Nahrmahn agreed. He sipped wine and squinted out across the sunlit gardens from the terrace's shade. "I'll try to bear it in mind," he promised, although Pine Hollow had no great expectation that he'd succeed. Nahrmahn probably didn't even tell *himself* about all of his various plots.

"But you said there were two points Hektor wasn't aware of," the earl prompted after a moment, and Nahrmahn chuckled nastily.

"I know Hahl hasn't had very much luck rebuilding his agents in Tellesberg," he said. "But whatever may be happening to him there, he's doing quite well other places. Which is one reason," the prince's voice turned somehow subtly darker, "I'm being patient with him about Charis."

Pine Hollow nodded. Baron Shandyr's every effort to replace the departed Braidee Lahang's operation in Charis had failed. Every attempt seemed to be detected almost instantly, and Shandyr had lost at least a half-dozen of his better people trying to figure out what was going wrong.

"Among the things he's done right," Nahrmahn continued more lightly, "is to establish contact with Baron Stonekeep."

Pine Hollow's eyes narrowed once more; Edymynd Rustmyn, Baron Stonekeep, was not only King Gorjah of Tarot's first councillor, but also his equivalent of Hahl Shandyr.

"Stonekeep is keeping us informed about Gorjah's negotiations with Hektor. His services aren't coming cheaply, but when the time's ripe, we'll use him to tell Gorjah what Hektor really has in mind for Tarot. Which is for it to get exactly nothing out of the deal, except relief from its treaties with Charis. I'm sure Gorjah won't care for that, at all. Especially if we offer to support his claim to at least a chunk of Charisian territory of his own. We're providing Stonekeep with some of our homing wyverns, as well, which may come in handy if quick political decisions have to be made."

Pine Hollow nodded again, this time in unalloyed approval, although he was tempted to point out that this was another of those little stratagems which Nahrmahn might have wanted to bring to his first councillor's attention.

"And, as a measure of last resort, as it were," Nahrmahn continued, "Hahl has a man in place in Manchyr. In fact, he has two of them. In a worst-case situation, Hektor's health may turn out to be much more fragile than he assumes it is."

The prince smiled again, then nodded at one of the serving platters.

"Pass the rolls, please?" he requested pleasantly.

JUNE, YEAR OF GOD 891

✦

.I.
Tellesberg

S o what's this all about?"
Zhaspahr Maysahn knew he sounded just a bit testy as he sat across the table from Zhames Makferzahn, but that was perfectly all right with him. Makferzahn hadn't been due to make contact with him for another two days under their agreed-upon schedule. Given Oskahr Mhulvayn's hasty departure and the fact that he and Maysahn had met fairly regularly—and publicly—Maysahn had ample reason to feel decidedly unhappy at the prospect of frequent meetings with Makferzahn.

"I know we're off schedule," Makferzahn said now, "but this is important, I think."

"I hope so, anyway," Maysahn grumped, then shrugged.

Part of it, he knew, was that he and Makferzahn sat in the same sidewalk café—at the exact same table, in fact—as they had on the day of Cayleb's attempted assassination. That struck him as a potentially bad omen, but he told himself he was being silly. In fact, he'd picked the site and the table deliberately. It was one of the places he used regularly for business meetings in his shipping house owner's persona, after all, and Makferzahn—whose cover was that of a purchasing agent for a Desnairian merchant house which was constantly hiring cargo vessels—had a perfectly logical ostensible reason for meeting with him.

"All right," he said after moment. "What's so important it couldn't wait two more days?"

"I finally got one of my people into the King's Harbor dockyard," Makferzahn said, and despite himself, Maysahn sat a bit straighter, eyes narrowing. "I know it's taken longer than either of us hoped it would," Makferzahn continued, "and he was only there for a few hours, but he managed to pick up at least a little information."

"And?"

"And I'm not sure what to make of it," Makferzahn admitted.

"Well don't just sit there," Maysahn commanded.

"Sorry." Makferzahn gave himself a little shake and sipped from his chocolate cup. Then he set the cup back down and leaned a bit closer to his superior.

"They've got half a dozen new ships under construction in the yard," he said. "Not galleys—galleons."

"Galleons?" Maysahn frowned in perplexity. What in Langhorne's name could the Royal Charisian Navy want with *galleons?*"

"I know." Makferzahn's small shrug was eloquent with frustration. "It doesn't make a lot of sense, but that's what they're doing."

"Did your man manage to pick up any indication of why?"

"No one's talking about it very much, even in the taverns and bars," Makferzahn said. "But according to the gossip he did overhear, they're arming them with cannon. *Lots* of cannon. According to one fellow he got drunk enough to risk pumping a bit, they're putting as many as thirty or even forty guns aboard some of them."

Maysahn's frown deepened. That was as silly as anything he'd heard lately. Oh, it might explain why they were building *galleons*, since he couldn't think of any practical way to put that many guns aboard a galley. But it didn't explain why they wanted to mount that many guns in the first place. No doubt they'd be able to fire a devastating broadside before boarding, which would certainly be worthwhile. But they wouldn't have time for more than a single broadside each, and given how clumsy and unmaneuverable galleons were, closing with a galley in the first place would be all but impossible.

"Whatever they're up to," Makferzahn continued, "they seem to think it's pretty important. My man managed to confirm the rumors about Cayleb. He's taken personal charge of their efforts out there, and he's pushing hard. Seems to be doing a damned good job of it, too, I'm afraid."

"I wish I could say I was surprised by that," Maysahn said sourly. "Unfortunately, he's a lot like his father in that regard. Life would be so much simpler if they were both just idiots. But then the Prince probably wouldn't need us here, would he?"

"Probably not," Makferzahn agreed. "But what do you make of it?"

"I'm not at all sure, either," Maysahn admitted.

He leaned back in his chair, drumming lightly on the tabletop while he watched the hucksters in the square across the street hawking their wares. A huge, articulated eight-wheeled freight wagon rumbled past, big enough to require two draft dragons, and one of the big six-limbed lizards snuffled wistfully as it smelled the fresh vegetables on display.

"You're right about the importance they must attach to whatever it is they're doing, especially if that's where Cayleb's disappeared to," he said finally. "And I suppose those new rigging plans Olyvyr has introduced could have something to do with it, too. Every report about them indicates that even the square-riggers he's been experimenting with are lots more maneuverable. Maybe they actually think they can get a galleon into effective artillery range of a galley."

"I just don't see them doing it without getting swarmed," Makferzahn objected. He wasn't rejecting Maysahn's theory out of hand, but clearly he wasn't convinced, either. "I could believe they thought they could get into range to smash *one* galley, but an entire fleet? What do they think all the *other* galleys are going to be doing in the meantime? And how do they expect to coordinate their own galleys with galleons?"

"I didn't say *I* thought they could do it." Maysahn shrugged. "I'm just trying to figure out what they could possibly be thinking. And," he continued a bit reluctantly, "the fact that I can't makes me very nervous. Whatever else the Charisian Navy may be, it's not exactly run by fools."

Makferzahn nodded in emphatic agreement. Like Maysahn, the more Makferzahn saw of the Royal Charisian Navy, the more he came to appreciate its quality. The Corisandian navy was one of the best in the world, but it wasn't in the Charisian Navy's league. No one else's Navy was, and Makferzahn had found himself sharing Maysahn's concern over the fact that not even Prince Hektor seemed to realize just how true that was.

But the immediate point, he reminded himself, was that Charisians normally didn't do stupid things where their navy was concerned.

"There were two other tidbits of information," he offered. Maysahn quirked an eyebrow at him, and he shrugged. "First, Olyvyr seems to think he's finally worked out a way to sheath a ship in copper without having it fall apart. At any rate, according to my man, the ships they're building are all supposed to be coppered when they're finished."

He and Maysahn looked at one another thoughtfully. Sir Dustyn Olyvyr's mania for finding some way to protect his ships' hulls from the depredations of borers was well known. Not that he was alone in that, of course. The several varieties of shellfish and worms which fell under that general heading could literally devour a ship's timbers in a matter of only a few months, and every attempt to stop them with pitch or some other form of protective coating had failed. If Olyvyr truly had managed to solve the problems which had so far stymied his efforts to use copper, the long-term implications would obviously be significant. But at this particular moment, Zhaspahr Maysahn was rather more concerned with *short-term* implications.

"You said two tidbits," he observed. "What's the other one?"

"The minor fact that they appear to have assembled a squadron of galleons to practice whatever it is they're up to," Makferzahn said grimly. "It's only five ships, but it seems to spend a fair amount of time out on exercises. And it anchors in the Citadel Basin, well away from any other shipping, whenever it's in port. According to the fellow my man got drunk, it's commanded by a Commodore Staynair."

"Staynair?" Maysahn repeated slowly. The last name was scarcely unique in Charis, but it wasn't especially common, either. "Would that be Sir Domynyk Staynair?"

"The Bishop's younger brother," Makferzahn agreed with a nod.

"Now *that's* interesting," Maysahn murmured while his brain raced.

On one hand, it was reasonable enough, he supposed. If this mysterious project of theirs was important enough for Cayleb to take personal command of it, then they'd want one of their best naval officers working with him on it, and everything he'd ever heard about Commodore Staynair suggested the commodore certainly fell into that category. But there was also the connection to Tellesberg's bishop. Rumor had it that Bishop Executor Zherald had been known to express more than a few qualms about Staynair's ultimate loyalties. If his younger brother was this deeply involved in whatever Haarahld and his son were up to, then Bishop Maikel probably knew all about it, too. Which meant the Church—or, at least, the *Charisian* branch of the Church—also knew about it. Although that didn't necessarily mean the bishop executor did.

"I wonder," Makferzahn said. His thoughtful tone drew Maysahn's attention back to him, and the younger man shrugged. "I was just wondering," he continued once he was certain he had his superior's ear, "about those galleons Olyvyr is building right here in Tellesberg."

"What about them?"

"Well, it just occurred to me while we were sitting here that he has a dozen of them under construction for eight different owners. That's in addition to all these 'schooners' of his, of course."

"Every shipyard in the Kingdom's laying down ships right and left," Maysahn pointed out dryly. "The yards that aren't actually building are all busy rerigging existing ships to take advantage of the new sail plans. And it's all Olyvyr's fault, one way or another. Well, his and Howsmyn's."

"I know. But apparently all these new galleons of his are identical to one another. And according to a couple of carpenters working in Howsmyn's Tellesberg yard, there are some significant changes in their design. For one thing, they're a good twenty or thirty feet longer and a hell of a lot more heavily built than any galleon those carpenters have ever worked on before. I know Olyvyr's reputation, and I know these new rigging notions of his have only strengthened that reputation. Still, doesn't it strike you as a bit odd that eight different shipowners should simultaneously order a dozen new ships, all built to a new and untested design?"

"That does sound a bit peculiar," Maysahn acknowledged. He sipped chocolate thoughtfully, gazing out at the busy street scene once more.

"You'd think they'd be a little bit more conservative, wouldn't you?" he mused aloud. "Maybe let Olyvyr build a couple of these new designs of his, get them into service and see how they actually performed, before they sank that much money into them."

"That's exactly what I was thinking," Makferzahn agreed. "At the same time, as you just pointed out, he has stood the entire Charisian shipbuilding business on its ear. At the moment, people are so busy throwing money at him if he'll just design a ship for them that these people may've simply decided that if they want an Olyvyr-designed a ship at all, they have to take what they can get. And," the younger spy admitted, "they've already seen plenty of evidence that his new ideas about rigging work pretty much as advertised."

"That's all true enough. But I think the possibility that he's actually building them for the Navy needs to be considered seriously," Maysahn said. "And if that's true, we'd better report that possibility to the Prince while we work on either confirming or denying it."

He sat for a moment longer, contemplating the news, then shrugged.

"It may not make a lot of sense to us right this minute, but at least we know a bit more than we did. Good work, Zhames. I'll get a dispatch off to Manchyr with Captain Whaite tomorrow morning."

▼   ▼   ▼

"—with Captain Whaite tomorrow morning."

Merlin Athrawes frowned as Owl played back the day's take from the bug assigned to follow Zhaspahr Maysahn around.

The endless hours he was investing in what he'd come to think of as "Project Bootstrap" left him far less time than he would have preferred to deal with things like monitoring Maysahn's whereabouts. He'd had to leave virtually all of that sort of activity up to Owl, and that made him nervous.

To be fair, the AI seemed to be handling the task adequately so far. It was Owl who'd identified Makferzahn as Mhulvayn's replacement, and the computer did an excellent job of keeping anyone in its sights after Merlin had tagged that individual for surveillance. But Owl remained hopelessly literal-minded and unimaginative, and Merlin had no choice but to allow the AI to sort and analyze the take from the majority of the SNARCs and hope nothing critical got lost. Some of the SNARCs Merlin continued to monitor personally—those watching Hektor, Nahrmahn, and Archbishop Erayk, for example—but even there he was forced to rely on Owl's recognition of critical keywords to direct his attention to relative bits of information.

Which category the afternoon's conversation between Maysahn and Makferzahn certainly fell into.

Merlin leaned back in his chair in his darkened quarters while he pondered. The fact that he could get along with so little "sleep" helped some, at least, although he had to remember to disarrange his bedding every night.

Should I take this information to Wave Thunder? he mused. *It had to happen sooner or later, and at least they don't seem to've picked up on the changes in the artillery itself. But just what they already know is going to start someone like Hektor asking questions I'd really prefer not get asked just yet.*

If he told Wave Thunder about this particular "vision," the baron might just feel inclined to pick up Makferzahn and all of his identified agents. In many respects, Merlin wouldn't have minded shutting down Hektor's network again. But if they did that, Hektor was going to wonder just what had inspired them to do so. And if they didn't shut down his *entire* network, then the information Makferzahn had already picked up would probably get through to Corisande anyway. Which would almost certainly start Hektor's agile mind down the same path.

Of course, there is *another possibility,* he thought more grimly. *Nothing says "Captain Whaite" has to survive to get Maysahn's dispatches to Hektor.*

Given the voyage time between Tellesberg and Manchyr, *Sea Cloud*'s failure to arrive on schedule would probably throw at least some serious delay into Hektor's information loop. The transit time was almost forty days either way for the disguised courier. If she should suffer a mischief, it would be eighty days, at the earliest, before Maysahn learned of her loss, and then it would take his replacement dispatch another forty days or so to reach Hektor.

It was tempting. In fact, it was *very* tempting, and the recon skimmer could eliminate *Sea Cloud* almost effortlessly. Doing so would require the deaths of "Whaite" and his entire crew, of course. That thought was enough to make Merlin hesitate, but it wasn't as if they were exactly innocent bystanders. Every one of them was a member of the League Navy, and arguably all of them were spies, as well.

Which, Merlin admitted to himself, was really largely beside the point, except for his own desire to justify the action he was contemplating.

He replayed the entire conversation between Makferzahn and Maysahn one more time, then shrugged.

Destroying Sea Cloud *wouldn't really do that much for us*, he decided. *Maysahn's obviously going to be sending follow-up dispatches as he and Makferzahn turn up additional information, anyway. So taking out* Sea Cloud *would only delay things a bit, unless I'm prepared to start picking off every courier Maysahn and Hektor send back and forth.*

He grimaced distastefully at the thought and shook his head.

No. I need to discuss this "vision" with Wave Thunder and Haarahld. They've still got a lot better "ear" then I do for how Hektor's likely to respond. Besides, it's not going to be all that much longer before Erayk gets here for his pastoral visit. That's going to cause more problems than letting this snippet of information get through to Hektor ever could.

And this way, he admitted to himself, *at least I won't have to feel like I'm shooting fish in a barrel.*

He stopped shaking his head and nodded, satisfied with his conclusion, and turned his attention to the SNARC which kept tabs on Prince Nahrmahn.

JULY, YEAR OF GOD 891

✦

Good morning, Your Majesty," Father Zhoshua Makgregair murmured, bowing deeply as the chamberlain ushered him into the private audience chamber.

"And to you, Father," King Gorjah of Tarot replied.

Gorjah was a slender man, especially compared to Makgregair's solid, broad-shouldered bulk. He was also barely into his mid-thirties, with dark hair and a complexion substantially darker than Makgregair's, and he was dressed in loose robes of silk. He also wore the "kercheef"—the traditional bandana-like head-dress of Tarot—instead of the heavy three-cornered cap of the priesthood, and he looked irritatingly comfortable despite the weather.

As if thoughts of the weather had summoned it, thunder rumbled once more out over Thol Bay, gentle with distance and almost lost in the sound of rain. The equatorial downpour pounded heavily outside the audience chamber's open windows, beating on the tile roof of Gorjah's palace. Waterfalls spilled from the eaves and ran gurgling down the gutters, and the warm air was heavy with moisture. It was also curiously still, despite the thunderstorm, settling about Makgregair like a humid fist, and his undergarments were damp with sweat.

Tarot's no assignment for a boy born in Northland, he reflected, thinking back to his boyhood in the Republic of Siddarmark's Northland Province. He'd grown up fishing in the cold, deep waters of Hsing-wu's Passage—when the ice melted enough to let him—and this wet tropical oven pressed down on him with an almost physical weight. *It's amazing to me that any of them have working minds, putting up with this kind of heat. I'd think just the mold would be enough to rot their brains!*

At least his summer-weight cassock was made of cotton instead of the traditional wool, but that was relatively little comfort at the moment, and a part of him looked longingly at Gorjah's even lighter silken robes.

"Thank you for making time in your busy schedule for me. And for agreeing to see me privately," he said as he straightened his back once again, just a bit more quickly than most diplomats would have. Gorjah was a king, whereas Makgregair was a mere upper-priest. But that upper-priest was here as the direct representative of God's holy Church, and he looked Gorjah squarely in the face. There was nothing disrespectful about it, but it was always best to make one's status clear from the outset.

"It's my pleasure to adjust my schedule in order to meet with Mother Church's representative at any time," Gorjah said. He actually sounded as if he meant it, too, Makgregair noted. On the other hand, kings got a great deal of practice sounding as if they meant things.

Almost as much as those of us who serve as diplomats in the Chancellor's service, he thought with a small inner smile.

"That's the sort of thing any priest is happy to hear, Your Majesty." He allowed himself an outer smile, as well, but then his expression sobered. "I'm grateful for it, nonetheless, Your Majesty. Indeed, I only wish all of Safehold's princes and kings were equally mindful of their responsibilities to God and His Church."

Gorjah's expression seemed to freeze, and his eyes narrowed.

"Excuse me, Father," he said after the briefest of hesitations, "but what prince or king could be so lost as to forget those responsibilities?"

"Mother Church, and the Holy Inquisition, must be always mindful of the fashion in which the duties and responsibilities—and temptations—of worldly power may draw a ruler away from his duty to God," Makgregair said gravely. "Not all of them are as scrupulous as you when it comes to the observation those duties, Your Majesty."

"I find that thought distressing, Father," Gorjah said slowly. "And, to be honest, a little frightening, since I must assume you're telling *me* this for a reason."

"Don't be concerned that anyone is displeased with your own respect for Mother Church, Your Majesty," Makgregair's tone was reassuring, and he smiled once more, albeit a bit sadly. "Yet you're quite correct. I am here to see you because of the failings of princes. Specifically, Vicar Zahmsyn's grown increasingly and deeply concerned about another ruler. One whose preoccupation with worldly power and wealth has led him perilously far from the path of obedience to God and His Church. And one with whom, I fear, you are closely associated."

Gorjah's swarthy complexion paled ever so slightly, and a few fine beads of sweat which had nothing to do with the morning's heat and humidity appeared on his forehead.

"I assure you, Father, that I would never associate myself with anyone who would defy God!" He shook his head emphatically. "If I believed for a moment that Prince Hek—"

"Forgive me, Your Majesty," Makgregair broke in gently. "I had no intention of implying that you or anyone in Tarot was guilty of any such thing. Indeed, I ought to have made it clear from the beginning that you yourself are not responsible for your relationship with him. It was your father who signed the treaty of alliance with *his* father."

Gorjah had opened his mouth, but he closed it again with an all but audible click. Makgregair could almost literally see the thoughts chasing one another through his brain and waited patiently while the King of Tarot worked his way through them.

It didn't take very long, and Gorjah's shoulders straightened as if a weight had been removed from them. Obviously, he'd feared that Makgregair was in Tranjyr because the Council of Vicars had learned about his secret negotiations with Hektor of Corisande. It was far from unheard of for the Chancellor to use the Church's priestly diplomats to warn secular rulers away from alliances of which the Church disapproved. And under normal circumstances, the Temple would have been most unhappy with Hektor's machinations. The combination of his obvious ambition and the skill with which he'd been manipulating the situation would have made him a substantial threat to the balance the Church sought to maintain to prevent any one secular ruler from growing too powerful.

Gorjah was as well aware of that as Makgregair. Just as he was also aware the Temple had, on more than one occasion, *encouraged* the ambition and avarice of a secular ruler as a counter to the power of someone else of whom the Council of Vicars disapproved even more strongly. So if the Chancellor's personal representative wasn't trying to warn Gorjah away from *Hektor* . . .

"Father," the king said after a moment, "from what you've said, I can only assume you're referring to Haarahld of Charis."

"Alas, I fear I am," Makgregair replied gravely.

"I'm . . . shocked to hear that," Gorjah said, and rubbed his short-trimmed beard thoughtfully. "While I've always known Haarahld was . . . deeply aware, let's say, of the opportunities his kingdom's wealth and naval power make available to him, I'd always believed he was equally aware of his responsibilities before God and His Church. I assure you, if I'd believed for a moment that he wasn't, it would have caused me to think very seriously and critically about the treaty between Tarot and Charis."

"Vicar Zahmsyn fears that the temptation of worldly power, coupled with his no doubt genuine sense of responsibility to his dynasty, is leading Haarahld astray." Makgregair stressed the noun "dynasty" ever so slightly, and watched Gorjah's eyes narrow as he recognized the implication.

Odd, Makgregair thought, *how well the vicars can differentiate between someone else's responsibilities to the land he rules and those to the ambition of his dynasty.*

It wasn't the sort of thought a priest was supposed to think, but those who served as Mother Church's diplomats required an appreciation of the realities behind their missions. Makgregair had that appreciation, but he allowed no trace of his reflections to touch his expression as he shook his head sadly.

"We're hearing some disturbing reports out of Charis," he continued. "Obviously, there's always been some cause for concern, given Charis' distance from the Temple. These latest 'innovations,' are most disquieting, however. While none of them appears to violate the Proscriptions, change begets change, and it cannot be long before violations *do* occur."

"May I ask if Mother Church intends to take action?" Gorjah asked diffidently.

"However concerned Mother Church may be, or may become," Makgregair replied, "she must be always mindful of her responsibility to act only after careful deliberation and mature consideration. Nor must she ever forget she is governed by mortal men, and that mortal men—even those called to the orange—are always fallible. Because of that, she hesitates to unsheathe her sword until and unless she knows beyond a shadow of a doubt that transgression has occurred. With Mother Church's enormous power, and her equally great responsibility to exercise that power judiciously and in accordance with God's will, comes an obligation to be certain beyond question that the line between darkness and light has truly been crossed before she may act. What we may fear lies in Charis' future cannot justify Mother Church in taking official action if no offense has yet been committed."

"I see." Gorjah leaned back slightly on his throne, the fingers of his right hand drumming lightly on the upholstered armrest as he gazed at Makgregair.

"Should I understand, then, Father," he said after a few seconds, "that the reason for your visit is primarily to warn me? To alert me to the Church's concerns so that I don't follow in Haarahld's wake if he does cross that line?"

"That is, indeed, a major portion of the reason for my visit, Your Majesty," Makgregair agreed, bowing slightly but gravely. "And I don't believe the Chancellor would be upset with me if I added that other princes and rulers will be receiving similar . . . alerts."

Gorjah's eyes flickered visibly at that, and Makgregair hid a smile of satisfaction.

"I am, of course, deeply distressed to learn that a ruler and a kingdom with whom I've been so closely associated has come to cause God's shepherds such concern," the king said. "Obviously, given how many years Tarot and Charis have been allied, it's difficult for me to believe Haarahld could be so lost to his duty to God. But I thank you and Vicar Zahmsyn for the warning. However distressing it may be, it's far better to be forewarned. I fear it will behoove me to very seriously reconsider my relationship with Charis in light of what you've told me."

"You must, of course, act as your own sense of responsibility to God and your realm requires," Makgregair said gravely. "I'm merely Vicar Zahmsyn's messenger, and it would be inappropriate for me to urge any specific course of action upon you without instructions to that effect from the Chancellor. I will say, however, speaking strictly for myself, that I believe it would, indeed, be wise to review your relations with Charis, and your treaty obligations, most carefully."

"I appreciate such wise counsel," Gorjah said with matching gravity. "Please tell the Chancellor I'm most grateful for his timely warning, and that I'll be thinking very seriously about all you've told me this morning."

"I feel confident nothing could please Vicar Zahmsyn more than to hear that, Your Majesty," Makgregair said with another bow. "And now, having discharged my instructions from the Chancellor, I'll bid you farewell and allow you to return your attention to the pressing matters from which my visit must undoubtedly have distracted you. With your permission, Your Majesty?"

"Of course, Father." Gorjah waved his right hand in a graceful gesture of permission. "Thank you."

"You're most welcome, Your Majesty," Makgregair murmured, and withdrew from the presence chamber with yet another bow.

.II.

The Galleon *Blessed Langhorne,*
Markovian Sea

G ood afternoon, Your Eminence."

"Good afternoon, Captain Braunyng." Archbishop Erayk Dynnys smiled pleasantly at Ellys Braunyng, the captain of the galleon *Blessed Langhorne,* although he didn't feel particularly pleasant.

It wasn't Captain Braunyng's fault, nor was it the fault of the weather. Although the Markovian Sea could be as rough and treacherous as any body of water in the world, especially in the late spring and early summer, it had been kind to them for this voyage—so far, at least. The water was a deep, sparkling blue; the heavens were a crystalline vault of lighter blue, banded with billows of white cloud; and the sun shone with surprising warmth as the crisp northwest wind, just cool enough to bite, came whipping briskly in over *Blessed Langhorne*'s starboard quarter.

Unfortunately, Dynnys had rather more to worry about than the current weather.

He'd left Home Port on Temple Bay aboard one of Vicar Allayn's dispatch galleys almost a full month before, as soon as the ice had sufficiently melted, and made a swift transit of Hsing-wu's Passage. The dispatch boats carried very large crews for their size so that they could change off rowers regularly and maintain a high rate of speed. But their shallow, lightly built hulls were poorly suited to open water, and the archbishop had transferred to the slower but more seaworthy galleon five days ago. Which meant he was only another five or six five-days from Tellesberg.

Another thing those idiots like Cahnyr who think I should spend more time in Charis don't think about, he thought grumpily. *Making my "one-month" pastoral visit uses up four months just in transit time! I spend half an entire year either in Tellesberg or traveling back and forth between it and the Temple.*

At least the semaphore chain along the shore of Hsing-wu's Passage had let him stay in touch with the Temple until he'd hit the open sea. But that was hardly the same thing as being able to attend personally to his archbishopric's business. Semaphore messages were, by their very nature, short and terse, and there was always the risk any cipher one used might be broken by someone who wished one ill.

He was fairly confident he could rely upon Mahtaio Broun to interpret even his briefest semaphore messages correctly, and to manage his affairs as well as anyone below the ranks of the episcopate could, yet he couldn't quite feel totally comfortable about it. He'd certainly trained the upper-priest carefully enough, and he had no doubts about Broun's intelligence or competence. But the Council's attitude towards Charis had grown even more suspicious and hostile over the winter, and if the Group of Four decided it was necessary to take action against Charis, Dynnys' own position in the Temple hierarchy would be severely damaged, at the very least. Broun was as aware of that as anyone, which meant any of Dynnys' rivals might scent an opportunity to entice his aide into betraying him.

All of which helped to explain his unhappy mood, despite the stiff, invigorating breeze and fresh sea air, as he leaned on his silver-headed ironwood cane.

"I trust lunch was satisfactory, Your Eminence?" Braunyng continued, and Dynnys hid an unwilling smile. The captain seemed . . . uncomfortable. Obviously, he'd realized Dynnys was feeling less than cheerful, yet he had no choice but to offer at least some small talk. The captain of a Temple galleon couldn't very well simply ignore an archbishop who arrived on his poop deck for a post-luncheon constitutional.

"Your cook manages surprisingly well, actually, Captain," Dynnys said, taking pity on the man. "I have to confess that I'd never make a good sailor, though. I miss fresh vegetables too badly for that!"

"I appreciate the compliment, Your Eminence, and I'll pass it along to the cook, with your permission. As for fresh vegetables"—Braunyng shrugged with a smile—"I can only agree with you heartily. In fact, the first thing I do whenever I return to Port Harbor is to take my wife to one of our favorite restaurants and sit down to the biggest, freshest salad I can find."

"Please, Captain!" Dynnys half-laughed. "Don't get me started on missing fresh lettuce!"

"Forgive me, Your Eminence." Braunyng inclined his head in a half-bow, clearly relieved by the genuine humor in the archbishop's response. Then he straightened, and his expression was rather more serious.

"Still, Your Eminence, as boring as our diet may be at sea, at least it keeps us healthy, thank Pasquale." He touched his heart and then his lips, and Dynnys repeated the gesture. "I hate to think what my men's state would be without Pasquale's teachings."

"I certainly agree with you there, Captain," Dynnys said with complete sincerity. The Archangel Pasquale's dietary laws were particularly ironclad for those—like men who spent five-days on end at sea—who lacked ready access to fresh provisions. On the occasions when those laws had been inadvertently or unavoidably broken, the consequences had been . . . ugly.

Dynnys recalled one instance from not too many years ago when a Dohlaran galleon had been all but dismasted by a terrible storm which had blown her far into the trackless depths of the Southern Ocean. Her surviving crew had managed to contrive a jury rig and had somehow found their way home once more, but her speed had been slowed to an agonizing crawl, and most of her provisions had been lost or ruined by the storm. By the time she'd finally managed to crawl into port on Westbreak Island, two-thirds of her crew had been dead of scurvy, for they'd been unable to keep Pasquale's laws and, as always happened, disease had followed quickly.

At least the unfortunates in her crew had still had water. They'd managed to catch some of the torrential rain in funnels made of old sails in order to refill their water tanks, and whatever might have happened to their provisions, those tanks had been intact, thank Pasquale!

Dynnys remembered a classroom experience from his own youth. Regardless of the order for which a churchman was destined, he was expected to be at least generally familiar with the basic teachings of the other orders. That particular day, an upper-priest of the Order of Pasquale had demonstrated why Pasquale required ships to store their water in iron tanks rather than wooden casks. The casks would have been far cheaper, but one look at the slimy green algae which had turned the water in the demonstration cask into a thick, stinking semi-sludge had been more than enough to make the point to young Erayk. Shipboard water might sometimes taste a little rusty, but he was perfectly prepared to put up with that. Just as he was prepared to dutifully consume his daily ration of lemon juice, or eat his bean sprouts.

Of course, an archbishop had rather more dietary options than a common seaman. The fresh eggs from the chicken coop on the main deck were reserved first for Dynnys and his clerical staff, and then for *Blessed Langhorne*'s officers. The petty officers and common seamen wouldn't taste eggs—or chicken—before they made land once more. And there were still five sheep in the pen beside the chicken coop, as well.

"What's your best estimate for our arrival in Tellesberg, Captain?" Dynnys asked after a moment.

"We're actually making better time than usual, Your Eminence," Braunyng said. "This time of year, the wind's mostly out of the northwest, like today, which puts us on our best point of sailing. It won't be quite as favorable once we pass Hammer Island and get out into the Anvil, but it should still be more with us than against us. One of those new 'schooners' I've been hearing about could make the passage more quickly, I'm sure, but by the Master's best reckoning, we're only about twenty-four days out of Tellesberg."

Dynnys suppressed a grimace, his mood darkening once again at Braunyng's reference to the new ship type. The captain was obviously blissfully unaware of the Church's reservations about Charisian innovation, or he would have watched his words much more carefully with Charis' archbishop.

Still, Dynnys reflected, *perhaps it's as well he didn't. He's a professional seaman, so maybe his reaction might provide a more realistic measure of the threat the Council sees coming out of Charis.*

"Have you actually seen one of these—'schooners,' did you call it?—yourself, Captain?"

"Indeed I have, Your Eminence." Braunyng's eyes brightened, and he reached out to lay one hand on the poop-deck rail. "Mind you, I love *Blessed Langhorne.* She's a good, stout ship, and she's been good to me and given the Temple good service. But while I know the *Writ* teaches envy is a sin, I'm only mortal. When I saw that schooner standing so much closer into the wind than any ship *I've* ever sailed in could have done—!"

He shook his head, smiling in memory.

"Any seaman worth his salt would love to get his hands on a vessel like that, Your Eminence," he finished simply.

Dynnys nodded slowly, smiling back at the captain even as he felt his own heart sink.

The messages which had arrived from Ahdymsyn as steadily as the weather permitted had made it increasingly clear Charis was becoming even more of a hotbed of innovation and new concepts than initial reports had suggested. Dynnys' own sources in the Temple and in Zion strongly suggested that accounts from other sources—like Prince Nahrmahn and Prince Hektor—were deliberately and severely exaggerated, but he couldn't simply ignore *Ahdymsyn's* correspondence. And if Ahdymsyn was to be believed, then the "schooner" which so entranced Captain Braunyng was only the tip of the iceberg.

"If you'll excuse me, Captain," he said courteously to Braunyng, "I believe I'd like to spend some time meditating while I walk off a little of that excellent luncheon your cook served us."

"Of course, Your Eminence. I'll pass the word to see to it that you aren't disturbed."

"Thank you, Captain. I appreciate that."

The captain bowed once again, and withdrew, leaving the windward side of the narrow poop deck to the archbishop. Dynnys composed his expression into one of suitable gravity, adjusted the light cloak he wore over his cassock, and paced slowly up and down, up and down, with the dragging limp his broken leg had left as a permanent legacy, leaning on his cane against the roll of the ship.

Twenty-four days, Braunyng estimated. The next best thing to five whole five-days. And who knew what was happening in Tellesberg—or the Temple—while *Blessed Langhorne* inched across the thousands of miles between Haven and Charis?

He remembered the meeting in which he'd steered the ecclesiastical court into settling the dispute over the Hanth succession in favor of Tahdayo Mahntayl. The proposition had seemed so simple then. Simply a routine matter, a decision rendered in return for a generous personal gift. But that decision loomed much larger now. Then, it had been no more than one more step in the well understood dance of Temple insiders. Now it was clear to Dynnys his archbishopric's future was far more fragile than he'd ever thought before, and that his own action, however innocuous and routine it had seemed at the time, had served the interests of the men who wanted to see that archbishopric's wealth and power broken forever.

He thought back to his winter conversation with Vicar Zahmsyn. The Chancellor's concern had been evident, yet the Vicar's reassurances that no decision about Charis was imminent had calmed the worst of Dynnys' worries. But that calm had been seriously undermined as spring crept steadily closer and the ice in Hsing-wu's Passage had begun to melt. And Dynnys' final interview with Trynair before his departure for Tellesberg had been anything but reassuring. Not because of what the Vicar had said, but because of what he *hadn't* said.

There was no question in Dynnys' mind that the Chancellor—probably the entire Group of Four—were taking their own steps to deal with any threat arising from Charis. But none of his sources had been able to tell him just what sort of "steps" they might have in mind, and Trynair's failure to tell him anything at all about the Group of Four's plans took on ominous overtones.

He paused for a moment, staring out to sea, eyes unseeing. Try as he might, he could think of only two things which might stave off the storm which loomed steadily closer.

One was to demonstrate his own firm control by taking decisive action. If the more worrisome of the new innovations could be ruled violations of the Proscriptions—or even if they could be ruled simply to *approach* violations—and he ordered their attestations revoked, it might convince the Group of Four he could control the situation without their intervention. It was by no means certain it would have that effect, but it might.

Failing that, the only option he saw was to convince them their dire interpretation of events in Charis was in error. If they could be brought to the conclusion that they'd overreacted, that the reports from places like Emerald and Corisande had, in fact, been grossly exaggerated, then they might well step back from taking active steps against the kingdom. At the very least, they were certainly aware of how much Charis' tithes contributed to the Church's coffers every year. Surely they'd hesitate to destroy that revenue stream unless they felt they absolutely must!

He hoped they would, at least, because if the Church, or even "just" the Council of Vicars acting in its secular role, decided Charis must be destroyed, Charis *would* perish. And if Charis perished, the career of the archbishop who'd been responsible for its orthodoxy would come to a sudden, shattering stop. Erayk Dynnys would lose his archbishopric, the wealth it represented, and at least two-thirds of his power and prestige, and he'd suddenly discovered that beside that, the bribe he'd pocketed from Hektor was meaningless.

How can they do this to me? his mind demanded harshly. *For years, I've been their archbishop, looked after them, protected them from the Inquisition and those on the Council who are automatically suspicious of any change. And how do they repay me? By embracing all of these damnable new notions of theirs! By walking straight into the dragon's lair—and taking* me *with them—because they're too stupid to see what they're doing!*

He gazed out over the rolling blue water of the Markovian Sea, and deep inside his heart railed at the unfairness of a world in which God permitted this to happen to him.

.III.
Royal Palace,
City of Gorath,
Kingdom of Dohlar

N ow, Father Ahlbyrt," Samyl Cahkrayn, the Duke of Fern, said to Ahlbyrt Harys as the palace footman showed the young priest into his private office in the Royal Palace. "What can I do for you today?"

"First, Your Grace, let me thank you for agreeing to see me," Harys said. "I know how busy you are as the Kingdom's First Councillor, and I, alas, am only an under-priest." He smiled charmingly. "Believe me, I'm only too well aware of what a small fish that makes me!"

"Nonsense, Father!" Fern smiled back at him, considerably more broadly. "You serve the Council of Vicars. Indeed, your letters of introduction are signed by the Chancellor himself. That makes you a rather larger fish than you may believe it does."

"That's kind of you, at any rate, Your Grace," Harys replied. In fact, as both of them understood perfectly well, it made him a very big fish indeed. But both of them knew how the game was played, and so both of them were also aware that his junior status allowed him to be an *unofficial* big fish. The one difference between them was that Harys knew why that was important.

"The Chancellor's letter implied you were here to discuss some diplomatic matter, Father?"

"Actually, Your Grace, it might be more accurate to say I'm here in an advisory capacity. Vicar Zahmsyn is rather concerned about certain developments—not here in Dohlar, of course—which could have . . . unfortunate implications for God's Plan, and my instructions are to share his concerns with you."

Fern had been listening with a grave smile. That smile disappeared with Harys' last few words, and he straightened a bit abruptly in his chair.

"That sounds ominous, Father," the duke said after a moment into the small silence Harys had allowed to fall, and his tone was cautious.

"It's always possible the Chancellor's concerns are misplaced," Harys said with precisely metered reassurance. "And, of course, I myself am not so experienced as he in matters such as this. It's possible my understanding of those concerns is less than perfect. I may be overreacting to what he said to me when he briefed me for this journey."

"That's always understood, of course," Fern murmured, but his sharp eyes told Harys he knew better. That he perfectly understood the diplomatic camouflage of the priest's last two sentences, even if he didn't yet know the reason for it.

"Well, having said that," Harys continued, "I'm afraid there are persistent reports of disquieting changes and initiatives coming out of Charis. At this stage, there's no concrete evidence any of the Proscriptions have been violated, of course. If there were, Mother Church and the Inquisition would already have acted. However, there's a growing level of concern, let us say, that the Proscriptions are being more and more closely approached."

"I see," Fern said, although it was clear to Harys he *didn't*—not yet, at least.

"Mother Church cannot take action based upon mere suspicion," the underpriest continued. "That, as I know you're aware, is a fundamental principle which was established long ago. But what's binding upon Mother Church in a corporate and temporal sense, as the anointed guardian of God's Plan, is less restrictive when the Church's servants discover they must act in a more secular role."

Fern nodded silently, this time in genuine comprehension.

"In a sense," Harys said, just to make sure they truly did understand one another, "I'm here not in the service of Vicar Zahmsyn or the Chancellor of the Council of Vicars so much as in the service of the Knights of the Temple Lands as they seek to discharge their responsibility for the secular administration of the Temple Lands. Of course, the Knights also sit upon the Council of Vicars, so there must be a certain commonality between their responsibilities as rulers in this world and the Church's temporal responsibility for men's souls in the next. Still, that which is binding upon Mother Church must not be lightly set aside by any of her servants, whether they act in the secular or the temporal role."

"I've often thought it must be extraordinarily difficult for the Vicars to discharge all their heavy responsibilities," Fern observed. "Obviously, as King Rahnyld's first councillor, my own duties are only a shadow of those which fall upon *their* shoulders. Despite that, there are times when I find myself torn between conflicting obligations, and that must be far worse for someone like the Chancellor. On the one hand, he has all of the responsibilities of any secular ruler, but on the other, he must be eternally vigilant against even the suggestion of capriciousness in how he might go about meeting them because of his even graver responsibilities to God and Mother Church."

"That, unfortunately, is only too true, Your Grace," Harys said with a sad little smile. "And in the case of Charis, the situation is further complicated by the fact that neither Mother Church nor the Temple Lands maintains any great strength at sea. Should it happen that . . . direct action against Charis became necessary, neither the Church nor the Temple Lands would have the means for it."

"Does the Chancellor think such an eventuality is likely?" Fern asked, his voice was calm, merely thoughtful, but his eyes were very narrow, and Harys shrugged.

"Again, Your Grace, you must remember my relative youth and inexperience. I may very well be reading more into the Chancellor's instructions than he intended. However, my own interpretation is that he does, indeed, fear such a day of direct conflict may dawn. How *likely* it is, I'm in no position to say. But the Chancellor will have been derelict in his duty if it happened such a terrible situation should arise, despite all his earnest prayers, if he's taken no steps to prepare against it. Hence my visit to Gorath."

"Indeed?" Fern cocked his head to one side.

"Your Grace, unlike the Temple Lands, Dohlar has a powerful fleet," Harys said frankly. "Moreover, without wishing to suggest that considerations of material gain could drive your Kingdom's policy, Charis' maritime strength is a direct threat to Dohlar's own needs and aspirations. In light of those considerations, the Chancellor has asked me to point out to you that the Temple Lands and Dohlar share a natural common interest. While the Chancellor's concerns are a direct reflection of his duties as one of God's senior shepherds, he's also well aware of the fashion in which Charis' growing wealth and power menace Dohlar's future. The primary reason for my mission here is to alert you to his growing disquiet . . . and to assure you that he—and Mother Church—understand any reservations you and King Rahnyld may feel about Charis."

Duke Fern's eyes were very narrow indeed now.

"And is the Chancellor preparing to take action if it should become necessary?" he asked.

"As I say, Your Grace, he has no naval forces at his command. Or, rather, no naval forces sufficient for a threat such as this. Nor is there likely to be time for the Temple Lands to increase their naval strength to that point. However—" Harys looked Fern directly in the eye. "—the Temple Lands' treasury is deep. Should it become necessary to take action, I feel confident the Chancellor and the Grand Vicar would recognize Mother Church's responsibility to support the sword arm of any prince or king acting in defense of God's Plan."

There was silence in the chamber for several seconds, and then Fern nodded slowly.

"I thank you for bringing this matter to my attention, Father. I assure you I'll inform His Majesty as promptly as possible about the Chancellor's concerns, and also about your own analysis of the . . . constraints under which he must address them. While I certainly can't speak for the King at this time, I'm sure he'd want me to ask you to inform the Chancellor that, as a loyal son of Mother Church, he stands, as always, ready to defend her against any threat."

"Your Grace, I see your reputation for graciousness and piety is well deserved." Harys bowed again. "I'll relay your words directly to the Chancellor. And, of course"—he looked up and met the duke's eye once again—"I'll keep you informed of any new messages I receive from him."

AUGUST, YEAR OF GOD 891

✦

Your Eminence." Bishop Executor Zherald Ahdymsyn bowed to kiss Archbishop Erayk Dynnys' ring as the archbishop was shown into the Archbishop's Palace. Although the Palace was officially Dynnys' residence, it was Ahdymsyn's *home*, and the bishop executor always felt just a bit odd when the archbishop arrived. As always, he'd met Dynnys in the entry hall, whose black and white marble squares stretched away, glistening in the sunlight pouring through the wide, deep set windows.

"Welcome to Tellesberg," he continued, straightening from his bow.

"Thank you, Zherald," Dynnys responded with a somewhat tart smile. "I appreciate the welcome, although, to be frank, I'd rather be in Zion."

"That's understandable, Your Eminence." Ahdymsyn returned his superior's smile, but inwardly he was somewhat shocked by Dynnys' appearance. It wasn't the ironwood cane and the hipshot stance, obviously designed to relieve pressure on the archbishop's right leg. Those he'd expected, more or less, following the dispatches about Dynnys' injuries. What he *hadn't* expected was the semipermanent vertical furrow between the archbishop's eyes. Or, for that matter, the worry in those eyes themselves.

"We have much to discuss," Dynnys said, then glanced over his shoulder as the rest of his party filed respectfully into the entrance hall behind him. Ahdymsyn recognized most of them, but there were a few new faces. There always were.

He was a bit surprised by Mahtaio Broun's absence, but only for a moment. Broun's steady climb in the archbishop's service and confidence made him the logical choice to be left home to see to Dynnys' interests in the Temple in his absence, and Ahdymsyn cocked his head with a slightly inquisitive expression as Dynnys waved one of the new faces—a young under-priest—forward.

"Zherald, this is Father Symyn Shumakyr, my new secretary. Symyn, Bishop Zherald."

"An honor, Your Eminence," Shumakyr murmured, bending to kiss Ahdymsyn's ring.

"Welcome to Tellesberg," Ahdymsyn responded.

Shumakyr was a personable-looking young man, in the habit of the Order of Langhorne with the white crown of a prelate's secretary on his sleeve. His eyes were bright and alert, and after his introduction, he stepped back into precisely the right position, one pace behind and to the left of his patron. On first impression, at least, he seemed a more than adequate replacement for Broun.

"I'm sure that after the fatigue of your long journey, you need an opportunity to rest and refresh yourself, Your Eminence," the bishop executor said, turning back to Dynnys.

"I certainly do," the archbishop agreed. "At the same time, thanks to my accident, I've been absent from Charis for much too long." He gave Ahdymsyn a sharp, straight look. "I'd like to get right to work, make up some of that lost time. I thought we might take time for a fairly leisurely lunch, then begin immediately with a general overview of the Archbishopric's affairs."

"Of course, Your Eminence," Ahdymsyn replied, not really surprised, given the anxiety in the archbishop's eyes and body language. He gestured to a liveried servant. "Hauwyrd will escort you to your chamber so that you can refresh yourself before lunch. We'll get the rest of your people settled in, as well."

"Thank you, Zherald," Dynnys said with a genuinely grateful smile. "That sounds excellent."

▼   ▼   ▼

"So, while I'm not totally easy in my own mind over this recent spate of new ideas, Father Paityr assures me there's absolutely no evidence of a violation of the Proscriptions."

"I gathered as much from your dispatches. And, of course, from young Wylsynn's reports," Dynnys said. He leaned back in the comfortable chair behind the desk in the large office permanently reserved for his exclusive use on his visits to his archbishopric. Ahdymsyn sat in a facing chair, and Father Symyn sat at a smaller desk to one side, the nib of his pen scratching as he took notes.

"As you, I'm more than a little uneasy over the abruptness with which all these . . . innovations have emerged," the archbishop continued. "That was why I requested Father Paityr to revisit his original evaluations of them."

He paused, then grimaced and glanced at his secretary.

"I think we'll go off record for a moment, Symyn," he said.

"Of course, Your Eminence," Shumakyr murmured, laying down his pen and folding his hands on his desk.

"To be totally candid, Zherald," Dynnys said then, "I'm not the only person in the Temple or in Zion who's been anxious about reports coming out of Charis. The Chancellor himself has expressed his concerns on more than one occasion."

He paused, and Ahdymsyn nodded very slightly. There was no need for the archbishop to explain that if Vicar Zahmsyn had expressed an opinion, it was actually that of the Group of Four.

"My impression is that those concerns encompass more than simply these new ship designs, or the new spinning and weaving machines, or new ways of counting," Dynnys continued after a moment. "Nonetheless, all those things are symptomatic of what appears to be worrying him. So I very much hope it will be possible to put his mind at ease over these matters. We need to reassure him that we're aware of our responsibilities, both to the Council and to God, and that we're meeting them with vigilance and forethought. And we also need to demonstrate that we're determined to keep an open mind—to continue to test, and to withdraw the certification of suspect devices or processes if we subsequently determine that the original attestation was in error."

"I understand, Your Eminence," Ahdymsyn assured him.

"Good. In that regard, I'd like you to arrange a personal interview for me with Father Paityr as early as possible tomorrow morning."

"Of course, Your Eminence."

"Thank you." The archbishop nodded to Shumakyr, who picked up his pen once again, then looked back at Ahdymsyn.

"And now, Zherald, please continue."

"Of course, Your Eminence." Ahdymsyn cleared his throat. "I have been a little concerned over a few minor points of doctrinal interpretation on the part of some of our local priesthood," he said carefully. "While I've seen no signs of any deliberate or intentional challenge to orthodoxy, there are some points upon which I think it might be well for you to counsel our priests and bishops, Your Eminence."

Dynnys' eyes narrowed slightly, and Ahdymsyn continued in a deliberately unhurried voice.

"Such minor matters of correction are far from uncommon, of course, and I've dealt with them as they arose. Nonetheless, while you're here in Charis, I feel it would be most appreciated by all of our priesthood to hear a frank expression of your own views and to receive your pastoral instruction."

"I'm sure you're right," Dynnys agreed after a moment. "Please see to working that into our schedule. And perhaps it would be well for me to meet privately with Bishop Maikel first?"

"I think that might be wise, Your Eminence, as well as courteous," Ahdymsyn said with a nod.

"See to that, as well, then, too."

"Of course, Your Eminence."

Ahdymsyn cleared his throat once more.

"One of the brighter spots has been the readiness with which the archbishopric's tithes have come forward," he said much more cheerfully. "That's not to say there hasn't been a certain degree of grumbling—there always is—and pleas for extenuating circumstances. I've granted a few commutations, subject to your approval, of course.

"The Church's estates and manors, not to mention the monasteries and convents, are generally in good order. I'm a little concerned about the management of one or two of our manors in Margaret's Land, but over all I have few complaints or criticisms. In the case of—"

▼   ▼   ▼

"Your Eminence."

Father Paityr Wylsynn crossed Archbishop Erayk's large, luxuriously furnished office with quick, brisk strides. He went to one knee before the archbishop and bent his head to kiss Dynnys' ring, then remained kneeling until Dynnys touched him lightly on the shoulder.

"Rise, Father," the archbishop said, and Wylsynn obeyed.

He folded his arms in the sleeves of his cassock, waiting silently, his expression both attentive and respectful, and Dynnys studied him thoughtfully.

He had the Wylsynn look, the archbishop thought. That strong nose and the stubborn, one might almost say mulish, set of the mouth were all too familiar, but there was something else about this youngster. Something in the gray eyes . . . or perhaps the set of the shoulders. It wasn't defiant, or disrespectful. Indeed, it was almost . . . serene.

Whatever it was, it made Dynnys uneasy, and he smiled a bit more broadly than usual to conceal it.

"I appreciate the promptness with which you responded to my request for a reexamination of your conclusions concerning the new processes and devices introduced here in Charis over the past year or so, Father."

"I'm gratified that I was able to meet your requirements, Your Eminence."

"Yes. Well," Dynnys turned and limped around behind his desk and sank into the comfortable chair, "while I appreciate how quickly you responded, it occurred to me that it was possible I might have rushed you just a bit. Do you feel confident you were able to take sufficient time to be certain in your own mind of your conclusions?"

He met the young upper-priest' eyes steadily. Any cleric of Wylsynn's seniority in the Temple or Zion would almost certainly have taken the hint. Wylsynn only looked back calmly and nodded.

"Yes, Your Eminence, I am, thank you."

"So you remain of your original opinion that there are no violations involved? No need for the Church to issue any cautionary notices? Revoke any attestations?" Dynnys asked pleasantly.

"Yes, Your Eminence, I do."

"I see."

Dynnys continued to gaze at the red-haired young intendant with a pronounced sense of frustration. Wylsynn couldn't possibly be as blind to the Church's political realities as he chose to appear, but his serenity was a shield, impervious to the archbishop's prods.

The Group of Four wanted proof Dynnys was *doing* something . . . and that

Charis was sufficiently obedient to its archbishop that *they* need not take action. And if he ordered the revocation of an attestation and Charis accepted it—which he was certain the kingdom would—he would have convincing evidence the situation was under control. But if Wylsynn gave him no opening, there was no way he could act.

With another intendant, Dynnys might have been tempted to order him to rewrite his initial evaluations to give him what he needed. With *this* intendant, that was out of the question. Besides, when it came right down to it, Dynnys wasn't truly certain he really wanted Wylsynn to disallow any of the Charisian innovations.

Or I think I'm not, anyway, he told himself. *Of course, that might be no more than putting the best face on it, since the stubborn little bastard isn't going to give an inch. On the other hand, as long as Wylsynn stands firm—which he obviously intends to do—even Clyntahn's going to find it hard to move against Charis for heresy. And if I emphasize his confidence in my "everything's all right down here, really" reports to the Temple . . .*

"In that case, I suppose there's nothing more to be said on that head," he resumed aloud after a moment. "However, I would like to ask you for your personal impression of this Merlin Athrawes. I read your dispatch, of course, but I've found the written word frequently fails to convey all of the nuances."

"Of course, Your Eminence," Wylsynn said when Dynnys paused with one eyebrow arched. "As I wrote in the dispatch to which you just referred, I personally interviewed Lieutenant Athrawes. Although you hadn't specifically requested me to, I felt the stories flying about required a closer look. Of course, all manner of wild rumors about him were undoubtedly inevitable, given the part he played in saving the Crown Prince's life. And then again, in that matter of the Duke of Tirian's treason.

"In light of those rumors, however, I specifically raised the point of whether or not he was a *seijin*. He told me he does possess at least some of the abilities attributed to the *seijin*, as the result of many years of study. It was scarcely necessary for him to tell me he had the *seijin*'s martial-arts abilities, of course, given what he's already reputed to have accomplished. But he also told me he doesn't claim that title for himself."

Wylsynn shrugged.

"My own study of the accounts concerning the *seijin* as a group indicate that very few supposedly genuine *seijin* have ever claimed that title for themselves. It seems to be awarded to them after the fact, based upon their accomplishments. Bearing that in mind, my own judgment is that Lieutenant Athrawes probably *is* a *seijin*, in the sense that his skill as a warrior will cause him to be so regarded in the fullness of time."

"And this business with the children he saved from the kraken attack?" Dynnys pressed.

"My best estimate, Your Eminence, is that the children involved were understandably hysterical and grossly exaggerated what happened. It's true the authorities in King's Harbor recovered one kraken which had been killed with a harpoon. No others were recovered, however, and according to Crown Prince

Cayleb, who's an experienced naval officer in his own right, and who also had by far the best view of what actually happened, the youngsters were much closer to the wharf than they believed they were.

"As closely as I can reconstruct what probably really happened, they were close enough for Lieutenant Athrawes to make what probably *was* a fairly remarkable cast with the harpoon. That would be in reasonable accordance with his previously displayed abilities as a warrior. He then dove into the water and swam to the boat, where the kraken he'd harpooned continued to attack the children until the mortal wound it had already suffered overcame it. The lieutenant may have helped to fend off the dying creature, but I suspect he was actually most concerned with getting the children out of the water, onto the overturned boat, where the wounded kraken would be less likely to attack them.

"Without wishing in any way to detract from the lieutenant's undeniable courage, I believe that must constitute the probable extent of his actions. And, to his additional credit, he's never claimed to have done more than that. At any rate, and making all due allowance for the fundamental truthfulness of the children involved, I sincerely doubt that even a *seijin* could throw a harpoon a hundred and fifty yards, swim the same distance in the twinkling of an eye, and then strangle three or four krakens with his bare hands! Indeed, I'm somewhat inclined to the opinion that there's a snowballing effect at work here. Lieutenant Athrawes initially appeared under rather dramatic circumstances, after all. With that in mind, it's not surprising the gossip of the uninformed attributes all sorts of semi-miraculous capabilities to him."

"But you believe it *is* 'the gossip of the uninformed'?"

"Probably not entirely, but in the main, yes, Your Eminence."

"And his purpose here?" Dynnys asked, eyes narrowing very slightly.

"I believe his purpose here is to offer his services as a warrior—an extraordinary one, perhaps, but still a warrior—to the House of Ahrmahk. I believe he genuinely . . . admires King Haarahld, and it's readily apparent that he's deeply attached to young Cayleb."

"You have no evidence of anything . . . deeper than that?" Dynnys pressed.

"None, Your Eminence," Wylsynn said firmly. "I realize there have probably been reports and rumors—some of which may have reached clear to the Temple—of some malevolent purpose on his part. Given the obvious trust he's won from Haarahld and Cayleb, jealousy and spite would certainly have produced those rumors, whether there was any foundation to them or not. And to be realistic, it's unlikely Lieutenant Athrawes is a complete stranger to ambition. He's certainly in an excellent position to rise quite high in the Royal Guard, for example, and I doubt he'd refuse promotion or wealth if they were offered to him.

"On the basis of my own conversations with the man, and with King Haarahld and Crown Prince Cayleb, though, I feel quite confident he has no more malign purpose than that. Indeed, my considered opinion is that this man has a profound respect for God and would never dream of defying God's will."

Dynnys blinked. He couldn't help it. There was a note of absolute certitude in Wylsynn's voice, as if God Himself had whispered in the under-priest's ear. He might be wrong, but there was no way Dynnys was going to shake his belief in this Lieutenant Athrawes' worthiness.

And, truth to tell, the archbishop thought wryly, *if a Wylsynn is prepared to vouch for the man, who are we mere fallible mortals to question that vote of confidence?*

"I see," he said again, after a moment. "Well, Father, I must say you've put my mind at ease on several points this morning. I appreciate that, just as I appreciate your devotion and zeal in attending to these matters."

"I'm very happy to hear that, Your Eminence. And I hope that if there's any other way in which I can be of service to you during your pastoral visit, you'll call upon me."

"Of course, Father." Dynnys rose, extending his right hand across his desk, and Wylsynn bent to kiss the episcopal ring once more. "Go with my blessing, Father."

"Thank you, Your Eminence," Wilson said.

Dynnys reseated himself as the under-priest withdrew, closing the door quietly behind him. The archbishop sat gazing at that door for a few seconds, then turned to Father Symyn at his own desk.

"Well, Symyn, what's next on the morning's agenda?"

▼   ▼   ▼

"This is a really excellent brandy, Zherald," Archbishop Erayk commented, inhaling deeply as he passed the deep, tulip-shaped glass under his nose.

"Yes, it is," Ahdymsyn agreed. "It was a gift from the Prior of Saint Trevyr's." He smiled slightly. "I didn't ask the Prior where it came from."

"Probably just as well," Dynnys agreed with a chuckle, and glanced over his shoulder.

"I think you've put in enough hard work today, Symyn," he told his secretary. "Put down your pen and pour yourself a glass."

"If you're certain, Your Eminence. I don't mind taking a few more notes," Shumakyr said.

"Nonsense!" Dynnys shook his head. "You may be willing to continue making notes, but *I've* put in a long, hard day. I don't intend to discuss anything else on the record tonight."

"Of course, Your Eminence."

The secretary carefully cleaned his pen and put it away, then capped his inkwell and straightened his papers with equal care before closing the cover on his own desk. Then he crossed to the side table and poured himself a glass of brandy as instructed.

The sun had almost disappeared beyond the western horizon outside the windows of Dynnys' office. The archbishop had been in Tellesberg for eighteen days now, and they truly had been arduous ones. Ahdymsyn was forced to concede that Dynnys had applied himself to the many problems facing him with a degree of energy and intensity the bishop executor had never seen out of him before.

"I must say," the archbishop said after a moment, propping his feet on an embroidered ottoman, "that I feel considerably relieved on several fronts. Which isn't to say—" He shot Ahdymsyn a sharp look. "—that I'm not still a little anxious about others."

"Isn't it always that way, Your Eminence?" the bishop executor allowed himself a small, weary smile.

"Yes. Yes it is," Dynnys sighed.

For just an instant, his face looked years older, worn with worry as well as the fatigue of the pace he'd set himself over the past three and a half five-days. Ahdymsyn, to his own surprise, felt a twinge of sympathy which actually had nothing at all—or very little, at least—to do with his own position and ambitions.

"I've drafted my preliminary report," Dynnys continued after another sip of brandy. "I'd appreciate it if you'd glance over it in the morning. Give me the benefit of your own perspective."

"Of course, Your Eminence." Ahdymsyn managed to keep any surprise out of his voice, but the request was unusual, to say the least.

Of course, it's probably not that surprising given how . . . carefully he has to have written it, the bishop executor thought after a moment. *And at least he's not asking me to cosign it!*

He felt a brief flicker of something almost like shame. Whatever else might be true, at least a large part of Dynnys' potential problems were none of his making. He'd never asked for this sudden, unsavory rush of inventiveness.

At least he could say honestly that his intendant had no qualms at all about all of the new devices and ideas. That should help quite a lot, in Ahdymsyn's opinion. Perhaps it wouldn't suit the more vengeful members of the Office of the Inquisition as much as making a few sharp examples would have, but it should at least pour a little water on that particular fire.

As for the other, more fundamental problems of the archbishopric, those had begun before Dynnys ever assumed office. Perhaps he should have dealt with them sooner, but that was a case of being wise after the fact, Ahdymsyn thought. For that matter, he himself clearly hadn't been sufficiently proactive in dealing with Bishop Maikel, not that he intended to admit it to anyone.

Ahdymsyn hadn't taken part in Staynair's private meeting with Dynnys. Only Father Symyn had been present for that in his role as the archbishop's secretary. The bishop executor's impression was that it might have gone better, but at least Staynair couldn't have offered any open defiance. If he had, Dynnys would have had no option but to discipline him, which—thank God!—he hadn't. The last thing anyone needed was for the Group of Four to add concerns over the doctrinal reliability of the local priesthood to the pot, and if the kingdom's senior *bishop* had to be disciplined—!

But they'd manage to avoid that, at least. And if the Group of Four's current worries could just be allayed, even temporarily, they might manage to save the situation after all. The archbishopric only needed a little time—a year or two, perhaps, without the Group of Four intervening to make the situation still worse—to put its house in order. That was all they really needed, he thought, and found himself wondering just how the archbishop had dealt with his own concerns about Bishop Maikel.

Well, I suppose I'll find out tomorrow, won't I? he told himself, and lifted his own brandy glass appreciatively.

.II.

King's Harbor,
Helen Island

H ow does Domynyk feel about Captain Maylyr?" Merlin asked.

He and Cayleb sat at a table under an awning atop the citadel, enjoying a brisk afternoon breeze as they gnawed on spider-crab legs. Gahlvyn Daikyn, Caleb's valet, had a particularly tasty recipe for them, and Merlin had found he was genuinely fond of the local delicacy, although he didn't think he could have matched Cayleb's prodigious, barely-post-adolescent appetite for them even if he'd had a full-sized flesh and blood "stomach" to pack them into.

Now the crown prince took time to swallow—and wash the swallow down with a long draft of beer—before he responded.

"I think he's reasonably satisfied," he said then, and shrugged. "Maylyr's only had a couple of five-days to settle in, after all."

"But Domynyk has a point about how long we've got to let people 'settle in,'" Merlin pointed out in his best devil's advocate manner, and Cayleb's teeth flashed in a smile.

"Yes, he does," he agreed. "And, no, I'm not prepared to override him on a whim. But I think we can give Maylyr another day or so before I order him fed to the krakens."

Merlin chuckled, although mention of feeding anyone to the krakens didn't really strike him as the most humorous possible joke.

"Time really is getting short, I'm afraid," he said after a moment, and Cayleb nodded soberly, his own mood darkening.

"You haven't had any more 'visions' of Gorjah or Rahnyld?" he asked.

"Not of their having any more conversations with representatives of the Council of Vicars." Merlin shook his head. "But Gorjah's been spending a lot more time chatting up Hektor's ambassador. And Rahnyld's had Admiral Gardynyr very quietly getting his navy ready to move if it has to."

"None of which is really much of a surprise," Cayleb pointed out in a voice which sounded much less concerned than Merlin knew he actually was.

"Perhaps not. But the fact that the Council's involved at all is hardly what I'd call good news, Cayleb!"

"Agreed. Agreed! But you heard what Rayjhis had to say right here on this very roof." Cayleb's expression was much grimmer for a moment. "Sooner or later, the members of the Council who fear us would've come out of the shadows, anyway. At least now, thanks to you, we know they're doing it."

"Thanks to me" in more ways than you know, Cayleb, Merlin thought with a spasm of guilt, then shook himself.

"I don't like the odds if they do bring Dohlar in," he said frankly.

"I can't say I'd care for them a lot, myself," Cayleb conceded. "Still, even adding Dohlar and Tarot to the balance sheet, Hektor wouldn't have much better than a three-to-two advantage in hulls."

Merlin gave him a skeptical look, and the crown prince snorted. In fact, as Cayleb knew perfectly well, the official strength of the Royal Charisian Navy, when fully mobilized, was a hundred and thirty galleys, including the fifty in the reserve fleet. Hektor of Corisande had an active-duty strength of fifty, with another thirty in reserve. Nahrmahn of Emerald had forty-five in permanent commission and another twenty-five or thirty in reserve. That gave the two of them a combined active-duty strength of ninety-five with another sixty or so in reserve, or a total of a hundred and fifty, although almost all of them were indivdually smaller and less powerful than their Charisian counterparts.

Tarot's fleet was smaller, with only thirty galleys in permanent commission and no reserve worth mentioning. But the Dohlaran Navy had sixty in permanent commission and another *seventy* in reserve, and their galleys were big, powerful ships, although they were very definitely designed as a coastal force, not for the high seas. So, if Tarot and Dohlar were added to the ranks of Charis' enemies, King Haarahld's hundred and thirty galleys could find themselves opposed by well over three hundred.

"All right," Cayleb said after a moment. "I'll grant you that if they got every hulk in their reserve fleet into commission, they'd have us by better than two to one. But, first, it's unlikely they will manage to get all of them into commission. And, second, Dohlar is over seven thousand miles from here as the wyvern flies . . . and over twenty-three thousand as the ship sails. That's a Shan-wei of a voyage for a batch of coastal galleons, Merlin! And Charis—and our entire navy—is squarely between Dohlar and Corisande. They'd have to get past us before they could combine."

"Which doesn't mean they won't try," Merlin pointed out.

"No, but if they don't coordinate things carefully, we'd be able to smash each wing of their strategy separately. And even using the Church's semaphore, it's going to take time for any operation that complex to be coordinated. You were there when I discussed it with Father and Rayjhis."

Cayleb shrugged.

"I agree with them. It's already early August. We're into midwinter down here, and by the time Erayk's report gets back to the Temple, it's going to be the end of the month, or even September. That means they're going to be heading into fall up north. It takes over a month for even the semaphore system to get a message from the Temple to Manchyr, and from your visions, they haven't even spoken to Hektor yet. So let's say they spend a five-day or two thinking things over, then send a message to Hektor. That means it's going to be somewhere around the middle of November by the time they can hear back from him. And *that* means it's going to be the end of February by the time they can get a second message to him. So, the earliest they should be able to move is going to be very late February or March, which is the middle of winter in Dohlar. Then it's going to take at least seventy days or so for the Dohlaran navy to get any of its ships as far as Charis. So if they get underway by the middle of March, they'll get here sometime in May. Which is the middle of fall again, and only an idiot would fight a sea war in these waters in the middle of storm season."

He shrugged again.

"If I were running the Temple, I'd accept that I was going to have to wait at least another two or three months, which would mean the earliest we'd see them down here would be sometime in the spring. Say October of next year."

"That all sounds perfectly reasonable and reassuring," Merlin said. "The only thing that bothers me about it is that it requires the other side to be smart enough to see the same objections *we* see."

"Granted." Cayleb reached for another spider-crab leg and waved it at Merlin. "At the same time, they don't know about Domynyk and his little surprise."

"No," Merlin agreed. "At least, not so far as I can tell."

"Well, there you are." Cayleb shrugged again and cracked the spider-crab leg to get at the succulent inner meat.

"And how many galleons do we have?" Merlin asked.

"Not as many as I'd like," Cayleb agreed rather indistinctly, then swallowed.

"Not as many as I'd like," he repeated, more clearly. "But if they'll hold off until spring, that will change."

It was Merlin's turn to nod. Commodore Staynair—except it was going to be Admiral Staynair very soon now—had his squadron of galleons up to fifteen, six of them converted merchantships armed solely with carronades. By November, that number would have just about doubled, although many of the additional ships would just be starting their working up exercises at that point. And by next March, the total should be up to almost fifty, many of which—especially the purpose-built units—would carry many more guns than the original Experimental Squadron's units. In addition, Haarahld and High Admiral Seamount had already earmarked almost a dozen largish schooners building in Tellesberg for impressment into naval service.

Unfortunately, it was far from certain they'd be able to effectively arm all their new units as soon as they were built. Howsmyn was working not so minor miracles at the vastly expanded King's Harbor foundry, and his new foundry at Delthak would be pouring its first run of artillery by late October, if all went well. Even so, things were going to be tight, and they'd been forced to effectively strip the entire reserve fleet of its heavy armament already. Which meant that adding fifteen galleons had reduced the Navy's effective strength by fifty galleys.

It also meant they were becoming increasingly strapped for competent galleon captains. Dunkyn Maylyr was a case in point. He was an experienced naval officer, who'd commanded his own ship for over five years, but he was a *galley* captain. He thought like a galley captain, and although he was in the process of becoming an enthusiastic recruit to the concept Merlin had described as "peace through superior firepower," he didn't have very much experience yet in commanding a galleon. Still, he was working hard, and they'd managed to quietly recruit several merchant skippers with previous naval experience. They had plenty of experience managing galleons; it was their *naval* skills which had gotten rusty.

At least Staynair's unyielding concentration on merciless gun drill had paid off. He'd insisted, with Cayleb's strong support, on training every member of every one of his original gun crews as a fully qualified gun *captain*. As a result, they'd been able to provide each ship with a nucleus of trained gun captains as it commissioned, and the Royal Charisian Navy's current gunnery standards were on a totally different plane from anyone else's.

Now if we only had more guns for them to shoot with, he thought sardonically.

"At least Erayk seems to be trying to keep the lid on the pot," he said to Cayleb after a moment.

"I know." Cayleb grimaced. "I'd call the man a toad, if it wouldn't be an insult to all toads. Still, at the moment his own motives are pushing him to do what we want. And Father Paityr's position hasn't hurt anything. All we can do now is wait and see. But if the Council only listens to him for a couple of more months, I'm pretty sure we'll have that break until next year. At which point," the crown prince's smile was not a pleasant expression, "we'll have enough galleons in commission to make them very unhappy."

.III.
Vicar Zahmsyn Trynair's Suite, The Temple

Vicar Zahmsyn Trynair spooned up the last bit of his dessert custard and swallowed it with a sigh of pleasure. A mouthful of water cleansed his palette, and he sat back from the table sipping his wine with a feeling of profound satisfaction.

The August day had been warm, the reports from his bailiffs all indicated his manors were likely to enjoy bumper harvests, and the year's tithing was almost an entire month ahead of schedule. It had been his turn to host the Group of Four's once-a-five-day working supper, and for once, he'd looked forward to it without worrying that anything would affect his digestion afterward.

He'd taken extra pains with this five-day's supper, and his chef had done him proud. Everyone except Clyntahn had obviously reached the point of repletion, and the only flaw in his own pleasure was the reflection that next five-day it would be Magwair's turn to feed them. And Magwair's idea of properly cooked vegetables required them to be boiled into an unappetizing pulp.

"Well," he said in his role as host, "I suppose it's time we got to business." He took another sip of wine. "Personally, I have to say I'm rather relieved by the tenor of Dynnys' dispatches."

"You are, are you?" Clyntahn half-grunted. He leaned forward and helped himself to one of the unclaimed rolls, spreading it liberally with butter and stuffing half of it into his mouth in a single bite.

"I have to agree with Zahmsyn, Zhaspyr," Duchaïrn said mildly. "I know you're not particularly fond of the entire Wylsynn family, but according to Dynnys, Father Paityr went back and reconsidered his original findings very carefully. He continues to insist there's no violation of the Proscriptions. To me, that strongly suggests the reports we've been getting—a lot of them from enemies of Charis, I think it should be noted—truly are exaggerated."

"I see." Clyntahn's response was indistinct. He swallowed the mouthful of bread, washing it down with a hefty gulp of Trynair's expensive wine, and shook his head.

"I might be willing to agree with you, Rhobair," he said then. "If, of course, our *good* Archbishop had told us the truth in his dispatches."

"What?" Trynair sat up straighter, aware Duchairn and Magwair had done the same thing, and looked demandingly at the Grand Inquisitor. "What do you mean, Zhaspyr?"

"I mean I've never trusted that little snot Wylsynn as far as I could spit," Clyntahn replied. "And I had my doubts about Dynnys' reliability, if it came right down to it. So, unbeknownst to our beloved Archbishop of Charis, his new secretary, Father Symyn, is an agent of the Inquisition. And *his* report covers a few things Dynnys inexplicably . . . overlooked."

The Inquisitor's smile was ugly, his eyes bright, and Trynair felt his stomach clench. Clyntahn's hatred for Charis had been bad enough before Paityr Wylsynn was assigned as its intendant. Since then, it had grown even more virulent, but he hadn't mentioned to any of the rest of the Group of Four that he intended to plant one of his own agents on Dynnys. Then again, his office gave him the authority to place agents and investigators anywhere he chose, any time he chose, and Trynair suddenly found himself wondering just how many others he had scattered about. And just whom they were keeping watch on.

Which was all somewhat beside the point at the moment, he supposed.

"Should we gather from what you've just said that your agent—Father Symyn, was it?—disagrees with Dynnys' appraisal of the situation?" he asked.

"Oh, yes, I think you could gather that," Clyntahn said sarcastically.

He finished the wine in his glass picked up the bottle, and poured another glassful, then leaned back in his chair with an expression which mingled triumph, hatred, and genuine worry.

"According to Father Symyn's observations and quiet investigation, Wylsynn's 'reconsideration' of his original findings was limited to a single interview with Haarahld and Cayleb. One at which, I might add, Maikel Staynair was also present . . . having been *invited* by our *dear* Father Paityr.

"Not only that, Archbishop Erayk somehow neglected to mention to us that this same Maikel Staynair has been preaching sedition from Tellesberg Cathedral itself."

"That's a rather serious charge, Zhaspyr," Duchairn observed, after a moment or two, into the sudden silence around the table.

"Staynair should never have been confirmed as Bishop of Tellesberg in the first place," Clyntahn half-snapped. "That position's far too important to be left in the hands of a *Charisian*. But," he waggled one hand, showing his teeth in a caricature of a smile, and his eyes were ugly, "that's all water under the bridge, I suppose. Except that Staynair's been preaching sermons about the fallibility of the Inquisition's judgment."

"Forgive me, Zhaspyr," Trynair said, "but I find that a bit difficult to believe. Surely, Bishop Zherald would have reported any such sermons! And whatever your opinion of young Wylsynn, I can't believe *he* would have allowed such a challenge to Mother Church's authority to pass unreported."

"Oh, you can't, can't you?" Clyntahn's laugh was as ugly as his eyes. "Well, Father Symyn was able to absolutely confirm that Ahdymsyn sent for Staynair following one of his heretical sermons and gave him a royal tongue-lashing. So obviously Dynnys' bishop executor was aware of the problem. And Dynnys had his own little discussion with Staynair, one Father Symyn was present for. Neither Dynnys nor Staynair came right out and admitted what was going on, but it was obvious Dynnys was warning him to keep his mouth shut . . . and that Staynair wasn't what you might call penitent, either. But Dynnys certainly didn't report anything about his need to 'counsel' Staynair to *me*. And I think you'll all agree it's significant that neither he nor Wylsynn has reported a word about it to us even now."

Trynair frowned. Even allowing for Clyntahn's hatred for all things Charisian, he had a point.

"There's another possible aspect to all of this," Magwair said after a moment, and all eyes turned to him.

"What sort of 'aspect,' Allayn?" Duchairn asked.

"I've received a handful of reports about the Charisian Navy." The Temple's captain general shrugged. "Most of them are coming out of Emerald and

Corisande, so I've tended to discount them somewhat. But in light of what Zhaspyr's just said, and particularly in light of the possibility that Wylsynn's been less scrupulous in the discharge of his duties than we'd thought, perhaps I shouldn't have been so quick to do that."

"What sort of reports?" Trynair managed to keep his tone short of an impatient demand, but it wasn't easy.

"Apparently the Charisians have undertaken some major changes in their navy," Magwair replied. "Details are sketchy, but they all agree that in addition to these new rigging plans of theirs, and this new 'cotton gin,' and all of the other . . . innovations they've introduced, they've obviously done something we *don't* know about where their navy is concerned. It's the only explanation for how secretive they're being, or, for that matter, for why they should suddenly be building *galleons* instead of galleys."

There were several moments of intense silence, and then Clyntahn belched. The sound was startling, and Trynair twitched in surprise.

"So," the Grand Inquisitor said, without bothering to apologize, "what do we have here? We have a bishop who's preaching sedition. We have this huge spate of changes and new techniques. We have a kingdom in the process of some sort of secret military buildup. We have a king whose family has a tradition of defiance towards Mother Church, and whose own policies have scarcely been accommodating to her just demands. We have a bishop who's preaching heresy and sedition from his own cathedral. We have an archbishop who's concealing information from us—probably just to cover his own arse, although I wouldn't be prepared to bet *my* soul on that. And we have a so-called intendant who hasn't reported *any* of this to us. What does that sound like to the rest of you?"

"Not good," Magwair grunted. Duchairn and Trynair said nothing, but Clyntahn's venomous summation had shaken them, as well.

"I'm still not convinced the situation is quite that bad," Duchairn said after several seconds. "Still, I'm certainly willing to concede that I'm not as confident of that as I was a few minutes ago. Assuming all of your assumptions are correct, Zhaspyr, what do we do about it?"

"If Staynair's truly preaching sedition, and if neither Ahdymsyn nor Dynnys has reported it to us, I see no option but to summon him—and them—to appear before a proper tribunal," Trynair said.

"And that young whippersnapper Wylsynn, as well," Magwair growled, but Clyntahn shook his head.

"I'm not sure that's the wisest course," he said, and all three of his colleagues looked at him in disbelief.

"Oh, I'm not saying they shouldn't all face the Inquisition, eventually. Or that they shouldn't suffer the full penalty for their actions. But if we summon Staynair to the Temple and he refuses the summons, what happens?"

"He *can't* refuse the summons," Duchairn protested. "The entire matter comes under the authority of the Church's justice."

"And if Haarahld, who's already defied the Church's obvious desires by insisting this man be made Bishop of Tellesberg in the first place, intervenes and prevents the Church courts in Charis from remanding Staynair to the Temple?"

"Surely he's not prepared to go that far," Trynair argued, yet he heard a certain lack of certitude in his own voice.

"He's making preparations for *something*," Clyntahn pointed out. "And don't forget how many of the clergy in Charis are native Charisians. I've argued for years that we should have assigned more non-Charisians to that pesthole, but would anyone listen? No. And now what do we have? Barely the tenth part—if that much—of the clergy is from outside Haarahld's kingdom. If he should choose to defy Mother Church, at least a sizable minority of those Charisians are likely to support him. And then what do we have?"

A fresh, even more profound, silence descended upon the dining room.

It was amazing, Trynair thought, how swiftly his own mood had gone from one of pleasant content to something very, very different. But if Clyntahn was correct, if his worst-case assumptions proved accurate, they would be looking at a nightmare the Church had never confronted before: the armed resistance of an entire kingdom to God's will. And if that resistance prospered, or even if it simply took some time to quell—which was scarcely unlikely, given Charis' sheer physical distance from the Temple and the Temple Lands—its example might well spread.

The Chancellor shuddered at the thought of what might happen if Siddarmark, for example, were to fall prey to the same madness. And if Charis were allowed to continue its military expansion—an expansion which, it now seemed, might be violating the Proscriptions after all—it might well seize Emerald, Corisande, and even Chisholm by force of arms before the Church could mobilize against it in sufficient strength. And if *that* happened . . .

"So how do we avoid all of that, Zhaspyr?" he asked finally, and Clyntahn shrugged.

"I think the answer to that is fairly simple, really."

His colleagues' surprise was obvious, and he chuckled, the sound harsh, almost hungry.

"Of course it is. Zahmsyn, you yourself started putting the pieces into place to support Hektor if it proved necessary. Well, I submit that it *has* proven necessary. I think our simplest, safest, and best course is to go ahead and support Hektor and Nahrmahn, but as the Knights of the Temple Lands, not the Council of Vicars. Bahrmyn's in Manchyr on his own pastoral visit right this minute, so tell him to . . . speak frankly with Hektor. Then bring in Dohlar and Tarot—and Chisholm, for that matter—but Mother Church stays out of it. The Temple Lands can support our friends—just forgiving Rahnyld the interest on all the loan payments he still owes the Treasury would be more than enough to buy *his* support—but the Church and the Inquisition will have nothing to do with it. Until, of course, Haarahld's been defeated."

"And then?" Trynair asked, trying to ignore the queasiness stirring in the pit of his stomach.

"I think we can count on Hektor and Nahrmahn to wreak sufficient havoc on Charis. If necessary, we can . . . encourage them just a bit. But by the time Tellesberg and most of their other major towns and cities have been burned, and their precious merchant fleet's been destroyed, what's left of Charis will be destitute, desperate for aid. At which point, Mother Church's loving arms will reach out to her distressed children. The Treasury will pour gold into rebuilding their shattered homes, and in the process, the Office of Inquisition will be perfectly placed to purge the unreliable elements of the priesthood."

He smiled with cold, vicious satisfaction.

"In short, I believe we're in a position to solve the Charisian problem for generations to come, my friends."

SEPTEMBER,
YEAR OF GOD 891

Prince Hektor of Corisande watched with carefully hidden anxiety as Borys Bahrmyn, the Archbishop of Corisande, strode past the throne room guards and paced gravely down the runner of carpet towards his throne. The guards watched him pass with carefully expressionless faces, although the stiff set of their spines showed how little they cared for their instructions, then closed the throne room doors behind him . . . from the other side.

The ragged ends of a late-winter thunderstorm had cleared earlier in the day, and sunlight through the stained glass windows threw flowing patterns across the floor. The gems on the archbishop's formal priest's cap sparkled whenever he stepped through one of those pools of light, and his expression was solemn.

Bahrmyn reached the foot of the dais and bowed his head gravely. Then he straightened, and Hektor inclined his own head in a gesture of respect.

"I must admit, Your Eminence," he said, "that I was a bit startled, and more than a little apprehensive, when I received your message."

"I apologize for that, Your Highness," Bahrmyn said. "Only the most pressing circumstances would have led me to request an audience on such short notice."

"I realize that. Which explains my apprehension," Hektor replied, showing his teeth in a slightly tight smile, although "request" was a pale choice of verb. The archbishop's message had been a none too thinly veiled peremptory demand for an immediate—and completely private—meeting.

Had he been anyone else, Hektor would have told him, none too politely, what he could do with his "request." Since he was who he was, however, the prince had had no choice but to comply. Which explained his guardsmen's unhappiness.

And his own.

"The world knows that you are your own first councillor, Your Highness." Bahrmyn produced a small smile of his own. "Were you not, I would undoubtedly have made whoever served you in that capacity . . . apprehensive instead of yourself."

"An excellent point, Your Eminence. Perhaps I should consider changing my arrangements."

Bahrmyn chuckled dutifully, and Hektor drew a deep breath.

"Nonetheless, Your Eminence, you did request the audience, and you're here now. So, how may the League of Corisande assist Mother Church?"

"Actually, Your Highness," Bahrmyn said slowly, "I'm not really here in Mother Church's name this morning." Hektor's eyes widened in surprise, and the archbishop shrugged slightly. "I *am* here on behalf of Chancellor Trynair, but not in his capacity as Vicar Zahmsyn."

Hektor's widened eyes narrowed in sudden speculation as he recognized Bahrmyn's distinction. As Chancellor, Trynair might speak officially for the Council of Vicars, or for the Knights of the Temple Lands; as Vicar Zahmsyn, he could speak only for the Church. Which put an abruptly different face on Bahrmyn's "request" for a completely private audience.

"I see," he said, after a moment. "In that case, how may be League serve the Chancellor?"

"In point of fact, Your Highness, I'm here to discuss how the Chancellor can be of assistance to *you*."

"Indeed?" Hektor kept his voice and expression alike under careful control, but it was hard.

"Your Highness," Bahrmyn said, "I've been instructed to speak very frankly, without the normal diplomatic circumlocutions. With your permission, that's precisely what I intend to do."

He raised his eyebrows, and Hektor nodded.

"Thank you, Your Highness." Bahrmyn bent his head once more, then cleared his throat.

"Your Highness, all the world knows that you and Prince Nahrmahn have, for some years now, found yourselves increasingly at odds with Haarahld of Charis. Mother Church, of course, must always be grieved when those she's anointed as secular rulers view one another with enmity. Nonetheless, Chancellor Trynair recognizes, as one charged with heavy secular responsibilities of his own in the Temple Lands, that even reasonable men may sometimes find themselves on opposite sides of irreconcilable differences. When that happens, it may result in open war. Other times, it may result in an ongoing, festering wound which poisons all about it."

The archbishop had Hektor's undivided attention. The prince made himself sit calmly in his throne, listening only attentively, but if Bahrmyn was headed where he *appeared* to be headed . . .

"Although both Corisande and Charis are far from the Temple Lands, the fact that between your lands—and, of course, Emerald—your ships carry so much of the world's cargoes means that any quarrel between you affects everyone who depends upon that shipping. The Knights of the Temple Lands are no different from any other rulers in that respect, and they've watched with increasing alarm as the hostility between you and Haarahld has deepened.

"Until recently, however, they've embraced a policy of neutrality in this particular dispute. That seemed the most reasonable course for them to pursue. But in recent months, the Knights of the Temple Lands have become aware of what they believe represents a dangerous shift in policy on Charis' part. Since the ecclesiastical courts decided against Haarahld's protégé, Breygart, in the matter of the Hanth succession, he appears to have resolved to settle the quarrel between you—and, no doubt, to 'avenge himself' for the part he seems to feel you played in the succession dispute—by force of arms."

Hektor managed not to blink. Despite his own concerns over the reports from Maysahn and Makferzahn, he rather doubted, as he'd told Earl Coris, that Haarahld had any intention of attacking Emerald or Corisande anytime soon. If nothing else, fear of the Church's possible reaction would have to hold him in check.

"Under most circumstances, I suppose," Bahrmyn continued, "any quarrel, even a war, fought this far from the Temple Lands might not appear to be of great consequence to the Knights of the Temple Lands. Given, however, Haarahld's obvious resentment of Mother Church's decision against him, and the fact that he's clearly contemplating a war of conquest against his neighbors, and the fact that should he succeed in defeating you and Nahrmahn, he would acquire near dictatorial control of so much of the world's seagoing trade, they simply can't view his clear intentions with equanimity. Indeed, they believe Haarahld's ambition poses a clear threat to that peaceable state of relations Mother Church is charged to maintain between all lands.

"Mother Church herself may not, of course, take sides in a purely secular conflict, unless one side should be proven to be in violation of God's law or plan. No one would suggest those circumstances apply at this time. But in their capacities as rulers, the Knights of the Temple Lands would be derelict in the discharge of their responsibilities to their own lands and subjects if they allowed such aggression to prosper.

"Therefore, Chancellor Trynair has charged me to inform you that the Knights of the Temple Lands have decided the time to restrain Charisian aggression has come. They are prepared to assist you and Prince Nahrmahn against Haarahld's overweening ambitions."

Bahrmyn paused, and it was Hektor's turn to clear his throat.

"Obviously, Your Eminence," he said, "I must welcome this evidence of the Chancellor's support. I do, I assure you. However, gratifying though it is, I fear the Knights of the Temple Lands are far away. And even were they not, they possess but little naval strength."

"Of themselves, that's certainly true, Your Highness," Bahrmyn agreed. "However, you aren't the only prince to whom the Chancellor has communicated his concerns over Charis. It's become obvious to him that Charis' ultimate ambition is to secure control of all the world's maritime trade for its own selfish profit. Accordingly, the interests of other lands, beyond Corisande and Emerald, are equally, if less immediately, threatened. In the Chancellor's view, it would be only just for those other lands to bear their fair share of the burden of defeating that ambition."

"I see."

Hektor could scarcely believe what he was hearing, and he cautioned himself to go slowly. This totally unanticipated offer went far beyond anything he'd ever dared allow himself to hope for, and the temptation to seize it instantly was overwhelming. But he had no idea what had prompted Trynair to send Bahrmyn to him, nor did he see where the Chancellor's own ultimate objectives might lie. On the other hand . . .

"May I know which 'other lands' the Chancellor has in mind, Your Eminence?"

"Of course, Your Highness. I'm instructed to tell you that the Chancellor has been in contact with King Rahnyld of Dohlar. He's also suggested to King Gorjah of Tarot that he might, perhaps, positively consider any initiatives your ambassador might extend. And it's also my understanding that Archbishop Zherohm has been charged to deliver a message to Queen Sharleyan, as well, urging her to support your efforts in this matter."

Despite all he could do, Hektor's jaw dropped slightly. Probably the only person in the entire world who hated him more than Haaralhd of Charis did was Sharleyan of Chisholm, yet even she would be unable to defy a "suggestion" from Trynair to support him. Which only made the Chancellor's offer even more breathtaking. An alliance of virtually *every* other maritime power against Charis? With the backing of the Temple Lands and their enormous wealth? And, whatever fiction Trynair might choose to maintain, the implicit support of the Church itself?

"Your Eminence, I'm . . . I'm stunned," he said, with total honesty. "I had no idea the Chancellor was so well informed on affairs so far from the Temple Lands. Nor did I realize how clearly he saw the ambitions of Charis. Obviously, if he feels this strongly about it, I would be eternally grateful for any assistance he or the Knights of the Temple Lands might be able to provide."

"Then should I inform the Chancellor you accept his offer?"

"Of course you should, Your Eminence!"

"I'm sure he'll be overjoyed to hear that, Your Highness." Bahrmyn smiled broadly. "And he's instructed me to tell you, should you accept his offer of assistance, that the messengers of the Temple will be at your disposal for coordinating with your new allies."

"Please tell him I am deeply, deeply grateful for all he's so generously offered," Hektor said sincerely.

"I will," Bahrmyn said. "And now, Your Highness, I'm sure you have a great deal to attend to, and with your permission, I'll leave you to it."

Queen Sharleyan of Chisholm stormed into the council chamber like a hurricane. Sharleyan wasn't a particularly tall woman, but at the moment, that was easy to overlook. Her dark hair seemed to crackle, her dark brown eyes flashed with fury, and her slender, petite frame seemed coiled like an overstrained cable as her quick, angry stride carried her across the chamber to the chair at the head of the table.

She seated herself, half-crouched forward in her chair, and glared at the two men who had awaited her. Neither one of them was at all happy to find himself the object of their youthful monarch's furious gaze, although both of them knew her anger wasn't directed at them.

She sat without speaking for perhaps ten seconds, then made herself draw a deep breath and sit back.

"Mahrak, Sir Lewk." Her voice was sharp, clipped. "I suppose I ought to say good afternoon, not that there's anything *good* about it."

Mahrak Sandyrs, Baron Green Mountain and First Councillor of the Kingdom of Chisholm, winced slightly. He knew that tone, not that he blamed her for it today.

"Has Mahrak brought you up to date, Sir Lewk?" the queen asked.

"Not really, Your Majesty," Sir Lewk Cohlmyn, the Earl of Sharpfield, replied cautiously. Sharpfield was the senior admiral of the Chisholm Navy, and he was more at home on a galley's quarterdeck then he was with the political maneuverings which routinely went on at court. "I arrived only a few moments before you did, and he hasn't had time to give me more than the very bare bones. I know there was some sort of message from the Church, and that whatever it was affects the Navy, and that's about all."

"Then let me give you the summary version," Sharleyan said harshly. "This morning, Archbishop Zherohm requested—no, *demanded*—an audience. Obviously, I granted it. And at that audience, he informed me that Chancellor Trynair *requires* us to support Hektor of Corisande against Charis."

"*What?*"

Surprise startled the question out of Sharpfield. He gawked at his queen, then turned to stare at the first councillor. After a moment, he shook himself and turned back to Sharleyan.

"Your pardon, Your Majesty. That was . . . unseemly of me." He seemed to take a certain comfort from the familiar veneer of courtesy. "Mahrak—Baron

Green Mountain—had told me the Archbishop's message was insulting and demanding, but I had no idea Vyncyt had said anything like *that!*"

"Well, unfortunately, he did," Sharleyan grated. Fresh fury flickered in her eyes, but then her nostrils flared and she inhaled once more.

"He did," she said, more calmly. "And he wasn't especially polite. Obviously, he knows how we feel about Hektor here in Chisholm, but it's clear the Chancellor—speaking, of course, for the Knights of the Temple Lands, not for Mother Church—doesn't care."

"What sort of 'support' are we expected to provide, Your Majesty?" Sharpfield asked warily, and the queen smiled thinly.

"Exactly what you're obviously afraid we are, judging by your tone," she said. "We are required to provide our maximum possible naval support, under Hektor's command, against the Royal Charisian Navy."

"That's insane!" Sharpfield said. "We're probably the only people Hektor hates as much as he hates Haarahld!"

"Probably not quite that much," Green Mountain disagreed. "But I'll grant you, we're almost certainly second on his list. Or possibly third. He has to have a slot in his plans for betraying Nahrmahn, after all."

"But they're asking us to help our worst enemy destroy our most likely ally!" Sharpfield protested.

"No, they aren't asking us to," Sharleyan said. "They're *ordering* us to. And, unfortunately," some of the fire seemed to leak out of her eyes, and her slender shoulders slumped, "I don't think we have any option but to obey."

"Your Majesty," Sharpfield said, "if we have no choice but to obey, then, obviously, I'll follow whatever orders you give me. But Mahrak is right. If Hektor succeeds in defeating Charis—and with the Temple Lands backing him, ultimately, I don't see how he can fail to—then he'll turn on us as soon afterward as he can. He'll be planning for that from the outset, and if he can, you know who he'll arrange to have suffer the heaviest losses. His navy's already bigger than ours, and his building capacity's greater, as well. If we take significant losses against Charis, it will only be a matter of time, and not much of it, before he attacks *us*."

"I know, I know," Sharleyan sighed. She leaned forward, propping her elbows on the polished table, and massaged her closed eyelids. Then she lowered her hands and looked at Green Mountain.

"Have you thought of any way out, Mahrak?" she asked, and for just a moment she looked even younger than her age.

The silver-haired first councillor had been almost a surrogate father to the barely teenaged girl who'd inherited the throne of Chisholm eleven years before, following her father's death in battle against a Trellheim piracy confederacy subsidized (unofficially) by Corisande. The two of them had weathered more than one potentially deadly crisis during that time, but now his expression was grim as he looked back at her.

"No, Your Majesty," he said heavily. "I've considered every alternative I could think of, and none of them will work. We can't possibly defy Trynair and the Group of Four over this."

"But Sir Lewk is right," she said almost desperately. "If—when—Hektor wins, he'll turn on us the moment he can. And without Charis to offset his power, we can't possibly defeat him. So whether we obey Traynyr's orders or not, we'll still lose in the end."

"I understand, Your Majesty."

Green Mountain rubbed his forehead. Very few people had expected young Queen Sharleyan to *stay* on her father's throne. That was partly because they'd underestimated her, but even more, perhaps, because they'd left Mahrak Sandyrs out of their calculations. But this time, not even the first councillor could see a way out.

"I understand," he repeated, "but if we defy Trynair, we know what will happen. If we obey him, there may still be some way we can stave Hektor off afterwards. If nothing else, it's possible Trynair will be unwilling to allow Hektor to become too powerful. In that case, we'll almost certainly be the only kingdom they could support as a counterweight."

"Forgive me, Your Majesty," Sharpset said, "but it's not that certain a thing that Hektor and Nahrmahn can defeat Charis, even with our support. Our combined fleets would outnumber Haarahld's by a considerable margin, but his galleys are bigger and individually more powerful. And, much as it pains me to admit it, his captains and crews are better than ours are. He'll try to catch isolated detachments of our fleet and chop them up. Even if he's forced to offer battle against unfavorable odds, he'll probably give at least as good as he gets. And if nothing else, he could choose to remain in port, behind the Keys and Lock Island, and engage only to defend the straits. We won't have enough of an advantage to fight our way through such narrow passages. If he holes up in the Throat, he can stay there until we're forced to disperse our forces once more, in which case the odds of Hektor's dealing him a knockout blow would be less than even, at best."

"I'm sorry, Sir Lewk," Sharleyan said. "I forgot to tell you. According to Vyncyt, we're not the only 'allies' Trynair's providing for Hektor. He's also adding Tarot and Dohlar to the list."

Sharpset looked at her for a moment, then shook his head slowly.

"What in Heaven's name could Charis have done to provoke this sort of reaction?"

"I don't know," Sharleyan said frankly. "The official line is that Haarahld intends to attack Hektor, and the Knights of the Temple Lands are concerned by his plans of aggression and evident desire to secure total control of all the world's merchant shipping."

Sharpset's eyes widened in disbelief, and she gave a sharp, harsh crack of laughter.

"It's all dragon shit, of course, My Lord!" she said scornfully. "My best guess is that Clyntahn's really behind it. He doesn't trust *any* of us, this far away from the

Temple, and all these new departures coming out of Charis—the new ships, the new spinning and weaving, the new numbers—have to've flicked him on the raw. So this is his response. What else should we expect out of that fornicating pig?"

"Your Majesty," Green Mountain said quietly. She looked at him, and he shook his head.

"Very well, Mahrak," she said after a moment, her tone less caustic but heavier, "I'll watch my tongue. But that doesn't make anything I just said untrue. Nor does it change the fact that if they actually do manage to combine our fleet with Hektor's, Nahrmahn's, Dohlar's, and even Tarot's, Charis is doomed."

"No, it doesn't," Green Mountain agreed. He sat back in his own chair, bracing his forearms on the armrests. "On the other hand, with that much other naval strength committed, even Hektor shouldn't need our full fleet to defeat Haarahld."

"And?" Sharleyan prompted when the first councilor paused.

"And over half our fleet is laid up in reserve, Your Majesty. Nor did we have any advance warning that we were going to be required to support our good friend and neighbor against the vicious aggression of Charis." Green Mountain's smile would have curdled fresh milk. "Under the circumstances, I don't see how anyone could find it surprising if we were to . . . experience some difficulties mobilizing our strength."

He paused again, and there was silence around the table once more. But this time, it was a thoughtful, calculating silence.

"That could be a risky game, Mahrak," Sharpfield said finally. "This business about the Knights of the Temple Lands is nonsense. It's the *Church* behind this, and that means every under-priest and sexton in the Kingdom would be a potential spy. If Trynair—or, worse, Clyntahn—decides we've deliberately held back . . ."

He let his voice trail off, and shrugged.

"Yes, it could be risky," Sharleyan agreed. "On the other hand, Mahrak has a point. You were just telling Parliament last month what poor shape the reserve is in, how far our supplies of spars and cordage have been drawn down to meet the active fleet's needs. All of that's on the official record."

"And, Lewk," Green Mountain said, "you've been complaining for years about all the incompetent grafters in the Navy's administration. Look at it this way. If we see to it that the directives go to those incompetents you've been trying to get rid of for so long, they're *bound* to screw up, even without a little judicious assistance from us. And when they do, not only will it keep a sizable chunk of our own Navy right here, safely out of harm's way, but when Trynair demands to know what happened, we'll simply tell him." The first councillor smiled unpleasantly. "Do you really think the patrons who've been protecting them this far will do the same thing when we offer them up to appease Mother Church's ire?"

"You make it sound very tempting, Mahrak," Sharpset said with a chuckle which carried at least some genuine, if grim, amusement.

"I think Mahrak's right." Sharleyan tossed her regal head. "It's not much, but it's the best we can do. And I think we'll probably be able to get away with it. Which may let us stave off disaster for at least a little while. But if the Church is willing to do this to Charis for no better reason than the Grand Inquisitor's temper, then, ultimately, no one is safe. And when Clyntahn doesn't have *Charis* to suspect anymore, he's going to fasten on someone else, equally far away."

"You may be right, Your Majesty," Green Mountain said heavily. "In fact, you probably are. It's not like we haven't seen this situation building for a long time now, however little we might have expected it all to explode like a powder magazine right this moment. But all we can do is the best we can do."

"I know." Sharleyan sighed again, her expression sad. "You know," she said, almost whimsically, "if I had my choice of who to support, I'd pick Haarahld in a heartbeat. In fact, if I thought he had a single chance of surviving, I'd be very tempted to throw my lot in with his right now, even with the Church on the other side."

"Then perhaps it's just as well he *doesn't* have a chance of surviving, Your Majesty," Green Mountain said gently. She looked at him, and his smile was as sad as her own had been. "He might have a *single* chance of beating off this attack, Your Majesty. But ultimately, with the Church against him—?"

The first councillor shook his head.

"I, too, respect Haarahld," he said. "And I would infinitely prefer an alliance with him to one with Hektor. But Charis is doomed, Your Majesty. We can't change that."

"I know," Sharleyan said softly. "I know."

.III.
Royal Palace,
Tellesberg

How bad is it?" Earl Gray Harbor asked.

Oil lamps burned brightly, illuminating the Privy Council chamber, and a huge chart was spread out across the table. Copied from the "Archangel Hastings'" maps, it showed all of Charis and stretched as far east as the western coast of the island of Zebediah. To the west, it showed the Kingdom of Tarot, the eastern coast of Armageddon Reef, and most of the Sea of Justice.

Gray Harbor was there, and King Haarahld, but most of the Council was absent. Wave Thunder sat in his accustomed place, and Bishop Maikel sat to the king's left, while Merlin and Cayleb sat together, facing the king down the length of the polished table. Lieutenant Falkhan stood at Cayleb's shoulder, and the prince wore a scruffy-looking tunic and well-worn trousers. They'd made a fast passage back from Helen Island aboard one of the Navy's new schooners, and Cayleb hadn't bothered to change into court dress.

Aside from the six of them, the council chamber was empty as Gray Harbor's question hung in the air.

"About as bad as it could be," Cayleb said grimly, after a moment. He nodded sideways at Merlin. "According to Merlin's visions, the Group of Four's obviously decided it's time to eliminate Charis once and for all."

"What have you seen, *Seijin* Merlin?" Bishop Maikel asked softly, and Merlin looked at him.

"Go ahead and answer him, please, Merlin," Haarahld said. Merlin looked at the king, in turn, and Haarahld smiled wearily. "I keep no secrets from my confessor. Of course, I understand *he* keeps a few from his religious superiors."

"The seal of the confessional is inviolable, Your Majesty," Staynair said serenely.

"Even against the demands of your own archbishop?" Haarahld's tone was that of a man engaged in a long-standing discussion.

"The conscience of a priest, and what he believes God requires of him, outweigh the demands of any mortal power," Staynair replied. Merlin's eyes widened slightly at hearing such a statement out of a bishop of the Church, even now, but Staynair continued in that same, calm voice. "That would be true even if the archbishop demanding I violate the seal of the confessional were worthy of the ring he wears. Which, unfortunately, he isn't."

"You see, Merlin?" Haarahld produced another smile. This one looked genuine, almost lighthearted. "What's a monarch to do when he falls into the hands of a spiritual counselor like this one?"

"I don't know, Your Majesty," Merlin said, after a moment. "But a king could find himself in far worse company, I believe." He half-rose and bowed to the bishop.

"I would prefer to hope we won't all find ourselves giving a personal account to God 'in my company' in the immediate future, *Seijin* Merlin," Staynair said dryly. "So, if you please, tell us what you've seen."

"Of course, Your Eminence."

Merlin seated himself once more, then cleared his throat.

"I don't know what exactly was in Archbishop Erayk's dispatches," he began. "Based on what I'd seen and heard during his pastoral visit, it seemed clear he intended to be as reassuring and placating as possible, if only to protect himself. If that's what he meant to do, though, he obviously failed. Chancellor Trynair's agents have been in contact with Hektor, Sharleyan, Rahnyld, and Gorjah. They *haven't* contacted Nahrmahn yet, but I expect they intended to. There was a nasty storm in the Chisholm Sea last five-day. My guess is that the courier boat crossing the water gap from Chisholm to Eraystor got caught in it. At any rate, I can't see them putting this together without bringing him in on it, especially since

Archbishop Borys specifically suggested that they concentrate their forces forward at Eraystor Bay."

He shrugged, and continued.

"Hektor, obviously, was delighted to hear from the 'Knights of the Temple Lands' and fell all over himself accepting their offer of support. Sharleyan was less pleased about it. In fact, she was furious, but she and Green Mountain can't see any way to refuse and survive.

"Gorjah's not quite so indecently happy about it as Hektor, and he probably wouldn't have had the courage to contemplate switching sides on his own. But with Makgregair leaning on him for Trynair, he's informed Hektor's ambassador that Hektor can count on the Tarotisian Navy, as well."

"And Rahnyld?" Staynair asked as Merlin paused.

"And Rahnyld is almost as delighted by the prospect as Hektor," Merlin said flatly. "He's up to his eyebrows in debt to the Temple, and Trynair's agreed to forgive the interest on almost all his loans. Not only that, but the Knights of the Temple Lands have offered lucrative subsidies to Dohlar, Tarot, and even Chisholm to help defray their military expenses. As Rahnyld sees it, he gets plenty of return for virtually no out-of-pocket expenses of his own—aside, of course, from any of his subjects who may happen to get killed along the way—plus removing Charis from the list of competing maritime powers."

"I'll wager his navy commanders are less delighted than he is," Haarahld said with a grim smile.

"Malikai thinks it's a splendid idea," Merlin replied. "Thirsk is a lot less enthusiastic. Not that he's going to say so, when the King's so pleased about the entire thing."

"That's because Thirsk is a seaman, and Malikai isn't, even if he is Rahnyld's 'high admiral,'" Haarahld said.

"I'm afraid I really know very little about the two of them, Your Majesty," Merlin said, and Haarahld snorted.

"The Earl of Thirsk is about as sound a sailor as you're going to find in most navies. In my opinion, which is admittedly biased, I don't think he's as good as *my* admirals, but he's no fool, and he recognizes exactly what Trynair and Clyntahn are telling his navy to do. And how ill-suited his ships are to the task.

"Duke Malikai, on the other hand, *isn't* a seaman. He doesn't need to be; he has the birth and connections to command their navy, anyway. At heart, he thinks like an army commander, not an admiral. In fact, their navy's officially under their army's orders, and I'm sure he doesn't have the least conception of what a voyage of fourteen or fifteen thousand miles is going to be like."

"It may not be as bad for them as we'd like it to be, Father," Cayleb said quietly. The king looked at him, and he shrugged unhappily. "The Council's representatives have also been in touch with the Emperor, and with the Prince of Selkar and the Prince of Maratha. They've 'requested' permission for Dohlar to use their harbors along the way."

"I see." Haarahld sat back and inhaled deeply. Then it was his turn to shrug.

"I see," he repeated, "and it will make a difference. But they're still going to be operating at the end of a supply line—and a line of retreat—thousands of miles long. That's going to have an effect, especially on their morale and aggressiveness, and so is the sheer wear and tear their ships are going to experience. Especially after they clear Samson's Land and have to cross the Sea of Justice." He smiled thinly. "Their galleys are less well suited to blue water even than ours are, and ours would have a hard enough time in those waters. And even without that, their bottoms are going to be foul, their gear's going to be worn, and unless I'm seriously mistaken, they're probably going to have managed to lose at least a few ships in transit, even if they have good weather all the way."

"That's true enough, Your Majesty," Gray Harbor said, "but it sounds as if the Group of Four's moving much faster than we'd allowed for."

"They are," Merlin agreed. "In fact, that's what disturbs *me* the most, in a lot of ways, My Lord. Archbishop Zherohm called on Sharleyan on the same day Archbishop Borys broached the entire idea to Hektor. They may want to preserve the illusion that Hektor's in charge, but it's obvious Trynair and the others are the puppetmasters. The Group of Four is telling Hektor's new 'allies' what to do before Hektor even knows he *has* them, and when the time comes, someone—probably Magwair—is going to be the one really giving their navies their orders."

"Which suggests they've decided they have to move much more rapidly than we'd believed they could," Gray Harbor said, nodding sharply.

"Which, in turn, suggests we'll have less time to prepare than we'd hoped," Cayleb added harshly.

"You're right." His father nodded in turn and puffed out his cheeks thoughtfully.

"All right," he said after a moment. "Let's assume Trynair and Magwair set this whole plan they and their cronies have come up with—and I'll bet you it was really Clyntahn's idea—into motion as soon as they hear back from Hektor. It's the middle of September. Hektor's acceptance can be back in the Temple by early October. If Magwair immediately sends the order to Rahnyld to get his fleet underway, it could be at sea by the third five-day of October."

He ran a fingertip across the chart, north and west of Armageddon Reef, and his eyes were intent.

"Assuming it doesn't run into any storms or other misadventures along the way, it could be as far as the Cauldron by, say, the end of November or the first couple of five-days of February. What they *ought* to do is take their time and bring them up the Howard and Haven coasts, then in across the north coast of Tarot. They're going to take a beating, whatever happens, and any seaman would know they're going to need to refit before they're really fit for battle. So they ought to send them to Tarot and allow a month or so for them to recover there before continuing on across the southern stretches of the Anvil and around to Eraystor."

He tapped the waters between Tarot and Charis with his finger, then paused. He looked around the table for any disagreement with his calculations, but he saw only nods.

"In that respect, the fact that Magwair's no seaman and they're in such a hurry may work for us. I'm not going to count on that until we know more, but if we're really, really lucky, he'll try to send them across the Parker Sea to come down around MacPherson's Lament.

"As I say, I'm not going to count on that, but I am going to assume Hektor's already started fully manning his active galleys and mobilizing his reserves," he continued. "And Nahrmahn's going to do the same, as soon as they get around to telling him about the new arrangement. Assuming the fat little bugger doesn't do us all a favor and drop dead of apoplexy when he finds out, at least.

"That's unlikely to happen, unfortunately. But he and Hektor will both probably need at least two months to fit out and man the reserves. So, Hektor can probably be ready to move at least a couple of five-days before Thirsk and Malikai could rendezvous with Gorjah's ships. Nahrmahn's probably supposed to be ready by the same time, under Magwair's plans. Unless they get word to him quickly, though, he's going to be late getting his full strength manned and ready. On the other hand, he's a lot closer to us, so he's got less passage time to worry about."

The king paused again, eyes thoughtful as he brooded down at the chart. Those eyes moved back and forth for several seconds, and then he nodded yet again.

"Since we're not supposed to know anything about this, and since the people planning this have even less naval experience than Malikai, they'll probably expect to have the advantage of strategic surprise. There's virtually no chance anyone could actually manage to move something the size of the Dohlaran Navy all the way to Charis without our finding out about it well before it got here, but they won't think that way. So, what they'll probably do, is use Nahrmahn's, Hektor's, and Sharleyan's forces to occupy our attention and tie us down defending Rock Shoal Bay and the Throat. Hopefully with a threat sufficiently serious to keep us from diverting any of our own strength from the immediate confrontation even if we figure out Dohlar and Tarot are coming."

His fingertip moved back to the Charis Sea, between Margaret's Land and Emerald.

"If they're feeling really clever, they may try to pincer us between—let's call them the 'Northern Force' and the 'Southern Force'—at sea. That sort of thinking would appeal to a planner who's basically a land animal and who's accustomed to passing messages between widely separated locations faster than anyone else can.

"If they're *smart*, on the other hand, they'll simply combine everything they've got into one huge fleet and throw it straight at us."

His right hand clenched into a fist and thumped the waters off Rock Shoal Bay.

"How bad would the odds be in that case, Haarahld?" Bishop Maikel asked quietly.

"Bad," the king replied frankly, sitting back from the table and laying his forearms on his chair's armrests. "Assuming Hektor and Nahrmahn are able to get all their reserve galleys manned, and that Rahnyld and Gorjah can do the same, they can muster about three hundred and twenty between them. Chisholm has thirty in active service, and another fifty in reserve, so if Sharleyan's entire fleet comes in, they'll have roughly four hundred.

"We, on the other hand, are down to the eighty galleys of the active fleet, with no remaining reserve fleet, and right this minute we have a total of fifteen galleons in full service and another six, all converted merchantmen, in the process of working up. Assuming the Dohlaran Navy doesn't arrive in our waters until the first five-day of February, we'll have somewhere around thirty-five or thirty-six in service and another fifteen or sixteen working up. So call it a total of a hundred and twenty or so of all types, galleys and galleons combined."

"Don't forget the schooners, Father," Cayleb said. "We'll have at least twelve of them, as well."

"True." Haarahld nodded. "On the other hand, they won't be very heavily armed, and they don't have ships' companies the size of the galleons."

"And even *with* them, we'll still be outnumbered on the order of four-to-one," Staynair said.

"Exactly, Maikel," the king agreed.

"If we concentrate on defending the Bay, we could offset a lot of their numerical advantage," Gray Harbor observed, gazing down at the chart. "If we concede Rock Shoal Bay and make our stand at Lock Island, they'll only be able to come at us head-on in restricted waters."

"No." Haarahld shook his head decisively. "Oh, I agree with what you just said, Rayjhis. But if we concede the initiative to them, we lose. If we get a strong easterly—unlikely, I'll admit, but more likely in the spring than any other time—we could be pinned inside Lock Island and the Keys. Besides, a close action in the North Channel would be so constricted it would deprive us of most of the advantages Seamount, Olyvyr, and Merlin built the galleons to exploit. They're designed to stand off and pound galleys with artillery, not for that sort of close-in melee. If we could suck them in—convince them to attack us head-on, as you say—*before* they know about the galleons, the sheer shock of our firepower *might* be able to wreak enough damage—and inflict enough panic—to drive them off. But it might not, too, and if they keep coming, they'll have the numbers to absorb all the damage we can hand out and still beat us. They'll pay a heavy price, but they can do it.

"Or, if they're smarter than that, they may simply refuse to cooperate by seeking battle at all. They'll have the numbers to blockade us where we are and ignore us, *and* they'll have the shipping available to lift an entire army from Emerald and Corisande and land it in Rock Shoal Bay to attack the Keys from the landward side without ever facing us ship-to-ship at all."

"But if we don't stand on the defensive there, Your Majesty, where can we?" Gray Harbor asked reasonably.

"We can't stand on the defensive *anywhere* and win," Haarahld said. "The only chance we have is to take the battle to *them*."

"I beg your pardon, Your Majesty?" Gray Harbor sounded as if he wasn't entirely certain he'd heard his monarch correctly, and Haarahld gave a harsh bark of laughter.

"Wondering if I've finally lost my senses, are you, Rayjhis?" he asked.

"By no means, Your Majesty." Gray Harbor still sounded more than a little dubious, but there was a flicker of humor in his eyes.

"Oh, yes, you are," Haarahld told him roundly. "And, hopefully, the other side's going to agree with you."

"Just what *do* you have in mind, Father?" Cayleb asked, regarding the king intently.

"I doubt very much that Sharleyan's going to be an enthusiastic member of our 'Northern Force,' " Haarahld said. "And if she's cooperating grudgingly, against her will, her admirals aren't exactly likely to throw themselves wholeheartedly into operations to accomplish Hektor's plans. Which means that, in practical terms, adding her squadrons to Nahrmahn's and Hektor's navies isn't going to affect the balance of power here in home waters nearly as severely as the raw numbers might indicate."

"I think you have a point there, Your Majesty," Merlin put in. "I believe Queen Sharleyan intends to drag her heels just as hard as she thinks she can get away with."

"Hardly surprising, given her history with Hektor," Gray Harbor agreed, and Haarahld nodded.

"Exactly. So, in realistic terms, until Dohlar and Tarot arrive, what we'll really be facing will be the hundred and fifty or so galleys we always expected Nahrmahn and Hektor to be able to mobilize against us. And, of course, there's the question of just how many of Nahrmahn's will be available, given the apparent interruption of their mail. So the numbers could actually be quite a bit better than that.

"I also doubt that the clever little 'puppetmasters,' as you put it, Merlin, in the Temple are going to commit Tarot's ships immediately. They're going to rely on the fact that we don't know what they're up to. Gorjah's going to go right on being our loyal ally up until the coin actually drops and they tell him to turn his coat. So, they're probably going to plan on the Dohlarans making rendezvous with the Tarotisians somewhere in the Sea of Justice before either of them enters our waters."

Merlin sat back in his own chair, nodding thoughtfully. Nimue Alban had been a tactical specialist, and a good one. But Merlin recognized his clear superior as a strategist—at least in this particular sphere of operations—in King Haarahld VII.

"Which route would you expect them to take *after* they make rendezvous, Father?" Cayleb asked.

"That's harder to say." Haarahld shrugged. "Hopefully, Merlin's visions will tell us that. And also, hopefully, keep track of where they actually are at any given moment."

He looked at Merlin and raised his eyebrows, and Merlin nodded back.

"I can't guarantee how close a watch I'll be able to keep on all their various fleet commanders, Your Majesty," he said, "but I ought to be able to track the fleets themselves fairly well."

"Good," the king said. "But to get back to your question, Cayleb, the shortest route would be the northern one, up through the Cauldron and the Tranjyr Passage and around the Stepping Stones."

His finger traced the route as he spoke.

"But that's also the route they'll expect us to be scouting most carefully," he continued, "so they might opt for the southern passage, especially with the prevailing northeasterlies in the Sea of Justice that time of year." His finger moved back to the south, down along the eastern coast of Armageddon Reef, across the Parker Sea west of Tryon's Land, and then up past MacPherson's Lament and across Linden Gulf. "It's the longer route, but they might actually make a faster passage. And February's the start of summer in these latitudes, so they'll have the best weather they're likely to get for the crossing. For all the good it's likely to do a fleet of Dohlaran galleys."

He paused again, gazing down at the map, then looked up, eyes gleaming in the lamplight, and smiled. It was not a pleasant expression.

"But it doesn't really matter which route they plan on following," he told them. "Either way, they still have to get across at least the southern reaches of the Sea of Justice, and they still have to make rendezvous somewhere. And they don't know Merlin will be able to tell us where they are and when. Which means they won't be expecting us to intercept them several thousand miles from their destination."

"*Intercept* them, Your Majesty?" Gray Harbor didn't really sound very surprised, Merlin noticed.

"It's the last thing they'll be looking for," Haarahld said, "and reasonably so. Even assuming we knew they were coming—which I'm sure the geniuses planning this operation will expect we *don't* know—there shouldn't be any way we could even find them. And they won't expect us to split our forces just to run the risk of missing them at sea and letting them past us unintercepted, even if they thought we'd have enough strength to make the attempt."

"Which means we'll turn *their* surprise around on them," Cayleb said, and as his eyes brightened, he looked more like his father to Merlin than he ever had before.

"Precisely," Haarahld agreed. "Sea battles aren't fought by ships, Rayjhis; they're fought by *men*. And the men commanding and crewing those galleys will be dumbfounded when they see Royal Charisian Navy ships standing in to attack them five-days away from Charisian waters. That's likely to produce the sort of panic that takes a fleet halfway to defeat before the enemy fires a single shot."

"With all due respect, Your Majesty, it had better produce it," Gray Harbor said wryly. "I'm assuming you're planning on using the galleons for this?"

"It's the sort of blue-water battle they were designed to fight," Haarahld said. "It would play to their advantages—and the galleys' *disadvantages*—more strongly than we could arrange anywhere here in home waters."

"I agree. But to get them there, assuming your worst-case estimate that the 'Southern Force' could be in our waters by the second five-day in February, the galleons would have to sail by the middle of November. How many of them will we have *then?*"

"Merlin? Cayleb?" Haarahld looked at them, and Merlin glanced at Cayleb.

"What if we abandon work on the ships furthest from completion and concentrate on the ones closest to launch and the conversions?" Cayleb asked him.

"That . . . might work." Merlin stroked a mustachio for a moment, then nodded. "If we do that, we could probably have thirty of them ready to sail by the middle of November. Maybe one or two more. But they're still going to be pretty green, Cayleb."

"The gun crews will be the *least* green," the prince countered. "And they'll have at least four or five five-days for sail drill—and more gun drill—before we can reach the enemy."

"That's true enough." Merlin considered it for a moment, and then they turned as one to face the king.

"I think we might count on thirty, Your Majesty," Merlin said.

"Against somewhere around a hundred and sixty galleys," Gray Harbor said.

"Just comparing the numbers looks bad," Haarahld said. Gray Harbor gave him a politely incredulous look, and the king snorted once more. "All right," he conceded, "it looks bad because it *is* bad. But it's not *as* bad as it looks. Either this entire new concept of ours works, or it doesn't. And if it's going to work, these are the best conditions we're going to be able to come up with. And don't forget that element of surprise."

"Indeed," Bishop Maikel put in. "As you've already pointed out, Your Majesty, surprise begets panic. If the galleons can inflict sufficient damage, and create sufficient panic, the Southern Force may well turn back even if its actual losses are less than crippling. At which point, the galleons can return to home waters, allowing you to concentrate your full strength against the Northern Force."

"Assuming our own galleys can successfully play tag with them until the galleons *get* back," Gray Harbor said. The bishop looked at him, and the first councillor smiled crookedly. "I used to be a sea officer, Your Eminence, and every sea officer knows the first law of battle is that what can go wrong, *will* go wrong."

"True," Haarahld said. "But that law applies to *both* sides."

"That's fair enough," Gray Harbor acknowledged.

"I must be on to something if *you're* prepared to admit that much, Rayjhis!"

the king said with a laugh. Then he shook himself and looked around the council chamber more soberly.

"I'm sure there are a lot of points we'll need to refine," he said, "but I've been thinking about how to deal with Dohlar ever since Merlin first warned us Trynair was talking to Rahnyld. I'm convinced this is our best response. And I'm also convinced that it's imperative that our captains and our crews be as confident and motivated as possible. Especially given the possibility that the fact that the Council of Vicars is really behind all of this, whatever it says, may leak out. Even the most stouthearted are going to feel a few qualms if they think Mother Church has decided we need to be crushed.

"Bearing that in mind, I think it will be necessary for me to take personal command of our galley fleet. Oh," he waved one hand as Gray Harbor stiffened in his seat, "I know it's been *years* since my own Navy days, Rayjhis! I won't attempt to exercise actual tactical command. That will be up to Bryahn—that's why he's High Admiral! But it's going to be important for our people to know I'm there with them, live or die."

"Your Majesty, if something were to happen to you—" Gray Harbor began, but the king shook his head.

"If we don't manage to defeat this combination of forces, and defeat it *decisively*, it's over, Rayjhis," he said quietly. "We've got to at the very least win another six months or a year, more preferably two or three years, to get more of the new ships into commission. And, if *they* defeat *us*, it doesn't matter where I am when it happens. If having me there, if knowing I'm with them, helps our people fight more effectively—and you know as well as I do that it will—then that's where I have to be."

Gray Harbor stared into his monarch's hard, unyielding eyes for a long, silent moment. Then his own eyes fell.

"And me, Father?" Cayleb asked, breaking the silence.

"And you, my son," King Haarahld said soberly, meeting Cayleb's gaze steadily, "will be with Admiral Staynair—and Merlin—with the galleon fleet."

Cayleb's eyes brightened. Gray Harbor, on the other hand, seemed to hover on the brink of a fresh protest, and the king smiled at him without any humor at all.

"Everything I just said about the importance of our galleys' morale is even more true of the galleon fleet, Rayjhis," he said. "However confident they may be, no one's ever fought a battle like this one will be, and they'll be outnumbered much more heavily than the galley fleet will be. They'll *need* to have someone from the royal house there, and Cayleb's spent the last year learning everything there is to know about the new ships and the new artillery."

"And me, Your Majesty?" Gray Harbor asked very quietly. "Where do *I* fit into this master strategy of yours?"

"Exactly where you're afraid you do," Haarahld said sadly. "Right here in Tellesberg, as the head of the Privy Council and as Zhan's regent if something should happen to Cayleb and me."

"Your Majesty, please, I—" Gray Harbor began, but Haarahld shook his head once more.

"No, Rayjhis. I *need* you here."

Gray Harbor seemed prepared to continue, but then he stopped himself and bent his head in silent submission.

"Thank you," Haarahld said quietly. Then he chuckled harshly. Gray Harbor looked up again at the sound, and the king smiled at him.

"I know that wasn't what you wanted to hear, Rayjhis," he said. "So, I have a little treat for you. Well, you and Bynzhamyn."

He smiled at Wave Thunder, who'd sat silent so far. The baron's expertise lay in other areas than grand naval strategy, and he knew it. But now his eyes brightened and he sat straighter in his chair, and the king chuckled again at the evidence of his eagerness.

"Under the circumstances," he said, "I see no particular advantage in allowing Hektor's and Nahrmahn's spies to continue to operate in Charis. I'd like to wait another two or three five-days, just in case we miss someone who manages to go scurrying off to Emerald before we're ready. But, as of . . . twelve days from today, the two of you have my permission to pick up every single spy you and Merlin have been able to identify."

OCTOBER, YEAR OF GOD 891

✦

Trumpets sounded across the dark blue water of Gorath Bay, and harsh, answering shouts of command rang out across the decks of the gathered strength of the Dohlaran Navy. White storms of seabirds and many-hued clouds of coastal wyverns swept back and forth across the crowded harbor in a ruffling thunder of wings, shrill cries, and high-pitched whistles. Brisk wind and thin, high bands of cloud polished a sky of autumn blue, and the broad waters of the bay had never before seen such a concentration of warships. The green wyvern on red of the kingdom's banners snapped and cracked sharply in the brisk wind, command streamers flew from the mastheads of the squadron flagships, and, despite himself, Admiral Lywys Gardynyr, the Earl of Thirsk, felt a stir of pride at the sight of such massed power.

It faded into something much less pleasant a moment later, however, as he turned his eyes to the galley *King Rahnyld*. The towering, high-sided vessel flew the command streamer of "Admiral" Malikai, and Thirsk felt a sudden temptation to spit over the side at the sight.

Shouted commands swept over his own flagship, and the capstan's pawl clanked steadily as the crew of *Gorath Bay* hove her anchor short. *Gorath Bay* was smaller and older than *King Rahnyld*, with less gilding, and her carving was far less intricate and ornate, while her figurehead was a simple carved kraken, rather than the half-again lifesized, magnificently painted and gilded figure of King Rahnyld which graced the fleet flagship. She was also lower to the water and far handier than the huge, lumbering white dragon of the fleet flagship. Malikai's ship had been built as an exercise in royal ego, plain and simple, as far as Thirsk could tell. Which, of course, made it unthinkable that Malikai should fly his streamer from any other ship.

Gorath Bay curtsied suddenly as the flukes of her anchor broke out of the sandy bottom of her namesake anchorage. The men on the pump heaved the handles up and down, and a stream of water gushed from the hose, sluicing mud and slime off the anchor hawser as it came steadily up out of the water.

The anchor had held the galley's head to the wind; now she fell off, and fresh orders rang out and the row master's drum began its deep, steady beat as her oars dipped. The bay's waters were ruffled with white, and the rowers had to lean hard into the sweeps before they could get steerage way on her and the helmsman could bring her back up into the wind.

That wind was out of the southwest, which meant it was almost directly into the fleet's teeth as it headed out of the bay. The galleys would leave the anchorage under oars, and stay that way until they cleared Lizard Island and turned northwest. After that, the wind would be almost broad on the beam, at least until they had to turn due west for the run down the Gulf of Dohlar to the Sea of Harchong. That promised to be an exhausting ordeal, given the prevailing winds this time of year.

Thirsk grimaced at the thought and folded his hands behind him as he strode briskly to the after rail and gazed back at the rest of the fleet. *King Rahnyld*, predictably, was slower and clumsier getting underway than almost any of the other ships. Not that it mattered all that much. A fleet of over a hundred and twenty galleys, accompanied by twenty-six clumsy transports and supply ships, wasn't going to get out of the bay in a tearing hurry. There'd be time for Malikai's lumbering flagship to tag along with the others.

Now if the "Admiral General" only had the least damned idea of what he was supposed to *do* with all these ships.

Thirsk stood atop the aftercastle, watching the panorama of the huge harbor as *Gorath Bay* moved slowly past the breakwater. The Dohlaran capital's walls gleamed in the sunlight, and the massive crowd of shipping made a splendidly stirring sight. But despite the dutifully cheering crowds which had seen Thirsk's crews off, and despite the stern proclamation from the king setting forth Dohlar's reasons for enmity with the distant Kingdom of Charis, none of the seamen and soldiers aboard the galleys really seemed to understand exactly where they were going, or why.

Which doesn't make the poor bastards so very different from me, *does it?* he thought mordantly. *Of course, I do understand whose idea this really is. That puts me at least a little up on them, I suppose.*

His lips tightened at the thought, and he spread his feet a bit further apart, balancing easily as *Gorath Bay*'s motion freshened.

Magwair, he thought. *That's who came up with this. And Rahnyld and Malikai actually think it's a* good *idea, Langhorne save us all!*

He drew a deep breath and commanded himself to stop fretting. It was an order more easily given than obeyed, but he was a disciplined man. Besides, if he didn't get a grip on his temper, sheer spleen was going to carry him off long before they reached the Straits of Queiroz. Still, only a landsman—and an idiot general, at that—could have come up with this brilliant idea.

We're supposed to "sneak up" on Haarahld, he thought disgustedly. *As if anyone could move a fleet this size through the Harthlan Sea without every trading vessel west of Tarot knowing all about it! And what* they *know, Haarahld will know within five-days. Certainly, he's going to know we're coming long before we get there.*

Well, he supposed surprise wasn't really essential when you'd been able to assemble four times your enemy's maximum strength. But committing a fleet of coastal galleys to the passage of the Sea of Justice wasn't exactly an act of genius.

Left to himself, and assuming he'd had no choice but to carry out these lunatic orders and attack a kingdom which had never threatened his own, he would have gone about it quite differently.

Their orders were to follow the eastern coast of Howard as far as Geyra, in the Desnairian Empire's Barony of Harless, then swing due east for the rendezvous off Demon Head, at the northern tip of Armageddon Reef. *He* would have hugged the coast all the way up to the Gulf of Mathyas and then around southern East Haven to reach *Tarot,* without going anywhere near the Reef. It would have added five-days to the journey time, but it would also have gotten them there without facing the Sea of Justice. And he would have taken his fleet straight from Tarot to Eraystor Bay, around the Stepping Stones and the southern part of the Anvil, and availed himself of the Emerald Navy's yard facilities to scrape his bottoms and get his galleys fit for combat once more before he went picking any fights with the Royal Charisian Navy in its own waters.

Unfortunately, he was only a professional seaman, not important enough to be consulted over minor matters like choosing the fleet's course or deciding upon its tactics.

Well, that's probably not entirely *fair, he told himself. Obviously, they've got some sort of wild hair up their arses about Charis—Langhorne knows why! Whatever it is, though, they want Haarahld smashed fast, which means there's no time to follow a coastal passage all the way. Still, I wish to hell they'd let me stay out of the middle of the Sea of Justice! If we have to use the southern route, then I'd prefer to stay still farther east, closer to Armageddon Reef, all the way.*

His lips twitched as he realized what he'd just thought, but it was true. Just thinking about Armageddon Reef made him . . . nervous, but not as nervous as the thought of crossing through the heart of the Sea of Justice outside of sight of land.

He blew air through his mustache and gave himself a shake.

If it worked, everyone was going to call Magwair's plan brilliant. If it didn't work, Malikai would undoubtedly blame *Thirsk* for failing to execute it properly. And whatever happened, when they got to the other end—in whatever shape they were in when they arrived—they were going to have to take on a Royal Charisian Navy fighting in defense of its own homes and families and with it's back to the wall.

Which, he thought grimly, *is going to be about as ugly as it gets. And all because Trynair offered our useless sot of a King a break on his loan payments.*

He grimaced and gave himself another, harder shake. That sort of thought was dangerous, not to mention being beside the point. King Rahnyld was his sovereign, and he was duty and honor bound to obey his king's orders, whatever he thought of the reason they'd been given. Which was why it was also his job to do whatever he could to rescue this campaign from Admiral General Duke Malikai.

It promised to be an . . . interesting challenge.

They're on their way," Merlin said grimly as he nodded to the Marine sentry and stepped through the doorway.

Cayleb looked up from the big table in the large, lamp-lit chamber Merlin had dubbed their "Operations Room." The table was completely covered by a huge chart, pieced together out of several smaller ones. Now Merlin crossed to the table and grimaced down at the chart. Big as it was, it would be five-days before the Dohlaran fleet reached the area it covered, but the campaign's opening move had begun.

"Any more indication of their course?" Cayleb asked, and despite his own grim mood, Merlin's lips quirked in a small smile.

Cayleb hadn't discussed Merlin's more-than-mortal nature with him since the night after he'd killed the krakens. Not explicitly, at any rate. But by now, the crown prince took the "*seijin's*" abilities so much for granted that he didn't even turn a hair over them anymore. Still, however . . . blasé Cayleb might have become, he realized exactly how valuable Merlin's "visions" truly were.

"Unless something changes, they're almost certainly going to follow the southern track," Merlin replied. "Thirsk doesn't like it. He'd really prefer to stay in coastal waters all the way to Tarot, but since he can't do that, he's trying to convince Malikai to at least pass to the east of Samson's Land and hug the east coast of Armageddon Reef."

"Because he's not an idiot," Cayleb snorted, walking around the table to stand beside Merlin and gaze down at the chart. "Mind you, there's something to be said for not going any further south than you have to, and *I'd* just as soon not try looking for an emergency anchorage on the Reef, given what it would be likely to do to my crews' morale. On the other hand, at least you could count on finding one if you needed it. And a fleet of galleys trying to cross those waters probably *will* need one at some point."

"That's basically what Thirsk is saying," Merlin agreed. "Malikai's opposed because he thinks it will take longer. Besides, it's going to be late spring by the time they reach the Sea of Justice, right? That means the weather should be fine."

"You know," Cayleb said, only half whimsically, "having Malikai in command of the Southern Force is one of the reasons I'm inclined to think God is on our side, whatever the Council of Vicars might think."

"I know what you mean. Still," Merlin shrugged, "he's got a lot of ships. And it looks to me as if Thirsk's squadron, at least, is going to be well drilled and ready to fight when they get here, regardless of how rough the passage is."

"I don't doubt it. But he still going to be hampered by Malikai."

Merlin nodded, and Cayleb cocked his head, frowning.

"And how does Admiral White Ford feel about all this?" he asked, after a moment.

"White Ford, and Gorjah, both agree with Thirsk, whether they know it or not," Merlin said. "They'd far rather have the Dohlarans make straight for Tarot, then either cross the Cauldron or sail up and around through the Gulf of Tarot. Unfortunately for them, Magwair—and Malikai—are convinced that would cost them the element of surprise."

Cayleb's laugh sounded like the hunting cough of a catamount. It also showed remarkably little sympathy for Gorjah and Gahvyn Mahrtyn, the Baron of White Ford, who commanded his navy.

"Well, if we were deaf, dumb, blind, and as stupid as Rahnyld, they *might* be able to surprise us, even without you," he said.

"You're probably right," Merlin said. "But you might want to reflect on just how big a stretch of water they have to hide in. As it is, you know they're coming, and you know the Tarotisians are supposed to rendezvous with Thirsk and Malikai off Armageddon Reef. But even armed with that knowledge, pulling off an interception that far from your own harbors wouldn't exactly be a walk in the park for most navies, now would it?"

"Not a walk in the park, no," Cayleb conceded. "On the other hand, assuming we could have known they'd be taking the southern route without you, we'd still have had a pretty fair chance. They're going to want to stay close to the coast, at least until they get south of Tryon's Land, and that would tell us where to find them. With the schooners to do our scouting, we could cover an awful lot of coastal water, Merlin." He shook his head. "I fully intend to make the best use I possibly can of your visions, but you've already done the most important thing of all by telling us they're coming and what course they're likely to follow."

"I hope it's going to be enough," Merlin said soberly.

"Well, that's up to us, isn't it?" Cayleb showed his teeth. "Even without the galleons and the new artillery, they'd have had a fight on their hands. As it is, I think I can safely predict that win or lose, they aren't going to enjoy their summer cruise."

Merlin returned his tight, hungry grin for a moment, then sobered once more.

"Cayleb, I have a favor to ask of you."

"A favor?" Cayleb cocked his head. "*That* sounds ominous. What sort of favor?"

"I've got some . . . equipment I'd like you to use."

"What kind of equipment?"

"A new cuirass and hauberk. And a new sword. And I'd like to get your father into new armor, as well."

Cayleb's face smoothed into non-expression, and Merlin felt himself tensing mentally. Cayleb might have accepted his more-than-human capabilities, but would he be able—or willing—to accept this, as well?

Merlin had thought long and hard before making the offer. He himself was, if not indestructible, at least very, very hard to destroy. His PICA body wasn't simply built out of incredibly tough synthetics, but incorporated substantial nanotech-based self-repair capabilities. Very few current-generation Safeholdian weapons could realistically hope to inflict crippling damage. A direct hit by a round shot could undoubtedly remove a limb, or even his head, but while that might be inconvenient, it wouldn't "kill" him. Even a direct hit by a heavy cannon couldn't significantly damage his "brain," and as long as his power plant remained intact—and it was protected by a centimeter-thick shell of battle steel—and as long as his nannies had access to basic raw materials (and lots and lots of time), they could pretty much literally rebuild him from scratch.

But his friends, and there was no point pretending these people hadn't become exactly that, were far more fragile than he was. He'd accepted his own potential immortality when he first awoke in Nimue's Cave and realized what he was. But until he'd become close to Cayleb, Haarahld, Gray Harbor—all the rest of the Charisians he'd come to know and respect—he hadn't realized how painful immortality could be. Even now, he knew, he'd only sensed the potential of that pain. Over the centuries, if he succeeded in Nimue's mission, he'd come to know its reality, but he was in no hurry to embrace it.

Even if that hadn't been a factor—and it was; he was far too honest with himself to deny that—he'd also come to recognize just how important Haarahld and Cayleb were to the accomplishment of that mission. He'd been extraordinarily fortunate to find a king and a crown prince intelligent enough and mentally flexible enough—and aware enough of their responsibilities to their kingdom—to accept what he'd offered them. Even from the most cold-blooded perspective, he couldn't afford to lose them.

And so, he'd instructed Owl to use the fabrication unit in Nimue's Cave to manufacture exact duplicates of Cayleb's and Haarahld's personal armor. Except that, instead of the best steel Safehold could produce, this armor was made of battle steel. No blade or bullet could penetrate it. Indeed, it would resist most round shot, although the kinetic transfer of the impact from something like that would undoubtedly kill its wearer, anyway.

He'd already replaced his own Royal Guard–issue armor. Not because he needed it to keep him alive, but to avoid any embarrassing questions about why he *hadn't* needed it. It would be much easier to explain—or brush off—a bullet that failed to penetrate his breastplate when it should have than to explain why the hole that same bullet had left in his torso wasn't bleeding.

But now he was asking Cayleb to accept what the prince had to think of as "miraculous" armor of his own. And flexible though he might be, Cayleb was still the product of a culture and a religion which had systematically programmed their members for centuries to reject "forbidden" knowledge on pain of eternal damnation.

Silence hovered between them for several seconds, and then Cayleb smiled crookedly.

"I think that's a favor I can grant," he said. "Ah, are there any . . . special precautions we should take with this new armor of ours?"

"The only real thing to worry about," Merlin said, trying—not completely successfully—to restrain his own smile of relief, "is that it won't rust. That may require just a little creative explanation on your part. Oh, and you might want to be a little careful with the edge of your new sword. It's going to be quite sharp . . . and stay that way."

"I see." For just an instant, Cayleb's expression started to blank once more, but then the incipient blankness vanished into a huge, boyish grin.

"So I'm getting a magic sword of my very own, am I?"

"In a manner of speaking," Merlin said.

"I always wanted one of those. I was younger than Zhan is now the first time I read the tale of *Seijin* Kody and the sword Helm-Cleaver."

"It's not quite *that* magical," Merlin told him.

"Will *I* be able to slice right through other people's swords now?" Cayleb demanded with a laugh.

"Probably not," Merlin said in long-suffering tones.

"Pity. I was looking forward to it."

"I'm sure you were."

"Well, does it at least have a *name?*"

Merlin glowered at him for a moment, then laughed.

"Yes, Cayleb," he said. "Yes, as a matter of fact it does. You can call it 'Excalibur.'"

"Excalibur," Cayleb repeated slowly, wrapping his tongue around the odd-sounding syllables. Then he smiled. "I like it. It sounds like a proper prince's sword."

Merlin smiled back at the youngster. Who really wasn't all *that* much younger than Nimue Alban had been, he reminded himself once more. Cayleb's reaction was a huge relief, but Merlin had no intention of telling him about the other precaution he'd taken.

He'd found a use for the med unit Pei Kau-yung had left Nimue, after all. He couldn't have offered Cayleb or Haarahld the antigerone drug therapies even if he'd trusted the drugs themselves after so many centuries. Having Cayleb running around at age ninety still looking like a twenty-something would have been just a bit awkward to explain. But he'd been able to acquire a genetic sample from the prince, and the med unit had produced the standard antigerone nanotech.

Merlin had injected it one night, five-days before. Keyed to Cayleb's genetic coding, the self replicating nano-machines would hunt down and destroy anything that didn't "belong" to him. They wouldn't extend Cayleb's life span—not directly, at any rate—but he would never again have a cold, or the flu. Or cancer. Or any other disease or infection.

Injecting it without Cayleb's informed consent had been a serious breach of the Federation's medical ethics, not to mention a violation of Federation law. Under the circumstances, Merlin had no qualms about either of those. What mattered was that the young man whose survival he'd come to recognize as critical to the success of Nimue's mission had been given the best chance *of* survival he could possibly provide.

And if, in the process, Merlin Athrawes had selfishly prolonged the life and health of someone who had become personally important to him, that was just too bad.

.III.
Royal Palace,
Manchyr

Prince Hektor of Corisande reminded himself that the Knights of the Temple Lands were doing exactly what he wanted them to do.

It wasn't easy.

"Excuse me, Father," he said, "but I'm not at all certain we can be ready to move that quickly."

"Your Highness must, of course, be better informed upon these matters than I am," Father Karlos Chalmyrz, Archbishop Bahrmyn's personal aide, said politely. "I merely relay the message I was instructed to deliver to you."

Which, as he carefully did not point out, came directly from Vicar Allayn Magwair.

"I understand that, Father Karlos." Hektor smiled just a little thinly at the upper-priest. "And I appreciate all your efforts deeply, truly I do. I'm simply concerned about the ability of my admirals and captains to meet the . . . proposed schedule."

"Shall I inform Vicar Allayn that you can't do so, Your Highness?" Chalmyrz asked politely.

"No, thank you."

Hektor smiled again, and reminded himself it truly wasn't Chalmyrz' fault. But assuming Dohlar had been able to obey *its* marching orders from the Temple, the Dohlaran Navy had been in motion for almost two five-days already. The fact that it was going to be hugging the coast all the way across the Harthlan Sea meant the Church's semaphore system could get a message to Duke Malikai from the Temple in no more than a few days. So, technically, Magwair could always adjust its progress at any point up to Geyra, when it was due to head out across the Sea of Justice. Unfortunately, it would require over a month for any message from Hektor to reach *Magwair*, or the reverse, which made any notion of close coordination a fantasy.

"I'll consult with Admiral Black Water this afternoon, Father," the prince said after a moment. "I'll know better then if it will be necessary to send any messages to the Vicar."

"Of course, Your Highness." Chalmyrz bowed. "If it should prove necessary, please don't hesitate to inform me."

"I won't, Father," Hektor promised.

▼   ▼   ▼

"I can't do it, Your Highness," Ernyst Lynkyn, the Duke of Black Water, told his sovereign prince. He was a compact, muscular man with a short, salt-and-pepper beard and an expression which had become increasingly harassed over the past several five-days. "I'm sorry, but a month isn't long enough. It simply can't be done that quickly."

"I already knew that, Ernyst," Hektor said. "What I need to know is how much of the fleet we *can* have ready to move by then."

Black Water squinted his eyes and scratched at his wiry beard. Hektor could almost feel the painful intensity of the duke's thoughts. Black Water wasn't the most brilliant of Corisande's nobles, but he was reliable, phlegmatic, and—normally—unflappable. Hektor had summoned him as soon as Chalmyrz had departed, and the duke had arrived with commendable speed. Now he looked very much as if he wished he hadn't.

"We've got the active-duty galleys almost completely manned now, Your Highness," he said, thinking aloud, "but at least a half-dozen of them are still in dockyard hands. Mostly for fairly minor things. We should be able to have all of them ready to sail. It's the reserve ships that worry me."

Hektor simply nodded and waited as patiently as he could.

"Most of the reserve's going to need at least another four or five five-days, minimum, to refit. Then we're going to have to put the crews aboard them, and it's going to take them at least another several five-days to work up. I don't see any way we could have more than ten of them ready to move within the time limit. So, call it sixty galleys. The rest won't be available—not fit to fight, at any rate—for at least another five five-days after that."

"I see."

Hektor was scarcely surprised. Galleys laid up in reserve always deteriorated to at least some extent, however careful the maintenance effort. It wasn't at all unheard of for them to become completely rotten in an amazingly short time. Assuming Black Water's estimate was accurate, the dockyard would be doing extraordinarily well to get the entire reserve ready for service once again that quickly.

"Very well, Ernyst," he said, after a moment. "If that's the best we can do, it's the best we can do. And if everything goes according to plan, it's going to be two months yet before we actually have to commit them to battle."

"I understand that, Your Highness. It's that bit about 'going according to plan' that worries me." Black Water shook his head. "With all due respect, the timing's too tight on all of this."

"I tend to agree," Hektor said with massive understatement. "Unfortunately, there's not very much we can do about that. And at least Haarahld's going to have even less notice than we do. I'm sure he has his agents here in Corisande, but by the time they realize we're mobilizing the fleet and get the message to him, we'll already be on our way."

"I can't say I'm sorry to hear that, Sire," Black Water said frankly.

.IV.
Port Royal,
Kingdom of Chisholm

A month?" Admiral Zohzef Hyrst looked at the Earl of Sharpfield and shook his head. "That's not very long," he observed mildly, and Sharpfield chuckled sourly.

"That's what I've always liked about you, Zohzef," he said. "That gift for understatement."

"Well, at least it's going to make it easier for us to leave most of our reserve at home," Hyrst pointed out.

"True." Sharpfield nodded. "Even without our handpicked idiots."

He walked across to the window of his office and gazed out across the city of Port Royal and the sparkling water of Kraken Bay. Port Royal had been founded almost a hundred years ago expressly to serve as the Chisholm Navy's primary base. From where he stood, he could see the dockyard crews swarming over the nested together reserve galleys like black insects, tiny with distance. Yard craft of every description dotted the harbor beyond them, tied up alongside other galleys, or plying back and forth between them and the shore establishment.

It was a scene of bustling activity which had been going on at full tilt for over three five-days now. And one which, he hoped, looked suitably efficient, even if it wasn't. Or, perhaps, especially *since* it wasn't.

"What sort of idiot thinks you can move a navy from a peacetime footing to a war footing, without any prior warning, in less than two months?" Hyrst asked.

"No doubt the esteemed Vicar Allayn," Sharpfield replied.

"Well, I guess that explains it. He probably thinks putting a galley to sea is as simple as hitching draft dragons to army freight wagons."

"I doubt he's quite that uninformed about naval realities," Sharpfield said mildly. "And, while I'm sure his lack of sea experience is playing a part, it's really not as stupid as it may seem to us."

"With all due respect, My Lord," Hyrst said, "expecting us to produce our full strength, 'ready for battle in all respects,' if I remember the dispatch correctly, off the coast of Charis two months from today is about as stupid as it gets."

"If he really expected us to be able to do it, it would be," Sharpfield agreed. "I doubt very much that he does, though. He's not going to admit that to *us*, of course. The whole object is to get us to Charis with as many ships as humanly possible, and making impossible demands is supposed to inspire us to do better than we think we can. But the main thrust of his strategy is to get us, Hektor, and Nahrmahn concentrated as *quickly* as possible, as well. He's figuring Haarahld won't even know we're coming until we're already there, which means it will be *our* active strength against *his* active strength. That gives us a better than three-to-two advantage, even assuming not a single one of his active galleys is in yard hands. And our reserve units will have at least a two-month head start over his."

"It would still be smarter to wait until more of our full strength was ready," Hyrst said. "Three-to-two sounds good, but two-to-one sounds a Shan-wei of a lot better against someone like Charis."

"Agreed." Sharpfield nodded. "I didn't say I agreed with him, only that his strategy's basically sound—or, at least, sounder than it might appear at first glance. And don't forget, Zohzef, we're not really supposed to take Haarahld on until Dohlar and Tarot arrive."

"Then we should be waiting until they get here before we move at all," Hyrst argued.

"Unless it turns out we catch Haarahld badly enough off guard to get past Lock Island and the Keys before he knows we're coming," Sharpfield pointed out. "I'll admit it's unlikely, but it *is* possible."

"I suppose *anything* is possible, My Lord." Hyrst grimaced. "Some things are more *likely* than others, though."

"Granted, but if you don't try, you'll never know whether it was possible or not, will you?"

T hat was a nasty thing to do to my bishop, dear."

"Nonsense." Prince Nahrmahn chuckled as he fitted the onyx bishop into the proper niche in the velvet-lined case. "It's simply retribution for what you did to my castle two moves ago."

"Then if it wasn't nasty, it was at least ungallant," his wife said.

"Now that," he conceded with the sort of smile very few people ever saw from him, "might be a valid accusation. On the other hand," he elevated his nose with an audible sniff, "I'm a prince, and princes sometimes have to be ungallant."

"I see." Princess Ohlyvya gazed down at the inlaid chessboard between them, and a smile of her own lurked behind her eyes. "Well, in that case, I won't feel quite so bad about pointing out to you that it was not only ungallant, but also unwise."

Nahrmahn's eyebrows rose, then lowered in sudden consternation as she moved one of her knights. The move threatened his queen . . . which he could no longer move to a position of safety, because the knight's move also cleared the file it had occupied, exposing his king to a discovered check from her remaining bishop. Which was only possible because capturing her other bishop had moved *his* remaining castle out of position to block the check.

He sat looking at the situation for several seconds, then sighed and moved his king out of check. At which point her knight swooped in and removed his queen from play.

"You know," he said, sitting back as he contemplated his next move, "by now I should realize that whenever you offer me a nice, juicy prize like that, there's always a hook somewhere inside the bait."

"Oh, no," she said demurely. "Sometimes I leave them out there with no hook at all. Just to encourage you to bite the *next* time."

Nahrmahn laughed and shook his head, then looked around the library.

Princess Mahrya was bent over a history text in one of the window seats. At almost eighteen, she was approaching marriageable age, although there were no immediate prospects on the horizon. Fortunately, as the graceful profile etched against the glow of the lamp at her shoulder proved, she took after her petite, attractive mother more than her father. She also had her mother's mischievous personality.

Prince Nahrmahn, her younger brother, at fourteen, looked like a much younger—and slimmer—version of his father and namesake. He, however, wasn't interested in a history text. He was buried in a novel, and judging from his intent expression it must contain quite a bit of derring-do. Not to mention swords, mayhem, and murder.

Their youngest children, Prince Trahvys and Princess Felayz, were up in the nursery in the nannies' care. It would be a few years yet before they were trusted among the library's expensive volumes.

There were moments, like this one, when Nahrmahn almost wished he weren't so deeply involved in the great game. Unfortunately, he was, and he intended to leave Nahrmahn the Younger a much larger and more powerful princedom than he himself had inherited. Besides, whatever its drawbacks, it was the only game truly worth playing.

His smile went just a bit crooked at the thought. Then he shook himself and returned his attention to his wife.

Ohlyvya smiled fondly at him, accustomed to the way his mind sometimes wandered. Theirs was not a marriage of towering, passionate love. Ohlyvya was a daughter of a collateral branch of the previous ruling house, and her marriage to Nahrmahn—arranged when she was all of four years old—had been part of the glue binding the old régime's adherents to the new dynasty. She'd been raised to expect exactly that, but Nahrmahn knew she was genuinely fond of him, and he'd often been surprised by how deeply he'd come to care for her. He wasn't, as he'd realized long ago, the sort of person who allowed people close to him, but somehow Ohlyvya had gotten inside his guard, and he was glad she had. Raising four children together had helped bring them even closer, in many ways, and he had great respect for her intelligence. Indeed, he often wished he'd been able to name her to his Privy Council, but that would have been unthinkable.

"Are you going to move sometime this evening, dear?" she asked sweetly, and he laughed.

"As soon as I recover from the shock of your perfidious ambush," he told her. "In fact, I think I've just about—"

Someone rapped sharply on the library door. Nahrmahn's head turned towards the sound, eyebrows lowering. All of the palace servants knew his evenings with Ohlyvya and the children were never to be disturbed.

The door opened, and one of the palace footmen stood in the opening, bowing deeply.

"Your pardon, Your Highness," he said, just a bit nervously. "I deeply regret disturbing you, but Bishop Executor Wyllys has just arrived at the palace. He says it's most urgent that he speak with you."

Nahrmahn's lowered eyebrows shot upward, and he heard Ohlyvya' little gasp of surprise. Mahrya looked up from her history text, her own expression one of astonishment, and not a little apprehension. The younger Nahrmahn was far too deeply buried in his novel even to notice.

"I'm sorry, my dear," Nahrmahn said to Ohlyvya after a heartbeat or two. "It looks like we'll have to finish this game later. Tomorrow evening, perhaps."

"Of course." Her voice was calm, almost tranquil, but he saw the questions burning in her eyes. Questions, he knew, she wouldn't ask.

"Forgive me for rushing off," he continued, rising and bending to kiss her forehead. "I'll be along to bed as soon as I can."

"I understand, dear," she said, and watched him stride rapidly out of the library.

▼   ▼   ▼

"Your Highness, I apologize for arriving in such unseemly haste at such an hour," Bishop Executor Wyllys Graisyn said as he was ushered into the small, private presence chamber.

The footman withdrew, and the bishop executor was alone with the prince and only a single bodyguard.

"Your Eminence, I'm sure no apology is necessary," Nahrmahn said, sparring politely for time. "I doubt very much that you would have come to call at such an hour without formally informing me you were coming except under pressing circumstances. Please, tell me what I can do for you."

"Actually, Your Highness, this is somewhat awkward," Graisyn said. His tone was simultaneously apologetic, embarrassed, and excited, and Nahrmahn's own curiosity—and apprehension—burned hotter.

"A Church dispatch boat arrived here in Eraystor less than three hours ago, Your Highness," the cleric continued. "It carried dispatches, of course. But when I opened them, I discovered that apparently a *previous* dispatch boat had been sent to me. That vessel never arrived, and I can only assume it foundered somewhere in the Chisholm Sea in that storm last month."

The bishop executor paused, and Nahrmahn's spine stiffened. He sat straighter in his chair, and his face, he was well aware, was an only too accurate an indicator of his suddenly spiking apprehension. Whatever the lost dispatch boat's messages might have contained must have been vital for a follow-up dispatch to get Graisyn over to the palace at this late an hour. Especially if the follow-up itself had arrived less than three hours earlier.

"As I'm sure you must have guessed, Your Highness, the earlier dispatch boat carried critically important messages. Messages addressed both to you and to me from Chancellor Trynair and Archbishop Lyam. Fortunately, when the dispatch boat failed to return to Traylis on schedule, duplicate dispatches were sent. They've now arrived."

"I see," Nahrmahn said. Then he cocked his head. "Actually, Your Eminence, I *don't* see. Not yet."

"Forgive me, Your Highness." Graisyn smiled almost nervously. "I'm afraid this is rather different from the sorts of business I normally discharge for Mother Church. Although, actually, as I understand my instructions, I'm not here on Mother Church's behalf. I'm here on behalf of Chancellor Trynair in his role as Chancellor of the Knights of the Temple Lands."

Nahrmahn felt his breathing falter.

"Your Highness," Graisyn began, "the Chancellor's become increasingly concerned by the apparent ambition of Haarahld of Charis. Accordingly, speaking for the Knights of the Temple Lands, he's instructed me to tell you that—"

▼　　　▼　　　▼

The moon was high in a cloudless sky, spilling gorgeous silver light down over the palace gardens. A small group of the carefully bred night wyverns for which Emerald was justly famed trilled and whistled sweetly in the fronds of the trees, and a cool breeze drifted in through the open window of the council chamber.

The gardens' tranquillity was in pronounced contrast to the occupants of that chamber.

"I can't believe this," Earl Pine Hollow said. "I simply can't *believe* this!"

"That, unfortunately, doesn't change the situation, Trahvys," Nahrmahn said rather tartly.

"I know." The first councillor gave himself a visible shake and smiled crookedly at his cousin. "I'm sorry. It's just that without any warning at all, having it just dropped on us in the middle of the night . . ."

"If you think it came as a surprise to *you*, you should've been there when Graisyn dropped it on *me*."

"I'd prefer to not even imagine that, if it's all the same to you," Pine Hollow said in a more natural tone.

"The thing that occurs to me, My Prince," Hahl Shandyr said, "is to wonder what could have set this off. None of our contacts in Zion or the Temple even suggested that the Group of Four might be contemplating something like *this*. May I ask if the Bishop Executor gave any indication that *Hektor* might have been behind this?"

"I don't think he has the least idea himself," Nahrmahn said frankly. "Personally, I'd be inclined to doubt Hektor set it up. Mind you, it sounds like it's designed to give him everything he's ever wanted—or, at least, to make him *think* that's what it's going to give him—but there's no way he could have that much influence with the Group of Four. No," the prince shook his head, "my guess is that this is Clyntahn. Haarahld must have finally done something to push him over the edge, and it must at least seem threatening enough to let him carry the other three along with him."

"My Prince," Shandyr said, in an unusually quiet voice, "I apologize."

Nahrmahn looked at him sharply, his expression a question, and his spymaster drew a deep breath.

"I ought to have been able to reestablish at least a handful of agents in Charis, Your Highness," he said. "If I had, we might at least know what's inspired this. And," he drew another, deeper breath, "we might have known in time to see it coming."

"I won't pretend I'm happy about the situation in Charis," Nahrmahn told him. "But judging from the tone of Trynair's messages, even if we'd had agents in place, they might not have realized this was in the wind. In fact, I doubt anyone in Charis has the least idea of what's about to happen."

"I'm sure that's part of their thinking, My Prince," Gharth Rahlstahn, the Earl of Mahndyr, said. Mahndyr was Nahrmahn's senior admiral, and his expression was grim.

"I'm sure that's part of their thinking," he repeated, once he was certain he had Nahrmahn's attention. "But this puts us in a Shan-wei of a spot. It would've been bad enough if the original dispatches had gotten through, but we've lost the better part of an entire month."

"Frankly," Pine Hollow said, "the whole tenor of this . . . correspondence, if I can call it that, worries me. We aren't being offered assistance, Your Highness; we're being ordered to do what Trynair and Clyntahn *want* us to do. And from the way *I* read these messages," he tapped the elaborately illuminated letter in question, lying on the council table in front of him, "Hektor's the senior partner as far as the Group of Four is concerned. It isn't an alliance of equals. We're *required* to support Hektor . . . and to place our fleet under the command of *his* admirals."

"I assure you, it does more than simply 'worry' *me*," Nahrmahn replied.

He started to say something more, then stopped and swallowed the words unspoken. Even here, among his closest advisers, he didn't quite dare to express the full, scathing fury he'd felt as he realized the Group of Four saw his entire princedom as a footpad it could whistle up on a whim and command to cut the throat of someone who'd irritated it.

"But," he continued after a moment, "however I may feel about it, we're stuck with it. Unless anyone here thinks refusing Chancellor Trynair's 'assistance' in this matter would be advisable?"

No one spoke, nor did they have to, and Nahrmahn's alum-tart smile held at least some genuine amusement.

"In that case," he said, "the really important question is one for you, Gharth. Is it possible for us to meet this schedule?"

"I don't know, Your Highness," Mahndyr said frankly. "I won't know until I've had a chance to kick some of my staff awake and get them started asking the right questions down at the dockyard. Off the top of my head, though, it's unlikely we can get the reserve activated in time. We're supposed to have our entire fleet ready for battle by early November, but nobody warned us it was coming. Just fully manning our active-duty galleys is going to stretch our current manpower to the breaking point. We'll have to send out the press gangs to man the reserve, and every merchant seaman who can see lightning or hear thunder's going to realize the press is coming as soon as we start refitting the reserve. So they're going to make themselves scarce. Which doesn't even consider where we are in terms of the supplies we need."

He shook his head.

"Your Highness, I'll do my best, but I'm not sure we could have had the entire reserve manned and worked up within the *original* time schedule. With the time we've lost just finding out about it—"

He shook his head again.

"I can't say I'm surprised to hear it," Nahrmahn said. "And, to be totally honest, I'm not certain I'm *unhappy* to hear it."

Mahndyr's surprise showed, and the prince chuckled harshly.

"Hektor's known about this longer than we have," he said. "That much is obvious from the nature of Trynair's dispatches. So he's going to've already started bringing his fleet to a war footing. Well, if we're going to be obliged to follow his orders, then I'd just as soon see his admirals forced to take the lead. He's going to be thinking in terms of his own advantage out of this. All right, let *him* pay the price for it. It's not our fault no one told us about this soon enough. We'll do our best, of course," he smiled thinly, "but surely no one will be able to blame us if we can't get the majority of the reserve fitted out and manned in the unfortunately short time available to us."

NOVEMBER,
YEAR OF GOD 891

The spring night was warm and humid, and distant lightening flickered far to the west, over Howell Bay, as the fleet weighed anchor.

Merlin stood beside Cayleb on the quarterdeck of HMS *Dreadnought*, with Ahrnahld Falkhan just behind them. Harsh commands cut through the darkness, but they were hushed somehow, as if the people giving them believed that if they were all *very* quiet, no one would notice what they were doing.

Merlin smiled slightly at the thought, despite the tension coiling within. All around him, a total of thirty-two galleons were getting underway. Thirty of them were warships of the Royal Charisian Navy; the other two were impressed merchantmen assigned to serve as supply ships. Unlike anyone else, his artificial eyes could pick every one of them out clearly, and a part of his tension stemmed from the very real possibility of collisions as, one by one, the fundamentally clumsy square-riggers raised their anchors and set sail. Fortunately, the wind was with them, blowing steadily, if not overly strongly, out of the west.

But that natural fear of accidents was only a part of his tension, and not the greatest one.

Inevitably, word of the mobilizing navies of Corisande, Chisholm, and Emerald had gotten out, carried by nervous merchant skippers to every port from Manchyr to Tanjyr. As the news reached Charis, Haarahld had responded by closing his waters and expelling all foreign shipping. His enemies had expected that response. In fact, they might have been suspicious if he hadn't done it, and if he was a bit less than gentle with Corisandian or Emerald-flagged merchantmen, who could blame him?

He'd also sent a request for assistance to his "ally," King Gorjah, as provided for by their treaties. That request had been carefully timed so that its arrival would indicate Haarahld had had no idea Corisande and her allies were mobilizing until barely three five-days ago. And before their departure, none of the crews of those expelled merchant ships had seen the least evidence that the Royal Charisian Navy was fitting its reserve galleys for war. As they'd departed, some of them had seen signs of a frantically rushed, last-minute mobilization effort, but it was obvious Hektor of Corisande and his allies had managed to take Haarahld by surprise.

At this very moment, Merlin knew, the combined strength of Chisholm and

Corisande was underway, headed for Eraystor Bay and the formation of what Haarahld had dubbed the Northern Force. The galleys of the Charisian Navy had already assembled to defend Rock Shoal Bay, and a screen of scouting vessels had been deployed to keep distant watch over Eraystor Bay.

That, too, was no less than Charis' enemies had anticipated.

But behind that screen, concealed from any hostile eyes, the galleon fleet moved slowly but steadily out of the crowded harbor of Lock Island, and *its* business was with the *Southern* Force.

Lock Island was the most important single naval base of the Kingdom of Charis. Located almost exactly in the middle of the long, narrow passage known as The Throat, it was heavily fortified and separated from the mainland by two channels.

The South Channel was twenty-four miles wide at high water, but it narrowed to only twelve at low water, when the mudbanks were exposed, and most of those twelve miles were too shallow for seagoing craft. The main shipping channel, marked by several sharp bends, was as little as two miles across at some points, and it passed within barely two thousand yards of the Lock Island batteries.

The North Channel was the deeper of the two, although it was under eighteen miles wide at high water. At low tide, it was less than fifteen, but the main shipping channel was almost eight miles wide at its narrowest, and it was also far less twisty than the one to the south. That meant even deep-draft ships could use it without passing within range of the shore batteries on either side. Which made the North Channel the one which required warships for protection . . . and also explained why the galleons, sailing with the falling tide, were passing between Lock Island and North Key, the matching fortress on the far side of the channel.

The geography of The Throat was both a tremendous strategic advantage and an almost equally tremendous handicap for Charis. It made the entire extent of Howell Bay the next best thing to impregnable as long as the Charisian Navy held Lock Island and the Keys, but it also meant a strong easterly wind could effectively close The Throat to all sail-powered traffic. A strong enough wind could close it even to galleys, which—as Haarahld had noted—could pin an entire defending fleet behind Lock Island.

Fortunately, the prevailing winds were from the north and northwest. That was the case tonight, although spring was the season when Rock Shoal Bay was more likely to get occasional strong easterlies. Even then, however, the wind was more often out of the north-northeast than straight out of the east, thanks to the sheltering landmasses of Silver and Emerald.

The cramped waters of even the North Channel might be enough to cause some anxiety, but it also meant the lights of the fortresses, and especially the hundred-foot beacon tower on the highest point of Lock Island, were very visible. They gave the pilots conning the galleons down the channel in line ahead excellent navigational landmarks, despite the darkness, and Merlin reminded himself of that repeatedly as it was *Dreadnought*'s turn to begin forging ahead.

"I suppose I ought to say something along the lines of 'We're underway at last!'" Cayleb said beside him as a mustache of white began curling back from the galleon's cutwater. The crown prince's voice would have sounded remarkably calm to people who didn't know him well.

"You could say that," Merlin replied judiciously. "Unfortunately, if you did, Ahrnahld and I would be forced to strangle you and throw your body over the side."

Cayleb chuckled, and Merlin smiled.

"At least the fleet doesn't think we're crazy," the prince said.

"There is that," Merlin agreed. "In fact, I think your father came up with just about the perfect cover story."

"And it's going to make *so* much trouble for Gorjah when it finally gets back to the Temple, too," Cayleb observed with a beatific smile.

"That does lend it a certain added savor, doesn't it?" Merlin said with a broad smile of his own.

The official explanation for how Haarahld had known to get his galleons to sea—and where to send them—was that one of Baron Wave Thunder's spies in Tarot had discovered the Group of Four's plans. He'd supposedly bought them from someone at court, which, as Cayleb had observed, ought to make things . . . interesting for Gorjah and his closest advisers when word inevitably got back to Clyntahn and his associates. And it very neatly provided an explanation—other than the mysterious visions of one *Seijin* Merlin—for how Haarahld could have planned his counterstroke.

He and the prince stood smiling at one another for several seconds, but then Cayleb's expression sobered.

"All of us—all of *this*—really depends on you, Merlin," he said softly, and Merlin could see his expression clearly, despite the darkness. "Without you, none of these ships would be here. And without you, we might have been just as surprised by this attack as we hope they'll go on thinking we are. In case I haven't said this in so many words, thank you."

"Don't thank me," the man who'd once been Nimue Alban said. "I told your father in our very first interview. I'm using Charis, Cayleb."

"I know that," Cayleb said simply. "I've known it from the beginning. I would've known it even if Father hadn't told me what you said that morning. And I know you feel guilty about it."

Merlin's eyes narrowed. Cayleb's eyes had none of Merlin's light-gathering capability, but the prince smiled anyway, as if he could see Merlin's expression.

"Rayjhis and I tried to tell you that day on the Citadel," he said. "You didn't cause this, Merlin; you only brought it to a head a bit sooner than it would have happened anyway. And, along the way, you've given us at least a chance of surviving."

"Maybe I have," Merlin replied after a few seconds, "but that doesn't change the fact that a lot of people are about to be killed."

"A lot of people would have been killed without you, too," Cayleb said. "The difference—and I hope you'll forgive me for saying it's a difference I approve of—is in exactly *who's* going to be killed. I'm selfish enough to prefer for it to be Hektor of Corisande's subjects, not my father's."

"And, speaking for those subjects, if I may," Falkhan put in from behind them, "I approve just as strongly as you do, Your Highness."

"There, you see?" Cayleb was almost grinning at Merlin now.

Despite himself, Merlin found himself smiling back. Then he shook his head and patted Cayleb on the shoulder. The prince chuckled again, more softly, and the two of them turned back to the rail once again, watching the night as the galleons forged steadily ahead into the darkness.

.II.
Judgment Strait,
Southern Ocean

The Earl of Thirsk found himself panting with exertion as he hauled himself through the entry port on to *King Rahnyld*'s deck, and he took a minute to catch his breath after scaling the battens on the huge galley's towering side. It was a long climb for a man in his fifties who no longer got as much exercise as he probably should, but he'd made it often enough over the weary five-days of this long, creeping voyage to be used to it by this time. And at least this time he felt a certain grim confidence that his idiot "Admiral General" was going to have to listen to him.

The ship, he noticed, was no longer the immaculate showpiece of the fleet which had departed Gorath Bay in mid-October. She was salt stained, now, her gilding and splendid paintwork battered by spray and weather, and her single sail had carried away in the recent gale. Her crew had done well to save the mast, but the replacement spar was shorter than the one which had carried away with the sail, and she looked awkward, almost unfinished.

It didn't help that the starboard bulwark and the gangway above the oar deck had been crushed for a length of over twenty feet where one of the mountainous seas had slammed into her. There were other signs of damage around the decks, including at least one stove-in hatch cover. The ship's carpenter and his mates would have plenty of repairs to occupy them, and he could hear the dismal, patient clanking of the pumps. He could also hear the moans of injured men floating up through the canvas air scoops rigged to ventilate the galley's berth deck, and he knew she'd suffered at least two dozen casualties, as well.

Frankly, he was astonished the lumbering confection had survived at all. Her captain must be considerably more competent than he'd thought.

"My Lord," a voice said, and he turned to find one of the flagship's junior lieutenants at his shoulder.

The young man had the look of one of the overbred, undertrained sprigs of the aristocracy who'd attached themselves to Malikai's "staff." But his red uniform tunic was water-stained and torn on one shoulder, and both his hands were heavily bandaged. Apparently he'd found something useful to do with himself during the storm, and Thirsk smiled at him rather more warmly then he might have otherwise.

"Yes?" he asked.

"My Lord, the Duke and the squadron commanders are assembled in the great cabin. May I escort you to the meeting?"

"Of course, Lieutenant."

"Then if you'll come this way, My Lord."

▼   ▼   ▼

King Rahnyld's great cabin was as splendidly overfurnished as the galley herself had been, although the boards hastily nailed over one of the storm-shattered stern windows and the general evidence of water damage rather detracted from its splendor. Duke Malikai was a tall, florid-faced man, with the fair hair and light complexion of his Tiegelkamp-born mother. Unlike the water-damaged cabin, or the lieutenant who'd guided Thirsk here, he was perfectly groomed, with no outward sign of the storm his flagship had survived. A carefully trimmed beard disguised the possible fault of a slightly receding chin, but his shoulders were broad, his physique was imposing, and he had what the court ladies persisted in describing as a high and lofty brow.

Actually, Thirsk thought, *he's probably even got a working brain in there somewhere. It's just hard to tell from the outside.*

Malikai looked up from a discussion with two of the more junior commodores as Thirsk was escorted into the cabin.

"Ah, My Lord!" he said, beaming as if Thirsk were one of his favorite people. "It's good to see you here."

"Thank you, Your Grace," Thirsk replied with a more restrained, but equally false, smile. "And may I say I was most impressed with Captain Ekyrd's handling of his ship under extremely adverse circumstances."

"I'll pass your compliment on to the Captain," Malikai assured him, but the duke's smile seemed to thin just a bit at the reminder of the violent weather the fleet had encountered. Or, perhaps, the oblique reminder of *where* the fleet had encountered it. Then he looked around the cabin—crowded, despite its luxurious size—and cleared his throat loudly.

"Gentlemen, gentlemen!" he said. "I believe we're all present, now, so let us to business."

It wasn't quite that simple, of course. There was the inevitable jockeying for position around the splendid table. Then there were the equally inevitable bottles of fine brandy, not to mention the obligatory fulsome compliments on its quality. One or two of the commodores around the table looked as impatient as Thirsk felt, but most of these officers were senior enough to know how the game was played, and so they waited until Malikai put down his glass and looked around.

"I'm sure we were all rather dismayed by the weather last five-day," he said, and Thirsk managed to suppress a harsh bark of laughter at the understatement.

"Obviously, the storm, and its consequences, require us to reevaluate our planned course," Malikai continued in his deep, resonant voice. "I realize there's been some difference of opinion about our best route from the beginning. Given the firm instructions issued by His Majesty before our departure, and repeatedly reconfirmed by semaphore dispatch since, we clearly were obligated to attempt the initial course. Not only that, but the Tarotisian fleet will be expecting to make rendezvous with us on the basis of our having followed our original routing.

"Despite that, I believe it's become incumbent upon us to consider alternatives."

He sat back, satisfied with his pronouncement, and Thirsk waited a moment to see if anyone else cared to respond. Then he cleared his own throat in the continuing silence.

"Your Grace," he said, "no one could dispute that it was our duty to follow our original orders insofar as practicable. However, all of the reports I've been able to collect from local pilots and ship masters on our voyage so far indicate that Schueler Strait is by far the harder of the two passages around Samson's Land, particularly at this time of year. The combination of current and the set of the prevailing winds creates exactly the sort of conditions we confronted last five-day, when we attempted that passage. I think, therefore, that we have little option but to consider the relative merits of using Judgment Strait, instead."

To Malikai's credit, no one could actually hear him grinding his teeth. On the other hand, there was no way anyone—including the duke—could realistically dispute what Thirsk had just said, either. If they'd wanted to, the loss of four galleys and one of the fleet's supply ships would have been a fairly powerful rejoinder. And the fact that they'd been forced to run before the wind, until they'd been blown well south and west of Samson's Land would have been another.

"Your Grace," Commodore Erayk Rahlstyn spoke up, "I believe the Earl's made a valid point. And I'd also like to point out, if I may, that we're supposed to make rendezvous with the Tarotisians off Demon Head. If we follow our original route, we'll be forced to cross over two thousand miles of the Sea of Justice, directly into the prevailing winds. Making back the distance we've lost, we'd have a total voyage of around fifty-two hundred miles.

"On the other hand, we're already in the approaches to Judgment Strait. If we continue through that passage, Samson's Land will cover us against the worst of the weather coming in off the Sea of Justice. And we can hug the western coast of Armageddon Reef for additional protection once we're through the strait. And, finally, it's less than thirty-eight hundred miles to Demon Head from our current position via the strait."

Malikai nodded gravely, as if every one of those points hadn't been made to him by Thirsk at least two dozen times in private conversations. But those conversations had taken place before his stubborn adherence to orders which had been written by landsmen who'd simply drawn a line on a chart without regard to wind, weather, or current had cost him five ships destroyed, another dozen or more damaged, and over four thousand casualties.

"You and Earl Thirsk have both made cogent arguments, Commodore," the duke said after a sufficiently lengthy pause to make it clear he'd considered those arguments carefully. "And, while it's never a light matter to set aside royal instructions, still, an officer's true duty is sometimes to . . . reinterpret his instructions in order to accomplish their purpose and intent even if changing circumstances require that he go about it in a slightly different manner. As you and the Earl have pointed out, this is one of those times."

He looked around the table and nodded firmly, as if it had been his idea all along.

"Gentlemen," he announced in a firm, commanding tone, "the fleet will proceed by way of Judgment Strait."

.III.
Eraystor Bay,
Emerald

Prince Nahrmahn gazed out his palace window at the crowded harbor and tried to analyze his own emotions.

On the one hand, he'd never expected to see so many warships in Eraystor Bay, and certainly not to see them there for the express purpose of helping him conquer the kingdom whose steady expansion had posed such a threat to his own princedom for so long. On the other hand, just arranging to feed their crews was going to be a logistical nightmare, and there was the interesting question of what that fleet's commander intended to do *after* Charis was defeated.

He frowned moodily, munching idly on a slice of melon, and contemplated the rapidly approaching admirals' meeting. At least the fact that it was taking place in the land *he* ruled should give both him and Earl Mahndyr a certain added weight in the various councils of war.

On the other hand, Duke Black Water could always point out that he'd brought seventy galleys with him, compared to Emerald's fifty and Chisholm's forty-two. Another ten Corisandian galleys were due to arrive over the next couple of five-days, as well, whereas it would be at least another four five-days before Nahrmahn was able to produce any additional ships. And he had only twenty more available, at most.

It should at least be an interesting discussion, he thought sardonically, and popped another slice of melon into his mouth.

▼   ▼   ▼

Lynkyn Rahlstahn, Duke of Black Water, looked around the council chamber with a dignified expression. He couldn't fault the arrangements Nahrmahn's people had made, much as a part of him would have liked to. The spacious chamber had been cleared of whatever other furniture might once have occupied it and outfitted with a single huge table, surrounded by comfortable chairs. The wall opposite the windows now boasted charts of Eraystor Bay, the Charis Sea, Rock Shoal Bay, and The Throat, and a long, low side table didn't quite groan under the weight of appetizer delicacies, wine bottles, and crystal decanters heaped upon it.

Black Water would infinitely have preferred to host this meeting aboard *Corisande*, his flagship galley. It would have placed it firmly on *his* ground and emphasized his authority, but he could never have crammed this many officers and their aides into *Corisande*'s great cabin. And perhaps that was for the better. It might make it more difficult for him to impose his will, but he had to be mindful of Prince Hektor's instructions to avoid stepping on other people's toes any more obviously then he had to.

On the other hand, he thought, *there's not much question who the Church— I mean, the Knights of the Temple Lands, of course—wants in charge of this entire affair. That should be worth at least as much as a council chamber, however fancy it is.*

He waited patiently while Nahrmahn finished making polite conversation with Sharleyan's Admiral Sharpfield. The prince took his time—possibly to make the point that it was *his* time—about it. Bishop Executor Graisyn was also present, staying close to Nahrmahn, but smiling at anyone who came in range. If the bishop felt out of place surrounded by so many military officers he showed no sign of it.

Finally, though, Nahrmahn crossed to the chair at the head of the table and seated himself. Graisyn followed him, sitting at his right hand, and everyone else began flowing towards the table, as well.

Black Water took his own chair, facing Nahrmahn down the length of the table, and once the two of them were seated, the rest of the horde of flag officers and staffers found *their* seats.

The prince waited again, this time for the scuffing of chairs and the rustle of movement to fade away, then smiled around the table.

"My Lords, allow me to welcome you to Emerald. I'm sure all of us are well enough aware of our purpose to require no restatement of it by me. And, truth be told, my own naval expertise is limited, to say the very least. Earl Mahndyr will represent Emerald in your discussions and planning sessions. Please be assured that he enjoys my complete confidence, and that he speaks for me."

He smiled again, this time with a hint of steel, despite his rotundity. Black Water doubted anyone around that table was stupid enough to misunderstand the prince's implications.

"Before you begin your discussions, however," Nahrmahn continued after a moment, "I'm also sure all of us would appreciate the blessing of Mother Church upon our efforts."

A quiet murmur of voices agreed with him, and he gestured gracefully to Graisyn.

"Your Eminence," he said, "if you would be so gracious as to invoke God's good graces upon the warriors assembled here in His name?"

"Of course, Your Highness. I would be honored."

Graisyn stood, raising his hands in benediction.

"Let us pray," he said. "O God, Creator and Ruler of the universe, we make bold to approach You as Your servant Langhorne has taught us. We ask Your blessings upon these men as they turn their hearts, minds, and swords to the task to which You have called them. Do not—"

▼   ▼   ▼

". . . so all the indications are that Haarahld never saw this coming until about four five-days ago." Baron Shandyr looked around the table, then bowed slightly to Black Water.

"That completes my report, Your Grace," he said, wrapping up a terse, well-organized thirty-minute briefing.

"Thank you, Baron," Black Water replied. "And may I add that your very clear and concise summation accords quite well with all the other information which has so far reached me."

"I'm glad to hear that, Your Grace," Shandyr said. "To be honest, our agents in Charis haven't been . . . as productive as we might have wished over the past year or so."

"Our own nets were badly damaged in that same shakeup, My Lord," Black Water said with a thin smile, forbearing to mention whose botched assassination plan had occasioned the shakeup in question. One must, after all, be polite. "It took months for us to begin putting them back together."

"A great deal of the information which has come to us here in Eraystor is primarily observational," Shandyr admitted frankly. "We don't have anyone inside Haarahld's palace or navy at this point. Not anyone reliable, at any rate. But we've been interviewing the crews of the merchant ships he's expelled from Charisian waters since he learned of our own mobilization. It seems clear he hadn't even begun overhauling his own reserve galleys until about three five-days ago."

"That's true enough," Earl Sharpfield said. "But I have to admit, Your Grace, that I'd feel much more comfortable if we knew more details about these *galleons* of Haarahld's we've been hearing so many rumors about."

"As would all of us," Black Water agreed with another, even thinner smile. "According to the last report we received from our own agents in Tellesberg, they probably have as many as fifteen to twenty of them in service, and all indications are that they're much more heavily armed with cannon than any of our galleys. They may represent a significant threat, although it seems unlikely. While I'm willing to concede that they can probably fire a heavy broadside, they won't have time for more than one or, at most, two before we get alongside them. At which point it's going to be up to the boarders, not the cannoneers."

A rumble of agreement ran around the table, and Black Water's smile grew broader. No one with a working brain was going to take the Royal Charisian Navy lightly, but there was an undeniable echo of confidence in that rumble. However good the Charisians might be, eighty of their galleys and fifteen or twenty galleons would be no match for his own hundred and sixty. Which didn't even count what was going to happen when the Dohlarans and Tarotisians arrived with *another* hundred and sixty.

The . . . lack of alacrity displayed by Chisholm and Emerald, while irritating, was really relatively insignificant in comparison to numbers like that.

"Bearing in mind that these galleons of theirs *are* going to have a powerful broadside armament," Earl Sharpfield said, "I think we might be well advised to consider how best to approach them before we actually meet them."

"I think that's an excellent idea, My Lord," Black Water agreed. "May I assume you've already had some thoughts on the subject?"

"I have," Sharpfield replied with a nod.

"Then please share them with us," Black Water invited. "I'm sure they'll provoke other thoughts as we discuss them."

"Of course, Your Grace," Sharpfield said. "In the first place, it seems to me that—"

Black Water nodded thoughtfully, but even as he listened to the Chisholm admiral laying out possible tactics, a corner of his mind remained busy, pondering Shandyr's report . . . and the maddening silence of his own agents in Charis.

He hadn't known about Maysahn and Makferzahn until he sailed, but Hektor and the Earl of Coris had seen to it that he was fully briefed before his departure. He'd been impressed by the amount of information Coris' agents had been able to assemble, but he'd also expected more information to be awaiting him here, in Eraystor.

Unfortunately, it hadn't been.

One of his staffers had very quietly made contact with Coris' man in Eraystor, who should have been the recipient of any reports from Maysahn or Makferzahn. But he hadn't heard a word from them.

No doubt Haarahld's decision to close his waters would make it difficult for any dispatches to get through, but there should have been *something* waiting for him. He supposed it was possible Maysahn hadn't gotten the word in time, and that the last reports he'd gotten out before Haarahld sealed off Charis had gone to Manchyr instead of Eraystor. It didn't seem very likely, though, which made the man's continued silence even more irritating.

On the other hand, Black Water had never really bought into the notion of secret agents creeping about in the background with vital military information. While he was perfectly willing to admit that spies could be invaluable in peacetime, once the fighting actually started, their value dropped steeply. When the swords were out, it was the information your own scouts provided that mattered, not reports from unknown people whose veracity you couldn't prove.

He grimaced internally, shoved the concern over the oddly incommunicado spies back into its mental cubbyhole, and began actually concentrating on what Sharpfield was saying.

.IV.
Grand Council Chamber,
The Temple

Archbishop Erayk tried very hard to conceal his nervousness as he was escorted into the Grand Council Chamber.

He was fairly certain he'd failed.

The taciturn Temple Guard colonel who'd awaited him on the dock as his galley rowed into Port Harbor through snow flurries and the crackle of thin surface ice hadn't informed him of why the archbishop was to return immediately to Zion with him. He'd simply handed him the message—simple, stark, and to the point—requiring him to appear before a committee of the Council of Vicars for "examination." That was all.

The colonel was still with him . . . and still hadn't explained.

The two of them stepped past the statue-still Guardsmen outside the Grand Council Chamber's door, and the archbishop swallowed as he saw the four vicars of the "committee" waiting for him.

Ancient tradition said the Archangel Langhorne himself had sat in council with his fellow archangels and angels in that chamber, and it was certainly spacious enough to have served that purpose. Its walls were adorned with magnificent mosaics and tapestries. Portraits of past Grand Vicars hung down one enormous wall, and a beautifully detailed map of the world, four times a man's height, had been inlaid into the facing wall. The entire Council of Vicars could be accommodated comfortably, along with their immediate staffs, within its immensity and the four men actually waiting there seemed small, almost lost.

They weren't seated at the raised table on the dais reserved for the Grand Vicar and the senior members of the Council on formal occasions, although any one of the four of them could have claimed a seat there. Instead, they'd chosen to sit behind a smaller, plainer table, one obviously brought into the Council Chamber for the occasion and set up in the center of the vast horseshoe shape of the richly inlaid tables where their fellows would have sat, had they been present. Nor were they completely alone, for two silent upper-priests in the habit of the Order of Schueler stood behind the Grand Inquisitor's chair.

Erayk Dynnys did not find that fact comforting.

The colonel escorted him down the long, crimson runner of carpet to the table, then stopped and bowed deeply.

"Your Grace," he said, directing his words to Allayn Magwair, who was the Temple Guard's commanding officer, "Archbishop Erayk."

"Thank you, Colonel. You may go," Magwair replied, holding out his ring hand. The colonel bowed once more, kissed the sapphire stone, and departed without another word, leaving Dynnys alone before the four most powerful men in the entire Church.

"How may I serve the Council, Vicar Zahmsyn?" he asked. He was pleased that there was no quaver in his voice, but no one responded. They only gazed at him, their eyes cold and thoughtful, and he felt sweat beading his scalp under his priest's cap.

They let him stand there for altogether too many seconds. His stomach churned, knotting itself in anxiety, and *still* they let him stand.

Then, finally, Zhaspyr Clyntahn tapped a folder on the table in front of him.

"This, Archbishop Erayk," he said softly, eyes glittering, "is a copy of the dispatches you and Bishop Executor Zherald sent by courier and semaphore from Tellesberg. We read them with considerable interest. Particularly since they seem to be in sharp disagreement with other reports we've received from that city."

He paused, waiting, and Dynnys swallowed as unobtrusively as he possibly could.

"May I ask what other reports you've received, Your Grace?" he asked.

"You may not," Clyntahn said coldly. "The Inquisition has its own sources, as you well know. They may not be challenged."

Dynnys' heart seemed to stop beating for an instant. Then he drew a deep breath.

"In that case, Your Grace," he said with a steadiness which surprised him just a bit, "may I ask what portions of my dispatches . . . conflict with those reports?"

"There are several points," Clyntahn said, still in that cold, precise voice. "We note, for example, that you allowed your intendant to skimp scandalously on his so-called reexamination of potential violations of the Proscriptions. We note that you failed even to rebuke him for permitting a local—and, I might add, suspect, on the basis of his own preaching—cleric to be present during his interrogation of the King of Charis, where he might influence or affect that examination. We note also that you failed to discipline the Bishop of Tellesberg for the crime of preaching heresy from the pulpit of his own cathedral. And we note, in addition, that you somehow inexplicably failed to mention any of these . . . minor difficulties in your dispatches to the Temple, despite the fact that your attention had been specifically directed to those matters by no less than Vicar Zahmsyn himself before your departure."

Dynnys tried to swallow again. This time, his mouth was too dry.

"These are serious charges, Archbishop," Trynair said. His voice was only marginally less cold than Clyntahn's. "Should they be sustained before a Court of Inquisition, the penalties which attach to them will be severe."

"Your Grace," Dynnys replied hoarsely, "it was not my intention to mislead you or the Council, or the Inquisition. My judgment, formed there in Tellesberg, was that Father Paityr had, indeed, very carefully considered his initial rulings. And while Bishop Maikel may have chosen his words poorly in one or two of his sermons, my reading of the text of those sermons was that they did not approach the threshold of *heresy*. I assure you, if they had, I would have removed him from his see immediately."

"It was indeed your intention to mislead us." Clyntahn's voice was no longer cold; it was harsh, biting. "What remains to be discovered is whether it was no more than an effort to protect your own incompetent arse or whether it goes deeper than that. In either case, *Archbishop*, you've lied to Mother Church, and you *will* suffer the consequences for your actions."

Dynnys looked at the Grand Inquisitor mutely, unable to speak. Then his head snapped back around to Trynair as the Chancellor spoke once more.

"You will face the consequences here," he said in a voice like doom itself, "but the consequences for Charis will be equally severe."

Dynnys' eyes widened.

"Within the month—two months, at the most—" Magwair said harshly, "the Kingdom of Charis will be destroyed. The canker of heresy and defiance will be cut out with fire and the sword, and the archbishopric which once was yours will be purged once and for all of these dangerous, heretical elements you have allowed to flourish."

"Your Grace," somehow Dynnys found his voice once more, "I beg you. I may have failed in my responsibility to the Temple. It was never my intention to do so, but it may be that I failed despite that. But I swear to you, on my own immortal soul and my own hope of Heaven, that nothing I saw in Charis merits punishment such as that!"

His words hung in the air, almost as surprising to him as to the seated vicars. But the men behind the table only gazed at him, their eyes flat, their expressions unyielding. Then Clyntahn turned and looked over his shoulder at the two waiting Schuelerite upper-priests.

"Escort Archbishop Erayk to the suite prepared for him," he said coldly.

Haarahld VII looked up from the correspondence on his desk as the Marine sentry outside his cabin door slammed the butt of his half-pike on the deck.

"Midshipman of the watch, Sire!" he announced loudly.

"Enter," the king replied, and a very youthful midshipman came just a bit timidly through the door, his hat clasped under his arm, and snapped to attention.

"Captain Tryvythyn's respects, Your Majesty," the youngster half-blurted, "but *Speedy* reports the enemy is coming out!"

"Thank you, Master Aplyn," Haarahld said gravely.

At eleven, Master Midshipman Aplyn was the youngest of HMS *Royal Charis'* midshipmen. That was a heavy burden to bear aboard any Navy ship, and it was made worse in Aplyn's case by his first name: Hektor. Haarahld was quite certain the boy had been teased unmercifully ever since reporting aboard, but he'd borne up under it well. He was also remarkably serious about his duties, and the king suspected that Captain Gwylym Tryvythyn had sent him with the sighting report as a reward.

"Ah, was that the Captain's entire message, Master Aplyn?" Haarahld asked after a moment, and the boy blushed fiery red.

"No, Your Majesty," he said, blushing even more darkly. "The Captain asks if you'd care to join him on deck."

"I see."

Aplyn looked as if he would have much preferred to evaporate on the spot, and the king was hard put not to laugh outright and complete the boy's destruction. Somehow, calling on decades of experience dealing with foreign diplomats and ambassadors, he managed not to.

"Very well, Master Aplyn. My compliments to Captain Tryvythyn, and I'll join him on deck directly."

"Yes, Sir—I mean, Your Majesty!" Aplyn got out. He whirled to flee the cabin, but Haarahld cleared his throat.

"A moment, Master Aplyn, if you please," he said gravely, and the youngster froze statue-still.

"Yes, Your Majesty?" he replied in a tiny voice.

"Master Aplyn, you delivered the Captain's message speedily and well. I don't believe it will be necessary to mention any small . . . irregularities about our exchange. Do you?"

"No, Your Majesty!" the midshipman blurted gratefully.

"Then you may go, Master Aplyn."

"Yes, Your Majesty!"

This time, Aplyn did flee, and Haarahld heard something remarkably like a smothered laugh from behind him. He looked over his shoulder and saw Sergeant Gahrdaner. The Guardsman's face was creased in a grin, and Haarahld cocked one eyebrow at his bodyguard.

"Something amuses you, Charlz?" he asked mildly.

"Oh, nothing in the world, Your Majesty," Gahrdaner replied earnestly. "Nothing in the world."

▼   ▼   ▼

Haarahld arrived on deck ten minutes later. He climbed the ladder to the conning position atop the galley's aftercastle, moving slowly but steadily with his stiff knee. Sergeant Gahrdaner followed him, and Captain Tryvythyn was waiting when he reached the top.

"Good morning, Your Majesty," the captain said.

"Good morning, Captain," Haarahld replied formally. He drew a deep breath of the fresh spring air, then raised one hand to shade his eyes and looked into the northeast.

Royal Charis was just south of the chain of islands off Triton Head, leading the centermost of the five columns into which the galley fleet had been deployed. All five columns were barely making steerage way under oars alone, moving just fast enough to maintain formation in the face of the steady breeze out of the northwest.

East Cape, the easternmost of the two capes guarding the entrance to Rock Shoal Bay lay just over four hundred miles west-northwest of their present position, and a chain of scouting vessels extended another sixty miles to the northeast, keeping an eye on the approaches to Eraystor Bay.

That chain was composed of schooners, specifically designed for the Navy by Sir Dustyn Olyvyr, although the shipyards building them hadn't known it. They were shallow-draft vessels, fitted to row if necessary, and small enough to row better and faster than the vast majority of galleys. Armed only with from six to twelve carronades, depending on their size, they were designed specifically to be used as scouts. They were fast, nimble, weatherly, and under express order to run away from any threat.

Now HMS *Speedy*, the northernmost schooner in the chain, had hoisted the signal that the combined Northern Force was sortieing. Haarahld could just see the topsails of HMS *Arrow*, the closest of the four schooners making up the entire chain. The midshipman perched in the lookout platform high up on *Royal Charis'* single mast, on the other hand, had one of the long, heavy spyglasses with which to read the colorful flags which repeated *Speedy*'s original signal.

"So, our friends are coming south, are they?" Haarahld was careful to project a note of amusement. "Odd. I'd started to think they were too shy to come to the dance, Captain."

One or two of the seamen and Marines stationed on the aftercastle smiled, and Captain Tryvythyn chuckled. Like Haarahld, he knew the king's joke, small as it was, would be repeated all over the ship within the hour.

"They aren't in any hurry about it, Your Majesty," he replied after a moment. "*Speedy* reports their speed at no more than five knots, despite the wind. She also says their formation is . . . disorderly."

"At that rate, they won't be up to us before dark," Haarahld reflected aloud, and Tryvythyn nodded.

"That's my own conclusion, Your Majesty."

"Well," the king said slowly, thoughtfully, "I suppose the prudent thing to do is to avoid a decisive action until Prince Cayleb and Admiral Staynair can return. Still, I think it's time we showed our hesitant dance partners the steps, Captain. Be so good as to signal *Tellesberg*. Inform Admiral Lock Island that we intend to pass within hailing distance, and then shape your course for her, if you would."

"Of course, Your Majesty. Master Aplyn!"

"Yes, Sir!"

"Signal *Tellesberg* that we intend to pass within hailing distance."

"Aye, aye, Sir!"

"Lieutenant Gyrard."

"Yes, Sir."

"Come four points to port, if you please. Lay us within hailing distance of *Tellesberg*."

"Aye, aye, Sir."

Orders rang out, and *Royal Charis'* oars quickened their stroke as the royal flagship altered course to close with *Tellesberg*. The columns were only seven hundred and fifty yards apart, and it didn't take long for the two flagships to find themselves side by side, separated by barely thirty yards of water.

"Good morning, Your Majesty!" Earl Lock Island called through his leather speaking trumpet. "How may I serve you this morning?"

"I believe it's time to go and see if these shy and retiring gentlemen are serious about venturing out of their nice, snug harbor, Admiral," Haarahld called back. "Be so good as to see to that for me, if you would."

"Of course, Your Majesty. With pleasure." Lock Island bowed across the gap, then turned to his own officers. A moment later, signals began to break from *Tellesberg's* yardarm while *Royal Charis* turned to resume her original station, leading her own column.

"Well, Captain Tryvythyn," Haarahld said, watching *Tellesberg* pick up speed as she and the twenty-nine other galleys of the fleet's two port columns headed off to the northeast, "I'm afraid I have some letters and reports I need to deal with. Please inform me if there are any additional signals."

"Of course, Your Majesty."

▼   ▼   ▼

Duke Black Water stood atop *Corisande's* aftercastle, hands clasped behind him, and concentrated on not cursing.

He hadn't really expected today's sortie to go smoothly, but he'd hoped it might go more smoothly than it actually had.

Yet another example of hope triumphing over experience, he thought sourly.

But that wasn't really fair, and he knew it. No one *had* any actual experience at hammering together three totally separate navies, two of which were accustomed to thinking of one another as mortal enemies, on less than three months' notice. With the greatest goodwill in the world, getting three different fleets coordinated would have been extraordinarily difficult, considering the inherent differences in signals, structure, tactics, and seniority.

Given the fact that "goodwill" was conspicuously lacking, just getting all their ships moving in the same direction on the same day was something of an accomplishment.

He snorted in wry amusement at the thought. Biting as it was, it at least restored some badly needed perspective to his current predicament. And however reluctant this particular arranged marriage might have been, the fact that it had been made by Mother Church (whether she admitted it or not) meant all of its participants had damned well better dig in to make it work. Which they undoubtedly would, given time.

Which, in turn, brought him back to the point of today's exercise.

Prince Hektor, he knew, would be simply delighted if an immediate opportunity to crush the Royal Charisian Navy should present itself. Well, Black Water would, too, but he wasn't going to hold his breath waiting for the chance. He estimated that he had a superiority of approximately two-to-one in hulls over Haarahld's active galley fleet, but there were still those galleons to worry about. And, whatever his theoretical numerical advantage might be, until he could count on his various squadron commanders to at least understand what he wanted them to do, numbers as such didn't mean a great deal.

He turned and gazed out over the panorama which underscored that brutal fact.

His huge force of galleys was spread out across the rolling blue plain of Eraystor Bay in a mob-like formation. The Triton Peninsula lay about twenty miles to starboard; to port, the nearest land was the big near-island known as The Wyvernry, almost four hundred and fifty miles to the southeast. The wind was out of the northwest, brisk enough to lift whitecapped waves of about four feet and move the galleys much more rapidly than they *were* moving. Few of his subordinate commanders, however, seemed to feel any particular need to take full advantage of that wind, despite any exhortations from him. The fleet was like some vast gaggle of sea wyverns bobbing on the surface of the waves and drifting leisurely along. Most of its units appeared to be on approximately the right heading, but that was about the best he could say.

It was relatively easy to pick out the divisions between his and his "allies'" galleys; theirs were the ones falling steadily farther behind. His own squadrons formed the vanguard, exactly as planned, although he was forced to admit that even their stationkeeping was far from perfect. His lead squadron was well in advance of his main formation, for example, and he shook his head.

Donyrt Qwentyn, Baron Tanlyr Keep, was an aggressive, thrusting officer, not the sort to let sailing conditions like these go to waste. Those qualities were to be encouraged, but Tanlyr Keep's disdain for what he considered Emerald's tardiness and lack of enthusiasm was only too evident, and his dislike for Corisande's traditional Chisholmian foes was equally pronounced. Which probably had something to do with the baron's determination to get his ships out in front and keep them there while he showed Mahndyr, Sharpfield, and their "laggards" how a *real* admiral did things.

Black Water had chosen him to command his own vanguard specifically because of those qualities, and Tanlyr Keep had responded by getting *his* ships to sea almost a full hour before dawn, well before anyone else had even cleared the breakwater. He'd opened the gap between him and the rest of the fleet steadily since then, and the hulls of his ships were only intermittently visible from deck level now.

Black Water made a mental note to discuss the concept of coordination and at least outward respect for allies with his subordinates. Not just Tanlyr Keep, either.

"I beg your pardon, Your Grace," a voice said, and he turned to find one of *Corisande's* lieutenants at his elbow.

"Yes?"

"Captain Myrgyn asked me to inform you, Your Grace, that Baron Tanlyr Keep is signaling that a sail is in sight to the southwest."

"Only one?"

"That's all the Baron has reported, Your Grace."

"I see."

Black Water considered for a moment, then shrugged. They knew Haarahld had been keeping scout ships spread across the approaches to Eraystor Bay. It was the only sensible thing for him to do, after all, and Black Water wouldn't be a bit surprised to discover he was using those infernally weatherly schooners of his for the task. If that was the case, no galley was going to catch one on a day with winds as brisk as today's, but that might not always be the case. For now, it was simply confirmation of what they'd anticipated all along.

"Thank the Captain for keeping me informed," he said.

"Of course, Your Grace."

The lieutenant bowed and withdrew, and Black Water returned to his earlier thoughts. He was tempted to signal the straggling components of "his" fleet to keep better station. The probability of any signal from him accomplishing any good, however, had to be weighed against the querulousness it would reveal.

Nagging ineffectually at them to close up their formation would only make it more difficult in the long run to exercise effective command.

Whatever he might think of Sharpfield and Admiral Mahndyr, both of them were experienced men, he reflected. They had to be as well aware as he was of what they were seeing, and it would be far more effective to discuss that with them face to face than to fire off signals which probably wouldn't be obeyed, anyway. Assuming, of course, that their signal officers could even recognize them as signals in the first place!

He sighed and shook his head. No doubt this had all looked far simpler from the comfort of a planning session somewhere in the Temple.

▼   ▼   ▼

Earl Lock Island stood in his chart room, contemplating the various ships' positions marked on the chart spread out on the table before him while he scratched his chin. His aide, Lieutenant Tillyer, stood quietly to one side, watching and waiting.

The earl gazed at the chart for several more seconds, his eyes focused on something only he could see, then nodded.

"I think it's time to go back topside, Henrai."

"Yes, My Lord." Tillyer reached the chart room door before the earl and stood aside, holding it open for his superior. Lock Island smiled at him and shook his head as he stepped through it, but the smile faded quickly as he climbed the short ladder to the aftercastle.

"My Lord!"

Captain Sir Ohwyn Hotchkys, *Tellesberg*'s commanding officer, saluted as Lock Island appeared. The earl returned his salute a bit more casually, then gazed up at the masthead pendant.

"Any change in our friends' formation?" he asked.

"No, My Lord. Not according to the schooners' reports, at any rate."

"Good." Lock Island turned away from the pendant and smiled unpleasantly at the captain. "In that case, Ohwyn, I believe it's time to put your signal parties to work. Here's what I want to do. . . ."

▼   ▼   ▼

"Pardon me for interrupting, Your Grace, but I think Baron Tanlyr Keep's sighted something else."

Black Water looked up from his belated breakfast as Sir Kehvyn Myrgyn stepped into *Corisande*'s great cabin.

"What do you mean, 'sighted something else,' Captain?" the duke asked, chocolate cup hovering in midair.

"I'm not certain, Your Grace," Myrgyn said a bit apologetically. "He's shaken out the reefs in his squadron's sails, and he's gone to oars, as well."

"Did he make any signals at all?" Black Water demanded, setting the cup down.

"Not that we could make out, Your Grace. Of course, he's far enough ahead of us that he might have signaled *something* without our spotting it."

Black Water scowled and pushed his chair back from the table. He'd known Tanlyr Keep was edging steadily, if gradually, further and further ahead, but he hadn't expected the baron's squadron to get *that* far out in front.

He strode on deck, Myrgyn following at his shoulder, and climbed to the top of the aftercastle.

Tanlyr Keep's ships were completely hull-down over the horizon from Black Water's position on *Corisande*'s deck. All the duke could see was their sails, and even they were dipping towards the hard, clear line of the horizon, but it was obvious the baron had, indeed, shaken the reefs out of his galleys' big, single square mainsails. With the wind out of the northwest, it was broad on Tanlyr Keep's starboard quarter, and he was taking full advantage of it.

"He's under oars, as well, Captain?" Black Water asked.

"Yes, Your Grace," Myrgyn confirmed, and the duke grimaced. That meant Tanlyr Keep was probably moving almost twice as fast as any of the rest of the allied force.

"Signal him to return to his station," he said.

"At once, Your Grace," Myrgyn replied, and turned to give the orders.

Another of the flagship's lieutenants sprang to obey the instructions, but Myrgyn's expression wasn't hopeful when he turned back to Black Water.

"He's far enough ahead I don't know if he'll even see the signal, Your Grace."

"I know." Black Water gripped his hands together behind him, rocking gently up and down on his toes while he considered. Then he looked astern, where the Emerald and Chisholm contingents had strayed even further out of position. Finally, he looked up at the sun.

The basic plan for today's sortie called for the fleet to return to its anchorage before nightfall. To do that, especially with the wind where it was, they were going to have to reverse course within the next three hours, at the outside. Given the speed Tanlyr Keep's squadron was making, *Corisande* and the rest of the Corisandian galleys wouldn't be able to overtake him, no matter what they did, and the baron knew when he was supposed to return to port.

The duke growled a silent mental curse. It was a comprehensive curse, directed at his laggardly allies, his . . . overly enthusiastic squadron commander, and at himself, for not keeping Tanlyr Keep's leash shorter. But curses wouldn't undo anything that had already happened. Signaling the baron to resume his station was all he could do, since he couldn't overtake Tanlyr Keep, anyway. And that being the case, he might as well do what he could to bolster his own reputation for phlegmatic confidence.

"Well, Captain Myrgyn," he said, after moment. "If he sees the signal, he sees the signal, and if he doesn't, he doesn't." He shrugged. "We'll be reversing course in the next few hours, anyway, and I still have an appointment with breakfast. If you'll excuse me?"

"Of course, Your Grace."

The captain bowed, and Black Water produced a confident smile as he headed back towards the breakfast which no longer seemed nearly so appetizing. But, appetizing or not, he intended to eat every last bite of it . . . and make certain everyone aboard his flagship knew he had.

▼   ▼   ▼

"We've just received another signal from Commodore Nylz, My Lord," Lieutenant Tillyer said.

"Ah?"

Earl Lock Island looked up from the fried chicken he was hungrily contemplating. The fleet hadn't been at sea long enough yet for fresh food to become a dreamed of, unobtainable luxury, but no seaman worth his salt ever turned up his nose at a decent meal.

"Yes, My Lord. He reports that the squadron pursuing him is still overhauling. In fact, it's into long cannon shot."

"I see." Lock Island rose from the table and stepped out onto *Tellesberg*'s spacious sternwalk. The railed platform ran the full width of the galley's high, ornate stern and wrapped around either quarter. The admiral stood for a moment, gazing up at the sky, gauging visibility and the remaining hours of daylight.

"I believe it's time, Henrai," he said, returning to the table and reaching for a drumstick as he seated himself once more. "Signal Commodore Nylz to engage at his discretion."

▼   ▼   ▼

"My Lord, the enemy—"

Donyrt Qwentyn, Baron Tanlyr Keep, had been gazing astern, where the white sails of Duke Black Water's main body had disappeared into the whitecapped blue of the bay, while he wondered why the duke hadn't cracked on more speed in response to his own earlier signals. Now he wheeled towards the lieutenant who'd spoken just as a sudden dull thud sounded across the water. Sudden clouds of smoke from the sterns of the six Charisian galleys he'd been pursuing for the last several hours, and the white, skipping splashes of round shot plowing across the waves obviated the report the lieutenant had been about to make.

"Good!" the baron barked, and wheeled to *Thunderbolt*'s commander. "It looks like they've figured out they can't get away, Captain. Now let's go get them!"

▼   ▼   ▼

Commodore Kohdy Nylz watched critically as his stern chasers opened fire. Despite the whitecaps, it was easy to spot where the shots had plunged into the sea, quite close to their targets, and he nodded in satisfaction.

"I hope the gun crews remember to fire slowly," one of HMS *Kraken*'s lieutenants murmured.

The commodore glanced at the youthful officer, but it was evident the lieutenant didn't realize he'd spoken aloud. Nylz considered replying to him anyway, then changed his mind. It would only embarrass the youngster, and the lieutenant hadn't said anything Nylz wasn't thinking.

His squadron had been selected for this particular maneuver because its artillery had been improved considerably. When Prince Cayleb and Admiral Staynair concentrated their efforts on the most advanced galleons, work on less advanced ships had been temporarily abandoned. The guns for some of those incomplete galleons had already been delivered, however, and Earl Lock Island and King Haarahld had seen no reason to leave them sitting uselessly ashore in an arsenal somewhere. Which meant *Kraken* and the other five galleys of her squadron had traded in their old-fashioned guns for the new-model weapons, with long krakens mounted fore and aft and carronades replacing falcons on their broadsides.

If everything went according to plan, the ten Corisandian ships pursuing him were going to find out about that shortly, but it wouldn't do to alert them *too* soon.

The commodore looked astern at his enemies, and his smile turned nastier as he thought about what was coming up from the east-southeast under oars alone.

▼   ▼   ▼

"We've got the bastards now!" Tanlyr Keep exulted.

The Charisian galleys had obviously been assigned to keep a protective eye on their scout ships in case Duke Black Water had decided to send out a few fast ships of his own to pounce upon them. But the "protectors" clearly hadn't realized the allied fleet was actually at sea. They'd continued towards him, as if seeking to make positive identification, until he'd managed to close to within no more than ten miles.

They'd turned to run then, but one of them had suffered damage aloft making the turn. It looked as if her weather sheet had carried away, and her single big sail had flogged and flapped furiously for several minutes before her crew had been able to get it back under control. That had cost her precious speed, and his own ships had charged forward in pursuit.

Her consorts, instead of abandoning her to her own resources, had reduced speed to stay in company with her. They shouldn't have. The six of them were each individually bigger than any of Tanlyr Keep's ships, but he had ten galleys to their six, and heavy drafts from the Corisandian Army had been put aboard to serve as marines. More than that, his ships' smaller size made them faster under oars.

He'd taken advantage of that, going to the sweeps and adding their power to the power of his ships' sails, and the gap between him and the fleeing Charisians had slowly but steadily narrowed. Now it was time to—

"Deck, there!" The shout echoed down from the crow's-nest atop the mast. "More ships, bearing east-southeast!"

Tanlyr Keep froze, staring up at the lookout.

"I make it at least fifteen galleys!" the seaman shouted down. "They're coming up fast under oars!"

▼   ▼   ▼

"Ah, they've seen the Earl!" Commodore Nylz observed as the galleys which had been pursuing him so doggedly suddenly wavered in their steady course. They were swinging wildly around, turning back up to the north, but that took them almost directly into the wind.

"Turn us around, Captain," he said to *Kraken*'s commander.

▼   ▼   ▼

"It looks like it worked, My Lord," Captain Hotchkys observed.

"So far, at least," Lock Island agreed.

The pursuing Corisandian galleys had dropped their masts. Lock Island's own ships had been waiting with their sails already down while Commodore Nylz' squadron baited the trap. With their sails and yards sent down to leave only their bare, white-painted masts, Lock Island's twenty-four galleys had been far harder to spot; indeed, they'd been effectively invisible at any range much over ten miles or so. And, as Lock Island had anticipated, the Corisandians' attention had been focused upon their intended prey. No one had even noticed him until he'd closed to a range of less than seven miles, sweeping in on the Corisandians from their eastern flank.

Nylz' ships were turning upon their pursuers, as well. The range there had fallen to under *two* miles even before Nylz opened fire. And, just as Lock Island had hoped, the Corisandian rowers were already badly fatigued from their long, grueling pursuit. Apparently it hadn't occurred to them to wonder why Nylz hadn't been rowing nearly as hard as they had.

The Charisian ships had cleaner bottoms, as well as fresher rowers, and Nylz was closing quickly. Lock Island wouldn't be able to get into action with the Corisandians as soon as the commodore, but his galleys—coaxed carefully into position by signals from the scouting schooners and Nylz himself—would be up with the enemy within two hours. Probably less, if Nylz could manage to slow them down a bit.

Kraken and her squadron mates had increased their rate of fire now that the trap had sprung. They were careful not to fire as rapidly as they *could* have—Lock Island and Nylz had no intention of letting Black Water realize just how dangerous Charisian artillery had just become—but as Lock Island watched, one of the Corisandian galley's starboard oars flailed in sudden confusion as a round shot pitched into them in an eruption of spray and splinters. At least four of the long sweeps shattered, splintered ends flying, and the earl could picture only too well what the butt ends of those shattered oars must have done as they flailed wildly about, breaking ribs and arms and cracking skulls.

The confusion was only brief, but more round shot were plunging into the water around their targets, or striking home with deadly force.

"Signal from *Speedy*, My Lord," one of *Tellesberg*'s midshipmen announced.

"Read it," Lock Island commanded.

" 'Enemy van bears north-northwest my position, distance eighteen miles, speed seven knots,' " the midshipman read from the piece of paper in his hand.

"Thank you," Lock Island said, and cocked his head as he consulted his mental chart. He couldn't see the schooner himself from deck level, but the masthead lookout and signal party could. She was still too far away for her signals to be read directly, so they were being relayed by her sister ship *North Wind*. Which put the main body of the straggling enemy fleet at least twenty-five miles—probably more—astern and directly to windward of Nylz' pursuers.

Those ships were making possibly three or four knots, while his own were moving at at least six, and cutting the angle to boot. If the rest of the enemy fleet was making good the seven knots *Speedy*'s captain estimated, then it would take at least two and a half hours for its most advanced units to reach the ships he was pursuing.

If they realized what was happening in time—and moved quickly and decisively enough—it could get tight, but not, he thought grimly, tight enough to save his intended prey.

▼   ▼   ▼

"That's the last of them, Your Grace," Captain Myrgyn grated as a fresh pillar of smoke billowed upward.

"So I see, Captain," Duke Black Water replied.

He forced his own voice to come out calm, but he knew he wasn't fooling anyone. Especially not Myrgyn.

He gripped his hands together behind him tightly enough to hurt and inhaled deeply.

"Very well, Captain," he said, "there's no point continuing the pursuit. Take us home."

"Yes, Your Grace," Myrgyn said heavily, and turned away to begin giving the necessary orders.

Black Water glared across the miles of water still separating him from the last of Tanlyr Keep's galleys. It would take him a good hour and a quarter to reach that flaming hulk, by which time it would have burned to the waterline and vanished beneath the waves. Nor was there any point in pursuing the Charisians, who'd already turned for home with the wind behind them, a good headstart, and—for all he knew—the *rest* of their accursed fleet waiting to ambush anyone who pursued *them*.

Even assuming he could overtake them at all, it would be a night battle, with all the confusion and chaos that implied. And it would have been his galleys—his sixty *remaining* galleys—alone against whatever he encountered, because neither the Emerald nor the Chisholm squadrons could possibly have made up the gap which had opened between them and him.

A part of him cried out to continue the chase anyway, to avenge the losses and humiliation which had been visited upon him. But the coldly logical part of him knew better.

They say you learn more from a defeat than from a victory, he thought grimly. *Well, in that case we've learned a lot today, and I intend to see to it that* all *of us "allies" draw the same conclusions from our lesson.*

What had happened to Tanlyr Keep this afternoon would serve as a very pointed reminder of the need for all of them to learn to function as a single, coordinated force. That would probably be worth what it was going to cost him and Corisande in prestige and moral authority.

Probably.

FEBRUARY,
YEAR OF GOD 892

.I.
Broken Anchor Bay,
Armageddon Reef

U nknown ships entering the anchorage!"
        Gahvyn Mahrtyn, Baron White Ford, jerked upright in his chair as
the lookout's shout echoed down through the open skylight. *King Gorjah II*, the
flagship of the Tarotisian Navy, moved uneasily to her anchor even here, in the
shelter of Demon Head. Which was fair enough; everyone *aboard* her was much
more than merely uneasy just to be here.

Someone knocked sharply at the great cabin's door, and he heard his valet
open it. A moment later, one of the flagship's lieutenants appeared in his private
chart room.

"Excuse me for disturbing you, My Lord, but—"

"I heard, Lieutenant Zhoelsyn." White Ford smiled thinly. "Should I assume
our unknown visitors are our long-awaited Dohlaran friends?"

"That's what it looks like, My Lord," Zhoelsyn acknowledged with a smile of
his own.

"Well praise Langhorne," White Ford said lightly. "Please tell Captain Kaillee
I'll be on deck in about fifteen minutes."

"Of course, My Lord."

Lieutenant Zhoelsyn withdrew, and White Ford raised his voice.

"Zheevys!"

"Yes, My Lord?" Zheevys Bahltyn, the baron's valet since boyhood, replied.

"My new tunic, Zheevys! We have a duke to impress."

"At once, My Lord."

▼   ▼   ▼

Two hours later, White Ford stood on *King Gorjah II*'s aftercastle in the cool
spring sunlight and watched the Dohlaran Navy rowing slowly and heavily into
Broken Anchor Bay. The bay, even though sheltered from the northeast wind by
the projecting finger of Demon Head, was no glassy mirror. Outside the bay, ten-
and-a-half-foot waves, whitecaps, and spray showed only too plainly what sort of
weather awaited the combined fleets.

Not that White Ford had needed the reminder. He'd lost two galleys, with
all hands, just getting here. And from the looks of the Dohlaran galleys straggling

into the more sheltered waters of the bay, they'd had an even worse time of it than he had.

Several of the ships he saw flew command streamers, but none of them showed the red and green stripes of the fleet flagship. Then, finally, he saw a mammoth galley, dwarfing those about her, creeping around the southern headland. The single yard her mast crossed was too small, obviously a jury-rigged replacement for the original, and she towered above her smaller consorts. In fact, she was double-banked, something White Ford hadn't seen in at least twenty years, and he shook his head in disbelief as he watched waves sweep higher than the lower oar bank while jets of white water cascaded from her pumps.

"What *is* that thing, My Lord?" Captain Zhilbert Kaillee asked quietly beside him, and the baron snorted.

"That, Zhilbert, is the flagship of the Dohlaran Navy. The *King Rahnyld*."

"*King Rahnyld*," Kaillee repeated, and White Ford chuckled.

"At least we named *our* flagship for a *previous* king," he said. "And unless I miss my guess, that monstrosity must've cost almost as much as two more reasonably sized galleys. Not to mention the fact that she has to be Hell's pure bitch to manage in a seaway."

"To say the least," Kaillee murmured as white water burst over the enormous galley's cutwater and swirled back around her struggling sweeps.

"But they got her here somehow," White Ford pointed out. "Even if they are a five-day late."

"For my money, My Lord, they did a damned incredible job to get her here at all."

The baron nodded, gazing at the sea-slimed hulls, the occasional empty oarport, the patches of bare planking which marked hasty repairs. Just watching the way the Dohlarans moved through the water, it was obvious their bottoms were badly fouled from the long voyage, which must have reduced their speed even further.

He wondered once again what lunacy had possessed the genius who'd planned this campaign. It would have made so much more sense to send the Dohlarans up the western coasts of Howard and Haven, then straight to Tarot, where the host of minor repairs they so obviously required could have been seen to. But, no, they had to come *here*, to the most haunted, ill-fated, unlucky place on the face of Safehold, and sail directly from here against their enemies.

"Well, I suppose the *real* fun starts now," he told Captain Kaillee, and there was no more humor in his tone.

▼   ▼   ▼

Earl Thirsk watched from his place behind Duke Malikai as Baron White Ford and his flag captain were shown into *King Rahnyld*'s great cabin.

The Tarotisian admiral was a small man, shorter even than Thirsk himself and slender, with dark eyes and dark hair, just starting to silver. Zhilbert Kaillee, the commander of his flagship, could have been specifically designed as a physical contrast. Nearly as tall as Malikai, he was far more massive, almost block-like, with enormous shoulders, and probably outweighed the duke by at least fifty or sixty pounds, none of it fat.

The two of them were followed by a small cluster of more junior captains and senior lieutenants, and Malikai greeted them with a broad, welcoming smile. Thirsk doubted the duke was even aware of that smile's patronizing edge.

"Admiral White Ford," Thirsk murmured as it was his turn to clasp the Tarotisian's hand, and a flicker of amusement danced in the smaller man's dark eyes.

"*Admiral* Thirsk," he replied, and Thirsk's mouth twitched in an effort not to smile at the Tarotisian's slight but unmistakable emphasis. White Ford had greeted Malikai as *Duke* Malikai, which was certainly correct, but obviously he'd recognized that however nobly born Malikai might be, he was no seaman.

Thirsk and the baron stood there for a few seconds, hands clasped, each recognizing a fellow professional, and then the moment passed and White Ford moved on. But Thirsk treasured that brief exchange, which seemed to promise a potentially sane ally. He hoped it did, at any rate, because he suspected he was going to need one.

▼   ▼   ▼

"I apologize for our tardiness, Baron White Ford," Duke Malikai said, as the formal after-dinner council of war got down to business. "I'm afraid the weather on our original route was worse than anticipated. I was forced to choose an alternate passage."

"I anticipated that that was the probable cause, Your Grace," White Ford said. "As you know, the semaphore system kept us reasonably well apprised of your progress. Given the weather we encountered on our own passage here, I wasn't surprised you were delayed. Indeed, I'm gratified you lost as few ships as you did."

"That's very understanding of you, Baron." Malikai smiled. "I'm sure I speak for all of us when I say I hope the worst of the weather is behind us now, and—"

"I'm sure we all do hope that, Your Grace. Unfortunately, it's most unlikely that it is."

Malikai closed his mouth with an expression which was both surprised and perhaps a bit affronted by White Ford's polite interruption. He looked at the Tarotisian for a moment, as if unsure how to respond, and Earl Thirsk cleared his throat.

"I'm sure you and your navy are much more familiar with the weather in these waters, Admiral White Ford," he said, and White Ford shrugged.

"We seldom come this far south, ourselves, of course. No one comes to Armageddon Reef unless he has to. But we are rather familiar with weather in the Parker Sea and the Cauldron. And at this time of year, weather seems to beget weather, as they say. This northeasterly may veer, possibly all the way round to the northwest, but it isn't going away. Or, rather, there's going to be another one, probably at least as strong, on its heels."

"That sounds . . . unpleasant," Thirsk observed in a carefully neutral tone, not even glancing at Malikai. For once, the duke appeared to have enough sense to keep his mouth shut, and the earl devoutly hoped it would stay that way.

"It's not that bad for galleons," White Ford said with a casual little wave of his hand. "It's not often we get seas much over fifteen or sixteen feet. But it *can* get a bit—what was the word you used, My Lord? Ah, yes. It can get a bit *unpleasant* for galleys."

There was a sudden, thoughtful silence from the Dohlaran end of the great cabin, and Thirsk had to raise his own hand to hide his smile.

"We do get the occasional full gale, as well, of course," White Ford continued. "When that happens, the waves can hit as much as thirty feet, but they're more common in the fall than in the spring. And you practically never see a hurricane in these waters, even in the fall."

"Since you're so much more familiar with the weather in these latitudes, My Lord," Thirsk said, choosing his words and his tone with care, "would you care to comment on our course from this point?"

"Well, since you ask, Admiral," White Ford said, "I'm afraid I feel we would be ill advised to cross the Parker Sea north of Tryon's Land, as our original orders specify. The weather's unlikely to cooperate with us, and we've both already lost ships and men. I'm no fonder of Armageddon Reef than any other sane human being, but my advice would be to continue around Demon Head, then pass between Thomas Point and the most southern of Shan-wei's Footsteps and hug the eastern coast of the Reef through Doomwhale Reach and the Iron Sea until we're at least as far east as MacPherson's Lament."

"Excuse me, Baron," Malikai said, "but that would add many miles to our voyage, and wouldn't we risk being caught on a lee shore if the wind does stay in the northeast?"

At least, Thirsk thought, it was a question, not an arrogant statement of objection.

"Yes, it would add some miles to the trip, Your Grace," White Ford conceded. "But the weather in the Parker Sea isn't going to moderate very much, whatever we want. And the weather south of MacPherson's Lament is going to be worse—considerably worse. We don't have any choice about swinging south of the Lament, into the Iron Sea, and while there's something to be said for skirting around through Tryon Sound and avoiding as much as possible of the Iron Sea, we'd still have to cross the *Parker* Sea to get there."

He paused, as if to see if his explanation was being followed. Malikai said nothing, and the Tarotisian continued.

"We're going to be looking at foul weather, whichever route we take, Your Grace, and while we'll certainly find ourselves traveling along a 'lee shore,' the entire coast of the Reef is broken up by bays and inlets. If we hit the sort of weather that's already cost us so many ships, we'll probably be able to find cover, someplace we can anchor and ride it out." He shrugged once more. "As I say, Your Grace, these waters aren't kind to galleys."

There was silence in the great cabin. *King Rahnyld*'s massive bulk shifted uneasily, even here, at anchor, as if on cue, and every ear could hear her the steady sound of the pumps, still emptying her bilges of the water she'd taken on through her lower oarports.

Thirsk knew Malikai couldn't be pleased to hear White Ford say exactly what Thirsk had been arguing all along. Still, the long, painful voyage to this point seemed to have been capable of teaching even the duke a little wisdom. It was a pity he hadn't had enough of it earlier to gather the sort of information Thirsk had before they ever set out. He might even have had the wit to argue against their proposed route from the outset. Still, Thirsk was a great believer in the proposition that it was better for wisdom to come late than never to come at all.

Of course, the fact that White Ford was an allied fleet commander, not simply one more subordinate, even if the entire Tarotisian Navy amounted to less than a quarter of Malikai's fleet, probably gave his words additional weight.

"Baron White Ford," Malikai said finally, "I bow to your greater familiarity with conditions in these waters. What matters most is that we reach our destination in a battle-ready condition, and from what you've said, it would seem to me your proposed route is more likely to deliver us in that condition."

Thank you, Langhorne, the Earl of Thirsk thought very, very sincerely. *And thank* you, *Admiral White Ford*.

▼   ▼   ▼

"What do you think, My Lord?" Captain Kaillee asked as he and White Ford stood on *King Gorjah II*'s aftercastle and watched the long chain of galleys rowing out of Broken Anchor Bay.

"Of what?" the baron asked mildly.

"What do you think of our allies?"

"Oh."

White Ford pursed his lips thoughtfully, studying the fleet as he considered his flag captain's question.

His flagship's motion was uneasy, to say the least, but at least the seas had moderated a bit in the two days since the Dohlarans' arrival. The galley's bows threw up a cloud of spray as she drove into a wave, but her sweeps moved steadily, strongly.

The bigger Dohlaran galleys coming along astern moved more heavily. In some ways, their larger size helped, but it was obvious to White Ford that they'd never been designed for the open sea. Their narrow, shoal hulls, typical of coastal-water designs, produced a vessel which was fast under oars but dangerously tender under sail . . . and less than stable, even in seas this moderate. He doubted they'd ever been intended to operate outside the Gulf of Dohlar, and by his estimate, the odds of their losing at least another half-dozen of them before they reached MacPherson's Lament were at least even.

"I'd say," he told Kaillee judiciously, "that the sooner that ridiculous flagship of theirs sinks, the better."

The flag captain's eyebrows rose. Not so much in surprise at White Ford's judgment, but at how openly his admiral had expressed it. White Ford saw his expression, and chuckled without very much humor.

"This entire notion of our 'sneaking up' on Haarahld from the south is ridiculous," he said. "Only an idiot would think he isn't going to have scouts posted all along the passage between Silver and Charis. So, in the end, it's going to come down to our combined strength against his combined strength in a head-on attack. Would you agree with that much?"

"Of course, My Lord."

"Well, if *Thirsk* had been in command of the Dohlarans, he would have found some plausible reason his ships had to continue clear up the coast to the Gulf of Mathyas. Which would have meant we could have taken the entire fleet up through the Anvil, in which case we probably wouldn't have lost *anyone* to simple bad weather. But Malikai's going to stick by his orders, come hell or high water. He's already done that, and I don't see any reason to expect him to change his style now. Which means he's going to command his forces like the landlubber he is. And *that* means Haarahld's people are going to ream us all new ones. Oh," he waved one hand, "we'll take them in the end. The odds are just too heavy for it to come out any other way. But we're going to lose a lot more ships, and a lot more people, with that idiot giving the orders."

Kaillee sat back on his mental heels, chewing on his admiral's acid analysis, then sighed.

"What?" White Ford asked.

"Nothing, really, My Lord." Kaillee shook his head. "I was just thinking how nice it would be if I could come up with a reason to disagree with you."

The Earl of Thirsk watched the clouds of seabirds and wyverns following the fleet like banks of gunsmoke. He had no idea how many of them made their nests along the deserted coasts of Armageddon Reef, but he'd never seen so many of them in one spot in his entire life. They wheeled and climbed, swooped and dove, exploring the ships' wakes for any scrap of garbage, and the mingled cries of the birds and the high, somehow mournful whistles of the sea wyverns came clearly through the sound of wind and wave, the occasional order and response, the creak of timbers.

The sun was settling into the west, beyond the barely visible smudge of Armageddon Reef. White Ford's warning that more heavy weather was coming had been justified, but they'd been past Demon Head and closing on Anvil Head, heading across the hundred and forty-mile mouth of Rakurai Bay, by the time the fresh heavy swell came rolling in. It had still been more than Thirsk's own galleys and crews were accustomed to—or, at least, than they *had* been accustomed to before beginning this insane trip—but at least they'd had the wind broad on the port beam. That meant they'd been able to ship oars and hold a reasonably steady course under double-reefed sails alone, despite the galleys' heavy rolling.

The difference that had made, even for the lumbering bulk of *King Rahnyld*, had been remarkable. Thirsk still felt like a new-hatched wyvern who'd strayed out into water too deep for it, but he was beginning to think White Ford's advice might actually get them all the way to MacPherson's Lament without losing another ship. They'd already passed Thomas Point, passing between it and the southernmost of the islands known as Shan-wei's Footsteps, which had made everyone happy. *No one* had wanted to take cover in Rakurai Bay if they had any choice at all.

He gazed up at the sky and frowned, wondering if perhaps he'd tempted fate by allowing himself such a dose of optimism. Clouds were building up along the eastern horizon. The breeze had freshened noticeably since noon, as well, and it felt chillier than their steady progress towards the colder waters of Doomwhale Reach could explain.

It was possible the weather was about to turn nasty again, but at the moment, *Gorath Bay* was about thirty miles off the coast, and they should make Rock Point before dawn. Once they'd cleared the point, the coast would curve away from them to the west, giving them more sea room if they needed it. Even better, they were only a couple of hundred miles from Cape Ruin, and the vast stretch of Demon Sound and Heartbreak Bay cut deep into Armageddon Reef south of the cape. The names were far from reassuring, but between them, they offered a shel-tered anchorage ample to the needs of a fleet ten times the size of their own, or a hundred . . . and without stirring up the ghosts which undoubtedly inhabited Rakurai Bay.

Still, he'd *prefer* not to have to anchor anywhere, and—

"*Sail ho!*"

Thirsk jerked as if someone had just poked a particularly sensitive part of his anatomy with a well-heated iron. He wheeled around to stare up at the masthead lookout, and even as he did, he sensed the same incredulous reaction out of every other man on *Gorath Bay*'s deck.

The man had to be mistaken, the earl thought. There was absolutely no rea-son for *anyone* to be traveling through these ill-fated waters unless they'd been or-dered to by a lunatic like the one who'd written *his* orders.

"Where away?" Lieutenant Zhaikeb Mathysyn, who had the watch, bellowed.

"Broad on the port beam, Sir!" the lookout shouted back down.

"The man's drunk!" one of the army officers serving as a marine muttered.

Mathysyn appeared torn between irritation at the landsman's criticism and matching incredulity. He glowered at the army officer for a moment, then snapped his fingers and pointed at one of the flagship's midshipmen.

"Take a glass and get aloft, Master Haskyn!" he snapped.

"Yes, Sir!"

Haskyn seized the heavy spyglass, slung it across his back on its carrying strap, and scampered up the ratlines with the nimbleness of his fifteen years. He clambered into the crow's-nest, unslung the glass, and rested it on the crow's-nest rail for steadiness while he peered through it for several minutes. Personally, Thirsk suspected the youngster was spending at least part of that time catching his breath.

"It's a single ship, Sir!" Haskyn shouted down finally. "She's making almost straight for us on the wind!"

Thirsk frowned in fresh consternation. Even if a merchant ship had been passing through these waters for some unimaginable reason of its own, no mer-chant skipper could have a legitimate reason to make for Armageddon Reef. And even if he'd *had* such a reason, a single ship could hardly have failed to spot the galleys' miles-long, straggling formation before he was spotted in turn! Which should have sent him heading in the opposite direction at the best speed he could manage.

Unless, of course, it was a courier ship sent to find them?

He shook his head almost as quickly as that thought occurred to him. They were over five hundred miles south of the course they'd been ordered to follow, and almost three five-days behind schedule. Even if someone had wanted to send them a courier, it would never have looked for them *here*. So what—?

"She's schooner-rigged, Sir!" Haskyn shouted, and Thirsk's heart seemed to skip a beat.

"Repeat that!" Mathysyn's bellow sounded disbelieving, but Haskyn stood his ground.

"She's schooner-rigged, Sir!" he repeated. "I can see her topsails clearly!"

"Get down here!" Mathysyn ordered, and Haskyn obeyed. He didn't bother with the ratlines this time; he reached out, caught a backstay, wrapped his legs around it, and slid down it to thump solidly on the deck almost at Mathysyn's feet.

"Yes, Sir?" he said.

"Are you *sure* it's a schooner?" the lieutenant demanded, almost glaring at the young man.

"Yes, Sir."

"Why?"

"Don't you remember that Tarot-owned schooner we saw when we made port at Ferayd in Delferahk, Sir?" The midshipman shook his head. "There's no mistaking *that* rig, Sir."

Mathysyn had opened his mouth. Now he shut it again and nodded slowly, instead.

"Very well, Master Haskyn. Present my respects to Captain Maikel and inform him of your observations."

"Yes, Sir!"

Haskyn bowed in salute and headed for the aftercastle ladder at a run.

▼　　▼　　▼

"I beg your pardon, Your Highness, but we've just received a signal from *Spy*," Captain Manthyr said as he stepped past Lieutenant Falkhan into the chart room.

"Have we?" Crown Prince Cayleb asked calmly, turning from the chart table to face him.

"Yes, Your Highness. 'Enemy in sight,'" he read from a notepad. "'Bearing from my position west-southwest, distance eighteen miles. Enemy course southwest, estimated speed six knots. Thirty-plus galleys in sight.'"

He lowered the notepad, and the expression on his face was a curious mix of awe and intense satisfaction.

"Thank you, Gwylym," Cayleb said, without even glancing at Merlin. "Please make certain Admiral Staynair has that information, as well."

"Yes, Your Highness."

"Also, request the Admiral to come on board and bring Captain Bowsham with him, please."

"Yes, Your Highness."

Cayleb nodded, and Manthyr came to attention and touched his left shoulder in salute, then departed. Cayleb waited until the chart room door had closed behind him, then, finally, turned to look at Merlin.

"So here we are," he said.

"Here we are," Merlin agreed.

"You know, don't you," Cayleb said with a crooked grin, "that the fleet's starting to think I'm almost as peculiar as you are?"

"Nonsense." Merlin shook his head with a chuckle. "You explained your logic perfectly."

"Sure." Cayleb rolled his eyes, and Merlin chuckled again, louder.

All of Cayleb's captains were already convinced Wave Thunder's putative Tarotisian spies had gotten inside information on the course the Southern Force had been ordered to follow. The tricky part had been allowing for the possibility—probability, really—that Thirsk and White Ford would be able to talk Duke Malikai into following the southern course, instead of the one they'd actually been given, in a way which would explain any changes in their own course which Merlin's "visions" might require.

Cayleb had simply observed at one of the early captains' conferences that only a lunatic would sail directly across the Parker Sea in a fleet of coastal galleys. He'd commented that he himself would have ignored his orders and stayed closer to Armageddon Reef. And, when Merlin confirmed that Thirsk and White Ford *had* managed to talk Malikai around, Cayleb decided during the next meeting with his captains that they were going to "play his hunch" and cover the Armageddon Reef route, instead.

It was unlikely Manthyr was particularly astounded by the fact that the Southern Force had, indeed, followed Cayleb's predicted route, although that obviously didn't keep him from deeply respecting Cayleb's iron nerve in playing his "hunch." What *had* surprised the prince's flag captain was the unerring—one might almost say uncanny—accuracy with which the prince's "seaman's instinct" had permitted the galleons to intercept that galley fleet on a course which left them perfectly placed to run down on the enemy force.

Of course, he didn't know Cayleb, courtesy of Lieutenant Merlin Athrawes, had the benefit of satellite reconnaissance.

"I hope *Spy* doesn't get too enterprising," Merlin said, after a moment. Cayleb looked at him, and he shrugged. "She doesn't know she's only out there to explain how we found them. If her skipper gets too close trying to maintain contact overnight, he could find himself in trouble."

"He knows his job, Merlin," Cayleb replied. "And it's not as if we've got much choice. Domynyk would probably accept your visions without turning a hair, after this long, and so would most of the original squadron's captains. But the rest wouldn't."

"And even if they would, all the reasons for not telling anyone else still apply," Merlin agreed with a sigh.

"Exactly." It was Cayleb's turn to shrug. "And even more so, now that the Church has declared war on us. We don't need to give them any ammunition for declaring that we associate with demons! As for *Spy*, I don't expect her to get into any trouble, Merlin. But, if she does, she does. Things like that happen in wars."

Merlin regarded him with a carefully hidden sardonic amusement—and sorrow—Cayleb would never have understood. The crown prince wasn't being callous, just realistic, and for all his youthfulness, he truly did understand the difference between the realities of war and the romanticism of heroic ballads. He simply had no way of knowing that the man to whom he was talking was the cybernetic avatar of a young woman who'd seen her species' entire civilization go down in fire and destruction. If anyone on the entire planet of Safehold knew that "things happened" in war, it was Merlin Athrawes.

"So," he said, changing the topic, "you feel confident enough to take time to bring Domynyk aboard for a last-minute discussion?"

"Yes," Cayleb said. "I'm assuming that if *Spy's* sighted them, they've probably sighted her. But even if they have, they can't do a lot about it. I'm sure Father was right about the impact our sudden appearance is going to have on their morale, but they really have only two choices: fight us at sea, or try to find some place to anchor in order to force us to come to them.

"Given how scattered you say their fleet is, they aren't going to *want* to fight us at all. Not until they get themselves reorganized, at any rate, and if *Spy's* estimate of their speed is accurate, just closing up their formation would probably take most of a full day." The crown prince shook his head. "If that's the best they can manage in this wind, then their bottoms must be even fouler than I'd thought."

Merlin nodded, reminding himself that "five knots" on Safehold wasn't quite the same thing as "five knots" would have been on Earth, where the nautical and statute miles had been different lengths. For Nimue Alban, "five knots" would have been the equivalent of just over nine and a quarter kilometers per hour or five and three quarters miles per hour. Here, "five knots" was exactly five miles per hour, and that was that.

Given that the current wind conditions hovered between Force Four and Force Five from the old Beaufort scale, that was pretty poor performance. Wind speed was fairly steady at around eighteen or nineteen miles per hour, and Cayleb's galleys could easily make good a speed of nine to ten knots under those conditions.

"The best way for them to get themselves back into some sort of order would be to find someplace to anchor, at least long enough to get their squadrons reorganized," Cayleb continued. "But there's no place for a fleet to anchor between Thomas Point and Rock Point. In fact, if they're looking for a *sheltered* anchorage, there's no place between Rock Point and Crag Hook.

"So, their choices are to continue on their present heading, at least as far as Crag Reach or to try to turn around and go back the way they came. If they get as far as Crag Reach, they might be able to get in behind Opal Island and anchor there. For that matter, the Reach is going to be much more sheltered than the open water, which would suit their galleys a lot better if they want to fight under oars.

"Given how little daylight's left, I doubt they've got time to pass the necessary orders to coordinate any major change of plans, which effectively rules out turning around. So, they're probably going to stay on their present course, spend the night doing the best they can to tighten their formation, and hope we're far enough behind *Spy* that they can get as far as Crag Reach before anything nasty catches up with them. If I'm right, we're going to know exactly where to find them in the morning, and it's important for me to go over our plans with Domynyk one last time and make sure we're in position by dawn to have all day to work on these people.

"And, of course," he grinned, "if I'm *not* right, it's going to be up to you to tell me about it so I can think up some semi-plausible reason to change *our* course."

"Don't forget the weather," Merlin cautioned.

The clouds coming in from the northeast marked the leading edge of a series of low-pressure fronts. His satellite observation indicated that the leading front, which was already almost upon them, was a fairly mild one, without the violent thunderstorms such fronts frequently brought. It was going to dump quite a bit of rain, and the wind was going to strengthen, but it should have passed through by sometime before dawn. His best current estimate was that it would push weather conditions to about Force Six, with winds of around twenty five or twenty-six miles per hour, and ten to thirteen-foot seas.

But the front coming on its heels was more powerful, with winds which might reach Force Seven and seas as high as seventeen or eighteen feet.

"I'm not forgetting it," Cayleb assured him, and smiled unpleasantly. "But Malikai isn't going to know it's coming, so it's not going to affect any orders he may try to pass before nightfall. And if the weather makes up, it's going to favor us over them."

▼   ▼   ▼

"Any changes in the standing orders, Sir?" Lieutenant Zhoelsyn asked. He had to speak loudly to make himself heard over the sound of the cold, steady rain, but he tried to keep any anxiety out of his voice as he relieved *King Gorjah II*'s first lieutenant, Leeahm Maikelsyn.

"None," Lieutenant Maikelsyn replied. He gazed at Zhoelsyn for a moment, then shrugged. "There's not very much we can do but hold our present course, Phylyp."

Zhoelsyn started to say something, but he stopped himself and simply nodded, instead. It was a pitch-dark, moonless night, the wind was freshening, the sea was making up, everyone on deck was soaked and miserable, despite their oilskins, and the lookouts could barely see the poop and masthead lanterns of the closest ships through the falling rain. It was possible Duke Malikai could have ordered a course change before nightfall, if he'd responded promptly to the sighting report, but he hadn't. Now it had become a physical impossibility. All they could do was hold their present course through the rain and hope.

Everyone knew that, but no one knew where that schooner had come from. Or how it could possibly have found them *here*.

It's probably just a scout, Zhoelsyn told himself for the thousandth time. *For that matter, it might even be no more than one of their merchant ships, swinging wide of the normal shipping routes because there's a war on. A lot of their merchant masters are ex-naval officers, after all. If one of* them *stumbled across us completely by accident, he'd know how important it was to get closer, find out everything he can before he heads back to Charis with his warning.*

Whatever it was, surely the Charisians couldn't possibly have diverted enough of their naval strength to waters this far from Rock Shoal Bay to threaten the combined fleet! The very idea was so insane that there was no wonder Malikai had felt no need to risk the confusion of trying to turn his spread-out fleet around. And yet, there that sail had been, heading straight towards them.

"Very well, Master Maikelsyn," Zhoelsyn said formally. "I relieve you."

▼ ▼ ▼

"All right, then. We all understand what we need to do tomorrow," Cayleb said.

He, Sir Domynyk Staynair, their flag captains, Merlin, and Lieutenant Falkhan sat around the dining table in HMS *Dreadnought*'s flag cabin while rain drummed on the cabin skylight and pattered against the stern windows.

Cayleb had no idea of the real reason Merlin had suggested that particular name for the first of the purpose-built gun-armed galleons, but he and his father had both agreed it fit perfectly. *Dreadnought* was almost forty feet longer than the Charisian Navy's older galleons. Admiral Staynair had retained HMS *Gale* as his flagship, but *Dreadnought* carried fifty-four guns to the older ship's thirty-six. She'd also been designed from the beginning with an unbroken sheer, without the exaggerated castles at either end. Her forecastle and quarterdeck were only about six feet higher than her maindeck, connected by bulwarks and spar decks for line handlers, and she carried all of her guns at maindeck level or higher. Despite the fact that she was generally sleeker and lower slung than her older sister—in proportion to her length, at least—the lower sills of her gunports were almost fifteen feet above her waterline, compared to only nine feet for *Gale*. And her greater ratio of length to beam and more powerful sail plan meant she was faster, as well.

Her greater size had also made her a logical choice as a flagship, and she'd been provided with the sizable (for a cramped, crowded, sail-powered ship, at least) quarters to accommodate an admiral. Or, in this case, a crown prince acting as an admiral.

"I think we understand, Your Highness," Admiral Staynair replied. He looked a great deal like a younger version of his older brother, although his beard was considerably less luxuriant. Indeed, he favored a dagger-style rather like Merlin's, except for Merlin's waxed mustachios. Now he smiled at his crown prince.

"If we don't, it's not because you haven't made it sufficiently clear, at any rate," he added.

"I don't mean to nag, Domynyk," Cayleb said with a rueful smile of his own. "And I'm not trying to pretend I know your job as well as you do. It's just—"

"It's just that the ultimate responsibility is yours, Your Highness," Staynair interrupted, and shook his head. "I understand that, too. And, believe me, I don't feel at all as if you don't trust me. For that matter, you've probably got as much experience in handling squadrons of gun-armed galleons as *I* do! But, all the same, it's time for you to relax as much as you can."

Cayleb looked at him in surprise, and the admiral shrugged.

"You need to have your head clear tomorrow, Your Highness," he said firmly. "And you need to remember it's not just your squadron commanders and captains who understand what we have to do. By this time, every man in the fleet understands, just as they know you've led them straight to the enemy. Believe me, they also know just how close to impossible that was. They have complete confidence in you and in their weapons, and they know exactly what the stakes are. If mortal men *can* win this battle, they *will* win it for you."

He held Cayleb's eyes for several seconds, until, slowly, the prince nodded.

"So, what *you* need to do right now, is to get as much sleep as you can," Staynair continued then. "You're going to have decisions to make tomorrow. Be sure your mind is fresh enough to make the decisions worthy of the men under your command."

"You're right, of course," Cayleb said after a moment. "On the other hand, I don't know how much sleep I *can* get tonight. I'll do my best, though."

"Good. And now," Staynair glanced up at the cabin lamp, swaying on its gimbals above the table, and listened to the sound of the rain and steadily freshening wind, "I'd best be getting back to *Gale* before the sea gets any higher."

He grimaced as a harder gust of rain drove against the skylight, then smiled at Captain Bowsham.

"Khanair and I are going to get soaked enough as it is," he added.

"Of course," Cayleb agreed. He glanced around the table one more time, then picked up his wineglass and raised it. "Before you go, though, one last toast."

All the others reclaimed their own glasses and raised them.

"The King, Charis, victory, and damnation to the enemy!" Cayleb said strongly.

"*Damnation to the enemy!*" rumbled back at him, and crystal sang as the glasses touched.

Merlin Athrawes stood with Ahrnahld Falkhan and Captain Manthyr behind Crown Prince Cayleb on HMS *Dreadnought*'s quarterdeck in the strengthening gray light and windy predawn chill as Father Raimahnd raised his voice in prayer.

Raimahnd Fuhllyr was Charisian-born. As such, it was unlikely he would ever be permitted to rise above his present rank of upper-priest, but he was still an ordained priest of the Church of God Awaiting. And he was also a priest who knew, just as Cayleb had made certain everyone else aboard his ships knew, who had truly orchestrated this unprovoked attack upon Charis. Not just upon their king, but upon their homes and families, as well.

Now Merlin watched the flagship's chaplain's back carefully. Fuhllyr stood beside the ship's bell at the quarterdeck rail, facing out towards the assembled ship's company, which meant Merlin couldn't see his face and expression. But what he saw in the under-priest's ramrod-straight spine, and heard in Fuhllyr's voice, was satisfying . . . and perhaps as troubling as it was reassuring to the man who'd brought such changes to Charis.

"And now," Fuhllyr brought his prayer to a close, his voice firm and strong against the wind's whine through the rigging, "as the Archangel Chihiro prayed before the final battle against the forces of darkness, we make bold to say: O God, You know how busy we must be this day about Your work. If we forget You, do not You, O Lord, forget us. Amen."

"Amen!" rumbled back from the assembled crew with an angry ardor.

Merlin's amen sounded right along with the others, as fervent as any he'd ever uttered, despite the reference to "the Archangel Chihiro's" plagiarization of Sir Jacob Astley's battle prayer. Yet Fuhllyr's very sincerity, the fact that there'd been no reservations in any of his sermons to *Dreadnought*'s company from the day they sailed, only underscored something he felt certain the Group of Four hadn't counted on.

Merlin didn't know how much of their decision to destroy Charis had sprung from genuine concern about the kingdom's orthodoxy and how much had been simply the cynical power calculation of an arrogant, thoroughly corrupt hierarchy. He suspected that *they* probably didn't know. But one thing he did know, was that it had never occurred to them for an instant that their plan to crush Charis might not succeed. Nor, whatever they might have *thought* they feared, did they have any true conception of what a genuine religious war might entail. But if they'd been able to hear Father Raimahnd this morning, perhaps they might have recognized in the sound of his firm, angry, *consecrated* voice, the death knell of their undisputed mastery over Safehold.

It was exactly what Merlin had wanted, although he'd never wanted it this soon, before he—and Charis—had had time to prepare for it. But Nimue Alban had been a student of military history, and so, unlike the Group of Four, Merlin *did* know what all-out religious war could be like, and as he listened to that hard, powerful "Amen!" and joined his own to it, the heart he no longer had was cold within him.

Cayleb turned his head, surveying his flagship one last time. The decks had been sanded for traction. The guns had already been run in, loaded with round shot and a charge of grape, and run back out. Marines, armed with the new muskets and bayonets, were positioned along the spar deck hammock nettings and in the fighting tops, along with sailors manning the swivel guns Safeholdians called "wolves" which were mounted there. Buckets of sand and water for firefighting, should it prove necessary. Boat chocks, empty where the boats had been swayed out to tow astern. Above the deck, the rigging and sails stood in sharp, geometric patterns, capturing the power of the wind itself. And *below* decks, Merlin knew, as he watched one of the younger midshipmen swallow hard, the healers and surgeons waited with their knives and saws.

"Very well, Captain Manthyr," Cayleb said finally, deliberately raising his voice for others to hear as he turned to his flag captain. "Please hoist that signal for me."

"Aye, aye, Your Majesty!" Manthyr replied crisply, and nodded to Midshipman Kohrby. "Hoist the signal, if you please, Master Kohrby."

"Aye, aye, Sir!" Kohrby saluted, then turned to issue sharp, clear orders of his own to the signal party.

The hoist rose quickly to the yardarm just as the rising sun, with perfect timing, heaved itself over the cloud-girt eastern horizon. It illuminated the signal flags in rich, golden light, and a huge, hungry cheer went up from *Dreadnought*'s company. Few of them could read that signal hoist, but all of them had been told what it said, and Merlin's lips twitched under his mustachios.

If I'm the only person on this entire planet who remembers any of Old Earth's history, he thought, *I might as well go ahead and crib all the good lines I can think of!*

Cayleb had loved the message when Merlin had suggested it to him last night, following Staynair's departure.

"Charis expects that every man will do his duty," those flags said, and as the rising sun picked out the signal, Merlin heard *Dreadnought*'s cheer echoing wildly from her next astern, frayed by the wind but powerful.

Cayleb turned to him with a smile.

"Well, you were certainly right about that," he said. "In fact, I—"

"Sail ho!" The shout from the lookout echoed down.

"Enemy in sight!"

▼   ▼   ▼

Earl Thirsk heaved himself up into *Gorath Bay*'s crow's-nest, panting from the exhausting climb up the ratlines. He was too old—and too out of shape—for that sort of exertion these days, but he had to see this for himself.

He settled his back against the vibrating tree trunk of the mast, and forced himself not to wrap one arm about something to steady himself. The galley's roll was far more pronounced this high above the deck, and the crow's-nest seemed to be swooping through an even wide arc than he knew was the case.

It's been too long since I had to climb up here, a corner of his mind thought, but it was only a very distant reflection as his own eyes confirmed the lookout's impossible reports.

The wind had freshened steadily overnight and veered around perhaps one point to the north. The waves were high enough to make rowing far worse than merely awkward, especially for the Dohlaran galleys, with their lower oarports, and shallower hulls. In fact, he knew he was driving *Gorath Bay* harder than was really safe under these conditions, and if he'd dared, he would have considered ordering his squadron to take a third reef to reduce sail area further.

But the one thing he couldn't possibly do was to reduce speed. Not when there was already such a gap between his squadron and Duke Malikai's flagship. *King Raynahld* was hull-down from *Gorath Bay*'s deck, almost completely out of sight, and White Ford's ships were even further ahead. This was no time to let the gap between them widen . . . especially not when at least twenty-five galleons of the Royal Charisian Navy were bearing down upon the spread out, straggling "formation" of the combined fleet.

They couldn't be here. Despite the evidence of his eyes, despite the golden kraken on black flying from their mizzen peaks, his mind insisted upon repeating that disbelieving thought. Even if Haarahld had known what was coming, he couldn't possibly have predicted where to find the combined fleet! And only a madman would have sent so much of his own navy out into the middle of this vast wasteland of saltwater on some quixotic quest to find the enemy.

And yet, there they were.

The rain which had soaked the fleet all through the night had started to taper off as the overcast began breaking up shortly before dawn. There were still a few lines of showers following behind it, though, and fresh clouds were billowing up along the eastern horizon, promising still more rain by nightfall. And the earlier rainfall had reduced visibility to no more than a few miles until it cleared, which explained how those galleons could have gotten so near without being spotted.

Of course, it *didn't* explain how those same galleons could have known exactly where the fleet was through that same curtain of rain.

He drew a deep breath and raised his spyglass to examine the enemy.

He'd never seen sailing ships hold such precise formation. That was his first thought, as the lead ships of the two columns bearing down upon him swam into focus through the spyglass.

I've never seen that many gunports *before, either,* he thought a moment later as he watched them surging boldly through the whitecaps and ten-foot waves in explosions of flying spray. Obviously the rumors about how many guns the Charisians were putting aboard their galleons had been accurate. In fact, it looked as if they'd probably *understated* the ships' armaments.

As he continued to study them, he began picking out differences between the individual ships. At least half of them must be converted merchant ships, he decided. All of them had the new, Charisian-invented sail plans, but the conversions were smaller, although some of them seemed to have more gunports even than ships considerably bigger than they were. He was willing to bet they didn't all handle equally well, either, although there was no evidence of that yet. Still, they were approaching at least half again his own ships' speed, and they were doing it under topsails and headsails alone. It was obvious they still had speed and maneuverability in reserve . . . unlike his own laboring, foul-bottomed galleys with their single sails.

His mouth tightened at the thought. These weather conditions hugely favored the more seaworthy, more weatherly galleons. Almost worse, he knew his own stunned disbelief at seeing those ships here must be echoing through the entire fleet as the sighting reports were confirmed, demoralizing his officers and crews. The morning's prayers and exhortations from his ships' chaplains, for all the fervor with which they'd been delivered, weren't going to change that. And when those already frightened and apprehensive crews realized just how great a maneuver advantage the enemy held, their demoralization was going to get still worse.

Stop that! he told himself. *Yes, it's going to be bad. Accept that. But you've still got over a hundred and fifty ships against no more than thirty! That's an advantage of five-to-one!*

He nodded sharply, crisply, and lowered his spyglass, then swung down from the crow's-nest and started clambering back down the ratlines to the deck. All the way down, he repeated the numbers to himself, over and over again.

It didn't help.

His feet finally touched the deck, and he handed the spyglass to a white-faced midshipman, then walked gravely, calmly, across to Captain Maikel.

"There are twenty-five or thirty of them," he said levelly, waving one hand in the direction of the clutter of topsails appearing against the blue-patched, shredding gray rain clouds to the northeast. "They're formed in two columns. It looks to me as if they're planning to cut straight through our line—such as it is, and what there is of it"—his mouth twitched in a smile which held at least a ghost of genuine humor—"and then try to chew up whatever they catch between them."

He paused, and Maikel nodded in understanding, his expression strained.

"If they hold their present course, their weather column's going to cut across *our* course at least five or six miles ahead of us. I suspect—" he smiled again, tightly "—that *King Rahnyld*'s sheer size has attracted their attention and they're planning to make her their first objective. If that happens, all we can do is maintain our present heading and try to come to the Duke's aid as quickly as we can."

"Yes, My Lord," Maikel said when the earl paused once more.

"Signal the rest of the squadron to maintain course and close up on us. I know most of them won't be able to, but every little bit will help."

"At once, My Lord." Maikel nodded to Lieutenant Mathysyn. "See to it," he said.

"After that, Captain," Thirsk said, "all we can do is prepare for battle."

"Yes, My Lord." Maikel bowed, and as Thirsk walked across to the weather bulwark and gazed up to windward at those oncoming topsails, he heard the deep-throated drums booming out the call to battle.

▼   ▼   ▼

"Well, they've seen us," Cayleb commented as a final line of showers poured rain across *Dreadnought*'s decks.

The prince ignored the water dripping from the brim of his helmet while he frowned thoughtfully.

The rain was clearing, but if Merlin's prediction was accurate, fresh, heavier rain—and still stronger winds, veering yet further around to the north—would make themselves felt no later than midafternoon. He had perhaps six hours before visibility began to deteriorate once more.

He could see the nearest galleys quite clearly now from deck level. The entire western horizon, as far north and south as he could see, was dotted with more sails, and he grimaced. Despite Merlin's descriptions and the sighting reports from *Spy* and her consort *Speedwell*, he hadn't truly visualized just how enormous—and spread out—his target was.

He considered what he could see, wondering if he ought to adjust his battle plan. The six schooners attached to his fleet were up to windward, under orders to stay out of the battle but remain close enough to see and repeat signals from or to *Dreadnought* or *Gale*. If he wanted to order any changes, he still had time, but not a great deal of it.

Dreadnought was the lead ship in the weather column. In some ways, it would have made more sense to put the flagship in the center of the line, where Cayleb would be better placed—at least in theory—to see more of the engagement and coordinate at least its opening stages more closely. Unfortunately, once the gunsmoke started billowing, *no one* was going to be able to see very much, even with this wind; that much had become painfully clear from Staynair's work with the Experimental Squadron. So both Cayleb and Staynair were leading their respective columns, which gave them the greatest degree of control over where those columns went before action was joined. And as long as the ships in line behind them followed in their wakes, it would give them the greatest control over where the action went *after* battle was joined, as well.

His frown deepened. Each column was almost three miles long, and Staynair's fifteen ships were about six miles to leeward of his own as they angled towards the enemy. *Dreadnought* was creeping just a bit to the north of the point Cayleb had originally selected, but that didn't bother him. Captain Manthyr had spotted the enormous galley flying the command streamer of a Dohlaran admiral and adjusted his course to pass astern of it accordingly.

Spurts of dirty, gray-white smoke began to erupt from some of the nearer galleys. The probability of anyone hitting anything from that range, especially with pre-Merlin artillery, was as close to nonexistent as anything Cayleb could think of. He couldn't even see the splashes where most of the round shot—which had to be aimed at *Dreadnought*—hit the water.

He pondered the situation for a moment longer, then shrugged. The plan he and Staynair and Merlin had put together was the best they'd been able to come up with between them. He wasn't going to start mucking about with it simply because he had a bad case of first-battle nerves.

He snorted quietly, amused by his own thoughts, and didn't even notice how his sudden smile relaxed the shoulders of the officers standing about him on the flagship's quarterdeck.

"About fifteen minutes, I make it, Captain Manthyr," he said conversationally.

"About that, Your Highness," Manthyr agreed.

"Very well, then, Captain," Cayleb said more formally. "Engage the enemy."

"Aye, aye, Your Highness!"

▼   ▼   ▼

Faidel Ahlverez, Duke of Malikai, stood on *King Rahnyld*'s aftercastle and watched the column of galleons headed towards his flagship. The lead ship in the enemy line was one of the largest in the Charisian formation, and Malikai's jaws clenched as it drew close enough for him to see the coronet above the golden kraken flying from its mizzen peak. Only one person in all of Charis was entitled to fly that flag: the heir to the throne.

Cayleb, he thought. Crown Prince Cayleb Ahrmahk himself, bearing down upon him like the get of some demon. Malikai hadn't placed much faith in the Church's obvious suspicions about Charis' orthodoxy, but how else to explain those galleons' presence, better than seven thousand miles' sail from Rock Shoal Bay? How else to explain how they could even have *found* his fleet, much less appeared in exactly the right position to press home their attack?

Cold, dull terror burned deep inside him, made still worse by the proximity of Armageddon Reef. He should never have allowed Thirsk and White Ford to talk him into staying so close to this accursed land! He should have sailed as he'd always intended to, as he'd been *ordered* to. Far better to have risked losing his entire fleet to wind and storm than to have it destroyed by the legions of Hell!

Captain Ekyrd stood by the port bulwark, watching the oncoming enemy intently, and Malikai glared at his flag captain's back. Ekyrd had recommended ordering the fleet to put about, even if it had to do so under oars, after the first unknown sail had been sighted. Malikai had brushed the suggestion aside, of course. The sighting report had probably been in error, and even if it hadn't, there couldn't possibly have been anything else behind that lone sail—certainly not anything capable of threatening a fleet the size of *his!*

Now his own flag captain was ignoring him.

Malikai glared at Ekyrd's straight spine, then touched the hilt of his sword. He eased it in its sheath, making certain it moved freely, and then looked at the gunners crouching above the breeches of their cannon.

Ekyrd had argued against Malikai's orders this morning, as well. He'd wanted to try to stay away from the Charisians, far enough that the guns of his lofty ship could at least hope to hit them, rather than close straight into their own guns, but Malikai had overruled him harshly. Those galleons might have more artillery than any of his ships did, but his galleys each carried enormous crews, buttressed by heavy drafts on the finest regiments of the Royal Army. If they could ever lay one of those galleons alongside, sweep over its decks with their boarding pikes, swords, and axes, it wouldn't *matter* how many guns the accursed thing had! And whatever Ekyrd might think, Malikai had five times as many galleys as they had galleons.

He bared his teeth, matching anger at his flag captain's cowardice against the cold poison of his own fear, as more guns began to fire aboard other galleys and the Charisians drew implacably closer and closer.

▼　　▼　　▼

The first few round shot whimpered through the air above *Dreadnought* like lost, damned souls. One of them hit the main topsail and punched through the wet canvas with the slap of a giant's fist. Another skipped across the ship's bows barely five feet in front of her, and then she took her first true hit.

A round shot, probably an eight-pounder from a long falcon, slammed into her below the spar deck hammock nettings and just forward of the mainmast. It erupted through the starboard bulwark in a burst of jagged splinters and cut a standing Marine in half in an explosion of blood. Yells and a few screams announced that the splinters had inflicted wounds of their own, and more than one member of *Dreadnought's* crew flinched. But she continued to forge steadily ahead, and the massive bulk of *King Rahnyld* was less than seventy yards away.

▼　　▼　　▼

"Stand ready to port your helm!" Captain Ekyrd said to his first lieutenant. "Our best chance is going to come after they pass astern of us!"

"Yes, Sir."

Malikai's lips twisted with contempt as he heard the faint quaver in the lieutenant's voice. The other man's obvious fear was a welcome distraction from his own, and he drew his sword as the end of *Dreadnought*'s long bowsprit began to pass across *King Rahnyld*'s wake barely fifty yards behind the flagship.

▼   ▼   ▼

"Fire as you bear!" Captain Manthyr bellowed as *Dreadnought* presented the muzzles of her forward guns to her target.

King Rahnyld's high, massive stern towered above the low-slung galleon. Despite the wear and tear the galley had suffered over the thousands of miles she had voyaged to reach this point, despite the sea slime and tendrils of weed along her waterline, traces of gilding still clung to the magnificent carving, gleaming against the vibrant color of broken gray cloud and bright blue sky in the morning light. Green water and white spray curled back from her hull as the seas washed higher than her lower bank of oarports, and the rows of her vast stern windows flashed back the sun, despite the rime of salt which encrusted them. Helmets could be seen above the aftercastle's bulwark, glinting dully with the sheen of steel, and more sunlight glittered from the points of boarding pikes and the blades of axes and halberds, the barrels of matchlock muskets. The galley's reefed replacement sail, patched and worn, bellied out like a shield, and shouts of defiance rang out.

But those shouts sounded halfhearted, and they were met only by silence from *Dreadnought*'s disciplined crew.

Fire flashed in *King Rahnyld*'s stern gunports, but the ports were too high, the gunners had mistimed the ship's motion, and *Dreadnought* was too close to her. Her guns, unlike Charisian artillery, couldn't be depressed, and the balls screamed across *Dreadnought,* without hitting a thing, and plunged uselessly into the water far beyond her.

And then the galleon's forward guns came to bear.

Gun by gun, the muzzles belched flame and choking smoke as the captains jerked their firing lanyards. The range was less than sixty yards, and unlike *King Rahnyld*'s gunners, the gun crews had timed their own ship's motion almost perfectly. Gunport by gunport, down the full length of the galleon's side, guns lurched back, recoiling in a mad chorus of squealing gun trucks, as their round shot—each shot with a charge of grapeshot for good measure—smashed into *King Rahnyld* like an iron avalanche.

The galley's stern windows disappeared, blotted away as *Dreadnought*'s raking fire turned that magnificent sternwork into the mouth of a gaping cave of horror. Roundshot and grapeshot ripped down the full length of the ship. Splin-

ters flew, men screamed, and the billowing smoke of the broadside hid the carnage of its impact.

There was time for only one shot from each gun as the galleon crossed *King
Rahnyld*'s stern, but Captain Manthyr's voice rang out.

"Off sheets and braces! Starboard your helm!" he shouted.

▼   ▼   ▼

Duke Malikai's world disintegrated in a stunning eruption of devastation. He'd
never imagined, never dreamed of, anything like the long, unending bellow of
Dreadnought's broadside. Twenty-seven guns hurled round shot six and a half
inches in diameter, each weighing over thirty-eight pounds and accompanied by
twenty-seven inch-and-a-half grapeshot, into his ship. They came crashing in
through the galley's stern, totally undeterred by the flimsy glass and carved planking, and smashed clear to the bow, killing and maiming anyone in their path.

That carefully aimed and timed broadside killed or wounded over a hundred
and thirty of *King Rahnyld*'s crew. Men shrieked as round shot, grapeshot, and
splinters of their own ship ripped into them. Blood sprayed across deck planks in
great, grotesque patterns, and men who'd never imagined such a hurricane of
fire—men already demoralized and frightened by the inexplicable appearance of
their enemies so many thousands of miles from Charis—stared in horror at their
mangled crewmates.

Most of *Dreadnought*'s fire went in below the level of *King Rahnyld*'s aftercastle. Half a dozen round shot crashed directly through the galley's great cabin, ex-
ploding out from under the break of the aftercastle and cutting great,
blood-splashed furrows through the men packing her deck. But at least two shots
ripped upward, directly through the aftercastle, and Malikai staggered as a bliz-
zard of splinters howled through the officers gathered there.

Something big, heavy, and fast-moving slammed into his own breastplate,
nearly knocking him from his feet. But the armor held. The impact spun him
around, just in time to see Captain Ekyrd stumble backward, clutching at the
thick splinter which had driven into the side of his neck like a jagged-edged harpoon. Blood sprayed around the splinter, like water from the nozzle of a pump,
and the captain thudded to the deck.

Malikai fought for balance as the final shots of *Dreadnought*'s thundering
broadside hammered into his flagship. His mind seemed stunned, as if it were
caught in some thick, dragging quicksand. He stared about wildly, and saw
Dreadnought passing clear of his ship to starboard.

The galleon put her helm over, turning steadily to port, taking the wind
broad on her beam rather than directly astern. Her yards moved smoothly, with
machinelike precision, as she settled on the port tack, a hundred yards to leeward,
between *King Rahnyld* and Armageddon Reef, like a kraken between a new-
hatched sea wyvern and the land.

The confusion and carnage her fire had wreaked paralyzed *King Rahnyld*. The galley's captain was dead; her first lieutenant was mortally wounded; her helmsmen lay bleeding their lives out on the deck. By the time her second lieutenant could begin reasserting control, *Dreadnought* had settled on her new heading and her broadside thundered again.

Fresh round shot battered into the galley's towering starboard side, not her flimsier stern. The thicker planking offered little more resistance to the galleon's heavy shot, but it provided more and bigger splinters to slice lethally into her crew. And as *Dreadnought* fired into her yet again, HMS *Destroyer*, *Dreadnought*'s next astern, crossed *King Rahnyld*'s wake and raked her all over again.

Malikai turned back from *Dreadnought* as *Destroyer* opened fire, and in the second galleon's thundering guns he saw the destruction of his fleet. None of his galleys could begin to match the concentrated firepower of Cayleb's galleons; they were hopelessly spread out and disordered while the Charisian ships were in a compact, well controlled formation, firing their guns with impossible rapidity; and galleys were at a hopeless maneuver disadvantage in the existing sea conditions. Numbers meant nothing unless they could be brought to bear, and his couldn't be.

He heard the flagship's second lieutenant shouting orders to the replacement helmsmen, fighting desperately to at least turn *King Rahnyld*'s stern away from that terrible, raking fire. But even as the lumbering galley began finally, reluctantly, to answer to her helm, a round shot cut away her mainmast below deck level. It came thundering down, spilling over the side in a tangle of shattered timber, flailing canvas, and broken rigging. It smashed across the deck and into the water, and the galley lurched wildly, indescribably, as she found herself suddenly helpless. The wreckage alongside acted like a huge sea anchor, dragging her around, and *still* that merciless fire smashed into her again and again and again.

Malikai stared aft, his stunned brain reeling, as the *third* ship in Cayleb's line came crashing in. *King Rahnyld* had turned enough for HMS *Daring*'s fire to hammer into her quarter, instead of directly into her stern, but the flagship wasn't really her primary target.

Duke of Fern, the next galley astern of *King Rahnyld*, had shaken out one of her reefs as she fought to come to the fleet commander's assistance. She heeled dangerously under the greater sail area, but she also drove through the water faster . . . only to find herself driving straight into the fire of *Daring*'s starboard broadside, as well.

Malikai cringed as the volcanic fury of the galleon's fire erupted. He could hardly see through the choking pall of gunsmoke, but the wall of smoke lifted on the fiery breath of yet *another* galleon's broadsides as HMS *Defense* came into action, as well. She blasted her fury into his ship, and into *Duke of Fern*, and behind her came HMS *Devastation*.

All he could hear was the thunder of Charisian artillery. It seemed to come from every direction—from *all* directions—as *Dreadnought*'s consorts followed her around, pushing steadily southwest. They were faster—much faster—under sail than any of his galleys, and their guns fired steadily, mercilessly, with that same impossible rapidity, as they overtook ship after ship.

King Rahnyld's motion was growing heavier and heavier. Her hull must be filling with water, Malikai thought vaguely as he staggered to the side. He leaned on a shattered bulwark, aware of the heaps of bodies and parts of bodies littering the aftercastle. The main deck was a chaos of corpses where the men Captain Ekyrd had assembled for the boarding attempt which had never happened lay piled in mangled drifts, and he looked over the side at the thick tendrils of blood oozing from the galley's scuppers. It was as if the ship herself were bleeding, a corner of his brain thought. And then something made him look up as *Devastation* swung around the shattered, slowly foundering hulk which had once been the pride of the Dohlaran Navy.

He raised his head just in time to see the thunderous flash of the galleon's guns.

It was the last sight he ever saw.

▼   ▼   ▼

Dreadnought forged steadily south, leaning to the press of the northeasterly wind. The thunderous cannonade astern of her continued unabated as the other ships of her column crossed the Southern Force's line of advance, then turned to follow in her wake.

The strong breeze rolled a billowing fog bank of gunsmoke towards the barely visible smudge of Rock Point, and the ferocity of the fire still roaring behind her indicated that at least some of the galleys north of Malikai's sinking flagship continued trying to fight their way through to the duke's side with futile gallantry.

Neither Cayleb nor Merlin was much concerned by that possibility. The entire enemy fleet was too spread out and straggling to concentrate enough ships for the sort of hammer blow it would take to break past the galleons' broadsides. If they wanted to come in ones and twos, Cayleb was content to leave the problem of their destruction to his captains' discretion while he concentrated on the rest of the Southern Force.

"I think we need a little more speed, Gwylym," he said, glancing up from the billow of smoke still two miles ahead, where Admiral Staynair's column had also broken across the enemy's course, to check the sun's height.

Captain Manthyr glanced upward at the topsails and masthead pendant, gauging the strength of the wind, then waited while a fresh broadside thundered. The galley which had tried to break west, away from *Dreadnought*, staggered as the galleon's starboard guns hammered her from astern. Rigging parted, her single mast crashed over the side, and she rounded to as the wreckage dragged at her.

"Set the topgallants?" the captain suggested.

"For now," Cayleb agreed.

"Aye, aye, Your Highness." Manthyr lifted his leather speaking trumpet. "Master Gyrard! Hands to make sail, if you please! Let's get the topgallants on her!"

"Aye, aye, Sir!" the first lieutenant acknowledged the order and started giving orders of his own, and seamen from the port gun crews went scampering up the ratlines to lay out along the topgallant yards while others raced to the forecastle and afterdeck and along the spar decks above the guns to the pinrails to cast off sheets, buntlines, and clewlines.

"Loose topgallants!" Manthyr bellowed through his speaking trumpet, and the hands aloft ungasketed the sails, untying the gaskets which fastened the canvas to the yards. The captain watched them critically, fingers of his left hand drumming slowly against his thigh while his ship's guns put another bellowing broadside into the galley to starboard.

"Let fall the topgallants!" the captain shouted, and the hands aloft pushed the canvas off the yard into its gear.

"Sheet home the topgallants!" Manthyr commanded.

"Sheet home!" the officer in charge of each mast echoed.

"Ease the buntlines and clewlines!" the pinrail captains commanded, and the topgallant sails fell like vast curtains, billowing above the already drawing topsails as the powerful wind filled them.

"Haul around on the sheets!"

Dreadnought leaned harder to the press of her increased canvas as her topgallants were braced round. She drove across the beam sea in sharp, white explosions of spray, and her starboard gunports dipped closer to the water. But the same increased angle of heel lifted her weather gunports higher, and she bore down upon the galleys ahead of her like a stooping hawk.

A final broadside from her starboard guns slammed into the galley to leeward, and Cayleb looked astern. *Destroyer* was setting her own topgallants to match the flagship, and beyond her, above the billows of smoke as she fired into the same hapless galley, he could see more canvas blossoming from the other ships in his column.

He glanced at Merlin with a tight, kraken-like grin, then turned back to the south as Captain Manthyr altered course very slightly to bring his port guns to bear upon yet another Dohlaran galley.

▼   ▼   ▼

Gahvyn Mahrtyn, Baron White Ford, stood like a statue atop *King Gorjah II*'s aftercastle. Captain Kaillee stood beside him, and both of them stared up to the north. The Tarotisian galleys had been leading the combined fleet, and *King Gorjah II* was near the head of the entire formation. White Ford was too far south to

see clearly what was happening, but his lookouts left him in little doubt of the to-
tality of the disaster.

"How did they *do* it, My Lord?" Kaillee muttered beside him, and the baron
shrugged.

"I have no idea, Zhilbert," he admitted candidly. "But how they did it doesn't
really matter at the moment, does it?"

"No, My Lord," Kaillee agreed grimly, and turned to look at his admiral.

White Ford continued gazing northward. The wind carried the intermittent
rumble of the heavy cannonade to him, and the sound was growing both steadier and louder as it drew closer. His lookouts had reported "many" galleons, but
he was quite certain they hadn't seen all of them yet. If Haarahld of Charis had
run the insane risk of sending any of his galleons this far from Rock Shoal Bay,
he would have sent *all* of them. And just from the weight of fire White Ford
could hear, they had to be steadily reducing the Dohlaran ships astern of him to
wreckage.

He looked up at the sky. The sun had moved well to the west of noon, and
the clouds which had hovered on the eastern horizon earlier in the day were
sweeping steadily—and rapidly—closer. Indeed, their outriders were already
overhead. More rain, he thought. Soon. And judging by how quickly it was coming on, the wind was going to increase still further, as well.

He turned and looked to the west. Crag Hook, the finger of rocky cliffs
reaching out to the southwest to shelter Crag Reach, was broad on his starboard
beam, and he felt a deep, burning temptation to alter course. If he passed between
Crag Hook and Opal Island into the sheltered waters of the reach, his ships
would be protected from the weather rolling in from the west. And in those sheltered waters, they'd be able to maneuver under oars, able—in theory, at least—to
give a better account of themselves against the vengefully pursuing galleons.

But . . .

"We'll hold our course," he said, responding to Kaillee's unasked question.
"And we'll shake out a reef, as well."

Protest hovered behind the flag captain's eyes, and White Ford's bark of
laughter was harsh.

"It's tempting," he admitted, waving his right arm at the passage into Crag
Reach. "It's very tempting, and I know I'm risking the ship by increasing sail in
this wind. But if we take shelter in the reach, they'll either come straight in after
us or else hover off Opal Island to keep us penned up like sheep until they're ready
to attack. And when they do, those guns of theirs will chop us up for kraken bait."

Kaillee looked rebellious, and White Ford shook his head.

"I know what you're thinking, Zhilbert, but *listen* to that." The wind brought
the thunder of cannon to them more clearly, and the baron grimaced. "They
don't just have more guns; they're firing them much more rapidly, as well. It's the
only explanation for how they can be producing that much fire. And"—he smiled

grimly—"it also explains why they were putting so many guns aboard galleons in the first place, doesn't it?"

"Yes, My Lord. I suppose it does."

Kaillee's look of rebellion faded, but one of deep concern remained, and White Ford understood perfectly. They were still almost two hundred and fifty miles north of Cape Ruin, and there was no protected anchorage between Crag Reach and Demon Bay.

"I imagine we're going to lose some more galleys, if the wind makes up the way it looks like it's going to," the baron said unflinchingly. "But bad weather will make it harder for them to run any more of us down, and we'll have a better chance against the sea than we will against *that*."

He jerked his head back to the north, and finally, slowly, his flag captain nodded not just in acceptance, but in agreement.

"Yes, My Lord," he said.

"Good, Zhilbert." White Ford laid one hand lightly on Kaillee's shoulder, then inhaled deeply. "And make a signal to all ships in company to make more sail, as well."

.IV.
HMS *Dreadnought*,
Off Armageddon Reef

Secure the guns, Captain," Crown Prince Cayleb said.

"Aye, aye, Sir," Captain Manthyr replied. "Master Sahdlyr, secure the guns."

"Aye, aye, Sir," Lieutenant Bynzhamyn Sahdlyr was *Dreadnought*'s second lieutenant, but he was acting as first. Lieutenant Gyrard was among the ship's nineteen wounded.

All along the ship, bone-weary seamen ran the guns in one last time, cautious with their two-ton charges on the pitching deck. Handspikes under the cascabels heaved up, depressing the guns' muzzles until the loaded round shot rolled out onto the deck, pushing the wads before them. Then hook-headed staffs were used to extract the powder cartridges before the guns were wormed to scrub away the worst of the built-up powder fouling and vent holes were thoroughly cleaned. Gun captains inspected the pieces carefully, then tampions and vent aprons were replaced and they were hauled back up to the closed gunports and secured for sea.

While the guns crews worked, Cayleb strode to the taffrail and looked astern. *Destroyer* still forged along in *Dreadnought*'s wake. She'd fallen farther astern—at six hundred yards, the interval between them had grown to twice what it had been at the start of the action—but she was making up the lost ground steadily.

It was hard to make out very much beyond her. The setting sun was invisible beyond the thick cloud cover, foam was beginning to blow in streaks, and what had begun as gusting showers of rain was turning into a steady downpour. The sails of *Destroyer's* next astern were dimly visible through the rain and spray, but the ship herself was impossible for Cayleb to identify, and he couldn't see the other ships of his column at all.

The crown prince turned his head as Merlin stepped up beside him. Lieutenant Falkhan stood between them and the rest of the quarterdeck, affording them privacy and serving as a discreet suggestion to others that they should do the same.

"Are they all still back there?" Cayleb asked. He had to raise his voice to a near shout to carry through the tumult of rain, wind, creaking timbers, and waves.

"Not quite." Merlin raised his own voice as he gazed out into the darkening rain. But his eyes were unfocused as he studied not *Destroyer*, but the overhead imagery Owl was feeding him from his SNARC. "The column's not as neat as it was. *Dagger* and *Dreadful* are sailing almost abreast, and most of the ships have changed their relative positions. All of them left the line at some point to deal with a cripple or someone trying to run, and *Damsel* and *Torrent* never managed to rejoin—they're making for Samuel Island—but we didn't lose any of them. The other twelve all got back into formation somehow, and they're still back there."

"I can hardly believe it," Cayleb confessed. He turned to look forward along *Dreadnought's* decks. "I mean, I knew the new guns were going to give us a tremendous advantage, but still . . ."

His voice trailed off. Merlin nodded, but his expression was shadowed with more than rain and spray.

"We may not have actually lost a ship, but didn't get off scot-free," he pointed out, and it was Cayleb's turn to nod grimly.

Dreadnought herself had taken sixteen hits, nine of them from guns at least as heavy as her own. She'd been holed below the waterline twice, but the carpenter and his assistants had hammered wooden shot plugs into the holes to stop the leaks. One of her foredeck carronades had been dismounted, and most of its crew had been killed by the same hit. Another round shot had taken a bite out of her mainmast. That, fortunately, had been a glancing hit, and before he'd been wounded, Lieutenant Gyrard had "fished" the wounded portion of the mast by lashing spars into place to stiffen it, like a splint on a broken arm.

The port anchor had been shot away, as well, and there were dozens of new splices in the running rigging, not to mention holes in almost every one of her sails. But despite all that, and despite her seventeen dead and nineteen wounded, the majority cut down by flying splinters, she was in incredibly good shape.

Other galleons, Merlin knew, had been less fortunate. HMS *Typhoon*, from the original Experimental Squadron, in Admiral Staynair's column, had found herself running along between two particularly ably handled Tarotisian galleys.

She'd hammered both of them into wrecks, but a lucky hit from their own artillery had cut her mainmast no more than a dozen feet above the deck. Worse, the collapsing mast had fallen across the Tarotisian to leeward, and the surviving members of the galleon's crew had stormed across the tangle of fallen spars in a desperate boarding attempt.

It had failed, amid horrendous casualties, inflicted in no small part by the flintlock muskets and bayonets of *Typhoon*'s eighty Marines. But it had inflicted even more losses on *Typhoon*'s company, as well. The galleon's total casualties amounted to over two hundred, better than half her total ship's company, and she'd lost contact with the rest of Staynair's column. But Captain Stywyrt was still on his feet, despite having suffered a minor wound of his own during the boarding attempt, and he had the situation under control. Despite the damage to her masts and rigging, she was still seaworthy, and he was conning her carefully through the rain and steadily rising wind towards the prearranged rendezvous off Samuel Island where the two supply ships awaited the rest of the fleet.

Very few of Cayleb's ships were undamaged, but none of the others had been as badly hurt as *Typhoon*. In fact, *Dreadnought*'s damages were worse than most, probably because she'd been at the head of her column.

"What can you tell me about Domynyk and the other side?" Cayleb asked, leaning closer, until their heads were only inches apart.

He still had to raise his voice to be heard through the noise of wind and sea, but not even Ahrnahld Falkhan could have overheard him, and this time Merlin turned his head to look at him levelly. He raised one eyebrow, and Cayleb showed his teeth in a tight grin.

"It's a bit late for either of us to be pretending you need to withdraw to your quarters and meditate, Merlin," he said, eyes flickering with humor.

"All right," Merlin agreed, then stroked one of his mustachios thoughtfully for a moment.

"*Traveler* and *Summer Moon* are waiting at the rendezvous with *Intrepid*," he said, beginning with the supply ships and their escorting schooner. "All the other schooners are still in good shape, but they're worrying more about the weather than anything else right now. I imagine most of them will make for Samuel Island, too, as soon as they can.

"Domynyk's column is pretty much intact. *Typhoon*, *Thunderbolt*, and *Maelstrom* have all gotten separated from his formation—they're proceeding independently to Samuel Island, like *Damsel* and *Torrent*—but the others are still in company with him. Domynyk himself is still in action with the trailers from White Ford's formation, but I think at least ten or twelve of the Tarotisians are going to evade him in this stuff," he waved an arm at the weather. "White Ford's leading them, and he's driving them awfully hard for these conditions. He's also well past Cape Ruin. I think he's making for Dexter Point at the moment, but whether he's thinking in terms of Demon Reach or continuing to run I couldn't say.

"There're another five or six galleys to the east," he continued, gesturing at the almost pitch-dark eastern horizon, and his expression was grim. "Two of them are pretty badly damaged; I don't think they'll survive the night. The others may, but two of *them* are Dohlarans, and they're already in trouble."

He paused for a moment, staring off into the darkness where the men crewing those galleys fought for their lives against the hunger of the sea beyond even the sight of his eyes, then looked back at Cayleb.

"Earl Thirsk's in command of what's left," he said. "He's got about sixty galleys and all the remaining store ships, and he's rounding Crag Hook right this minute. He'll be safely anchored in Crag Reach within another two or three hours."

"I see."

Cayleb frowned, staring at nothing while he considered what Merlin had told him. He stayed that way for several seconds, then looked back at Merlin.

"What's our own current position?" he asked.

"So, now I'm your navigator, as well, am I?" Merlin retorted with a smile.

"When a wizard—or a *seijin*—appears to offer you his services, you might as well take full advantage of them," Cayleb replied with another of those tight grins.

"Well, for your information, we're about thirty-three miles south-southeast of the northern tip of Opal Island."

"And is Thirsk anchoring behind Crag Hook or in the lee of Opal?"

"Behind Crag Hook," Merlin replied.

Cayleb nodded again, obviously thinking hard, then grimaced.

"I can't remember the chart well enough," he admitted. "Could we make the passage between Opal and Crag Hook from here in a single tack?"

It was Merlin's turn to frown as he studied the satellite imagery relayed to him from the overhead SNARC.

"I don't think so," he said after a moment, speaking just a bit more slowly. "The wind's veered too far round."

"I was afraid of that. Still, it may be for the best. The men can use the rest."

Merlin turned to face the prince squarely.

"Cayleb, you aren't thinking about going into Crag Reach after them *tonight*, are you?"

"That's exactly what I'm thinking," Cayleb said, and Merlin's frown deepened.

"Cayleb, you've got only thirteen ships—assuming none of the others lose contact on the way, and you're talking about threading a needle in the dark! The passage between Opal and Crag Hook is barely twenty-two miles wide; it's raining hard; night's falling; the wind's still rising; we've got sixteen-foot seas; and every depth your charts show is eight hundred years out of date!"

"Agreed," Cayleb said calmly. "On the other hand, according to the charts, the main channel's over nine miles wide and almost sixty feet deep until you're past the northern tip of the island. Things may have changed since Hastings created the original charts, but there should be enough margin to let us in."

"In the middle of a rainy night?" Merlin demanded. "Without waiting for Domynyk or any of the stragglers?"

"We'll lose at least a couple of days making rendezvous with Domynyk and then getting back into position," Cayleb pointed out.

"Which doesn't change the fact that it's going to be darker than the inside of a barrel by the time we can get there. Your lookouts won't even be able to *see* Crescent Island, much less avoid running into it!"

"Ah, but I have the aid of a wizard, don't I, *Seijin* Merlin?" Cayleb replied softly. "*You* can see Crescent Island, and probably Opal Island and Crag Hook, all at the same time. So *Dreadnought* will take the lead, and the others will follow in our wake."

"But why run the risk of having one of them go astray?" Merlin argued. "If one of our galleons goes ashore in weather like this, we'll probably lose her entire company, and Thirsk isn't going anywhere. Certainly not before daylight!"

"No, he isn't," Cayleb agreed. "But I'll tell you what he is going to be doing." Merlin raised both eyebrows, and Cayleb shrugged. "He's going to be putting springs on his anchor cables. He's going to be ferrying as many of his heavy guns as he can ashore and setting them up as shore batteries. He's going to be thinking about what we did to him, and thinking about the fact that Crag Reach is a lot better suited to his galleys than the open sea was. And he's going to be doing everything he can to offset his men's panic and shock. He's going to use every single day—every *hour*—we give him to make arrangements to kill as many of *my* men as he can when we finally attack."

"But—" Merlin began, and Cayleb shook his head.

"I know that if we wait for Domynyk, we can still destroy every ship Thirsk has, whatever he does in the meantime. But if we give him the time to prepare, we're going to lose ships of our own. Nowhere near as many as he will, I'm sure, but we'll be forced to come to him on far less favorable terms, and there's no way he'll give in without a fight—probably a nasty one, at such close quarters.

"On the other hand, if we go in *tonight*, while his men are still exhausted and terrified, while he himself is probably still trying to grapple with what we've already done to him, the momentum will all be on our side. His men will feel trapped and helpless, and men who feel that way are a lot more likely to simply surrender instead of fighting to the bitter end."

Merlin had started to open his mouth in fresh protest, but now he closed it. He still thought Cayleb's scheme was risky, but he had to admit the prince appeared to have adjusted quite nicely to the notion that the more-than-human abilities of his *seijin*—or wizard—were there to be used. And given Merlin's own capabilities, the notion of entering Crag Reach in the middle of a near gale, wasn't *quite* as insane as it had appeared at first glance.

Yet that wasn't what chopped off his protest. No, what did that was the realization Cayleb was right.

It wasn't really something which would have occurred to Nimue Alban, for there'd been no surrenders in the war *she'd* fought. There'd been only victors and the dead, and the very concept of quarter had been meaningless. Merlin had allowed for the effects of demoralization and panic on the combat capability of the enemy, but he hadn't gone the one step further and remembered that honorable surrender was a deeply enshrined part of Safeholdian warfare.

And, he admitted to himself, he'd been too concerned with the potential difficulties of simply penetrating Crag Reach to consider how terrifying a night attack in a "secure anchorage" must be. Especially on a night such as this one promised to be . . . and on the heels of the sort of nightmare day the men on the receiving end of it had just endured.

It was still a questionable decision, he reflected. It could be argued either way, and rightfully so. Yet he was coming to suspect that Cayleb Ahrmahk would always prefer the more audacious solution to almost any problem. That could be a bad thing, but only if the prince allowed his instincts to overrule his cold calculation of potential advantages and disadvantages. And despite Merlin's initial reaction, that wasn't what was happening here.

It looks like he's inheriting more than just a throne from his father, Merlin thought, remembering Haarahld's cool, calculating response to the horrendous odds against his kingdom. *I wonder if there's a gene for this sort of thing?*

"All right, Your Highness," he said finally, his tone rather more formal than had become the norm. "If you're determined to do this, I suppose the least your tame 'wizard' can do for you is help."

"That's the spirit!" Cayleb said, smacking him on the water-streaming backplate of his cuirass, and turned to look over his own shoulder.

"Captain Manthyr! General signal: 'Form line astern of me. Prepare for night action. Repeat to all units.' Then let's get our night lights lit and hoisted while we've still got a little daylight. After that," he bared his teeth at the flag captain, "I want you to change course."

.V.
Crag Reach,
Armageddon Reef

Earl Thirsk stifled a groan of pure exhaustion as he lowered himself into the chair. His belly rumbled, with a sudden sharp pang, as the aroma of the hot food his valet had managed to put together reminded him he hadn't eaten since breakfast, the better part of thirty-six hours ago.

He started to reach for his wineglass, then stopped, and his mouth twitched wryly. The last thing he needed on a completely empty stomach was wine, and he picked up a large buttered roll, instead.

He bit into it, and at that instant, it was the most delicious thing he had ever tasted. He forced himself to chew slowly, savoring it rather than wolfing it down like a half-starved slash lizard, then swallowed with a sigh of pleasure.

He leaned forward, gathering up his fork and knife, and cut a piece of the broiled mutton on his plate. It followed the roll into his mouth, and he closed his eyes, chewing blissfully.

It was a small enough pleasure after a day like this one, he thought, and swallowed. He allowed himself a small sip of wine, and grimaced as it washed the mutton down.

He didn't know even now exactly how many ships he still had under his command. The best estimate he'd been able to put together was that there were between forty-five and eighty, including what he thought were all the surviving supply ships. That wasn't very much out of a combined fleet which had numbered over a hundred and seventy only that morning.

He forked up a steaming bite of buttered potato, although the food suddenly seemed less tasty, despite his hunger, as he contemplated the day's endless chain of disasters.

He didn't know how many of the other ships of the fleet had actually been lost, but he knew the number was high. He'd personally seen *King Rahnyld*'s corpse-littered wreck—and the wave-washed bodies floating away from it—just before the shattered hulk rolled over and sank. He'd seen the funeral pyres of at least another dozen ships, billowing up where they'd either taken fire in the midst of combat or been set ablaze by the Charisians. He hoped the enemy had at least allowed their crews to take to any surviving boats before firing their ships behind them, but he wasn't even certain of that.

He paused a moment, then shook his head, irritated with himself.

Yes, you know they did *allow the crews of at least some of their prizes to abandon first,* he told himself. *Hell, you've got over a hundred and ninety survivors aboard* Gorath Bay, *alone!*

Which was true enough. But the number his own ship had picked up only underscored all of the hundreds—thousands—of other men who'd been aboard Malikai's other galleys.

He cut another piece of mutton and put it in his mouth, chewing methodically.

He'd seen nothing but sinking wrecks and blazing hulls as his flagship sailed along in the wake of the running battle. The Charisian galleons appeared to have left no surviving galleys behind them. They'd been twice as fast as his own ships, especially after they'd set their topgallants, and they'd used that speed to chase down their prey relentlessly, steadily overtaking—and sinking—every galley in their path. There'd been nothing at all he could do about that, but it was probably just as well they'd been too fast for him to catch, he told himself grimly, remembering the old story of the hunting hound who'd "caught" the slash lizard.

He shook his head again, this time in still-stunned shock. The survivors *Gorath Bay* had picked up had confirmed what he'd already realized. Somehow, the Charisians had figured out a way to fire heavy cannon three or four times as rapidly as anyone else in the world. He was still trying to get his mind wrapped around the consequences that implied for the art of naval war, but Prince Cayleb—and several of the survivors had identified the Charisian crown prince's flag aboard one of those deadly galleons—had delivered a brutal demonstration that those consequences would be . . . profound.

At least Thirsk had managed to get the ships still in company with *Gorath Bay* into the shelter of Crag Hook. Even here, behind the stony barrier of the curved headland, his flagship jerked and snubbed harshly, uneasily, at her anchor. Pelting rain drummed on the skylight overhead and ran gurgling off the decks and through the scuppers, and he could hear the wind whining in the galley's shrouds and lifting blowing spray.

The lamps swayed on their gimbals above him, flooding the familiar comfort of his great cabin with warm light, and he remembered other nights. Remembered sitting here, smoking his pipe, enjoying a cup of wine or a tankard of beer, warm and comfortable and made even more aware of it by the sound of rain or the sigh of wind.

But there was no comfort tonight. There was only the awareness that he'd won no more than a breathing space. Cayleb would deduce where he was without any difficulty. And having deduced it, he would do something about it.

From the survivors' stories, and his own observations, he doubted very much that Cayleb had lost more than one or two of his galleons, at most. The young Charisian prince had just won what was undoubtedly the greatest, most one-sided naval victory in history, and unlike Malikai, Cayleb was a seaman. The Royal Charisian Navy knew about finishing the tasks to which it set its hand, and the prince was unlikely to pass up the opportunity to make his victory complete. Within a day or two, Thirsk would see those galleons standing into Crag Reach, and when he did, it would be his turn to see his ships shot to pieces in front of his eyes.

But they won't win as cheaply against us *as they did against Malikai*, he promised himself.

He'd already issued orders for every galley to rig springs to their anchor cables as soon as it was daylight. The springs—hawsers led out of gunports and attached to the ships' anchor cables at one end and to their capstans at the other—would allow any of his ships to turn in place by simply winding the hawser around the capstan. It would enable them to aim their guns in any direction, which was about the best he could hope to do. His artillery still wouldn't be able to fire as quickly as Cayleb's obviously could, but Cayleb wouldn't be able to bring all of his firepower to bear simultaneously, either.

And next time, Thirsk thought grimly, *what he can do to us won't come as a complete surprise, either.*

He stabbed his fork into another potato and bared his teeth.

As soon as it was light, he would start putting parties ashore to find suitable spots for shore batteries, as well. It wasn't going to be easy, but he was confident he could find at least some—and given the steepness of the hillsides rising beyond the beach, probably high enough to give his guns greater reach. Once *they* were in place, the price Cayleb would pay for any victory would climb steeply.

It was even possible, he told himself, that if he could make the probable price high enough, Cayleb might decline to pay it. After all, he'd already shattered this prong of the allies' planned offensive, and his galleons had to represent a huge part of Charis' total naval strength. Given the choice between heavy losses in return for the destruction of an already defeated foe or returning with his own ships intact to support the rest of the Charisian Navy against the combined forces of Corisande, Emerald, and Chisholm, he might well choose the latter.

And you really *want to* convince yourself of that, *don't you, Lywys?* he told himself with a sour snort.

He swallowed yet another bite of potato, then blinked in groggy surprise as he realized it was the *last* bite. He'd also managed to consume the entire thick slice of mutton and the side of green peas. And, he discovered, peering into the empty bread basket, at least another three rolls.

He laughed and shook his head tiredly. Clearly, he was even more exhausted than he'd thought he was, and it was time he got some desperately needed sleep.

Things may not look any better in the morning, he thought, *but at least a few hours of sleep on a full belly will leave me in better shape to deal with them.*

He finished the glass of wine, stood, and stumbled off to his sleeping cabin.

.VI.
HMS *Dreadnought*,
Off Armageddon Reef

Merlin Athrawes stood in the mizzenmast ratlines, eight feet above the quarterdeck, and peered into the darkness.

The wind, as he'd predicted, had continued to rise, but it actually seemed to be tapering off slightly now. It was down to "only" about thirty-four miles per hour, but the rain was even heavier then it had been earlier. Even his artificial eyes couldn't see very far through the almost solid wall of rain and spray.

It was a pity, he thought, that PICAs didn't come equipped with radar. Still, he supposed it would've been a bit much to put radar emitters powerful enough to do him much good under these conditions into PICAs intended to wander around the environs of a high-tech civilization.

"Owl," he subvocalized, climbing back down to the deck and grasping one of the lifelines rigged across it.

"Yes, Lieutenant Commander?"

"I need that imagery now."

There was no response, and Merlin grimaced.

"Begin feeding the previously specified imagery," he said, quite a bit more snappishly.

"Yes, Lieutenant Commander," the AI replied, totally unperturbed by his tone, and a detailed, see-through schematic blinked into existence across his field of view.

Unlike Merlin's eyes, the SNARC's sensors were perfectly capable of penetrating the stormy darkness, and Merlin felt an undeniable surge of relief as he saw the icons of all thirteen of Cayleb's galleons. Precisely how the merely mortal lookouts aboard any one of those ships had been able to keep sight of the poop lanterns and the additional lanterns suspended from the mizzen peak of the ship in front of them was more than Merlin was prepared to explain. But somehow, they'd done it.

Now it was up to him to get them into the sheltered waters of Crag Reach.

He considered the schematic's terrain imagery. It looked as if *Dreadnought* was just about on the proper heading, but "just about" wasn't nearly good enough.

"Owl," he subvocalized once more.

"Yes, Lieutenant Commander."

"Add current wind vector and vector and course projections for *Dreadnought* to the imagery and update continuously."

"Yes, Lieutenant Commander."

The requested arrows and dotted line appeared effectively instantaneously, and Merlin snorted. Then he made his way across the steeply tilted, pitching quarterdeck, moving hand-over-hand along the lifeline, to where Cayleb stood with Captain Manthyr beside the helmsmen. There were two men on the wheel, and a third seaman stood ready to lend his weight, as well, if it should prove necessary.

Manthyr really should have been getting some rest of his own, Merlin thought, but the flag captain hadn't even considered the possibility. *Dreadnought* was his ship. Everything about her was his responsibility, and now that he'd seen to the immediate needs of his men, he was undoubtedly standing there silently praying that his crown prince wasn't quite as insane as he seemed.

Merlin's mouth quirked at the thought, but perhaps he was doing the captain an injustice. What Cayleb had accomplished already this day (with, of course, Merlin's modest assistance) seemed to have given every man aboard the flagship a near idolatrous faith in the prince's seaman's instinct. If he wanted to sail them straight towards a cliff-girt lee shore in the middle of a midnight gale, they were prepared to do just that . . . although Manthyr obviously intended to stay right here and personally keep an eye on the entire process.

Cayleb himself appeared totally unworried by anyone's possible concerns about his mental stability. The prince's feet were spread wide apart as he clung to another lifeline for balance with his right fist, and he'd draped an oilcloth poncho over his cuirass and mail. The wind whipped the loose fall of the poncho, rain and spray ran from the rim of his morion-like helmet like a waterfall, and the light gleaming up from the binnacle's illuminated compass card lit his face from below. There were lines of fatigue in that face, and his cheekbones were gaunt, etched against the tight skin, yet his mouth was firm and confident, and the glow in his brown eyes did not come solely from the binnacle light.

He might, Merlin realized, be a very young man, but this was the sort of a moment for which he'd been born.

Cayleb looked up at his approach, and Merlin leaned close, half-shouting in his ear.

"We're pointing too high! The wind's backed a little to the east, and we need to come about a point and a half to leeward!"

Cayleb nodded, and Merlin walked over to where Ahrnahld Falkhan stood, half his body illuminated by the glow of the great cabin skylight, watching Cayleb's back even here.

Cayleb waited several minutes, then bent deliberately over the binnacle, squinting at the compass. He straightened and gazed up at the set of the barely visible sails, then stood in obvious thought for a second or two before he turned to Manthyr. No one could possibly have heard what he said to the flag captain, but the conversation lasted only a minute or so. Then Manthyr leaned close to his helmsmen.

"Make your course southwest-by-west!" he bawled through the tumult.

"Aye, aye, Sir!" the senior helmsman shouted back. "Sou'west-by-west, it is!"

He and his companion eased the wheel, spoke by spoke, eyes locked to the compass card. Holding an exact heading under any conditions was impossible for any sailing vessel. In *this* weather there wasn't any point even trying, but they were highly experienced helmsmen. They'd stick as close to it as anyone could, and Merlin smiled in satisfaction as *Dreadnought*'s projected track extended directly into the deepwater channel north of Opal Island, between Crag Hook and the much smaller Crescent Island.

Or, he reminded himself, *into what* was *a deepwater channel eight hundred years ago, at least.*

"He did that well!"

Merlin turned to look at Falkhan as the Marine shouted in his ear. They could see one another's faces clearly in the glow of the skylight, and Merlin raised one eyebrow.

"Who did what well?" he asked.

"Cayleb," Falkhan replied with a grin. He wiped water from his face and shook his head. "Those men will never guess you gave him the course correction!"

"I don't know what you're talking about!" Merlin replied as innocently as anyone could under the current conditions of wind and sea.

"Oh, of course not, *Seijin* Merlin!" Falkhan agreed with an even broader grin, and Merlin laughed. Then he sobered.

"You're right, he did do it well!" he shouted back. "And that's more important than ever!"

"Agreed!" Falkhan nodded vigorously. Then he glanced at the prince, and his smile was deeply approving. "He's growing up, isn't he?" he said to Merlin.

"That he is!" Merlin agreed. "That he is!"

Falkhan was right, he reflected, and in more ways than one. Cayleb had already demonstrated his own tactical and strategic insight, and also his willingness to back his own evaluation of a situation. He wasn't deferring to Merlin's suggestions—not unless he happened to agree with them, at least. He was using Merlin's *abilities* . . . then making his *own* decisions.

And the young man was showing an impressive attention to detail, as well. He'd deliberately sailed further east than he had to before turning back towards Armageddon Reef. He'd added at least two more hours to the total transit time, and Captain Manthyr had used that time to get the galley fires relit and feed every man as much hot soup, stew-thick with rice and vegetables, as he could eat.

It was impossible to estimate how much that hot food was going to mean to men who'd already had an exhausting day and faced an even more exhausting night. But Manthyr had also managed to give each man at least two hours in his hammock, as well. *Dreadnought*'s seamen and Marines would be going back into combat as well fed and rested as they could possibly be, and the captain had even managed to rig canvas scoops to gather rainwater to replenish their water tanks, then ordered the cooks to prepare gallons of hot tea before they doused the galley fires once more.

The men aboard *Dreadnought* recognized all of that, and word had gotten around that the prince had deliberately given them the time for it. That was the sort of consideration—and preparation—they weren't going to forget.

Those of them who survived the night, at least.

"Thank Langhorne we're not out in *that*," Lieutenant Rozhyr Blaidyn observed, listening to the storm.

It was blacker than the inside of a boot, but the regular, savage pounding of the heavy surf on the far side of Crag Hook and Opal Island could be heard even through the wind and rain. Of course, the wind—like the waves—was far weaker here, inside the sheltered waters of Crag Reach. Not that those waters were precisely what Blaidyn would have called "calm."

The anchorage was deep, with its walls rising sheer-sided out of the water, especially on its eastern side, where deep water ran to the very foot of the hundred-foot cliff which formed Crag Hook's western face. On the western side, the shore was less vertical and the water shoaled much more sharply. There were actually some smallish rocky beaches in pockets scalloped out of the feet of the steep hills on that side. But the shallower water was also rougher, and most of the fleet's captains had opted to anchor further out, in deeper water which gave them more safety room if their ships should happen to drag their anchors.

Blaidyn's ship, the *Royal Bédard*, had been one of the last galleys to reach safety. Visibility had been worse than bad by the time she arrived, and she'd collided with her consort, *Royal Champion*, on their way into the reach, losing one of her bow anchors in the process. Given her late arrival and the gathering darkness, she'd been forced to find the best spot to anchor she could, effectively on her own, and her captain had felt his cautious way as far into the reach as he'd dared, then dropped his remaining bow anchor. As a result, she was one of the southernmost of the huddled fleet's ships, and also one of the furthest east, separated from *Paladin*, the next nearest galley, by about a hundred and twenty yards. She was well into the lee of Crag Hook, but more exposed than many of the other ships, and even now she seemed to jerk nervously, as if frightened by the fury of the weather outside the anchorage, as she snubbed and rolled to her single anchor.

"I didn't realize you were so devout, Rozhyr," Nevyl Mairydyth said in response to his remark.

He and Blaidyn stood sheltering from the wind and rain in the lee of the forecastle, at the foot of the starboard forecastle ladder. Mairydyth was *Royal Bédard*'s first lieutenant, while Blaidyn—who'd just completed a personal check of the anchor watch—was the galley's second lieutenant. The first lieutenant was due to relieve him as officer of the watch in another ten minutes or so. After which Blaidyn would finally be able to stumble below, find something to eat, and get at least a few hours of desperately needed sleep.

"After a day like today?" Blaidyn grimaced at his superior. "Every damned man aboard is a hell of a lot more devout tonight than he was this morning!"

"Summed up like Grand Vicar Erayk himself," Mairydyth said sardonically.

"Well, would *you* rather be out there, or safe and sound in here?" Blaidyn demanded, waving one arm in the general direction of the seething white surf invisible through the thick, rainy night.

"That wasn't exactly my point," Mairydyth replied. "My point was—"

He never completed the sentence.

▼　　▼　　▼

The three-man anchor watch saw it first.

They weren't stationed in *Royal Bédard*'s bows as lookouts. They were there solely to keep an eye on the anchor cable, to be sure the galley wasn't dragging and that the cable wasn't chafing—a point which had assumed more than usual importance, given that it was now the only anchor she had. There *was* a lookout stationed in the galley's crow's-nest, but not because anyone—including him— really thought there'd be anything for him to spot. He was there solely because Earl Thirsk had ordered every ship to post lookouts, and the unfortunate seaman in *Royal Bédard*'s crow's-nest deeply resented the orders that put him up on that cold, vibrating, rain and wind swept perch for absolutely no good reason.

He was as wet, chilled to the bone, miserable, and exhausted as anyone else, and his body's need for rest was an anguished craving. He huddled in the crow's-nest, his oilskin draped to protect him as much as possible, and concentrated upon simply enduring until he was relieved and could finally collapse into his own hammock.

In fairness, even if he'd been fresh and alert, it was unlikely, given the visibility conditions, that he would have seen anything, despite the low range, more than a handful of seconds before the anchor watch did. But that was because HMS *Dreadnought* had extinguished all of her lanterns and running lights except for a single shaded poop lantern whose light was directed dead astern.

Unfortunately for *Royal Bédard*, she—like every other vessel anchored with her, and *unlike* Cayleb's flagship—was illuminated by anchor lights, poop lanterns, and lanterns at entry ports. More lights burned below deck, spilling illumination out of stern and quarter windows, out of oarports, deck hatches, and opened scuttles. Despite the darkness, and the rain, she wasn't at all hard to see.

One of the anchor watch straightened up suddenly, peering into the night as a shadow seemed to intrude between him and *Paladin*'s stern windows, almost due north of his own ship.

"What's that?" he demanded of his fellows.

"What's *what?*" one of them retorted irritably. He was no fonder of the weather, or any more rested, then any of them, and his temper was short.

"*That!*" the first man said sharply as the vague shadow became suddenly much clearer. "It looks like—"

▼   ▼   ▼

Captain Gwylym Manthyr stood very still by the quarterdeck bulwark. Not a voice spoke as *Dreadnought*'s entire crew waited, poised statue-still at its action stations. The captain was aware of the crown prince, his Marine guards, and Lieutenant Athrawes standing behind him, but every ounce of his attention was focused on the lanterns, windows, and scuttles gleaming through the rain.

Even now, Manthyr could scarcely believe Prince Cayleb had brought them unerringly into Crag Reach with the flood tide behind them. The combination of tide, current, and wind had created a wicked turbulence, but the channel between Crag Hook and Opal Island was as broad as their charts had indicated. It was a good thing it was, too. The sudden blanketing effect of Crag Hook's towering height had robbed *Dreadnought*'s sails of power for several minutes before the inrushing tide and her momentum carried her out of its wind shadow.

In more cramped waters, that might well have proved fatal, but Cayleb had put them in what was, as nearly as Manthyr could tell, the exact center of the deepwater channel. And now they were about to reap the rewards of the crown prince's daring.

The captain discovered he was holding his breath, and snorted. Did he he expect the enemy to hear him breathing, despite the tumult of the storm outside the reach? He grimaced in wry self-amusement, but the thought was only surface deep as his ship crept between the galley so far to the south of the main enemy fleet and the next closest one, a hundred or so yards north of her. The gleam of the southern ship's anchor light stood out sharply at her bow, marking her out for his port gunners. Her consort to the north was even more visible, for her stern windows glowed like a brilliant beacon for Manthyr's *starboard* gunners.

Another few seconds, he thought, raising his right arm slowly, aware of the gun captains crouching behind their weapons in both broadsides. Another . . . few . . .

"*Fire!*"

His right arm went downward, and the darkness came apart in the thunderbolt fury of a double broadside.

▼   ▼   ▼

"It looks like—"

The alert seaman never had the chance to finish his observation. A thirty-eight-pound round shot came howling out of the sudden gush of smoky flame directly ahead of *Royal Bédard* and struck him just above the waist.

His legs and hips stood upright for an instant, thick blood splashing through the rain. Then they thumped to the deck as the screams began.

▼   ▼   ▼

"Port your helm!" Manthyr barked as the smoke-streaming guns recoiled and their crews hurled themselves upon them with swabs and rammers. "Bring her two points to starboard!"

"Aye, aye. Two points to starboard it is, Cap'n!"

"Stand by the stern anchor!"

▼   ▼   ▼

Lieutenant Blaidyn recoiled in horror as a screaming round shot ripped into the bows, punched through the break of the forecastle in a cyclone of lethal splinters, and struck Lieutenant Mairydyth like a demon. The first lieutenant literally flew apart, drenching Blaidyn in an explosion of hot, steaming blood so shocking he scarcely even felt the sudden flare of agony in the calf of his own right leg.

Dreadnought's guns had been double-shotted. The gun crews had prepared with exquisite care, taking the time to be certain everything was done right. Each gun had been loaded with not one round shot, but two, with a charge of grape on top for good measure. It decreased accuracy and put a potentially dangerous strain on the gun tubes, but the range was short, every one of her guns was new, cast to withstand exactly this sort of pressure, and the consequences for their target were devastating.

The range was little more than forty yards, and *Dreadnought*'s gunners might as well have been at target practice. It wasn't physically impossible for them to miss, but it would have been very, very difficult.

Twenty-seven guns hammered their hate into *Royal Bédard* with absolutely no warning, no time for the galley to prepare. Her own guns were secured. Her off-duty crew were in their hammocks. Her captain was asleep in his cabin. Her Marines were neither armed nor armored. That dreadful avalanche of cast-iron shot came howling out of the heart of the storm like an outrider of Hell, almost directly down the centerline of the ship, and the carnage it inflicted was unspeakable.

Paladin, thirty yards farther away, might have expected to fare better at the greater range, but her lighted stern windows offered an even better target . . . and far less protection than *Royal Bédard*'s stoutly planked bows. The devastating broadside ripped into her, rending and killing, and the shrieks of the maimed and dying followed on its heels.

▼   ▼   ▼

Lywys Gahrdaner, the Earl of Thirsk, stirred in his sleep at the sudden rumble. He grimaced, not quite waking, his sleeping mind identifying the sound of thunder which might have accompanied any storm, far less one as strong as the one pounding at Armageddon Reef this night.

But then it came again. And again.

His eyes popped open . . . and it came *again*.

▼   ▼   ▼

Dreadnought answered to her helm. She swung to starboard under topsails and headsails alone, streaming smoke from both broadsides, as she turned away from *Royal Bédard* and deeper into the main anchorage. Her long bowsprit thrust into the Dohlaran formation like a lance, and her starboard battery roared again as she swept around *Paladin*'s port quarter. She pushed between her target and *Archangel Schueler*, lying almost directly west of her. The two of them, like every other ship in the Dohlaran force, had been carefully anchored far enough apart to allow them to swing to their anchors without risk of collision, and that left ample room for *Dreadnought* to slide between them.

Captain Manthyr stood behind his helmsmen, one hand resting on each seaman's shoulder, almost crooning his orders into their ears. He conned his ship with exquisite care, and smoke and thunder jetted from either broadside, blasting into the anchored ships whose crewmen were only just beginning to rouse from exhausted slumber.

Behind her, HMS *Destroyer* followed her as she threaded her way deeper and deeper into the mass of anchored galleys. And behind *Destroyer* came *Danger*, and *Defense*, and *Dragon*.

"All hands, stand by to anchor!" Manthyr shouted.

"Stand by to reduce sail!" Lieutenant Sahdlyr barked through his speaking trumpet, while Midshipman Kohrby crouched beside the anchor party in the stern.

"Let go the stern anchor!" Manthyr commanded, and Kohrby echoed the order. The anchor disappeared into the whitecaps, and the cable led aft down the center of her berthdeck smoked as it burned across the sill of one of her after gunports.

"Clew down!" Sahdlyr shouted.

The officers in charge of each mast repeated the order, and the seamen at the pinrails eased the halyards, lowering the topsails' yards into their lifts and spilling their wind. Other seamen tended the buntlines and leechlines as the yard came down, and Sahdlyr watched closely.

"Round in the lee brace! Clew up the topsails!"

The canvas disappeared as the hands on the clewlines hauled it up to the yards and belayed. More men on the foredeck took in the jibs while the anchor hawser ran out, and the ship came to a stop as the flukes of her anchor dug into the bottom of Crag Reach.

"Clamp on the spring!" Manthyr ordered, and Kohrby's seamen made the already prepared bitter end of the spring cable fast to the anchor hawser just outside the gunport.

"Hands to the after capstan!" the captain shouted, and the seamen previously detailed went running to the capstan to take tension on the spring.

▼   ▼   ▼

Earl Thirsk stumbled out of his cabin into the rain, barefoot, wearing nothing but his breeches, as still more cannon began to thunder. He hurled himself up the ladder to the top of the aftercastle, ignoring the icy water sluicing over his naked torso as he stared in horrified disbelief at the savage flashes lighting up the rain.

It was a sight such as no Safeholdian had ever seen before. The Charisian cannon rumbled and roared, the muzzle flashes impossibly long and brilliant in the darkness. Smoke gouted, fuming up in sulfurous clouds reeking of Shanwei's own brimstone. Each muzzle flash etched every plunging raindrop against the night, like rubies, or diamonds of blood, and the banks of smoke towered up, lit from below, like the fumes above erupting volcanoes.

And there was nothing at all the Earl of Thirsk could do about it.

▼   ▼   ▼

Royal Bédard lurched as yet another galleon—the sixth, Lieutenant Blaidyn's cringing mind thought—swept slowly past her bow, cannon thundering. The lieutenant stood at the top of the port forecastle ladder—the starboard ladder was a shattered ruin, like the mast whose broken stump stood ten feet off the deck—clinging to the forecastle rail for support, and the calf of his right leg had been laid open by a splinter as if by a sword. He felt hot blood sheeting down his leg but ignored it as he ignored the rain while he shouted encouragement to the seamen trying to get two of the galley's bow chasers loaded despite the round shot howling around their ears.

But then he smelled the smoke. Not powder smoke, rolling on the rain-slashed wind from the enemy guns, but a far more terrifying smoke. The smoke of burning wood.

His head snapped around, and he blanched in fresh horror. The severed mast had fallen across the decks at an angle, draping the broken yard and its burden of sodden canvas across the midships hatch. But now smoke billowed up out of the half-blocked hatch, funneling through the fallen rigging and wreckage, thickening into a dense, flame-lit pillar as it streamed up around the yard and mast.

He didn't know what had happened. Most likely, one of those lighted lanterns below decks had been shattered, spilling flaming oil across the decks. Or it could have been an accident by one of the powder monkeys trying to carry ammunition to the guns. It might even have been a flaming wad, hurled out of one of the Charisian cannon.

But it didn't really matter how it had started. Wooden ships' worst enemy wasn't the sea; it was fire. Built of seasoned timbers, painted inside and out, caulked with pitch, rigged with tarred cordage, they were tinderboxes awaiting a spark, even in this sort of weather, and *Royal Bédard*'s spark had been supplied.

Under other circumstances, the fire might have been fought, might have been contained and extinguished. But not under *these* circumstances. Not while round shot continued to crash through the ship's hull, mangling and disemboweling terrified crewmen whose exhausted brains were still clawing their way out of sleep and into nightmare.

"Abandon ship! *Abandon ship!*"

Blaidyn didn't know who'd shouted it first, but there was no fighting the panic it induced. For that matter, there was no *point* fighting it, and he dragged himself the rest of the way up the ladder and across to the port bulwark. He peered down over it, and his jaw clenched. The galley's boats had been lowered when she anchored, and men were flinging themselves over the side, struggling through the water, trying to reach that at least temporary sanctuary.

Blaidyn turned at the bulwark. One of the gun crews was still fighting to get its weapon loaded, and he limped back over to grab the closest man by the arm.

"Forget it!" he shouted. "There's no time! Over the side, boys!"

The rest of the gun crew stared at him for a moment, wild-eyed. Then they were gone, scrambling over the bulwark. Blaidyn watched them go, then turned to take one last look around the deck, to be sure everyone was gone or going.

Flames were beginning to spurt out of the hatchway. He could feel their heat on his face from here, even through the rain, and he tried to close his ears to the agonized shrieks of men trapped below in that blazing inferno.

There was nothing more he could do, and he turned to follow the gun crew . . . just as a single round shot from a final thundering broadside struck him squarely in the chest.

Fourteen minutes later, the flames reached his ship's magazine.

▼   ▼   ▼

At least three of the anchored galleys were on fire now, illuminating the anchorage brightly despite the rain. Merlin stood beside Cayleb on *Dreadnought*'s quarterdeck as the galleon's guns continued to rave at their targets, and the wild vista of destruction all about him dwarfed anything Nimue Alban, who'd warred with the power of nuclear fusion itself, had ever seen with her own eyes.

The ship was no longer moving. She was motionless—not as stable as a shoreside fortress in these whitecapped waters, perhaps, but close enough to it for gunners accustomed to the rolling, pitching motion of a ship at sea. Scoring hits on equally anchored targets was child's play for them under these conditions, and their rate of fire was far higher than it would have been from a moving ship's deck. They loaded and fired, loaded and fired, like automatons, reducing their targets to shattered, broken wrecks.

Steam curled from the hot gun tubes between shots, hissing up like tendrils of fog to be whipped away by the wind. The reek of powder smoke, blazing wood, burning tar and cordage raced across the waves in spray-washed banners of smoke, twisted and broken above the whitecaps, starkly silhouetted against the flash of guns and flaming ships.

One of the blazing galleys drifted free as her anchor cable burned through. The wind sent her slowly in *Dreadnought's* direction—not directly towards her, but close enough—wreathed in the fiery corona of her own destruction. Captain Manthyr saw her, and his orders sent the capstan around, tightening the spring until the galleon's starboard broadside bore on the fiery wreck.

He stood ready to cut his own cable and make sail, if necessary, but three quick, thunderous broadsides were enough to finish the already sinking galley. She settled on her side in a huge, hissing cloud of steam as water quenched flame, a hundred and fifty yards clear of his ship, and another snarling cheer of victory went up from his gunners.

▼   ▼   ▼

Royal Bédard exploded.

The deafening eruption when the flames reached her magazine dwarfed every other sound, even the brazen voices of the Charisian guns. The tremendous flash seemed to momentarily burn away the spray and rain. It illuminated the bellies of the overhead clouds, flashed back from the vertical western face of Crag Hook, and hurled flaming fragments high into the windy night, like homesick meteors returning to the heavens.

The fiery debris arced upward, then crashed back, hissing into extinction as it hit the water, or smashing down on the decks of nearby galleys and galleons alike in cascades of sparks. Crewmen raced to heave the burning wreckage over the side, and here and there small fires were set, but the pounding rain and wind-blown spray had so thoroughly soaked the topsides of both sides' vessels that no ship was seriously threatened.

Yet the furious action paused, as if the galley's spectacular, terrifying disintegration had awed both sides into a temporary state of shock.

The pause lasted for two or three minutes, and then it vanished into renewed bedlam as Cayleb's gunners opened fire once more.

▼   ▼   ▼

Earl Thirsk stared helplessly at the hellish panorama.

He had no idea how long he'd stood on *Gorath Bay's* aftercastle. It seemed like an eternity, although it couldn't really have been much longer than two hours, possibly a bit more. Someone had draped a cloak over his shoulders—he had no idea who—and he huddled inside it, holding it about him, while he gazed upon the final ruin of his command.

The Charisians had split into at least two columns, or perhaps three. They were deep inside his anchored formation, firing mercilessly, and everywhere he looked the rain was like sheets of bloody glass, lit by the glare of burning galleys and flashing artillery.

He'd underestimated his enemy. He'd never *dreamed* Cayleb would have the insane audacity to lead an entire fleet of galleons into Crag Reach *at night* through the fury of a near-gale. He *still* couldn't believe it, even with the devastating evidence burning to the waterline before his very eyes.

Royal Bédard was gone, taking her flames with her, but a half-dozen of his other ships blazed brightly, and even as he gazed out at the carnage, another kindled. He watched flames shooting up out of its holds, licking up its tarred shrouds, and silhouetted against the light he saw crowded boats pulling strongly away from the inferno. As far as he could tell, no Charisian had even been firing at the blazing ship, and his teeth ached from the pressure of his jaw muscles as he realized the crew had deliberately fired their vessel and then abandoned ship rather than face the enemy.

He turned away from the sight, only to see another of his as yet undamaged galleys getting underway. Not to close with the enemy, but to row directly towards the western shore of the anchorage. Even as he watched, she drove herself bodily up onto the rocky beach, and her crew flowed over her sides, splashing into the shallow water, stumbling ashore, fleeing into the darkness.

Part of him wanted to curse them for their cowardice, but he couldn't. What else could anyone have expected? Destruction was upon them all, appearing out of the night like the work of some demon, and were they not anchored in the waters of Armageddon Reef itself?

That was the final straw, he thought. This very land was cursed. Every single one of his men knew the story of the monumental evil which had been birthed here so long ago and the terrible destruction which had been visited upon it, and that was enough, added to the terror of the totally unexpected attack, the sudden explosion of violence, and their completely unprepared state.

Another galley flamed up, fired by its own crew, and a second started moving towards the beach. And a third. And beyond that, silhouetted against the smoky glare of their burning sisters, he saw other galleys hauling down their flags, striking their colors in token of surrender.

He stared at them for a moment longer, then turned away. He climbed down the aftercastle ladder slowly, like an old, old man, opened his cabin door, and stepped through it.

E arl Thirsk is here, Your Highness," Ahrnahld Falkhan announced with unusual formality as he opened the door to HMS *Dreadnought*'s flag cabin.

Cayleb turned from the vista of whitecapped water beyond the stern windows to face the door as his senior Marine bodyguard ushered the Dohlaran admiral through it.

"Your Highness," Thirsk said, bending his head.

"My Lord," Cayleb returned.

The Dohlaran straightened, and Cayleb studied his face thoughtfully. The older man was soaking wet from the rough passage in an open boat, and he looked worn and exhausted, but more than fatigue was stamped upon his features. His dark eyes—eyes, Cayleb suspected, which were normally confident, even arrogant—carried the shadows of defeat. Yet there was more to it even than that, and the crown prince decided Merlin had been right yet again when Cayleb explained what he had in mind. Not even this man, confident and strong minded though he was, was immune to the reputation and aura of Armageddon Reef.

Which was going to make this morning's conversation even more interesting.

"I've come to surrender my sword, Your Highness," Thirsk said heavily, as if each word cost him physical pain.

He reached down with his left hand, gripping not the pommel, but the guard of the sword sheathed at his hip. He drew it from its scabbard, ignoring the eagle eye with which both Falkhan and Merlin watched him, and extended it to Cayleb, hilt-first.

"No other man has ever taken my sword from me, Prince Cayleb," the Dohlaran said as Cayleb's fingers closed upon the hilt.

"It's the sword of a man who deserved a better cause to serve," Cayleb replied quietly. He looked down at the weapon in his hand for a moment, then handed it to Falkhan, who set it gently on Cayleb's desk, in turn.

The crown prince watched Thirsk's face carefully for any reaction to his comment. He thought he saw the Dohlaran's lips tighten slightly, but he couldn't be positive. After a moment, he gestured at one of the pair of chairs set ready on opposite sides of the dining table.

"Please, be seated, My Lord," he invited.

He waited until Thirsk had settled into the indicated chair before seating himself on the opposite side of the table, and Merlin, in his bodyguard's role, moved to stand behind him. A decanter of brandy sat on the linen tablecloth, and the prince personally poured a small measure into each of two glasses, then offered one to Thirsk.

The Dohlaran commander accepted the glass, waited for Cayleb to pick up his own, and then sipped. He drank very little before he set the glass back on the table, and Cayleb smiled wryly as he set his own beside it.

"I've also come, as I'm sure Your Highness has deduced, to discover what surrender terms the remainder of my fleet may expect," Thirsk said in a flattened voice.

Cayleb nodded and sat back in his chair.

Nineteen of Thirsk's galley's had been sunk or burned. Another three had been battered into shattered, foundering wrecks which had barely managed to beach themselves before they went down. Eleven more had struck their colors, and eight had driven themselves ashore, undamaged, before their crews abandoned them. Yet a third of Thirsk's total warships remained, along with all his supply ships, and Cayleb had paid a price of his own for that victory.

HMS *Dragon* had found herself in the path of one of the burning galleys after the Dohlaran ship's anchor cable burned through. The blazing wreck had drifted down upon the galleon, and though *Dragon* had cut her own cable and tried to evade, she'd failed. The two ships had met in a fiery embrace, and both had been consumed in a floating, roaring inferno which had eventually engulfed two more of Thirsk's anchored ships.

Over two-thirds of *Dragon*'s company, including her captain and all but one of her lieutenants, had been lost, killed when their ship's magazine exploded, or else drowned before they could be plucked from Crag Reach's waters.

Despite that, Thirsk's remaining twenty-one warships were helpless. Cayleb's surviving twelve galleons were anchored in a somewhat ragged line between them and any hope of escape. After what those galleons' guns had already done, none of those galleys' crews—or the admiral in command of them—had any illusions about what would happen if they tried to attack the Charisians or break past them to the open sea.

"My terms are very simple, My Lord," the crown prince said finally. "I will expect the unconditional surrender of every ship in this anchorage."

Thirsk flinched, not so much with surprise, as in pain.

"I might point out, Your Highness," he said, after a moment, "that you don't begin to have sufficient men aboard your ships to take my own as prizes."

"True," Cayleb conceded, nodding equably. "On the other hand, I have no intention of taking them with me."

"No?" Thirsk gazed at him for a moment, then cocked his head. "Should I assume, then, that you intend to parole them and my surviving men?"

"You should not," Cayleb said in a far, far colder voice.

"Your king sent his navy to attack the Kingdom of Charis in time of peace," he continued in that same icy voice, aware of Merlin standing at his back. "Charis did nothing to offend or harm him in any way. He made no demands upon us, nor did he declare his intent. Instead, like an assassin, he dispatched Duke Malikai—and *you*, My Lord—to join with the forces of one of our own allies to treacherously attack a land over six thousand miles from his own."

Surprise, and perhaps a flare of anger at Cayleb's biting tone, flickered in Thirsk's eyes, and Cayleb snorted.

"We weren't as unsuspecting as you—and your masters among the 'Knights of the Temple Lands'—expected, My Lord. Our agents in Tarot knew all about your plan to attack us. How else do you think we could have known which waters to watch for your approach? And never doubt, Earl Thirsk, that Gorjah of Tarot will pay for *his* treachery, as well.

"But what matters to us at this moment is that your king neither deserves, nor can be trusted to honor, any parole you or your men might give. And so, I regret to say, you won't be offered that option."

"I trust," Thirsk said through tight lips, "that in that case you aren't so foolish as to believe my men won't attempt to take back their ships from whatever prize crews you may be able to put upon them, Your Highness?"

"There will be no prize crews," Cayleb informed him. "Your ships will be burned."

"*Burned?*" Thirsk gaped in shock. "But their crews, my men—"

"Your men will be put ashore," Cayleb said. "You'll be permitted to land supplies, materials from which shelters may be built, and provisions from your vessels, including your supply ships. You will *not* be permitted to land any weapons other than woodcutter's axes and saws. Once all of your men are ashore, all of your vessels, except a single, unarmed supply ship, will be destroyed. That vessel will be permitted to sail wherever you wish to send it with dispatches for your king."

"You can't be serious!" Thirsk stared at him, his expression horrified. "You can't put that many men ashore and simply abandon them—not here! Not on Armageddon Reef!"

"I'm entirely serious," Cayleb replied mercilessly, holding the older man's eyes with his own and letting Thirsk see his angry determination. "You brought this war to *us*, My Lord. Don't pretend for a moment that you were unaware of the plans the 'Knights of the Temple Lands' had for my kingdom's total destruction and what that would mean for my father's subjects! I can, and will, put you and your men ashore anywhere I choose, and I *will* leave them there. Your choice is to accept that, or else to return to your flagship and resume the engagement. If, however, you choose the latter course, no further surrenders will be accepted . . . and no quarter will be offered."

Merlin stood behind Cayleb's chair, his own face an expressionless mask. He heard the absolute, unyielding steel in Cayleb's voice and prayed that *Thirsk* heard it, as well. The terms Cayleb had offered were the crown prince's, and no one else's. Merlin had been only slightly surprised by what Cayleb had decided to do with Thirsk's surrendered personnel, but he'd felt an inner chill when Cayleb explained what he intended to do if Thirsk rejected those terms.

Now Thirsk gazed at Cayleb Ahrmahk's unyielding face and recognized the youthful prince's total willingness to do precisely what he'd just said he would. Cayleb might not like it, but he *would* do it.

"Your Highness," the earl grated, after a long, tense moment of singing silence, "no commander in history has ever made a threat such as that against enemies who have offered honorable surrender."

"No?"

Cayleb looked back at him, then showed his teeth in a smile his dynasty's kraken emblem might have envied and spoke with cold, deadly precision.

"Perhaps not, My Lord. Then again, what other commander in history has discovered that no less than five other kingdoms and princedoms have leagued together to destroy his own, when his king's done no harm to any of them? What other commander has known his enemies intend to burn his cities, rape and pillage his people, for no better reason than that someone's offered to hire them like the common footpads they are? I told you our agents in Tarot know what your paymasters had in mind, and honorable and generous terms of surrender are for honorable *foes*, My Lord. They are not for hired stranglers, murderers, and rapists."

Thirsk flinched, his face white and twisted, as Cayleb's savage words and vicious contempt bit home. But his eyes flickered, as well—flickered with the knowledge that those words, however savage, however contemptuous, were also true.

Cayleb let the silence linger for a full minute, then looked Thirsk squarely in the eye.

"So, now you know the conditions under which your vessels and their crews will be permitted to surrender, My Lord. Do you wish to accept them, or not?"

▼   ▼   ▼

Merlin stood with Cayleb on *Dreadnought*'s sternwalk, watching as Thirsk's launch rowed away through the still rough waters of Crag Reach.

"You were a bit harsh with him," the man who had once been Nimue Alban observed.

"Yes," Cayleb conceded. "I was, wasn't I?"

He turned to face Merlin squarely.

"Do you think I was harsher than he deserved?" he asked.

It was a serious question, Merlin realized, and he considered it seriously before he responded.

"Actually, I do think you may have been harsher than *he* deserved," he said after a moment. "Which isn't to say King Rahnyld didn't deserve everything you said. Although you might want to think about the potential diplomatic consequences of flaying him quite as thoroughly as he deserves."

"After what we've done to him—and what he's *tried* to do to us—I don't really think it's very likely even Father or Rayjhis could negotiate any sort of treaty with him, whatever *I* said or didn't say," Cayleb said with a snort. "Even if Rahnyld had any desire to forgive and forget—which he won't have—Clyntahn and the rest of the Group of Four wouldn't let him. And unlike Charis, Dohlar is effectively right next door to the Temple. So I might as well tell him what I really think of him."

"I'm sure it was personally satisfying," Merlin said mildly, and Cayleb barked a laugh.

"Actually, it was *extremely* personally satisfying," he corrected. "That wasn't why I did it, though." Merlin quirked an eyebrow, and the crown prince shrugged. "Thirsk's going to report this conversation when he finally gets home. And when he does, Rahnyld's going to be absolutely livid. Well, that was going to happen anyway, no matter how 'diplomatic' I might have been. But now two other things are going to happen, as well.

"First, in the impetuousness of my youth and immature anger, I've 'let slip' the penetration of our agents in Tarot. That should serve as an additional layer of protection for your 'visions,' Merlin. But, possibly even more importantly, Rahnyld—and, hopefully, the Group of Four—are going to believe *Gorjah* was responsible for letting out the information that allowed us to intercept the Southern Force. Either he deliberately fed it to us, or else he was criminally careless, and the fact that the only survivors of this entire debacle are all going to be *Tarotisian* galleys may help convince his 'friends' he set the whole thing up intentionally. In either case, it's going to leave him just a tiny bit of a problem, don't you think?"

Cayleb's evil smile made him look remarkably like his father in that moment, Merlin reflected.

"Second," the crown prince continued, "what I said to Thirsk, and what he's going to repeat to Rahnyld, is going to get out. Don't think for a moment it won't. And when it does, it's going to affect the thinking of all Rahnyld's nobles. It's also going to get out to all the other rulers of Howard and Haven, as well, and I suspect that's going to make it a bit more difficult for the Group of Four to arrange a repeat performance of this. They certainly won't be able to approach it as if it were no more than 'business as usual.' And if their next batch of potential catspaws understand exactly how we're going to regard them, and what can happen to *their* navies if they lose, it may make them just a bit less eager."

Merlin nodded slowly. He wasn't at all certain he agreed with everything Cayleb had just said, but the decisiveness it reflected was typical of what he was coming to expect out of the youthful heir to the throne.

As far as the effect on Tarot and King Gorjah was concerned, he probably had an excellent point, Merlin reflected. It was the other side of it Merlin found worrisome. Yes, it might make it more difficult for the Group of Four to marshal the forces for their next attack, but the stark ruthlessness of Cayleb's expressed attitude might also provoke a matching response from future opponents.

Still, Merlin asked himself, *how much worse could it get? Cayleb's absolutely right about what the Group of Four wanted to happen to Charis* this *time. Is it really likely their objectives are going to get* less *extreme after their tools got hammered this way the first time around?*

"Well," he said aloud, "at least Thirsk accepted instead of forcing your hand."

"Yes." Cayleb nodded. "And you were right this morning when you suggested offering him the option of putting his men ashore on Opal Island, instead of the mainland. Personally, I don't think I'd find putting Crag Reach between me and the demons he expects his people to be so worried about would be all that reassuring. But I'm just as glad *they'll* find it that way, if it makes them happier about accepting and means I don't have to kill them all after all."

"I'm glad to have been of service," Merlin said dryly. "And, now that he's accepted, what are your other plans?"

"Well," Cayleb said slowly, turning to look out across the water at the tree-covered slopes of Opal Island's three thousand-plus square miles, "I'd really prefer to head back home immediately. But if *Typhoon's* as badly damaged as you say, she's going to need time for repairs. We've got damage to other ships, as well, and all of us used a lot of powder and shot. We need to get *Traveler* and *Summer Moon* in here and replenish our ammunition. And I'm thinking that before we burn Thirsk's galleys, we'll strip them of anything we can use, as well—especially spare spars, lumber, cordage and canvas, that sort of thing—then stay here long enough to complete at least our major repairs."

"Is that wise?" Merlin asked in a deliberately neutral tone.

"I'll discuss it with Domynyk, get his suggestions and advice, of course," Cayleb said, "but I don't think we have a lot of choice. We can't leave just one or two ships here to repair by themselves, not when Thirsk's going to have several thousand men right here on Opal Island to try something with. So, either we burn our worst-damaged ships right along with the galleys—which, much though I don't want to, may turn out to be our best choice—or else we all stay here long enough to repair them and take them with us when we leave."

The crown prince shrugged unhappily.

"I'm not delighted with either option, Merlin. But whatever we do, we're still the better part of a month's hard sail away from Charis. Taking another five-day or two to make repairs isn't going to add very much to how long it takes us to get home. And, for that matter, Hektor and Nahrmahn won't be expecting Malikai for almost another month, anyway. Your own 'visions' say they're still waiting under the original timetable, and they aren't going to be that surprised if

Malikai and his fleet are later even than that. Not after traveling that far in Dohlaran galleys.

"So, unless Domynyk comes up with some compelling argument which hasn't already occurred to me, I think it's more important for us to fully repair all of our surviving galleons than it is to try to get home a couple of five-days earlier."

MARCH, YEAR OF GOD 892

✦

.I.

HMS *Dreadnought,*
Off Armageddon Reef

Merlin gazed across the hammock nettings as the southern tip of Opal Island passed slowly to port.

The schooner *Spy* led the line of Charisian ships, moving with saucy grace as her more ponderous consorts followed heavily in her wake. The summer sun shone brightly out of a blue sky polished by a handful of fair-weather cumulus clouds, while torrents of the gulls, puffins, and sea wyverns which nested in the cliffs of Crag Hook circled and dove. A gentle surf broke against Sand Islet, off the port bow, and the lower line of cliffs leading the way to Bald Rock Head, to starboard.

Nothing, he thought, could have presented a greater contrast to their arrival in Crag Reach.

"I can't say I'm sorry to be going," Cayleb remarked from beside him, and Merlin turned his head to look at the prince.

Cayleb wore a tunic and trousers, not the armor and helmet he'd worn that violence-wracked night, and he ran a hand over his bare head as he, too, looked across at Opal Island.

"You do realize this is going to go down as one of the greatest naval battles in the history of the world, don't you?" Merlin said quizzically.

"And rightly so, I suppose." Cayleb shrugged. "On the other hand, I did have certain . . . unfair advantages."

He smiled, and Merlin smiled back.

"I do feel sorry for Thirsk, though," Merlin said after a moment, his smile fading. "You were right when you said he deserved a better cause to serve."

"He'd be more likely to find one of those if he'd find a better *king*," Cayleb said tartly. "Trust me. That's something I know a little about."

"Yes, you do."

Merlin turned his eyes back to the island's forested slopes. Earl Thirsk and his survivors should be just fine until someone sent the necessary ships to take them home again. Opal had plenty of fresh water, they'd already erected sufficient shelter, especially for the summer, and landed enough provisions to carry them for at least six months, even if they were unable to add anything by hunting and fishing. And Cayleb had relented, just a bit, and left a small store of cap-

tured matchlocks and arbalests on the beach when his ships weighed anchor this
morning.

Of course, what's going to happen to Thirsk when he gets home *may be something else
entirely,* Merlin thought grimly. *He's the senior Dohlaran admiral who's coming home
after the worst naval disaster in Dohlar's history, and what I've seen of King Rahnyld suggests he's going to be looking for scapegoats, more than explanations.*

He thought about it for a moment longer, then put the matter of Earl
Thirsk's future away and leaned out across the hammock nettings to look back at
the line of sails following along astern of *Dreadnought.*

The last thick, dark pillars of smoke from over fifty blazing ships still trailed
across the sky, following the galleon fleet out of its anchorage. The line of ships
looked impressive and proud after two five-days of repairs, with the brooms
lashed to the heads of their main topgallant masts. Cayleb had laughed out loud
when Merlin suggested that gesture and explained the symbolism behind it, but
then he'd sobered as he realized how apt it was. His galleons certainly *had* swept
the sea clean of their enemies.

Merlin's lips twitched in a remembered smile of his own, but then it faded,
for three sails were missing, and he felt a fresh stab of grief for the schooner
Wyvern.

He didn't know what had happened to her. She'd been there, riding the fury
of the gale, in one SNARC pass; in the next, she'd simply been gone. He'd been
able to locate no survivors of her ninety-man crew, not even any wreckage.

Then there was *Dragon*, lost so spectacularly in the final stage of the Crag
Reach action. And HMS *Lightning*, one of the converted merchantmen, from Sir
Domynyk Staynair's column, had taken more damage in the action off Rock
Point then Merlin had first thought. She'd made it to the rendezvous in the lee of
Samuel Island with the rest of Staynair's ships, but then she'd slowly foundered
over the course of that long, stormy night. The good news was that they'd at least
gotten almost all her people safely off before she finally went down.

Typhoon's repairs had taken the full two five-days Cayleb had predicted, but
she had a brand new mainmast, and the rest of the fleet had made good use of the
time it had taken to replace the original. They'd replenished their water from
Opal Island, their provisions from captured stores, and their magazines and shot
lockers from *Traveler* and *Summer Moon*, and all of the other galleons had been
able to repair their own battle damages while Captain Stywyrt worked on his.
The survivors from *Dragon* and *Lightning* had been distributed throughout the
rest of the fleet, making up the worst of their personnel losses, as well, so at least
all of the surviving galleons were combat-ready.

"I wish we could have gotten out of here sooner," Cayleb muttered. The
prince was talking to himself, but Merlin's hearing was rather more acute than
most, and he gave Cayleb another look.

"You were the one who said we needed to make good our damages," he
pointed out. "You had a point. And Domynyk agreed with you."

"But you didn't," Cayleb said, turning to face him fully while the steady, gentle breeze ruffled his hair.

"I didn't *disagree*, either," Merlin responded, and shrugged. "You were right when you pointed out that there wasn't a perfect decision. Somebody had to choose, and you happen to be the Crown Prince around here."

"I know," Cayleb sighed. For just a moment, he looked twice his age, then he shook himself and produced a wry smile. "You know, usually being Crown Prince is a pretty good job. But there are times when it's really not so much fun."

"So I've observed. But the important thing, I suppose, is that you need to remember you *are* the one who has to make the decisions, and you aren't usually going to have lots of time to sit around and ponder them. By and large, the people who're going to second-guess and criticize you after the fact are going to be doing it from someplace nice and safe, with all the advantages of hindsight and plenty of time to think about what *you* did wrong."

"That's more or less what Father's said, once or twice," Cayleb said.

"Well, he's right. And the good news, you know, is that when you do get it right, like the decision to go straight into Crag Reach, you also get all the credit for it." Merlin grinned. "Just think—now you're a certified military genius!"

"Yeah, sure." Cayleb rolled his eyes. "And I can already hear Father cutting me back down to size when I get too full of myself over it, too!"

.II.
Eraystor Bay,
Princedom of Emerald

Whats's so important you have to drag me out of bed in the middle of the night?" Duke Black Water demanded irritably, tying the sash of a light robe as he glowered at Tohmys Bahrmyn, Baron White Castle.

The baron rose from the chair in *Corisande*'s great cabin as the duke stamped in from his sleeping cabin. Black Water had been in bed for less than three hours after yet another contentious conference—or perhaps "acrimonious debate" might have been a better term—with his unwilling allies.

He was *not* in a particularly good mood.

"I apologize for disturbing you, Your Grace," White Castle said, bowing respectfully. "I think, however, that you'll agree this is something you need to know about now."

"For your sake, I hope you're right," Black Water growled, and waved the baron brusquely back into his chair.

The duke snapped his fingers, and his servant appeared as if by magic, carrying the brandy decanter and glasses on a silver tray. He poured two glasses, handed one to each nobleman, and then disappeared just as expeditiously.

"All right," Black Water said, a bit less snappishly, as he lowered his half-empty glass a moment later. "Tell me what's so important."

"Of course, Your Grace." White Castle leaned forward in his chair, clasping his own unsampled glass in both hands. "As you know, of course, I've been stationed here as the Prince's ambassador to Emerald for over four years now. During that time, by and large, he's been very careful to keep me separate from Earl Coris' operations here in the princedom."

He paused, and Black Water grimaced, waving impatiently for him to continue, yet White Castle noticed that a spark of interest had begun to glow in the duke's eyes.

"That's just changed," he said in response to the duke's gesture. "I was contacted this evening—less than two hours ago, in fact—by a man I'd never met before, but who had all of the correct codewords to—"

"Correct codewords?" Black Water interrupted.

"Yes, Your Grace." If White Castle was irritated by the interruption, he was careful not to show it. "When I was first sent to Emerald, my instructions included a sealed envelope to be opened only under certain specific conditions. That envelope contained a series of codewords to be used by especially trusted agents of Earl Coris."

Black Water was listening very intently now, leaning slightly forward while he rested one elbow on the table beside him.

"This man, who correctly identified himself, was placed in Tellesberg over twelve years ago, Your Grace. He was placed in complete isolation, totally separate from any other agents in Charis. None of Earl Coris' other agents knew him; he knew none of them. His job—his sole job—was to be a good, loyal Charisian, hopefully employed in or near the royal dockyards, until and unless war broke out between the League of Corisande and Charis. Apparently, Earl Coris assumed that in the event of a war he'd lose access to at least a portion of any spy web he'd established, and this man was part of his insurance policy."

He paused again, and Black Water nodded.

"Continue, Baron," he said. "I assure you, you have my attention."

"I rather thought I might, Your Grace." White Castle finally allowed himself a small smile. Then his expression sobered once more.

"Apparently, Wave Thunder and his people knew a great deal more than any of us had imagined about Earl Coris' 'official' spies in Charis. And, it would appear, Wave Thunder—and Haarahld—also knew what was coming quite a bit earlier than we thought they did."

"Why?"

"Because, Your Grace, they very, very quietly arrested virtually all foreign spies in Tellesberg, and apparently everywhere else in the entire kingdom, clear back in early October."

"*October?*"

"Yes, Your Grace. Obviously, they must have realized at least part of what was coming much earlier than we've been assuming they did. And I think that probably accounts for the silence from Earl Coris' other agents which you've mentioned."

"But they missed this man because not even Coris' other agents knew about him," Black Water said slowly.

"That's certainly what appears to have happened, Your Grace."

"But," Black Water's eyes sharpened, "I'm willing to guess he didn't come to you just to tell you all the rest of our spies had been arrested three months ago. So, Baron, what brought him to your door at this particular time?"

"Actually, Your Grace, he's been trying to get to me for over two months now, but it hasn't been easy. The Charisians have put an iron clamp on traffic through The Throat and around Lock Island, and they've got light units patrolling the Charis Sea north of Rock Shoal Bay. He had to travel overland to avoid The Throat, then find a smuggler willing to run him across to Emerald. In fact, it took him three tries to get across, because the smuggler in question turned back twice after sighting a Charisian schooner.

"But you're quite correct that he didn't come on a whim. In fact, he came to tell us the entire Charisian galleon force left Charis, under Crown Prince Cayleb's personal command, in October."

"What?" Black Water blinked in surprise, then half-glared at the ambassador. "That's ridiculous! Our scouts have seen their topsails behind Haarahld's galleys!"

"Not according to this man, Your Grace," White Castle said diffidently. "He's been a ship's chandler, supplying ships in the Royal Dockyard in Tellesberg, for over five years. And according to what he's picked up from 'friends' he's cultivated in their navy, thirty of the galleons the Charisians have been working so hard to arm sailed from Lock Island five-days before you reached Eraystor Bay. *And*," the baron said, "also according to what he's learned, the Charisians still haven't activated their reserve galleys. Not only that, but King Haarahld's chartered two or three dozen merchant galleons for unspecified purposes. While he wasn't able to absolutely confirm that, he did observe himself that at least a dozen merchant ships which had been idled by the war have left Tellesberg flying the royal banner. No one seems to know exactly where they are."

Black Water's jaw clenched. Was it truly possible—?

"You say he says they sailed in October. He doesn't have any idea where?"

"None," White Castle admitted.

"Well, they wouldn't have sailed without *some* destination in mind," Black Water said slowly, thinking aloud. "I wonder . . ."

He glowered at the floor, rubbing his chin, then shook his head and looked back up at White Castle.

"We've all been assuming Haarahld didn't know what was coming until shortly before we sailed. But if he got those galleons to sea that early, he *must* have known something, and he probably knew it almost as soon as we did. But he couldn't have found out about it from spies in Corisande; there wasn't time for anyone to get a message to him all the way from Manchyr that quickly. And he couldn't have found out about it that early from spies in Emerald, because *Nahrmahn* didn't know that soon, thanks to those lost dispatches. Which means he could only have found out from Tarot."

The ambassador frowned for a moment, obviously considering Black Water's analysis, then nodded.

"I think you're right, Your Grace. But how much did anyone in Tarot know?"

"I can't answer that," Black Water admitted. "Obviously, Gorjah had to know at least the bare bones of what we were going to be doing, because he had to coordinate what *he* was supposed to do with it. But I don't have any idea how fully informed he may have been about our plans. And," his mouth tightened, "it doesn't really matter. Not if the galleons sailed that long ago and Haarahld's been using the sails of chartered merchantships to fool our scouts—and me—into thinking they're still with him."

"Your Grace?" White Castle looked confused, and Black Water laughed harshly.

"He sent his galleons off somewhere his galleys didn't have the seakeeping ability to go, My Lord," he said. "And if he learned what was happening from agents in Tarot, I can only think of one thing that would have taken them away so soon and prevented them from returning by now."

The duke shook his head, his expression bemused, almost awed.

"He's decided to risk an all-or-nothing throw of the dice," he said. "He's sent his galleons—and his son—off to intercept the Tarotisians and the Dohlarans. He doesn't have them here, not protecting Rock Shoal Bay. They're off somewhere with Cayleb in the Sea of Justice, or the Parker Sea, depending on how good his spies' information really was, hoping to find Duke Malikai and stop him from ever getting here."

"That's cr—" White Castle began, then stopped. He cleared his throat. "I mean, that strikes me as a very risky thing for him to have done, Your Grace."

"It's an *insane* thing for him to have done," Black Water said flatly. "At the same time, it's the only possible answer for where his galleons have really been all this time. And . . ."

His voice trailed off again, and his expression darkened.

"Your Grace?" White Castle said quietly after several moments.

"It's just occurred to me that there could be one way for him to pull it all together with a fair degree of confidence." Black Water's lips twitched in something that was much more snarl than smile. "If his spies in Tarot were good enough, or if someone highly enough placed were deliberately feeding him information, he could have learned from the Tarotisians where *they* were supposed to find the Dohlarans."

"Your Grace, are you suggesting Gorjah himself might have delivered the information to Charis?" White Castle asked in a very careful tone.

"I don't know." Black Water shrugged. "At first glance, I can't see any reason for him to have done it—certainly not to have risked angering Vicar Zahmsyn or the Grand Inquisitor! But that doesn't mean someone else highly placed in his court couldn't have done it."

The duke glowered at the deck again for several more seconds, then gave his entire body a shake.

"We may never know the answer to your question, My Lord. But if your man's report is accurate, what matters is that at this moment there are only eighty galleys or so between us and control of Rock Shoal Bay. And if we can defeat those galleys and take control of Rock Shoal Bay, we can both hold it against his galleons, if and when they finally return, *and* bring in troops to besiege the Keys from the land side."

"Those numbers assume their reserve fleet truly hasn't been activated, Your Grace," White Castle pointed out, and the duke snorted.

"If I'm prepared to believe this spy of yours really knows his business and risk trusting what he's said about the galleons, I may as well believe him about the galleys, as well!" Black Water shrugged. "And, to be honest, we've seen no sign of the Charisian reserve galleys. I've been assuming all along that the manning requirements of their galleons prevented them from manning the galleys, as well. So I'm strongly inclined to believe he is right about that."

"And what do you intend to do about it, if I may ask, Your Grace?" White Castle asked. The duke quirked an eyebrow at him, and it was the baron's turn to shrug. "I *am* Prince Hektor's ambassador, Your Grace. If whatever you decide to do requires Prince Nahrmahn's support, then I may be in a position to help nudge him into doing what you want."

"True enough," Black Water conceded. "As for what I intend, though, that's going to depend on what I can talk my gallant allies into."

.III.

HMS *Dreadnought*,
The Cauldron

Crown Prince Cayleb sat up in the box-like cot suspended from the low beams of his sleeping cabin's deckhead as someone rapped sharply on the cabin door.

"What?" he said, rubbing his eyes before he glanced out the opened stern windows into the warm, clear night. The moon hadn't even risen yet, which meant he'd been in bed only an hour or so.

"I'm sorry to wake you, Cayleb," a deep voice said, "but we need to talk."

"Merlin?" Cayleb swung his legs over the side of the cot and stood. There was a note in Merlin's voice he'd never heard before, and he crossed the cabin in two strides and yanked the door open. "What is it? What's happened?"

"May I come in?"

"What?" Cayleb gave himself a shake, then grinned crookedly as he realized he'd opened the door without bothering to dress. In fact, he was stark naked, the way he habitually slept on such warm nights, and he stepped back with a chuckle, despite the tension in Merlin's voice.

"Of course you can come in," he said.

"Thank you."

Merlin stepped past Sergeant Faircaster, the sentry outside Cayleb's door, bending his head to clear the deck beams, and closed the door quietly behind him.

"What is it?" Cayleb asked, turning away to pick up the tunic he'd discarded when he turned in and drag it over his head.

"I've . . . just had a vision," Merlin said, and Cayleb turned back quickly at his tone, waving sharply at a chair.

"What sort of vision?"

"A vision of Duke Black Water in Eraystor Bay," Merlin said, his voice almost flat as he settled into the indicated chair. "It seems Bynzhamyn and I missed at least one of Hektor's spies, and he's just reported to Black Water that—"

▼   ▼   ▼

"—so that's about the size of it," Merlin finished grimly several minutes later.

Cayleb sat on the edge of his cot, his face almost totally expressionless, as he concentrated on what Merlin had just told him.

"What do you think he's going to do?" the prince asked now, and Merlin shook his head.

"I think he was right when he told White Castle that depends on what he can convince his allies to do, Cayleb. All I can tell you right now is that Corisande's finally managed to get practically its entire reserve sent forward. Emerald has about sixty of its galleys into full commission, too, and despite everything Sharleyan, Sandyrs, and Sharpfield have been able to do, they've been forced to send another twenty of their galleys forward to Eraystor, as well. Even with the losses Bryahn and your father inflicted on them, that brings them up to a hundred and eighty to your father's eighty. Well, seventy-six, given the four he lost on the reef off Crown Point last five-day."

"Better than two-to-one," Cayleb muttered.

"And," Merlin added, "given that Black Water knows—or strongly suspects—that we're somewhere else, he's almost certainly going to be tempted to try to strike before we can get back. *If* he can talk his 'allies' into it."

"Fifteen days, if the wind holds steady," Cayleb grated. "Three five-days." He slammed his right fist into his left palm suddenly. "*Damn!* I should have started home without making repairs!"

"Remember what I said about hindsight," Merlin told him. The youthful crown prince glared at him, and he gave a small shrug. "You made a decision. You didn't know this was going to happen. Right now, you need to concentrate on what we do *next*, not on what we've already done."

"What *I've* already done, you mean," Cayleb said bitterly. Then he threw back his shoulders and inhaled deeply. "But whoever did it, you're right. The problem is, there doesn't seem to be a lot we *can* do."

Merlin tried to think of something to say, but there wasn't much he could. The surviving galleons were already making their best speed, driving hard as they close-reached across the Cauldron on a steady wind out of the east-northeast at almost ten knots. They *might* be able to squeeze a little more speed out of some of the ships, but the merchant conversions had the typical high-capacity hulls of their merchant ancestry. They tended to be shorter and tubbier than naval galleons—especially Olyvyr's designs, like *Dreadnought*. They were already carrying virtually all the canvas they had, just to stay with their special-built consorts. If the fleet tried to sail faster, it could only be at the expense of leaving its slower ships behind. And it probably would shave no more than a day or two off its total transit time, anyway.

"If only *Father* knew about this," Cayleb said softly to himself, pounding his fist gently but rhythmically into his palm once more. "If only—"

His hands suddenly stopped moving, and his head came back up, his eyes locking on Merlin in the dimly lit sleeping cabin.

"Can you tell him?" he asked softly, and Merlin froze.

He looked back at the young man sitting on the cot, and his thoughts seemed to grind to a complete halt.

"Cayleb, I—" he began, then stopped.

How much was Cayleb *truly* prepared to accept about him? The prince had already taken far more in stride than Merlin would ever willingly have shown him, but where were the limits of Cayleb's flexibility? He might half-jestingly refer to Merlin as his "wizard," and he might have accepted Merlin's more-than-human strength and vision. He might even have recognized the inevitable clash between his kingdom and the corrupt men sitting in power in the Temple. But he was still a Safeholdian, still a child of the Church of God Awaiting, which was the very reason he was so angry about the corruption which afflicted it. And he'd still been steeped from birth in the belief that Pei Shan-wei was the mother of all evil and that the angels who'd fallen into evil with her had become demons, determined to tempt humanity into following Shan-wei's thirst for forbidden knowledge into damnation.

"Do you really want me to answer that question?" he asked after a long, still moment. Cayleb started to answer, but Merlin raised one hand. "Think first, Cayleb! If you ask and I answer it, you'll never be able to un-ask it."

Cayleb looked at him for perhaps three heartbeats, then nodded.

"I want you to answer it," he said steadily.

"All right, then," Merlin replied, just as steadily. "The answer is yes." Cayleb's expression started to blossom in relief, and he opened his mouth once more, but Merlin shook his head. "I *can* tell him this very night, even though he's four thousand miles away," he continued, "but only by physically going to him."

Cayleb's mouth snapped shut.

Silence hovered once more in the sleeping cabin. A taut, singing silence, enhanced but not broken by the background sound of water sluicing around the hull, the bubble of the wake below the opened stern windows, the creak of rigging and hull timbers, and the occasional sound of the rudder.

"You can *go* to him?" Cayleb said finally.

"Yes," Merlin sighed.

"Merlin," Cayleb said, gazing at him levelly, "*are* you a demon, after all?"

"No." Merlin returned his gaze just as levelly. "I'm not a demon, Cayleb. Nor am I an angel. I told you that before, in King's Harbor. I'm—" He shook his head. "When I told you then that I couldn't explain it to you, I meant I literally *can't*. If I tried, it would involve . . . concepts and knowledge you simply don't have."

Cayleb looked at him for fifteen endless, tense seconds, his eyes narrow, and when he spoke again, his voice was very soft.

"Would that knowledge violate the Proscriptions?" he asked.

"Yes," Merlin said simply, and if he'd still been a creature of flesh and blood he would have held his breath.

Cayleb Ahrmahk sat very, very still, gazing at the being who had become his friend. He sat that way for a long time, and then he shook himself.

"How can you say you stand for the Light when your very existence violates the Proscriptions?"

"Cayleb," Merlin said, "I've told you before that I've never lied to you, even when I haven't been able to tell you *all* the truth. I won't lie to you now, either. And if there are still things I simply can't explain, I *can* tell you this: the Proscriptions themselves are a lie."

Cayleb inhaled sharply, and his head flinched back, as if Merlin had just punched him.

"The Proscriptions were handed down by God Himself!" he said, his voice sharper, and Merlin shook his head.

"No, they weren't, Cayleb," he said. "They were handed down by Jwo-jeng, and Tsen Jwo-jeng was no more an archangel than I am."

Cayleb flinched again, and his face was pale. Merlin's eyes—his *artificial* eyes—could see it clearly, despite the dim light.

"How can the Proscriptions be a lie?" the prince demanded hoarsely. "Are you saying *God* lied?"

"No," Merlin said again. "God didn't lie. *Jwo-jeng* lied when she claimed to speak for Him."

"But—"

Cayleb broke off, staring at Merlin, and Merlin held out his right hand, cupped palm uppermost.

"Cayleb, you know the men who currently rule the Temple are corrupt. They lie. They accept bribes. They use the Proscriptions to extort money out of people who try to introduce new ideas, or from people who want new ideas suppressed. You yourself told me, standing on top of the citadel with Rayjhis, that the vicars are more concerned with their secular power than with saving souls. They're willing to destroy your entire kingdom—burn your cities, murder and terrorize your subjects—when you've done nothing at all wrong! Is it so inconceivable to you that other men have also used God, and twisted His purpose, for ends of their own?"

"We aren't talking about 'men,'" Cayleb said. "We're talking about the *archangels* themselves!"

"Yes, we are," Merlin acknowledged. "But the beings who called themselves archangels weren't, Cayleb. They were men."

"No!" Cayleb said, yet his voice's certitude wavered, and Merlin felt a small flicker of hope.

"If you want me to, I can show you proof of that," he said gently. "Not tonight, not here, but I can show it to you. You've seen the things—some of the things—*I* can do. The men and women who claimed to be archangels could do the same sorts of things, and they used that ability to *pretend* they were divine beings. I can prove that to you, if you're willing to let me. The problem, Cayleb, is that if your faith in the lie you've been taught all your life is too strong, you won't believe any proof I could show you."

Cayleb sat motionless, his jaw clenched tightly and his shoulders hunched as if to ward off a blow. And then, slowly—so slowly—his shoulders relaxed just a bit.

"If you truly are a demon, despite whatever you say," he said at last, "then you've already tempted me into damnation, haven't you?" He actually managed a twisted smile. "I've known for months now that you were more than mortal, and I've used you—and your . . . abilities—for my own ends and against the princes of the Church. And that's the definition of heresy and apostasy, isn't it?"

"I suppose it is," Merlin said, his voice as neutral as he could make it. "In the eyes of the Temple's present management, at least."

"But you didn't have to tell me you could warn Father, any more than you *had* to save those children in King's Harbor. Or to save Rayjhis from Kahlvyn. Or to lead me to Malikai's galleys, or into Crag Reach."

"I suppose not. But, Cayleb, if I *were* a demon out to tempt you into damnation, I'd do it by appealing to your desire, your *need*, to protect the people and kingdom you love. You aren't Hektor, or even Nahrmahn. I couldn't appeal to your greed, your hunger for power, so I'd tempt you through the goodness of your own heart, your fear for the things you care so deeply about."

"And probably tell me you would have done exactly that, on the assumption that I'd believe it proved you *hadn't*," Cayleb said, nodding with that same crooked smile. "But you missed my point. Perhaps you *are* a demon, or what the *Writ* calls a demon, at any rate. And perhaps you *have* tempted me—after all, you always told Father and me you were using us for your own ends. But if you've tempted me into the damnation of my soul, Merlin Athrawes, then so be it, because you've never asked me to do one single thing which wasn't what a just and loving God would have had me do. And if the God of the *Writ* isn't a just and loving God, then he isn't mine, either."

Merlin sat back in his chair, gazing at the young man in front of him. The young man, he realized, who was even more extraordinary than Merlin had believed.

"Cayleb," he said finally, "in your place, I doubt I could reach beyond everything I'd been taught the way you just have."

"I don't know if I really have," the prince replied with a shrug. "You say you can prove what you've said, and someday I'll hold you to that. But for now, I have to make decisions, choices. I can only make them on the basis of what I believe, and I believe you're a good man, whatever else you may be. And I believe you can warn my father."

"And how do you think your father will react if I suddenly simply appear aboard his flagship, four thousand miles from here?" Merlin asked wryly.

"I don't know," Cayleb said, then grinned suddenly, "but I'd dearly love to see his expression when you do!"

.IV.
The Cauldron

Merlin Athrawes lay stretched out, swooping up and down with the swell as he floated on his back, watching the moon.

Somewhere beyond his toes, invisible from his present water-level position, HMS *Dreadnought* and her consorts continued on their course, unaware one of their crewmen was missing. Hopefully, they'd stay that way.

This, he thought philosophically, gazing up at the stars, *is probably the . . . least wise thing I've done yet. Aside from the krakens, maybe, anyway. No matter how well Cayleb took it, there's no way of telling how Haarahld is going to react.*

Still, right off the top of his head, he couldn't come up with any alternative course of action which offered a better chance for Haarahld's survival.

In cold-blooded terms, now that he'd had a chance to think about things a bit more, it probably didn't matter to the long-term survival of Charis what happened to King Haarahld and his galleys. What Cayleb and Sir Domynyk Staynair had already done to one galley fleet promised they could do the same to another, if they had to. Especially one which was going to take losses of its own—serious losses—if it pressed an attack home against the Royal Charisian Navy. So even if Black Water succeeded in gaining control of the Charis Sea and Rock Shoal Bay, it would be only a temporary possession, lasting just long enough for Cayleb to get home and take them back again. And however badly Haarahld's death might hurt the rulership of Charis, Merlin felt confident of Cayleb's fitness to take the crown, especially with Gray Harbor and Wave Thunder to advise him.

But while Charis might survive King Haarahld's death, Merlin had discovered he wasn't prepared to do that himself. Or to see Cayleb forced to do it. Not without doing everything he possibly could to prevent it.

It was odd, he reflected as he rose high enough on the swell to glimpse the lights of one of the galleons in the distance, but when he'd first set out to shape Charis into the tool he needed, it hadn't occurred to him how close he might come to the Charisians themselves as people, as individuals he cared about. Haarahld Ahrmahk wasn't simply the King of Charis; he was also Merlin Athrawes' friend, and the father of another, even closer friend, and the man who had once been Nimue Alban had lost too many friends.

Is that the real reason I let Cayleb "talk me into" telling him I could do this in the first place? Or, he frowned as another thought occurred to him, *was it because I'm so lonely? Because I need someone to know what I'm trying to do? How far from home I truly am? These people may be my friends, but none of them know who—or what—I really am. Do I have some sort of subconscious need to know that someone who considers me a friend knows the truth—or as much of the truth as he can comprehend, anyway—about me?*

Perhaps he did. And perhaps that need was a dangerous chink in his armor. No matter how Cayleb, or even Haarahld, might react, the vast majority of Safeholdians, even in Charis, would, indeed, regard him as the very spawn of Hell if they discovered even a tenth of the truth about him. And if that happened, everything which had ever been associated with him would be tainted, rejected with horror. So, in the final analysis, if he allowed a need for friendship to lure him into revealing the truth to someone not prepared to accept it, or simply to someone who might inadvertently let the secret slip, everything he'd accomplished so far—and all the people who'd died along the way, and who were still going to die—would have been for nothing.

All of that was true. He knew that, but he wasn't prepared to psychoanalyze himself in an effort to parse his motivation, even assuming a PICA was subject to psychoanalysis. Because, in the end, it didn't matter. Whatever the reasons for it, this was something he had to do. Something he couldn't *not* do.

He rose to the top of another swell. This time, there were no lights in sight, and he gave a mental nod of satisfaction as he checked the overhead visual imagery being relayed from the stealthed recon skimmer hovering above him. The fleet was moving along nicely, drawing steadily further away from him as he floated alone in the immensity of the sea.

Getting someone off a crowded, cramped sailing vessel without being noticed, he'd discovered, was only marginally less difficult than he expected getting someone *onto* a crowded, cramped galley without being noticed to be. The fact that the full moon had risen now only made the task even more challenging.

Fortunately, he and Cayleb had already put a defense in depth into place, even if they'd never contemplated using it for exactly this purpose. Ahrnahld Falkhan, and the other members of Cayleb's Marine bodyguard detachment, all knew the "truth" about "*Seijin* Merlin." Every one of them knew Merlin had visions, and that it was necessary for him to retire and meditate in order to see them. And every one of them knew that concealing the fact of his visions from anyone outside King Haarahld's or Cayleb's innermost circle was absolutely essential.

And so, Merlin, as an officer of the Royal Guard and Cayleb's personal guardsman, had been provided with his own small private cabin. It was right aft, just below Cayleb's quarters. It even had its own stern window, and Falkhan and the other Marine sentries who guarded Cayleb were well placed to intercept anyone who might have disturbed the *seijin* during his meditations.

They were also well accustomed to leaving Merlin to those same meditations themselves. All of which meant it had been relatively simple for him to crawl through that window and lower himself hand-over-hand down a rope into the water. Once in the water, he'd submerged and swum the better part of a half-mile, then surfaced and waited while the fleet sailed past him.

He was down-moon from them, and he'd probably been far enough away when he surfaced that no one would have noticed anything, but he felt no great urge to take any chances. The night was as clear as only a tropical night could be, with glowing phosphorescence spilling back along the ships' sides as they sailed along the silver moon path, their canvas like polished pewter, their ports and scuttles glowing with the lamps and lanterns within. The odds against anyone happening to glance in exactly the right direction to see something as small as a human figure floating into the heavens was undoubtedly minute, but he had plenty of time. Certainly enough to avoid taking any chances.

Or, he corrected himself wryly, *any more chances, at least.*

He checked the visual imagery one last time, then activated his built-in communicator.

"Owl," he said, speaking aloud for a change, still contemplating Safehold's alien heavens.

"Yes, Lieutenant Commander?"

"Pick me up now."

"Yes, Lieutenant Commander."

 King Haarahld VII waved his valet out the door.

"Are you sure you won't need me any more tonight, Sire?"

"Lachlyn, you've already asked me that three times," Haarahld said affectionately. "I'm not yet so feeble that I can't climb into bed by myself, even at sea. So go. Go! Get some sleep of your own."

"Very well, Sire. If you insist," Lachlyn Zhessyp said with a small smile, and obeyed the command.

Haarahld shook his head with a chuckle, then crossed the great cabin, opened the lattice-paned door, and stepped out onto *Royal Charis*'s sternwalk.

He stood there, gazing off into the west, as if watching the setting moon slide the rest of the way below the horizon could somehow bring him closer to his son.

It was even harder being separated from Cayleb than he'd expected it to be. It wasn't like the year Cayleb had spent aboard ship as a midshipman. Then all he'd really had to worry about were the risks of disease, accidents, or shipwreck. Now he'd knowingly sent his elder son off to battle against an enormously numerically superior foe *seven thousand miles* away. If all had gone well, the battle Cayleb had been sent to fight was long over, but had his son won, or had he lost? And in either case, had he survived?

Not for the first time in the long, hard years of his kingship, Haarahld Ahrmahk found that knowing he'd made the right decision could be very cold comfort, indeed.

"Your Majesty."

Haarahld twitched uncontrollably, then whirled, one hand dropping to the hilt of the dagger he wasn't wearing. He half-crouched, despite his bad knee, his incredulous eyes wide, as he saw the tall, broad-shouldered man standing in the shadows at the far end of the sternwalk.

Disbelief and shock held him motionless, paralyzed as a statue, staring at the man who could not possibly be there.

"I apologize for startling you, Your Majesty," Merlin Athrawes said calmly and quietly, "but Cayleb sent me with a message."

▼　　▼　　▼

The Ahrmahk Dynasty, Merlin decided, must have some sort of genetic defect. That was the only explanation he could think of, because something was obviously badly wrong with its "fight or flight" instincts.

King Haarahld should have reacted by at least shouting for the guards, assuming he hadn't simply bolted for the cabin, or even flung himself over the sternwalk to escape the apparition. In fact, Merlin had brought along a stun pistol for the express purpose of dealing with any such perfectly reasonable reaction, although he hadn't looked forward to explaining its effect to an irate monarch afterward.

But, instead of doing any of those things, Haarahld had simply stood there for almost exactly ten seconds by Merlin's internal chronometer, then straightened and cocked his head to one side.

"Well, *Seijin* Merlin," he'd said with appalling calm, "if Cayleb sent you with a message, at least I know he's still alive, don't I?"

And he'd smiled.

Now, twenty minutes later, the two of them stood together, still on the sternwalk, the one place on the flagship where they could hope to find true privacy. The noise of wind and sea as *Royal Charis* and her squadron moved slowly along with the rest of the fleet neatly covered their voices, as well.

"So Cayleb sent you to tell me Black Water's seen through our little masquerade, did he, Master Traynyr?" Haarahld asked, and Merlin chuckled, shaking his head, as he remembered the first time Haarahld had called him that.

"Yes, Your Majesty." Merlin inclined his head slightly, then snorted gently. "And, if you'll permit me to say it, Your Majesty, you've taken my . . . arrival rather more calmly then I anticipated."

"Over the last year, Merlin, I've come to expect the unexpected from you. And don't think I missed how carefully you answered Father Paityr's questions when he brought his truth stone with him. Or the way Cayleb watched you while you did it. Or any of several other . . . peculiar things you've accomplished over the months. All the interesting bits and pieces of knowledge you've produced. The fact that, despite your rather glib explanation at the time, there's not really any way you could've gotten to Kahlvyn's townhouse as quickly as you did."

The king waved one hand in an oddly gentle gesture of dismissal.

"I decided long ago," he said calmly, "that you were far more than you chose to appear, even to me, or possibly even to Cayleb. And, yes," he smiled, "I know how close you've become to my son. But as I believe I mentioned to you once before, a man—*any* man, regardless of his . . . abilities—must be judged by his actions. I've judged you on the basis of yours, and, like my son, I trust you. If I'm in error to do so, no doubt I'll pay for it in the next world. Unfortunately, I have to make my decisions in *this* one, don't I?"

"Your son is very like you, Your Majesty." Merlin inclined his head once more, this time in a bow of respect. "And I can think of few greater compliments I might pay him."

"In that case, now that we've both told one another what splendid people we are," Haarahld said with a smile, "I suppose we should decide what to do with this latest information of yours."

"It's not certain yet what use Black Water will be able to make of his spy's report," Merlin replied. "From what I've seen of him, however, I expect him to bring the other admirals around to his own view. He has a more forceful personality than I'd first expected, and the fact that all his 'allies' know he's being backed by the Group of Four gives him a powerful club whenever he chooses to use it."

"In that case, he certainly will try to press the attack, and as quickly as possible." Haarahld gazed up at the stars where the moon had finished setting while he and Merlin spoke. He frowned, stroking his beard.

"He can't know how much time he has before Cayleb's return," the king continued, obviously thinking aloud. "So he'll probably try to press an attack directly into Rock Shoal Bay. He'll expect us to either stand and fight, or else retreat behind Lock Island and the Keys. In either case, he'll have control of the Bay, and the Charis Sea, at least until Cayleb gets home."

"That's essentially what Cayleb and I decided his most likely course of action would be," Merlin agreed.

"And Cayleb's suggestion was?" Haarahld looked back at Merlin.

"He suggests that you go ahead and concede the bay." Merlin shrugged. "As long as you still control The Throat, even if you were to lose one or both of the Keys, they aren't going to be able to press a serious attack on any of your vital areas. And Cayleb's only fifteen days away. If they're deep enough into the bay when he arrives, they'll be trapped between your forces and his."

"I see my son is concerned about his aged father's survival," Haarahld said dryly.

"Excuse me, Your Majesty?"

"I've already discovered that Black Water, while he may be lumbered with allies who aren't exactly the most cooperative ones imaginable, is no fool, Merlin. He knows Cayleb's going to be coming home. If he sends his fleet into Rock Shoal Bay, he's not going to send it so deep he can't get it out again in a hurry. Nor is he going to neglect the elementary precaution of picketing the approaches. Whether Cayleb comes south, from Emerald Reach, or north, from Darcos Sound, he'll be spotted long before he can trap Black Water in the bay. So what Cayleb's strategy would really accomplish would be to keep *me* safely behind Lock Island while almost certainly affording Black Water the time to fall back on Eraystor Bay, or even retreat past Emerald to Zebediah or Corisande, to avoid *him* when he arrives. And, of course, my own forces would take so long to clear the bottleneck between Lock Island and the Keys that we'd never be able to stop Black Water before he ran."

"If we approached under cover of night," Merlin began, "then—"

"Then, if everything went perfectly, you *might* be able to pull it off," Haarahld interrupted. "But, as Rayjhis pointed out, what can go wrong in a battle plan, will. No. If we want to *finish* Hektor's navy, hiding behind Lock Island is the wrong way to go about it."

"It sounds to me as if you plan to do something else, Your Majesty," Merlin observed with a slight sense of dread.

"I do, indeed." Haarahld showed his teeth. "I have no intention of allowing myself to be penned up in The Throat. Nor do I intend to give Black Water the battle he wants. However, I do intend to dangle the *possibility* of that battle in front of him."

"How, Your Majesty?"

"I'm about to shift my main base of operations south from Rock Shoal Bay to Darcos Sound. Darcos Keep isn't as well suited as a major fleet base as Lock Island, but it will serve well enough for long enough. When Black Water manages to launch his offensive, I'll dance and spar for time, and I'll withdraw south, *away* from the bay. He's smart enough to recognize that my navy is his true objective. Once the fleet's out of his way, he can do basically whatever he wants; as long as the fleet exists, his options are cramped, at best. So, unless I miss my guess, he'll be so happy to have shifted me away from a well fortified bolthole like Lock Island and The Throat that he'll follow me up."

"You're planning to draw him south of the Charis Sea," Merlin said. "Away from his shortest line of retreat."

"Precisely." Haarahld nodded. "I'm sure he'll cover his rear with picket ships, but he'll only have so much reach. If I can pull him far enough south, keep his attention firmly enough focused on *me*—and the fact that my standard will be flying from this ship should certainly help to do that—then when Cayleb comes down from the north behind him, you'll be between him and retreat."

"Cayleb won't like it, Your Majesty."

"That's unfortunate," Haarahld said calmly. "As it happens, I'm King, and he's Crown Prince. Which means we'll do it *my* way."

"But if you move your fleet south," Merlin said, searching for counter arguments, "you'll expose The Throat. The North Channel's broad enough they could slip galleys right through it, if you're not there to stop them."

"Not anymore." Haarahld chuckled. "I see you haven't managed to keep an eye on quite everything, *Seijin* Merlin."

"Your Majesty?"

"Baron Seamount and Sir Dustyn have been busy in your absence. It was Seamount's idea. The two of them have thrown together what Seamount calls 'floating batteries.' They're basically just rafts—big ones, but just rafts—with solid, raised bulwarks about five feet thick and gunports. They've got fifteen of them, each with thirty carronades and a half-battalion of Marines to discourage boarders, anchored on springs squarely across North Channel, directly between Lock Island and North Key's shore batteries."

The king shrugged.

"I don't believe anyone's likely to get past them, do you?"

"No, but—"

"Then we'll do it my way, won't we?" Haarahld asked inflexibly.

Merlin looked at him for a long moment, then nodded heavily.

"Yes, Your Majesty."

"The one thing I wish we could do," Haarahld said thoughtfully, "is find some way for Cayleb and me to coordinate our movements. If what I've got in mind works, Black Water's going to be directly between Cayleb's galleons and my galleys when you turn up in his rear. That means he'll see you, know you're there, before I do. If there were some way—aside, of course, from this rather dramatic personal visit of yours—for you to let me know when Cayleb is about to make contact with him, it would be an enormous help."

He cocked his head again, looking at Merlin with an expression so much like that of a hopeful little boy that Merlin chuckled.

"As a matter of fact, Your Majesty, I've given a little thought of my own to that possibility. Here."

He held out a small object. Haarahld gazed at it for an instant, then took it just a bit hesitantly, and Merlin was hard pressed not to chuckle again. Apparently even an Ahrmahk's imperturbability had its limits.

"That's a pager, Your Majesty."

"A 'pager'?" Haarahld repeated the bizarre word carefully.

"Yes, Your Majesty."

Merlin had considered providing the king with a full-capability communicator, but he'd decided against it. Given how well Haarahld had handled his appearance on *Royal Charis'* sternwalk, his concern that the king might have found voices coming out of a tiny box more than he was prepared to accept had probably been misplaced. Unfortunately, he'd selected the pager instead, before he left the skimmer.

"It's set to vibrate when I need it to," he said now. "May I demonstrate?"

"Of course," Haarahld said.

"Then put it on your palm, please, Your Majesty. No, with the flat side down. That's right. Now—"

Merlin used his internal com to trigger the pager, and the king's hand jerked as the vibration tingled sharply against the palm of his hand. He looked up at Merlin, and his eyes were wide—with as much delight as surprise, Merlin realized.

"You felt that, Your Majesty?"

"I certainly did!"

"Well, what I'd like you to do, is to carry that under your clothing somewhere," Merlin said. "I was thinking you might use the wristband—its adjustable, Your Majesty, like this"—he demonstrated—"to wear it on your forearm, under your tunic. If you do, then I can signal you when we sight Black Water's ships. I was thinking I might cause it to vibrate one time when we first sight one of his scout ships, then twice when we sight his main body, and three times when we're prepared to engage."

"That sounds as if it should work quite well," Haarahld said, gazing down at the pager now strapped to the inside of his left forearm.

"Next time," Merlin said dryly, "I'll try to provide something a bit more . . . exotic, Your Majesty."

Haarahld looked up sharply, then laughed.

"Point taken, *Seijin* Merlin. Point taken."

He gave the pager one last look, then smoothed the sleeve of his tunic over it.

"I suppose it's time you were getting back to Cayleb now, Merlin." He reached out, resting his hands on Merlin's shoulders. "Tell him I'm proud of him, very proud. And that I love him."

"I will, Your Majesty. Not that he needs to be told."

"Maybe not, but sometimes it's as important to say it as to hear it. And," Haarahld gazed directly into Merlin's sapphire eyes, "for yourself, accept my thanks. The thanks of a king, for helping him to protect his people, and of a father, who knows you'll do all you can to keep his son safe."

"Of course I will, Your Majesty." Merlin bowed again, more deeply than ever, then straightened. "And now, as you say, it's time I was getting back to Cayleb."

He boosted himself up to the sternwalk's rail, gazing down at the water below.

"Do you really have to leave that way?" Haarahld asked.

"Excuse me, Your Majesty?"

Merlin looked back over his shoulder in surprise, for the king's tone had been almost wistful.

"I was just thinking it would be marvelous to see someone fly," Haarahld said in an undeniably wheedling tone.

"I wish I could do that for you, Your Majesty," Merlin said, and almost to his surprise, he meant every word of it. "Unfortunately, I'm afraid your officers and seamen aren't quite ready for flying *seijin*. Maybe another time, but if one of them happened to look in exactly the wrong direction at exactly the wrong moment tonight . . ."

He shrugged, and Haarahld nodded.

"I know, and you're right," the king said. "But one of these days, when there's no one else about, I'm going to hold you to that 'maybe' of yours!"

"Somehow, I'm sure you will, Your Majesty," Merlin said with a laugh, and dropped into the night with a quiet splash.

Duke Black Water sat in his chair at the head of the table in *Corisande*'s great cabin, his face impassive, as he listened to Sir Kehvyn Myrgyn's voice. After careful consideration, he'd decided to allow his flag captain to present the new information to his allies instead of doing it himself. He couldn't change the fact that it was coming from one of Prince Hektor's spies, but he could at least try to minimize the sense that he was personally ramming it down their throats.

Not that he expected to fool anyone about that.

He considered the faces of his two fellow admirals. Sharpfield looked skeptical, but then, Sharpfield *always* looked skeptical. None of Black Water's spies had been able to intercept any of Queen Sharleyan's dispatches to her fleet commander, despite their best efforts, but the duke was privately certain of what he would have found if he had been able to read any of them. And, to be honest, he didn't blame Sharleyan a bit. In her shoes, *he* would have done everything he thought he could get away with to minimize his own exposure and losses in the service of one of his most bitter enemies. Not that understanding her motives made their consequences any more pleasant.

Still, Sharpfield was also a considerably more experienced naval commander then Prince Nahrmahn's Earl Mahndyr. And however unwillingly his queen had been compelled to support this entire campaign, Sharpfield was far too intelligent to do anything overt to which the Group of Four might take exception.

Mahndyr was another matter. Unlike Sharleyan, Nahrmahn had every reason to want this campaign to succeed. Well, to see it avoid *failure*, which wasn't precisely the same thing, perhaps. Black Water, now that he'd met the Prince of Emerald, had come to the conclusion that his own ruler had underestimated him. Nahrmahn was anything but the fool Black Water had been warned to expect, and, the duke was quietly certain, he'd made arrangements of his own to protect himself from the consequences of a victory by Prince Hektor. Whether or not those arrangements would work was another matter, of course. But, either way, he was even more certain Nahrmahn would prefer to take his chances against a victorious Hektor rather than against a victorious—and enraged—Haarahld.

That would definitely appear to be the case judging by the way Nahrmahn's navy had responded to Black Water's orders in the two months since the destruction of Baron Tanlyr Keep's squadron, at any rate. Mahndyr had pitched in and goaded his own captains and crews into energetic—if not necessarily wildly enthusiastic—cooperation with Black Water's rigorous training exercises.

Sharpfield's cooperation had been less enthusiastic than Mahndyr's, but, by the same token, his captains had been better trained to begin with. And Black Water had taken Sharpefield's own experience into consideration and sought his advice in planning the fleet's exercises, which actually appeared to have gotten the senior Chisholm officer actively involved in the process. The duke had also been careful to stay fairly close to home during those two months, unwilling to offer the Charisians the opportunity to lure another detachment into a trap until he'd whipped his command into something a bit more cohesive, and his efforts had borne fruit.

There were still weak spots, of course. Black Water suspected there would have been in any coalition this diverse, even if all of its members had wanted to join it in the first place.

The worst weakness of all was that the components of the fleet were still organized on a national basis. Black Water would really have preferred to break up all three of the allied fleets and recombine their units into integrated squadrons. Not even Mahndyr was going to agree to *that* one, though.

Short of achieving that particular impossible goal, the duke was about as satisfied with his command as he had any right to expect in this less-than-perfect world. It wasn't going to get much better, at any rate, and at least he could count on its doing pretty much what he asked it to at sea. The problem was convincing his fellow admirals that what he wanted to do needed doing before they *put* to sea.

"Thank you, Sir Kehvyn," Black Water said as the flag captain completed his briefing. Then he looked down the table at Sharpfield and Mahndyr.

"I believe this information puts rather a different complexion on our own situation," he said. "Clearly Haarahld's known a great deal more about our plans—and our capabilities—than any of us had believed was possible. Exactly how that information came into his hands is something I'm sure all of us would like to know. What matters for our purposes right this minute, however, is what we do now that we know what he's apparently done on the basis of his knowledge."

"With all due respect, Your Grace," Sharpfield said, "do we *really* know what he's done? We have a single report from a single one of Prince Hektor's spies. Even granting that the man is completely honest, and that the information he's reported is true to the best of his own knowledge, he could be in error on some—or all—of the points in his report. And even if every word of it's completely accurate, we have no way of knowing what's come of Haarahld's actions."

The Chisholm admiral shook his head with a half-snort.

"Personally, I think Haarahld would have to have been out of his mind to try something this idiotic, and I can't remember the last time someone accused Haarahld of Charis of stupidity. The chances of his even *finding* Malikai and White Ford at sea, whether he knew the originally proposed location for their rendezvous point or not, would be minute. And, even if Cayleb did find them, his galleons would have been outnumbered by something like six-to-one when they engaged."

He shook his head again.

"I simply can't see Haarahld taking that sort of chance with that big a piece of his total navy—and his own son's life—when he'd have to be shooting almost completely blind."

"Then what *do* you think he's done, My Lord?" Black Water asked courteously.

"I don't have the least idea," Earl Sharpfield said frankly. "I suppose it's remotely possible he's trying some sort of complicated double bluff. If he ostentatiously sent his galleons off early, counting on us to still have at least some spies in Charis to report the fact, he could want us to believe the topsails we've been seeing belong to merchantmen, when they're actually the sails of his war galleons. On the other hand, I'd have to admit that trying something like that doesn't strike me as a great deal more reasonable than sending his entire force of galleons haring off into the middle of the Parker Sea!"

"Well, he's obviously done *something* with them," Mahndyr said, "and I, for one, am inclined to trust your man's information, Your Grace." He inclined his head in Black Water's direction. "I'll defer to Earl Sharpfield's greater experience at sea and agree it seems like a remarkably foolhardy risk on Haarahld's part. Still, if he did have better knowledge of our plans than we believed he did, he must have known the odds, the forces being assembled against him. He may have calculated that he couldn't hope to defeat our combined forces after all of them were joined together and decided that *some* chance—even if it were a slim one—of preventing us from ever uniting all of our ships at all was better than a certainty of seeing his own fleet destroyed after we did."

"That's certainly possible," Sharpfield acknowledged a bit grudgingly. "It just seems so . . . unlike Haarahld. He's very like his father was. I met the old king when I was a captain. The Queen's father chose my ship to transport a diplomatic mission to him, and my impression of him was that he was always ready to take chances, even bold ones, but only when the possible return outweighed the risk and the odds were in his favor. Everything I've ever heard about Haarahld says he thinks exactly the same way, and that isn't—can't—be the case here, whatever this report seemed to indicate."

"I would tend to agree with you, under normal circumstances, My Lord," Black Water said. "In this case, though, I believe we have to at least tentatively accept that the information is correct. And if it is, then I think we must also assume that either Cayleb managed to intercept Duke Malikai, or else he didn't. If he did, they've fought a battle, which one of them won. If Cayleb won—or even if he simply failed to make contact at all—he should be back sometime in the next two to four five-days. If Duke Malikai won, he should be here within the same timeframe. If he slipped past Cayleb without making contact at all, he should be here within no more than the next two five-days. What we have to do is to decide how to proceed until one or the other of them turns up."

"I'm very tempted to suggest we do nothing to bring on a general engagement until Duke Malikai arrives," Sharpfield said. "That was the original plan for the campaign, and it would offer at least some protection against the possibility that Haarahld truly is trying some sort of complicated misdirection with the movements of his galleons. And," he added, looking Black Water straight in the eye, "if Duke Malikai and Baron White Ford *don't* arrive, that should be a fairly pointed indication of what will happen to our galleys in a battle against these new galleons of theirs."

"I disagree, Sir Lewk," Mahndyr said in a courteous tone. "I believe we should do our very best to provoke, even force, a general engagement as soon as possible. If Duke Malikai won against Cayleb, then we'll be in an even better position to proceed after his arrival if we've managed to defeat Haarahld, in the meantime. If he lost, but still managed to inflict heavy losses on Cayleb, then it's important that we neutralize Haarahld's galleys to prevent them from supporting and covering Cayleb on his return. And if Cayleb won without suffering significant losses, it's more important than ever that we not have to worry about facing Haarahld's galleys at the same time we confront him."

"I find myself in agreement with Earl Mahndyr, My Lord," Black Water said to Sharpfield. "I'll confess that I myself would feel much more comfortable if we had some independent confirmation of this single report. Nonetheless, it seems to me we have to at least probe to see whether or not Haarahld's galleons are in company with the rest of his fleet.

"If it turns out they are, our information is obviously in error. If it turns out they *aren't*, then I think Earl Mahndyr's suggestions will have considerable merit. While it's true the original plan for this campaign required us to wait for the arrival of the Tarotisian and Dohlaran squadrons, it's also true the reason we were waiting for them was to attain a decisive numerical superiority over the Charisians. If all we face is the eighty galleys of Haarahld's peacetime navy, then we *have* a decisive superiority at this moment."

There was silence for a moment, and then, almost as if against his will, Sharpfield nodded slowly.

.VII.
Off Triton Head,
Charis Sea

They *are* coming south, Your Majesty."

Captain Tryvythyn gave King Haarahld a rather peculiar look. The sort, Haarahld reflected, which was normally reserved for prophets, madmen . . . or *seijin*.

"Are they, indeed, Dynzyl?" he responded mildly, looking up from his lunch.

"Yes, they are, and in considerable strength," his flag captain said. "According to *Flash*, it looks like their entire fleet, in fact."

"I see."

Haarahld picked up his wineglass and sipped, then wiped his lips with a snowy napkin.

"Well, Dynzyl," he said then, "if they seem intent on offering battle, I suppose they have a reason to. We, on the other hand, do not."

"Not an *immediate* reason, Your Majesty, no," Tryvythyn agreed. The emphasis on the adjective was slight, but unmistakable, and Haarahld smiled.

"Dynzyl, Dynzyl!" The king shook his head. "I know giving ground against these . . . people goes against the grain. And I know Bryahn kicked their arses for them the last time they came this far south. But you and I both know they wouldn't be here if Black Water didn't feel fairly confident we wouldn't be doing that to them again. And whatever they may want, what *we* want is to continue to buy time until Cayleb returns."

"True enough, Your Majesty," Tryvythyn conceded.

He did not, Haarahld noticed, point out that no one in the Charisian fleet knew whether or not Cayleb *was* returning. The king felt a sudden, powerful temptation to tell his flag captain what he knew, but he suppressed it easily enough.

"Pass the word to Bryahn," he directed instead. "Tell him to execute the plans we discussed yesterday."

▼　　▼　　▼

"Well, *this* is unexpected," Duke Black Water commented, and Sir Kehvyn Myrgyn chuckled beside him.

"I hadn't realized what a gift for understatement you have, Your Grace," the flag captain said, when Black Water looked at him, and the duke smiled. But then the smile faded, replaced by a thoughtful frown, as he considered the report.

"South," he murmured, scratching the tip of his nose while the brisk northeasterly ruffled his hair. "Why *south?*"

"It does seem peculiar, Your Grace," Myrgyn observed. "I would have expected him to fall back towards Rock Shoal Bay, if he was intent on avoiding action."

"So would I," Black Water agreed.

He cocked his head and clasped his hands behind him, standing by the starboard bulwark of *Corisande*'s aftercastle, and rocked up and down on his toes for several seconds.

"Whatever he's up to, Your Grace," Myrgyn offered, "it does look as if he wants to avoid a general engagement."

"Which would appear to confirm the report that his galleons are somewhere else." Black Water nodded. "If all he has is eighty galleys, of course he doesn't want to fight our combined strength. But this business of falling back *away* from Rock Shoal Bay . . . *That* bothers me."

"You think he's trying to draw us into some sort of ambush, Your Grace?"

"An ambush by *what?*" Black Water asked. The frustration in his question wasn't directed at his flag captain, as Myrgyn understood perfectly, and the duke flung out one arm in a sweeping gesture at the long columns of allied galleys forging steadily southwest.

"If our information's correct, he doesn't have anything he could 'ambush' us *with!* And if our information *isn't* correct, what point would be served by moving clear down into Darcos Sound before offering battle?"

"Perhaps he's simply trying to avoid being trapped inside the Bay, Your Grace," Myrgyn suggested after a moment. Black Water looked at him, one eyebrow raised, and the flag captain shrugged.

"We've always assumed the Charisians would fight to hold the bay, Your Grace. What if we were wrong? What if Haarahld's willing to let us have the bay, if that's what it takes to prevent us from pinning him down?"

"In theory, if he did that, it would give us the opportunity to send a raiding force past Lock Island," Black Water said thoughtfully. "Would he run that risk?"

"That depends on how great a risk it would be, doesn't it, Your Grace? If we got even a few galleys loose in Howell Bay, we could do a *lot* of damage. But if he has a few galleys of his own waiting there, or just on the other side of Lock Island, covering North Channel, we'd have to commit a much larger force if we hoped to break through successfully."

"Which might give him the opportunity to come in behind our main force after we've weakened it by detaching a big enough squadron for the job," Black Water said, nodding slowly.

"There's this, too, Your Grace," Myrgyn said. "If he's waiting for his galleons to come back from wherever they've been, he'll try to avoid a fight to the finish until they get here. And he won't want to be stuck in a pocket like Rock Shoal Bay if his son needs his help out in the Charis Sea."

"I was thinking the same thing." Black Water frowned some more.

"If he *is* waiting for Cayleb's return," he went on after a few seconds, "then perhaps the fact that he's falling back to the south indicates the direction from which he expects Cayleb to appear. The last thing he'd want would be for our complete fleet strength to be between him and Cayleb, where we'd have the best chance of defeating either of his two forces in isolation."

"Unless he's thinking in terms of a converging attack," Myrgyn pointed out, and Black Water laughed harshly.

"Sharpfield hates our guts, Kehvyn, but he's got a point about Haarahld and the sort of risks he's likely to take. Try to catch us between two widely separated fleets, each of them weaker than we are? When he can't even be certain when the other fleet is going to arrive?" Black Water shook his head. "Neither one of them would even know we were engaged with the other until after the battle was over!" He shook his head again, even more firmly. "No, that's the sort of over-clever plan someone like Magwair might come up with. Haarahld's too good a seaman to try something that foolish."

"I didn't say it was likely, Your Grace," Myrgyn pointed out. "I simply threw it out as one possibility."

"I know." Black Water reached out and patted his flag captain on the shoulder in a rare public display of affection. "And I do think you have a valid point about the reasons he'd want to stay out of Rock Shoal Bay, especially if he *is* expecting Cayleb's return."

"How far south to you think he'll go before standing and fighting?" Myrgyn asked.

"Probably no further than Darcos Strait," Black Water replied after a moment. "Darcos Keep's nowhere near as good a base as Lock Island, but it would do in a pinch, at least for a while. And the passage between Darcos Island and Crown Cape is less than thirty miles wide at high water. At low water it's a lot narrower, and the safe channel's even narrower than that. He could fall back into the strait, and we'd play hell trying to follow him up."

"But we could always circle around through Silver Strait and come up behind him," Myrgyn pointed out.

"Not without splitting our own forces," Black Water countered. "We'd have to leave someone to keep him from simply heading north again, which would give him the opportunity to defeat one of *our* forces in isolation. Or that's what he may be thinking, at least."

"And what are *you* thinking, Your Grace?" Myrgyn asked, looking at him shrewdly.

"I'm thinking that if he's foolish enough to let himself be trapped inside Darcos Strait, I'll go ahead and split my forces," Black Water replied. "If we drive him back into the narrows, then *we* can afford to reduce our forces north of the the strait, because we'll have the same narrow front to protect he does. Which means we can probably hold any attempt of his to break back out into the Sound with no more than a quarter or a third of our total strength while we send all the rest around behind him."

"Do you really think he'll be that foolish, Your Grace?"

"No, he probably won't. But I can always hope. In the meantime, it's the next best thing to six hundred miles to Darcos Island. At our present speed, that's almost a five-day. And however shy he's being right now, I think we can count on him to do his best to make our lives miserable between now and then. The next several days ought to be interesting.

Haarahld of Charis stood on his flagship's aftercastle, gazing towards the eastern horizon, where summer lightning seemed to flash and blink through the darkness.

It wasn't lightning, of course, and his jaw tightened as he wondered how many of his subjects were dying out there.

Not many, if it's going according to plan, he told himself. *Of course, it never* does *go "according to plan," does it?*

"Commodore Nylz knows his business, Your Majesty," Captain Tryvythyn murmured, and Haarahld turned to look at the flag captain.

"Do I look *that* anxious?" he asked wryly, and Tryvythyn shrugged.

"No, not really. But I've come to know you rather better than most, I think, Your Majesty."

"That's certainly true," Haarahld agreed with a chuckle. "Still, you're right. And someone had to do it."

"Exactly, Your Majesty," Tryvythyn agreed.

The flag captain bowed slightly and turned away, allowing his king to return to his own thoughts. Which, Haarahld discovered, were somewhat lighter after Tryvythyn's intervention.

The king drew a deep breath and made himself consider the last eleven days.

Black Water was clearly determined to pin him down and destroy his fleet once and for all. To be honest, Haarahld was a bit surprised by the Corisandian's tenacity and the degree of tight control he seemed able to maintain over his composite fleet. After Haarahld had used the cover of night to slip his entire fleet around Black Water's right flank and break back north of the duke, Black Water had simply turned around and started following him back towards Rock Shoal Bay.

He'd refused to spread his units in an effort to cast a wider net, which was what Haarahld had more than half-hoped he might do. Instead of offering up more isolated squadrons for the Charisians to snap up, however, Black Water had maintained his concentration—except for his scouting ships—and continued his dogged pursuit. Clearly he wanted a decisive battle, but, equally clearly, he wasn't prepared to court a defeat in detail in his efforts to get one.

And despite all Haarahld's maneuvers, all the wiles and cunning he could bring to bear, the Corisandian had gradually closed the distance between their two fleets.

Haarahld's galleys were individually bigger than their opponents, and better designed for open water. But that also meant they were at least marginally slower under oars at the best of times, and they'd been continually at sea for almost three months now, except for brief returns to port on a ship-by-ship basis to replenish their water tanks. Their bottoms had become foul, which was making them even slower.

Under sail, that wasn't much of a problem, because they also had bigger, more powerful sails. But working to windward under oars, it was. Which was why Black Water's fleet had been less than twenty-five miles south of Haarahld's flagship at sundown.

I've got to get back south of him again, where I can run on the wind, Haarahld told himself yet again, watching the gun flashes grow in intensity. *But at least this should be the last time I need to.*

He wanted to go below, to the refuge of his cabin, away from that silent "heat lightning," but he couldn't. Commodore Kohdy Nylz was out there with his squadron, attacking a force many times his own strength, solely to convince Black Water that Haarahld was trying to break past him to the *east*, not to the west.

The least the king who'd sent them out could do was stand here and watch.

.IX.
Galley *Corisande*,
Darcos Sound

The Duke of Black Water walked on deck after an abbreviated breakfast and looked sourly over the bulwark.

Under normal circumstances, he conceded, the sight before him would have caused him considerable pleasure. Two big galleys lay on *Corisande*'s port quarter. The nearer ship flew the gold-on-black standard of Charis under the white-on-orange of Corisande; the other flew the Charisian colors under the silver doomwhale and royal blue field of Chisholm. They were the first two important prizes Black Water's fleet had captured, and it was already obvious from the preliminary reports that there were some significant peculiarities about the way their guns were mounted.

"Peculiar" or not, he thought grimly, *they obviously* work *well enough, don't they?*

Capturing those two ships—and destroying a third—had cost him four of his own galleys. Actually, it had cost him six, but the damage to two of them was repairable. Of the other four, one had been sunk outright, and the other three had been reduced to such shattered wrecks that he'd ordered them burned himself, after taking off the survivors of their crews.

And after all of that, almost two-thirds of the Charisian force had actually managed to disengage and run.

Two-to-one losses, he reflected. *And we'll probably never know why the third one caught fire and blew up, which means we can't exactly count on doing it again.*

He didn't much care for the implications. Of course, he *had* more than twice as many galleys as Haarahld, but having a dozen or so battered ships left after finishing off the last Charisian wasn't exactly likely to delight Prince Hektor.

"Good morning, Your Grace."

"Good morning, Kehvyn." He turned to face the flag captain, whose breeches were soaked to well above the waist. "Have you had an adventure this morning?" the duke asked mildly, raising one eyebrow.

"I mistimed it when I jumped for the entry port ladder, Your Grace."

Myrgyn grimaced humorously, and Black Water snorted, although it wasn't always funny, by any means. Mistiming the transfer from a small boat to the ladder-like battens fastened to a galley's side for the steep climb to its deck could have fatal consequences. More than one man had been crushed against the side of his own ship when an unanticipated wave slammed the boat he'd just left into him. Others had been washed off their perch by similar waves, sucked under the bilge, and drowned. Black Water had almost suffered that fate himself when he was a much younger man.

"I'm glad to see you're no worse for wear," he told the flag captain, then jerked his head at the two prizes. "What do you make of them?"

"I'm . . . impressed, Your Grace," Myrgyn said soberly. "And I understand what happened to Tanlyr Keep much better now. They're bigger than our ships, which I expected, of course. But those guns of theirs." The flag captain shook his head, his expression half-admiring and half-chagrined. "I don't know why no one else ever thought of it, Your Grace. Their broadside weapons are much shorter than our guns, and lighter—lots lighter. They're like sawed-off krakens mounted where only a *falcon* ought to be able to go. And *all* their guns have these . . . these *pivot* things on the sides of the barrel, almost like the sheaves in a block." Myrgyn's hands moved, as if trying to twist something invisible in the air in front of him. "It lets them actually elevate and depress their guns. And there's something different about their gun powder, too."

"Different? Different how?"

"It's like . . . grains, Your Grace. Grains of sand. Or maybe more like coarse-ground salt."

"Hmmm." Black Water frowned, trying to visualize what Myrgyn was describing.

"I found out how they're managing to fire that quickly, as well, Your Grace," Myrgyn told him, and the duke's eyes sharpened.

"It's another thing I can't understand why nobody else ever thought of," the flag captain said. "They've simply sewn the charges for their guns into cloth bags. They ram the entire bag down the barrel with one shove, instead of using ladles. And they've got some sort of . . . thing mounted on the gun. It's like a little hammer with a piece of flint stuck onto it and a spring. They pull the hammer back, and when they're ready to fire, the spring snaps it down and strikes sparks onto the priming, instead of using slow match or an iron."

Black Water grimaced. He'd always known Charisians were irritatingly innovative. After all, that was a big part of what the Grand Inquisitor had against the kingdom. But from even his present grasp of Myrgyn's explanation, which he knew was imperfect at this point, he began to understand how eight galleys had done so much damage before they were driven off.

No, he told himself harshly. *Not "driven off"; the other five voluntarily* disengaged *after they'd done what they came to do.*

"That's all very interesting, Kehvyn. I mean that, and I'd appreciate it if you could sketch some of the things you're talking about for me, so I could look at them over lunch. But for right now, what do we know about the rest of Haarahld's ships?"

"About what you'd surmised at sunup, Your Grace," Myrgyn replied, and it was his turn to grimace. "You were right. It was a diversion, and while we were all looking *east,* Haarahld slipped back past us to the west. His main body's about twenty miles south of *our* main body and opening the range, slowly but steadily, with these wind conditions."

"Shan-wei seize the man," Black Water said, far more mildly than he felt, and shook his head in grudging admiration. "Now we'll have to chase him all the way to Darcos Island all over again."

"Do we really want to do that, Your Grace?" Myrgyn asked diffidently, and Black Water looked at him sharply. "What I mean, Your Grace, is that as you yourself pointed out when we began pursuing them, if they're expecting Cayleb to return from the south, and if they've managed to make us spend this long chasing them, we may not be able to catch up again before he gets here."

"Or before *Duke Malikai* gets here," Black Water said. "He's supposed to be coming from the same direction, if you recall."

"With all due respect, Your Grace, Duke Malikai is already the better part of a month overdue. He may still be coming, but if they've managed to put as many guns like the ones I was just examining aboard their galleons as our spies had reported, and if they actually managed to intercept Malikai, then the Duke's taken *significant* losses. Those galleys—" He waved at the two prize ships. "—only have six guns in each broadside. According to our spies, their galleons have as many as *twenty.*"

"I know."

For a moment, Black Water's expression showed a bleakness he would not have permitted anyone else to see. Then he drew a deep breath and shook himself.

"I know," he repeated. "But we did manage to take or sink a third of their galleys last night, and Cayleb would have been outnumbered by Duke Malikai by an even greater margin than they were outnumbered by the column they attacked. You're probably right about what galleons with that much firepower could do, but surely they would have suffered losses of their own, and they didn't have that many galleons to begin with."

"With all due respect, Your Grace, I certainly hope you're right about that," Myrgyn said with a wry smile.

"So do I," Black Water admitted. "Still, whatever their galleons look like, they can't have these new guns of theirs widely distributed through their *galleys*. If they did, they'd have sent more of them along last night. For that matter, if *all* their galleys had them, they wouldn't have bothered to run away from us in the first place!"

He snorted with bleak humor and glowered at the prizes, then shook his head.

"I expect they concentrated on putting all the new guns they had aboard the galleons," he said. "Which should mean that if we can ever get to grips with that slippery bastard Haarahld, we should still be able to crush him. And if they do have galleons headed back this way from the Parker Sea, we'd *better* deal with Haarahld before they get here."

"To be honest, Your Grace," Myrgyn said slowly, his expression troubled, "I'm not at all sure the galley hasn't just become thoroughly out-of-date."

"I think you're probably right about that," Black Water said grimly. "And the bad news is that we don't have any galleons of our own. But the good news is that the Charisians don't have a *lot* of them, and we can start building them from an almost even footing, now that we've figured out how they're mounting their guns."

"Exactly, Your Grace." The flag captain nodded. "And what I'm wondering, if that's true, is whether or not there's any point in engaging Haarahld."

Black Water looked at him sharply, and Myrgyn shrugged.

"Even if we completely destroy Haarahld's fleet, we'll only be capturing—or sinking—ships nobody's going to want in another year or two," Myrgyn pointed out.

"Oh. I see what you're thinking now," Black Water said, but he also shook his head.

"I see two reasons to go ahead and smash Haarahld," he said. "First of all, we don't know what's happened to Cayleb. He may have been badly defeated by Malikai and White Ford, despite all our present doom and gloom. Even if he won, he's probably taken losses—quite possibly enough losses that even with all the wonderful new guns he could put aboard his remaining ships, we could still beat him.

"But, second, even if Cayleb is coming back with a fleet we can't possibly face in battle—at least until we've built ourselves a fleet just like it—we still need to destroy *this* fleet. Their king's aboard one of those galleys, Kehvyn. If we kill him, or even better, *capture* him, the consequences will be enormous. And even if we fail to do that, those ships have got thousands of trained officers and seamen aboard them. Those are the men they'll use to crew any more galleons they might build. We need to kill as many of them as we can now, while our ships are still equal to theirs, to deprive them of all that experienced manpower."

Myrgyn looked at him for several seconds, then nodded slowly with an expression of profound respect.

"I wasn't thinking that far ahead, Your Grace. Perhaps," he smiled thinly, "that's why you're an admiral, and I'm not."

"Well," Black Water said with an answering, somewhat crooked, smile, "*one* of the reasons, anyway. Perhaps."

"Of course, there's still the little problem of what happens if Cayleb turns up at an inopportune moment, Your Grace," Myrgyn pointed out.

"We've got picket ships out to the north," Black Water countered, "and Haarahld is south of us. If Cayleb turns up from the south, then we turn around and run north. And while I realize these new rigging ideas of theirs make their galleons more weatherly, I strongly doubt that they can sail straight into the wind the way we can row."

"And if we're wrong, and he turns up from the *north*, Your Grace?"

"Then our pickets will tell us he's there long before Haarahld can know anything about it," Black Water replied. "In that case, we make straight for Silver Strait and run for it. We'll probably have enough forewarning to get around Haarahld before he realizes what's happening, if we stop chasing him and just concentrate on running. And if Haarahld does get in our way—" The duke shrugged. "—we cut our way through him and inflict all the damage we can in the process."

.X.
Darcos Sound

"You hardly touched your supper," Lachlyn Zhessyp observed.

King Haarahld turned from his contemplation of the stern windows at his valet's complaint.

"Was there something *wrong* with it, Your Majesty?" Zhessyp inquired with a certain hurt dignity as he gathered up the dishes on his tray, and Haarahld shook his head with a smile.

"No, there wasn't anything wrong with it," he said patiently, ignoring the grin on Sergeant Haarpar's face as the guardsman watched from the great cabin door he'd opened for Zhessyp. "And, no, I have no complaints for the cook. And, no, I'm not ill. And, no, you can't bring me a snack later tonight."

Zhessyp regarded him with the mournful, martyred eyes only the most loyal and trusted of retainers could produce, and the king sighed.

"*But,*" he said, "I promise to eat a simply *enormous* breakfast. There. Are you satisfied now?"

"I'm sure," Zhessyp said with enormous dignity, "that it's not *my* place to be extracting promises from you, Your Majesty."

He picked up his tray, elevated his nose ever so slightly, and left the cabin. Haarpar held the door for him, and his grin got even bigger as the departing valet stepped past him.

"You know, Gorj," the king said dryly, "the frightening thing is that he really thinks he means that."

"Aye, Your Majesty, he does," the guardsman agreed. "Still and all, down inside somewhere, he knows better."

"Yes, he does." Haarahld smiled fondly, then shook his head. "Goodnight, Gorj."

"Goodnight, Your Majesty." The guardsman touched his left shoulder in salute, then shut the door.

Haarahld gazed at the closed door for the better part of a minute, then rose, his smile fading, and stepped out onto *Royal Charis'* sternwalk.

He gazed up at the sky, where the fingernail paring of a new moon gleamed faintly in the east. The musical bubble of the galley's wake came to him from below, coupled with the rhythmic sound of water sluicing along the sides of his flagship's hull. Stars burned brightly high overhead, and the following wind had freshened slightly and veered a bit back towards the west.

It was a beautiful night, if a little on the dark side, and he gazed astern at the running lights of the other ships in *Royal Charis'* column. The men aboard those galleys were every one of them obedient to his orders. And, he knew, they executed those orders willingly, by and large, trusting him to get it right. But beyond the running lights he could see were those of the fleet he *couldn't* see, yet which was once again creeping closer.

Soon now, very soon, he was going to have to decide whether to fall back south of Darcos Island or try to break around Black Water's flank once more. He didn't want to go any farther south than he had to—if nothing else, there wasn't another base as good as Darcos Keep once he got down into the Middle Sea. But Black Water was staying close to his heels, and the chances of his bamboozling someone as shrewd as the Corisandian duke got slimmer each time he had to make the attempt.

That's not what's really worrying you, though, he told himself, gazing out at the night. *What's worrying you is that according to Cayleb's and Merlin's estimate, and even allowing for how much further south we are right now, they should have made contact with Black Water's picket ships no later than day before yesterday.*

He smiled without a great deal of humor and braced his forearms on the sternwalk railing as he leaned over it to take some of the weight off of his right knee.

He was certain the rest of the fleet must be beginning to wonder exactly what he had in mind with all this bobbing and weaving about the Charis Sea and Darcos Sound. He would have liked to have been able to tell them, too. But just exactly how was he supposed to inform even his most trusted officers that he'd decided to base his strategy—and, for that matter, his hope for the very survival of his entire kingdom, the lives of all their families, and very possibly their immortal souls—on the services of what might well turn out to be a demon?

He laughed softly, shaking his head, remembering Merlin's expression on this very sternwalk. Whatever else Merlin might be, he was clearly no omniscient being. In fact, that was one of the reasons Haarahld had decided to trust him, although he'd never told the *seijin*—or whatever he truly was—that.

Merlin could be surprised. Which undoubtedly meant he could also make mistakes. But what Merlin could not do was to conceal what he *felt*. Perhaps the *seijin* didn't realize that. Or perhaps it was only his friends from whom he couldn't hide. But Haarahld had long since realized Merlin was a deeply lonely man. One who'd been hurt, but refused to surrender to the pain. And whatever his origins, whatever his powers, he truly was committed to the purpose he'd explained to Haarahld in their very first interview.

I realize it's possible he really is a demon, God, Haarahld Ahrmahk thought, gazing up at the clean, untouched beauty of the glittering handiwork of the deity he worshiped. *If he is, and if I shouldn't have listened to him, then I apologize, and I ask for Your forgiveness. But I don't think he is. And if he isn't, then perhaps You truly did send him, whatever he is. He's not very much like what I always expected an archangel to be like, either, of course.* The king smiled wryly in the darkness. *On the other hand, I suppose You could send whoever You wanted to to teach those corrupt bastards in the Temple the error of their ways. If it's Your will that I live to see that happen, I'll die a happy man. And if it isn't, then I suppose there are worse causes a man could die serving.*

It wasn't the sort of prayer of which the Council of Vicars would have approved, and not just because of the content. But that was just fine with King Haarahld VII of Charis.

It was odd, he reflected. Despite his concern for Cayleb's tardiness, despite the fact that the Group of Four had decreed Charis' destruction, despite even the fact that he fully realized that the defeat of this onslaught would only prompt the Group of Four to try again, with even stronger forces, he felt a deep sense of content. He was far from blind to the realities of what was about to happen. If Charis lost this war, the consequences for all Haarahld cared for and loved would be catastrophic. And even if Charis won *this* war, it would only be to face another, and another beyond that.

Haarahld doubted he would live to see the end of the titanic conflict which he prayed nightly was only just beginning. But perhaps Cayleb would. Or Zhan and Zhanayt. Or his grandchildren. And at least he'd taken a stand. At least he'd provided for the possibility that those grandchildren he hadn't met yet would live in a world in which evil and venal men, hiding their avarice and corruption behind the face of God Himself, could not dictate *their* beliefs, exploit *their* faith in God for their own vile purposes.

Poor Merlin, he thought. *So afraid I'd see where his purposes must ultimately lead! I wonder if he's started to figure out that I've been in front of him almost all the way?*

It was probably time he sat down and discussed the entire subject openly and frankly with Merlin, he decided. There was no longer any point pretending, after all. And once they could stop wasting time on all this diplomatic indirection, they could probably—

King Haarahld's thoughts broke off as the "pager" strapped to his forearm vibrated suddenly.

▼   ▼   ▼

Prince Cayleb and Merlin leaned over the chart table. The prince's frown was intense as he gazed at the copper coins Merlin had used as map tokens.

"So this is their main force over here," Cayleb said, tapping a roughly rectangular area of the chart delineated by the coins placed at each corner.

"Yes." Merlin stood back, folding his forearms and gazing at the prince's intent expression.

Despite the tension of the moment, Merlin felt a temptation to smile at Cayleb's almost absent tone. The prince's frustration as adverse winds delayed their passage had been palpable to all around him. Now that same frustration had transmuted itself into something else, and he was so focused on the task at hand that it clearly no longer even occurred to him to worry about where—and how—Merlin got his information. Just as he hadn't worried about how Merlin had just finished informing King Haarahld of their arrival.

"And these," Cayleb's hand swept over the arc of smaller coins scattered to the north of Duke Black Water's main fleet, "are his picket ships."

"Yes," Merlin said again, and the prince straightened, still frowning.

"If these positions are accurate, he's let his pickets get too far astern," he said. "And too far from one another, as well."

"True," Merlin agreed. "On the other hand, it's a clear night. Any cannon fire's going to be visible for a long way."

"Granted. But," Cayleb looked up with an evil smile, "there doesn't necessarily have to *be* any cannon fire, does there?"

"What do you have in mind?" Merlin asked.

"Well," Cayleb crossed his own arms and straightened up, settling back on his heels, "he's using light units. For all intents and purposes, they're basically no more than dispatch boats. At most, they've got a few wolves."

Merlin nodded. "Wolf" was a generic term for any Safeholdian naval gun with a bore of two inches or less. Such small pieces, like the ones in *Dreadnought's* fighting tops, were intended almost entirely as antipersonnel weapons—essentially, enormous single-shot shotguns—although they could also be used effectively against boats and launches.

"I'm thinking," Cayleb continued, "that if this picket here—" He unfolded his right arm to reach out and tap one of the coins with his forefinger. "—were to suffer a mischief sometime around Langhorne's Watch, it would leave a gap between *these* two." He tapped two more coins. "Not only that, but I'm betting it's the relay ship for both of them, so even if they did see us, they couldn't report it to Black Water. Which means we could get the main fleet to within ten miles of his main body, maybe even less, between moonset and dawn."

Merlin considered the chart, then nodded slowly.

"And just how do you intend to arrange for it to suffer that mischief?" he asked politely.

"I'm glad you asked that," Cayleb said with a toothy smile.

▼   ▼   ▼

I've really got to talk to this boy about appropriate risks for fleet commanders to run, Merlin told himself three hours later, standing on the afterdeck of the schooner *Seagull.*

Seagull was one of the larger of the schooners attached to Cayleb's galleons. She mounted twelve carronades, six in each broadside. Unlike *Dreadnought's,* the schooner's carronades' bores measured only five and a half inches, and the round shot they threw weighed just a bit over twenty-three pounds each. That was far lighter than her larger consorts' weapons, but much, much heavier than anything her size had ever been able to mount before.

At the moment, however, the weight of her broadside was irrelevant. The flush-decked schooner, barely ninety feet in length, was crammed with Marines. Cayleb had managed to pack an additional eighty men into her, plus Merlin, Cayleb's Marine bodyguards, and Cayleb himself.

"This is *not* something you should be doing," Merlin said quietly into the prince's ear. The two of them stood to one side of the helmsman as he leaned on the tiller bar.

"No?" Cayleb returned, equally quietly, and his teeth flashed white in the dim light of the setting moon as he smiled.

"No," Merlin said, as deflatingly as possible. "Getting yourself killed doing something as minor as this would be stupid, not gallant."

"Father always told me 'gallant' and 'stupid' usually meant exactly the same thing," Cayleb said.

"A smart man, your father," Merlin replied.

"Yes, he is," Cayleb agreed. "But as it happens, I think I *do* have to be here. Unless, of course, you're prepared to explain to the Captain just how it is that *you* know exactly where to go?"

Merlin had opened his mouth to respond. Now he closed it again, glowering at the prince. Unfortunately, Cayleb had a point. By now, every man in the galleon fleet was firmly convinced Cayleb could literally smell his way to the enemy. They were thoroughly prepared to follow his "instincts" anywhere, and not at all surprised when they found enemy warships wherever he took them, which neatly deflected any attention from Merlin's contributions. In the long term, that was undoubtedly a good thing, but in the short term, Merlin wasn't at all happy about Cayleb's risking himself on a harebrained stunt like this one.

Come on, he told himself. *It's not really a "stunt" at all, is it? Because Cayleb's right; if we pull this off, Black Water's going to be in for a really nasty surprise about sunrise.*

No doubt he would, but Merlin could think of all too many examples from Old Earth's history of essential men and women who'd gotten themselves killed doing important but not *essential* things.

"Well," Merlin murmured into the prince's ear now, "if you're the one doing all the explaining to the Captain, you'd better tell him to alter course about half a point to starboard."

"Aye, aye, Sir," Cayleb said with an ironic smile and crossed to where the schooner's captain stood watching his ship's sails.

▼   ▼   ▼

The light galley *Sprite* ghosted slowly along on one more leg of her endless patrol. *Sprite*'s Emeraldian crew wasn't especially fond of Duke Black Water. They hadn't particularly cared for the orders which subordinated their own navy to the Corisandian's command. And they especially hadn't cared for the orders which had kept them at sea for the last three and a half five-days.

Every member of the galley's seventy-five-man company knew they were out here primarily as an afterthought. Oh, it was always *possible* the mysteriously absent Charisian galleons might try to come creeping up behind the combined fleet from the north. It wasn't very likely, though. Especially not in light of how persistently the Charisian galleys had insisted on heading *south.* *Sprite*'s crewmen didn't object to the notion of having someone watch the main fleet's back; they simply didn't see why *they* should be stuck with the job.

Her captain had ordered a single reef taken in her sail just after sundown. Not because the wind had freshened enough to pose any sort of threat, but because he had to reduce sail if he wanted to maintain his assigned position to windward of the main fleet's bigger, slower galleys. He'd also turned in after supper, leaving the deck to his second lieutenant, and most of the rest of his ship's company was working assiduously to get all the sleep it could before yet another boring day of playing lookout.

▼   ▼   ▼

"There," Cayleb whispered into the ear of *Seagull*'s captain, and pointed to leeward.

The schooner was on the starboard tack, broad reaching with the wind coming in over her starboard quarter. And there, almost precisely where the prince had predicted, were the running lights of a small vessel.

The moon had set, and the schooner, all of her own lights extinguished, was sliding along under jibs and foresail alone as she crept stealthily closer to the galley.

The picket boat was even smaller than *Seagull*, little more than sixty feet in length, if that. Her stern lanterns picked out her position clearly, and the schooner's captain nodded to his crown prince.

"I see her now, Your Highness," he whispered back, and Cayleb's lips twitched as he heard the semi-awe in the man's voice.

"Lay her alongside, just like we planned," he said, carefully suppressing the amusement in his own voice.

"Aye, aye, Your Highness."

The captain touched his shoulder in salute, and Cayleb nodded, then stepped back over beside Merlin and Ahrnahld Falkhan.

"And when he *does* lay us alongside," Merlin said just loud enough to be certain Falkhan could hear, "*you* stay right here aboard *Seagull*, Your Highness."

"Of course," Cayleb replied in a rather absent tone, watching as *Seagull* changed course very slightly, edging ever closer to the unsuspecting galley, now little more than a couple of hundred yards clear.

"I *mean* it, Cayleb!" Merlin said sternly. "Ahrnahld and I are *not* going to explain to your father how we managed to let you get killed taking a dinky little galley, is that understood?"

"Of course," Cayleb repeated, and Merlin looked across at Falkhan.

The Marine lieutenant looked back and shook his head, then jerked it to indicate Sergeant Faircaster. The burly, powerfully built noncom stood directly behind the crown prince, and he looked quite prepared to rap the heir to the throne smartly over the head if that was what it took to keep him aboard *Seagull*.

Which, Merlin reflected, suited him just fine.

▼   ▼   ▼

"*Now!*"

Seagull's helmsman put his tiller sharply up to windward, and the schooner slid neatly alongside *Sprite*. Someone aboard the galley spotted her at the very last minute and shouted in alarm, but it was far too late to do any good.

Grappling irons flew, biting into *Sprite*'s timbers as the two vessels ground together. The watch on deck—no more than a dozen men, all told—whirled, gaping in horror as *Seagull* came crashing out of the night. The schooner's side was a solid mass of rifle-armed Marines, bayonets gleaming with the dull, murderous reflection of *Sprite*'s running lights, and then those same Marines swept across *Sprite*'s deck.

Bayonets thrust. Clubbed musket butts struck viciously. There were a few screams and more shouts, but not a shot was fired, and it was over in less than thirty seconds. It took a little longer than that for the crew trapped below decks to realize what had happened, of course, and for *Sprite*'s captain to accept it and formally surrender his ship. But there were only seven casualties, all of them Emeraldians, and only two of them fatal.

It was a neat little operation, Merlin conceded. And, best of all from his perspective, there hadn't been time for Cayleb to get himself involved in the boarding action even if he'd wanted to.

"All right," the crown prince said now, standing beside Merlin on the afterdeck of the captured galley, where he'd just accepted the surrender of *Sprite*'s stunned, disbelieving captain. "Let's get the prize crew aboard. Then we've got to go back and get the rest of the fleet up here."

▼   ▼   ▼

King Haarahld lay in the gently swaying cot, dutifully pretending to sleep.

The fact that there wasn't very much else he could do didn't make it any easier. What he really wanted was to call Captain Tryvythyn into the chart room and begin discussing possible deployments. In fact, the temptation was very nearly overwhelming. Except, of course, that Tryvythyn would undoubtedly wonder what had inspired it. And except for the fact that although he knew Cayleb was almost certainly less than fifty miles from where he himself lay, that was *all* he knew.

It wasn't as if he and Admiral Lock Island and their commodores and captains hadn't discussed possible tactical situations and their responses to them exhaustively over the past months. Every one of his senior officers knew exactly what all of them were supposed to do, and Haarahld felt confident they would understand not simply his orders, but the purpose *behind* those orders, when the time came.

But the fact that there wasn't anything he needed to be doing didn't keep him from wishing there were.

He glanced at the stern windows, wondering if the sky beyond them really was just a bit lighter than it had seemed the last time he looked. It was possible, although it was more likely wishful thinking on his part.

He smiled at the thought, amused despite the tension coiling tighter and tighter inside.

Yes, the sky definitely *was* lighter, he realized, and—

The pager vibrated against his forearm again. This time, twice.

▼   ▼   ▼

"It's a good thing you're young enough to not need very much sleep," Merlin said a bit sourly, and Cayleb grinned at him.

"Be honest, Merlin," he said. "You're just pissed because I behaved myself last night and didn't give you anything to complain about."

"Nonsense. I'm not 'pissed'; just astonished," Merlin replied, and this time Cayleb laughed out loud.

"Do you think they've spotted us yet, Your Highness?" Falkhan asked, and the crown prince sobered.

"If they haven't yet, they will shortly," he said, rather more grimly, and Falkhan nodded.

Cayleb's galleons were formed into a single column this time, forging ahead with all sail set to the topgallants, and headed almost exactly southeast-by-east on the port tack. *Dreadnought* led the column, and the sails of the closest of Black Water's galleys were clearly visible from deck level against the steadily brightening sky to the east.

"We've still got a minute or two, I think," Merlin said quietly. "The sky's still dark behind us. But you're right, Cayleb. They're going to pick us up any minute now."

"Be ready with those signals, Gwylym," Cayleb said over his shoulder.

"Aye, aye, Your Highness," Captain Manthyr replied, and glanced at Midshipman Kohrby's signal party.

▼   ▼   ▼

The lookout in the Emerald Navy galley *Black Prince* stretched and yawned. His relief in the crow's-nest was due in another half-hour or so, and he looked forward to breakfast and some hammock time.

He finished stretching and turned, making a leisurely visual sweep as the sky in the east turned pale-cream and salmon colored. A few wisps of cloud were high enough to the north and west to pick up some of the color, standing out like misty golden banners against a sky of graying velvet, still pricked by stars.

He started to turn back to the east, then paused as something caught his eye. He frowned, peering more intently to the northwest. He was looking almost into the eye of the wind, and his own eyes watered slightly. He rubbed them in irritation and looked again.

His heart seemed to stop. For an instant, all he could do was stare incredulously at the impossible sight as the steadying light from behind him turned gray, weather-stained canvas briefly into polished pewter. Then he found his voice.

"Sail ho!" he screamed. "*Sail ho!*"

▼   ▼   ▼

"Well, they've seen us," Merlin commented quietly to Cayleb as the nearest ship, the rearmost galley in the Northern Force's westernmost column, flying the red and gold standard of Emerald, turned suddenly into a kicked ants' nest of furious activity.

He didn't need his SNARC's overhead imagery to see it, either. He could scarcely believe how close Cayleb had managed to get, although he knew Cayleb himself was more than a little frustrated.

The crown prince was running well over two hours behind his own original ambitious schedule. He'd hoped to overtake Black Water's fleet before dawn, announcing his arrival only with the first broadsides, delivered from total darkness. But even with perfect information on the relative positions of the two fleets, he'd been unable to allow properly for vagaries of wind and current.

His irritation at the delay was probably a bit more evident than he fondly believed it was, Merlin thought with a grin. For all he'd already accomplished, there were times when Crown Prince Cayleb was very young.

Fortunately, he'd allowed for at least some slippage in his original timing, and the weariness of the enemy's lookout, coupled with the poorer visibility to the west, had allowed *Dreadnought* to get to within less than six miles before being spotted. Black Water's nearer two columns were hull-up, clearly visible from *Dreadnought*'s deck, although no one else could see them quite as clearly as *he* could.

"Hoist the signal, Captain!" Cayleb snapped.

"Aye, aye, Your Highness! Master Kohrby, *if* you please!"

"Aye, aye, Sir!"

The colorful flags rose to *Dreadnought*'s yardarm, streaming out in the wind, repeated by the schooners stationed up to windward of the galleons' battle line, and a hungry cheer went up from Cayleb's men.

"Number One hoisted, Sir!" Kohrby reported. "Engage the enemy!"

▼   ▼   ▼

King Haarahld was half-finished dressing when the pager on his forearm vibrated yet again. This time there were three pulses, and he raised his voice in a shout to his cabin sentry.

"Charlz!"

The door flew open instantly, and Sergeant Gahrdaner stepped through it, sword half-drawn. His eyes snapped around the cabin, seeking any threat, and then he relaxed—slightly—when he found none.

"Your Majesty?" he said.

"Pass the word for Captain Tryvythyn," Haarahld said. "And then, get me my armor."

▼   ▼   ▼

Lieutenant Rholynd Mahlry spun in place, staring disbelievingly up at the crow's-nest.

"Ships on the starboard quarter!" the lookout bawled frantically. "*Many* ships on the starboard quarter!"

Mahlry stared for another heartbeat, then raced across *Black Prince*'s aftercastle to stare up to windward himself. For just a moment, he saw nothing—then he saw altogether too much.

"Beat to quarters!" he shouted, watching the endless line of galleons bearing down upon his ship. "Someone wake the Captain!"

▼   ▼   ▼

"Signal to *Gale*," Cayleb said, eyes fixed on the rapidly nearing enemy vessels.

"Yes, Your Highness?" Kohrby asked, chalk poised over his slate.

"Engage the enemy column nearest to windward," Cayleb said.

"Engage the enemy column nearest to windward, aye, aye, Sir!" Kohrby said, and turned to his signal party once more.

"Captain Manthyr, we'll pass astern of at least the two nearer columns, if we can."

"Aye, aye, Your Highness." The flag captain gazed at the nearest enemy galleys for a moment, then looked at his helmsmen. "Bring her head two points to port."

▼   ▼   ▼

Captain Payt Khattyr came bounding up *Black Prince*'s aftercastle ladder like a hedge lizard with its tail on fire. He hadn't waited for his armor, or even to dress, and he was bare to the waist as he arrived at Mahlry's side.

"Where—?" he began urgently, then chopped the question off as he saw the galleons for himself.

"They've altered heading in the last few minutes, Sir," Mahlry said, pointing at the lead ship. "They're edging further up to windward."

"Steering to cut us off from home," Khattyr muttered. Mahlry didn't know whether the comment was intended for him, or not, but he found himself nodding in grim agreement with his captain's assessment.

"Make the signal for enemy in sight," Khattyr said.

"I already have, Sir," Mahlry replied, and Khattyr spared him a brief glance of intense approval.

"Good man, Rholynd!"

The captain turned back to his perusal of the enemy, and his jaw tightened as he saw the lines of gunports opening and the cannon muzzles snouting out like hungry beasts.

He turned to stare south, along the line of his ship's column. *Black Prince* was the rearmost ship in the westernmost of nine columns. There were twenty galleys in her column, all of them Emeraldian, and the next two columns to eastward were also Emeraldian, with the nearer one headed by Earl Mahndyr's flagship *Triton*. The fourth column was headed by the last ten Emeraldian galleys, followed by nine Chisholmian ships. The fifth consisted of another twenty Chisholmian galleys, led by Earl Sharpfield, in *King Maikel*. Then came the sixth column, com-

posed entirely of Corisandian ships and led by Duke Black Water in the fleet flagship. Then another column of Chisholmians, and two final columns of Corisandians.

With an interval of two hundred yards between ships, even the shortest column was over two and a half miles long, and the the interval between columns
was three miles. That meant the entire formation stretched twenty-four miles
from east to west . . . and that a masthead lookout in *Black Prince* couldn't quite
see the ships in the farthest column at all.

It also meant it was going to take time for Black Water to receive word of
what was happening, and even longer for him to respond to it.

"Any signal from Earl Mahndyr?" he asked.

"No, Sir," Mahlry said tensely, and Khattyr swallowed a curse.

He looked back at the inexorably advancing Charisian galleons. They had to
be making good at least ten or eleven knots in the stiff breeze, he thought, watching them lean to the press of their mountains of canvas, probably more, and they
were slicing steadily eastward. In another fifteen minutes—twenty-five, at
most—they were going to be squarely across *Black Prince*'s stern, and the captain
felt his belly tightening down into a cold, hard knot at the thought. He'd seen
what *galleys* armed with the new Charisian artillery could do, and the nearest
Charisian galleons had at least twenty-five guns in her broadside, four times what
their galleys had mounted.

"Sir!" Mahlry said suddenly, pointing across at the Charisian leader. "That's
the Crown Prince's standard!"

"Are you certain?" Khattyr asked urgently. "Your eyes are better than mine,
boy—but are you *certain?*"

"Yes, Sir," Mahlry said firmly.

Khattyr slammed his balled fists together, wheeling to stare along the column once again. He could hear other galleys' drums beating to quarters, see
crewmen dashing about the decks of the nearer ships, but *still* there was no signal
from Earl Mahndyr.

He waited another five minutes, then drew a deep breath and nodded
sharply.

"Take in the sail!" he ordered harshly. "Out sweeps! Bring her about!"

▼　　▼　　▼

"There's someone with his wits about him, Your Highness," Captain Manthyr
observed as the northernmost galley in the nearest column suddenly brailed up
her single big sail.

Her oars thrust out of their ports, and she turned sharply, swinging out of her
column. One or two derisive taunts went up from some of *Dreadnought*'s seamen,
but that galley wasn't fleeing. As they watched, she turned into the wind and
steadied on her new course—straight for *Dreadnought*.

"They've seen your standard, Your Highness," Ahrnahld Falkhan said quietly as the galley's oars started to stroke.

"Yes, they have," Cayleb agreed.

He gazed at the oncoming galley for a moment, judging relative motions with a seaman's eye. Then shook his head slowly.

"They've seen it, but they didn't turn quite soon enough," he said.

"With your permission, Your Highness, I'd still prefer to give him a bit more sea room," Manthyr said. "The last thing we need is to have your flagship damaged or taken out of action early."

"Oh, no, we couldn't have *that*, Captain," Cayleb agreed, eyes glinting with amusement at his flag captain's careful choice of words.

"I'm glad you agree, Your Highness," Manthyr said gravely, and looked at his helmsmen again. "Bring her up another point to port."

▼   ▼   ▼

"Shan-wei seize it!" Khattyr snarled as the long line of galleons altered course slightly. His eye was as good as Cayleb's, and he could see clearly what was about to happen.

He'd waited too long, assuming there'd ever been any real chance of success at all. But the absolute necessity of maintaining formation had been drilled into every captain of Black Water's fleet. Leaving it without orders was a court-martial offense, and he'd taken too much time wrestling with himself before he acted.

Unfortunately, there wasn't much he could do about it now. Turning away would only make it worse, and there was always at least the chance he might actually be able to carry through despite their guns, still get to grips with the Charisian heir's flagship. If he could do that, then every Charisian ship in sight would swarm in to save Cayleb. The consequences for *Black Prince* would undoubtedly be fatal, but if he could just delay those galleons, just tie them up for an hour or two while the rest of the fleet reacted . . .

▼   ▼   ▼

"*Open fire!*"

Captain Manthyr's order rang out clear and sharp. The inevitable noises of a ship underway seemed only to have enclosed and perfected the taut silence of *Dreadnought*'s company, and despite everyone's tense anticipation, the command came almost as a surprise.

For one tiny slice of a second, nothing happened. And then, every gun captain in her starboard broadside yanked his lanyard simultaneously.

▼   ▼   ▼

"You wanted me, Your Majesty?"

Captain Tryvythyn had arrived quickly. Quickly enough, indeed, that he hadn't fully completed dressing and appeared in his cotton shirt, without his uniform tunic.

"Yes, Dynzyl."

Haarahld turned to face his flag captain as Sergeant Gahrdaner finished buckling his cuirass for him. The captain's eyebrows had risen in surprise at finding his king obviously arming for battle, and Haarahld smiled tightly.

"No, I haven't lost my mind," he said reassuringly. "But I've got a . . . feeling we're going to be busy today, and shortly."

"Of course, Your Majesty." Tryvythyn couldn't quite keep his mystification—and perhaps just a hint of skepticism—out of his voice, and Haarahld snorted in amusement.

"I don't blame you for cherishing a few doubts, Dynzyl, but trust me."

"I do, Your Majesty," Tryvythyn said, and there was no hesitation at all in that statement.

"Good. In that case—"

"Excuse me, Your Majesty," Midshipman Marshyl said from the cabin door. "We've just received a signal from *Speedy.*"

"What signal?" Haarahld asked.

"She reports hearing gunfire to the northeast, Sire. She's moving to investigate it."

Tryvythyn stared at the midshipman for a moment, then back at his king, and Haarahld saw the wonder—and the questions—in the flag captain's eyes.

"General signal, Dynzyl," he said. "Prepare for battle."

▼　　▼　　▼

The Charisian flagship disappeared behind a sudden blinding eruption of gunsmoke shot through with flashes of fire. The range was still almost two hundred yards, but these guns *weren't* double-shotted. The press of *Dreadnought*'s canvas heeled her to starboard, bringing the sills of her gunports closer to the water, but she had ample freeboard, and it actually made her a more stable gun platform. Better than half her shots still missed . . . but almost half of them *didn't.*

▼　　▼　　▼

Captain Khattyr saw the fiery blast of smoke an instant before the first round shot slammed murderously into his galley's port bow. It was a quartering broadside, coming in at an angle of perhaps sixty degrees, and splinters flew as thirty-eight-pound spheres of iron crashed through her timbers. Shrieks of agony came from the oardeck, and her forward sweeps flailed as the men manning them were smashed and mangled by cast-iron and the pieces of their own vessel.

More shots came in higher, slamming through the bulwarks, carving gory furrows through the borders still assembling on her forecastle and in the waist. Bits and pieces of men were snatched up in that iron hurricane, and blood sprayed as human bodies were torn apart.

Black Prince staggered, like a runner who'd caught his toe on some unseen obstacle, and Khattyr shouted orders to the helmsmen, trying to compensate for what had just happened to a third of his port sweeps.

▼   ▼   ▼

"What did you say?" the Earl of Mahndyr demanded of his flag captain.

"*Black Prince* reports enemy in sight, My Lord," Captain Nyklas Zheppsyn repeated.

"That's ridiculous!" Mahndyr said. "How could Haarahld have gotten clear around us that way?"

"My Lord, I don't know," Zheppsyn said. "We've just received the signal, and—"

"What was that?" Mahndyr snapped, cocking his head at the sound of distant thunder.

"Gunfire, My Lord," Zheppsyn said grimly.

▼   ▼   ▼

Dreadnought's gunners hurled themselves onto their recoiling guns, swabs and rammers jerking. Gun trucks squealed as carriages were hauled back into battery, and muzzles spewed fresh smoke and flame.

As always, the shorter, lighter carronades fired faster than the long guns on her main deck. Merlin stood well clear of the quarterdeck carronades, between Cayleb and the rail, and watched the heavy shot tear into the Emeraldian galley across the steadily shortening range.

Her port sweeps flailed in wild disorder as *Dreadnought*'s fire smashed into the crowded confines of her oardeck, and Merlin felt a mental chill as he pictured the butchery and carnage. A galley under oars depended on the intricate coordination of her rowers, and no one could maintain that coordination while everyone about him was being torn into bleeding meat.

The galley's forward guns managed to return fire, but their shots went wide, and *Dreadnought* was passing directly across *Black Prince*'s bows. Her fire ripped down the centerline of the galley, killing and maiming, and the sound of the Emeraldian crew's screams was clearly audible in the fleeting instants in which none of *Dreadnought*'s guns was actually firing.

▼   ▼   ▼

Captain Khattyr clung to the aftercastle's forward rail.

There was nothing else he could do. Even his worst nightmares had fallen short of what a galleon's broadside could do. *Black Prince*'s hatchways belched men, many of them bleeding from terrible wounds, as her panicked rowers boiled up through them. But there was no shelter from the Charisians' merciless fire on the open deck, either.

His ship was losing way, his people were dying for nothing, and he couldn't simply stand here and watch them be slaughtered for no return at all.

"Lieutenant Mahlry, strike—" he began, turning to the lieutenant. But the young man lay on the aftercastle deck, eyes already glazing, both hands clutching the spear-like splinter which had driven deep into his chest.

Khattyr's jaw tightened, and he grabbed a midshipman by the shoulder.

"Strike the colors!" he barked. "Get forward and—"

The thirty-eight-pound round shot killed both of them instantly.

▼   ▼   ▼

"Why doesn't he strike?" Cayleb muttered. "Why doesn't he *strike?*"

The galley wallowed helplessly, shuddering under the tempest of iron ripping her apart. *Devastation* and *Destruction*, the two galleons following in *Dreadnought*'s wake, were firing into her as well, now, and thick streamers of blood oozed down her sides. There was absolutely nothing that ship could do to hinder Cayleb's progress, but *still* her captain obstinately refused to haul down his colors in token of surrender.

"She's done, Cayleb!" Merlin half-shouted in his ear.

Cayleb looked at him for a moment, then nodded sharply. He crossed to Manthyr and gripped the flag captain's shoulder.

"Let her go, Gwylym!" he commanded.

Manthyr glanced at him, and the captain's eyes were almost grateful.

"Cease fire! *Cease fire!*" he shouted.

Dreadnought's guns fell silent, but *Devastation* and *Destruction* continued to fire for another minute or two. Then, finally, the savage bombardment trailed off.

The wind rolled the fog bank of smoke away, and more than one man aboard Cayleb's flagship felt a touch of horror as he looked at their target, heard the screams and moans of her broken and bleeding crew. The galley rolled heavily, oars smashed, mast leaning drunkenly, and it sounded as if the ship herself were crying out in agony.

The entire crew stared at the shattered hulk, and even as they watched, the tottering mast toppled wearily into the sea beside her. Then Captain Manthyr's voice cut through the stillness in a tone of unnatural calm.

"Let her fall off a point," he told his helmsmen, and *Dreadnought* altered course to starboard, closing on the second column of her enemies, now less than two miles ahead.

▼   ▼   ▼

"They took the *northern* passage?"

Duke Black Water looked at Captain Myrgyn in disbelief.

"That's what the signal says, Your Grace," the flag captain replied tautly.

Black Water turned away, staring out the great cabin's stern windows while his brain tried to grasp Myrgyn's message. *The north?* How could Cayleb—and it could *only* be Cayleb—have come at him from the *north* when Haarahld had been so stubbornly clinging to a *southern* position? And how had he gotten through Black Water's screen of picket vessels without being spotted? What demon had let him time his arrival so perfectly? Come sweeping in *exactly* with the dawn?

He clenched his jaw and shook himself viciously. *How* didn't matter. All that mattered was what he did about it.

His mind began to function once more, sorting out possibilities, options.

The initial sighting report had come in from one of the ships in his westernmost column. That meant Cayleb was either due west of him, or else coming down with the wind from the northwest. Given the limitations of his signaling system, Black Water couldn't be sure which, and it mattered.

A part of him insisted Cayleb couldn't possibly have placed himself north, as well as west, of the combined fleet. No one could have had *that* much battle luck! But, then again, no one could have enough luck to come straight to him like this in the first place.

In either case, Cayleb was going to hit Mahndyr's Emeraldians first, and he was going to hit them hard. Surprise was almost total, and that was going to produce panic. Mahndyr was no coward, and neither were most of his captains, but Black Water felt grimly certain he was going to lose at least one of Mahndyr's columns completely.

The question, he thought, *is whether I try to* fight *him or simply cut and run?*

Every instinct told him to turn towards Cayleb. To bring his entire fleet and its massive numerical superiority sweeping in on the Charisian crown prince's galleons and crush them. But intellect shouted in warning, remembering Myrgyn's descriptions and sketches of the new Charisian artillery . . . and what those outnumbered, far more lightly gunned galleys had done with it.

But if I run, this entire campaign's been for nothing, he thought grimly. *The Prince won't like that—and neither will Clyntahn and the Council. And I can't really* know *how effective their broadsides are without fighting them. Besides, at this point I'm only guessing about his actual position, his strength—everything! Heading north might actually be the best way to* evade *him.*

"General signal," he said harshly, turning back to Myrgyn. "Enemy in sight to windward. Prepare for battle. New course north."

▼　　▼　　▼

"Fire!"

Dreadnought swept across the second galley column, and her broadside bellowed yet again. The range was a bit shorter this time, and this galley was still headed almost due south, directly away from her. The Emeraldian vessel's stern windows and ornate carving shattered as the broadside slammed home, and more guns began to thunder from the west as Sir Domynyk Staynair's squadron separated from Cayleb's. Staynair's ships began forging down to the south, paralleling the rest of *Black Prince*'s column as it clung to its original course, away from Cayleb, and the outgunned galleys' fired back far more slowly.

Cayleb's decision not to reduce sail was paying a huge dividend, so far, at least, Merlin reflected. The prince's experience off Armageddon Reef had convinced him that old-style guns had very little chance of inflicting crippling hits on his galleons' rigging. They simply couldn't fire fast enough, couldn't be pointed high enough. And so, he'd opted to come in under all plain sail, without brailling up even his courses until he'd come fully to grips with the enemy.

That gave him a clear speed advantage, and he and Staynair were using it ruthlessly.

▼　　▼　　▼

"Anything more from *Speedy*?" King Haarahld asked as he finished the climb to *Royal Charis'* aftercastle.

"Yes, Your Majesty!" young Midshipman Aplyn replied with a huge grin. "*Speedy*'s just repeated a signal from *Seagull*! 'My position one hundred miles north Darcos Island with twenty-eight galleons. Enemy bears south-by-southeast. Engaging. Cayleb.' "

The cheer which answered the eleven-year-old's announcement ought by rights to have deafened Hektor all the way back home in Manchyr, Haarahld thought.

"Thank you, Master Aplyn," he said quietly through that torrent of shouting voices, resting one hand on the boy's slight shoulder. "Thank you very much."

He squeezed the midshipman's shoulder for a moment, then turned to Tryvythyn.

"If they have any sense at all, they're going to turn and run for Silver Strait."

"They still have him outnumbered at least six-to-one, Your Majesty," Tryvythyn pointed out, and Haarahld snorted with harsh, fierce pride.

"Cayleb is here, Dynzyl, with the loss of only two galleons, and Duke Malikai isn't. What do you suppose that means happened to the *last* galley fleet that outnumbered my son six-to-one?"

"A point, Your Majesty," his flag captain conceded. "Definitely a point."

"And one that won't be lost on Black Water," Haarahld said, his expression and voice grimmer. "I wish it would be. I wish he were stupid enough to stand and fight, but he's smarter than that, and I think he has the moral courage to run if that's the only way to save what he can."

"That's my own assessment of him, Your Majesty," Tryvythyn agreed.

"Well, in that case, I think it's up to us to argue with him about his choice of courses." Haarahld gazed up at the masthead pendant and the royal standard of Charis, then turned back to his flag captain.

"General signal, Dynzyl. Form in columns of squadrons, course east."

▼   ▼   ▼

The Emeraldian galleys in Black Water's two western columns never saw his signal. There was too much smoke, and they had other things on their minds.

Staynair's squadron forged steadily down the flank of Earl Mahndyr's column, pounding savagely. None of the other nineteen ships were hammered quite as brutally as *Black Prince* had been, but that was mostly because they were able to strike their colors while they still had at least some men on their feet. Staynair closed to within fifty yards, artillery bellowing, dismasting his targets, wreaking carnage on their crowded oardecks, slaughtering the hapless soldiers and seamen packed together on their decks and aftercastles for boarding attacks that never came.

Staynair had no time to take formal possession of the surrendered ships, but there wasn't much need. While some of them might violate the terms of their surrender, or claim they'd never struck their colors in the first place, and escape, most of them were too shattered and broken to do much more than tend their wounded as best they could until someone did arrive to take custody of them. And if Staynair and Cayleb didn't have sufficient ships to gather them all in, King Haarahld certainly did.

While Staynair finished crushing that column, Cayleb continued steadily to the east, angling slightly southward. He crossed the tracks of the third and fourth columns, close enough to rake the last ship or two in each column as he passed.

"Black Water's trying to break north!" Merlin shouted in Cayleb's ear as *Dreadnought* poured fire into yet another victim. "He's got four columns—about ninety ships—turning north-northwest!"

Cayleb glanced at him, then closed his eyes, obviously summoning up a mental chart. He studied it from behind his eyelids, then nodded sharply.

"Captain Manthyr!"

▼   ▼   ▼

Duke Black Water paced savagely back and forth atop *Corisande*'s aftercastle. He knew it wasn't doing a thing to settle the nerves of his flagship's officers and crew, but standing still was beyond his power.

He paused every so often, glaring west and north. The signaling procedures he'd worked out for his combined fleet were more sophisticated than those of most navies, but far inferior to the ones Staynair, Seamount, and Merlin had developed. They simply weren't up to the task of keeping him accurately informed of what was happening, even assuming any of his squadron commanders and captains had truly known in the first place.

What he *did* know was that at least one column of Sharpfield's Chisholmian galleys had failed to see—or chosen to ignore—his signal to turn north. It was continuing steadily to the south, taking a tenth of his total strength with it.

And he also knew he could hear the thunder-grumble of massed cannon fire, distantly and intermittently, but growing stronger and steadier.

The turn to the north had reversed the order of sailing in the columns which had obeyed. *Corisande* had been leading her column on its original heading; now she found herself the last ship in line, which meant the admiral supposedly commanding the fleet was going to be one of the last to find out what in Shan-wei's name was happening.

"Your Grace."

Black Water whirled and found himself facing Captain Myrgyn.

"What?" he managed—somehow—not to snap.

"Your Grace, the masthead's reported gunfire and heavy smoke to the west and north. I sent Lieutenant Wynstyn to the crow's-nest for a better evaluation."

The flag captain indicated *Corisande*'s first lieutenant, standing tight-faced at his shoulder, and Black Water turned to Wynstyn.

"Well?" he demanded.

"Your Grace, I couldn't see very much to the west, but the smoke extends from about one point abaft the port beam to about one point forward of the starboard bow."

Wynstyn's voice was steady enough, but Black Water heard the control it took to keep it that way, and he couldn't blame the lieutenant.

"Thank you, Master Wynstyn," he said, after a moment, and turned to the aftercastle rail, leaning on it with both hands while he considered what Wynstyn had said.

If the lieutenant's observations were correct, Cayleb must, indeed, have arrived in almost the perfect position. With the current brisk breeze, the far greater sail area of his galleons gave him a marked speed advantage, and he must have split his ships into at least two forces. One of them was obviously sweeping south, and if Wynstyn's bearings were accurate, it must already have overtaken the head of Black Water's most western column, which meant it was probably smashing Mahndyr's *Triton* even now. Even worse than that, it was also in a position to start curling around to the east, directly across his original line of advance.

That was bad enough, but the smoke to the north was even more frightening. Cayleb was casting his net about Black Water's entire fleet, despite the fact that he must be hugely outnumbered. And if he was already so far east, he'd already cut across at least a third of Black Water's formation, probably more.

The duke's hands clenched into fists on the rail, and he swore with savage, silent venom.

From the speed with which Cayleb's galleons were advancing, it was clear no one was even slowing him down. Surprise, and the resultant panic, could explain a lot of that, possibly even all of it, yet Black Water was sickly certain the true reason was far simpler.

He remembered again what the Charisian galleys had done, and the rumble of the galleons' guns came to him on the wind once more.

If he continued north, he would be heading directly into those guns, and his own flagship would be one of the last of his vessels to engage. It seemed obvious that Cayleb's northern division had the speed to get across in front of him whatever he did, and he could count on the force to his west to sweep in astern of him, as well.

It was possible his galleys would be able to absorb the galleons' fire and still close with them for a conventional boarding melee, but he doubted it. Even if the galleons' firepower advantage was less than he feared, he could already sense the incipient panic of his personnel, even here, aboard his own flagship. It took courage and determination to close with an enemy under the best of circumstances. Closing through the sort of rapid, rolling broadsides he heard echoing down from the north would require far more determination than usual. Determination his badly shaken officers and men almost certainly no longer had.

But there were still the comparative numbers to consider. Even if it proved impossible to bring on the sort of close action which was his galleys' only hope of victory, Cayleb simply didn't have enough ships to take or destroy *all* of Black Water's fleet. Some of them would have to break through, if only because the galleons would be too busy with other victims to stop them. Yet Cayleb was in a position to smash every ship he *could* engage, and Black Water's own words to Myrgyn came back to whisper viciously in the back of his brain.

You wanted to kill as many as possible of Haarahld's trained seamen even if their ships were *out of date*, he thought. *Now Cayleb's in a position to do that to you, isn't he?*

He looked at the sun's position, then back to the northwest.

If he held his present course, he would be feeding his ships directly into Cayleb's guns by the quickest possible route. He'd be giving Cayleb a gift of time. Time to shatter and splinter Black Water's galleys as they closed on him. Time for him to pursue anyone who managed to break past him. Time for Haarahld to bring his own galleys sweeping up from the south behind Black Water.

But if the duke turned southeast himself, made directly for Silver Strait, he'd be headed *away* from both of Cayleb's divisions. A stern chase was always a long chase, he reminded himself, even if the pursuer did have a significant speed advantage, and if he could stay away from Cayleb until nightfall, then order his remaining ships to scatter and evade pursuit individually . . .

Yet turning away from Cayleb would give *Haarahld* an opportunity to intercept him, assuming the king reacted quickly enough. Still, Haarahld's galleys were a known quantity, and surely Black Water still had the strength to fight his way through anything Haarahld might manage to put into his path.

Besides, he told himself grimly, *his galleys aren't those Langhorne-damned galleons. The men are less likely to panic at the thought of taking him on.*

"Captain Myrgyn," he said, turning from the rail to face the flag captain.

▼   ▼   ▼

Merlin watched yet another ship stagger as *Dreadnought*'s first broadside ripped into her. The sight was becoming horrifically familiar, like some infinitely repeating act of butchery. The galley's sweeps flailed wildly as the round shot slammed home among her rowers, and bits and pieces of her hull flew lazily through the air until they hit the water in white feathers of spray.

He looked away, concentrating once again on the SNARC's overhead imagery, and stiffened. Then he turned quickly to Cayleb.

The prince stood beside Captain Manthyr, his young face bleak as he watched his flagship's guns slaughtering yet another crew.

"Cayleb."

Cayleb turned at the sound of his name, and Merlin leaned closer.

"Black Water's changed his mind," he said, speaking as quietly as he could and still be heard. "He's turning his columns back around, heading southeast."

"Silver Strait," Cayleb said flatly.

"Exactly," Merlin agreed, and his expression was grim. Cayleb raised an eyebrow as his tone registered, and Merlin grimaced.

"Your father obviously anticipated what Black Water might do. He's already heading to cut them off short of the strait."

Cayleb's eyes widened, then they narrowed in comprehension, and he sucked in a deep breath and nodded. Not in approval, or even in simple comprehension of what Merlin had just told him. He nodded in decision and turned sharply to his flag captain.

"Captain Manthyr, we'll alter course to the south, if you please. General signal: engage the enemy more closely."

▼   ▼   ▼

"Your Grace, the Charisian galleys are standing directly into our path," Captain Myrgyn said harshly.

Black Water looked up from the chart before him. The flag captain stood in the chartroom door, and his expression was concerned.

The duke didn't blame him. The fleet's formation had become badly disordered when he turned it around yet again. The columns were still sorting themselves out, or attempting to, although the Chisholmian units didn't seem to be trying all that hard to obey his orders. Several of them seemed to have creatively

misconstrued—or simply ignored—his signals, depriving him of still more desperately needed strength. He was scarcely in the best possible condition for a
general engagement with Haarahld's fleet, and he'd hoped to break past the king
before Haarahld realized what he was about.

Obviously, that wasn't going to happen.

Still, he had at least a hundred galleys still under his own command, and
Haarahld had only seventy.

"Let's go on deck," he said quietly to Myrgyn, and the flag captain stood
aside, then followed him out of the chartroom.

The duke blinked in the bright sunlight. It was just past noon. The long,
running battle had raged for over eight hours now, and his jaw tightened as he
heard the continuing rumble of artillery from astern. It seemed to be growing
louder, and he smiled grimly. Cayleb couldn't know exactly what his father was
doing, but it was evident that the Charisian crown prince understood the importance of staying close on a fleeing enemy's heels.

Black Water looked up at the sky, then forward, to where a forest of galley
masts and sails loomed almost directly ahead. Even as he watched, sails were being furled and yards were being lowered, and he bared his teeth as he recognized
the traditional challenge to a fight to the finish.

Part of him wanted nothing more than to give Haarahld exactly that. But if
he did, Cayleb would close in from behind, and by this time, the Charisian galleys and galleons combined would actually outnumber the ships actually still under Black Water's command. His earlier huge numerical advantage had
evaporated, and a general engagement, especially with those galleons added to the
fray, could result only in his defeat.

"We'll hold our course, Captain Myrgyn," he said calmly. "Don't reduce sail."

▼   ▼   ▼

"They're going to try to break right past us, Your Majesty," Captain Tryvythyn said.

"What they *try* to do and what they actually do may turn out to be two different things, Dynzyl," Haarahld said calmly.

The king stood on *Royal Charis'* aftercastle, watching the clutter of enemy
galleys bearing down upon his own fleet. Unlike the four long, disordered lines
of Black Water's fleet, Haarahld's was formed into a dozen shorter, more compact
columns of a single squadron each, and despite himself, the king felt something
almost like satisfaction.

He was far too intelligent not to recognize the enormous advantages Merlin's
changes had conferred upon his navy. But the Royal Charisian Navy and the ferocity and deadly skill of the Charisian Marines had made themselves the terror
of their enemies long before Merlin and his new artillery ever came along. This
would be a battle in the *old* style, possibly the last one, and Haarahld had grown
up in the old school.

His flagship led her own squadron, but the King of Charis had no business in the first, crushing embrace of battle. Especially not of the sort of battle Charisian galleys fought.

"General signal, Dynzyl," he said as Black Water's fleeing squadron's bore down upon him. "Close action."

▼   ▼   ▼

Black Water's eastern column had drawn well ahead of the others. Now its lead galleys crunched into the Charisian formation like a battering ram.

That was what it might have looked like to the uninformed observer, at least. But what actually happened was that the Charisian squadrons swarmed forward like krakens closing on a pod of narwhales.

Traditional Charisian naval tactics were built uncompromisingly on ferocity and speed. Charisian Marines knew they were the finest naval infantry—the only *professional* naval infantry—in the world, and Charisian squadron commanders were trained to bring their ships slashing in on any opponent as a unit.

Admiral Lock Island's flagship led the first assault, crashing alongside one of Black Water's Corisandians. *Tellesberg*'s port oars lifted and swung inboard with machinelike precision as Lock Island's flag captain smashed his ship's side into the smaller, more lightly built galley *Foam* like a battering ram.

Foam's mast snapped at the impact, thundering down across her deck. Hull seams started, spurting water, and *Tellesberg*'s port guns fired into the mass of fallen cordage and canvas as she ground down *Foam*'s side. Lock Island's flagship swung clear, her sweeps snapped back out, and she gathered fresh momentum as she hurtled down on *Foam*'s consort *Halberd*. Behind *Tellesberg*, HMS *Battleaxe* hammered *Foam* with her own artillery, then launched herself at the Corisandian *Warrior*.

Tellesberg slammed into *Halberd* almost as violently as she'd collided with *Foam*. *Halberd*'s mast didn't quite come down, but the smaller, lighter galley staggered under the impact, and dozens of grappling irons arced out from the Charisian ship. They bit into *Halberd*'s bulwarks, and the first Charisian Marines swarmed across onto the Corisandian's deck behind the high, quavering howl of their war cry. No one who'd survived hearing that sound ever forgot it, and the well earned terror of the Royal Charisian Marines was borne upon its wings.

Most of the new muskets and bayonets had gone to Cayleb's galleons, but *Tellesberg*'s Marines didn't seem to mind. They swept across *Halberd* in a tidal wave whose very ferocity disguised its intense discipline and training. Boarding pikes stabbed, cutlasses and boarding axes chopped, and the first rush carried *Halberd*'s entire waist.

But then *Halberd*'s company rallied. Matchlocks and "wolves" fired down into the melee from aftercastle and forecastle, killing and wounding dozens of the Marines. Corisandian soldiers counter-charged with the power of desperation, slamming into the boarders violently enough to throw even Charisians back on their heels.

For a few minutes, the tide of combat swirled back and forth, first this way, then that, as men hacked at one another in a frenzy of destruction and slaughter. Then *Tellesberg*'s consort *Sword of Tirian* came thundering along *Halberd*'s other side, and a fresh wave of Charisian Marines overwhelmed the defenders.

▼   ▼   ▼

Duke Black Water watched bleakly as his fleeing galleys merged with their Charisian opponents.

It wasn't working. His jaw muscles ached as he recognized that. His own column, the westernmost of them all, had fallen perhaps a mile and a half behind the others, but he could see what was happening. The tangle of colliding galleys as the Charisians flung themselves bodily upon the ships of his first two columns was simply too thick for him to cut his way through them. As the second and third and fourth galleys in each long, unwieldy column caught up with the leaders, they were unable—or, in some cases, unwilling—to avoid the knots of vessels which were already grappled together. Some of them tried to, but there always seemed to be another compact Charisian column waiting, another Charisian galley perfectly placed to crash alongside them, grapple them, add them to the steadily growing barricade of timber, stabbing steel, and blood. It was like watching autumn leaves swirl down a racing stream until they encountered a fallen branch and, suddenly, found themselves piling up, heaping together into a solid mass.

And even as Haarahld's fleet threw itself in front of him, he heard Cayleb's guns growing louder and louder behind him as the galleons began savaging the rearmost ships of his own column.

He glared at the tangle of ships, fallen masts, smoke, banners, and wreckage, and saw the complete and total failure of his entire campaign. But then, to one side of the main engagement, he saw a single Charisian squadron, and his eyes flamed as he recognized the banner it flew.

The way his column had fallen a little behind the others was what had allowed Cayleb to get at its rearmost units. But it also meant his flagship, and the galleys behind it, hadn't yet been swept into the general melee.

Most of Haarahld's galleys *had*, however, and Black Water's lips drew back from his teeth. He grabbed Captain Myrgyn's shoulder and pointed at the royal standard of Charis.

"*There!*" he snarled. "There's your target, Kehvyn!"

▼   ▼   ▼

Captain Tryvythyn saw the line of Corisandian galleys sweeping down upon *Royal Charis*. There were at least fifteen ships in the column—he couldn't be certain of the exact number; there was too much smoke—and there was no question that they'd recognized the royal standard.

The rest of the flagship's squadron saw the enemy almost as soon as he did, and oarmasters' drums went to a more urgent tempo as the other five galleys swept forward, charging around *Royal Charis* to intercept the attack. Tryvythyn glanced at his king and half-opened his mouth, but Haarahld only looked back steadily, and the flag captain closed it once more.

"Better," Haarahld said with a thin smile, then nodded at the oncoming Corisandians. "If these people get past us, there's no one left to stop them."

"I realize that, Your Majesty," Tryvythyn said. "But I hope you'll forgive me for saying that I think you're worth more to Charis then all of those ships put together."

"I appreciate the compliment, Dynzyl. But no one man is essential, and victory *is*. And not just victory, either. This war's only just beginning, whatever happens here today, and our ability to control the sea is the only thing which may let us survive. We need a victory so complete, so crushing, the next admiral to think about fighting us will be half-defeated in his own mind before he ever leaves port. So devastating *our* men will know they can do *anything*, defeat anyone, no matter what the odds. And we need an example that will make them willing to *fight* at any odds. That's more important than the life of any one man—even a king. Do you understand me?"

Tryvythyn looked into his king's eyes for a moment, and then he bowed.

"Yes, Your Majesty," he said steadily. "I understand."

▼   ▼   ▼

Dreadnought overtook another galley.

Devastation had fallen astern, but *Destruction* had out sailed her and forged up almost abreast of the fleet flagship, and the two of them had spread further apart. *Destruction* lay further to the east than *Dreadnought*, passing down the galley *Scimitar*'s port side, and her starboard guns thundered. *Dreadnought* was still a ship's length ahead of her consort, and her port guns smashed in the galley's *starboard* side. A few of her shots missed, two of them whipping across *Destruction*'s bows at dangerously close range, but the concentrated fire, crashing in on *Scimitar* simultaneously from both sides, was devastating.

Cayleb glared at the crippled hulk as the Corisandian flag came down. *Dreadnought*'s gunners were too exhausted to raise a cheer this time, and ammunition was getting low. The gunner was almost out of made-up cartridges, and Captain Manthyr had detailed a long chain of Marines to pass more round shot up from the shot lockers. Despite that, the crown prince already knew Charis had won a crushing victory this day. He knew that, yet he fretted inside like a caged slash lizard as Manthyr tried to wring still more speed out of the flagship.

Cayleb's own squadron—more than a little disordered as the faster ships, like

Destruction, overtook and passed the slower ones in front of them, but still intact—was closing rapidly on Duke Black Water's fugitives. To the north, Staynair had wreaked dreadful havoc upon the western half of Black Water's original fleet, and over twenty Chisholmian galleys had surrendered with only minimal resistance. At least a few determined Emeraldian and Corisandian captains had managed to evade both squadrons of Cayleb's galleons in the smoke and confusion and break north successfully. There weren't more than a double handful of them, however, and at least two-thirds of the ships still with Black Water were locked in melee with the galleys of his father's fleet.

Only thirty or so Corisandians still had any hope of escape. They were trying to break around the western edge of the huge, confused hand-to-hand fight raging between their consorts and the main body of the king's fleet. Cayleb and his squadron were on their heels, already engaging their rearmost units, but some of them might yet win free.

Except for the six Charisian galleys steering to meet them head-on.

▼   ▼   ▼

Black Water looked astern. He could see the topgallants of the nearest galleons now, looming above the smoke. They were still well astern, but they were coming up fast, and there was plenty of daylight left.

His mouth was a hard, thin line as he glanced at Captain Myrgyn and he saw the same knowledge in the flag captain's eyes.

"At least we can take a few more of them with us," the duke said grimly, and Myrgyn nodded.

▼   ▼   ▼

HMS *Queen Zhessyka* charged to meet *Corisande* as Black Water's flagship led the attack. *Queen Zhessyka*'s captain judged relative positions and motion carefully, steering to lay his ship hard alongside the Corisandian flagship, but Captain Myrgyn stood tensely beside his helmsman, judging those same motions with equal care.

The two ships came together with a closing speed of at least fifteen knots, with *Queen Zhessyka* angling slightly to leeward, and Myrgyn showed his teeth in a thin little smile. He watched the Charisian unwaveringly, waiting for the moment when the other galley shipped its port oars. That would be the instant when her captain committed, and Myrgyn waited . . . waited . . . waited . . .

"*Now!*" he barked, and his helmsman put his helm a-lee.

Corisande turned sharply—not downwind, into the Charisian, but *upwind*, away from her. *Queen Zhessyka* tried to compensate, following her around, but the Charisian captain had expected an opponent under sail to turn with the wind, not against it. He still managed a glancing contact with *Corisande*'s port quarter, and at least a dozen grappling irons slammed across the gap. But the momentum of two thousand-plus tons of wooden galleys, moving in different directions, snapped the irons' lines like thread.

Corisande staggered and timbers screamed as her quarter gallery was smashed in, and twenty-five feet of the aftercastle's bulwark went with it. Five of the army troopers put aboard as marines were killed, crushed by the same impact which demolished the bulwark, and at least another half-dozen crewmen were injured. Two planks were stove in below the waterline, and water began gushing into her hold. But her mast held, she was still underway, and Myrgyn's crisp orders brought her quickly back under control.

She was past the rest of *Royal Charis*'s squadron, and King Haarahld's flagship lay almost dead ahead, rushing to meet her.

▼   ▼   ▼

Haarahld watched the other five galleys of his squadron as the hammer blow came down. *Corisande* might have gotten past *Queen Zhessyka*, but the next seven galleys in line were all intercepted.

HMS *Rock Shoal Bay* sideswiped the galley behind *Corisande*, crashing into her hard enough to bring down her mast, then staggered directly across the path of *Confederate*, the third ship in Black Water's line. Galleys might no longer mount rams, but *Confederate*'s bows slammed into *Rock Shoal Bay* like an ax, cutting a third of the way through the bigger Charisian ship in a dreadful rending, tearing crunch of shattered timbers. Mortally wounded, *Rock Shoal Bay* began to fill rapidly, leaning against her opponent and trapping *Confederate*'s bow in the wound it had torn. At least thirty of *Rock Shoal Bay*'s rowers were killed by the impact, and dozens more of them were injured, many hideously. Their companions struggled to pull them out of the in-rushing water as their ship began to settle, but the Charisian gunners fired a deadly salvo of grapeshot down the length of *Confederate*'s deck, and *Rock Shoal Bay*'s howling Marines charged across onto the other ship in an unstoppable flood of edged, thrusting steel.

Queen Zhessyka recovered way quickly after her grazing collision with *Corisande* and swerved to meet the oncoming *Harpoon*. This time, *Queen Zhessyka* made no mistake, turning neatly onto the same heading as her intended victim and allowing *Harpoon* to run up alongside *her*. Grappling irons flew a second time, and this time the two ships were headed in the same direction. They ground together, timbers groaning and shuddering under the impact, and another tide of Charisian Marines streamed across onto *Harpoon*'s decks.

The other three Charisian galleys—*Sand Island*, *Margaret's Land*, and *King Tymythy*—picked their own opponents with care. They each crashed into their chosen victim, deliberately fouling the enemy column's line of advance, and at least two more Corisandian ships plowed into the sudden roadblock which had materialized before them.

But *Corisande* was already past them, and eighteen more galleys were streaming down upon them.

▼   ▼   ▼

This time, *Corisande*'s mast went down.

Captain Myrgyn's ship slammed alongside *Royal Charis* with a rending, grinding shriek of timbers. Grappling irons flew in both directions; matchlocks, wolves, and cannon thundered; and men screamed and died. Haarahld's flagship had replaced her original broadside falcons with carronades, and the carnage they wreaked splashed *Corisande*'s decks with blood. *Royal Charis*' Marines had been issued the new flintlocks, as well, and a deadly volley added its share to the butchery.

For a moment, it looked as if the battle had been decided in that single cataclysmic moment, but then Black Water leapt up onto the aftercastle bulwark, drawn sword flashing in his hand.

"*After me, lads!*" he bellowed, and a savage roar of anger went up from *Corisande*, overpowering even the screams of the wounded.

The duke leapt across the gap between the two ships, landing all alone in an open spot where one of *Corisande*'s own guns had heaped the Charisians in a mangled pile of bodies. His boots slipped on the blood-slick deck, and he sprawled backward, which undoubtedly saved his life. The closest Charisian Marines were still turning towards him when the rush of additional boarders from *Corisande* swept over him.

His surviving soldiers and seamen abandoned their own ship, hurling themselves across onto Haarahld's flagship, half-crazed with terror, desperation, and a fiery determination to reach the man whose standard *Royal Charis* flew. They slammed into the defenders like a human tidal wave, and even Charisian Marines were forced to give ground before such fury.

The attackers drove clear across *Royal Charis*' waist, then most of them turned aft, fighting their way towards the aftercastle, while the remainder tried to hold off the Marines counterattacking from the forecastle.

The battle swayed desperately back and forth for several endless minutes, but *Corisande*'s people had taken too many casualties before they ever closed, and Charisian Marines were simply the best in the world at this sort of fight. They regained the momentum Black Water's reckless gallantry and courage had won and drove the Corisandians steadily back.

And then, suddenly, the Corisandian galley *Sea Crest* came crashing in on *Corisande*'s disengaged side, and a fresh tide of attackers flooded across Black Water's flagship, using her like a bridge, and hurled themselves into the fray.

▼   ▼   ▼

Cayleb Ahrmahk's face was a mask of grim, savage determination as *Dreadnought* drove into the rear of the disintegrating Corisandian column. He could see the tangled knot of intermixed Charisian and Corisandian galleys coming up quickly on *Dreadnought*'s port bow, but at least three more enemy ships had evaded the massed melee. They were charging down on his father's flagship, already engaged with two opponents.

There was no need for him to exhort Captain Manthyr to greater efforts. That was Cayleb's father up there, but it was also Gwylym Manthyr's king, and Merlin, standing behind the two of them, could almost physically feel Manthyr leaning forward, as if to add his own weight to the wind driving his ship.

Yet they could only move so quickly, and *Dreadnought*'s guns blazed on either broadside. The only way to reach *Royal Charis* was directly through the Corisandian ships in front of them, and Manthyr took his galleon in among them under full sail, as if she'd been a ten-meter sloop at a racing regatta back on Old Earth.

Guns fired at ranges as low as twenty yards. Flintlocks barked, swivels banged from the fighting tops, and return fire came back from Corisandian wolves, matchlocks, and cannon.

At that range, even the slow-firing Corisandian artillery could inflict dreadful wounds, and one of *Dreadnought*'s maindeck guns took a round shot almost directly on its muzzle. The entire gun and carriage flew backward, the gun tube flipping up like a terrestrial dolphin standing on its tail. Then it crashed down, like a two-ton hammer, crushing the members of its crew who hadn't been killed outright by the round shot into gruel.

A section of hammock nettings flew apart as a charge of grapeshot blew through the tightly rolled hammocks stowed there to stop bullets and splinters. Those hammocks had never been intended to stop grapeshot, though, and the deadly missiles killed six Marines and three seamen and wounded five others. Screams told of other casualties, and a round shot chewed a splinter-fringed bite out of the mainmast, but *Dreadnought*'s gunners ignored the carnage around them. It wasn't simply courage, nor training—it was also exhaustion. They'd been reduced to automatons, so focused on what they were doing that nothing else was really quite real.

▼   ▼   ▼

"Fall back! *Fall back to the aftercastle!*"

Captain Tryvythyn's desperate order cut through the chaos as yet another Corisandian galley, the *Doomwhale*, surged alongside *Royal Charis*. His ship was bigger than any of its opponents, with a larger crew and more Marines, but no less than five of the Corisandians had managed to get to grips with him.

The enemy had completely overwhelmed the defenders of *Royal Charis*' forward third. Perhaps half his Marines and a quarter of his seamen were still on their feet aft of the forward hatch, but they were being driven back, step by bloody step, by an ever mounting flood of enemies. Dynzyl Tryvythyn watched their stubborn retreat, and his eyes were desperate. Not with fear for himself, but for the king who stood behind him.

"Hold the ladders!" he shouted. "Hold—"

A musket ball from one of *Doomwhale's* embarked musketeers struck him at the base of the throat. It flung him backwards, and he went down, choking on his own blood as the boots of desperately fighting men stamped all about him.

The King, he thought. *The King.*

And then he died.

▼   ▼   ▼

Dreadnought passed down the leeward side of another galley. Her guns savaged the fresh target, and she shuddered as more shots slammed back in reply. Her fore topgallant mast quivered as its shrouds were shot away, then toppled slowly forward to hang like a broken cross, canvas billowing. But then she was past her enemies, her gunports streaming smoke, as she bore down on the galleys grappled to *Royal Charis* at last.

"Lay us alongside!" Cayleb snapped, drawing the sword Merlin had given him, and his eyes blazed coldly.

▼   ▼   ▼

Duke Black Water stared about wildly. The crews of his galleys were hopelessly intermixed. All unit organization had disappeared into the indescribable confusion of savage hand-to-hand combat, but he found himself briefly behind the battle driving steadily aft.

He didn't understand why he was still alive. His breastplate was battered and scarred from blows he scarcely remembered, and his sword was red to the hilt with the blood of men he hardly recalled killing. He could hear the ongoing thunder of artillery even over the screams and shouts around him, and as he turned to look up into the north, he saw Cayleb's galleons bursting out of the smoke and confusion at last.

They hadn't fought their way through his entire fleet unscathed. He saw missing topmasts and sails pocked and torn by splinters and round shot, saw broken rigging blowing on the wind, saw shot holes in bulwarks and sides, saw bodies lying across hammock nettings and hanging in their fighting tops. But they were still there, still intact, their gunports still streaming smoke, and he bared his teeth in hatred.

He snarled, then began pushing his way through the men about him, elbowing them aside as he forced his way towards *Royal Charis'* beleaguered aftercastle.

▼   ▼   ▼

A musket ball screamed off Haarahld Ahrmahk's breastplate as he leaned on the half-pike for support with his left hand. He grunted and staggered under the rib-snapping impact, but the ball whined away, leaving not even a dent, only a smear of lead, on Merlin's gift to mark its passing. He held his feet, and his right hand drove his sword into the chest of a Corisandian seaman trying to claw his way up the ladder from the maindeck. The man fell back with a bubbling scream, blood spraying from his mouth and nose, and Haarahld grunted at the fresh stab of pain from his bad knee as he recovered.

Sergeant Gahrdaner dropped his own opponent with a two-handed blow and then shoved the king unceremoniously aside, taking his place at the head of the ladder. Haarahld grimaced, but he knew better than to argue, and he fell back, panting heavily as he watched his bodyguard's back.

The aftercastle was an isolated island of resistance, and it couldn't hold much longer. Haarahld hadn't seen Tryvythyn die, but he'd seen the captain's body, along with those of at least three of *Royal Charis*' lieutenants. Midshipman Marshyl was down, as well, lying across the body of Major Byrk, the commander of the flagship's Marines. Gahrdaner was the last of Haarahld's guardsmen still on his feet, and the knot of defenders around the king was contracting steadily under the unremitting savagery of their attackers.

Midshipman Aplyn stood beside him, his face pale and tight with terror. Yet the boy's eyes were determined, and he clutched a seaman's cutlass in both hands, like a two-handed sword. He hovered there, as if trapped between the compulsion to fling himself forward and the desperate need to live, and Haarahld released his grip on the half-pike to grip the boy's shoulder, instead.

Aplyn jerked as if he'd just been stabbed, then whipped around to look up at his king.

"Stay with me, Master Aplyn," Haarahld said. "We'll have work enough soon."

▼   ▼   ▼

Dreadnought smashed into the tangle of grappled galleys. Gwylym Manthyr wasn't worrying about damage to his ship—not now. He refused to reduce sail until the very last moment, and wood splintered and screamed as he drove his ship squarely into *Doomwhale*'s starboard side

Dreadnought's bowsprit loomed over the galley's waist, driving forward until her jibbom shattered against *Royal Charis*' taller side. Her cutwater sliced into *Doomwhale*'s hull, crushing timbers and frames. Her entire foremast, already weakened by the topgallant mast's fall and two other hits, just above deck level, toppled forward, crashing across her target in an avalanche of shattered wood, torn cordage, and canvas. The Marines and seamen in the foremast fighting top went with it, and the main topgallant mast and topmast came toppling down, as well.

Men stumbled, fell, went to their knees, as the impact slammed through both ships. Others were crushed by the falling masts. But then every one of *Dreadnought*'s surviving Marines was back on his feet. They stormed forward, dodging through the broken spars and rigging, muskets firing, and crashed into the backs of Corisandian boarders still pushing towards *Royal Charis*. Gleaming bayonets thrust savagely, then withdrew, shining red, and Marine boots trampled the bodies underfoot as they drove furiously onward.

Even as the Marines charged, Merlin went bounding forward along the starboard hammock nettings, katana in one hand, wakazashi in the other. Cayleb, Ahrnahld Falkhan, and the prince's other bodyguards charged on his heels, but they were merely human, and he left them far behind.

Most of the wreckage had gone to port, and the two or three seamen who got in his way might as well have stood in the path of a charging dragon. They went flying as he slammed past them, and then he launched himself in a prodigious leap across at least twenty-five feet of trapped water, churning in the triangle between the two locked hulls.

He landed all alone on *Doomwhale*'s deck amid a solid mass of Corisandians. Three of them had seen him coming and managed to turn around in time to face him . . . which made them the first to die.

▼   ▼   ▼

Sergeant Gahrdaner went down with a pikehead in his thigh. He pitched forward to the maindeck, and the swords and boarding axes were waiting as he fell.

Howling Corisandians stormed up the ladder he'd held, and the remaining handful of Charisians fell back to the after rail, forming a final, desperate ring around their king. For a fleeting instant, there was a gap between them and their enemies as the Corisandians funneled up the two ladders they'd finally taken.

Haarahld had lost his helmet somewhere along the way, and the wind was cold on his sweat-soaked hair. He and Midshipman Aplyn were the only officers still on their feet, and he heard his last defenders' harsh, gasping exhaustion. He looked at their enemies, and for a moment, he considered yielding to save his men's lives. But then he saw the madness in the Corisandians' eyes. They were in the grip of the killing rage which had brought them this far; even if they realized he was trying to offer his surrender, they would probably refuse to accept it.

I ought to come up with something noble to say. The thought flashed through his brain, and to his own amazement, he actually chuckled. Aplyn heard it and glanced up at him, and Haarahld smiled down at the white-faced boy.

"Never mind, Master Aplyn," he said, almost gently. "I'll explain later."

And then the Corisandians charged.

▼   ▼   ▼

Merlin Athrawes crossed *Doomwhale* in an explosion of bodies, then vaulted up onto *Royal Charis'* deck and charged aft, killing as he came.

The Corisandians who found themselves in his path had no concept of what they faced. Very few of them had time to realize that they didn't.

He was, quite literally, a killing machine, a whirling vortex of impossibly sharp steel driven by the strength of ten mortal men. His blades cut through flesh, armor, pike shafts, and cutlasses, and no one could face him and live. Bodies and pieces of bodies flew away from him in spraying patterns of blood and severed limbs, and he went through his enemies like an avalanche, more hampered by their corpses than by their weapons.

But there were hundreds of those enemies between him and *Royal Charis'* aftercastle.

▼　　▼　　▼

Cayleb couldn't follow Merlin's leap. No one could have, but he and his bodyguards continued their own charge along the hammock nettings. Faircaster managed to get in front of the prince somehow, and the burly Marine led the way onto *Doomwhale*. The Marines already aboard the galley recognized the prince and his bodyguards, and they redoubled their efforts, fighting to stay between him and his enemies.

They failed.

Cayleb, Faircaster, and Ahrnahld Falkhan were the point of the Charisian wedge hammering its way across *Doomwhale* to *Royal Charis*, and the sword Merlin had called "Excalibur" flashed in the crown prince's hand as it tasted blood for the first time.

▼　　▼　　▼

The Corisandians hit the thin ring of Marines and seamen protecting Haarahld. For a few incredible moments, the defendeus held, throwing back their enemies. But then one or two of them went down, and Corisandians flooded through the gaps.

The Charisians gave ground. They had to. They broke up into small knots, fighting back to back, dying, still trying desperately to protect the king.

Haarahld braced himself against the after rail, bad knee afire with the anguish of supporting his weight, and his sword hissed. He cut down an attacking seaman, then grunted under a hammer-blow impact as a Corisandian soldier swung the spiked-beak back of a boarding ax into his chest with both hands. That awl-like spike was specifically designed to punch through armor, but it rebounded, leaving his breastplate unmarked, and the Corisandian gawked in disbelief as Haarahld's sword drove through his throat.

He fell aside, and for a moment, there was a gap in front of the king. He looked up and saw a Corisandian with a steel-bowed arbalest. Somehow, the man had actually managed to respan the weapon before he leapt up onto the aftercastle bulwark. Now he aimed directly at Haarahld.

"*Your Majesty!*"

Hektor Aplyn had seen the arbalest as well. Before Haarahld could move, the boy had flung himself in front of him, offering his own body to protect his king.

"*No!*" Haarahld shouted. He released the after rail, his left hand darted out and caught the back of Aplyn's tunic, and he whirled, yanking the midshipman back and spinning to interpose the backplate of his cuirass.

The arbalest bolt struck him squarely in the back and screamed aside, baffled by the battle steel plate. He felt its hammering impact, then gasped with pain as something else bit into his right thigh, just above the knee.

At least it's not the good leg!

The thought flashed through his mind as he turned back towards the fight. The Corisandian seaman who'd wounded him drew back his boarding pike with a snarl, shortening for another thrust, but Aplyn hurled himself past Haarahld with a sob. The slightly built boy darted in below the pike, driving his cutlass with both hands, and the Corisandian screamed as the blade opened his belly.

He collapsed, clutching at the mortal wound, and Aplyn staggered back beside the king.

They were the only two Charisians still on their feet, and Haarahld thrust desperately into the chest of a seaman coming at Aplyn from the right, even as the sobbing midshipman slashed at another Corisandian threatening the king from his left. The boy cried out as a sword cut into his left shoulder. He nearly fell, but he kept his feet, still slashing with the heavy cutlass. A sword cut bounced off Haarahld's mail sleeve, and the king slashed that seaman aside, as well, yet he felt himself weakening as blood pumped down his right leg.

▼   ▼   ▼

Some instinct warned the Corisandian soldier at the top of *Royal Charis'* starboard aftercastle ladder. His head turned, and he had one instant to gape at the blood-soaked apparition which had suddenly vaulted all the way from the deck below to the bulwark beside him. Then he died as a battle steel katana went through his neck in a fan of blood.

"*Charis!*"

Merlin's deep voice boomed the battle cry, cutting through all of the other noises, and then he was onto the aftercastle itself. One or two of the men facing him managed to launch defensive blows of their own. He ignored them, letting them rebound from his armor as he hacked his way towards the king.

"*Charis!*"

He carved a corridor of bodies through the Corisandians, sapphire eyes merciless, katana and wakazashi trailing sprays of blood, and panic spread from him like a plague.

And then, somehow, he was through the final barrier between him and Haarahld. He whirled, facing back the way he'd come, and for a long, breathless moment, not one of the forty or fifty Corisandians still on the aftercastle dared to attack.

Behind him, Haarahld went to his left knee, sword drooping, and Aplyn thrust himself in front of the king.

"Take him, you fools!" a voice shouted, and the Duke of Black Water shouldered through the frozen ranks of his surviving boarders.

His armor was hacked and battered, and he bled from half a dozen shallow cuts of his own. His sword's point dribbled tears of blood, and his eye were mad, but his hoarse voice crackled with passion.

"*Take him!*" he bellowed again, and charged.

His men howled and followed him, hammering straight at Merlin, and Merlin met them with a storm of steel. He never moved. His feet might have been bolted to the bloody planking, and his eyes never blinked.

Black Water had one instant to realize he faced something totally beyond his experience, and then he, too, went down under Merlin's merciless steel. At least a dozen more of his men fell to the same blades. Most of them never even had the chance to scream. They were like a stream of water, hurling itself against a boulder only to splash from its unyielding strength.

No man could enter Merlin's reach and live, and after ten shrieking seconds of slaughter, the survivors drew back in terror from the breastwork of bodies he'd built before the wounded King of Charis.

▼   ▼   ▼

Hektor Aplyn felt something touch the back of his leg.

He whirled, cutlass raised, then froze. It had been the king's hand, and Aplyn's eyes widened in horror as he saw the steadily spreading pool of blood around him.

"Your Majesty!"

The boy fell to his knees, eyes searching frantically for the king's wound, but Haarahld shook his head. The motion was terrifyingly weak.

"I'm sorry, Your Majesty," the bleeding young midshipman sobbed. "*I'm sorry!* You shouldn't have pulled me out of the way!"

"Nonsense," the king said. His voice was weak as his life flowed out of him with the blood still pumping from the deep wound in his thigh. "It's a king's duty to die for his subjects, Master Aplyn."

"*No!*" Aplyn shook his head.

"Yes," Haarahld said. It was amazing, a distant corner of his mind thought. There was no pain anymore, not even from his knee. Not physical pain, at any rate, and he reached out an arm which had become impossibly heavy and put it around the weeping boy rocking on his knees beside him. About the child who had become so important to him . . . and for whom he might yet do one more service, as a king should.

"Yes," he whispered, leaning forward until his forehead touched Aplyn's. "Yes, it is. And it's a subject's duty to serve his new king, Hektor. Can you do that for me?"

"Yes," the boy whispered back through his tears. "Yes, Your Majesty."

"It's been . . . an honor . . . Master Aplyn," Haarahld Ahrmahk murmured, and then his eyes closed. He slumped forward against Aplyn, and the boy wrapped his arms around him, put his face down on his armored shoulder, and sobbed.

APRIL, YEAR OF GOD 892

✦

King Gorjah III's expression was stony as Edymynd Rustmyn, the Baron of Stonekeep, stepped into the council chamber.

"You sent for me, Your Majesty?" Stonekeep said calmly, keeping his face expressionless, despite the other two men already waiting with the king. Baron White Ford sat on Gorjah's left, but the Earl of Thirsk sat to the king's right, in the place of honor.

"Yes, I did," Gorjah said, and his voice was much colder than Stonekeep's had been. "Be seated."

The king pointed at the chair at the far end of the council table, and the tall, silver-haired Stonekeep seated himself in it, then cocked his head interrogatively.

"How may I serve you, Your Majesty?" he asked.

Gorjah glowered at the man who was both his first councillor and the man in charge of his own spies. Under normal circumstances, Stonekeep was one of the very few men who enjoyed the king's near total confidence, which made him far too valuable to sacrifice. But these circumstances were far from normal, and Gorjah wondered just how clearly the baron understood that.

"I've just been discussing certain matters with Earl Thirsk," the king said coolly. "In particular, he's been kind enough to share with me what Prince Cayleb had to say to him. Just before he put him ashore on Armageddon Reef."

Stonekeep simply nodded silently, but his eyes were intent. Thirsk's arrival in Tranjyr was hardly a secret from him, although the rest of the court had yet to discover it. King Gorjah's senior councillors had known for almost two five-days, ever since White Ford's *King Gorjah II* had limped back into port, that Cayleb had managed to intercept the combined fleet off Armageddon Reef with disastrous consequences. Stonekeep had argued successfully in favor of keeping that news to themselves until they knew precisely *how* disastrous those consequences might have been.

Apparently, they'd been even more disastrous than Stonekeep had feared from White Ford's initial reports.

"Cayleb," Gorjah continued, pronouncing the name as if it were a curse, "took and destroyed every ship remaining under Earl Thirsk's command. It would seem the six galleys which have so far returned, and the single store ship upon which Earl Thirsk sailed to Tranjyr, are the only survivors of the entire combined fleet."

This time, despite all of Stonekeep's formidable self-control, he blanched.

"The question which exercises my mind at this particular moment," the king said, "is precisely how Cayleb and Haarahld managed this miraculous interception of theirs. Would you have any thoughts on that subject, Edymynd?"

White Ford simply looked at the first councilor thoughtfully, but Thirsk's eyes could have bored holes in a block of stone. Which, coupled with the fact that the Dohlaran was present at all for what was becoming an increasingly unpleasant conversation, warned Stonekeep that things were about to get ugly. Or, perhaps, *more* ugly.

"Your Majesty," he said reasonably, "I'm not a naval man. The deployment and utilization of fleets is far beyond my own area of competence. I'm sure Baron White Ford or Earl Thirsk is far better qualified than I am to suggest answers to your question."

A slight flicker in White Ford's eyes, and the tightening of Thirsk's mouth, suggested he might have chosen a better response.

"Interestingly enough," Gorjah said, smiling thinly, "Gahvyn, the Earl, and I have already discussed that point. According to them, Cayleb couldn't possibly have done it."

Stonekeep considered that for a moment, then looked Gorjah straight in the eye.

"Your Majesty, I can only assume from what you've said, and the fact that you've said it to *me*, that you believe I may have been in some way responsible for what happened. So far as I know, however, I had virtually nothing to do with any of the decisions about the fleet's organization or movement. I'm afraid I'm at something of a loss to understand how I might have contributed to this disaster."

What might almost have been a shadow of grudging respect flickered across Thirsk's face. Gorjah, however, only regarded Stonekeep coldly for several seconds. Then the king gestured at the Dohlaran admiral.

"According to Prince Cayleb," he said, "Haarahld's known our plans for months. His 'failure' to mobilize his reserve galleys, his 'assistance request' under the treaty, were both ruses. In fact, Cayleb must have already sailed by the time Haarahld's messages arrived here in Tranjyr. Both Baron White Ford and Earl Thirsk have confirmed to me that Cayleb couldn't possibly have reached Armageddon Reef when he did unless that were true, so I think we must assume Cayleb knew what he was talking about. Wouldn't you agree, Edymynd?"

"It certainly sounds that way, Your Majesty," Stonekeep said cautiously. "Of course, as I said, my own familiarity with such matters is limited."

"I'm sure it is." The king's smile was even thinner than before. "The problem, however, is just how Haarahld came by that information. And according to Cayleb, he got it from *us*."

Stonekeep's belly seemed to tie itself into a knot, and he felt sweat breaking out under his kercheef.

"Your Majesty," he said, after a mouth-drying second or two, "I don't see how that could be possible."

"I'm sure you don't," Gorjah said.

"I understand now why you summoned me," the baron said, speaking as calmly as he could, despite the king's tone, "and I also understand why Earl Thirsk is as angry as he appears to be. But I literally don't see how it could be possible."

"Why not?" Gorjah asked coldly.

"Because so far as I'm aware, no one outside this council chamber at this very moment, aside from one or two of Baron White Ford's subordinates, knew where the fleets were to rendezvous, or what route they would follow from the rendezvous to Charis. For that matter, *I* didn't know the route."

Gorjah's eyes flickered, and Stonekeep permitted himself a tiny sliver of relief. But Thirsk shook his head.

"Baron Stonekeep," he said, "*someone* must have known and passed that information on to Charis. As a foreigner here in Tarot, I have no idea who that someone might have been. But the timing indicates that Tarot is the only possible source. No one else could have told them in time for them to get their fleet into position to intercept us."

"Forgive me, My Lord," Stonekeep replied, "but unless I'm very much mistaken, King Rahnyld and his court knew about this proposed operation long before anyone here in Tarot did."

"But we didn't know the rendezvous point or the course we were to steer after it until just before our fleet actually departed," Thirsk said. "And there wasn't time for that information to reach Haarahld from Dohlar early enough for him to respond this way."

"I see." Stonekeep managed to maintain his outward aplomb, but it wasn't easy.

"As for the exact route we followed after the rendezvous," White Ford said, speaking for the first time, and sounding as if he truly wished he didn't have to, "I'm afraid someone as experienced as Haarahld wouldn't have needed exact information. In fact, we didn't follow the course laid down in our original orders. The one we did follow was dictated by sailing conditions, and Haarahld is fully capable of predicting what changes sea and wind would be likely to force upon us. And of dispatching Cayleb's fleet accordingly."

"So, you see, Edymynd," Gorjah said, drawing the baron's eyes back to him, "all the available evidence suggests Haarahld did get the information from us."

Stonekeep might have debated the use of the word "evidence" to describe what they had to go on, but he knew better than to make that point just now.

"And if he did get it from us," Gorjah continued, "Vicar Zahmsyn and Vicar

Zhaspyr are going to be *most* displeased. And if they're displeased with *me*, I'm going to be . . . displeased with whoever allowed that to happen."

He held Stonekeep's eyes levelly, and for once, the baron could think of absolutely nothing to say.

.II.
Royal Palace,
Eraystor,

Your Highness."

Nahrmahn of Emerald gave a most un-prince-like snort, then sat up in bed. It looked rather like a particularly round narwhale or an Old Earth walrus rising from the depths, and his expression was not happy.

"I'm sorry to wake you, Your Highness." The night chamberlain's words came out almost in a gabble in response to that expression. "I assure you, I wouldn't have done it if I'd had any choice at all. I know you don't wish to be dist—"

"Enough," Nahrmahn didn't—quite—snarl, and the man chopped himself off in midsyllable.

The prince rubbed his eyes, then drew a deep breath and gave the chamberlain a slightly less hostile look.

"Better," he said. "Now, what is it?"

"Your Highness, there's an officer here from the dockyard. He says—"

The night chamberlain broke off for an instant, then visibly steeled himself.

"Your Highness, there's been a battle. From what the officer says, we lost."

"Lost?"

Nahrmahn's irritation disappeared into shock. How could they have lost a battle when they outnumbered their enemy by almost three-to-one?

"The dockyard officer is waiting for you, Your Highness," the chamberlain said. "He's far better qualified than I am to explain what happened."

"Bring him," Nahrmahn said harshly, swinging his legs over the edge of the bed.

"Shall I send for your body servants, first, Your Highness?"

The chamberlain seemed almost pathetically eager to fasten upon some reassuringly normal routine, but Nahrmahn shook his head angrily.

"Bring him!" he snapped, and stood, reaching for the robe laid ready beside the bed.

"Yes, Your Highness!"

The chamberlain scurried out, and Nahrmahn fastened the robe's sash, then turned to face the bedchamber door, waiting impatiently. Less than two minutes later, the chamberlain returned with a naval officer who looked even less happy than the chamberlain did. The officer wore no sword, and his dagger sheath was empty, but a quick shake of Nahrmahn's head told the guardsman outside his bedchamber door to stay there.

"Captain Tallmyn, Your Highness," the chamberlain said, as the officer bowed deeply.

"Leave us," Nahrmahn told the chamberlain, who promptly disappeared like a wisp of smoke in a high wind.

The door closed behind him, and the naval officer straightened his spine and met Nahrmahn's eyes, although he clearly would have preferred not to.

"Captain Tallmyn," Nahrmahn said. "And you would be—?"

"Captain Gervays Tallmyn, Your Highness." Tallmyn had a deep voice, undoubtedly well suited to bawling orders. At the moment there was an echo of shock in its depths, and Nahrmahn's lips tightened as he heard it. "I have the honor to be the assistant commander of the Royal Dockyard here in Eraystor."

"I see. And what's this about a battle?"

"At the moment, Your Highness, our information is far from complete," Tallmyn said a bit cautiously, and Nahrmahn nodded impatient understanding of the qualification. "All we really knew so far is that *Sea Cloud*'s returned to port. According to her captain, she's the only survivor of her entire squadron. And—" The captain inhaled, visibly bracing himself. "—she may be the only survivor of our entire fleet."

Nahrmahn's round face went pale.

"I don't say she is, Your Highness," Tallmyn said quickly. "I said she *may* be. At the moment, she's the only ship which has returned, but her captain is obviously badly shaken. It's entirely possible, even probable, that even though he's being as honest as he possibly can, his own experiences are causing him to overestimate our total losses. But"—the captain's voice went lower and darker—"even if they are, there's no question that we've suffered a very serious defeat."

"How?" Nahrmahn demanded.

"I'm afraid it's going to be some time before we can really answer that question, Your Highness. However, it appears from *Sea Cloud*'s report that Cayleb and the Charisian galleons have returned. Apparently, they struck our fleet from behind, just at dawn, and their gunfire was even more effective than Duke Black Water's last reports suggested it might be. *Sea Cloud* managed to escape to windward, but her captain personally saw at least eleven of our galleys, including every other ship in his own squadron, strike."

Nahrmahn simply stared at him for several seconds. Then he nodded slowly and walked across to gaze out his bedchamber's window across the palace gardens.

King Haarahld VII's body lay in state before the high altar in Tellesberg Cathedral. Six halberd-armed men of the Royal Guard surrounded the bier, gazing rigidly in front of them, the heads of their weapons draped in the black of mourning. By King Cayleb's orders, Sergeant Gahrdaner and Sergeant Haarpar lay on either side of the king they'd died to protect, and Midshipman Hektor Aplyn sat at his dead king's feet, one arm in a snow-white sling, keeping watch over King Haarahld's sword.

Aplyn was one of only thirty-six survivors of *Royal Charis*' entire crew. Every one of the survivors had been wounded. Some of them might yet die, despite all the healers could do.

For four days now, King Haarahld's people had shuffled quietly, reverently, through the enormous cathedral to bid their old king farewell. Many had sobbed, most had wept, and all had been grim faced with grief.

Yet there'd been little or no despair.

Merlin Athrawes stood behind King Cayleb, gazing over the young monarch's shoulder as he sat in the royal box with his younger brother and sister, waiting for the funeral mass to begin. Zhan and Zhanayt looked as if they were still trying to comprehend the enormity of their father's death. Cayleb's expression was less stunned and far, far harder.

And that, Merlin thought as he, too, gazed sadly at Haarahld's body, summed up the mood of most of Charis quite well. The death of their beloved king tempered the Charisians' joy and pride in the victories their navy had won, but nothing could erase their understanding of what those victories meant.

Nineteen of Haarahld's galleys, a quarter of his entire fleet, had been sunk or so badly damaged that Cayleb had ordered them burned; *Dreadnought*'s bow had been so shattered by the collision with *Doomwhale* that it had been impossible to keep her afloat; and casualties throughout the galley fleet had been heavy. But as compensation, a hundred and seventeen of Black Water's galleys, most badly damaged, but including thirty-six Chisholmian galleys which had surrendered virtually undamaged, were anchored in Tellesberg's harbor under Charisian colors. Another forty-nine had been sunk in action or burned afterward. Only seventeen—less than ten percent of the fleet Black Water had taken into action—had managed to escape.

Of the total combined force of over three hundred and fifty warships the Group of Four had assembled for the attack on Charis, less than thirty had escaped destruction or capture. It was, by any measure, the most one-sided naval victory in Safehold's history.

The Kingdom of Charis' pride in its navy was like a bright, fierce flame, one which burned even more brilliantly against the darkness of its dead king, and Merlin understood that only too well. He wished, with all his molycirc heart, that Haarahld hadn't done it. Wished he himself had reached the aftercastle of *Royal Charis* even a minute earlier. Wished he'd realized how serious the king's wound had been, or that he'd been able to somehow treat that wound while simultaneously holding the Corisandian boarders at bay.

But none of those things had happened, and so the king he had come to admire and respect so deeply—had come, without even realizing it, to love—had died behind him in the arms of an eleven-year-old midshipman.

It was a tragedy made even greater and far more painful because the victory had already been won. If every single ship in Black Water's column had escaped, Darcos Sound would still have been a crushing triumph. And yet . . .

Merlin stood behind King Cayleb, watching, listening, and he knew that whether or not Darcos Sound would have been a victory anyway was really almost immaterial. The SNARC he'd had monitoring Haarahld had recorded the king's conversation with his flag captain, and he knew the king's death had purchased exactly what Haarahld had flung his life into the scales to buy. The entire Kingdom of Charis knew King Haarahld could have avoided action. It knew he'd *chosen* to engage at odds of six-to-one rather than turn his back and let those ships escape, and that he'd done it because Charis needed far more in *this* war than mere victories. Just as it knew his flagship's crew had fought literally to the last man, building a ring of their own bodies about their king. And just as it knew that in the final decision he would ever make, its king had lost his life protecting an eleven-year-old midshipman. Young Aplyn had told Cayleb the last thing his father had ever said. The words had come hard from an officer who was also a boy, trying desperately not to weep, and they had already spread throughout the entire kingdom.

Charis knew as well as Merlin did that Haarahld hadn't had to meet the enemy head on. That, in many respects, it had been the wrong decision for a king to make. But it had been the right decision for a *man* to make, and Charis knew that, too . . . just as it would always treasure the last words he had said to an eleven-year-old boy. He had become a martyr and, even more importantly, an example, the yardstick against which his navy would forever be measured, and the legend of HMS *Royal Charis*' last battle would do nothing but grow with time. Haarahld had provided that legend by showing what he had expected of himself, showing his people the measure to which they must now hold themselves if they would be worthy of their dead king.

Merlin had no doubt that they would hew to the standard Haarahld had set.

Nor was that example all Haarahld had left his people, for he'd left them a new king, as well, and the Charisians' pride in him burned as bright as their pride in his father. They knew it was Haarahld who'd planned the Battle of Darcos

Sound. The entire campaign had been his strategic concept, and his had been the mind—and courage—which had made it so decisive, even at the cost of his own life. But it was King Cayleb who had won the crushing victories of Rocky Point and the Battle of Crag Reach in the demon-haunted waters off Armageddon Reef, and it was Cayleb whose arrival and ships had made Darcos Sound possible. They were united behind their young monarch as very few kingdoms in human history had ever been.

And that was a good thing, because they also knew now who had orchestrated the attack upon them.

Cayleb and Gray Harbor had decided to make that information public, and Merlin thought they'd been right to do so. It wasn't a secret which could be kept for long, anyway, and it was time for the people of Charis to know what their kingdom truly faced. Time for them to know that the rulers of the Church of God Awaiting had decreed their destruction.

That information was still sinking in, Merlin knew. It would be five-days, probably months, before it sank fully home, but the reaction of Cayleb's subjects to the news was already clear.

As was Cayleb's.

King Haarahld's funeral mass would not be celebrated by Bishop Executor Zherald. The bishop executor was currently Cayleb's "guest" in a comfortable palace suite. No bishop in the history of Safehold had ever been arrested or imprisoned by a secular ruler. Technically, that was still true, but no one doubted the reality behind the polite pretense. Just as no one doubted that the true prelate of all Charis was now Bishop Maikel Staynair.

It would take some time, but Merlin could already hear the echoes of Henry VIII. Whether or not Cayleb would formally assume the position of the Church's head in Charis remained to be seen, but the Charisian Church's separation from the Temple was an accomplished fact which awaited only official ratification.

It was not a fact which had met with universal approval. Almost a quarter of the kingdom's clergy, including its native Charisians, were outraged and horrified by the very suggestion. So was at least a portion of the general population, but the percentage there was much smaller, so far as Merlin could tell.

There was quite a lot of fear and concern, not to mention confusion, but the vast majority of Cayleb's subjects had never been especially fond of the corrupt men in Zion. The fact that the Council of Vicars had launched an overwhelming attack upon them when they'd done nothing to deserve it had turned that lack of fondness into virulent hatred. The fact that it was actually the Group of Four, and not the entire Council of Vicars, was at best a meaningless, artificial distinction for most of them, nor had Cayleb and Gray Harbor gone out of their way to emphasize it.

The Safeholdian Reformation which Merlin had hoped to delay until Charis was ready for it was already a fact. There was nothing he could do to undo that, nor would the white-hot anger of Charis and its new monarch have permitted him to, even if he could have.

And at least for now, the initiative lay firmly in Cayleb's hands. Despite its own losses, the Royal Charisian Navy held uncontested command of the sea, for there was quite literally no other navy in existence.

God only knew what the Group of Four would do when it discovered that fact. In the short term, there wasn't very much it *could* do without a fleet. In the long term, the Temple controlled somewhere around eighty-five percent of the total planetary population and a huge proportion of the planet's total wealth. Those were daunting odds, but if they dismayed Cayleb Ahrmahk, Merlin had seen no sign of it. And Cayleb was already working to improve them.

Queen Sharleyan's distaste for the orders forced upon her by the Group of Four offered him an opening, and the fact that so many of her warships had surrendered offered him a lever. He'd already dispatched a special ambassador to Cherayth with an offer to return her vessels, along with all of her personnel, in return for a formal end to hostilities.

That was the *official* message. The private letter from Cayleb to Sharleyan which accompanied it suggested a somewhat closer relationship. It very carefully did *not* mention the fact that the Group of Four was likely to be rather upset with her kingdom and her navy's performance against Charis. Nor did it even hint that Cayleb's return of her surrendered ships would almost certainly make the Group of Four even angrier. Which, of course, only emphasized those facts more strongly. It *did* specifically point out all of the reasons to hate and despise Hektor of Corisande which Charis and Chisholm had in common, however, and suggest that they do something about them.

And, of course, there was always Nahrmahn of Emerald. Who now found himself on the other side of the Charis Sea with no navy, no allies, and very little in the way of an army.

But that could wait, Merlin thought, as the organ music swelled and the cathedral doors opened. The time would come when all those other threats must be dealt with. The time for analysis, planning, the identification of opportunities and perils. But that time was not now, and even if it had been, Merlin would not have cared.

Perhaps it was as "wrong" of him to feel that way as it had been for Haarahld to steer to meet Black Water's flagship instead of turning away. Merlin Athrawes, after all, was a creature of circuitry and alloys, of the cool whisper of electrons and not flesh and blood, or the beating of a human heart. It was his duty to look to those threats, to scent those opportunities, to determine how best to turn even King Haarahld's death to advantage. And he would discharge that duty.

But not today. Today belonged to the man who had become his friend. The man who'd trusted him with his own life, and his kingdom, and his son, and died without ever truly knowing what Merlin was. This day belonged to Haarahld Ahrmahk, and to all the other men who had died in a war whose true objectives had never been explained to them. It belonged to their memory, to Merlin's own prayers for forgiveness as he contemplated the blood upon his hands and the greater tides still waiting to be shed.

As he gazed at Haarahld's bier and the wounded midshipman at its foot, Merlin Athrawes tasted the full, bitter weight of immortality. Of knowing how many endless years stretched out before him, how many more men and child-officers—and women, in days to come—would die in the war *he* had begun.

He felt that weight, saw it in his mind's eye, looming before him like an Everest of the soul, and it terrified him. But Haarahld's example—and Pei Kau-yung's, and Pei Shan-wei's, and even Nimue Alban's—burned before him, as well. That Everest was his, and he would bear it, for however long it took, for however far he must journey. He knew that. But for today, it could wait while the Kingdom of Charis—and the man who had been Nimue Alban—said their final farewell to King Haarahld VII.

It could all wait.

Characters

AHDYMSYN, BISHOP EXECUTOR ZHERALD—Archbishop Erayk Dynnys' chief administrator for the Archbishopric of Charis.

AHLBAIR, LIEUTENANT ZHEROHM, ROYAL CHARISIAN NAVY—first lieutenant, HMS *Typhoon.*

AHLVEREZ, ADMIRAL-GENERAL FAIDEL, DOHLARAN NAVY—Duke of Malikai; King Rahnyld IV of Dohlar's senior admiral.

AHRMAHK, CROWN PRINCE CAYLEB—Crown Prince of Charis, older son of King Haarahld VII.

AHRMAHK, KING HAARAHLD VII—King of Charis.

AHRMAHK, KAHLVYN—Duke of Tirian, Constable of Hairatha, King Haarahld VII's first cousin.

AHRMAHK, KAHLVYN CAYLEB—Kahlvyn Ahrmahk's younger son.

AHRMAHK, RAYJHIS—Kahlvyn Ahrmahk's elder son and heir.

AHRMAHK, PRINCE ZHAN—Crown Prince Cayleb's younger brother, youngest child of King Haarahld VII.

AHRMAHK, PRINCESS ZHANAYT—Crown Prince Cayleb's younger sister, second eldest child of King Haarahld VII.

AHRMAHK, ZHENYFYR—Duchess of Tirian, wife of Kahlvyn Ahrmahk.

AHZGOOD, PHYLYP—Earl of Coris, Prince Hektor's spymaster.

ALBAN, LIEUTENANT COMMANDER NIMUE, TFN—Admiral Pei Kau-zhi's tactical officer.

ALLAYN, VICAR—see also Allayn Mahgwyr.

APLYN, MIDSHIPMAN HEKTOR, ROYAL CHARISIAN NAVY—junior midshipman, HMS *Royal Charis.*

ATHRAWES, LIEUTENANT MERLIN, CHARISIAN ROYAL GUARD—Nimue Alban's male persona.

AYMEZ, MIDSHIPMAN BARDULF, ROYAL CHARISIAN NAVY—a midshipman, HMS *Typhoon.*

BAHRMYN, ARCHBISHOP BORYS—Archbishopric of Corisande.

BAHLTYN, ZHEEVYS—Baron White Ford's valet.

BAHRNS, KING RAHNYLD IV—King of Dohlar.

BORYS, ARCHBISHOP—see Archbishop Borys Bahrmyn.

BAHRMYN, TOHMYS—Baron White Castle, Prince Hektor's ambassador to Prince Nahrmahn.

BAYTZ, PRINCESS FELAYZ—Prince Nahrmahn of Emerald's youngest child and second daughter.

BAYTZ, PRINCESS MAHRYA—Prince Nahrmahn of Emerald's oldest child.

BAYTZ, PRINCE NAHRMAHN II—ruler of the Princedom of Emerald.

BAYTZ, PRINCE NAHRMAHN GAREYT—second child of Prince Nahrmahn of Emerald.

BAYTZ, PRINCESS OHLYVYA—wife of Prince Nahrmahn of Emerald.

BAYTZ, PRINCE TRAHVYS—Prince Nahrmahn of Emerald's third child and second son.

BÉDARD, DR. ADORÉE, PH.D.—Chief Psychiatrist, Operation Ark.

BISHOP EXECUTOR ZHERALD—see Bishop Executor Zherald Ahdymsyn.

BISHOP EXECUTOR WYLLYS—see Bishop Executor Wyllys Gryrsyn.

BISHOP MAIKEL—see Bishop Maikel Staynair.

BLAIDYN, LIEUTENANT ROZHYR, DOHLARAN NAVY—second lieutenant, galley *Royal Bédard*.

BLACK WATER, DUKE—see Ernyst Lynkyn.

BOWSHAM, CAPTAIN KHANAIR, ROYAL CHARISIAN MARINES—CO, HMS *Gale*.

BRADLAI, LIEUTENANT ROBYRT, CORISANDIAN NAVY—true name of Captain Styvyn Whaite.

BROUN, FATHER MAHTAIO—Archbishop Erayk Dynnys' senior secretary and aide; Archbishop Erayk's confidant and protégé.

BROWNYNG, CAPTAIN ELLYS—CO, Temple galleon *Blessed Langhorne*.

BREYGART, FRAIDARECK—fourteenth Earl of Hanth; Hauwerd Breygart's great-grandfather.

BREYGART, SIR HAUWERD—the rightful heir to the Earldom of Hanth.

BYRK, MAJOR BREKYN, ROYAL CHARISIAN MARINES—CO, Marine detachment, HMS *Royal Charis*.

CAHNYR, ARCHBISHOP ZHASYN—Archbishop of Glacierheart.

CHALMYR, LIEUTENANT MAILVYN, ROYAL CHARISIAN NAVY—first lieutenant, HMS *Tellesberg*.

CHALMYRZ, FATHER KARLOS—Archbishop Borys Bahrmyn's aide and secretary.

CHARLZ, CAPTAIN MARIK—CO Charisian merchant ship *Wave Daughter*.

CLAREYK, MAJOR KYNT, ROYAL CHARISIAN MARINES—a Marine expert in infantry tactics.

CLYNTAHN, VICAR ZHASPYR—Grand Inquisitor of the Church of God Awaiting; one of the so-called "Group of Four."

COHLMYN, ADMIRAL SIR LEWK, CHISHOLMIAN NAVY—Earl Sharpfield; Queen Sharleyan's senior fleet Commander.

CORIS, EARL—see Phylyp Ahzgood.

CAHKRAYN, SAMYL—Duke of Fern, King Rahnyld IV of Dohlar's first councillor.

DAIKYN, GAHLVYN—Crown Prince Cayleb's personal valet.

DAYKYN, PRINCE HEKTOR—Prince of Corisande, leader of the league of Corisande.

DRAGONER, CORPORAL ZHAK, ROYAL CHARISIAN MARINES—a member of Crown Prince Cayleb's bodyguard.

DUCHAIRN, VICAR RHOBAIR—Minister of Treasury, Council of Vicars; one of the so-called Group of Four.

DYMYTREE, FRONZ, ROYAL CHARISIAN MARINES—a member of Crown Prince Cayleb's bodyguard.

DYNNYS, ADORAI—Archbishop Erayk Dynnys' wife.

DYNNYS, ARCHBISHOP ERAYK—Archbishop of Charis.

EKYRD, CAPTAIN HAYRYS, DOHLARAN NAVY—CO, galley *King Rahnyld*.

ERAYK, ARCHBISHOP—see Erayk Dynnys.

FAHRMAHN, PRIVATE LUHYS, ROYAL CHARISIAN MARINES—a member of Crown Prince Cayleb's bodyguard.

FAIRCASTER, SARGEANT PAYTER, ROYAL CHARISIAN MARINES—senior noncom, Crown Prince Cayleb's bodyguard.

FATHER MICHAEL—parish priest of Lakeview.

FERN, DUKE OF—see Samyl Cahkrayn.

FALKHAN, LIEUTENANT AHRNAHLD, ROYAL CHARISIAN MARINES—commanding officer, Crown Prince Cayleb's personal bodyguard.

FOFÃO, CAPTAIN MATEUS, TFN—CO TFNS *Swiftsure*.

FUHLLYR, FATHER RAIMAHND—chaplain, HMS *Dreadnought*.

FURKHAL, RAFAYL—second baseman and leadoff hitter, Tellesberg Krakens.

GAHRDANER, SERGEANT CHARLZ, CHARISIAN ROYAL GUARD—one of King Haarahld VII's bodyguards.

GARDYNYR, ADMIRAL LYWYS, DOHLARAN NAVY—Earl of Thirsk; senior professional admiral of the Dohlaran Navy; second-in-command to Duke Malikai.

GRAND VICAR EREK XVII—secular and temporal head of the Church of God Awaiting.

GRAY HARBOR, EARL—see Rayjhis Yowance.

GREENHILL, TYMAHN—King Haarahld VII's senior huntsman.

GREEN MOUNTAIN, BARON—see Mahrak Sandyrs.

GUYSHAIN, FATHER BAHRNAI—Vicar Zahmsyn Trynair's senior aide.

GYRARD, LIEUTENANT ANDRAI, ROYAL CHARISIAN NAVY—first officer, HMS *Dreadnought*.

GRAISYN, BISHOP EXECUTOR WYLLYS—Archbishop Lyam Tyrn's chief administrator for the Archbishopric of Emerald.

HAARPAR, SERGEANT GORJ, CHARISIAN ROYAL GUARD—one of King Haarahld VII's bodyguards.

HOTCHKYS, CAPTAIN SIR OHWYN, ROYAL CHARISIAN NAVY—CO HMS *Tellesberg*.

HAHLMAHN, PAWAL—King Haarahld VII's senior chamberlain.

HALMYN, ARCHBISHOP—see Halmyn Zahmsyn.

HASKYN, MIDSHIPMAN YAHNCEE, DOHLARAN NAVY—a midshipman aboard *Gorath Bay*.

HANTH, EARL—see Tahdayo Mahntayl.

HARRISON, MATTHEW PAUL—Timothy and Sarah Harrison's great-grandson.

HARRISON, ROBERT—Timothy and Sarah Harrison's grandson; Matthew Paul Harrison's father.

HARRISON, SARAH—wife of Timothy Harrison hand and an Eve.

HARRISON, TIMOTHY—Mayor of Lakeview and an Adam.

HARYS, FATHER AHLBYRT—Vicar Zahmsyn Trynair's special representative to Dohlar.

HAUWYRD, ZHORZH—Earl Gray Harbor's personal guardsman.

HENDERSON, LIEUTENANT GABRIELA ("GABBY"), TFN—tactical officer, TFNS *Swiftsure*.

HOWSMYN, EHDWYRD—a wealthy foundry owner and shipbuilder in Tellesberg.

HUNTYR, LIEUTENANT KLEMYNT, CHARISIAN ROYAL GUARD—an officer of the Charisian Royal Guard in Tellesberg.

HYNDRYK, CAPTAIN SIR AHLFRYD, ROYAL CHARISIAN NAVY—Baron Seamount, the Royal Charisian Navy's senior gunnery expert.

HYRST, ADMIRAL ZOHZEF, CHISHOLMIAN NAVY—Earl Sharpfield's second-in-command.

KAILLEE, CAPTAIN ZHILBERT, TAROTISIAN NAVY—CO, galley *King Gorjah II*.

KHATTYR, CAPTAIN PAYT, EMERALD NAVY—CO, galley *Black Prince*.

KING GORJAH III—see Gorjah Yairayl.

KING HAARAHLD VII—see Haarahld Ahrmahk.

KING RAHNYLD IV—see Rahnyld Bahrns.

KOHRBY, MIDSHIPMAN LYNAIL, ROYAL CHARISIAN NAVY—senior midshipman, HMS *Dreadnought*.

LAHANG, BRAIDEE—Prince Nahrmahn of Emerald's chief agent in Charis.

LANGHORNE, ERIC—Chief Administrator, Operation Ark.

LAYN, LIEUTENANT ZHIM, ROYAL CHARISIAN MARINES—Major Kynt Clareyk's aide.

LOCK ISLAND, HIGH ADMIRAL BRYAHN—Earl of Lock Island, CO Royal Charisian Navy, a cousin of King Haarahld VII.

LORD PROTECTOR GREYGHOR—see Greyghor Stohnar.

LYAM, ARCHBISHOP—see Archbishop Lyam Tyrn.

LYNKYN, ADMIRAL ERNYST, CORISANDIAN NAVY—Duke of Black Water, CO, Corisandian Navy.

MAHGENTEE, MIDSHIPMAN MAHRAK, ROYAL CHARISIAN NAVY—senior midshipman, HMS *Typhoon*.

MAHKLYN, DR. RAHZHYR—head of the Royal Charisian College.

MAHLRY, LIEUTENANT RHOLYND, EMERALD NAVY—a lieutenant aboard galley *Black Prince*.

MAHNDYR, EARL—see Gharth Rahlstahn.

MAHNTAYL, TAHDAYO—usurper Earl of Hanth.

MAHRAK, LIEUTENANT RAHNALD ROYAL CHARISIAN NAVY—first lieutenant, HMS *Royal Charis*.

MAHRTYN, ADMIRAL GAHVYN, TAROTISIAN NAVY—Baron White Ford; senior admiral of the Navy of Tarot.

MAGWAIR, VICAR ALLAYN—Captain General, Council of Vicars; one of the so-called Group of Four.

MAIKEL, CAPTAIN QWENTYN, DOHLARAN NAVY—CO, galley *Gorath Bay*.

MAIKELSYN, LIEUTENANT LEEAHM, TAROTISIAN NAVY—first lieutenant, *King Gorjah II*.

MAIRYDYTH, LIEUTENANT NEVYL, DOHLARAN NAVY—first lieutenant, galley *Royal Bédard*.

MAKFERZAHN, ZHAMES—one of Prince Hektor's agents in Charis.

MAKGREGAIR, FATHER ZHOSHUA—Vicar Zahmsyn Trynair's special representative to Tarot.

MALIKAI, DUKE—see Faidel Ahlverez.

MANTHYR, CAPTAIN GWYLYM, ROYAL CHARISIAN NAVY—CO, HMS *Dreadnought*.

MARSHYL, MIDSHIPMAN ADYM, ROYAL CHARISIAN NAVY—senior midshipman, HMS *Royal Charis*.

MASTER DOMNEK—King Haarahld VII's court arms master.

MATHYSYN, LIEUTENANT ZHAIKEB, DOHLARAN NAVY—first lieutenant, galley *Gorath Bay*.

MAYLYR, CAPTAIN DUNKYN, ROYAL CHARISIAN NAVY—CO, HMS *Halberd*.

MAYSAHN, ZHASPAHR—Prince Hektor's senior agent in Charis.

MAYTHIS, LIEUTENANT FRAIZHER, CORISANDIAN NAVY—true name of Captain Wahltayr Seatown.

MHULVAYN, OSKAHR—one of Prince Hektor's agents in Charis.

MYCHAIL, RAIYAN—a major textile producer and sailmaker in Tellesberg.

MYLLYR, ARCHBISHOP URVYN—Archbishop of Sodar.

MYRGYN, SIR KEHVYN, CORISANDIAN NAVY—CO, galley *Corisande*.

NYLZ, COMMODORE KOHDY, ROYAL CHARISIAN NAVY—CO of one of High Admiral Lock Island's galley squadrons.

NYOU, KING GORJAH III—King of Tarot.

OARMASTER, SYGMAHN, ROYAL CHARISIAN MARINES—a member of Crown Prince Cayleb's bodyguard.

OHLSYN, TRAHVYS—Earl of Pine Hollow, Prince Nahrmahn's of Emerald's first councillor and cousin.

OLYVYR, AHNYET—Sir Dustyn Olyvyr's life.

OLYVYR, SIR DUSTYN—a leading Tellesberg ship designer; chief constructor, Royal Charisian Navy.

OWL—Nimue Alban's AI, based on the manufacturer's acronym: Ordoñes-Westinghouse-Lytton RAPIER Tactical Computer, Mark 17a.

PEI, ADMIRAL KAU-ZHI, TFN—CO, Operation Breakaway; older brother of commodore Pei Kau-yung.

PEI, COMMODORE KAU-YUNG, TFN—CO, Operation Ark final escort.

PEI, DR. SHAN-WEI, PH.D.—Commodore Pei Kau-yung's wife; senior terraforming expert for Operation Ark.

PHONDA, MADAM AHNZHELYK—proprietor of one of the City of Zion's most discrete brothels.

PINE HOLLOW, EARL—see Trahvys Ohlsyn.

PRINCE CAYLEB—see Cayleb Ahrmahk.

PRINCE HEKTOR—see Hektor Daykyn.

PRINCE NAHRMAHN—see Nahrmahn Baytz.

PROCTOR, DR. ELIAS, PH.D.—a member of Pei Shan-wei's staff and a noted cyberneticist.

QUEEN SHARLEYAN—see Sharleyan Tayt.

QWENTYN, COMMODORE DONYRT, CORISANDIAN NAVY—Baron Tanlyr Keep, one of Duke of Black Water's squadron commander's.

RAHLSTAHN, ADMIRAL GHARTH, EMERALD NAVY—Earl of Mahndyr, CO, Emerald Navy.

RAHLSTYN, COMMODORE ERAYK, DOHLARAN NAVY—one of Duke Malikai's squadron commanders.

RAICE, BYNZHAMYN—Baron Wave Thunder, King Haarahld VII's spymaster and a member of his Privy Council.

RAYNO, ARCHBISHOP WYLLYM—Archbishop of Chiang-wu; adjutant of the Order of Schueler.

RHOBAIR, VICAR—see also Rhobair Duchairn.

ROPEWALK, COLONEL AHDAM, CHARISIAN ROYAL GUARD—CO, Charisian Royal Guard.

ROWYN, CAPTAIN HORAHS—CO, Sir Dustyn Olyvyr's yacht *Ahnyet*.

RUSTMYN, EDYMYND—Baron Stonekeep; King Gorjah III of Tarot's first councillor and spymaster.

SAHDLYR, LIEUTENANT BYNZHAMYN, ROYAL CHARISIAN NAVY—second lieutenant, HMS *Dreadnought*.

SANDYRS, MAHRAK—Baron Green Mountain; Queen Sharleyan of Chisholm's first minister.

SEAFARMER, SIR RHYZHARD—Baron Wave Thunder's senior investigator.

SEAMOUNT, BARON—see Sir Ahlfryd Hyndryk.

SEATOWN, CAPTAIN WAHLTAYR—CO of merchant ship *Fraynceen*, acting as a courier for Prince Hektor's spies in Charis. See also Lieutenant Fraizher Maythis.

SHANDYR, HAHL—Baron of Shandyr, Prince Nahrmahn of Emerald's spymaster.

SHARPFIELD, EARL—see Sir Lewk Cohlmyn.

SHUMAKYR, FATHER SYMYN—Archbishop Erayk Dynnys' secretary for his 891 pastoral visit; an agent of the Grand Inquisitor.

SMOLTH, ZHAN—star pitcher for the Tellesberg Krakens.

SOMERSET, CAPTAIN MARTIN LUTHER, TFN—CO, TFNS *Excalibur*.

STAYNAIR, BISHOP MAIKEL—Bishop of Tellesberg; King Haarahld VII's confessor and adviser.

STAYNAIR, COMMODORE SIR DOMYNYK, ROYAL CHARISIAN NAVY—specialist in naval tactics; CO Experimental Squadron; Crown Prince Cayleb's second-in-command; younger brother of Bishop Maikel Staynair; later admiral.

STOHNAR, LORD PROTECTOR GREYGHOR—elected ruler of the Siddarmark Republic.

STONEKEEP, BARON—see Edymynd Rustmyn.

STYWYRT, CAPTAIN DAHRYL, ROYAL CHARISIAN NAVY—CO HMS *Typhoon*.

SYMMYNS, TOHMAS—Grand Duke of Zebediah, senior member and head of Council of Zebediah.

TALLMYN, CAPTAIN GERVAYS, EMERALD NAVY—second-in-command of the Royal Dockyard in Tranjyr.

TANLYR KEEP, BARON—see Donyrt Qwentyn.

TAYT, QUEEN SHARLEYAN—Queen of Chisholm.

THIESSEN, CAPTAIN JOSEPH, TFN—Admiral Pei Kau-zhi's chief of staff.

THIRSK, EARL—see Lywys Gardynyr.

TOHMYS, FRAHNKLYN—Crown Prince Cayleb's tutor.

TILLYER, LIEUTENANT HENRAI, ROYAL CHARISIAN NAVY—High Admiral Lock Island's personal aide.

TIRIAN, DUKE—see Kahlvyn Ahrmahk.

TRYNAIR, VICAR ZAHMSYN—Chancellor of the Council of Vicars of the Church of God Awaiting; one of the so-called Group of Four.

TRYVYTHYN, CAPTAIN SIR DYNZYL, ROYAL CHARISIAN NAVY—CO, HMS *Royal Charis*.

TYRN, ARCHBISHOP LYAM—Archbishop of Emerald.

URVYN, ARCHBISHOP—see Urvyn Myllyr.

WAVE THUNDER, BARON—see Bynzhamyn Raice.

WHAITE, CAPTAIN STYVYN—CO, merchantship *Sea Cloud*, a courier for Prince Hektor's spies in Charis. See also Robyrt Bradlai.

WHITE CASTLE, BARON—see Tohmys Bahrmyn.

WHITE FORD, BARON—see Gahvyn Mahrtyn.

WYLLYM, ARCHBISHOP—see Wyllym Rayno.

WYLLYMS, MARHYS—the Duke of Tirian's majordomo.

WYLSYNN, FATHER PAITYR—a priest of the Order of Schueler, the Church of God Awaiting's intendant for Charis.

WYNSTYN, LIEUTENANT KYNYTH, CORISANDIAN NAVY—first lieutenant galley *Corisande*.

YOWANCE, EHRNAIST—Rayjhis Yowance's deceased elder brother.

YOWANCE, RAYJHIS—Earl of Gray Harbor, King Haarahld's first minister and head of the Privy Council.

ZEBEDIAH, GRAND DUKE—see Tohmas Symmyns.

ZAHMSYN, ARCHBISHOP HALMYN—Archbishop of Gorath; senior prelate of the Kingdom of Dohlar.

ZAHMSYN, VICAR—see Zahmsyn Trynair.

ZHANSAN, FRAHNK—the Duke of Tirian's senior guardsman.

ZHASPYR, VICAR—see Zahmsyn Clyntahn.

ZHASYN, ARCHBISHOP—see Zhasyn Cahnyr.

ZHEPPSYN, CAPTAIN NYKLAS, EMERALD NAVY—CO, galley *Triton*.

ZHESSYP, LACHLYN—King Haarahld VII's valet.

ZHOELSYN, LIEUTENANT PHYLYP, TAROTISIAN NAVY—second lieutenant, *King Gorjah II*.

Glossary

Anshinritsumei—literally "enlightenment," from the Japanese. Rendered in the Safehold Bible, however, as "the little fire," the lesser touch of God's spirit. The maximum enlightenment of which mortals are capable.

Borer—a form of Safeholdian shellfish which attaches itself to the hulls of ships or the timbers of wharves by boring into them. There are several types of borer, the most destructive of which actually eat their way steadily deeper into a wooden structure. Borers and rot are the two most serious threats (aside, of course, from fire) to wooden hulls.

Catamount—a smaller version of the Safeholdian slash lizard. The catamount is very fast and smarter than its larger cousin, which means that it tends to avoid humans. It is, however, a lethal and dangerous hunter in its own right.

Commentaries, The—the authorized interpretations and doctrinal expansions upon the *Holy Writ*. They represent the officially approved and sanctioned interpretation of the original scripture.

Choke tree—a low-growing species of tree native to Safehold. It comes in many varieties, and is found in most of the planet's climate zones. It is dense-growing, tough, and difficult to eradicate, but it requires quite a lot of sunlight to flourish, which means it is seldom found in mature old-growth forests.

Cotton silk—a plant native to Safehold which shares many of the properties of silk and cotton. It is very light weight and strong, but the raw fiber comes from a plant pod which is even more filled with seeds than Old Earth cotton. Because of the amount of hand labor required to harvest and process the pods and to remove the seeds from it, cotton silk is very expensive.

Council of Vicars—the Church of God Awaiting's equivalent of the College of Cardinals.

Doomwhale—the most dangerous predator of Safehold, although, fortunately, it seldom bothers with anything as small as humans. Doomwhales have been known to run to as much as one hundred feet in length, and they are pure carnivores. Each doomwhale requires a huge range, and encounters with them are rare, for which human beings are just as glad, thank you. Doomwhales will eat *anything* . . . including the largest krakens. They have been known, on *extremely* rare occasions, to attack merchant ships and war galleys.

Dragon—the largest native Safeholdian land life forms. Dragons come in two varieities, the common dragon and the great dragon. The common dragon is about twice the size of a Terran elephant and is herbivorous. The great dragon is smaller, about half to two-thirds the size of the common dragon, but carnivorous, filling the highest feeding niche of Safehold's land-based ecology. They look very much alike, aside from their size and the fact that the common dragon has herbivore teeth and jaws, whereas the great dragon has elongated jaws with sharp, serrated teeth. They have six limbs and, unlike the slash lizard, are covered in thick, well-insulated hide rather than fur.

Five-day—a Safeholdian "week," consisting of only five days, Monday through Friday.

Fleming moss—(usually lower case). An absorbent moss native to Safehold which was genetically engineered by Shan-wei's terraforming crews to possess natural antibiotic properties. It is a staple of Safeholdian medical practice.

Grasshopper—a Safeholdian insect analogue which grows to a length of as much as nine inches and is carnivorous. Fortunately, they do not occur in the same numbers as terrestrial grasshoppers.

Group of Four—the four vicars who dominate and effectively control the Council of Vicars of the Church of God Awaiting.

Hairatha Dragons—the Hairatha professional baseball team. The traditional rivals of the Tellesberg Krakens for the Kingdom Championship.

Insights, The—the recorded pronouncements and observations of the Church of God Awaiting's Grand Vicars and canonized saints. They represent deeply significant spiritual and inspirational teachings, but, as the work of fallible mortals, do not have the same standing as the *Holy Writ* itself.

Intendant—the cleric assigned to a bishopric or archbishopric as the direct representative of the Office of Inquisition. The intendant is specifically charged with assuring that the Proscriptions of Jwo-jeng are not violated.

Kercheef—a traditional headdress worn in the Kingdom of Tarot which consists of a specially designed bandana tied across the hair.

Knights of the Temple Lands—the corporate title of the prelates who govern the Temple Lands. Technically, the Knights of the Temple Lands are *secular* rulers, who simply happen to also hold high Church office. Under the letter of the Church's law, what they may do as the Knights of the Temple Lands is completely separate from any official action of the Church. This legal fiction has been of considerable value to the Church on more than one occasion.

Kraken—generic term for an entire family of maritime predators. Krakens are rather like sharks crossed with octupi. They have powerful, fish-like bodies, strong jaws with inward-inclined, fang-like teeth, and a cluster of tentacles just behind the head which can be used to hold prey while they devour it. The smallest, coastal krakens can be as short as three or four feet; deep-water krakens up to fifty feet in length have been reported, and there are legends of those still larger.

Kyousei hi—literally "great fire" or "magnificent fire." The term used to describe the brilliant nimbus of light the Operation Ark command crew generated around their air cars and skimmers to help "prove" their divinity to the original Safeholdians.

Langhorne's Watch—the thirty-one-minute period immediately before midnight in order to compensate for the extra length of Safehold's 26.5-hour day.

Master Traynyr—a character out of the Safeholdian entertainment tradition. Master Traynyr is a stock character in Safeholdian puppet theater, by turns a bumbling conspirator whose plans always miscarry and the puppeteer who controls all of the marionette "actors" in the play.

Narwhale—a species of Safeholdian sea life named for the Old Earth species of the same name. Safeholdian narwhales are about forty feet in length and equipped with twin horn-like tusks up to eight feet long.

Prong lizard—a roughly elk-sized lizard with a single horn which branches into four sharp points in the last third or so of its length. They are herbivores and not particularly ferocious.

Proscriptions of Jwo-jeng—the definition of allowable technology under the doctrine of the Church of God Awaiting. Essentially, the Proscriptions limit allowable technology to that which is powered by wind, water, or muscle. The Proscriptions are subject to interpretation, generally by the Order of Schueler, which generally errs on the side of conservatism.

Rakurai—literally "lightning bolt." The Holy Writ's term for the kinetic weapons used to destroy the Alexandria Enclave.

Sand maggot—a loathsome carnivore, looking much like a six-legged slug, which haunts beaches just above the surf line. Sand maggots do not normally take living prey, although they have no objection to devouring the occasional small creature which strays into their reach. Their natural coloration blends with their sandy habitat well, and they normally conceal themselves by digging their bodies into the sand until they are completely covered, or only a small portion of their backs show.

Sea cow—a walrus-like Safeholdian sea mammal which grows to a body length of approximately ten feet when fully mature.

Seijin—sage, holy man. Directly from the Japanese by way of Maruyama Chihiro, the Langhorne staffer who wrote the Church of God Awaiting's Bible.

Slash lizard—a six-limbed, saurian-looking, furry oviparous mammal. One of the three top predators of Safehold. Mouth contains twin rows or fangs capable of punching through chain mail; feet have four long toes each, tipped with claws up to five or six inches long.

SNARC—Self-Navigating Autonomous Reconnaissance and Communication platform.

Spider-crab—a native species of sea life, considerably larger than any terrestrial crab. The spider-crab is not a crustacean, but rather more of a segmented, tough-hided, many-legged seagoing slug. Despite that, its legs are considered a great delicacy and are actually very tasty.

Spider rat—a native species of vermin which fills roughly the ecological niche of a terrestrial rat. Like all Safehold mammals, it is six-limbed, but it looks like a cross between a hairy gila monster and an insect, with long, multi-jointed legs which actually arch higher than its spine. It is nasty tempered but basically cowardly, and fully adult male specimens of the larger varieties of spider rat run to about two feet in body length with another two feet of tail. The more common varieties average between 33 percent and 50 percent of that body/tail length.

Steel thistle—a native Safeholdian plant which looks very much like branching bamboo. The plant bears seed pods filled with small, spiny seeds embedded in fine, straight fibers. The seeds are extremely difficult to remove by hand, but the fiber can be woven into a fabric which is even stronger than cotton silk. It can also be twisted into extremely strong, stretch-resistant rope. Moreover, the plant grows almost as rapidly as actual bamboo, and the yield of raw fiber per acre is seventy percent higher than for terrestrial cotton.

Surgoi kasai—literally "dreadful (great) conflagration." The true spirit of God, the touch of his divine fire which only an angel or archangel can endure.

Tellesberg Krakens—the Tellesberg professional baseball club.

Testimonies, The—by far the most numerous of the Church of God Awaiting's writings, these consist of the firsthand observations of the first few generations of humans on Safehold. They do not have the same status as the Christian gospels, because they do not reveal the central teachings and inspiration of God. Instead, collectively, they form an important substantiation of the *Writ*'s "historical accuracy" and conclusively attest to the fact that the events they collectively describe did, in fact, transpire.

Wire vine—a kudzu-like vine native to Safehold. Wire vine isn't as fast-growing as kudzu, but it's equally tenacious, and unlike kudzu, several of its varieties have long, sharp thorns. Unlike many native Safeholdians species of plants, it does quite well intermingled with terrestrial imports. It is often used as a sort of combination of hedgerows and barbed wire by Safehold farmers.

Wyvern—the Safeholdian ecological analogue of terrestrial birds. There are as many varieties of wyverns as there are of birds, including (but not limited to) the homing wyvern, hunting wyverns suitable for the equivalent of hawking for small prey, the crag wyvern (a small—wingspan ten feet—flying predator), various species of sea wyverns, and the king wyvern (a very large flying predator, with a wingspan of up to twenty-five feet). All wyverns have two pairs of wings, and one pair of powerful, clawed legs. The king wyvern has been known to take children as prey when desperate or when the opportunity presents, but they are quite intelligent. They know that man is a prey best left alone and generally avoid areas of human habitation.

Wyvernry—a nesting place and/or breeding hatchery for domesticated wyverns.

A Note on Safeholdian Timekeeping

The Safeholdian day is 26 hours and 31 minutes long. Safehold's year is 301.32 local days in length, which works out to .91 Earth standard years. It has one major moon, named Langhorne, which orbits Safehold in 27.6 local days, so the lunar month is approximately 28 days long.

The Safeholdian day is divided into twenty-six 60-minute hours, and one 31-minute period, known as "Langhorne's Watch," which is used to adjust the local day into something which can be evenly divided into standard minutes and hours.

The Safeholdian calendar year is divided into ten months: February, April, March, May, June, July, August, September, October, and November. Each month is divided into ten five-day weeks, each of which is referred to as a "fiveday." The days of the week are: Monday, Tuesday, Wednesday, Thursday, and Friday. The extra day in each year is inserted into the middle of the month of July, but is not numbered. It is referred to as "God's Day" and is the high holy day of the Church of God Awaiting. What this means, among other things, is that the first day of every month will always be a Monday, and the last day of every month will always be a Friday. Every third year is a leap year, with the additional day— known as "Langhorne's Memorial"—being inserted, again, without numbering, into the middle of the month of February. It also means that each Safeholdian month is 795 standard hours long, as opposed to 720 hours for a 30-day Birth month.

The Safeholdian equinoxes occur on April 23 and September 22. The solstices fall on July 7 and February 8.

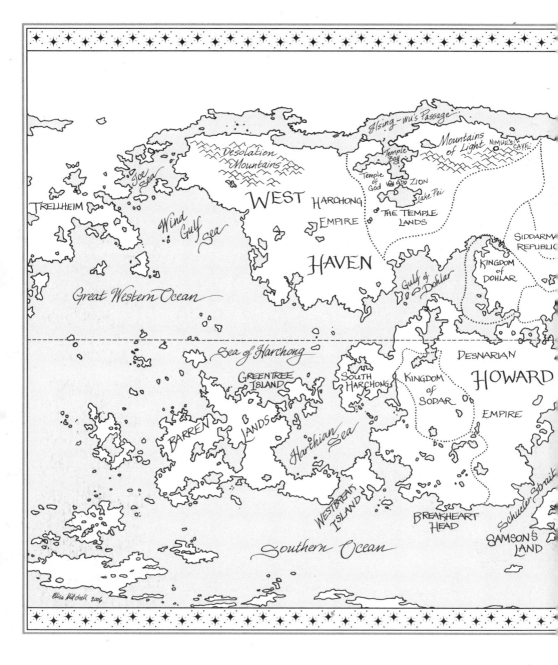